Ex-National Hunt
voted TV's most
broadcasting for ... has established
himself as one of the front runners in the racing thriller stakes. He lives in Berkshire.

Praise for John Francome's novels:

'Follows in the footsteps of Dick Francis . . . the story races along, with plot twist succeeding surprise revelation . . . descriptions of the races, from the jockey's saddle, are realistic enough to excite a confirmed non-racegoer' *Scotsman*

'Francome provides a vivid panorama of the racing world . . . and handles the story's twist deftly' *The Times*

'Francome brings authenticity to tales of the horse-racing circuit and, like Dick Francis, goes beyond the thunder of the turf to the skulduggery of the trading ring . . . the twists and turns of the last few hundred yards prove Francome to be a winner on the home stretch' *Mail on Sunday*

'Thrills to the final furlong . . . Francome knows how to write a good racing thriller' *Daily Express*

'Pacy racing and racy pacing . . . Francome has found his stride as a solo novelist' *Horse and Hound*

Also by John Francome

Stone Cold
Stud Poker
Rough Ride
Outsider
Safe Bet
Tip Off
Liefline
Dead Weight
Inside Track
Stalking Horse
Back Hander

Also by John Francome and James MacGregor

Eavesdropper
Riding High
Declared Dead
Blood Stock

High Flyer

and

False Start

John Francome

headline

HIGH FLYER first published in Great Britain in 1997
by HEADLINE BOOK PUBLISHING

FALSE START first published in Great Britain in 1996
by HEADLINE BOOK PUBLISHING

First published in this omnibus edition in 2005
by HEADLINE BOOK PUBLISHING

A HEADLINE paperback

10 9 8 7 6 5 4 3 2 1

ISBN 0 7553 2656 3

Typeset in Times by Avon DataSet Ltd,
Bidford-on-Avon, Warwickshire

Printed and bound in Great Britain by
Mackays of Chatham plc, Chatham, Kent

Headline's policy is to use papers that are natural, renewable and recyclable products and made from wood grown in sustainable forests. The logging and manufacturing processes are expected to conform to the environmental regulations of the country of origin.

HEADLINE BOOK PUBLISHING
A division of Hodder Headline
338 Euston Road
London NW1 3BH

www.headline.co.uk
www.hodderheadline.com

High Flyer

Chapter One

Barry Mannion looked at his watch. It was eight-thirty on a warm Monday morning in late May, six days before the French Derby. He should have been getting back to his office but, shaking his head to dislodge a lingering hangover, he picked up the local paper and started to flip his way to the racing pages.

Halfway through, a headline caught his eye. He glanced at his employer, Joey Leatham, sitting on the other side of a green cast-iron table in Joey's garden.

'Freddie Fielding's Circus, didn't you used to work there?' Barry said in his soft, Tipperary accent.

Until Barry innocently asked the question, Joey had been sitting happily, dealing with his post and the day's business. Almost ten years had passed since the young jockey had last heard the name mentioned; a period which had helped slowly to numb his conscience without deadening it completely. As he looked up from the letter he was reading, his face showed none of the guilt that flooded into him. 'Yes. Whatever made you ask that?'

'They're mentioned in this rag.' Barry nodded at the paper.

'What does it say?' Joey didn't want to hear, whatever it was.

Barry chuckled. 'One of their giraffes escaped and fell into someone's swimming pool. They're only over in Cambridge. Did you know?'

News of the giraffe came as a relief. After all this time, Joey was certain no one would come looking for him, but the mere mention of the circus was enough to set his pulse racing.

He managed to smile. 'They never could keep their animals under control!' He was aware that his Scouse accent was stronger than usual in his effort to sound unruffled.

Barry didn't notice. He looked at his watch again. 'Ah, well, you'll have your work cut out keeping Isle de Rey under control.' He dropped the paper on the table and stood up. 'I'd better get back to the office to ring Zamowski and tell him you'll take the ride.'

Joey nodded absently. 'Okay.'

A look of concern came over Barry's broad, red face. 'Are you sure now? He is a bit of a monkey?'

Joey nodded again. 'Yeah. Sure.'

As his agent padded away across the velvet turf to his office beside the house, Joey's throat felt suddenly dry. He closed his eyes to wipe away a vision from his past. The action only made the scene worse – brought it back to haunt him, as vivid now as it had been ten years ago.

He snapped his eyes open and sought reassurance from the timeless view of flat meadowland beyond the brook which burbled along the eastern edge of his garden.

He had woken early to find a bright sun already shafting through the light mist over the water meadows. The weather was unusually hot and when Barry had arrived, they'd decided to have breakfast outside.

Joey's black and white springer spaniel, Roger, was flopped at his feet in semi-slumber with a lazy eye on the cereal bowl which would soon come his way – half full if he was lucky.

They were sheltered from the sun by a canopy of dangling yellow laburnum blossom and a row of young poplars. The rustle of tiny silver leaves provided a background to the spring song of thrushes and warblers hidden in the bushes around the finely mown lawn.

Joey pushed back a lock of his curly black hair from his forehead and turned to look at Roger. The animal wagged his shaggy tail and sprang to his feet.

Joey passed his untouched cereal bowl down to the dog, who buried his nose in it with noisy gratitude. He leaned back and wished that the memories of Freddie Fielding's Circus hadn't come back to spoil such a perfect morning.

A jay cried loudly in a stand of massive beeches in the corner of the garden. Joey stood up and walked out from under the laburnum. He drew in a lungful of meadow-scented morning air, his nostrils twitching appreciatively. He stretched and absently, almost unconsciously, threw back his arms in a routine exercise.

His well-tanned, hard-muscled figure showed beneath a light cotton shirt, giving the impression of a compact Roman sculpture, with almost implausibly fine features – features which, with his exceptional shortness, looked pretty rather than handsome, and had made him the butt of countless jokes for much of his young life in Liverpool.

Even now, at twenty-eight, his dark, tousled hair and sea-blue eyes set above high cheekbones gave him a look of guileless innocence which was not entirely false – an attribute which a lot of rivals envied.

Joey finished stretching and stood quite still while his eyes followed a heron flapping up the brook. When the bird had disappeared behind a clump of willows, he gazed around his garden, determined to dispel the sense of foreboding that had descended on him.

After all, he told himself, if he discounted his lack of height, life couldn't have been better at the moment. He was supremely fit, healthy and good-looking, and for the last two seasons had been one of the most sought-after jockeys in Europe. He had worked hard to get to the top, and he'd been lucky, too. Almost everything he'd touched – or, in his case, sat on – had turned to gold. As a result, he now lived in a beautiful old Suffolk farmhouse, drove a Ferrari Testarossa and owned a new Cessna 800 five-seater plane. He was, by almost any standards, a very wealthy man.

Taking a retainer with Dick Seabourn at Crowle House had been a major decision given the success Joey was already having as a freelance. But the first few months had worked out better than even Barry, the congenital optimist, could have predicted.

Dick's three-year-olds were on fire and Joey was reaping the benefits. Added to that, his appointment as senior jockey had attracted half a dozen more top-class horses to the yard. He'd already ridden thirty-eight winners that season; they'd had a runner in each of the Guineas and both had been placed. The colt Scaramanga had finished so strongly to take second that he was now favourite to win the Derby in a fortnight's time. And this morning Barry had announced that Joey was booked to ride Isle de Rey in the French classic, the Prix du Jockey

Club at Chantilly, the following weekend. Joey had never seen the colt race but if Barry had booked it then it was certain to be in with a chance. His agent and mentor from the days when they had been apprentices together was a wizard with the form book.

As he looked down at Roger pushing the empty bowl around the lawn, memories of Fielding's big top danced across his mind again and led, as they so often did, to bitter-sweet memories of Nina.

Joey wished, not for the first time, that somewhere among the thousands of beautiful women who had paraded past him at racecourses around the world, he could find just one to match her. Nina Korsakov had been very special to him.

For a moment he allowed himself to reminisce, then he shook his head and returned to the comfort of the present. He had no intention of letting a past that held so many unhappy memories spoil anything for him now. Barry returned a few minutes later, by which time Joey had his thoughts back on track.

'I don't suppose you'd want another, slightly tricky ride before the French Derby?' Barry said almost triumphantly. He swayed from side to side in an attempt to disguise his eagerness, then pulled up a chair.

Joey laughed. 'Why are you so keen?'

'Listen, Joey, it's up to you. But this is a horse called Sudden Spin – a six-year-old. He's been away at stud for the last two seasons.'

Joey nodded. He remembered the horse from the couple of times he'd been sent over to run in England. He'd been a top-class stayer and had won the Gold Cup at Royal Ascot. 'How come he's back in training?'

'I've just been talking to Michel Lacroix's assistant

and according to him, they'd nothing but problems with the horse. To begin with, he wasn't interested in any of the mares; then he turned the other way and didn't behave quite like a gentleman. He got so vicious they just couldn't handle him. Anyway, they decided not to cut him, and to put him back in training for a season or two to see if he calms down a bit.'

'How's he done so far?'

'He hasn't run yet, but if he starts in one piece, he'll walk all over the rest of them at Chantilly.' Barry paused and nodded. 'And if anyone can get him to the start, it's you.'

'I'll check him out and let you know,' Joey said. 'I'm not too keen on blind dates with loonies. You never know what they'll lead to.'

The racing was typically moderate for a Monday, and Joey had taken the day off – the first since early March. He felt that a morning doing nothing would freshen him up. Recharge his batteries. He pottered around the garden while Barry returned to his office to do his job of finding and booking rides for Joey and the four other jockeys he now handled. Joey was pulling some weeds from a bed of roses when he heard the familiar sound of his Range Rover scrunching across the gravel driveway.

Danny Leatham was returning from doing morning stables at Dick Seabourn's yard. He was looking forward to lunch. He'd been up since five-thirty, mucking out and riding work. Mondays were always harder than any other day of the week because with only half the staff working on Sundays, the stables were never mucked out properly.

He turned the vehicle into a courtyard with the buildings to three sides and parked it next to his brother's red Ferrari. To either side of him, thatched barns stood at right angles to the corners of the big timber-framed farmhouse. The barn on his left, Joey had converted into a cottage for Danny. The other served as a garage, beneath Barry's office.

Danny stepped out of the Range Rover and breathed in the quiet air. Until Joey had come along and his riding had taken off, Danny had resigned himself to living in Seabourn's hostel. Then, he'd shared a room with three other lads and struggled to run a clapped-out Mini. Now, he had a two-bedroomed cottage to himself and the use of either of Joey's cars. Life for the brothers these days was unrecognisable from their childhood.

He debated for a moment whether to go to his cottage or look for Joey. Making up his mind, he walked towards the sturdy oak front door of the house. He'd find his brother and give him the good news.

Roger spotted Danny's arrival first and bounded off across the lawn, barking hysterically with a frantic quivering of his body.

Danny fended him off with a laugh. 'Get down, you soppy bugger.'

The two brothers, handsome in their individual ways, bore little resemblance to one other. As well as being nine inches taller, Danny had a much heavier frame. His hair was fair, where Joey's was black as coal, and through years of careful eating, Joey's face had an altogether sharper look. The one feature that might have caused a stranger to connect them was a tiny upturned nose. Their looks were the only thing that their parents had ever given them.

Joey watched his brother walking towards him and wondered why he had come back from Crowle House in the middle of the day. Usually, if he wasn't at the races with a horse, Danny spent his lunch hour at the pub with the rest of Dick's lads.

Joey felt a twinge of concern. He'd learned from long experience that his brother was fine so long as he stuck to the routine of his job.

On the occasions – mercifully few – when he succumbed to a bout of gambling or drinking, everything got out of synch for a few days, and Joey would find himself having to make excuses for Danny.

Of course, people were inclined to accept Joey's apologies, though it made neither brother happy.

But that morning – Joey thought – Danny looked well enough. 'All right?' he called over Roger's noisy greeting. 'How's Scaramanga this morning?'

'If you don't win the Derby this year, I'll shag Dick Seabourn's donkey,' Danny said confidently, grinning at his own peculiar sense of humour.

Danny looked after Scaramanga and his excitement was because, for the first time that season, the colt had genuinely relaxed while cantering. 'Normally he's tugging on the bit and doing more than is necessary but if he settles like he did this morning, he'll win by a mile! I wish I was riding him.'

Danny often ribbed his younger brother that if he'd been his size, he would have been a top jockey too. He only ever said it in jest, but if he took it too far, Joey was quick to remind him that it had taken only one ride over hurdles to discover that, when it came to a race, Danny just didn't have the nerve. Despite this, he was an excellent work rider and knew what he was talking about when it came to judging a horse.

Joey was intrigued to know why Scaramanga had suddenly decided to settle. The colt had been keen since he'd first set a hoof on the Newmarket turf. Danny had done a good job with him, but up until now Scaramanga had never learned to relax completely and wasted valuable energy because of it. 'So, what do you put that down to?'

Danny held up his hands as if they were pieces of priceless porcelain. 'You couldn't buy a pair of these in the shops, Shorty.'

Joey winced. Even now, at the pinnacle of a career where his size was a vital asset, he was still hung up about his height. But he didn't like his feelings to show, not even to his brother, so he smiled broadly.

Danny spotted the cover-up. He shrugged and said more quietly, 'I think he must be growing up, that's all.' With that he turned and walked towards his cottage, taking Roger with him.

Michel Lacroix had been shocked when Sudden Spin had returned from stud at the end of the previous summer.

The horse had always been quite difficult to handle, but as Sudden Spin leaped from the horse-box that delivered him back to Lacroix's yard in Lamorlaye, the whites of his eyes flashed with an anger that the trainer had not seen in a horse before.

The stallion tugged menacingly on the bridle through an old leather muzzle strapped tightly to his head. He pounded the ground with his hooves, using every ounce of strength he could summon from his huge chestnut frame, and dwarfing the two grooms who struggled to hold him. '*Ce cheval est taré!*' the older groom yelled in fear and anger. He yanked the sharp steel bit harshly across the bars of the horse's mouth and managed to bring him back to his feet and under control.

Michel watched apprehensively as Sudden Spin snorted defiantly through the thick muzzle. The trainer had lived sixty-one years and spent the last fifty-five working with horses. He'd handled probably over two thousand in his time – everything from show-jumpers to trotters – but they could still surprise him. That, he admitted, was sometimes the pleasure and often the frustration of dealing with them.

As the two lads wrestled Sudden Spin across the yard towards his old stable, Michel guessed that getting this horse back on to a racecourse would test his skill to the limit.

He knew from the owner that the horse's problems had developed while he had been away at stud. It wasn't unusual for stallions to become aggressive when they covered mares, often kicking and biting them. For that reason, a mare was always protected with thick leather padding. But Sudden Spin had managed to rip off the pad and savage a mare viciously.

Thierry Grazac, the lad in charge of him, had panicked and lost his temper. He had picked up a mash pole and given the stallion such a violent thrashing that one of the other lads had had to drag him out of the covering shed.

As a result, Sudden Spin had become impossible to handle, and Thierry had been sacked. Soon after that, Michel had received a call telling him to expect the horse back at his yard.

Watching him now, nine months later, quietly picking

grass on the lawn beside the house, Lacroix wondered at the transformation.

It had taken over a month before anyone could go into his box without first hooking on a muzzle. But Marlon, the young Turkish lad now standing at the horse's head, had shown limitless patience with him. He had spent every spare hour talking to him, stroking him until he had begun to gain his confidence. No one but a fool would have trusted the animal completely, but at least he could now be handled more easily.

He was also working better. The year off had allowed him to mature, and he was much stronger.

Lacroix had just heard from Barry Mannion in Newmarket, confirming that Joey Leatham would ride the horse. With the little Englishman on board, he thought, the race at Chantilly would be simple.

Two days after Barry had booked Joey's rides at Chantilly for the following Sunday, he arrived at the house with a videotape of Isle de Rey's previous races.

He and Joey sat on the sofa in the study and played the tape until Joey felt as though he'd ridden the horse himself. He experienced a moment of sympathy for the young jockey who had ridden him in all his races but who was now sidelined with a broken ankle. The horse had an electric turn of speed and if he was close enough at the furlong pole, Joey doubted anything would be quick enough to go with him. It was also clear from each race that Isle de Rey had a mind of his own.

It was a fact that when people whom Joey had never ridden for contacted him out of the blue, it normally meant they had a talented horse but with a quirk. He knew how to ride a tactical race as well as any other jockey on the circuit; but it was his reputation for handling the tricky animals that made him a cut above the rest.

However, in the five years that Barry had been his agent, Joey had urged him always to weigh the odds between talent and danger and so far Barry hadn't let him down.

On the morning of the French Derby, Barry had arranged for Joey's pilot to pick him up in the Cessna 800 on Newmarket racecourse at nine-thirty. The flight to Chantilly would take a little under two hours, which would give Joey plenty of time to walk the course, and to relax before his two rides.

A friend of his who lived in the next village was booked to ride the pacemaker for an English runner. He had rung earlier in the week and asked if Joey could give him a lift to Chantilly. Johnnie Redmond was a good jockey, but wasn't a winner and would never be top-class. He was good company, though, and Joey had told him he'd be glad to have him on the trip.

Johnnie hadn't put the phone down at once.

Joey guessed what was coming. Since he'd owned the plane, he'd grown used to people asking outrageous favours.

'Is Barry coming too?' Johnnie had asked.

'No. Why?'

'Well, I wondered if there'd be room for one more?'

'Depends who it is.'

'You don't know her.'

'Oh, no,' Joey said, well aware of Johnnie's form. 'Not another of your conquests?'

'She's not,' he said quickly. 'I've never even . . . well, I hardly know her myself. She's a French girl who wants to get back to Paris. And I just said . . .'

'All right,' Joey agreed with a laugh. 'We'll squeeze her in.'

He had put the phone down wondering what Johnnie had got himself into this time.

Chapter Two

Joey's nose was buried in the sports section of *The Sunday Times* as Barry pulled up the Ferrari beside the small plane.

'Jesus! Would you take a look at that!'

Joey knew without raising his eyes that there had to be a girl nearby. He'd heard the lusty Irish voice produce similar invocations a hundred times before. Anything female in a skirt could set Barry off.

But this time Joey found himself gazing at a girl who could have stepped right off the cover of French *Vogue*. She was standing talking to Johnnie, but looked over and smiled as they arrived. She wore a fitted cream linen dress that stopped six inches above her knees. With a grin, Joey noticed Barry craning his neck to get a better view of her legs.

There was something about the way French girls dressed that always made them stand out. But this one had more. Joey couldn't decide whether it was her violet-blue eyes, her flawless, slender limbs, or her soft, full mouth that made the greatest impact.

She couldn't have been more than twenty, about five foot ten, with dark hair cut neatly to her shoulders. In her hand she held a wide-brimmed hat and a matching linen jacket, folded carefully to avoid creasing.

Embarrassed, Joey became abruptly aware that his eyes must have been popping out of their sockets. He blinked, blushed and turned away to stroke Roger who was squashed on to the back shelf, while Barry eased himself out of the driver's seat and ambled over to say hello.

Joey stayed where he was, looking around the inside of the car, self-conscious and nervous about meeting a woman who was just too beautiful for words. It was at times like this that he most wished he was taller. And it didn't do any good reminding himself that if he were, he'd probably still be living in the back streets of Liverpool.

Taking a deep breath, he swung open the car door, climbed out and walked the few yards to where the girl stood with Johnnie and Barry. Joey was determined not to let the difference in their height matter, though his eyes were at the same level as the simple pearl necklace that hung round her neck. It helped that Johnnie wasn't much taller, and didn't seem to be having any trouble communicating with her.

Joey gave her a grin. '*Bonjour. Ça va?*' Before she had a chance to reply, he added quickly, 'I'm Joey Leatham and I'm afraid that's all the French I know.'

She held out one slim, brown hand. 'That's not much,' she said with an upturn of her wide mouth. 'How are you going to tell the horse what to do?'

'With these.' Joey lifted his hands, much as Danny had to him at the beginning of the week.

'For me, you can speak in English . . . Stephanie Ducas.' She spoke in a soft French accent that made Joey's skin tingle. 'It is very kind of you to give me a lift.'

'No trouble. Do you have any bags?'

'Just that.' She nodded at the small briefcase by her feet.

The pilot had climbed out of the Cessna to join them. He picked up Stephanie's bag to stow it with the jockeys' kit-bags in the small hold and they all walked towards the plane.

Watching them, Barry wished he was going to Chantilly now, instead of returning to his office to book rides for the coming week. He waited to see the French girl negotiate the step up on to the wing of the plane, the two jockeys having gallantly let her go first. He was rewarded with a tantalising glimpse of stocking top. Johnnie caught his eye and grinned like a naughty schoolboy.

Barry let out a long sigh. 'Well, best of luck, boys. I'll be here this evening to pick you up at eight-fifteen, so don't be late.'

Joey gave him a wave, and clambered in behind Johnnie. Barry watched the plane taxi away across the turf and take off. He climbed back into the Ferrari, turned to Roger and sighed. 'Some guys have all the luck,' he chuckled and swung the car in a big arc across the grass and drove back to Three Elms Farm.

Joey found the journey to France passed quickly. Sitting opposite Stephanie, he realised she was just as beautiful as on first impressions.

She seemed relaxed and, to their surprise, was well informed about French racing. It turned out that her father had over a dozen horses in training with various yards around the French capital and one of them was racing that day – a four-year-old, Duveen, who was declared to run in the staying race against Sudden Spin.

He was already the top hurdler in France and if Joey's mount was still rusty after his lay-off, looked the most likely to win instead.

From the moment he had set eyes on Stephanie, Joey had accepted that, however friendly she might be, she was out of his league.

Girls like her had a queue of men to choose from, all at least as rich as he, more sophisticated, and almost certainly taller.

While Johnnie prattled on, Joey sat back in his seat and thought of Nina.

He remembered how the first time he'd seen her his heart had pumped so hard, he thought it would show. He was only fifteen when he'd first seen Freddie Fielding's Circus in Liverpool. He'd sneaked in without paying and found a spare seat right next to the tunnel. Nina had appeared riding a grey stallion which Joey had thought absolutely magnificent. As she'd waited her turn to enter the ring, she'd been so close he could almost have touched her.

Within a month, he'd joined the circus and she'd become his best friend. It was she and her mother who had taught him to ride – not just to sit on a horse, but to do anything he wanted with one. For two years, Nina had been the centre of his existence and although he'd never told her, she was the first and only person he had ever truly loved.

She wasn't as beautiful as Stephanie, but looking at the girl opposite him now, he decided that Nina was no less striking – unless time and memory were playing unfair tricks on him. After all, he hadn't set eyes on Nina in over ten years.

Since he'd left the circus, he'd often thought of going

to look for her, but every time he'd found an excuse not to. In his heart, he knew that the real reason was fear of rejection.

Another reason was guilt.

But maybe it was time he confronted it. Maybe this time he really would go to look for her. Perhaps when he got back from France . . .

Stephanie's laughter brought Joey back to the present. He looked at her and managed a smile.

'Tell me, Stephanie, what have you been doing in Newmarket?'

'I was only there for one night, staying with Lord Leamington.'

'Moving in the right circles, then.' The Leamingtons were owners and breeders who entertained on a grand scale.

Stephanie shrugged. 'He wants to sell some pictures to my father.'

'Her dad's got a big gallery in Paris,' Johnnie said. 'Specialises in sporting pictures. Leamington wants to sell him a pair of Herrings.'

'He'll be wanting a few bob for them,' Joey said, impressed. He'd looked at a lot of racing pictures himself over the last few years, since he'd had money to invest, and he'd taught himself a lot about the art market. 'Are you buying them?'

Stephanie smiled and tapped the side of her nose with her index finger.

'You work for your dad, then?' he asked.

'He says he works for me. Are you interested in paintings?'

'Yeah. I buy a few, but only when I know they're

selling for less than they should be.'

'Then you will not buy anything from us, but I'm going back into Paris straight after racing. Why don't you both come with me and have a look at the gallery, if you want?'

Johnnie looked eagerly at Joey, like a dog who was about to be thrown a bone.

Joey shook his head. 'Sorry, I'd like to, but I've got to get back tonight.' He didn't have to be anywhere that night, but he was certain he wasn't ready for Stephanie Ducas yet; he doubted that he ever would be.

Bitterness had been festering in Thierry Grazac since he'd been unfairly sacked by the stud where he'd looked after Sudden Spin.

But today he was going to exact his revenge. He'd found another job easily enough, but only as a stable lad. He'd always been a loner and at the stud he'd had a cottage to himself; now he was living in a hostel, sharing a room. His wages were a third of what they'd been. But he wasn't brooding about the money; in his time working with the stallions he'd saved most of what he'd earned and had the advantage of being single, with no one to support but himself.

What had incensed him was the injustice done to him; that he'd been dismissed for doing a job he was good at, which he loved and in which he took great pride.

Maybe he had gone a bit over the top with Sudden Spin, but he'd been around horses long enough to know just how much you could safely let them get away with.

He'd seen savage stallions before. He had previously worked at a stud with a stallion so unpredictable that no one ever went into his box. Once, when they were trying to shoe him, they decided to hold him secure between two heavy timber boards, but as the blacksmith stepped into the box, the horse had gone berserk; he'd bent the boards as if they were flimsy ply. Next, they'd attempted to lasso him and half suspend him from a beam over his stable. The lad with the rope had been tugged right off the stable floor, and the horse attacked him so viciously with hooves and teeth that he'd spent six months in hospital.

Thierry was in no doubt that the beating he'd given Sudden Spin was for everyone's protection. The horse was evil and if he'd let him get away with savaging one mare that way, he'd only have become worse and maybe ended up killing another.

He was angry, too, because after the incident he had told the stud manager that he thought the horse's behaviour had been triggered by the disinfectant they were using. He'd thought for some time it was making the stallion worse and had made no secret of his theory. Two months later, he was told by another lad that Sudden Spin had started to turn savage while he'd been at a spelling yard, before he'd come to the stud, and that his first real beatings had happened there. When Thierry also discovered that they'd used the same disinfectant, he was sure the horse associated its smell with serious pain.

Even after he had been fired, ignominiously and without notice or wages in lieu, he'd written to the stud owner, who also owned Sudden Spin, to tell him what he thought had happened. But, despite Thierry's five years' service at the stud, the owner hadn't even had the courtesy to reply.

Now Sudden Spin was due to run again, and Thierry

was looking forward to finding out if his theory about the disinfectant was right.

If it was, the owner could kiss goodbye any chances of winning. If the horse behaved badly enough he might even be warned off, which would make him worthless, and the arrogant pig who owned him would get what he deserved.

If Thierry was wrong and nothing happened, there'd be nothing lost; he'd soon find another way to repay his old boss.

His plan was simple, and depended on the network of lads who worked in the dozens of training yards around Chantilly.

Thierry had once worked with Georges Kerlidou, a wiry little Breton who was now travelling head lad for Eric Clauzel, and Clauzel's yard had a runner in Sudden Spin's race. Thierry found him in the racecourse stables.

'Georges, how's it going?'

'Fine, except for this bloody heat. How about you?'

'I'm still doing my two, and flogging fly repellent for some extra cash. Have you got anything you want to try some on? It's the best I've come across.' The enthusiasm in his voice sounded genuine.

'They'll all need some today, particularly Duveen. He's like a magnet to every insect in Picardy.'

'It's a disinfectant, actually, and I'm supposed to be flogging it on commission for the makers.'

'Sure, let's give it a try,' he agreed.

'If you think it's any good, get your guv'nor to buy some and we'll both make a few bob.'

'If it helps Duveen to calm down, I don't give a damn about any commission.'

★ ★ ★

Michel Lacroix had Joey's saddle and weight-cloth tucked neatly under his arm. He was looking around the pre-parade ring for Sudden Spin when the dapper figure of Freddie Long, his English travelling head lad, appeared, walking briskly towards him.

'The horse has started getting on edge and showing himself,' he told his boss anxiously.

Michel shook his head slowly, knowing that the news shouldn't have come as a surprise. 'Where is he?'

Freddie pointed to one of the enclosed saddling boxes. 'I put him in there, hoping he'd quieten down a bit.'

The two men walked across the neatly mown grass and into a dimly lit stable. Sudden Spin was on his toes, rattling the concrete floor and gazing wildly about him as his young Turkish lad struggled to calm him.

The trainer took one look at the stallion's extended penis and sent Freddie for a large bucket of cold water.

When his head lad returned, Michel made sure he closed the door and took the bucket from him.

'Right. Hold him tight.'

In a single, decisive movement, he threw every drop of water over the colt's genitals. Sudden Spin tried to rush forward but found nowhere to go. His head crashed into the thick wooden door. The deluge of cold water and hitting his nose seemed to shock him into temporary submissiveness. His penis retracted and he stood in the middle of the stable shaking.

'I just hope that keeps his mind on the job for a while,' Michel muttered as he stepped back. But he knew that all the valuable hours spent settling the truculent stallion had been undone in a few minutes. He watched the water forming a puddle around Sudden Spin's feet. 'What set him off?' he asked without looking up.

Marlon shook his head dejectedly.

'I don't know. As soon as we walked out of the stable yard, he was twitchy, and then he started to go mad, just like he used to when he first came back.'

For the next few minutes Sudden Spin stood still and allowed Michel and Freddie to saddle him and rinse his mouth and nostrils with water. But when Michel pulled the door open and let the bright sunshine flood in, the stallion immediately tried to bolt outside.

Michel snatched the bridle and yanked him back. Sudden Spin turned his head to bite him, but feinted at the last moment.

'Freddie,' Lacroix muttered through gritted teeth, 'get round the other side of him and keep a good hold of that chifney. If he steps out of line, let him have one. Marlon, take this side.' He handed the rein to the anxious Turkish lad.

'Do you want us to take him into the parade ring yet?' Freddie asked.

Michel thought for a moment, weighing up the options, watching Sudden Spin tugging on the bit.

'No. Lead him around here, away from the others. He'll be better off if we bring him into the paddock late.' He looked down through his race card. He didn't need to tell Freddie not to walk the stallion behind the one filly in the race, but he was looking for something he knew was quiet. 'Tuck him behind the hurdler, Duveen. Number four.'

Michel left the two lads hanging on to Sudden spin and started to walk towards the parade ring. He was thinking about the trouble they'd had when the horse had arrived back from stud. He stopped and for a moment considered going for a muzzle. But he decided against it. Once Joey Leatham was on board Lacroix was confident the horse would behave.

As Joey stepped into the tree-shaded paddock he glanced around for his trainer. There were twenty runners, the parade ring was crowded, and it was a few moments before he spotted Michel's silver hair.

Lacroix was with a group of people less than twenty yards away. As Joey walked towards him, he scanned the myriad colours in the ring, looking for an elegant splash of cream linen. But Stephanie was nowhere to be seen.

He was shaking hands with Sudden Spin's owner when he caught a glimpse of her walking into the paddock. Michel and his owner followed Joey's gaze. The trainer looked down at Joey with a grin on his face. 'So you've met Harry Ducas' daughter?'

'I gave her a lift from Newmarket this morning.'

As she walked in his direction with her head slightly bowed, Joey sensed that she was embarrassed by the number of people staring at her. This was something he'd experienced too, only in his case because he was so short.

Stephanie saw him, smiled and mouthed 'Hello' as she carried on to join some people nearby. She started chatting to a tall, greying man in a well-cut, light-weight English suit. As he listened, absorbed in every word she said, Joey guessed from the pride on his face that he was her father. Of the others in the group, Joey recognised only Duveen's trainer, Eric Clauzel.

'I would train Ducas' horses for nothing, with a daughter like that,' said Michel with a mischievous grin. Seeing that his owner wasn't amused, he quickly added that Duveen was a very versatile horse, and the one Sudden Spin had to beat.

Joey angled himself so that he could watch Stephanie while still listening to Michel. In the heat of the afternoon sun she was using her race card as a fan-cum-fly-deterrent. A welcome breeze briefly rippled the leaves of the trees but vanished almost as quickly as it had come. Eric Clauzel turned and uttered a few words to a skinny lad standing a couple of yards away with his hands behind his back.

Georges Kerlidou nodded and went off to draw Duveen into the middle of the ring. He removed the gelding's thin paddock sheet as he'd been told. He had previously dampened it with Thierry's disinfectant to keep the flies at bay, but now the heat was promising to be more of an irritant than the insects.

When the girl who looked after Duveen had led him away again, Georges carried the sheet and roller back to Clauzel who was still talking to Harry Ducas and Stephanie.

Another gust of wind brought some reprieve from the sticky heat. Most of the horses and jockeys had come in. Trainers were issuing final instructions and thinking about getting their jockeys mounted.

Suddenly, the quiet murmuring of pre-race speculation was rent by a thunderous roar. Every head turned to see a large chestnut horse charging into the paddock, completely out of control. Two lads were struggling to hang on to his bridle. The animal's neck was held high and his small ears lay flat against his skull.

The crowd scattered all over the parade ring in the rush to get out of his way. Two owners tripped and crashed into each other. One elderly lady slipped and fell to the ground in front of her trainer, who stooped to help her up. But the horse was already on top of them and trampled across them as if they weren't there. A scream of pain escaped the woman's lips as a large rear hoof crushed her ankle. The animal charged on as if locked on to some kind of homing device.

Georges Kerlidou stood for a moment wondering if there was anything hc could do. But the animal was rushing away from him and there were other lads closer, already running to help. Abruptly, he realised where the horse was heading. He screamed to Duveen's girl to look out.

An instant before the stallion hit the gelding head-on, two more lads and a tall, silver-haired man grabbed it and dragged it to a standstill.

The animal stood snorting noisily. His eyes rolled angrily at the restraint finally imposed by five men holding him. Georges arrived, panting, and yelled at the girl to get Duveen well out of the way. With the maverick horse apparently under control, other trainers quickly got their own horses mounted and clear of the paddock while a pair of paramedics ran in with a stretcher for the old lady, who was still lying on the ground, crying in pain.

Jocy had watched the whole scene with disbelief. If he hadn't thought he knew better, he'd have said that Michel Lacroix had known what was going to happen as soon as Sudden Spin entered the paddock. The trainer had moved almost before the stallion's roar had finished. By the time Joey and the owner had realised that it was their horse which was causing the fracas, Lacroix had got the animal under control, and it was all over.

They hurried across to where the trainer stood holding the quivering stallion.

'Get on him now.' Michel's voice invited no debate. 'He'll be fine once you're on him.'

Joey hesitated, feigning difficulty with the buckle of his helmet. He'd forged his career riding moody horses, but this one looked positively evil. There was something almost sinister about the animal – the way he strained at the reins while a lathery sweat drenched his massive frame. Every vein and muscle seemed to bulge in defiance and his manic eyes beamed pure hatred.

Joey had seen a horse behaving like this only once before, when he'd first arrived in Newmarket. The animal had developed an abscess which had been causing it pain for weeks. Joey was in charge when the vet came to treat him. With no warning, he had sunk his teeth deep into the man's side and lifted him right off the ground as if he were a doll.

Joey vividly remembered the vicious wound he had caused, the torn, ragged edges where the skin had been severed. He had wondered how any doctor was ever going to stitch it back together.

He looked at Michel, and shook his head. 'Forget it. I'm not riding him.'

Michel glared back at him in amazement. 'What do you mean?'

In a job where subservience to trainers, owners and stewards was second nature to every jockey, it took courage for Joey to say what he had. A lot of people who didn't know him would call him a fool.

But he knew that getting up on Sudden Spin was too great a risk to take. Damn what anyone else thought! he told himself, it was his neck!

'I mean what I say, and anyway, he's not going to run any sort of race now. Just look at him.'

The trainer continued to stare down at Joey. He realised that he had no choice. There was still a crowd of people in the paddock, waiting to see what Sudden Spin would do next.

'I'll see you never get another ride in France,' Lacroix hissed with such venom that Joey almost reconsidered. But the chance was lost. 'Take him back to the stables,' the trainer snapped at the horse's nervous young lad.

'Let me take my saddle first.' Joey slipped smartly round the seething trainer. He slid his tack off the stallion's still-heaving back and wrapped the girth and circingle neatly round the saddle. As he stepped away, he caught sight of Stephanie walking back from the course.

Joey felt his stomach turn at the idea of her seeing what had gone on and thinking him a coward. She had no idea how many horses he'd ridden that other jockeys had turned down – all those tearaways with nothing on their minds beyond getting the rider off their back and on to the ground; the horses on which he'd made his name.

He was rehearsing what he would say to her when Sudden Spin's anger seemed to be triggered again by another gust of wind.

He lunged forward half a stride, slackening the reins. Before the two boys holding him could adjust their grip, he snatched his head away to the right, knocking one of them over. Unrestrained on that side, he whipped his back-end round and lashed out his near-hind to land a hefty kick on the boy's thigh. The sharp crack of breaking bone filled the air, and was followed by the boy's terrified scream.

The other lad tried to yank the horse away but Sudden Spin sprang at him, using his head like a battering ram and lifting him off the ground. The lad's arms flailed through the air. He dropped the reins as he struggled to regain his balance, but failed.

The horse sensed at once that he was free and tossed his big head. The lead rein swung loose in a broad arc. Michel made a grab for it, but as his right hand got to within an inch of the leather, Sudden Spin thrust away and was gone.

Stephanie stood mesmerised, not knowing what to do. She'd watched Duveen go out on to the course, and had come back to see what had happened to Joey and Sudden Spin. After his kindness in giving her a lift that morning, she was concerned for his safety.

Coming back into the parade ring, she'd spotted Duveen's paddock sheet where Georges had dropped it earlier. She'd picked it up and taken a few paces towards the group beside Sudden Spin when the trouble had begun again. When she'd seen the lad being kicked she'd run forward, wanting to help, but common sense drew her up short. She wasn't used to dealing with horses, and their size frightened her.

She waited to see what would happen. Suddenly, without warning, she realised that the horse was loose and charging straight towards her.

Joey dropped his saddle and began sprinting the moment he realised Sudden Spin was free. His first few strides took him towards the paddock entrance to head off the horse and prevent him from getting in amongst the crowd.

But the horse had dropped his nose to the ground and

it was clear that he wasn't trying to get out. Roaring and snorting, he snaked across the ring towards his quarry.

Someone screamed at Stephanie to run, but her legs wouldn't work. Her brain told her to move, but she was paralysed with fear.

She could feel her grip tighten on the paddock sheet as she lifted it up in front of her to protect herself. But still she couldn't move until Sudden Spin was only a few feet away; then an inner will to survive took over and she spun round.

The stallion timed his attack to perfection, knocking her over as his toes stabbed into the turf, bringing his huge frame to a sudden halt. Stephanie crashed to the ground and winded herself. Sudden Spin's bulk cast a shadow over her where she lay, but she couldn't move. The horse raised his head in triumph and dropped to his knees.

Stephanie opened her mouth and screamed as the horse's weight pinned her legs to the ground. She struggled with every ounce of strength, utterly terrified now, as she felt his coarse sweaty hair press against her soft skin.

Her heart almost stopped as she wriggled her upper body round and came face to face with his gaping mouth and huge jagged teeth, inches from her face. She was still clutching Duveen's paddock sheet tightly in her hands; she pulled back, yanking it over her head, just as Sudden Spin took his first bite. The force of his assault drove her face into the grass with a thud. His weight as he thrust his mouth towards the back of her head kept her pinned there. He tugged the sheet violently, trying to tear it away.

Joey was in full flight as Sudden Spin opened his

huge jaws. He forced his legs to move faster as a vision of the vet's ravaged side flashed through his mind. Stephanie was screaming, twisting her body with only the sheet between herself and Sudden Spin's massive jaws. Joey was almost there when the animal snatched its head viciously towards him with the thin cotton material still between his teeth. The sheet had been pulled away enough to expose Stephanie's tangled dark hair. Joey dived forward and forced his strong fingers behind the rings of the bit. His right shoulder hit Sudden Spin just behind the ear, but the strength and momentum of the animal's downward lunge were too much for him.

Stephanie twisted her neck just as Sudden Spin thrust his mouth forward again. She yelled as she felt the sharp edges of his teeth scrape her ear. She sensed him turning his head to take a proper bite; then a hand slapped against her as more weight piled into her back.

Joey caught hold of the chifney with his left hand and pulled it as hard as he could, using the bottom half as a lever. The pressure inside Sudden Spin's mouth forced him to keep it open. The next moment Michel Lacroix had joined Joey, and they were both grappling to get the horse under control. But even their combined strength was no match.

Michel relinquished his hold on the reins for a second, drew his fist back and hammered the animal in the eye with an almighty punch. The horse hesitated for a moment, before springing up with the two men still clinging on to him.

Michel administered three ferocious jabs to Sudden Spin's mouth, bringing him to submission, and as suddenly as the drama had started it was over.

With the weight gone from her legs, Stephanie crawled painfully to her feet.

Joey was immediately by her side. 'Are you all right?' he asked, looking at her anxiously. Her face was pale with a wide graze down one side and there was blood on the other side of her head. She was obviously in shock; he wanted to hold her but felt too awkward. She sniffed deeply, trying to regain her composure.

'I'm fine,' she said, smoothing her grass-stained dress and combing her dishevelled hair with her fingers. She opened her mouth to speak again but instead burst into tears.

Joey stepped forward and wrapped his arms around her hunched shoulders. As her whole body heaved uncontrollably, he held her closer, oblivious of the watching public, the pressmen and the cameras until her father arrived and took his place.

Grateful for the smile that shone through her tears, as they walked away, Joey looked around and found that Sudden Spin had already been led out of the paddock. He collected his saddle from where he had dropped it and walked quietly back to the weighing room.

The story of Sudden Spin's attack spread rapidly, and for the remainder of the afternoon Joey found himself besieged by press and TV. Ironically, his subsequent win on Isle de Rey later on in the French Derby seemed of minor importance.

That evening, after he'd checked on Stephanie and was heading home, the story of an Englishman who refused to ride for a French trainer before courageously saving a beautiful girl was headline news. It was a story that would lead from bravery to blackmail.

Chapter Three

Joey looked out at the heat still shimmering above the runway at Bernes-sur-Oise. There was no one in the Cessna besides him and the pilot. Johnnie had disappeared after the races, leaving a message that he would be making his own way home. Joey sighed. He didn't even have a newspaper to read.

As they took off, he settled back, dozing, half dreaming of Stephanie. She had come looking for him in the weighing room to congratulate him on his win on Isle de Rey, and he'd thought he had detected a tear in her eye as she'd thanked him again for saving her life. She had repeated her invitation to come back to Paris with her, to look at some pictures and dine with her father, but he'd stuck to his original plan.

Now he was wondering why.

He pulled out his wallet and looked at the gallery business card on which she had written her home phone number. He gazed at it for a moment, before putting it back thoughtfully.

Among the bits of paper and receipts nestling in his wallet was a newspaper cutting. He plucked it out now and carefully unfolded it. It was the report about the runaway giraffe at Freddie Fielding's Circus which Barry had found. Joey read it, and his thoughts turned inevitably to Nina.

He hadn't seen her since he was eighteen. And in the few years he'd known her then, he hadn't so much as kissed her. Although on the flight over that morning he'd seriously thought about going to look for her in Cambridge, it seemed inconceivable that she wouldn't be married and even, perhaps, a mother by now. He wondered if she knew what he was doing, if she ever followed racing or had read about his success; if she was even aware that he was the same Joey Leatham who had turned up as an undersized fifteen-year-old at Freddie Fielding's Circus.

It was Nina who had first put him up on a horse – on one of the Lusitano stallions which her mother, Tatyana Korsakov, used in her troupe of Cossack Riders. Within two years of arriving at the circus, he could ride at a full gallop round the arena, hanging on to the underside of a horse's belly, then pull himself round until he was on its back. He could perform handstands on a horse's quarters, ride backwards, sideways, blindfold, and with his wrists and ankles bound and the reins between his teeth.

They didn't tell him at the time, but the Korsakovs had recognised as soon as they'd seen him on a horse that he was an intuitive rider. He loved the animals, and seemed to understand them instinctively. He had an extraordinary natural balance and a pair of hands that any horse could trust.

Looking down over the Channel at the English coastline appearing in the evening sun, Joey wondered if Nina knew that those same hands had gone on to steer more than six hundred winners past the post.

★ ★ ★

A few minutes before they landed, Joey picked out the red dot of the Ferrari, parked on the Newmarket turf beside the Rowley mile.

Barry was standing by the car, watching the small plane land and taxi to a standstill. He walked over as Joey climbed out and jumped to the ground. There was a huge smile on Barry's face. Above the smile, his eyes were dancing.

'Congratulations! How was La Belle France?'

'As belle as ever, but I'm glad to be back.'

Barry opened the boot in the front of the Ferrari and Joey dropped his bag into it. 'Do you want to drive?'

'No.' Joey shook his head and opened the passenger door. Roger, crammed into the tiny rear, stuck his head between the front seats and wriggled in ecstatic greeting.

Barry climbed in beside Joey. 'Are you okay?'

He nodded, but said nothing.

'So,' Barry went on. 'What on earth happened to Sudden Spin? I didn't see it on the telly, but I've heard he started misbehaving in the paddock.'

Joey grunted. 'What an understatement! He damn' near killed three people – including Stephanie.'

Barry started to drive the car slowly across the undulating turf. 'So what happened exactly?'

Joey told him, as objectively as he could.

'Well, I don't blame you for not riding him.'

Joey glanced at his agent. 'Thanks. I'm afraid Monsieur Lacroix wasn't so understanding, though I'm pretty sure he was expecting something like that to happen.'

'I won't book you for any of his horses again, I promise.'

'I don't think we'll be asked.'

Barry shrugged it off. 'Ah, well. So, how's Stephanie? Is she grateful to you?'

'I suppose so. She wanted me to have dinner with her and her father.'

'And you didn't go!'

Joey shook his head with a rueful grin. 'No, she gave me her number, though.'

'You lucky bastard. Mind, I reckon she fancied me more.'

Joey laughed, wondering if Barry was being serious. 'I'm not giving you her number then. By the way,' he wanted to change the topic, 'is that circus still in Cambridge?'

'What circus?'

'Freddie Fielding's. You told me about their giraffe falling into a swimming pool, remember?'

'Oh, yes. Your old outfit. I haven't got a clue. Why? Do you want to look up your old mates?'

'I just wondered, that's all.' Joey sat in silence as Barry drove out on to the road and headed for home.

'What have I got on for tomorrow?' Joey asked after a few moments.

'You should win the sprint. There's not much left in and Zapata Bianca's well drawn.'

Joey perked up. Barry seldom exaggerated their chances. 'You said she worked well last week?'

'Yeah, she did. The only thing is, Dick thinks she's better than she is. He's entered her in all the top races. Really he should keep her to Leicester and the smaller tracks. But then,' he shrugged, 'I'm just a humble jockeys' agent.'

'You're not humble.'

'No,' Barry agreed. 'It's the jockeys I'm referring to.'

'I suppose you told Seabourn what you thought?'

'I mentioned it.'

Joey grinned. Not many people told Dick Seabourn what to do.

Seabourn was an old-fashioned, gentleman trainer, in his late-fifties, who occupied one of the most venerable yards in Newmarket. Crowle House had been left to his wife by her late father, who had himself been one of the great racing names of the forties and fifties. It was Barry who had advised Joey to take up his retainership with the yard, while keeping it open-ended.

Seabourn had been spectacularly successful in his first dozen years, but more recently his yard had been plagued with a virus. Showing real grit, Seabourn never gave up, and after four wretched seasons, his fortunes had started to change.

He was hauling himself back into the limelight and the previous season had had an impressive crop of two-year-olds. But Graham Street, his stable jockey of six years' standing, had been beaten on some of them when it mattered. Barry had spotted a chance for Joey to move in. It hadn't taken him long to persuade the trainer to engage Joey as Graham's replacement. The move had benefited Seabourn in more ways than one. Joey's appointment as stable jockey had immediately attracted a handful of top-quality new horses to the yard.

'Doesn't he bite off your head when you try to tell him his job?'

Barry nodded with a grin. 'He does, but then I remind him that taking you on was my idea and he becomes more co-operative. After all, it's worked for him, and it's worked for you. I was totting it up while I was waiting for you this evening: it's nearly thirty winners you've ridden for Dick so far this year.'

The downside to the glory was the guilt Joey felt about replacing Graham as Seabourn's jockey. He knew that if it hadn't been him, it would have been someone else, but he hadn't realised until it was too late just how devious Barry had been in bringing it off.

Graham Street was a few years older than Joey, an apprentice already winning races when Joey had first turned up in Newmarket. A handsome, rough-hewn young man, full of natural verve and charm, he'd made Joey welcome, shared a room in his digs, and encouraged him in his pursuit of success on the racecourse. Their friendship had started to sour as Joey had begun to attain the success that Graham originally encouraged him to achieve.

Graham hadn't taken his dismissal at all well. He had blamed Seabourn's lack of winners on anything other than his own performance.

But whatever the cause, Joey had proved it didn't apply now, and, as a result, he was bearing the full brunt of Graham's resentment.

Graham was almost the first person Joey saw when he and Barry drove into Leicester racecourse the next afternoon.

As Joey climbed out of the passenger seat of Barry's car, Graham was in a huddle with Mike Wade, another jockey, not ten yards away. There was some kind of row going on, but whatever it was about, both men clammed up as soon as they saw Joey. Whatever their disagreement, there was no mistaking their joint feelings for him. Joey shied away from their scornful stares.

'Ignore the eejits,' Barry said, seeing them.

Although Mike Wade was a perfectly competent flat jockey – not one of the best, but not one of the also-rans – he was also thoroughly disreputable. For years, he had been known as the man to contact if a jockey wanted to earn a wedge for hooking up a horse. He had relationships with several heavy-weight punters and a few bookies. Now it looked as if Graham Street was going down the same road.

The Jockey Club had never been able to pin a single act of malpractice on Mike when he'd stopped horses himself; and even when other jockeys, acting on his instructions, had been caught and punished, they had never pointed the finger at him. Not because they liked Mike, but because they were afraid of the people he knew.

He had once, in carefully ambiguous terms, asked Joey to fail to win on a favourite in a handicap. Joey had always kicked any suggestion clean out of court. But having told Wade to get out of his life, Joey had failed to win on his horse and Wade compounded the loss by putting it around that he'd paid Joey. He made a show of handing him an envelope in clear sight of three or four other jockeys. But Joey had torn the envelope open, in front of everyone, and flung the thousand pounds it contained back into Wade's face.

Since then, Wade had been one of his most committed enemies. Joey always did his best to ignore him.

Ten minutes after he had seen Mike in the car park, he heard his voice, right beside him in the changing room.

'Fucking chicken.'

The words were hissed over Joey's shoulder, loud enough for most of the other jockeys in the changing room to hear.

Joey didn't let his head turn a single degree.

'You're giving us a bad name, bottling out of a ride like that. Lacroix says he'll never book an English jockey again.'

Joey thought of simply shaking his head, but Wade would consider even that a triumph. He carried on buttoning up his silk.

'Yeah, Joey.' He recognised Graham's hectoring tones. 'Call yourself a pro?'

A few other jockeys, smelling a good scrap in the air, tittered and waited for the follow-up.

But still Joey said nothing. There wasn't a sound as Mike and Graham waited for his response.

It was Johnnie Redmond who broke the silence.

'If either of you had been there, you'd have run a fucking mile. It was Joey who pulled the horse off the girl when it went berserk.'

'Only because he was getting jealous,' Mike guffawed, until he noticed he wasn't carrying the rest of the changing room with him.

Joey turned and stared at him. 'Piss off, Wade,' he said with disdain.

Barry watched Zapata Bianca canter to the start and marvelled at Joey's hands. He had set off with the normally flighty filly on a long rein and now she was on her way to the start like an old hack.

Barry had recognised Joey's special gift from the very first time he'd seen him ride at Sammy Samson's yard. When Danny had introduced them, announcing that Joey had spent the past three years in a circus, flying a trapeze and trick riding with Korsakov's Cossack Riders, the other lads had looked at him and laughed. Within a week, the laughing had stopped.

But Joey had never forgotten it.

He remembered it almost every day, and he saw each race as a way of proving that he was no joke, even now, after six hundred winners.

This was his first race on Zapata Bianca. He'd ridden work on her for Seabourn on Newmarket Heath, but her earlier runs had been under Seabourn's claiming jockey.

He pulled up as they approached the starting stalls and walked her the last fifty yards with his feet out of the irons and his legs hanging loose at her sides. Joey did everything he could to let her know she was in safe hands, talking to her all the time and patting her muscled neck until she was inside her stall.

When the gates sprang open, she half missed the break and Joey had her settled at once.

Barry Mannion stood alone, packed tightly among a crowd of spectators in the stand. He watched quietly without any display of raucous triumph as Joey and Zapata Bianca sneaked up and stole the race. He, like Joey, was a winner, but he'd had the sense to accept early in his career that he hadn't been born with the natural skills of a successful jockey. Besides, he liked his food and drink too much.

However, he possessed one characteristic that was essential in the racing world. He had the capacity to retain a clear mental picture of almost every race he'd ever seen. As soon as Joey's riding career had started to progress, Barry had appointed himself the young jockey's unofficial adviser, which had turned out to be a critical factor in a career where luck, timing and judgement were as important as talent.

As Joey brought Zapata Bianca to a trot, and winning punters whooped and congratulated themselves, Barry calmly calculated his winnings.

Joey had always liked Di Lambert and was glad to see her walking out on to the course with Zapata's lad to lead in the winning filly. She was Dick Seabourn's secretary, a strong fit, lively girl in her mid-twenties. Her long legs and spectacular shape made up for her mousy hair and a nose which was a little too long. In racing circles, she was known for her forthrightness. Among the devious and duplicitous, who made up a large part of Newmarket's racing community, Joey found her a breath of fresh air.

Dick and Veronica Seabourn often brought her with them to the races, where she enjoyed helping out. Like the daughters of thousands of English gentlemen farmers, she couldn't remember a time when she hadn't had a horse of her own to look after. Even now, she still kept a hack in a small stable on the edge of town and, on the long summer evenings when all the expensive bloodstock had been put to bed, she liked to ride out on the heath.

Today, at Leicester races, she looked up with a broad grin on her face as the lad clipped a leading rein on to the winner's bit.

'Brilliant riding, Joey,' she said. 'I thought you'd never get her through that gap.'

He smiled back.

'Thanks. It was probably wider than it looked from the stands. I was lucky.'

He always felt more secure, high on the back of a horse where his size didn't show – especially on a horse that had just won.

Di had never made him feel inadequate; in fact, he had had an almost adolescent crush on her earlier in the year, but somehow they'd never quite found themselves in a position where anything developed. Now, as Di walked with her long stride beside the filly and her hand on Joey's thigh, he felt a sudden rush of heat to his groin.

'You've recovered from France, then?' she asked, perfectly aware of the effect she was having on him.

Joey grinned. 'Just about.'

'It all looked very dramatic in the papers . . . and rather romantic,' she added wistfully.

Dick Seabourn had watched the race from a box lent to him by one of his owners. Today he had invited several others to join him – mostly well-heeled, old Etonian types like himself, who lived and hunted nearby. When he had arrived back from unsaddling Zapata Bianca, they were patting his back and booming congratulations which he accepted with typical modesty.

'It's the jockey you should be congratulating, not me. He's wonderful with a young horse.'

'That last chap of yours, Street, was a crooked little bugger, I'm certain,' a white-haired Lincolnshire landowner chortled tactlessly. 'I reckon he was stopping half the good horses he rode.'

'Not mine,' Seabourn said. 'I'm afraid last year they were more than capable of losing without any help from my jockey. The virus did a pretty good job all on its own.'

'I should think some of those big owners will come back, now the horses are winning for you again,' another man in the party suggested.

Seabourn's wife Veronica – grey-haired and neatly dressed in an emerald green linen suit – pursed her lips. 'I think not. Dick's rather burned his boats with most of them. Nearly all our new horses are owned by people we've gone out and found.'

Seabourn looked embarrassed. 'I did tell them what I thought of them, I must admit,' he said with a quick laugh.

Veronica raised her eyebrows almost imperceptibly and inwardly sighed. She looked out on to the course where the runners were being led out for the next race and spotted Graham Street leaning on the rails, watching them.

Chapter Four

Joey walked into the Seabourns' drawing-room at Crowle House in Newmarket, three hours after leaving Leicester races.

A hundred or so assorted friends, relations, owners, trainers and hangers-on were assembled with the Seabourns and their teenage daughter, Laura, to celebrate their twentieth wedding anniversary.

Dick Seabourn pressed a glass of champagne into his hand. 'Very well done, Joey,' he said.

'On Zapata?' he asked with a grin.

'Of course. She hardly knew she'd had a race. But I suppose we ought to drink to your French win, too. Next time, though, can you please make sure it's on one of ours?'

'Of course. By the way, Captain Zamowski sends his regards. He's a good trainer to ride for.'

'But not Michel Lacroix, what?' Seabourn laughed.

'No. I can safely say he's not my favourite!'

Barry Mannion joined them and they talked for a while about French horses and forthcoming racing events. As the party settled down, groups forming and dissolving, Joey found himself alone for a moment.

Laura Seabourn, seventeen and precociously confident, made her way through the crowd to him. She was wearing a little black dress so short that half her height seemed to consist of slender brown legs. She leaned down and kissed him on the lips, with a possessive air. Joey had the impression that she thought, because her father retained him, he was a piece of family property, available for her amusement.

'Bloody brill bit of riding in France, Joey,' she said in a public-school accent slurred by champagne. 'Did you get laid afterwards?'

'Of course not.' Joey smiled. He was not in the least bit interested in the likes of Laura Seabourn, but he knew it would be rude not to flirt back. 'There wasn't time, and I'm saving myself for you, aren't I?'

'Well, don't save yourself for too long, will you, or you might find someone else has got there first.'

'Don't worry. I'm good when it comes to a tight finish, you should know that.'

She gazed down at him with undisguised eagerness. 'Why don't you take me out to dinner tonight?'

'I expect your father will want you to eat here this evening.'

'For God's sake, Joey, I'm not a ten-year-old kid, you know,' she expostulated with a pout.

'I'm sorry, Laura,' he said, 'but tonight I feel like an old man. I'm exhausted and am going straight to bed as soon as I leave here.'

'God! You're so boring,' she said, trying to laugh off his rejection.

As she flounced off with an attempt at a steamy look over her shoulder, Dick Seabourn spoke from behind Joey.

'Don't encourage her, there's a good chap.'

'I wouldn't dream of it, sir,' he replied, and to himself

he thought, she doesn't need any encouragement.

The trainer shook his head in mock despair and turned away to talk to his vet.

Half an hour later, Dick stood on one of his wife's Chippendale dining chairs, brought the room to silence and delivered a short eulogy in praise of Veronica. He followed this up with a handful of compliments about Joey's riding skills and proposed a toast to his health.

Joey listened with the uncomfortable feeling that the trainer's heart wasn't quite in it; perhaps he was just peeved at Joey's winning a classic, albeit in another country, for another trainer.

By nine-thirty, Joey had spoken to almost everyone in the room; he'd done his duty and was ready to go. When he found a natural break in a conversation, he extricated himself and started to walk towards the door. He had nearly reached it unhindered when Veronica saw him and touched his arm, turning away from the group to whom she was talking.

'Are you off then, Joey?'

He nodded. 'Yes, I am. Thanks for a good evening.' He found that he always wanted to tell Veronica the truth; her manner was so unthreatening, one never felt the need to disguise anything. 'I don't want to make a fuss, and with my size, I can usually slip off without anyone seeing me.' He grinned.

'I don't blame you.' Veronica had changed from the green suit she'd been wearing at the races into a plain beige silk blouse and a skirt with a fine gold chain around her neck. She was at least ten years younger than her husband and still a good-looking woman in a traditional English way. 'Thanks for that win today; in fact, thanks for all the wins this season. It's been a huge boost to Dick's business.' Her voice dropped to a whisper. 'I'd been telling him from the word go that Graham wasn't up to the job.'

'He really used to work hard at it,' Joey said, being fair. 'I think he was getting frustrated. You know, weight problems and all that.'

'Frankly, Joey, you're being too kind, and you know it. Though why,' she went on with a hint of sadness, 'I should discourage a bit of kindness in this jungle, God knows. Anyway, you escape now, and thanks for coming.' Unexpectedly, she leaned down and gave him a gentle kiss on his cheek.

Joey stared at her for a moment, slightly embarrassed, before she turned away. Two minutes later, with a sense of relief, he steered his Range Rover out of the Seabourns' gates. He was grateful to them for inviting him to the party, but even after ten years in racing – the last two as a major figure – he still didn't feel comfortable with most of the people at that sort of function. Except Veronica, of course; he would always have time for her, though he suspected he'd read more into her kiss than he should have done.

He sighed to himself. It was time he got his love-life sorted.

There had been several girls – he was no saint; some he'd taken out three or four times. But in the end he always compared them to Nina, and often lost interest once that had happened. Sometimes, he dreaded the thought that maybe his memory was flawed and the Russian horsewoman would turn out to be nothing like the person he had so firmly fixed in his mind. He might find out if he could just pluck up the courage to look for the circus in the first place.

★ ★ ★

It was just before sunset when Joey parked his car in the courtyard at Three Elms Farm. He stood listening to the noises of roosting birds, took a deep breath and walked towards his front door. As he reached it a dark shape separated itself from the deep shadows in the far corner of the yard.

'Hello, Joey.'

'Danny? What are you doing lurking there?'

'I've just been for a stroll in the garden. Good party, was it?'

'Not really. Well, not the sort of party you'd have enjoyed.'

'I wouldn't know – lads never get asked to things like that.'

'Well, you weren't missing much. Do you want to come in and have a cup of coffee?' asked Joey, getting his keys out.

'Okay. But I'd rather have a drink.'

Joey didn't think Danny needed another drink but that wasn't his problem. As he unlocked the front door, he heard Roger snuffling and scratching in the kitchen. Joey let him out and the dog bounded towards them, leaping up at the two brothers.

'Fancy a game of snooker?' Joey asked, ruffling Roger's floppy ears.

'A pound a point and you're on,' Danny grinned.

They walked through into what had once been the farmhouse dairy, before Joey's predecessor had converted it into a grown-ups' games room. At one end of the long room was a fake rustic 'bar', which Joey hadn't got round to replacing. Joey poured them each a good measure of Jack Daniel's while Danny set out the snooker balls.

'So,' he said, swallowing a mouthful of whisky, 'they say you were a bit of a hero in France?'

Joey shrugged. 'Did you see the race?'

'Nope. I was busy trying to get a few quid from somewhere. Lenny Williams has taken a bundle off me in the last few weeks.'

'Come on, Dan. That's what bookies are for. Anyway, more likely you gave it to him.'

Danny laughed. 'Yer right. It's a joke, isn't it? The punters on the outside think we lads know it all.' He hammered the cue ball at the triangle of reds, scattering them all over the green baize, leaving his brother with a choice of half a dozen shots.

'The trouble with you,' Joey said, lining up an easy pot, 'is that you can judge a horse as well as the next man, but you don't spend enough time studying the races and the form. That's what Barry does, all the time, and he wins. But you'll never make money punting until you learn to work at it.'

'Yeah,' Danny sighed. 'I guess you're right.'

They played and gently ribbed each other until Joey had won and Danny was forty pounds down. Joey looked at him.

Danny shuffled his big feet and looked away from his brother's enquiring eyes. 'Double or quits?' he suggested.

Joey shook his head. 'Keep your money. Don't worry about it; it's only a game.'

Danny nodded gratefully. 'Say, Joey, I don't like to ask, but could you lend us twenty quid till Friday?'

Joey slipped a hand into his rear pocket and pulled out a bundle of notes. He peeled off a twenty and handed it to his brother. 'There you go. Don't spend it all at once!' There was neither accusation nor recrimination in his voice.

Danny sometimes wished there were.

'Thanks, Joe. Friday – I promise.'

Joey sighed as he shut the front door behind his brother, wondering for the umpteenth time how best to treat him.

Danny seemed to have no idea how to run his life and Joey seriously doubted he would ever survive on his own. He didn't want to put him down, but being a permanent soft touch wasn't going to help him, either.

The French Derby was followed by a normal enough week in the lead up to the English Derby. Scaramanga, the big prospect at Crowle House, had been visibly improving week by week since the Guineas.

Joey's arrival at the start of the season had given a real boost to morale in the yard and, for almost the first time in his life, he didn't feel that everyone around him was laughing at him or looking down on him.

Danny seemed extra buoyant when Joey turned up to ride work on Scaramanga two days later.

'How's he doing?' Joey asked as his brother legged him up on to the big, brown colt.

'He's brilliant. Doesn't he look great?'

Joey nodded. 'Let's hope he doesn't peak too soon.'

'Let's hope,' Danny agreed.

The larks were up, quivering their wings and trilling above Newmarket Heath. The morning sun, already strong, cast twenty-foot shadows behind the horses and riders as they hacked up from the stables in the town.

Dick Seabourn was on the Heath by the time his first

string arrived. He stood beside his spotless old Mercedes with a pair of battered binoculars in his hands, their case dangling at his hip. Tall – six foot three – and handsome in an unmistakably English way, he wore a flat cap over his tanned forehead and thick, dark grey curls, a tweed jacket, cavalry twill trousers and brown brogues. He squinted his clear blue eyes into the sun to watch his horses walk on to the Heath.

Scaramanga was an uncomplicated individual, a beautiful conformed animal who simply loved to gallop. After six furlongs at three-quarter speed, Joey pulled him up, as Seabourn had instructed, and trotted across to the trainer where a lad had turned up to ride the horse back.

Joey jumped down, feeling conscious of his size, as always, and losing confidence as soon as his feet touched the ground. Seabourn towered over him but, unlike many men, he seemed to understand Joey's complex about his height. He managed somehow to talk to Joey as if they were eye to eye.

'He's looking good. If we can win at Epsom . . .'

He seemed suddenly reluctant to tell Joey what the benefits would be – apart from the obvious ones – if Crowle House managed to send out the winner of the Derby. Joey didn't press him. If they pulled it off, he thought, that would do for him: two Derbys in one year.

'I think we might,' he said, without too much emphasis.

Seabourn nodded again. 'How does he feel?'

'Plenty in hand at the end, and I wasn't doing anything to help him.'

'Good. Well, let's keep our fingers crossed.'

★ ★ ★

Joey's last ride at York was at four-thirty-five. Forty minutes after he'd picked up his prize – his only trophy that day – he was strapping himself into a seat in the Cessna. The plane took off and followed the A1 south towards Newmarket.

By six-thirty, Joey was driving his Ferrari into the converted thatched barn beside his house, underneath Barry Mannion's office.

Barry's Porsche was still parked outside, along with the Range Rover and a BMW Joey recognised as Barry's old car.

He ran up an external wooden staircase and let himself into the office which was a large open room with exposed beams and rafters. There was an oak desk, where Barry sat, and a smaller pine one for his secretary, though currently occupied by Di Lambert. There were several indoor plants positioned between the desks and a long sofa in green and white checked linen, on which Danny was flopped with Roger curled up asleep beside him. A coffee table in the middle of the room was covered in magazines and newspapers.

A television opposite the sofa was tuned loudly to the Racing Channel. Barry was shouting happily down the telephone and Di Lambert was on another line, giggling to someone.

'Hello, team,' Joey called over all the noise. Hearing Joey's voice, Roger awoke, eased himself off the sofa and padded over to sniff approvingly at his master.

Barry glanced across and nodded with the phone wedged between his cheek and shoulder while he thumbed through a pile of papers. Di smiled at him and carried on her conversation.

'All right, Joey?' Danny said, without taking his eyes

off the TV screen. 'God! This guy's going to get a suspension! He's hit that horse ten times already.'

Joey pottered about while he waited for Barry to finish his call. For a couple of minutes he glanced at the next day's declarations before picking up a bundle of post lying on the coffee table. He pulled off the rubber band which was wrapped around it to see if there was anything interesting for him. At the bottom of the stack was a Jiffy bag bearing a French stamp, which made him think of Stephanie.

He peeled off the sticky tape and pulled apart the staples that secured the envelope.

As he'd assumed, there was a videotape inside.

Di finished her conversation and put the phone down. 'Hi, Joey! What've you got there?'

'It must be the French Derby. Zamowski said he'd send a tape.'

'Great. Can I have it after you?'

'We can watch it now, if you want?'

Di looked at her watch. 'I wish I could but I've got to run, I'm meeting my mother in Cambridge.'

Barry, at his desk, had also put down his phone. 'Well done, Joey boy. I didn't think you'd get the trip,' he said, referring to Joey's York winner.

'That horse'll go a mile and a half; I told you.'

'Well, I can't always be right.'

Joey laughed. 'I never thought I'd hear you admit it, though.' He waved the tape in his hand. 'Do you want to have a look at this?'

'Sure. I've been meaning to all day.'

'Danny?'

Danny was absorbed in the next race replay. 'What?' he grunted.

'Do you want to see my win at Chantilly?'

'There're a few more races I want to watch here first.'

'I'll take it back to the house and watch it there, then,' Joey said, resigned, and turned to Barry. 'Come over when you've finished, if you want?'

He nodded. 'Will do.'

'By the way, what's your old BMW doing outside? I thought you'd sold it?' Joey asked as he headed for the door with Roger bounding behind him.

'Graham wants to buy it,' Di said with a lift of her brows.

'Yeah,' Barry said. 'The cheeky bastard said he wanted to test drive it, so I brought it in specially, he took it for a spin and then dropped it back here saying he'd have to think about it first.'

Joey glanced at the old BMW as he walked across to his house. It must be worth about ten grand, he thought. Where the hell was Graham going to get that kind of money from?

Joey couldn't help feeling some sympathy for him, but Graham had ridden for the bookies too often recently. Good jockeys could get away with not trying occasionally, especially if they were also producing plenty of winners. Graham seemed to be doing it every afternoon. It was only a matter of time before his licence was rescinded.

Joey unlocked his front door and went in. He was always glad to get back home. The house was furnished in a simple, country style with old pine, oak and elm. The wife of one of the smaller trainers had set herself up as a decorator to supplement her husband's recession income. She had understood exactly what Joey wanted, and he was more than happy with what she'd done for him.

He made a cup of tea, took it through into his study and pushed the videotape into the VCR. He settled down on one of the sofas to watch himself winning the Prix du Jockey Club on Isle de Rey.

Eighty seconds later, he was staring at a blank, fizzing screen, limp and helpless with shock.

He had been expecting Chantilly and his first success in a French classic, but what he had just watched were two scenes from a world he'd hoped never to see again.

The first short clip provoked only a mild mood of nostalgia, even a smile, as he saw himself riding out into the arena beneath Freddie Fielding's big top in his first public performance as one of Korsakov's Cossack Riders. It wasn't a bad performance, either, he thought to himself, for a sixteen-year-old Liverpool kid who had never so much as touched a horse six months before. The sight of Nina Korsakov cantering round with perfect poise and a cool smile on her face evoked some unsettling memories, though.

But it was the second clip which left him shaking with horror. Starting with a sequence of shaky shots of him rehearsing a spectacular act with the Korsakovs' trapeze troupe, it turned into a replay of the worst, most terrifying event of his life.

Slowly, as his senses returned, so too did vivid memories which he'd been trying to wipe from his consciousness for years; memories of a time when he had been bullied and frightened, and desperate loneliness had clouded his judgement.

What he had seen was a minute from his past, recorded ten years before, caught and perfectly preserved like a specimen in formaldehyde – a minute that was the very nadir of the two lonely years he had spent with

Freddie Fielding's travelling circus.

In the final few seconds of the short sequence, the unsteady but sharply focused camera zoomed in on the floor of the big top, where a broken safety net lay, draped around the two inert figures of Mikhail Korsakov and his father Ivan.

Ivan Korsakov. Even now, the thought of the man made Joey shudder with fear.

Ivan was the first person he had seen when he'd crept into Freddie Fielding's Circus compound, plucking up the courage to ask if they had any work.

Joey had been to the circus a few days earlier in Sefton Park, near Liverpool, where he lived. A picture of the blonde goddess on the grey stallion, both with manes flowing, had never left his head since and that day he'd followed them to their next pitch on the edge of Stockport, just south of Manchester.

He had put on his best clothes – a white cricket sweater, a pair of almost new cord trousers, and his old shoes polished as bright as he could get them. He was feeling hot and awkward, dreading instant rejection, but had made up his mind that the circus was going to be his way out of Liverpool.

Danny had already gone, and had written to Joey from Newmarket – working with horses was a breeze and freedom was fantastic, he'd said.

It was mid-morning and several hours before the first performance when Joey wandered uncertainly from the road, in among the cluster of tents, pick-ups and trailers behind the big top. He saw no one until he rounded the corner of a large, grubby marquee emitting aromas of unfamiliar animal dung.

A tall man, stripped to the waist and wearing only black tights which showed every sinew of his well-muscled legs, was standing with his back to Joey outside a long, four-wheeled caravan. He was shaving in front of a mirror dangling from a hook on the side of his trailer.

Knees trembling, Joey walked up to him. He stood there unseen until he cleared his throat. The big man spun round. Joey couldn't help cowering at the sight of the hard, muscular torso and the cruel, flashing dark brown eyes. The man's sheer physical presence almost knocked him off his feet. Even his moustache was viciously pointed so that it seemed more of a weapon than an adornment.

'Who are you?' He towered over Joey's slender four feet ten inches. 'What do you want?'

'I want to work . . . with the horses, please?'

'What do you know about horses?' the big man challenged in a rumbling, foreign voice.

'Not much,' Joey admitted. 'I just know I like them.'

'Do you?' the man said with heavy cynicism. 'Many, many people want to work in the circus, you know.' He gazed down at Joey between the wings of his huge moustache. 'You are just a mouse of a boy, but you have something. Maybe I can use you on the trapeze. If I want you, the boss will have you. If not . . .' He heaved his shoulders dismissively. 'That's his trailer – over there. Tell him Ivan Korsakov sent you.' He nodded at a caravan elaborately finished in chrome and gold-flake paint. 'If I want you, you will be something. If I don't, you are nothing. And I won't ever let you forget it.'

And – Joey reflected bitterly now, stricken with horror in front of his television – he never had.

Even ten years after Ivan Korsakov's vicious bullying

had stopped for good, Joey felt a faint nausea at the memory. Automatically, he stumbled across his study to the television. He rewound the tape in the VCR, started it again and fell back on to the feather cushions of his chesterfield to gaze at the screen again in incredulous horror. Hard though he had tried to erase it from his memory, he found he hadn't forgotten a single second of the sequencc it showed.

The terror Joey felt now was as vivid and debilitating as on the day it had happened. When the film clip had finished for the second time, he leaned back his head and closed his eyes, drained, utterly appalled that the one discreditable moment in his personal history had been recorded and reproduced on videotape, capable of duplication for anyone to see.

He groaned and swore as the questions began to pound inside his head.

Who the hell had sent it?

Ginger Calaval?

No, Ginger had always been his friend.

But if not Ginger, who?

Who else could have done it?

Why had they sent it? Why now?

Who else had seen it?

He screwed up his face and gritted his teeth as the true horror of it hit him.

There was a loud bang on the front door.

Joey started. It would be Barry coming to watch the race. He gasped with relief that he'd managed to watch the tape before Barry had arrived.

He leaped to his feet and crossed to the television. He ejected the tape and stuffed it into a waste-paper basket. Going into the hall, he forced a smile on to his face before opening the front door.

Graham Street was standing on the door step, fastidiously picking fluff from the lapel of his smart blue blazer.

'Oh, hello, Joey,' he said, as if surprised to see him in his own home. He pushed a fringe of fine blond hair off his forehead. 'Can I come in? I want to ask you a favour.'

Joey wasn't feeling up to seeing anyone, least of all Graham, but he forced himself to open the door wider and let the other jockey in.

'Do you want a drink?' he asked, hoping he was making it clear he didn't want the offer accepted.

'Yeah. Brandy . . . please.'

Joey led him into his study where he'd just been watching the horror show on tape. He glanced guiltily at the waste-paper basket.

He poured his guest a much larger drink than he would normally have done, and a small one for himself.

He waved Graham into one of the easy chairs, and sat himself on a sofa. 'Well, what can I do for you?'

Graham took a noisy swig of his brandy and gazed at the blank television screen. He tried to look directly at Joey but turned his eyes away at the last moment. 'I was going to ride Sheila's Shebeen in the ten-furlong race at Epsom tomorrow.'

'I'm riding her now. But I didn't know you'd been jocked off. I'm sorry.' Joey shrugged his shoulders. 'What can I say? I didn't chase the ride.'

'No, I'm not saying you did. That fat bastard, Leeming who owns her wanted you.'

Joey made a regretful gesture with his hands. 'Not my fault, Graham.'

'Could you tell him you've changed your mind? Say

you can't ride her for some reason?'

'Why? I suppose you could do with a few winners.' Though Joey had already guessed that winning wasn't what Graham had in mind.

Graham looked at him for a few seconds, and Joey saw the shame in the other man's eyes.

'It's just that,' he forced the words out, 'I really need to ride her.'

'So you can stop her?'

Graham bit his lip nervously. 'I need the money, Joey.'

He hardened himself to the catch in Graham's voice and the desperation in his eyes.

'I can't do it. I'm sorry you're in trouble, but I'm not going to help you get yourself deeper into it by dealing with people like Lenny Williams. If you get really stuck, let me know.'

Graham flicked back his hair and glared at Joey. 'I don't want your fucking charity!' He drained the rest of the brandy from his glass and stood up a little unsteadily before walking out of the room.

Joey followed and said nothing as he watched him heave open the front door to let himself out.

Graham left the door ajar and strode across the yard to a clapped-out Subaru. He jumped in, revved up and drove out, narrowly missing Barry, who had just stepped down the stairs from his office.

Joey waited as he walked towards the house.

'What's up, Joey boy? You look as though you're about to throw up.' He nodded in the direction Graham had driven off. 'How he thinks he can afford to buy my BMW I'll never know,' he snorted. 'If that toe-rag's been giving you a hard time about Sheila's Shebeen, don't take any notice. He was on at me about it too – accusing me of nicking the ride for you.'

'That's not the problem. Maybe I ate something.'

'You want to take some medicine then. I'll leave you to it. I just came to say I haven't time to see that tape now. I'll have a proper look tomorrow, okay?'

He gave his customary nod and a wink, and walked over to his car.

Joey watched him go, glad of the extra time to think of a good reason why Barry couldn't see the video the next day either. He went back to his study and took it from the basket. He plucked at the tape with his fingers, pulling it from the spool until he'd extracted it all and scrunched it into an untidy bundle. He carried it through his kitchen to the back door, picking up a box of matches on the way, and took it out to the incinerator in the garden.

He dropped the tape in, lit it and watched it flare up. He knew that wasn't the end of it. There would be other copies of it somewhere, but the act relieved him for the moment, deluded him that any danger it threatened was past, for the time being at least.

He went back inside to change for a reception the auctioneers were holding at Tattersall's and tried to block out of his mind the agonising question of who had sent the tape.

Before he went out, he picked up the Jiffy bag in which the tape had been sent. It was post-marked Paris, 3 June 1996.

Chapter Five

For a brief moment, inside two furlongs from the Epsom finishing post, Joey thought he was going to land his Derby double. He was lying second and gaining ground when, despite Joey's intense efforts, the leader fought back and deprived Scaramanga by a short head.

For the next week and a half, Joey heard nothing from whoever had sent the tape. He felt like a man wandering through a minefield, waiting every second for the explosion that would inevitably finish him off.

He carried on his work automatically, giving scarcely any hint of the turmoil inside him. Dick Seabourn asked him once if something was the matter, but Joey fobbed him off with a story about a dose of food-poisoning.

On the tenth morning, he came home from riding work. There was a stack of post scattered on the sea-grass flooring in the hall.

He picked it up, carried it through to his kitchen and dropped it on the old pine table in the middle of the room. He ground some dark Costa Rican coffee beans and made himself a large espresso. He glanced at his watch: eight-thirty. Barry would be round in twenty minutes to go through the declarations with him.

It was Tuesday, the first day of the Royal meeting – the biggest week in the flat-racing calendar – and the bookies had made Joey Leatham favourite to win the jockeys' title.

Scaramanga's finish in the Derby, a few inches behind the winner, and comparable form among several of Dick's horses, made Joey optimistic about his fifteen chances over the next four days.

He turned the television on to the Racing Channel to see a preview of the day's events while he drank his coffee. At the same time, he started to open his post.

When he opened the fourth letter, it took him a fraction of a second to register that it was neither typed nor hand written, but scrappily composed with Letraset.

There was an accurate estimate of his earnings for the year, and a demand for £100,000, which was approximately twenty-five percent of that sum – followed by an uncompromising threat to despatch copies of the videotape to interested parties if he did not comply precisely with the instructions he would receive.

Joey read the scruffy message several times before he picked up the envelope. It was addressed by hand in block capitals, dated the previous day and stamped with a Nottingham post-mark.

Joey stared at it, absurdly trying to put a face to the sender. At the same time, he shook with a deep, physical fear of exposure, blame and public opprobrium for an eighteen-year-old's innocent prank that had ended in tragedy. For two weeks he'd been hoping and praying he wasn't going to hear anything more about the tape. Now, as he'd always known it would, it had come back to blight his life until somehow he could find who was responsible.

As Barry drove him to Ascot, he tried unsuccessfully to make a link between the two post-marks: Paris and Nottingham.

The first race of the Ascot meeting promised to have an extra edge to it. Graham Street was riding the favourite while Joey was on an unfancied outsider called Pistachio, from another yard.

In the absence of a Seabourn runner, Barry had persuaded the doubtful owner that he should run the colt, with Joey up.

As he cantered down to the start of the seven-furlong course, Joey acknowledged to himself, as he often had, how Barry's skill in spotting underrated horses had done so much for his own career. It was the first time the horse had run short of a mile.

He also knew that Barry had backed Pistachio to win a lot of money.

Joey pulled up behind the starting stalls beside Graham Street, who was already circling on an athletic chestnut colt. The animal had a lot of class and had already won two big races that season. Joey knew that Graham's winning percentage was more than he could have earned for stopping it.

As far as Joey knew it was Graham's only ride for the whole meeting. All the press had tipped the horse that morning; for once, he would be desperate to win. But Joey was determined to beat him – not out of any malice towards Graham, but simply because that's what gave him a buzz.

And a buzz was what he got, with Graham Street's mount half a length back in second.

★ ★ ★

Joey and Pistachio were led in by Samantha Peacock, whose Australian husband owned the exhausted, sweating colt. There was a ragged cheer for the jockey and his unexpected winner. After the first race of Royal Ascot, for a few untroubled moments Joey felt the same elation he had in his earliest wins for Sammy Samson. Then he saw Graham glowering at him from beneath his bushy eyebrows, and his thoughts sharply back-tracked to the letter that had arrived in the post that morning.

He'd had several hours to think about it, only half listening to Barry's analysis of every runner in every race that day as they'd driven down from Newmarket, and his head was full of possible suspects – dozens of people who he thought might be resentful enough, desperate enough, malicious enough, to want to damage him and benefit themselves.

Rationally, though, he concluded that it must have come from someone at the circus. But why had they waited so long? He had been earning good money for three or four years. However hard he tried to deny the possibility, Ginger was still the most likely culprit.

Ginger Calaval had been the elder of the two clowns at Freddie Fielding's. The pair performed their own crazy juggling act and filled in time between the others. When Joey had arrived at the circus, Ginger was living on his own in a small caravan. However, he had a spare bunk in a tiny compartment at the end of his trailer and when Ivan Korsakov had agreed to take Joey on, he had offered it to Joey.

Ginger was a Czech, a few inches taller than Joey and about fifty years old, though he could easily have been ten years more or less.

He greeted Joey with voluble irritation.

'Why on earth,' he asked in his thick accent, 'have you come to this bunch of wandering misfits?'

'I dunno. Maybe I'm a bit of a misfit meself,' Joey said. 'My mum came over from Ireland and dumped me and my brother. I don't even know what my real name is.'

'So you're an Irish boy?'

'I suppose so, I haven't a clue who my dad was. The council gave us our names. We were sent to an orphanage then fostered by some people called Mr and Mrs Roberts.'

'And now you've run away from them?'

Joey nodded. 'They're not like real parents; they were paid for keeping us and never let us do anything. We couldn't watch telly or go to the films. They're Methodists, ever so strict. I even had to sneak off to come to the circus.'

'But you should still be at school, shouldn't you?'

'Not for much longer. I'm sixteen next month. Our kid's gone off to work in Newmarket and I don't think the Robertses wanted me for much longer. Anyway, I hated school. I was smaller than everyone in my class and I kept getting thumped for it. It was all right for Danny . . .'

'Who's Danny?'

'My brother. He's a year older than me and twice the size. Anyway, I did a bit of a paper round so I had some money to come to the circus.' Joey shook his head. 'I'm glad I did. I was knocked out by it, you know. I mean – I couldn't believe the trapeze artists and the tigers! But it was the horses, the Cossack Riders, I liked the best.'

Ginger made a sour face. 'And the clowns?'

'Oh, yes, of course. D'you know, when I saw you and all those midgets, it made me feel better. You see, I'm never going to get any taller, for sure, but you're even smaller and it doesn't seem to matter to you.'

Joey had regretted the words as soon as he'd spoken them.

The hurt on the clown's face was almost tangible. 'Not now it doesn't. As you get older you learn there's no point denying the inescapable. It doesn't really make it any better, though.'

Ginger had been right about that, Joey thought. But what could have made the clown turn against him now?

The tape had been sent from France, which was why, when he'd first seen the package, he'd assumed it was the French Derby recording. Joey recalled that there'd been a rumour when Ginger had left the circus that he'd gone to join some old colleagues in France, though no one knew for sure.

He didn't want to believe that his old friend had harboured any kind of animosity towards him. After all, the whole plan to make Ivan Korsakov look a fool had been Ginger's. Finding him now was Joey's top priority.

'Are you all right, Joey?' Samantha Peacock asked, leading him into the paddock.

He forced a smile and glanced down. The owner's wife was regarding him with unexpected concern. 'Yeah, sure. Suffering from shock.' He grinned. 'Didn't think we'd that much of a chance.'

'Barry did.'

'Well, I hope you followed his advice.'

'We did.' She laughed happily. 'And you deserve a big thank you.'

Joey didn't answer. The trainer had joined them at the gate to the paddock and was patting the horse's neck, congratulating the jockey. They pulled up in the winner's slot; Joey jumped down and unbuckled his girth. He heaved the saddle over the horse's back, stopped for a moment for a photograph then hurried off to weigh in.

Afterwards, with no ride in the next race, he got a cup of tea from the small canteen in the changing room and tried to decide what his next move should be.

When Joey was still an apprentice, Jimmy McMahon had been the first owner to insist that Sammy Samson put Joey on his horses. He had recognised the young jockey's skill and grit right from the start and had moved six horses to Crowle House when Joey had taken his retainer there.

Over the years, they had become good friends with a strong mutual regard. It was now a tradition for Joey to spend Ascot week in the McMahons' house, a convenient few miles from the course.

Jimmy McMahon was the boss of a major construction company and a big character in every way: a first-generation Irish immigrant who disguised his shrewdness beneath eighteen stone of overindulged flesh and booming Celtic bonhomie.

If Joey had had a weakness for alcohol, he'd have been hard tempted during his four nights with Jimmy and his wife Molly, a tiny Kerry woman. Every evening was a party, whether they'd won money or lost; Jimmy McMahon never divulged which.

Getting back that evening, Joey managed to slip away

for the first hour with the excuse that he was going to take a nap in his room, which was furnished like a five-star hotel with phone, fax and modem.

He picked up the phone and asked directory enquiries to give him the number of Cambridge police.

As he had hoped, they were able to tell him at once where Freddie Fielding's Circus had gone. After Cambridge, they had a two-week run in Nottingham.

Joey dialled the number of the only man he knew in Nottingham – the retired cavalry officer who was clerk of the racecourse there. If he was surprised by Joey's question, he didn't show it.

'A circus performing near here, did you say?'

'Yeah, sounds a funny question, I know,' Joey said, 'but is there?'

'Yes, there certainly is.' The major gave a curt, faintly disapproving laugh. 'Right here on the racecourse, for the next ten days.'

'And what's it called?' Joey asked unnecessarily.

'Freddie Fielding's Cir—' The ex-soldier's faintly supercilious voice faded into an embarrassed grunt. 'Er . . . didn't I read that you were once with them?'

Joey laughed. 'Yes, you did. That's where I learned trick riding: with Korsakov's Cossack Riders.'

'They're still on the bill,' the clerk said. 'Lovely girl running the show.'

'Really?' Joey replied, finding it hard not to show his excitement. 'Not a girl called Nina?'

'That's the one.'

'Well, I may be up to see them soon,' Joey said. 'Thanks for your help.'

He put down the phone, wanting to jump into his car and leave at once.

Nina and the Cossack Riders, Ginger, Giulio and the midgets, Mr Wimsatt the ring-master . . . He hadn't seen any of them since he'd left the circus. Nina had been the only reason he might have gone back, but a nagging doubt that she would ever return his feelings had always stopped him. That and his own awful feeling of guilt. As soon as Royal Ascot was over, he was going to put that aside and go in search of her.

Joey decided he wasn't ready to put on a front for the party-goers downstairs. Instead, he lay on his bed and thought about Freddie Fielding's Circus.

He wondered if Ivor Wimsatt was still owner and ring-master. Wondered too what he would have made of Wimsatt if he had met him at this age, not as the completely unsophisticated fifteen-year-old he had been then. He recalled the first time he had met the strange little man . . .

After his encounter with Ivan Korsakov, Joey had knocked on the door of the trailer which the big Russian had pointed out.

It was opened by a woman with hair dyed the colour of straw. She was wearing leopard skin leggings and a short purple halter top. Joey thought he'd never seen so much make-up around a woman's eyes.

'Hello. I . . . I'm . . .'

'What is it, pretty boy?' the woman asked, not unkindly.

'I want to see Mr Wimsatt,' he said in a rush.

'He's not here.'

With a lurch of disappointment, Joey turned and saw the big Russian, fifty yards away, glance up from his shaving and stare at him.

Joey swallowed. If everyone in the circus was like that man, he was damn' sure he didn't want to stay.

He turned back to the woman. 'Oh, well, never mind. I think I'll leave it.' He started to climb down the steps.

'Hang on, love. They're not all like him, you know. If you want to see Mr Wimsatt, you come back up and stop here a few minutes.'

Joey looked at her for a moment before making up his mind. He clambered back into the caravan, amazed by the flashy luxury of the interior and its spaciousness.

The woman waved him to the sofa and gave him a can of Coke to drink. 'You'll be all right here,' she said with a wink, and clattered off down the steps in her high-heeled mules.

Joey gazed at the ornately framed photographs of circus acts that covered the walls, and wondered what Mr Wimsatt would be like, and what he should say to him. He remembered seeing the archetypal ring-master when he'd come to watch the circus perform; a man like Ivan but much smoother.

The reality was a disappointment. The only thing Mr Wimsatt had in common with the Russian was his moustache – and this was an insignificant little growth compared to Ivan's.

'Who are you? Sharon said you've come for a job.'

'I never said that,' Joey started, peeved that he had been pre-empted.

'Well, she didn't think you'd come to sell me life insurance.' Mr Wimsatt was a small, busy man, wearing tartan trousers and a red cardigan. He sat down at a table and shuffled through some papers as he talked, giving the impression that he was allowing the boy about a quarter of his attention. 'How old are you?'

'Fifteen, nearly sixteen.'

'You look about twelve. What's your act?'

'I . . . I haven't got an act,' he said. 'But I'll learn. I want to work with the horses and I'll do anything while I'm learning – for no pay,' he added recklessly.

'I've got plenty of people here already working for nothing,' Wimsatt said bluntly.

'Ivan said he could use me on the trapeze,' Joey offered reluctantly.

Wimsatt looked up from his papers and thoughtfully rattled a wooden pencil between his teeth. 'Did he? You look keen and fit. Maybe, if someone will give you some space in a van, we can find something for you – if Ivan wants you. If anyone'll teach you to ride, that'd be a bonus.'

Joey lay back in the luxury of the McMahons' Virginia Water mansion and found himself wondering, not for the first time, what his life would have been like if Ivan Korsakov had not wanted him.

After half an hour, his conscience got the better of him and, reluctantly, he started to dress. Putting on a classic Prince of Wales check suit, he tried to put a good face on his inner turmoil and went down to join the festivities below.

Joey had decided to ride at Warwick on the Saturday, rather than Ascot Heath. After racing on Friday, he hitched a lift back to Newmarket with Johnnie Redmond. He picked up Roger from Danny's cottage and, with a sigh of relief to be away from the permanent party atmosphere of Ascot, let himself in at his front door while the sun was still well above the horizon.

He walked through to his kitchen, dumped his bags on

the table and switched his television on to the Racing Channel to watch a replay of the day's races while he opened a tin for Roger.

It had been one of the best weeks ever in his career, and he'd crowned it with a double that day. He'd won the week's championship. Everyone wanted him to stay and celebrate. There was nothing he wanted less, not, at least, until he'd found out who had sent that tape, and with a demand for £100,000.

The phone trilled. A racing journalist wanted to interview him about his week.

Joey managed to answer his questions for five minutes and get rid of him without saying anything too personal. As soon as he'd put down the phone, it rang again.

'Hello?'

'Hello, Joey. Not out celebrating then?' He didn't catch the words at once, the sound was indistinct. 'No, maybe not. Got a pen and paper?'

Joey's blood chilled as he realised the significance of the whispering voice which had been deliberately distorted to avoid identification. He leaned over and picked up a Biro and the *Sporting Life* from the dresser. 'What is it?' he croaked.

As he listened, Joey tried to discern some recognisable characteristics or accent in the voice, but it was impossible through whatever device the man – if it was a man – was using.

He was told to deposit £100,000 into an account at any branch of the Southern Counties Building Society, by the following Tuesday. If the money didn't arrive, or he went to the police, the voice told him, he would find that every national newspaper's sports desk would receive a copy of the videotape.

Joey felt all the strength drain from his limbs. The phone line clicked and reverted to a dialling tone. He banged down the receiver and took a deep breath.

He tried to imagine the man, maybe ringing from Nottingham, somewhere near the circus.

He looked at his watch. It was after nine; too late to start out now. He would go after racing tomorrow.

The telephone by his elbow rang again.

He picked it up warily.

'Hello.'

'Hi, Joey. It's Di.'

A picture of Di Lambert instantly came to mind: bright-eyed, reliable, good-natured – and, above all, in possession of a fine body in full working order. Suddenly Joey realised how much he needed some female company to distract him from the looming crisis.

'Hi, Di.' Joey smiled to himself. 'Where are you?'

'At home . . . at a loose end. No one's back from Ascot.'

'You sound lonely. Come round and have a drink.'

'Can we have dinner first?'

' "First"? I like the sound of that. Sure I'll treat you to dinner. Book us a table at Le Picasso and I'll pick you up in twenty minutes.'

Joey studied Di in the candle-lit, Art Deco surroundings of Le Picasso. She wasn't as beautiful as Stephanie, or as striking as Nina, but tonight she was looking her very best. Carefully applied make-up made her eyes look bigger than normal, her nose more pert, and her chin smaller. A soft, smooth, well-tanned cleavage was clearly visible over the sheath of black silk-satin she wore. A sweet, musky scent wafted from her warm skin.

But Joey's natural diffidence wouldn't let him plunge straight into the kind of blatant innuendo other men might have been tempted to try on her.

Although they'd been to dozens of the same parties and had spent hours in the same bars and boxes at the races, this was the first time they'd had dinner alone together; the first time they'd really been one to one; and, as far as Joey could judge, she was as pleased to be there as he was.

But she sensed his reticence. 'Well, didn't you fancy staying in Ascot for a celebration with Mr McMahon?'

'No, I did not.' Joey grinned. 'Until you rang, I'd made up my mind to stay in and celebrate with Roger. I'm riding work first thing, I've got three rides at Warwick and then I'm driving to Nottingham.'

'Nottingham? But there's no racing there tomorrow night.'

'I'm not racing – I'm going to the circus.'

He got a perverse amusement from the effect this had on Di. His old life in the circus was fairly common knowledge; most people in Newmarket knew about it, but seemed to find the idea rather embarrassing and were reluctant to mention it or ask him about it.

'The circus?' Di said with surprise. 'What for?'

'Come on, don't tell me you didn't know I once worked in a circus?'

'Well, I suppose I had heard . . .'

'For God's sake,' Joey laughed, 'it's not as if it was a leper colony.'

'No, of course not.'

'I'm not ashamed of my time there.' This wasn't entirely true, but he had a point to make. 'It's where I learned to ride.'

'What – trick riding?'

'That's right.'

'Who taught you to race ride, then?'

Joey didn't answer at once. He gazed around the restaurant – a popular place but only half full that evening. A lot of Newmarket people weren't back from Ascot. A cross between folksy and minimalist in harebell blue and lemon yellow, the restaurant served expensive food in such small portions that even the most weight-conscious jockey could eat safely. But Joey was the only jockey there. As he thought about the answer to Di's question, his mind flashed back to his first few months in Newmarket.

'There's a touch of irony there, actually,' he said. 'It's funny how relationships – friendships – change over a few years. You wouldn't believe how terrified I was of this place when I first came here . . .'

'What? Of Le Picasso?'

'No. Of this town. It seemed to me like an entirely separate world, with its own rules and codes – its own language, almost – which you had to learn before anyone would take any notice of you. It makes outsiders feel very alien and unwanted. You wouldn't know that – you've been around here all your life. But people like Sammy Samson, Mick Mahoney – Sammy's first jockey then – Graham Street, were like people from another planet to me. Even Danny my brother, for God's sake.'

Joey didn't need to point out to Di the obvious reversal in their respective fortunes.

'And I couldn't believe the amount of money around – what the jockeys were paid, and driving around in Ferraris, and fellas paying millions for yearlings . . .

'The funny thing was, though, in a tacky sort of way

the circus was quite glamorous, too. You know – spotlights, sequins, cheering crowds and all. The main difference from racing was the performers earned a pittance. They'd have got more on the dole, half of them, but that didn't matter – not inside the circus. There was a kind of religious commitment to the way of life.

'But here, where there's all this money, bullshit and jargon – all this hierarchy and snobbery, as if they're dealing with matters of vital world importance – all it's really about is making your horse run faster than anyone else's. Not very important in the scheme of things, is it? But you get sucked up into it until it's the be-all and end-all.'

Joey looked at Di with a wry grin. 'You were asking who taught me to race ride. I don't suppose you knew Sammy Samson – my first trainer? He taught me a lot, but I learned most from Graham.'

'Who? Graham Street?' Di said, amazed. 'He never told me.'

'Didn't he?' Joey sounded surprised. 'Well, he was a bloody good teacher, and he really wanted me to succeed.'

'Not quite to the extent you have, though, I suspect.'

'No. I'm afraid he probably wishes he hadn't taught me a thing, especially after Pistachio's race on Tuesday. He didn't look too chuffed after.'

'He had all his punters on it, apparently.'

'You don't say.' Joey thought of Graham, dead broke, with a nag of a wife, two snotty-nosed kids, a mortgage you couldn't count the noughts on, and no regular income.

It wasn't the first time since the blackmail demand had come in that he'd thought of Graham – resentful, and certainly desperate, enough to look anywhere for a large lump of easy money. If Joey hadn't opened the French Jiffy bag himself, Graham would have been prime suspect. Logically, though, Joey was still convinced that if it wasn't Ginger, it must have been someone else from the circus. And he hadn't yet ruled out his old circus friend.

He shook his head.

'What?' Di asked.

'Sorry – thinking of something else. Did you get to know Graham well while he was at Dick's?'

Di seemed reluctant to admit it. Finally she said: 'Yes, I suppose so. He's had a tough time, really, and his wife's a bitch.'

'What did he marry her for, then?'

'God knows, but he did and they've got those kids, so he won't leave her now. And anyway, lots of men marry bitches. Don't ask me why.'

'You're right,' Joey mused. 'I've often wondered about that, too.'

'So,' Di said abruptly, reverting to their original conversation, 'how did you end up at Samson's?'

'Through my brother Danny. Then when Sammy gave up I persuaded Dick to take him on at Crowle House.'

'He's not at all like you, is he?'

'He is in some ways,' Joey said, automatically defensive. 'We were very close when we were kids.'

'Were you? But you're complete opposites now. He's big, thick and charmless.'

'Oh, come on, that's not fair. But I suppose the comparison's flattering for me – except for the size.'

'You're paranoid about being short, aren't you? I can't think why you're so worried about it; you wouldn't be where you are if it weren't for your height. Besides –' there was a mischievous gleam in her eye '– I hear you're not so small in certain other departments.'

'For God's sake,' Joey said. 'Who the hell told you that?'

'I've forgotten,' she laughed. 'Anyway, I thought I might find out for myself one of these days.' She opened her big, candid eyes and drank Joey in.

He succumbed, pouring himself a large glass of wine. 'Well, maybe you will.'

'Tell me something . . .' Joey was lying naked on his stomach, diagonally across his bed. He looked at the black dress and lacy underwear abandoned on the carpet and leaned over the edge of the bed to pick up a bottle of champagne from the floor. He topped up two glasses standing beside it and lifted them, turning over as he did. 'How did you learn to make love like that?'

'I don't know,' Di murmured with matter-of-fact confidence. 'It sort of came naturally.'

'Like you just did?'

'Mmmm. I can see why you get on so well with the fillies.'

Joey laughed out loud. 'I only talk to them, for God's sake.'

'Well, you're hung like a horse, so it wouldn't be a problem.'

He laughed again. 'Talking of horses, do you realise that in precisely two hours from now, I'm supposed to be galloping one across the Heath?'

'And you need some sleep. Okay, I'll go. But first, I'll just give you a little goodbye kiss.'

She turned and placed her left knee beside his right

ear, leaning forward until Joey felt her lips brush his stomach.

She crouched lower so her mound was a few inches above his face. He felt her hands on his hardening penis and the soft suction of her lips around it.

He reached up and wrapped his arms around her soft buttocks, drawing her down so his tongue could stretch up and probe, and she began to tremble again while her own busy mouth brought him to another shuddering climax.

Di's words the previous night came back to Joey as he walked his horse from the end of the gallop towards Dick Seabourn's waiting Mercedes. It had been a great evening but with all the hallmarks of a one night stand. Besides racing, he and Di had little in common.

She was a good-natured, well-constructed Sloane Ranger, who would probably revert to type and marry an Old Etonian banker, while he was a four-foot-ten-inch orphan from the wrong end of Liverpool.

Of course, since he'd arrived in the traditionally aristocratic world of flat-racing, he'd taught himself to fit in – or at least, not to stand out – in the Newmarket crowd. He didn't find it difficult to dress like something out of the Hackett's catalogue, not to hold his knife like a pen, and to tone down his native Scouse.

After ten years in the business, he realised he was actually more intelligent than many of the senior racing figures he met. Occasionally he would regret he'd left school before he'd had so much as a sniff of a GCSE paper, missing out on what minimal qualifications were on offer at his Liverpool comprehensive. But he wasn't so naive as to believe that paper qualifications were the only kind. On a racecourse, he knew, he could achieve things undreamt of by even experienced jockeys.

As he pulled up the young horse, relaxed and balanced now, he saw the appreciative look in Dick Seabourn's eyes.

'I think she could be a bit special. Did she feel as good as she looked?'

'Yeah. Brilliant. She stopped fussing after a furlong and settled beautifully.'

'Well done,' the trainer said as Joey took his feet out of the stirrups and swung his leg over the horse's quarters.

When his feet touched the ground, he handed the reins to a waiting lad, legged him up and watched him walk the horse over to the rest of the circling string. He unclipped his bobble-topped helmet and took it off with relief.

'You look a bit rough, Joey. I thought you missed all the celebrations in Ascot and went home early last night?'

'I did, but Di came round. We went to Le Picasso and . . . you know, one thing led to another.'

'Did they indeed?' Dick nodded his head. 'I wondered when you'd get round to it.'

Joey grinned, a little relieved. He'd thought his boss might be touchy about him sleeping with his secretary.

'At least it wasn't *my* daughter,' Seabourn went on. 'Mind you, Graham Street won't be too pleased.'

Joey stared at him. 'Graham? You're kidding! He's already married. I should have thought he had enough problems, and you wouldn't think he was her type, would you?'

★ ★ ★

It was only later, when Joey was alone in the house and the effects of his night with Di had worn off, that the menace of the blackmail threat crept back into the forefront of his mind. But now he'd worked out the beginnings of a campaign to deal with it. As he changed, he was almost looking forward to his visit to the circus.

Chapter Six

The familiar red and blue stripes of Freddie Fielding's Circus tent loomed inside the last long bend of the turf track as Joey drove his Range Rover into Nottingham racecourse.

The evening sun blazed obliquely across the faded canvas, exaggerating folds and ripples so the tent looked like a great colourful, wrinkled elephant, with its sides heaving perceptibly in a strong evening breeze.

Joey felt a surge of contrasting emotions: fear and nostalgia; affection and apprehension. He parked his car unobtrusively, some distance away.

He walked around the back of the stands and on to the course. He leaned on the running rail and gazed at the familiar bustle around the big top. It was ten years since he had last seen it, but suddenly it all came vividly back to him.

Joey could remember clearly how, once he had stowed his meagre possessions inside Ginger's caravan, he had gone off with a thumping heart to find the Korsakovs.

He couldn't guess what sort of reception he'd find. He knew only that Ivan had agreed with Wimsatt that he would see if Joey showed ability on the trapeze – which his size suggested – and, as they were short-handed, he could also help out with the horses.

Joey wandered among the lorries and trailers, looking at the bizarre collection of people who scurried about their business. Some cast him curious glances and faint nods of greeting. Most ignored him and he carried on until he reached the long khaki tent where Mr Wimsatt had told him he would find the Korsakovs with their horses.

He stopped at the entrance and drew a deep breath, sucking in through his nostrils for the first time the particular smell of horse dung and sweat which would pervade the rest of his days here.

Hoping that Ivan wouldn't be there, he walked into the gloom of the canvas stables and looked around. Eight white horses were tethered in temporary stalls made from timber panels and iron rails.

At first he couldn't see anyone until, in the darkness of the far end, he spotted the round denim-clad bottom of someone bending over, pulling apart a bale of hay.

Joey's pulse quickened. He couldn't deny that for him the biggest attraction of the Cossack Riders' show had been the fiery blonde girl who seemed to be the leader of the troupe. When he had seen the circus in Liverpool, he'd been struck by her skill and mesmerised by her coolness as she careered round the arena with her long golden hair flying behind her.

He knew at once that the firm shapely hips belonged to her. He stopped a few feet inside the tent and a moment later the girl straightened herself, holding a thick wedge of hay and an empty hay-net which she started to fill. She turned and walked towards one of the stalls near the entrance where Joey stood. She saw him at once, but acknowledged him with only a brief nod. She squeezed her way to the horse's head and tied the net on to an iron ring. When she edged out of the stall and walked up to Joey, he was still gazing at her with an awed expression which she ignored.

'Are you the boy my father took a liking to?' The girl spoke with a throaty accent which was a cross between Russian and rural English.

'Yes,' Joey said, coughing nervously. Close to, she looked more stunning than he'd dared imagine. Her dark eyes were set above soft, porcelain pale cheeks with just the hint of a flush from her exertions over the hay, and silver-gold hair fell in soft waves to her shoulders. An embroidered cotton top and denim jeans did nothing to hide the curves of a body in which not a single contour was overstated or out of place.

'What's your name?' she asked.

'Joey Leatham.'

'I am Nina Ivanovna Korsakov. My father . . .' Joey detected a hint of dislike in the two words '. . . says you will help with the horses until he has time to train you on the trapeze.'

'I'll do anything to help,' Joey blurted out eagerly, unable to believe his luck.

'Don't say that to people here or they'll all have you doing their jobs.' She turned and walked back to the stack of bales at the end of the tent. 'You can start by filling the rest of these hay-nets. I'll show you how to do it.'

As she demonstrated and Joey followed all her actions, she carried on talking – matter-of-factly, never losing a slight aloofness.

'Where are you going to live?' She asked the question as if she didn't much care.

'With one of the clowns.'

Nina stopped what she was doing to turn and look at him, and made a face. 'With Ginger?'

'Yes.'

'How old are you?'

'Nearly sixteen.'

'But you're so small,' she said with no attempt at tact. 'I thought you were about twelve.'

'That's just the way I'm made,' he said with rare defiance. 'How old are you then?'

'I'm nineteen, if you want to know. Anyway, don't worry about being small – it might help you,' she said. 'What do you know about horses?'

'Which is the head and which is the tail; not much else.'

'Have you ever ridden?'

'In Toxteth? No way.'

'You'll learn.'

Joey smiled, looking forward to it.

'You won't smile like that when my mother's teaching you,' Nina said, with her first sign of sympathy.

With these memories fresh in his mind, Joey walked across the Nottingham course where he'd ridden and won dozens of times and joined the short queue outside the circus box-office van.

When he came face to face with the well-remembered, elongated and slightly bulbous features of one of the midget clowns, it was as if he'd seen him just a few days before.

'Hello, Joey. Been on holiday then?' the little man said with a sardonic grin.

Joey smiled back. 'How're you doing, Charlie? You haven't changed.'

'You have. You look like a man with a few shillings in his pocket.'

Through the strange, faintly archaic accent and idiom which the circus seemed to foster in its performers, Joey thought he heard an edge of resentment which set his mind racing and reminded him why he was here.

'Here's your ticket,' Charlie said. 'No, you don't have to pay. I'll tell the others you've come.'

'Don't do that. I don't want to disturb anyone. I just want to watch, like an ordinary punter.'

'Mexican flyers we've got now. Brilliant – much better than those Russkis you were mixed up with.'

'That's good.' Joey hesitated a moment. 'What about the horses – the Cossacks?'

Charlie immediately picked up the nuance in Joey's voice. 'Oh dear, still in love, are we? Don't you worry. The lovely Nina's still with us. Her mum died, though.'

'Tatyana?'

'That's the one – tough old boot. But Nina's done a good job.'

'Is she . . . er . . .'

'Is she married?' the clown pre-empted him. 'Is that what you were going to ask? No. She was, mind, but it didn't last long. We didn't think it would. A great oaf, he was. Weight-lifter, waste of time. Magnificent physique and all that, handsome too, but, oh, was he dim!'

There was a perceptible grumbling from the queue piling up behind Joey.

'Right,' said Charlie. 'I'll see you later. I've got to deal with these eager punters.'

Joey took his ticket and gave a quick smile of apology to a mother and three children behind him.

'Hey! It's the jockey, Joey Leatham,' said a man

behind her. 'Come to ride them Cossack horses, I should think!' He cackled and beamed at his own joke.

Joey gave him a half a smile. Not enough to encourage him, but enough to stop him saying to his friends: "That Joey Leatham is a right miserable sod when you meet him. No sense of humour."

He was used to total strangers treating him with familiarity, assuming he'd know them simply because they'd recognised him.

Charlie, he'd noticed, had made no direct reference to his recent career. Joey still didn't know if the circus people knew what he'd been doing since he'd left.

He followed the steady trickle of people entering the musty gloom of the big top. The smell of elephant droppings, sawdust and damp canvas took him back ten years in an instant.

He climbed a few steps up one of the gangways in the bank of seating and sat down beside a group of children. He gazed around the tent, recognising almost everything as memories flooded in. Nothing seemed to have changed.

Even the diminutive Ivor Wimsatt, elongated by his top hat and red tails, looked the same as he'd always done while he announced the first act in his booming voice: Nina Korsakov and her Cossack Riders.

Joey held his breath as the six Lusitano horses cantered into the arena, ridden by five men followed by Nina.

She, like the others, wore Russian breeches and an embroidered jerkin, but where the men wore small fur *feskas* on their heads, her long blonde hair flowed free behind her.

Joey found that time stood still as he watched them

gallop through the routines he knew so well. A few manoeuvres and tricks had been added but generally the show was much the same as it had always been, until Nina got up to stand on her horse's back, without reins or any other support, and cantered her beautifully balanced animal around the ring. Her golden hair and high cheekbones showed clearly in the spotlights, and a broad confident smile revealed her gleaming teeth.

It came to Joey with a sharp jolt that this extravagantly beautiful and talented woman was pathetically wasted in a tacky, tawdry circus, performing every night to a few hundred punters who wouldn't have any idea of the quality they were watching.

Whatever else he was going to find out tonight, he'd at least had the satisfaction of seeing that Nina looked even better than he remembered.

When the Cossacks had cantered off to a burst of applause, Joey settled into a kind of reverie as he watched the other acts – including a few new ones – until at last Mr Wimsatt announced the men on the flying trapeze.

In the ten-minute interval before, while they were setting up the safety precautions, Joey watched with grim fascination as the guys and stays which supported the net were put in place.

The Flying Ferraras, a family of five Mexican brothers, had appeared earlier in the show, clowning around on a trampoline with comic skill. But on the trapeze, Joey had to agree with Charlie, they were at least as good as the Korsakovs, and a brilliant act.

For the twenty minutes the Mexicans' show lasted, Joey completely forgot his purpose in coming to the circus.

But by the time they had taken their last flamboyant bow and the ring-master was singing their praises before the final parade, Joey was waiting restlessly to get on with his investigation.

He left the big top with the public, but peeled off outside and made his way round the side to the encampment of tents and trailers at the back.

He guessed Nina would still be with her horses, checking that they had everything they needed for the night. He identified the long, low khaki tent – a relic of the days of cavalry warfare by the look of it – which would be the mobile stable block.

She was still there, and Joey was relieved to find her alone. She was strapping on the horses' rugs and settling them down for the night.

Joey watched her for a moment before he spoke.

'Hello, Nina.'

She glanced towards the entrance where he stood obscured by darkness.

'Who's that?'

Joey took a few paces in. Light from a dim, naked bulb dangling from the apex of the tent caught his face.

'Joey! My God! Little Joey Leatham!' She walked up to him with a beaming smile, flung her arms around him and hugged him. 'Where have you been?'

He breathed in the smell of her fresh cotton blouse and the light scent she wore. He hardly dared believe her apparent pleasure in seeing him again, but couldn't stop his pulse from racing.

'Don't you know?' he asked.

'No. Why should I? You never came back and told us anything. Someone said you went to ride racehorses, but I never knew for sure.'

'I did.'

'And now you're back?'

Joey shook his head, smiling, touched by her innocence of the outside world. He'd almost forgotten how insular circus life could be. 'No. I've only come to visit. Can I give you a hand?'

'I've just finished.' Nina hesitated for a moment. 'I was going to have something to eat. Do you want to join me?'

'Sure.'

'Come to my caravan then. There's goulash and Georgian wine.'

Joey had forgotten the strong Russian accent she'd inherited from her parents, and her husky voice, surely lower than it used to be. He followed her to what he recognised as Ivan's old trailer, transformed inside with Indian cottons, kilim rugs and a display of fine Russian pottery. Joey guessed from the look of the place that Charlie was right about her living alone.

'Here,' she said, handing him a bottle. 'Open that while I heat up the goulash.'

He filled two glasses of wine and sat on a tapestry-covered bench. Nina perched on a chair opposite. Joey had his first real chance to look at her. She must be about thirty now, and her looks had lost nothing since he'd last seen her. There was an clusive softness – perhaps an increased tolerance of others' failings – about her which he didn't remember.

She smiled at him. 'It's good to see you again, Joey. Why's it been so long?'

'There hasn't been a reason to come back – not really. I never belonged here, did I? And after your father and Mischa died, it didn't feel the same. I knew what happened was partly my fault . . .'

'Joey, no one ever blamed you. Accidents happen on the trapeze. Of course, I loved Mikhail – I still miss him.'

'And your father?'

'No,' she said without a moment's hesitation. 'In his case, it was an accident I'd been praying for.'

Everyone in the circus had known that Ivan beat his wife. Joey had suspected that Nina and Mikhail and their brothers had also been victims of this brutality. Although Joey had loathed Ivan, he hadn't realised that the big Russian had been so disliked by his own family. This no doubt explained why he himself hadn't suffered more recriminations at the time.

'What about your mother?'

'She despised him. Nobody missed him. Wasn't it obvious?'

'Maybe it was, but not to me. I was young; I don't think I really knew what was going on half the time and I could never relax after it had happened. When Ginger left, I just didn't feel like staying on. He was the person I knew best – I thought. Though maybe I didn't know him at all really.'

'I always thought he'd picked you up somewhere and brought you back to the circus.'

'How do you mean?' Joey asked, shocked and uncomfortable at the implication.

'I mean, I thought you were gay. Well, you were so pretty and . . . not very big.'

'You mean, a little squirt?'

Nina looked at Joey in a way that made his heart race. 'I never thought of you like that. But people believed you and Ginger were an item. It was only when he left that we found out he'd been carrying on with that partner of his, Giulio. Poor old Giulio was in tears for months afterwards. But Ginger had got upset because Giulio had a scene with someone else for a while.'

'Someone in the circus?'

'Yes,' Nina said with a grimace. 'My father,' she added with disgust. 'Now you can see why my mother wasn't unhappy when he died.'

'Are you saying your father was *gay*?'

'It's not unheard of, you know,' she said without any apparent embarrassment.

'But what happened to Giulio after that? I didn't see him tonight.'

'No. He went, only about a year ago. He was never the same after Ginger left.'

'I'd like to see him again.'

Nina looked surprised. 'Would you? Why?'

'Well,' Joey said carefully, 'he might know where I can find Ginger – for old times' sake. Unless you know?'

'No. No one knows where Ginger went. He had friends in France, though, and most people thought he'd gone there. But no one ever heard from him again as far as I know. Hang on.' She glanced at the gas range behind her, where a pot of stew was bubbling with spicy aromas. She got up and turned it off. She spooned some on to two big willow pattern plates. 'So, why have you come back now? What have you been doing since you went?'

'Don't you ever read the papers?'

'No, why should I?'

'Or watch the telly?'

'Only the soaps and old films. But what's that got to do with you?'

'Well, I haven't done too badly in racing. I won the

French Derby this year, and I rode the most winners at Royal Ascot this week.'

Nina stopped what she was doing, holding a spoon in mid-air. 'I don't believe it!' She dropped the spoon into the ghoulash and spun round to look at him. 'That's it! I heard them mention Joey Leatham. I never thought it was *you*, though. Fancy that – little Joey, a champion jockey!'

'I've never won the championship. But,' he added quietly, 'I am in with a chance this year.'

As they spoke, Nina put two plates and some fine silver knives and forks on the table, and he refilled their wine glasses.

'Then you're rich and famous now.' Nina looked at him with pride, and a little envy. 'And I taught you to ride! You didn't know which end the bit went when you came here.'

Joey laughed. 'I haven't forgotten that, but if you're after a percentage, you're too late. I've already got an agent.'

It was obvious to him that Nina was relaxed and happy in his presence and the easy rapport between them was stronger than ever.

She was looking at him now with wide eyes.

'It's funny,' she said. 'You haven't grown, but somehow you're bigger, more manly. Are you married to some beautiful model or something like that?'

'No.' He blushed. 'Of course not.'

'Oh, well, never mind.' Nina grinned. 'It's fantastic everything else has worked out so well for you, Joey. D'you know, I sometimes think I'm wasting my life here, but . . .' she heaved her shoulders philosophically '. . . my family's been in the circus for four generations and it's hard to break with tradition. Anyway, what else would I do?'

'You could do anything,' he said, 'with what you know about horses, and your grit and looks. You're not tied down by anyone, are you?'

Nina shook her head slowly. 'No. There was a guy, six years ago – Diego. I married him.'

'The weight-lifter?'

Nina nodded.

'Charlie told me,' Joey said. 'But he went?'

'Yes, he went.' She gave a short laugh. 'He was very good-looking, like Arnie Schwarzenegger, and very stupid, like a big baby. I was dumb, too, to marry him.'

Joey had the crazy idea of asking her, then and there, to leave the circus and marry him. He could almost have convinced himself she would do it, too.

But before he brought anyone else into his life – even if they wanted to come – he knew he had to get rid of the blackmail which was threatening to take it over and destroy all the fruits of his success – everything he'd achieved since he'd last seen Nina.

Instead, he asked her about the assorted bunch of eccentrics who went to make up the circus community, and sat only half hearing her answers. He could have stayed there all night, watching her, listening to her soft, throaty voice, but at one o'clock, after a couple of hours in the warmth of the caravan and Nina's personality, he eased himself off the plush bench and stood up. 'I'm going to have to go, but before I do, can you tell me where Giulio is now?'

Nina looked at him curiously. 'I don't know.'

'Is there anyone in the circus who does?'

'I'll ask, if it's important. Tell me where I can call you and I'll let you know.'

'That would be great! I was hoping you'd do that for me. I've got to find him – and not because he's an old boyfriend, either,' he added with a grin.

'I'm glad to hear it. I wish I'd never thought you were gay. But I suppose when people tell me things, I just believe them.'

'Now who's being naive?' Joey leaned over to give her a kiss on the cheek. 'It's been great to see you again, and give me a ring if you find out about Giulio. In fact,' he added with a faint blush, 'give me a ring anyway.'

'I promise.'

Joey successfully disguised his pleasure at her answer. He sensed she didn't want him to leave. 'Here's my phone number,' he said, scribbling on a card. 'Thanks for a fantastic dinner and a great evening. Talk to you soon, okay?'

Nina smiled at him and nodded slowly. 'Okay.'

Joey opened the door of the caravan, gave her a wave and jumped to the ground.

He strolled back through the tents, caravans and trailers, remembering all the sights and smells, and thought of how things had changed, and how they'd stayed the same.

He thought of Ivan Korsakov, and his wife Tatyana.

Joey had learned soon after meeting her that Nina's mother never smiled. She showed no obvious reaction when Nina had taken Joey to meet her in their caravan – merely looked him up and down and pronounced that he might be worth teaching.

She told Nina to tack up one of the white horses with

a lunging rein and take it to the scrubby patch of grass beside the camp. She and Joey followed more slowly while, in her strange guttural English, Tatyana began to lecture him on horsemanship.

They arrived at the little field at the same time as Nina, who gave Joey a leg up. Tatyana's manner once he was on the unfamiliar animal suggested that she considered him to be no different from a new horse that needed training.

She stood in the middle of a circle made by the horse trotting on the end of the long rein, giving an occasional flick of her long whip. Joey sat astride the horse, with no stirrups or saddle, clutching a neck rein while his mount trotted, walked, trotted again, was gingered into a canter by the hissing cord of the whip – and all the time the poker-faced Russian woman barked instructions at him to sit up, straighten his legs, push down his heels, keep his chin up and point his toes in.

She carried on mercilessly until unused muscles in his legs screamed for relief. Circus people passing saw him and smiled sympathetically, despite his unfamiliar face.

But together with all the discomfort and embarrassment, Joey was experiencing something entirely new, and unbelievably thrilling. Like millions of young people before him, he was relishing the sensation of being on an animal that moved and carried him, within the restrictions of the lunging rein, where and when he wanted in response to instructions from reins and legs.

When at last Tatyana told him to dismount, he felt a pang of disappointment, for despite his wobbling legs and the humiliation of having this crabby woman shouting at him, he'd loved every moment of his first ride.

Tatyana restricted her assessment of his efforts to a

few words. 'Maybe I can teach you something, if you will work hard.'

He couldn't wait for his next lesson.

Joey was still immersed in memories as he drove home from Nottingham. When his thoughts returned to the present, they careered between the sublime and the deeply depressing.

One thing was sure: until he found the blackmailer, his life was blighted by the fact that the damning videotape could end up in the wrong hands – like with the police or the national press – at any moment. And, although after the accident the police had let him go soon enough, on the tape, whose existence had been unknown at the time, it was patently obvious that Joey's actions had been deliberate. It would be only a step from there to the conclusion that he'd also been responsible for the collapsing net which had caused the death of the two men.

A good prosecuting counsel would have had no problem creating a plausible motive – from what Nina had just told him, a seamy one of homosexual liaisons and jealousies which would attract millions of tabloid words.

It made Joey tremble and sweat just imagining the results of an onslaught like that.

In contrast to this horrible prospect, though, was the amazing discovery that Nina had been pleased to see him again.

This made the need to deal with the blackmail threat even more urgent, for though she hadn't shown much regret over her father's death, she'd loved her brother Mikhail. Joey guessed that if she were to see the tape, she'd find it hard to forgive him for his part in her brother's death, however often he told her his intention had been merely to humiliate Ivan, never to kill him.

The next day was Sunday, and there was no racing. Joey thanked God. He was physically and mentally exhausted from the pressure of trying to win the jockeys' championship at the same time as coping with blackmail.

He slept late and spent an hour in a hot bath, purging himself of feelings of guilt he didn't deserve but couldn't get rid of.

He had planned to spend the day alone, but was just out of the bath when the phone rang.

Joey picked it up, still towelling himself.

'Joey? It's Dick Seabourn here. Veronica wondered if you'd like to come and have lunch with us? We'll be out in the garden, by the pool.'

Off the cuff, he couldn't think of a plausible reason not to go. Besides, he liked Veronica. 'Thanks. That'd be great. What time shall I come?'

'Any time after midday.'

'See you then.'

'By the way,' Seabourn added quickly before he hung up, 'there's a big article about you in the *Sunday Mirror*.'

Joey felt as if the blood had been drained from him. His mouth was suddenly dry.

'What does it say?' he asked nervously.

'Quite a good profile: the likely champion, all that sort of stuff.'

Joey let out a long breath. He had known it was ridiculous to expect any fall-out from the tape already, but this had brought sharply home to him just what role the press could play if the time ever came.

Joey put the phone down with a groan. Maybe lunch

at the Seabourns' would be better than brooding on his own all day.

But he felt stifled. He wanted air. He pulled on some clothes and called Roger, and they walked out into the garden and across a small bridge over the brook into the meadows beyond.

The walk and the peace of the morning helped to calm his fears until he was coming back through the courtyard, when the Ferrari powered through the gates and came to a slithering halt in front of the house, next to the Range Rover.

When he had come home at half-past two that morning, Joey had noticed that the car wasn't there, and recalled that Danny had asked if he could borrow it.

Despite his misgivings, and a tentative suggestion that it might be wiser to get a taxi home, he had let his brother take the Ferrari, on the understanding that he wouldn't get back into it if he was even slightly drunk.

At least it looked as though Danny had heeded the warning – something he wouldn't have done a year ago.

Danny opened the door of the car and heaved himself awkwardly from the low-slung seat. He banged the door shut and leaned against the roof of the car, apparently to keep his balance, then straightened himself with difficulty.

''Morning, Danny.'

He swung round, more rapidly than he should have done, and shook his head with pained regret. 'Hello, Joey.'

'Bloody hell, Dan, you're still plastered!'

'No, I'm not. I've just got a hell of a hangover. I wouldn't have driven if I was still pissed.'

Joey shook his head. 'At least you made it back in one piece. Come on in and have some coffee.'

Danny smiled his gratitude. 'I'm sorry, Joe, I won't do it again.'

'That's what you said last time.'

In the kitchen, Roger flopped into his basket and Danny sank into a venerable old elm carver at the head of the table while Joey shoved a kettle on the Aga and heaped a few spoonfuls of dark Costa Rican coffee into a cafetière.

'Where d'you go last night, then?' he asked.

'I promised a couple of lads I'd give them a lift to Cambridge. Billy's brother's got a tattoo place. They wanted to have it done, so I took 'em in.'

Joey poured a mug of coffee and slid it across the table to his brother. 'What the hell did they want to get tattooed for?'

'Why not? Why shouldn't they?'

'Because it'll cost a bomb and a load of grief to get it off once they're old enough to wish they'd never done it.'

'I had one done too.' Danny glowered into his coffee.

'Oh my God!' Joey laughed. 'What does it say?'

His brother sat back and rolled up his right sleeve to reveal a crudely drawn heart with the word 'Mum' in thin, curly letters.

Joey stared at it a moment and shook his head with a sigh. 'You're pathetic sometimes, Danny. You don't even know our mum.'

'So? Doesn't mean we haven't got one.'

'Oh, well, no more short-sleeved shirts for you,' Joey said with a laugh.

'It's my bloody arm!'

'You're right. It's none of my business.'

'No. And, anyway, where were you last night?' Danny asked.

Joey hesitated before he answered. He had never kept any secrets from his brother, except one.

'I went up to see Freddie Fielding's Circus.'

'Bloody hell! What for? Some nostalgia trip?'

'Something like that.'

'I'd have come with you, if you'd said. I never saw them, but I can remember you writing to me, soon after you'd run away there. I've still got the letter somewhere.'

Joey nodded. 'Yeah, I can remember writing it. I felt so lonely. It was strange really, in some ways I was in seventh heaven, being away from the Robertses, but I think I already knew I'd never really be one of the circus people.'

'Did you see that bloke you used to stay with? You said you liked him.'

'Ginger? No, he left before I did.' Joey laughed ruefully. 'Someone told me last night that he was gay – and I never knew.'

'What?' Danny expostulated. 'You lived in his caravan all that time, and he never tried anything?'

'No. Never even a hint. That caravan was a happy home to me. Ginger was tricky, mind; full of it one minute, gloomy as hell the next. If I ever did him favours – you know, did a bit of shopping for him without him asking – he used to look at me in a strange way, like I was the son he never had. I asked him once why he never married, but he just looked at his funny little body and shook his head. I thought he had a girlfriend in the circus because sometimes he didn't come back at nights. Now it turns out he was having it off with the other clown! I was so bloody innocent, in two years I never realised.'

'Where did he come from?' Danny asked.

'He was a Czech. Used to tell me fantastic stories about when he was a kid in Prague. I didn't believe half of them but they were great yarns, and bloody funny. Better than telly any day.'

'What do you think happened to him?'

'I don't know. They say he went to France.'

As he spoke, Joey was reminded of the post-mark on the package which had brought the videotape.

Joey drove the few miles to Crowle House wishing that he could have told Danny more. He longed to share his secret – and his guilt – with someone else, but he knew that he couldn't be sure who to trust.

He arrived at the Seabourns' to find Di Lambert already there.

'Hi, Joey,' she greeted him off-handedly, as if they hadn't been in bed together only two nights before.

In a way he was relieved, after seeing Nina and realising what he still felt for her, but like most people he didn't enjoy losing an admirer either. And he'd found Seabourn's suggestion that Di was having a scene with Graham Street – if it was right – oddly disturbing.

Di was pouring champagne at a table beneath a pergola of well-weathered wrought iron. Joey joked with her while he tried to avoid Laura Seabourn's advances, but her manner towards him didn't thaw for the rest of the afternoon.

He was relieved when Veronica appeared and kissed him, taking him by the arm to lead him out across a velvet lawn to a seat beneath the sprawling boughs of a large blue cedar.

The day passed comfortably enough between the tennis court and swimming pool. It was only as Joey drove home alone that his anxiety began to resurface.

His answerphone was flashing at him when he walked into his kitchen. He played back a few messages about his work, until his attention was grabbed by Nina's throaty Russian accent.

'Joey, this is Nina. I can tell you where Giulio is – it's not far. He's at Summertown Holiday Village at Great Yarmouth. He's a sort of compère there, poor man!' she added with feeling. 'Come and see me again soon. 'Bye.'

'I will.' Joey spoke aloud into the empty kitchen. 'For sure.'

He opened his diary. As if providence had arranged it specially, he was riding at Yarmouth the following Thursday.

But he couldn't wait that long.

He changed into a pair of worn jeans, a T-shirt and dark glasses, climbed into his Ferrari and headed for the Norfolk coast.

He knew it was a mistake to be so hasty and prepared himself to be disappointed. After all, on Sunday night there was a good chance Giulio would be in town, doing whatever off-duty clowns did in their leisure time.

He tried to think back, to remember what he could about the man.

During the season, from spring to autumn, the circus would move sites about once a week. When they were on the move, Ginger and Joey used to travel with Giulio, a lugubrious Italian who was the other half of Ginger's act. Joey couldn't imagine one ever performing without the other. Despite the ominous purpose of his trip, he was almost looking forward to seeing how Giulio coped on his own.

Summertown Holiday Village had the weary, unloved

look of a refugee camp, with a high chain-link fence, designed, pointlessly it seemed to Joey, to keep gate-crashing punters away from all the free rides and jollity within.

He parked his conspicuous car a long way from the holiday camp and walked up to the main gates.

If anyone recognised him, they gave no sign. He bought himself a day ticket and wandered over to the Pavilion where the evening's entertainment was due to start soon. He checked on the posters in the foyer to find that 'Giulio, Internationally Acclaimed Circus Clown' would kick off the proceedings in half an hour.

Joey went into a large auditorium where a virtue had been made of the heavy structural RSJs by painting them with thick coats of red gloss paint to match the steel-framed windows, which were themselves framed in orange folk-weave curtains thirty years out of date. He sat at a table, ordered fish and chips and buried his head in a paper, hoping he wouldn't be recognised.

When Giulio appeared, he looked much as he had when Joey had last seen him. His movements, always slow, were a little more ponderous and his lined face thinner and even more lugubrious, but his routine with a bicycle, which kept collapsing every time he mounted it, was the same, stroke for stroke. It was, Joey thought, still a brilliant piece of comic mime, and worthy of a far more appreciative audience than the Summertown holiday campers.

Since the first blackmail letter had arrived, Joey had considered the possibility that Giulio might have sent it. He, of all the people in the circus at the time, had perhaps been best placed to record Ivan's fall.

Alternatively, as he and Ginger had been in and out of

each other's pockets so much, he might simply have found a tape Ginger had made, and stolen it. Adding to this what Nina had told him about their long-standing relationship and the row over Ivan, Giulio became an even more likely prospect.

Joey slipped out of the garish room as soon as the clown's act was over and left the camp to find his car. He decided that it would be much more productive to wait and confront Giulio on Thursday, after the first blackmail payment had been made.

On the Monday morning, Joey deposited a bank draft for £100,000 in the building society account he'd been instructed to. Doing it, he was determined that he would see all or most of the money back. But in the meantime, he was taking a punt on having more chance of identifying the blackmailer by paying up now without a fuss.

He spent the day performing with a mechanical competence that evoked no particular curiosity in the people around him. He convinced himself that it was only a matter of time and determination before he identified his blackmailer. The field was so narrow. And in two days' time, he would be able to see for himself if Giulio had been a beneficiary of the £100,000. He couldn't reconcile the clown's heavy Italian accent and use of idiom with the distorted voice in the phone call, but it seemed possible, even likely, that the old clown would have an accomplice to make the calls for him.

Joey shook his head. It was hard to be certain of anything at this stage. He'd have to wait until Thursday, when he'd meet Giulio and confront him.

★ ★ ★

Joey rode a winner at Brighton the next day and afterwards joined Jimmy McMahon, the winning owner, at a French restaurant in Kemp Town. It was an expensive place, though not particularly exclusive; the first person Joey saw when he walked in was Mike Wade. And opposite him, beside a girl who looked as if she'd just walked off the Baywatch set, was Graham Street.

Joey tried to reach his table without being spotted, but Graham leered at him and beckoned him over.

''Ere,' he said to the girl, 'meet the man of the moment, Joey Leatham. This is Sammy.'

Joey saw that Graham was drunk, which wasn't unusual. He guessed that Wade was picking up the tab from the restaurant and Graham was making the most of it. Joey nodded at them both, and carried on to join Jimmy McMahon at his table.

'Who's the tart, then?' Jimmy asked.

Joey shook his head. 'Trouble, I'd say.'

'For me? A happily married man? No – my interest is academic. She's a rare species, in danger of extinction. I didn't know they still made women like that.'

'Whatever she is, she looks expensive to run,' Joey said thoughtfully. 'I wonder who's paying?'

The gateman at Summertown Holiday Village looked at the short, handsome Irishman with tousled hair and over-sized dark glasses. He didn't doubt that the little man was what he said he was – some kind of trick rider looking for a job. He was also pretty sure the so-called director of entertainments wouldn't want to see him. But that wasn't his problem. He nodded the man through and told him where to go.

Joey walked unnoticed among the crowds of holiday-makers, with just the glasses and an Irish accent for a disguise. He didn't go to the entertainment director's office, but asked a camp official where he could find the other performers. He found an old comedian he'd seen in the Sunday night show drinking in a staff bar which had clearly missed out on the last few camp refurbishments. The man was half-cut already, slouching at a table, nursing a bottle of Newcastle Brown. Joey guessed that he would be happy to talk as long as there was a steady supply of free drinks.

On the subject of Giulio, he was voluble in his disdain. 'Miserable sod! I don't know why they keep him on.'

'I saw him on Sunday night. He looked pretty professional to me,' Joey said.

'Maybe he is, but when you've seen his act four hundred times, you begin to wish he was a tad more versatile.'

'Do you see him around much?'

'Why? What do you want to know for?'

Joey shrugged. 'I was just interested in what happens to these old performers.'

'I see him most days, before the show. Had a drink with him today – I bought as usual and he was as gloomy as ever.'

'Where does he go after the show?'

'Look, what is this? Why the fascination for an old Italian poof? Or are you one of them too?'

'No, I'm not. It's like I said, I was just wondering how a fella like that copes.'

'Well, he usually goes straight back to his cabin.'

When Joey guessed he had teased as much useful information as he was going to get from the cantankerous old comedian, he didn't ask him which Giulio's cabin was. Anyone would be able to tell him that.

As he extricated himself from the comic, Joey was already feeling disappointed about his mission. It didn't sound to him as if Giulio was behaving like a man who had just come into substantial funds. Reluctantly, Joey was preparing to scratch him from the list of potential runners, as easily as he had made him favourite on Sunday night.

When he walked into the clown's stuffy room five minutes later and saw his face, Joey knew he had to discount him.

Giulio's cabin had the damp, musty smell of a badly built pre-fab occupied by a man less than diligent about washing. The squalid little room contained a rickety wardrobe, a chest of drawers and a narrow bed beneath a grimy Indian bedspread. The stained walls were well covered with framed photographs, which seemed to span half a century of Giulio's life in various circuses. A dusty bronze statuette of a classic clown – some kind of award – stood on the chest of drawers alongside a greasy comb and a half empty bottle of Grappa.

Joey had taken off the dark glasses just outside the cabin door. Giulio, sitting hunched on his bed, looked up to see him standing in the doorway.

'*Dio!*' he gasped, eyes momentarily animated as Joey closed the flimsy door behind him. 'Joey? What are you doing here in this Godforsaken corner of Hell?'

'Is it that bad, Giulio?'

'Oh, yes, and I don't care any more. That makes it even worse.' His face grew longer and his dark eyes misted over. 'But why have you come here? Not to work, I hope?'

'No. To see you.'

'Why do you want to see an old clown like me?'

'To tell you the truth, Giulio, I want to find Ginger.'

Giulio's face puckered, as if at some painful memory. He stood up and walked a pace to the chest. He opened one of the drawers and took out two small, beautifully cut crystal liqueur glasses. 'Have a little Grappa with me?' he pleaded.

'Sure,' Joey nodded. 'Do you know,' he said, when he'd taken a sip of the bitter, herby fluid, 'when I was at the circus, I never knew you and Ginger were lovers. I never even realised either of you was gay.'

Giulio looked back at him. 'I know. Ginger never wanted you to know or feel threatened. You were so innocent.'

Joey nodded. 'I don't think I even knew what gay meant.'

'Ginger liked you very much, you know, but he didn't want to frighten you away by telling you. He knew you weren't like us, nor ever would be.'

The idea that Ginger had been harbouring this affection for him all the time they had shared the trailer hit Joey hard and uncomfortably. And yet, if Giulio was telling the truth, Ginger had disguised his feelings very convincingly.

Joey tried not to think about Ginger's intentions. 'Where is he now?' he asked.

'Why do you want to know?'

'It's . . . something I gave him before he went. I need it back.'

Joey knew it sounded lame, but Giulio didn't press.

'I don't know for sure,' he said. 'But he went off to Le Grand Cirque Fantastique du Midi. There were people there he'd worked with in Czechoslovakia, but that was ten years ago. Now . . .' Giulio heaved his shoulders sadly. 'I don't know. I haven't seen him or spoken to him since he left. He never even wrote. It was someone else who told me where he'd gone.'

As Giulio talked, Joey thought.

The demands had been made over the phone, and could have come from anywhere; the letter was from Nottingham, where the circus was. But the tape had come from France, postmarked Paris, which still left a wide field of possibility.

But Le Grand Cirque Fantastique du Midi was surely not going to be too hard to find in France in mid-summer.

Without hurting the feelings of the old Italian, Joey managed to bring their conversation to an end. He even evoked a pathetic smile of gratitude from Giulio by producing two fifty-pound notes.

'Here, I've had a bit of luck recently. Get yourself a nice present.'

'*Grazie*, Joey. You are a fine boy.'

'I'll come and see you again.'

'I may not be here, though.'

'Why not?'

'Can't you see? I'm not well. Look how thin I am.' He extended a dry, sinewy hand on a bony wrist. 'I've got AIDS,' he whispered. 'Don't tell anyone here, please. They don't know yet. They'll throw me out when they do.'

'Giulio, I'm sorry.' Joey knew how inadequate it sounded but the old clown had caught him unawares. 'How long have you had it?'

'From Ginger. That's another reason he would never touch you. But he was a flirt, he went with other boys.

That's why I went with Ivan.'

Joey held his breath. He hadn't dared ask directly about that relationship.

'With Ivan?' he prompted.

'Don't act like you didn't know. Ginger told you for sure. That's why he asked you to play that trick on Ivan: because he knew Sol Werner would come to watch that new routine, and then Ivan would be made to look a fool.'

Joey's heart stopped. He said nothing. He looked straight into Giulio's black eyes and tried to quell his trepidation.

'What did he tell you?' Giulio went on.

'He just said Ivan was such a bullying bastard, he deserved to fall and look a fool. I thought he'd tumble into the net – with nothing hurt but his pride.'

Giulio nodded, and sighed. 'I saw Ginger unclip the guy ropes,' he said quietly.

Joey could hardly believe what he was hearing. 'Are you telling me Ginger planned Ivan's death?'

'Oh, yes. He admitted it all to me afterwards, when I told him I'd seen him with the ropes.'

Joey couldn't contain the surge of shameful relief that suffused him. 'Giulio, thank God you told me this. For years I've blamed myself for Ivan's death.'

'This is why you want to see Ginger, I suppose?'

Joey nodded.

The clown put his hand on Joey's arm.

'If you still want to, and you do find him, tell him you saw me looking well and happy – not like I really am. And don't say where.'

Joey nodded sympathetically.

'You know something else?' Giulio went on. 'Ginger

never told anyone, but he boasted to me afterwards that he filmed the whole thing.'

Joey's face turned ashen. 'But what did he do with it?'

'I don't know. I never saw it. Is that what you want to find?'

'But you said Ginger liked me? He wouldn't use it against me, surely?'

Giulio shrugged. 'Who knows? Sometimes the distance between love and hate is very small.'

Joey drove home with these words pounding in his brain as he tried to fathom an aspect of human behaviour he hadn't encountered before. At the same time he realised that Giulio had been honest with him, and if it ever came to defending himself against a charge of murder, the old clown was the one vital witness who could tell a court the truth about what had happened.

Joey was already five miles from Yarmouth when a sudden thought occurred to him. He turned the car around and went back to find the old man and persuade him to write down everything he had said.

But when Joey got back to the holiday camp, Giulio wasn't in his room and no one knew where he'd gone. After half an hour of fruitless search, Joey slipped a note under his door with his phonc number on it, asking him to get in touch.

It was after one, dark and moonless, when Joey reached home, but there were still several lights on in his house. As he put his car away in the garage, he guessed that Danny must be there.

He unlocked the front door and stood in the hall for a

moment to work out where he was, but only the ponderous 'tock' of a long case clock broke the silence.

The door to his drawing-room stood ajar, showing a crack of light.

Joey seldom used this room; it was more suitable for large gatherings. He wondered what Danny had been up to.

He walked across the oak floor of the hall as quietly as he could, pushed open the door and looked inside.

In the middle of the room, sprawled across a large kilim rug, was the body of a mini-skirted woman. She wasn't moving, and from where Joey stood, she wasn't breathing either. For a few seconds, he feared the worst.

With his heart pounding, he hurried across the room and crouched beside the slender female form.

With a flood of relief, he saw the girl's chest rise and fall, lightly but regularly, and a strong smell of alcohol suggested the cause of her condition.

The relief was short-lived when he saw that it was Laura Seabourn.

He stood up and looked around for her companion.

Danny was lying full-length on a deep chesterfield. His mouth was open, emitting stertorous breaths. Lodged beside his head was an empty bottle which had contained double strength Russian vodka, presented to Joey by some misguided owner.

Before he tried to wake his brother, Joey checked around to see if there were any obvious signs of damage or disaster. Nothing appeared to have been disturbed.

Joey sighed. He thought of leaving them both where they were and dealing with them in the morning, but didn't relish having to tell her father what had happened. The first priority was to get Laura home.

He knelt down beside her and shook her gently, until her eyes flickered open. The confusion that first showed turned quickly to pleasure.

'Joey, where've you been?' she murmured. 'I've been waiting for you for hours.'

'You chose a great place to go to sleep,' he said.

Laura looked around her. 'Oh my God! It must have been all that vodka Danny gave me. It was really strong.'

'You should be tucked up in bed by now.'

She nodded in mock remorse. 'Well, we can go up to your bed, if you like?'

'Oh no we can't,' he said as firmly as he could. 'I'll run you home, before your dad finds out you're missing.'

'For God's sake, Joey, I'm not a schoolgirl. He knows I stay out.'

'Maybe, but not with me. Come on.'

'Don't you want to sleep with me, then?'

'Not tonight, and not when you're drunk.' He helped her from the ground with his hands under her shoulders.

'I'm probably better when I'm drunk,' she said, half turning so her face was just under his.

Joey's more basic male instincts needed little encouragement, but he stopped himself.

One kiss, he knew, and he'd be in all sorts of trouble. At the back of his mind, he was glad he'd had no more than a single glass of Grappa all evening.

'Well, I'm not going to find out tonight,' he said wryly. 'Come on, let's go.'

He half led, half dragged her from the room and across the hall. Once the cool of the night air hit her, she woke up a little and seemed to accept the inevitable.

She sank into the passenger seat of the Ferrari without arguing. Coolly, she hunted in the glove box for a

CD she liked, slotted it in and leaned back as he drove the few miles to Crowle House.

'Is Danny *really* your brother?' she asked.

'Yes. At least, we had the same mother.'

'He's completely different from you. I mean, he's such a nerd. When I turned up at your place, he thought I'd come to see him. He insisted on staying with me while I waited for you. Still,' she added, overlooking his shortcomings for a moment, 'he had some bloody good drink.'

Joey swung the car into the Seabourns' drive and pulled up in front of the house. He turned and looked at Laura.

'Danny's got strengths you'll never have, but he's vulnerable too, so just leave him alone, okay? If you promise me you won't come round again, I won't tell your father I found you pissed on my drawing-room floor.'

Laura didn't say a word as she climbed out of the car and flounced up the steps to let herself in through her parents' front door. It closed behind her and Joey drove away, hoping he hadn't woken the Seabourns.

When he walked back into his drawing-room, Danny was stirring. Joey looked down at him, shook his head with a weary smile and tip-toed from the room.

Chapter Seven

''Allo, Joey?' said a French voice.

His nerves were so on edge he jerked the cup he was holding and splashed coffee on to his jodhpurs. His first thought was that it was his blackmailer.

'Yes,' he croaked, and cleared his throat.

'I 'ope you are not ill, Joey. I want you to ride Isle de Rey for me again.'

Joey was so wrong-footed for a moment, he didn't know who was speaking to him, or even who Isle de Rey was.

''Allo, Joey? Are you there?'

'Yes, yes. Sorry, Captain. I was miles away. Where do you want me to ride him?'

'In the Grand Prix de St Cloud, next Sunday.'

Joey didn't need to look in his diary. 'You're on. How is he?'

'Missing you,' the French trainer said with a laugh.

Joey checked the travel arrangements with the French trainer and loosely discussed the possibility of a few other rides for him during the long Deauville meeting in August, before ringing off.

Joey picked up the phone again and dialled Barry's home number.

The Irishman answered after one ring and didn't sound as happy as usual.

'Hi, Barry,' Joey said as brightly as he could. 'I'm just phoning to let you know I've told Captain Zamowski I'll ride Isle de Rey in Paris on Sunday, and I've decided to stay on in France for a couple of days afterwards.'

'What!' he exploded. 'You can't do that! How am I going to make you champion jockey if you're not here?'

'Barry, I'm going.'

'But . . . where exactly are you going?'

'It doesn't matter where. I've got a couple of things I have to do, that's all.'

'My God, it's that Stephanie!' Barry laughed.

'Don't be ridiculous, of course it isn't. Look, just fix it for me, please. Say I'm taking a short break.'

'Joey . . .'

'Barry, you're supposed to work for me, remember?'

Joey could almost hear the resentment crackling down the line. But Barry backed down.

Joey got up from the table. He had half an hour to spare. Normally he would have used the time to take Roger for a quick run through the beech woods opposite his front drive. He decided he was damned if he'd give in to the pressure he was under, and whistled to his springer spaniel.

Roger leaped to his feet and bounced around his master's legs all the way up the drive. They had reached the gate and were about to cross the road when Danny arrived in the Range Rover.

He stopped the car when he saw Joey and wound down his window, emitting a barrage of house music.

Joey winced. Danny switched off his ignition.

'What are you doing back here now?' Joey asked.

'I'm ill. I've got a thumping headache. I told Mickey I was coming home.'

Mickey was Seabourn's head lad.

'He won't let you off for a hangover more than a couple of times,' Joey warned.

'I haven't got a hangover,' Danny said.

'Well, you deserve one.'

His brother ignored him. 'What did you do with Laura last night?'

'I found her asleep on the floor, so I picked her up and took her home.'

Danny pulled a face. 'Thanks. Did her dad catch her?'

'I don't know.'

'He'll go ape-shit if he hears about it. He'll sack me – even though I'm your brother.'

'I'd keep out of her way in future, if I were you. She's trouble and always will be.'

'How do you know?'

'She's just the type of girl who thrives on other people's failings.'

'Thanks,' Danny muttered sarcastically. 'I know what you mean, but I still wish I hadn't passed out.'

'Don't worry, she was beyond any action by the time I found her.'

Danny laughed like a man who has failed to get his bet on a horse that has just lost and drove on down to the house.

Joey looked after him for a moment before he turned and crossed the road into the woods with Roger.

Half an hour later, he walked back through the front of his house. As he pushed it open, it brushed over a small envelope. He picked it up. It was addressed in thick marker pen with the single word "JOEY".

With a sinking stomach, he tore it open and pulled out the inevitable Letraset note.

'We've had one hundred grand but you earned seven and a half last week. We'll have three. Same place – by next Tuesday.'

Joey was still staring at the note, feeling as helpless as a man drowning in quicksand, when he heard a car drive up to the house and a knock on his front door.

He pulled himself together and, putting on a smile, went to answer the door. It was Di, looking vaguely sheepish.

'Hi,' she said, head drooping in obvious embarrassment. 'Are you in?'

'What's it look like?'

'I mean, are you alone? Do you mind if I come in?'

'No, why should I?' He opened the door wider and beckoned her in.

'I wasn't too friendly at lunch last weekend, was I?'

'Weren't you?'

'You know perfectly well I wasn't, but Dick had given me a hell of a bollocking.'

'He suggested to me that you're having a scene with his former jockey.' Joey shrugged.

Di had followed him into the kitchen by now.

'Joey, I can't think why he said that. Of course I'm not having any kind of scene with Graham. I did fancy him once, but nothing ever happened.'

'It's none of my business anyway. Do you want a drink?'

'A quick glass of wine?'

Joey nodded and took a bottle of Chablis from the fridge. 'Anyway, did you want anything in particular?'

'I was just passing so I thought I'd pop in and apologise.'

'Apology accepted.'

'Oh, come on, Joey, don't be so uptight. That was a great night we had and you know it.'

He smiled at the memory, despite himself. 'Yeah, it was.'

'I suppose you'll be seeing the lovely Stephanie when you're in France for the Prix de St Cloud?'

'Not necessarily.'

'You mean, you haven't arranged anything?'

Joey grinned. 'If I had, do you think I'd tell you?'

'Sorr-ee.' Di drained her glass. 'Don't worry, I'm going. Thanks for the drink.'

Through his study window, he watched her get into her car and drive off faster than she had to, and wondered why she had really come to see him.

At the last minute, Barry decided to come to Longchamps with Joey, who couldn't reasonably refuse him a seat on his plane.

Nevertheless, despite a rational deduction that Barry couldn't have any part in blackmailing him, Joey was feeling strangely uncomfortable about the Irishman's presence.

But Barry was in his usual ebullient form once they reached Paris on the Saturday evening before the race.

'Far be it for me to lead you astray, Joey boy,' he said as their taxi pulled up outside the Bristol, 'but I think I might treat myself to dinner at the Taillevent tonight. You can watch and I'll tell you what it tastes like. How does that grab you?'

'You greedy bastard,' Joey laughed, knowing he could eat what he liked and still draw the lightest weights. 'Serve you right if I have to put up overweight tomorrow.'

In the morning, he rode work for Captain Zamowski. Later, Barry and he went shopping before heading off to the race course.

'I wonder if the lovely Stephanie will be here? I see her old man's got two runners today,' Barry said as they pulled into the jockeys' car park. He glanced sharply at Joey for his reaction.

Joey shrugged. 'As long as that bastard horse Sudden Spin isn't.'

The principal race was the third on the card. Barry had managed to fix up three more rides for Joey, but it wasn't until the Prix de St Cloud that, with conflicting emotions, Joey saw Stephanie.

She looked every bit as stunning as she had at the Prix du Jockey Club. She caught Joey's eye and smiled. Without thinking, he found himself smiling back.

He had not thought about her a lot since their first meeting. There was no doubting his physical attraction to her, but he suspected it would be short-lived once he made the inevitable comparison to Nina.

The Russian girl was much more his type; so much so that he couldn't think of anything about her that he didn't like. He still wasn't sure, though, that she felt the same about him.

When he came face to face with Stephanie, he found a surprising paradox: the more politely and charmingly he kept her at bay, the more eager she seemed.

Isle de Rey won his race on the bit and was ready to go round again. Joey earned a five-thousand-pound bonus (including five hundred for Barry) and went to join Zamowski and the grateful owner in his box.

He wasn't surprised to find that Monsieur Ducas and his daughter were already there. Zamowski had told him

Ducas was an old friend. There were several other girls in the box who all seemed keen to try out their English on Joey. He obliged, but had to call in Barry to help him out.

As they talked and joked, he tried to imagine how Nina would have coped in these surroundings. He was determined to find out very soon. That evening, though, he was saved from any temptation to stray by Barry's announcement that he wanted to get back to England. Joey left with him to return to the Hôtel Bristol and then saw him off in a taxi to Charles de Gaulle airport for a scheduled flight.

Back inside the hotel where Isle de Rey's owner had put him up, he pushed thoughts of Stephanie to the back of his mind and settled down to ring round and find out where the Cirque du Midi was currently performing.

On a Sunday night, there was no official body operating to tell him. With growing frustration, he dialled Nina's mobile number in England.

She sounded pleased to hear from him.

'Did you find Giulio?' she asked.

'Yes. Thanks for the message. I meant to ring you before. He's not too well so it wasn't much of an evening, but he told me to look for Ginger in Le Grand Cirque Fantastique du Midi. I'm in Paris now, trying to find out where it's pitched, but I can't find anyone to tell me. Do you know anyone who'd know?'

'Sure. There's an agent called Sol Werner who always knows where everyone is. I've got his number in London.'

Sol Werner. Joey hadn't thought of Werner for years until his name had cropped up in the conversation with Giulio the other evening.

Sol Werner, who had come to watch the Korsakov trapeze troupe's new routine the night Ivan and Mikhail had died.

Joey rang him.

'It's Joey Leatham here, Mr Werner. Nina Korsakov gave me your number.'

'Joey Leatham? The boy who was in the accident with her father? What can I do for a jockey who's making millions? I'm just a humble circus agent.'

'I'm in France, and I want to visit the Le Grand Cirque Fantastique du Midi.'

'Why do you want to do that?'

'I'm looking for someone.'

'Are you? Who is that?'

'A clown from Freddie Fielding's called Ginger.'

'Ginger. Heinrich Calaval. He's not there any more.'

Joey's heart fell. 'Do you know where he's working now?'

'No. In fact, I doubt he works. He's very sick – AIDS.' Sol Werner hissed the word with distaste. 'People can't risk a man like that in the circus.'

'Have you any idea about where he went?'

'No. It's of no interest to me when people have left the circus.'

'Who would know, then?'

'Maybe someone at the Cirque du Midi.'

'Okay. So where's it pitched now?'

'Somewhere near Paris, I think. Hold on.' Werner was evidently consulting a calendar. 'Yes. Near Versailles – between St Germain-en-Laye and Versailles. It shouldn't be hard to find.'

'Thanks, Mr Werner.'

'Sol – call me Sol. And maybe you can do something

for me. I've got other boys from the circus who would love to do what you have done. Maybe you could come and see me sometime.'

'Maybe,' Joey said, without conviction.

'Good. I'll be in touch.'

Joey wished he'd spent enough time at school to have learned a few words of French, at least enough to have understood the various and apparently contradictory directions he was given from the centre of Versailles to the circus. It took him an hour to find it, pitched in a woodland glade on the edge of the town.

He parked his unobtrusive rented Peugeot among a sea of cars and walked across to join the noisy throng heading for the big top.

This French circus was a much bigger, more diverse affair than the smaller outfits that still toured Britain. There were fewer restrictions or public bodies in France imposing bans on wild animal acts, and the French still took the circus seriously.

Joey had arrived just before the afternoon show. He thought he might as well go in and watch it: maybe he would see someone he knew.

Once again, sitting inside the big top, he found vivid memories of his circus life flooding back – most potently when the trapeze artists finally took over.

Joey had never become a fully fledged flyer himself, though he was close to it by the time his career in the circus came to its ignominious end, but watching the lithe figures of the young men gliding so gracefully through the air, he was soon reliving his own experiences.

Joey had started on the trapeze at the same time as

Tatyana Korsakov had been putting him through his paces with the horses. Ivan had taken on the much lengthier and more dangerous process of teaching him how to fly.

It was unusual for one family to be involved in two such different acts, but Ivan Fedorovich came from a long line of trapeze artists and Tatyana's family had performed on horses for several generations. It would have been a waste not to use both skills. So the Korsakovs had strengthened their hand considerably by being able to offer circus bosses two pivotal acts.

On the trapeze, Joey's size was in his favour. Ivan ordered him to get up and swing until any residual fear of heights had evaporated and he could swoop across the big top like a swallow, almost to the highest point of the canvas.

He had learned a few beginner's steps in flying – like letting go of his trapeze to grab a static bar – but it would be several years before he could perform twists and somersaults well enough to fly effectively in public. But once he had experienced the intense thrill of flying and was beginning to get it right, Nina's brothers offered him the encouragement normally reserved for family members.

They also started to tease him about his crush on Nina. Their father, as he put Joey through his paces on the trapeze, took every opportunity to tell him what he thought of his romantic ambitions.

'Do you think I would let my daughter have anything to do with a midget like you? A menial with no circus blood in his veins? Forget it, you little shrimp!'

As a result, the resentment Joey had developed for Ivan deepened every day. There was no let up in the abuse. The big Russian was well established as the circus bully, by far the strongest man there and probably the worst tempered. It was tacitly accepted that no one ever pushed him too far.

Once, when Joey had been alone with Giulio during a stop-over between pitches, the Italian had muttered reluctantly that the jugglers in the trailer next to the Korsakovs had heard Ivan beating his wife, his sons, even his daughter. When Joey pressed him for details, the clown clammed up; if stories like that found their way back to Ivan, it would only mean trouble and pain for the informant.

There was another, better known story of his beating a man to death in a Hungarian circus, so that he and his family had been forced to run, even managing to dodge the wary border guards on their way to the West.

Tatyana never spoke of it and her children claimed they were too young to remember what had happened. Besides, Nina and Mikhail had been born later, in France.

But the stories about Ivan the Terrible had persisted.

When the tormenting became too much for Joey, he would tell his friend Ginger. Ginger's attitude was ambivalent. There was no doubt, he agreed, that Ivan was a bully, but the little clown seemed to take the view that he was such a magnificent man that he was entitled to be one.

As the performance of Le Grand Cirque du Midi came to an end, Joey emerged from his recollections, sweating at the thought of the man who had made life such hell for him. Now it seemed, even from the grave, he was going to do it again.

Joey shivered and looked at the audience around him.

They were cheering and clapping happily, reluctantly preparing to leave. Joey had other plans.

Although he had recognised no names or faces among the performers, he still felt he had something in common with them all. He had no trouble blagging his way into the camp with pidgin English and a lot of smiling and nodding.

Once he was among the caravans and trailers, he spotted one of the clowns, still in make-up and costume.

'Hello,' said Joey.

''Allo. Do you want something?' the clown asked with a thick French accent.

'Yes.' Joey grinned. 'I'm looking for another clown, one called Ginger. Do you know him?'

The man stopped and looked at him. 'Ginger?' he said. 'He was 'ere, but 'e 'as gone since. Maybe one year.'

'I have to find him, it's very important,' Joey said urgently.

The performer shrugged the pointed shoulders of his emerald satin costume. 'Maybe I can find out where he is. Come.'

The man, with a milk-white face and huge black semi-circles over his eyes, led Joey to a small trailer on the edge of the camp. He beckoned him up the steps. Inside, he took a bottle down from a shelf. 'Calva?'

Joey had never drunk Calvados, despite his annual visits to Deauville, but thought he'd risk a glass of the Normandy cider brandy, out of politeness.

The clown poured an inch of the clear, viscous fluid into a tumbler which he plonked on a table in front of Joey. He turned back to his shelves and took down one of the three books there and handed it over.

'I don't read good. Maybe you find his name. He write it for me when he went.'

Joey racked his brains, trying to remember the real name and surname that Sol Werner had used for Ginger.

'What was his real name?' he asked.

'Heinrich.'

'That's it,' Joey said with satisfaction. 'Heinrich Calaval.'

He thumbed to the 'C' section of the address book, which was full of names, addresses and telephone numbers – all in different hands and mostly with what looked like a job description; each, as far as Joey could tell, in a different language.

He found Calaval, scrawled in a script he recognised at once, with an address in an outer suburb of Paris.

Joey read it out.

The clown nodded. 'Yes 'e tell me. Is a cheap *pension* 'e used to stay.'

Joey copied the address into his diary then knocked back the Calvados at a gulp, and regretted it as soon as he had.

He thanked the clown warmly, resisted the offer of another drink, and walked from the circus compound as fast as he could.

He was standing in the crowded car park, trying to remember where he had put his car, when an old Citroën van, grey and corrugated and coming from the opposite direction, trundled past him and stopped.

Joey didn't give it a thought, until two pairs of hands grabbed him, spun him round and hurled him through the open back doors of the low-slung vehicle.

His face scraped along the dirty floor and he breathed

in familiar smells of hay and animal feed. The doors were banged shut behind him. Before he could turn, the weight of two men crashed down on his back and shoulders and an old hessian sack was pulled over his head.

Joey lay trembling in the dark, wondering what was going to happen. He tried to lift his head, despite knowing he couldn't see anything through the sack.

He lay there for a few moments, waiting for someone to say something, but no one spoke. The van was still jolting slowly across the lumpy field where the circus audience had parked their cars.

Abruptly and without warning the assault came. Joey was kicked viciously in the lower abdomen, below the diaphragm, until he was left gasping and helpless while his pockets were rifled. Then one of his attackers finally addressed him.

'You wanna be careful.' It was an Englishman – a voice Joey didn't know and a gravelly Essex accent. 'People don't want you to go looking for trouble in case you get hurt. But if you do, next time you won't go home alive.'

The doors were opened and a moment later he felt himself being picked up and heaved from the back of the moving van.

There was a split second before his head crashed on to the rutted track, then nothing.

He came round a few seconds later and dragged the musty sack off his head. His preliminary check for injuries identified nothing more serious than a sore shoulder and a headache. He looked around. There didn't seem to be anyone about to witness what had happened. He stood and searched through his pockets.

Everything had gone. Wallet, car keys, passport.

Joey looked up and gazed across the fast emptying car park. There was no sign of the van, and he hadn't seen any of the people who had attacked him. He hadn't heard them either; they had been very careful, very professional. He wondered who the hell they were.

If Ginger was the main man, it wasn't surprising he wanted to stop Joey pursuing any investigations in France.

But the only people who knew he was actively looking for Ginger and could have warned him were Giulio, Sol Werner and Nina. And at least one of the heavies had been English.

He bundled up the old sack and ran up to some higher ground to get a view over the remaining parked cars and orientate himself. He still couldn't see the Citroën van, or his rented Peugeot.

He thought for a moment before walking briskly towards the gate where the cars were still streaming out. He started thumbing a lift, and almost at once a Mercedes with two or three people in it stopped for him.

The driver, with his window down and a cigarette hanging from his lip, looked at Joey, making an instant appraisal. He nodded and muttered something over his shoulder. A back door was opened and a sultry, dark-haired girl beckoned Joey inside.

He leaped in gratefully and pulled the door shut just as the car reached the gate and turned on to the road.

'*Merci*,' he said, exhausting most of his vocabulary in one hit.

'English?' the girl asked at once.

Joey nodded.

'Are you with the circus?' she asked in an American

accent, indicating with her big black eyes that his size suggested it.

Joey shook his head. 'Not any more. I went to look up an old friend. Then I was mugged – just now. They took everything: money, passport, car, the lot. I need to get back to my hotel in Paris to make some phone calls.'

The driver turned and glanced at him in the mirror. 'Where are you staying?' Although obviously native French, he also spoke with a slight American accent.

'The Bristol,' Joey answered.

'We can take you there. But if you want to make some calls, use this.' He passed a cell phone over his shoulder.

'Thanks,' Joey said, and passed it to the girl. 'My French is lousy. Can you get the number of a place called the Ducas Gallery for me? It's in the Faubourg St Honoré.'

'Sure,' the girl said, and tapped into enquiries.

A minute later, Joey was talking to Stephanie, who sounded pleased he had rung, though surprised to hear he was still in France.

'Yeah,' he said, 'there were a couple of things I wanted to do, but I've got a bit of a problem. I hoped maybe you could help me out?'

'Of course I will – you saved my life. And you gave me a lift from Newmarket,' she laughed.

'I've been robbed, out near Versailles,' he said, feeling slightly foolish. 'They took everything. Of course, I could just go back to my hotel and get the plane to pick me up at Bernes but I've got a couple more things I need to check out first.'

'No problem. Where are you now?'

Joey turned to the girl beside him. 'Where are we?'

'On the A13 into Paris.'

'Whose car are you in?' Stephanie asked.

'Some good people who say they'll take me into Paris.'

'Put me on to the driver, I'll ask him if he can drop you at my father's place in St Germain-en-Laye and tell him how to get there. It's not too far. I'll meet you there in an hour. You could stay for dinner,' she added.

'Thanks.' Joey handed the phone to the driver.

Twenty minutes later, the Mercedes turned off a quiet tree-lined road into an elliptical drive that swept up to a classic French mansion in stone and slate. They stopped before a broad flight of stone steps leading up to the front door.

Joey was impressed. He'd been to dozens of big flashy houses – like the McMahons' – endowed with all the trappings of wealth: ostentatious pools, snooker rooms, cocktail bars, gyms and Jacuzzis. These were the things people had often already acquired before they started owning expensive racehorses. But this house, a kind of mini-château set in a story-book garden, showed impeccable taste.

Joey thanked the people who had driven him and got out of the car, just as the front door was opened by a tiny Indo-Chinese woman who appeared to be expecting him.

He waved goodbye to his rescuers and walked up the steps to the fine stone portico. When he reached the top, he found himself, for once, towering over the maid by an inch or so.

'Mam'selle Stephanie say you come.' She opened the door wider and led him across a wide hall into a pleasantly cool, dark salon where the smell of piquant pot pourri lingered.

The maid left him, to reappear five minutes later with a tray of tea and cakes.

Joey thanked her and drank the tea, wondering about Stephanie and her father. Monsieur Ducas was evidently a very wealthy man. The room in which Joey sat was full of exquisite furniture and pictures.

These were things that he had learned to appreciate in recent years, for themselves, not the mere possession of them. But these surroundings, the quiet air of old money, he knew he could never aspire to, and Stephanie was undeniably part of this world.

Nina, despite her exotic Slav origins, would always be closer to him in temperament and experience – though that didn't mean the French girl was without her attractions.

But for now he had more pressing problems to deal with.

He guessed that the attack in the circus car park was meant to be a low-key beating, just a warning to let him know that his blackmailer was keeping close tabs on him. While he hadn't personally told many people he was going to stay in France for a few days, his presence at Longchamps on Sunday would have been announced in the racing pages of hundreds of newspapers across Europe.

To have had someone follow him after racing the day before would have been easy to arrange, especially when he was off his guard.

But what was puzzling him was that the people who'd temporarily hijacked him must have assumed he hadn't found out anything. Or that they hadn't been concerned about any information he might have gathered at the circus.

He knew for certain that no one had followed him from the circus to St Germain-en-Laye. He'd had plenty of opportunities to check from the back seat of the Mercedes.

His next task was to trace the address he had been given for Ginger. He was hoping Stephanie would give some help with that.

He crossed the room to the sweeping floor-length windows which overlooked the drive. As he surveyed the formal beauty of the Ducas' garden, spread out below, a gleaming Aston Martin convertible appeared through the gates. Stephanie was driving, her hair loose and tangled from the wind.

Joey watched her park and run up the steps. He heard her footsteps click across the hall and a moment later she appeared in the doorway. A smile spread across her face. 'Oh, good. You're here.'

She walked over to Joey by the window and stood close to him, accentuating the difference in their heights.

'Hello,' he said. 'Thanks for letting me come. When I was in trouble, your name was the first that came into my head.'

'What happened to you?'

'I went out to Versailles to track down an old friend – and I got mugged when I was leaving.'

'They even took your car?' she asked.

'Yes.' Joey gestured helplessly. 'They dumped me out of a van. I hit my head and blacked out.'

'My God, some mugging! But they were crazy. They won't be able to use the car for ages after you've reported it.'

He shrugged. 'I don't know about that. They could change the number, respray it – whatever. Anyway, that's the first thing I have to do, report everything I lost: my passport, my credit cards, and ten thousand francs I'll never see again.'

'Use my father's office, if you like?' Stephanie showed him to a room across the hall. 'And you can stay the night here if you don't want to go back into Paris,' she added.

'Thanks, that'd be great, but I need to borrow a car as well. I got an address for this guy I'm looking for – a little hotel in Clichy – and I want to follow it up before . . .' Joey hesitated.

'Before what?'

'Just as soon as I can.'

'That's fine. Make your calls, have a shower and freshen up, then I'll drive you, Okay?'

Joey stripped off his clothes and stepped gratefully into the shower. He realised he was far better off staying away from the Bristol tonight. He must have been followed from the hotel this morning and it seemed more than likely that someone would still be watching for him there.

Back in the bedroom to which Stephanie had shown him, he checked himself for injuries. There was nothing worse than a few bruises. He'd hit his shoulder badly as well as his head when he'd been chucked out of the van, but it hadn't stiffened up. He lay down on his bed feeling that even if he hadn't won the first round, he hadn't lost it either.

His final show-down with Ginger, though, might turn out to be another matter altogether.

As dusk fell, Stephanie drove him up to Clichy on the western outskirts of Paris. Joey hadn't told her why he wanted to see his friend, but had warned her that there could be some trouble, and still she had insisted.

With Joey map-reading, she turned her car into a dull street of villas built in the early nineteenth century. The place had evidently taken a few steps down the social scale since then. The Aston Martin looked much too opulent among the old cars that lined the road. Joey checked the address he'd been given for the *pension*'s number. It was a house slightly larger than the others, with a freshly painted front door and respectably clean if fussy lace curtains in the front windows. Joey couldn't reconcile this fastidious gentility with his memory of the outspoken, rebellious Ginger.

Wondering if their arrival had already been observed, he asked Stephanie to carry on to the end of the street and park a short distance away. He let himself out of the big sports car and walked back but stopped a hundred metres short of the *pension*. The only other pedestrians were a pair of old women creeping home nervously with a bag of shopping. A few more people came and went but it was a quarter of an hour before anyone emerged from Ginger's lodging house. Then a middle-aged woman walked briskly towards Joey. She passed him with hardly a glance. He called after her.

'*Madame*?'

She turned warily, ready to run, until she took in his unthreatening size and appearance. '*Oui*?'

'Heinrich Calaval? You *connais*?'

'English?'

Joey nodded.

'You ask, do I know Heinrich Calaval?'

'Yes.'

'I did. He lodged in our house for a short time, about

one year ago. But he is ill. My mother send him to some other place, where they look after him.'

'Do you know where?'

'No. My mother has died now, but if you want I can find out. If it is important?'

'It is.'

The woman hesitated a moment then declared, 'Okay.'

Joey had to make up his mind, on the strength of this very brief acquaintance, if she could be trusted or was simply tricking him into coming into the house.

He decided to follow her back to the *pension*. Inside, she asked him to wait on an upright chair in an old-fashioned, brightly tiled hall. A minute or two later she reappeared with a small piece of paper on which she'd scrawled an address in a town on the Seine, fifty miles west of Paris.

'Thanks,' he said, and from his pocket pulled out one of the five-hundred-franc notes Stephanie had given him, which he handed to the astonished woman.

She was still staring at it as he turned and walked out of the front door, back to where Stephanie was waiting.

'Well?' she asked, excited by the prospect of a chase.

'He's gone – to some kind of hospice, fifty miles west of here.'

'Let's go, then,' she said eagerly.

Joey shook his head. 'No, not tonight. It's a convent. I'll go in the morning.'

'Okay. I'll take you.'

Joey wasn't so sure. 'You want to go and see some old guy dying of AIDS?'

'No, but I'll drive you there. Now if we go home, my father will be back and we can have dinner. He will be pleased to see you and talk about horses.'

Joey smiled to himself. He'd almost forgotten that he made his living riding horses.

He enjoyed dinner more than he had expected. They talked widely, all three of them, about pictures and racing. Monsieur Ducas was uncondescending about art and showed a genuine respect for Joey's own talents. No mention was made of a Madame Ducas – whether she was alive or dead – and Joey didn't ask, but he sensed that Stephanie and her father were very close.

After a large glass of the softest old Cognac Joey had ever tasted, he and Stephanie went upstairs. When they reached his bedroom door, Stephanie lingered only a moment and, unprompted, kissed him on the lips before slipping away.

In his room, Joey felt relieved. For though his physical excitement was undeniable, he couldn't ignore an absurd but deep sense of loyalty towards Nina. He lay in bed, thinking of her and longing to rid himself of the black cloud which hung over his future.

In the morning, Joey persuaded Stephanie that she wouldn't enjoy the next stage of the search for Ginger. Privately, he thought it more than possible that this was when things would get nasty.

She agreed reluctantly, but insisted that he keep in touch with her via her mobile. She gave him the keys to a small spare BMW, and he promised her he would be back again for dinner that evening.

Joey drove away from Paris against a fierce incoming tide of impatient commuters, but once he had broken free from the clinging suburbs, quickly reached the small town where the convent hospice stood, on the outskirts and set still further apart, as if the local people were anxious not to rub shoulders with a place dedicated to housing the incurably ill and dying.

Joey watched the building from a few hundred yards away before he made up his mind what to do.

It had occurred to him that someone might have become alerted to his presence after his visit to the *pension*. Although he had performed a few simple manoeuvres on the way and was sure that no one was behind him, they might still have pre-empted his journey here.

There were few people coming and going from the hospital besides the nuns who ran it. It was the sight of them, serene and at peace with themselves despite their daily contact with the terminally ill, which finally gave Joey the confidence to go in. It seemed to him very unlikely that he would be attacked in a place like this.

He had noticed a pair of nuns, surprisingly young, he'd thought, carrying a fork and hoe down to a vegetable garden.

Skirting round the perimeter of the convent's grounds, he found the two women with their habits tucked into rubber boots, hoeing between rows of healthy-looking onions.

'Hello, sisters,' he ventured. 'Does either of you speak English?'

'*Anglais*? *Non*.' Both of them shook their heads.

Joey's face must have shown his frustration.

'*Attendez*,' one of them said, and walked back up the path to the convent buildings.

Joey smiled with conscious restraint at the one who had stayed behind, and was relieved when a few moments later the other reappeared with a third nun, clearly older and presumably wiser.

'Hello? What can we do for you?' she asked him in fluent, lightly accented English.

'Well, sister,' he said, 'I had heard there's a man I want to see living here, but I hadn't arranged a meeting and didn't want to just arrive unannounced.'

'Who is it you want to see?'

'Heinrich Calaval.'

The nun shook her head slowly. 'I'm afraid he is no longer here.'

Joey panicked. Ginger must have heard that he was on his way.

'When . . . when did he go?'

'The first week of June.'

Before the first blackmail letter! No wonder the heavies at the circus hadn't bothered to stop him coming here. He guessed this must be where the trail stopped.

Unless this nun knew, and was prepared to tell him where Ginger had gone?

'Do you know where he went?'

She looked upward and pointed a finger at the thick grey clouds above them. 'To heaven, God willing. He had done everything to purge himself and make his peace with the Lord before he went.'

'You mean,' Joey said fatuously, 'he's dead?'

'Yes.' The nun nodded. 'He has gone to join his Lord; he is happy now.'

Joey's mind went blank.

For a few desperate, irrational seconds, he thought that maybe this beatific-looking woman was in on the blackmail plot. After all, he thought, it must cost a mint of money to keep a Gothic pile like this going.

He looked at her again, and rejected the thought.

But to learn Ginger had died five weeks ago!

'When was it exactly, sister?'

'I can tell you, because I know who you are now. Heinrich saw you on television, saving the young woman from the mad horse. He was so pleased and proud of you. You are Joey, are you not?'

He nodded.

'He didn't know until then that you had become a famous jockey. But he found out where you lived and asked me to post a parcel to you. Something very precious, he said. Something he wanted you to know that he was sorry for.'

'Yes,' Joey said. 'I got the parcel. But when did he die?'

'The very next day.'

The words hit him like a punch to the diaphragm.

Not only had Ginger never received the £100,000, but even if he had been responsible for the original blackmail letter, he was dead long before it was posted from Nottingham.

And from the way this nun was talking, he had hardly been in the frame of mind for blackmail. It seemed to Joey from her expression that she had been fond of Ginger, even approving, certainly prepared to forgive a man the kind of life that led to a death such as his.

The nun seemed to sense his surprise. 'He may have done some terrible things in his life, Joey, but in the end he found God, who forgave him. You must believe me, he died happy.'

He tried to understand what the nun was saying but couldn't make sense of it.

He had no doubt now that Ginger had sent the tape. But, if the nun was right, it was someone else who was extorting money from him. Somewhere, though, there had to be a connection with Ginger.

As Joey stared up at the grey stone walls of the convent, he felt the first drops of a summer shower fall from the heavy clouds overhead.

'Sister,' he said, 'Ginger was a good friend to me once. Will you tell me where he's buried?'

'Of course.' She glanced at the sky. 'Come inside.'

Ten minutes later, the rain had set in and Joey was in his car, following directions to the fourth and final address he'd been given for Ginger.

The cemetery was on the other side of the Seine. He drove through the damp little town, over an ancient bridge and up the bank on the far side to the walled graveyard perched near the top.

He parked outside a pair of high, rusty wrought-iron gates and got out of his car. The wind whipped up the river valley, howled up the bank and spat rain into his face. He pulled his jacket closer around him and let himself into the gloomy burial ground.

He found Ginger's grave where the nun had told him he would – a humble mound of earth still, with a small cross at one end. The remains of one modest bouquet of flowers drooped from a plastic vase – placed there, Joey guessed, by the saintly sisters.

No one else had been at the burial, the nun had told him. The tragic man must have led a life full of setbacks and disappointments. And yet, Joey realised now, Ginger had been nothing but kind and considerate with him, and had asked very few favours in return.

Help in getting his revenge on Ivan Korsakov had been one of those few.

Two years after Joey had joined the circus, it was pitched

on Putney Common. This was a popular site among the circus people. They played there for ten days and liked the chance to get into the middle of London. It was early autumn; the evenings were still mild but shortening fast – usually a good time for the circus.

Three days after they had arrived there and the big top was up, Ginger came back to the caravan late one night while Joey was watching television, exhausted from a strenuous day's rehearsal. The trapeze troupe had been working for over a year on a new, potentially spectacular routine in which two smaller 'flyers' – Joey and Mikhail – caught the big catcher – Ivan.

Although to aficionados of the circus the idea of the catcher himself flying and being caught was crazy enough to be exciting, the movement still lacked finesse and drama and Ivan was getting impatient, as much with his own performance as with the boys'. Nevertheless, the day before he had announced that he had persuaded Sol Werner, one of the leading London circus agents, to come for a private preview of the sensational new act.

Joey switched off the television when he saw Ginger's face. The clown looked as if he had seen his mother's ghost – simultaneously terrified and mystified.

'The shits . . .' he hissed. 'The lying, cheating, sons of whores!'

'Who? What?' Joey asked. He'd never seen Ginger so openly upset or heard him complain so bitterly.

'That big stupid bastard Ivan Fedorovich thinks he can take whoever he wants . . .'

'What's he done?' Joey asked, glad to hear anything disparaging about the man in the circus whom he most thoroughly disliked.

Ginger pulled himself up, as if abruptly aware of

having committed an indiscretion.

'I can't say, but I tell you, that man deserves to be completely humiliated.' Ginger fell silent and gazed speculatively at Joey. 'I have an idea,' he said slowly. 'Maybe you can help me.'

And Joey had helped.

Joey looked at the pathetic oblong of grey-brown earth and contemplated the irony of what Ginger had since, unwittingly, unleashed. He thought of that evening with him, and all the other long evenings when he had first arrived at the circus, and Ginger had told him story after story: of acrobats, elephant trainers, lion tamers and trapeze artists; of how he and his family had survived then fled the stifling communism of post-war Prague.

Joey found himself close to tears. Decisively, he turned and walked out of the cemetery to the BMW, drove back down to the town and found a florist's shop.

He managed to convey to a confused assistant that he wanted a dozen arum lilies and a tasteful disposable vase. Once he had them, he took them back to the cemetery and placed the vase in the middle of the hummock of earth that covered his dead friend.

He wondered why he was doing it. He didn't believe in life after death, but maybe Ginger did, and Joey was doing this for him.

Feeling better for leaving his tribute, he walked back through the drizzle to the car and set off for St Germain-en-Laye. He would see Stephanie to thank her, excuse himself from dinner, and arrange to go home on the next scheduled flight.

Now that he had traced Ginger, Joey was almost relieved he could scratch him from his list of suspects.

But he was still no closer to finding his blackmailer. With an effort, he resigned himself to starting the search all over again, back at square one, when all he had to go on was a Nottingham post-mark, an unidentifiable voice – and a list of people who might, just possibly, have played Ginger's video before he had.

Joey tried to reach Stephanie on her mobile phone and at the gallery, without success. To fill in time, he stopped at a riverside café for lunch. When he came out, the rain had blown off and the clouds had broken to unveil a strong sun. He tried Stephanie's number again. This time he got through.

'Hi,' he said. 'I've done all I can here.'

'Did you find your friend?'

'In a manner of speaking – in a cemetery.'

'Oh. What are you going to do now?'

'I have to get back to England and do some work.'

'I see.' Stephanie's disappointment was obvious. 'But I'll see you when you bring back the car?'

'Will you be there?'

'I will.'

She appeared at the front door as soon as he turned into the drive.

He left the car at the bottom of the steps and walked up to greet her. 'Thanks for all your help, you've been brilliant. You must tell me what I owe you?'

'A dinner, just the two of us, soon.' She walked before him into the cool of the dark hall.

Joey smiled. 'I think I could manage that. Sorry about this evening, but my agent's going mad that I'm not riding.'

'When are you leaving?'

'I couldn't get a scheduled flight tonight, so my plane's coming over to an airfield outside Versailles in about three hours. The Bristol is sending my bags over now.'

'Great! So you don't have to go right away?'

'Not for a couple of hours.'

'It's a beautiful afternoon. Would you like a swim?'

'Now that's a good idea.'

Joey glanced up at her. Just a slight wrinkling of her perfectly shaped nose gave the hint that, maybe, there was more than a swim being proposed.

'Got any spare swimming trunks?' he asked.

'Who needs them?' Stephanie half turned her head and raised her eyebrows a fraction. 'There's no one around. Come on.'

She glided down the hall to a grand old conservatory. They passed through the palms and spice bushes, out on to a broad, stone-flagged terrace. Beyond this, a large swimming pool had been situated unobtrusively, encompassed on all four sides by a high yew hedge. A margin of soft, beautifully tended grass surrounded the paving stones at the edge of the pool.

In one corner of the enclosure stood a mock Chinese pavilion which served as a changing room.

Stephanie evidently didn't need to use it. She reached one arm behind her back and unzipped her short chiffon dress. It floated down round her ankles on to the grass; she stepped out of it, kicked off her sling-back shoes, unclipped her bra and dropped it on the dress.

Joey had followed her through the gap in the perimeter hedge. Without realising it, he had stopped in his tracks and was gawping at her like a teenager. She wriggled seductively out of her pants and turned round to face him. He couldn't tear his eyes from the sight of her long, tanned body; the proud-nippled breasts, soft but self-supporting.

He had seen beautiful naked women before, but Stephanie's body had been presented to him so unexpectedly that, for a moment, he didn't know how to react.

She knew it, and grinned. She said nothing, though, just turned to take three quick strides and dive elegantly into the water. Joey still hadn't moved when her head broke the surface at the other end of the pool.

'Aren't you coming in?' she called.

Joey, embarrassed by his awkward reaction to her nakedness, was still rooted to the spot.

The girl had turned and was drifting in a leisurely back stroke. Joey felt excitement course through him at the sight of her legs lazily opening and closing; her nipples and pubis breaking the lapping surface of the water.

He turned away, acknowledging that, right then, the man in him wanted nothing more than to make love to her, as she evidently assumed he would.

But he resented that assumption; and the idea of his abandoning control before such unsubtle tactics. He turned and looked up at the magnificent house.

'Come on, Joey. It's lovely. It will cool you down,' Stephanie's voice floated to him across the water.

He looked back at her and shrugged. 'Okay. Why not?'

He took off his clothes until he was standing in a pair of sky blue briefs on the edge of the pool, presenting a well-tanned, hard-muscled figure.

'Joey,' Stephanie admonished, 'you can't swim in those.'

Ignoring her remark, he lifted himself on to his toes,

flexed his knees and sprang up to perform a neat jack-knife into the cool blue depths. Hugging the bottom of the pool, he looked up through the glittering water to where two long brown legs trod water. He swam well past the girl and broke the surface at the other end.

When he turned, there was no sign of her. The sun was striking the water and it was impossible to see through the glare.

Suddenly, the touch of her hands on his thighs had him caught between conflicting thoughts and desires. He used his hands to grab his pants as she tried to slip them down.

She tickled him under his arm. He laughed and let go. She had the pants down over his calves before he knew it and she faced him with a mischievous smile. Now, unlike on land, their eyes were level.

Stephanie put a hand on one of his buttocks and squeezed. 'What's the matter, Joey?'

He plunged sideways to escape her, reached the side of the pool and heaved himself up the ladder.

He snatched up his shirt and wrapped it round his waist to conceal the effect she had had on him. Part of him was thankful for his lucky escape from committing a major indiscretion; another longed to plunge straight back into the cool water.

She followed him up the steps, dangling his pants from her index finger.

Joey hesitated. To run would have been absurd, but he knew if she touched him again, his resistance would ebb.

He put up a hand like a policeman on point duty. 'Stephanie, I'm not ready for this, not now anyway. I've got too many other things on my mind.'

She stopped short as if she had walked into a wall.

Then, regaining her poise, she gave a small regretful pout and shrugged her shoulders. 'Okay. But I thought you wanted to.'

'Have you any towels?'

'In the pavilion.'

Feeling ridiculously guilty, Joey tried to walk with some semblance of dignity to the decorative building. He opened the door and found several towels on a rack. He wrapped one around himself, picked one up for Stephanie and went out to mend bridges, wondering what he had done to get himself into this position.

She was smiling, still naked, still holding his pants. He passed her the towel. When she started to rub herself down, he had to look away.

'Well,' she said, 'I guess the swim cooled you off more than I meant it to.' She started to walk back towards the house. 'We'd better get you packed and over to the airfield, or you might have to stay another night.'

Joey was relieved to find his pilot already waiting in the Cessna when he and Stephanie arrived at the small airfield.

He gave her an awkward kiss and mumbled that he would see her soon.

She gave him a wry smile and lifted one eyebrow a fraction. 'I hope so, Joey. Good luck.'

Ten minutes into his journey, he was hit by a thought that made him feel sick with anxiety. He had been so sure of finding Ginger, and that his old friend was the culprit, that he had done nothing about paying the additional three thousand pounds into the building society, as the blackmailer had instructed. And he'd been told to get it there by Tuesday at the latest. It was already

Tuesday, but he couldn't do anything over the phone; he didn't have the number of the building society account. And by the time they got back to Newmarket, the banks would be closed.

He realised with a sinking stomach that now he would find out just how serious these people were.

Chapter Eight

Joey arrived in Newmarket as the sun sank towards the dark ridge of the Devil's Dyke. A taxi was waiting at the racecourse to take him home.

He was thankful that neither Barry nor Danny was at the farm. He needed more time alone to sort out his thoughts.

There was a string of messages on his answerphone and half a dozen faxes waiting for him, but nothing from the blackmailer.

He looked up the account number of the building society and immediately faxed instructions to his bank for the transfer of three thousand pounds from his own account first thing next morning.

When he'd done that, he relaxed a little and rang back all the people who had left messages. The last call he made was to Dick Seabourn. Di Lambert answered.

'You're working late, Di.' Joey laughed to disguise the pressure he was under.

'Yes, there was a whole lot of entries to finish off. How was France?'

'Great,' he lied.

'I hope it was worth it. You missed two winners here.'

'I know, but you've got to leave a little for the rest.'

'Don't get too cocky.'

'Is Dick there?' asked Joey. 'I wanted a word about tomorrow.'

'No, but I'll ask him to call you as soon as he's back. He'll want you out in the morning, I expect.'

Joey put the phone down, wondering how the hell he was going to cope with riding while the threat was still hanging over him. He didn't want to sit on another horse or do anything else until he'd dealt with the extortionists. At that moment, more than anything, he wanted to confide in someone about the mess he was in.

He thought of Nina. He could have skirted round the facts and used her as a sounding-board, but he needed specific advice; as much as he longed for her comfort, he knew she wasn't the one to give it. In terms of wisdom and experience, Dick would have been the ideal person, but Joey could hardly go to his boss and tell him he was being blackmailed – for killing a former boss!

There was Giulio, of course. Although he hadn't contacted Joey since their conversation in Yarmouth, he had seemed sympathetic enough and knew exactly what had gone on at the circus. Joey still wanted to get his testimony down on paper and, besides, the clown might have an idea who else could have found out about the existence of the videotape.

The sad old clown wasn't an ideal candidate for a supportive role, but Joey ruefully had to accept that he was all there was. After racing at Yarmouth next day, Joey decided to go round to Summertown – assuming the tape hadn't been revealed to the world by then.

He switched on the TV but it failed to take his mind off the horrendous prospect of the tape's being released. He stood up and wandered about, trying to think what was missing, until he realised Roger wasn't there.

When Danny was looking after the dog, he usually took him into work with him, to exercise him during the day. If he went out in the evenings, he left him in his cottage, although sometimes he'd been known to forget about Roger and the poor dog had been found sitting by Joey's front door, waiting for his master's return.

Joey picked up a bunch of keys and walked out of the house and the few yards to the cottage. He let himself in, waiting for the usual noisy, hyperactive greeting. But there was no sign of Roger. He looked in the kitchen and saw that the dog bowl was empty. Danny would have filled it up earlier that evening before going out, so at least the dog had eaten; maybe Danny had taken Roger with him.

With a sigh of disappointment, Joey went out. Although the sun had set, it was still light, and instead of going back into his own house, Joey decided to walk round the outside to the garden and see how his roses were doing.

He found Roger on the stone-flagged path outside the back door, lying on his side, quite still.

Joey didn't have to look closer to know that he was never going to move again. With tears welling in his eyes, he ran the last few steps and knelt down beside him. A pair of opaque staring eyes seemed to reproach him as he stroked his hand across the shaggy coat and felt the body, still warm underneath.

Joey looked up and scanned the garden. It was empty, save for a few birds singing their evening finale.

'Bastards!' he hissed in fear and anger.

This was the next, inevitable development of the

endless nightmare he'd found himself in; he wondered where it would end.

Brimming over with guilt, he leaned down and slid his hands under the stiffening corpse. He lifted Roger and carried him slowly, almost ceremonially, to the large beech tree on the far side of the lawn.

He laid the dog gently on the ground beneath the spreading branches and walked back to fetch a spade from the garden shed.

When Joey had buried his old friend, he walked from the garden into the kitchen and heard his phone ringing.

'Found your dog yet?' Joey heard the distorted voice with a shudder of dread. 'I thought after Monday you'd have got the message. But you've been a naughty boy, haven't you? I said by Tuesday, remember? You must understand that I'm serious.' The strange distortion of the voice gave the words added menace. 'I don't know what you think you were up to in France yesterday, but you found you were wasting your time, didn't you? When you should have been doing as you were told. Now, I'm just putting a copy of the tape into a Jiffy bag but I can't decide whether to send it to the *News of the World*, the Jockey Club or the DPP. What do you think?'

'I transferred the money this evening,' Joey blurted, ashamed of his fear but with a picture of Roger in his head. 'It'll be in the account first thing tomorrow.'

'That's good.' Joey thought he detected relief in the hollow, grating voice. 'Don't keep me waiting, or next time it won't be just a lethal injection in a dog.'

When he'd put the phone down, Joey took a deep breath to calm his jangling nerves. He went back out to his garden and the warm dusk. He wanted to yell, to vent his frustration, grief, anger and shame in a mighty scream; instead, in silence, he walked across to Roger's freshly dug grave and stood for several minutes below the great beech.

It seemed impossible that a life could be turned upside down so suddenly and so completely by something that had happened more than ten long years before, but from where he stood now, Joey couldn't see any way out. He breathed deeply, hoping the evening air would calm thoughts that were running out of control. He wondered if now was the time to call the police. If he told them to go and see Giulio, the old Italian could tell them exactly what had happened in the big top the day Ivan Korsakov died.

Decisively, Joey walked back into the house. He picked up the phone while he pulled a directory from a shelf. He found the number of the police station in Newmarket; his finger hovered over the buttons. He thought of the police watching the tape, then remembered he didn't have a copy of it. There was no point going to them and saying someone was blackmailing him, without being able to show them why.

Of course, he could alert them that it was coming and get his defence in first. But, eventually, they would see the tape and Joey couldn't believe they'd be prepared to accept that his intention that day had been nothing more serious than to make the Russian trapeze artist look foolish.

He put the phone down without dialling.

Tomorrow he would go and see Giulio again, and tell him what had been happening.

In the meantime, he sat down and made a list of everyone he could think of who might be tempted to blackmail him, given the opportunity.

Ten minutes later, Joey gazed at the dozen or so names on the pad in front of him. It seemed to him that any of them could have been willing to extort money from him, and several were poor enough to need it badly. Although none of them had any connection with the circus, there was one, and only one, who knew that Ginger existed and that Joey had lodged in his trailer for nearly two years.

Danny, his brother.

Reluctantly, Joey turned over the possibility in his mind. In common with several other names on the list, Danny was also in a position to judge fairly accurately what Joey's earnings were; but then, anyone with a reasonable knowledge of racing and the daily papers could have done the same.

He sighed. Danny may have had his difficult moments, but Joey was sure that his heart was in the right place. He admitted that, as a lad who couldn't ride work, Danny was paid a wage which was less than he would have received in unemployment benefit. True, he was housed for free, but as far as Joey could see, most of what he earned went on drink, cigarettes and gambling.

Maybe, Joey found himself thinking, Danny had decided it was time to strike out for himself; but he stopped pursuing this line abruptly. Even if Danny was harbouring an unreasonable and well-disguised resentment, there was no way he could have got hold of a copy of the tape. It was impossible that he had been to France to see Ginger – he'd have been missed from the yard. And what would his relationship be with the man who had spoken to Joey on the phone?

With relief, he concluded that his brother simply was not a suspect.

He thought back to the moment he had first seen the tape. He had found it in a padded envelope which had not been open – or had it been and then carefully resealed? After the four weeks that had passed since he had destroyed it, he simply couldn't remember if it had shown any signs of tampering.

He wasn't in any doubt that it was Ginger who'd sent it; the nun at the French hospice had confirmed that.

He tried to remember who had been in Barry's office on the day the tape had lain about on the coffee table.

Barry, Di, Dick and Graham – maybe a few others, as well as Danny.

Graham Street was on Joey's list, and it wasn't the first time his name had featured in the parade of suspects. Graham was up to his neck in debt, and patently disliked Joey for taking his job.

But if Graham had opened the package and seen the tape on the day it arrived, he wouldn't have had the patience to wait three weeks before asking for money.

In the end, Joey came to the conclusion that there was no certainty that his blackmailers had anything to do with racing, although there was obviously a local contact.

At the same time, if it was someone from the circus, why had they only now decided to use their knowledge?

He was still sitting at the table in his kitchen, staring at the names he had scrawled, when Dick Seabourn rang.

'Hello, Joey. Feeling better?'

'What?'

'I thought you had the 'flu? Barry said that was why you didn't come back from Paris on Sunday night.'

'Oh, yes. I'm fine now, thanks. Di said you may need me tomorrow morning?'

'Yes, please. Scaramanga – first lot.'

'Fine. I'll see you then.'

'Are you all right, Joey? You sound rather agitated.'

'No. I'm fine, guv'nor, I promise.'

'Good. I'll see you tomorrow then.'

Joey put down the phone with a shaking hand and, breaking one of his own rules, took four sleeping pills and went to bed.

He went to see Giulio straight after racing the next day. He had taken the Range Rover and parked it in the town, not far from the holiday camp. He made his way to the old clown's cabin, unchallenged until he reached it.

There he found a policeman standing outside the flimsy door with its flaking paint.

'What's going on?' Joey asked.

'I'm sorry, sir, you can't go in there. There's been an accident.'

'But I've come to see Giulio. He's an old friend. What's happened?'

'I'm afraid Mr Santini was found dead in here this morning, sir. A murder enquiry is currently in progress. The DI looking after the case will want to talk to you if you were a friend of the deceased.'

Joey was still rocking on his heels from the shock.

'Are you all right, sir?' The policeman stepped forward solicitously.

'No,' he said. 'Of course I'm bloody not! What else do you expect? I've come to see an old friend for a chat, and you tell me he was murdered last night.'

'I'm sorry, sir. Though we're not confirming it was a case of murder yet,' the policeman backtracked. 'The medical officer said he died from cardiac failure, but someone was round earlier and gave him a thorough hiding which triggered the heart attack.'

'Oh my God!' Joey groaned. He already had a horrible suspicion that this was connected with his own recent visit. 'Where is he now?'

'They took him away, once they'd done the photos and that.'

'If I can help . . .'

'Hang on. I'll tell DI Jacobs about you. He's in one of the offices here.' The policeman unclipped his radio and got through to the detective. When he was finished, he told Joey how to get to the temporary incident room, where the DI was waiting for him.

As Joey followed the directions, he felt like a drowning man. In the last few days, he had built Giulio up as his principal witness for the defence, the lynch pin of the case for his innocence, not just in a court of law but in his own eyes, too, and ultimately Nina's. He cursed himself for not having come back sooner.

Joey was trying to face up to the fact that the only two people besides himself who'd known what had really happened to Ivan and Mikhail were now dead.

He pushed open the door to some kind of accounts office, furnished with a pair of steel desks and shelves full of files and cash books.

The policeman in charge of the investigation was sitting at one of the desks, with a junior plain clothes man at the other. DI Jacobs was a Londoner – an East Ender, Joey guessed, from his sharp, nasal accent. He had the fast talk and quick gestures of the inner city.

They seemed out of place in the sleepy semi-rustic air of the Norfolk coast.

As he waved Joey impatiently towards a battered metal chair, he seemed to be raking in every visible detail and nuance of his appearance.

'You're a jockey, aren't you? What's your name?'

'Joey Leatham.' He nodded at them both.

The detective constable gave an embarrassed smile.

'And what brings a top jockey to a seedy dump like this – to visit an elderly homosexual entertainer?'

'He was an old friend. I used to work with him years ago.'

'Where was that?'

'At Freddie Fielding's Circus.'

'You used to be in the circus?' Jacobs said with disbelief.

'He was, guv,' the DC butted in importantly. 'I read it once, in one of the papers.'

The DI raised his eyebrows. 'Really?' He turned back to Joey. 'Did you often come and see him?'

'No. When I visited him last week it was the first time in about ten years. I was trying to track down another fella I knew – he'd been a friend of Giulio's, too.'

'Okay,' Jacobs said. 'Now, I've dealt with a lot of enquiries like this in my time and I can tell you that when a man dies in these circumstances, and I hear someone who hasn't seen him for years has come visiting the week before, everything tells me there's a connection.' He looked straight into Joey's eyes without blinking.

Joey stared back. 'And is there always?'

The DI gave a hint of a smile. 'No, not always, but nearly always.'

'Well, this must be one of those rare exceptions.

Because my coming to see him, and his being attacked, are a total coincidence. There's nothing to connect the two.'

'And you've come back, which isn't par for the course,' the detective added. 'You knew Giulio, you say, though you hadn't seen anything of him in the last ten years? So, tell me, why do *you* think somebody might want to harm or frighten him?'

Joey shrugged his shoulders and shook his head. 'I haven't got a clue. He was gay, as you know. I suppose that might have something to do with it. Or maybe someone was trying to rob him.'

'There wasn't a lot to steal, was there?'

'I gave him a hundred quid last week. People have killed for less than that, haven't they?'

'Yes, Mr Leatham, they have,' Jacobs said impatiently. 'Now, let's get down to business. Where were you last night?'

Joey shivered and felt himself turn pale. He had seen and spoken to no one between talking to Seabourn on the phone at about eight-thirty and meeting him on Newmarket Heath just after seven the next morning.

'I was at home, alone. The last phone call I got was at eight-thirty and I didn't see anyone until about seven this morning.'

'So, you had plenty of time to drive up here, do the deed, and scarper off back home?'

'Yes.'

'Is that what you did?'

'No.'

DI Jacobs laughed. 'All right. Let's have your dabs. Constable?'

The junior officer opened an ink pad and placed a

pair of fingerprint cards on the desk in front of Joey.

'D'you mind, sir?'

He shook his head slowly and allowed his finger and thumb tips to be pressed on to the soft black pad and gently rolled from side to side on the small squares provided.

'And now, would you expectorate into this beaker, please?'

'Would I what?'

'Spit – into this plastic cup.'

'What for?'

'I don't have to tell you, Joey, but I will. It looks as though old Giulio had a drink with someone. There were a couple of glasses with the remains of some filthy Italian drink in them.'

'Grappa. I had a glass with him when I came to see him.'

'That was nearly a week ago, you said, wasn't it? I doubt we'll get much of a reading from them, then. Let's hope not anyway. Now, let's just get your version of events down on paper, to make sure I haven't made any mistakes.'

Twenty minutes later, inwardly in turmoil but calm on the surface, Joey left the stuffy office and walked to his car as quickly as he could.

He was back home in an hour – speeding seemed a negligible offence compared to the horror he was facing. As soon as he was in the house, he picked up the phone and dialled Nina's number.

'Nina? It's Joey.'

'Hello.'

He stiffened at the coldness of her voice. 'Are you okay, Nina?'

'I'm okay, but I just heard about Giulio.'

Joey didn't reply at once. He could tell that he would have to put his case very carefully if he didn't want a major misunderstanding to develop.

'That's what I was ringing about. I've just come back from Yarmouth.'

'What were you doing over there?'

'I went over to see Giulio again. When I got there, the police told me he'd been attacked and had died.'

'Look, Joey, you're going to have to tell me what's going on. Why you've been running around looking for him and Ginger when you hadn't been near the circus for years?'

'That's why I rang,' he said again. 'To tell you. I've found myself mixed up in something that goes back a long way – to when I was in the circus. I thought I could deal with it on my own, but now it's turned nasty.'

Nina didn't answer at once. 'Okay,' she finally relented. 'But I wish I hadn't heard about Giulio from someone else first.'

'Can I come up and see you tonight?'

'Do you know where I am?'

Joey had rung her mobile; it hadn't occurred to him that the circus might have moved on from Nottingham.

'No, I don't.'

'You'd better get your skates on, then. We've just arrived at a pitch in Lichfield, north of Birmingham. Do you know it?'

'I think so. I can look it up.'

'Are you still coming, then?'

He glanced at his watch. 'Yeah. I'll see you in an hour or so.'

'Don't kill yourself, Joey.'

The gently uttered words lingered in his mind as he powered his Ferrari up the Midlands motorways to the small Staffordshire city.

He found the circus in a municipal park near the town centre. It had only arrived that day and the big top was half up. He drove across the thin grass and stopped his car beside the collection of lorries and trailers that made a temporary village for the circus people.

He found Nina in her trailer.

She looked to him as spectacularly attractive as she had last time, but greeted him so icily that his heart sank.

'Come on, I'm taking you out,' he said as brightly as he could.

'But I've got to deal with the horses.'

He got the impression she was nervous of going outside the circus – surroundings which had always cocooned her from the real world. It had never occurred to him before that Nina could be nervous about anything.

'Get someone else to do it,' he suggested. 'I really need to talk to you away from here.'

She looked at him for a moment, undecided.

'I'll have a walk round for ten minutes while you change,' he urged.

Nina opened her mouth to object, then with a sigh changed her mind. 'Okay.'

Joey left her trailer knowing that she was going to want a plausible explanation for what he'd been doing – a convincing reason for his search for Ginger and Giulio.

He looked around, recognising many of the caravans and trailers from the old days. As on his last visit, a wave of intense nostalgia washed over him, but this time mingled with a dread of ever having to go back to make his living here, if the other, thriving career he had made for himself was brought abruptly to an end. And overall there was the nagging fear that somewhere within this strange nomadic community, someone was watching him; laughing as Joey waited, sick with frustration, for the next demand. Someone who had had no scruples about killing Roger, and Giulio.

He suddenly felt a fool for coming.

He couldn't tell Nina enough to answer her doubts about him – not without admitting his own part in the accident – and, if he was being watched by someone in the circus, it wouldn't help her if they thought she knew what was going on. He was going to have to pick his way very carefully through the truth.

'Still carrying a torch for Nina, then?' a familiar deep voice said just behind him. Joey spun round to find Ivor Wimsatt watching him.

He hadn't seen the ring-master closely or to speak to on his last visit. Wimsatt hadn't changed much; he had a few more wrinkles and the grey at his temples had spread to cover most of his head.

'Hello, Mr Wimsatt. I just thought I'd come and see how everyone was.' Joey tried to speak lightly.

'Didn't take too long to get up from Newmarket in that nice little red car, I shouldn't think. If you're waiting for Nina, come into my trailer.'

Joey didn't want to talk to Wimsatt, but couldn't think of an excuse fast enough so followed the boss into his lavish caravan.

'Drink?' Wimsatt's hand hovered in front of a cluster of bottles on a shelf.

'No, thanks. I haven't got time.'

Wimsatt shrugged off the refusal. 'I heard you were

back the other week,' he said, faintly accusatory, 'but you never came to see me.'

'That was a quick visit, too.'

As Joey's eyes ranged around the caravan, recalling the first time he'd seen it the day he'd arrived at the circus, they landed, almost without registering it, on a padded envelope with a French stamp and a Paris post-mark.

His heart lurched.

'Maybe I will have a drink,' he said huskily. 'A vodka.'

Wimsatt turned back to the shelf which contained bottles of every conceivable shape and colour.

Joey waited until Wimsatt handed him a glass of Stolichnaya.

He cleared his throat. 'What's this you've had from France?' he asked as lightly as he could, reaching over to pick up the package.

Wimsatt threw him a puzzled, faintly resentful look and took the package from him. He put in his hand, pulled out an unlabelled videotape and shrugged his shoulders.

'It's nothing; just a tape of an act I said I'd look at. Sol Werner said I should see it.'

Joey stiffened.

'Sol Werner?' he asked, almost unconsciously.

'You must remember Sol?' Wimsatt said testily. The tape is of a riding act – no use to me, of course, as long as I've got Nina. Anyway,' he went on brusquely, 'I heard last time you came you were looking for Ginger.'

'Yeah,' Joey answered blandly.

'And Giulio.'

He nodded.

'I could have told you Ginger was dead.'

'How come you knew when no one else here did?'

'He used to send me a card now and again. The nuns at the hospice wrote to me.'

'You mean, he kept in contact with you after he left?'

'We went back a long way, me and Ginger. But never mind that. What I want to know is what the hell happened to Giulio? I heard you were looking for him, too, then last night somebody beat him so badly he died, just after you'd been to see him for the first time in years. Why was that?' Wimsatt was glaring at Joey by the time he finished the question.

'That's what the police asked me, and I told them – God knows.'

'Oh, no.' Wimsatt shook his head. 'There's got to be a connection.'

Joey saw a sudden coldness in the ring-master's eyes and tried to hide his own uneasiness. 'All I did was ask him where I could find Ginger. I followed it up until I found the hospice outside Paris, but Ginger had died there about a month ago.'

'And why were you so keen to see him?'

'Because he wrote to me – it must have been just before he died. He'd seen me on French television, the nuns said. It was the first I'd heard of him in years. When I knew I had a few days to spare in France, it seemed like a good idea to look him up.'

'I didn't know jockeys could just take days off when they wanted?' Wimsatt said sceptically.

Joey dredged up another lie. 'I had the 'flu, not badly but enough to keep me off peak form.' He wondered why he owed Wimsatt an explanation. 'But I was sorry to miss Ginger; he was a good friend to me when I first came to this circus.'

'Maybe he wasn't such a good friend as you think.'

Joey looked sharply at Wimsatt who seemed to be having second thoughts about what he'd just said.

'What do you mean?' asked Joey.

'It doesn't matter. But I have to tell you, there are a lot of people here wondering who killed Giulio.' Wimsatt paused, eyes narrowed and knuckles protruding whitely. 'And if you don't want to make any more enemies than you've got already, take my advice and keep away from Nina Korsakov.'

Joey recognised that the chips were down.

'Thanks, Mr Wimsatt, but I don't think I'll listen to your advice.'

He turned and opened the door to let himself out. He didn't look back, stamping down the wooden steps, seething with angry suspicion.

Nina was overdressed, but Joey didn't care; with a woman as stunning as she, few men would have minded if she'd worn a ball gown to McDonald's.

She looked at the Ferrari distrustfully before lowering herself into the bucket seat. 'I hope this thing isn't as fast as it looks?'

'Only when I want it to be.'

They crawled out of the circus compound and on to the road outside the park. Joey headed for the centre of the small city. He'd looked up a guide and found a small Italian restaurant listed.

The waiters beamed when he walked in with Nina; beautiful women were always welcome, especially on a quiet Wednesday.

Joey wished their first dinner together could have been at a less fraught moment in his life, though he was well aware of the irony that it was precisely because of the blackmail threat that he had finally returned to the circus – and to Nina.

They sat either side of a small round table with a candlestick in a wax-dribbled bottle as the main source of light. When they'd dealt with the business of ordering dinner, Joey leaned back and looked at Nina.

She seemed surprisingly vulnerable – sad and uncertain.

'What's the matter?' he asked.

She forced a smile and straightened up. 'I'm okay, really. It's Ivor . . . the trouble is, ever since Diego went, he's been trying to get me to move in with him.'

'What happened to Sharon?'

'Oh, she walked out on him five or six years ago.'

Joey saw now why Wimsatt had been so hostile, and his hunch that the ring-master might have been behind the blackmail plot suddenly seemed less likely.

'Have you . . . you know, been out with him much?'

'You mean, have I been to bed with him?'

Joey nodded and held his breath.

She shook her head. 'No way. But he's been coming on very strong recently. He bought me this ring.' She waggled her right hand at him to show off a large diamond with a cluster of small rubies round it. Joey didn't know much about jewellery but he guessed he was looking at something worth several, if not tens of thousands of pounds.

'When did he give you that?'

'Last week. And he's booked a house in Barbados for a month in the winter, and wants me to come.'

'He's splashing out a bit! The old circus must be making a few bob at last.'

'I don't know about that. I think the audiences have been down, and they don't seem to be getting any better.'

Joey looked at her. He spoke as lightly as he could. 'Has he been buying much else for himself recently?'

Nina laughed. 'Yes, a bloody great car – a Bentley – and he was showing me pictures of a farm back in Essex he says he's going to bid for.'

'How the hell's he paying for all this?'

Nina shrugged. 'He'd never tell me anything like that. But there always was a rumour that he had money somewhere.'

'Would you choose this life-style, if you had money?'

Nina looked back at him, hurt. 'Do you think it's such a terrible life I lead?'

'I'd like to show you another one,' he said.

She didn't answer. A waiter had arrived with their first courses and placed them on the table with a lot of prattle. Joey acknowledged him, but didn't speak.

Nina's eyes had dropped to her hands for a moment. Joey saw her fists tighten before she lifted her eyes to meet his. 'Don't mess around with me,' she said quietly when the waiter had gone. 'I've found out more about you since you last visited. I could hardly believe it but they say you're a rich man now, and famous.'

He dismissed this with a shrug. 'Only to people who follow racing.'

'That's quite a lot of people. Anyway, you must be living a life-style that's miles from the circus. That's why I want to know why you suddenly turned up, and why Giulio's dead?'

'What makes you so sure I had anything to do with that?'

Nina looked guilty. 'Ivor – he said you had good

reasons for stopping Giulio talking about old times.'

'But, Nina, if I wanted to stop him talking, I'd have done it years ago, wouldn't I? Did you tell Wimsatt I was coming this evening?'

'No, but he knew you'd been before, to Nottingham.'

'Look, I've seen the police; they took my fingerprints and everything. They don't think I had anything to do with Giulio's death or they'd have charged me. If Wimsatt says I did, maybe it's because *he's* got something to hide.'

'Like what?' Nina asked.

'Well, there was a rumour that someone had deliberately loosened the guys to the safety net when your father and Mikhail were killed.' Joey felt guilty that he was suggesting Wimsatt was involved, when he already knew it had been Ginger.

Nina looked at him sharply, then shrugged her shoulders. 'There would be, wouldn't there? Anyway, if someone had loosened them on purpose, how the hell did they know he was going to fall that day? He hadn't fallen doing that act for a year or so, had he, since you'd first started practising it?'

'No . . .' Joey tried to think fast, ashamed that he still didn't have the courage to tell her the truth.

Nina shook her head. 'I think this is all a fairy story.'

'Then why did someone kill Giulio? I went to see him because Ginger got in touch with me just before he died, but he didn't tell me where I could find him. Remember, that's why I came back to the circus in the first place? So, Giulio tells me where I can find Ginger and I follow it up. But he also tells me his theory about those rumours and when I come back to tell him what I've found, he's dead. In other words, someone doesn't want him repeating what he'd told me.'

'Who do you think it is, then?'

'I don't know. I wish I did,' he added with feeling.

'Those poor old clowns,' Nina said. 'They were always such sad characters, weren't they? But to die like that, in a grotty little holiday camp, with no one around to care . . .'

'I care, and I'm going to find out who killed him,' Joey promised. 'If you hear anything about it, you'll tell me, won't you?'

'If it means I'll find out the truth about what happened to Mischa, then of course I will.'

Joey winced at that thought. Only when he was sure he could convince her of what he had agreed with Ginger at the time would he tell her the whole story, in the hope that he hadn't overestimated her capacity for forgiveness.

'Have you got a gap between shows coming up?'

Nina nodded. 'Yes, we've got three days off after we finish here. We've got to park up out in the country near Chester before we pitch there.'

'Come on down and see me then. Just ring me, and I'll pick you up from the station – unless you've learned to drive?'

'No, I bloody haven't.' She laughed at herself. 'The boys do it all for me.'

'The boys?'

'The Spanish boys who ride for me.'

'Are all the Cossack Riders Spanish, then?'

'Yes,' she laughed again.

After that, Joey tried to keep the conversation off the threat which had been looming over his life for the last month. To his surprise, it was easy to forget, for a while, that he wasn't just enjoying himself, catching up with an old friend with whom he'd shared a lot of youthful experiences.

They were the last customers lingering over a glass of Sambucca when Nina said they should go.

'Haven't you got to be up exercising some racehorse first thing in the morning?'

'Probably.' He grinned. 'You should come and do it too, some time.'

Nina nodded. 'Yes, I think I'd like that. I've started watching the racing on TV,' she admitted. 'Your riding's improved.'

'Thanks! Come on, I'll drop you back at your trailer.'

Joey stopped the Ferrari outside the park and turned off the engine. 'I hope I'll see you next week?'

Nina looked at him by the dim light of a street lamp twenty yards away. She leaned across and gave him a quick kiss on the cheek. 'You will.'

She turned and let herself out of the car and disappeared into the darkness with a little flick of her wrist in parting.

Barry Mannion let himself into Joey's house, wondering where his friend and client had gone. Joey had disappeared after his last ride at Yarmouth races without a word about where he was going.

Barry was nervous; Joey's behaviour had been strange recently. He seemed permanently distracted and kept forgetting what he had been told. He was producing results by instinct rather than design.

And then there was the bizarre business of Roger. The spaniel, Joey had said, choked on a bone and died. No vet had been involved. Danny said the animal was as right as rain when he'd gone out at eight-thirty on

Tuesday night, an hour before Joey himself had got back from France. And no one had left any bones out.

Barry rummaged around Joey's desk, trying to find the Ferrari's insurance policy which was running out, and which he had promised to renew for half the price.

On top of the desk, a parking ticket caught his eye.

It had been given in Yarmouth – three hours after Joey had left the racecourse that day, and on the other side of town.

Barry wondered what on earth he had been doing there, and out of habit tried to guess the reason.

He still hadn't thought of anything plausible by the time he was climbing into his old Porsche to head back to Newmarket for some rest and recreation. He let the problem drop.

In the big hotel in the town, where he regularly met a few like-minded friends for the first part of the evening, the subject of Yarmouth cropped up again.

'Evening, Barry.' Di Lambert was just leaving with a wad of papers under her arm. 'Have you seen Joey?'

'I have not. He left after the fourth and I never saw him again. Why?'

'One of his old colleagues has been in the news.'

'Who's that?'

'Some old clown – Giulio something or other – found beaten to death at a holiday camp in Yarmouth.'

Barry's eyes nearly popped out. 'Yarmouth? Good God!'

'What about it?'

'Well, we were racing there today, for God's sake.'

'So?'

'So, Joey disappeared early, and I know for a fact he was still in Yarmouth three hours later, and over the side of town where that place is.'

'Maybe he'd heard.'

'Then why didn't he tell me? I wonder what in hell he's up to?'

'Barry, what are you talking about? Why should he be up to anything?'

'Listen, let me get you a drink. I want a word. Do you have time?'

'Okay,' Di gave in. 'A large vodka and I'm all yours.'

A few moments later they were installed with drinks at a corner table.

'What did you want?' Di asked.

'The fact is, I'm worried about Joey. He's been acting really strangely for the last few weeks. Then he took those days off in France, and his dog died, and he shot off to that place where that fella was killed. And he keeps disappearing – being careful not to tell me where.'

'Come on, Barry – you're his agent, not his nanny. Why should he tell you everything he does?'

'It's just that he always used to.'

Di grinned at his forlorn expression. 'Look, Joey's riding as well as ever – better, if anything. I shouldn't worry about it. I'll keep an eye on him for you.'

Chapter Nine

'Joey, they want you up in the commentary box for an interview,' Barry said, poking his head round the door of the jockeys' changing room at Sandown. Joey got up from the bench and walked over to him.

'I told you, Barry, I don't want to do any interviews.'

He had had another phone call at six-thirty that morning. The blackmailer knew he'd been to Summertown; he felt as if he were living in a glass box, like a stripper he'd once seen in a club one of his owners had taken him to. It was as if the whole world was spying on him, watching everything he did, while under the spotlight behind the glass he couldn't look out and see the watchers.

'Come on, for Christ's sake!' Barry was saying, close to losing his temper – something he seldom did. 'You've just won a big race and you're twenty-four winners ahead in the championship. The punters have a right to hear what you've got to say.'

'Well, I'm not saying it today. Sorry, Barry. I told you this morning – no interviews for the time being.'

'But why the hell not?'

'Because I've got a few things on my mind that need sorting out.'

'Joey, you don't have that option. You're in the entertainment business now, and entertainers have to please their public.'

'That's crap, Barry. The punters are interested in what horses win, and marginally interested in who's ridden them. They couldn't give a damn about my views on the meaning of life. Now, I've got a big race to ride in a moment, so if you don't mind, I'll get changed.'

'. . . and this must be one of the most spectacular rides ever seen in British racing!' The television commentator took a deep breath and resumed his excited coverage of the race from the commentary box at Sandown. 'Joey Leatham was *spun round* Scaramanga by a slipping saddle! He ended up *under* his horse's belly! In the most dazzling piece of horsemanship I personally have ever witnessed, which must surely hark back to Joey's days as a circus rider, he pulled himself back on to Scaramanga's back and still managed to ride the finish of a lifetime, to force the colt home by a whisker!'

Nina gazed, incredulous, at the television in her caravan. She knew many circus riders but few who could have pulled off the stunt Joey just had – and on a galloping three-year-old thoroughbred, not a highly schooled, ten-year-old Lusitano.

She was more impressed by what she'd just witnessed than anything she'd heard about Joey's career.

She was almost scared by what she was feeling for him. It wasn't something that had happened to her before. Even with Diego, with whom she'd been briefly infatuated, she had always been in control, known that she called the shots and could choose to have him as and when she wanted.

But Joey, younger than she, and smaller, was so talented, positive and energetic, his compact physique at least as beautiful as Diego's. More than that, it was a new and exciting experience for her to talk to a man with an active mind, who listened to her and was ready to open up and be honest with her without making it seem like weakness.

Circus people tended to think that admitting a problem of any sort was admitting their own failure, and the whole ethos of the big top was centred on complete abnegation of the idea of failure.

Joey, Nina had noticed, wasn't scared to admit his problems, but didn't appear any less of a man because of that.

She was still thinking of him when she went to the stable tent later that evening. One of the Spaniards was already there, giving the horses a final check.

'It's all right, Miguel. I'll finish them off.'

'Okay, Señorita Nina. Two of them not too good; others fine.'

'I'll have a look.'

When he had gone, Nina took her time inspecting both ailing horses. She guessed they were suffering from a cold, which was easy to treat.

She enjoyed the smells and quiet sounds of the stable tent, and the distant sounds of the circus people enjoying their leisure for a few days while the circus wasn't performing.

She went to the back of the tent and opened up a trunk of animal medicines beside a stack of hay bales.

She ignored the sound of flapping canvas at the entrance to the old military marquee. The soft footfalls across the grassy floor were lost among the stamping and snorting of the ten horses.

It was only when she stood up with a bottle in her hand and turned around that she found herself looking straight into the staring, intoxicated eyes of Ivor Wimsatt.

'Hello, my beauty,' he hiccuped.

She winced at the waft of sour brandy on his breath. She took a step back and to one side, automatically lifting the bottle to protect herself. 'Mr Wimsatt! What do you want?'

'Don't call me *Mr* Wimsatt. I'm Ivor, remember?'

'Sorry, Ivor, but I'm busy. Two of my horses are sick.' She tried to step round him. He moved with her, blocking her way, advancing slightly so that she was pressed back against the hay bales. 'What are you trying to do?'

He chortled. 'You don't want to stop me. You know you want me.'

Nina squirmed between the stocky little man and the teetering pile of hay. 'For God's sake!'

'Come on.' Wimsatt's cajoling tone turned nasty. 'You can't stop me anyway.'

He grasped her blouse in both hands and tore it open. Nina dropped the bottle and tried to strike him. But Wimsatt was too strong; he thrust his hands clumsily behind her back, breaking the flimsy clip of her bra, dragging it off together with the blouse.

He almost drooled as he looked at her naked breasts jutting proudly. Before she had time to get her breath, he grabbed the waistband of her jeans and, with startling strength, ripped the zip apart.

She pummelled him with her fists but made no impression. He was leaning heavily against her now, and she felt the whole stack of bales begin to shift until suddenly they collapsed and he was horizontally over her, then leaning back briefly to snatch at her jeans and pants and pull them off her legs, taking her shoes with them.

She felt the hay scratching her legs and naked back under the impact of his body, crushing hers again as he fumbled with his flies in a lustful frenzy.

At the same time, he muttered a breathless litany of savage endearments, oblivious to her wildly hammering fists.

Grunting angrily, he was trying to thrust himself into her. She wanted to scream but gagged instead, almost choking in disgust, as he failed and semen spurted over the inside of her thighs.

Once spent, he collapsed, panting and wheezing, temporarily weakened. Nina grabbed the chance to heave him off and shove him to one side.

Her first instinct was to scream and beg for help from anyone who would come, until she stood up and looked down on her naked, degraded body, and shuddered with shame.

She turned and looked at the man who had all but raped her. The sight of his leering sweaty face was too much for her. She picked up the discarded medicine bottle, lunged forward and brought it smashing down on his head.

Wimsatt's eyes closed and he fell back, comatose.

In the brief respite that followed, she turned her attention to herself. She felt filthy; in urgent need of a wash. She grabbed the nearest water bucket and tipped the cold contents over her thighs, scouring herself afterwards with a rough cloth.

She dragged her clothes back on, praying that none of

the Spaniards would come in and see what had happened.

When she was dressed in her ruined jeans and ragged blouse, she looked down at Wimsatt who was beginning to stir. She picked up a metal feed scoop, crashed it down on his head and left him bleeding on the straw.

Later, on her own in her trailer, she let herself go. She sobbed until she was calm enough to pick up the phone and dial Joey's number in Newmarket.

To her bitter disappointment, she was connected to a recorded message with Joey's voice inviting her to ring a mobile number if she wanted to.

Joey was just starting up the M11 the next morning, on his way back from Jimmy McMahon's. He'd spent the night there after winning the Eclipse at Sandown.

'Hello?'

'Hello, Joey?'

'Nina?' He tried to keep a tremor of excitement out of his voice.

'Yes. Joey . . . something horrible's happened here.'

He heard the frightened note in her voice. 'What is it?' he said, brought down to earth at once.

'I was attacked last night.'

He immediately thought of Roger, and Giulio.

'Attacked? How? Why?'

Nina found she was struggling to explain. 'Sexually,' she said finally.

'Oh my God!' he gasped. 'I'll come up. Where are you?'

'Near Chester, on the Wrexham road. But don't come to the pitch. There's no point. I haven't told anyone here, and I don't want to.'

'But . . .' he started to protest.

'No,' she said. 'I beg you.'

Joey fought back his frustration. He burned to deal viciously with the man who could do this to Nina. 'Where can I meet you?'

'Outside Chester. There's a Little Chef on the ring road. How long will it take you?'

'I'll see you there at about one. Is that okay?'

'Yes, thanks – that's fine. And, Joey, I saw your ride yesterday afternoon. It was fantastic.'

He laughed, relieved that Nina could think of anything other than her own appalling experience. 'It's amazing what fear of fast-moving ground and galloping hooves will do!'

Joey drove home first, where he changed and checked his messages. He was on his way out of the house again when Danny left his cottage.

'Morning, Joey. Great ride yesterday! We all cleaned up in the yard.'

'I knew it was worth hanging on.' Joey grinned as he walked towards his car.

'Where are you off to now?' his brother asked.

'Just to see a friend. Why?'

'Di Lambert was round earlier, looking for you.'

'What did she want?'

'She didn't say, just asked me to let her know when you got back. I suppose the guv'nor wants to get hold of you.'

'I'll ring him from the car.' Joey opened the door of the Ferrari and got in. 'See you.'

Among the crowd of drab Sunday travellers, Nina stood

out like a beacon – looking even brighter when she saw Joey.

He sat down opposite her and ordered a cup of coffee, glad not to have been recognised.

Behind her smile, Joey could see she was really scared.

'What happened?' he asked quietly.

'Last night, when I was dealing with the horses, Wimsatt turned up . . .'

'I *knew* it! The bastard!' Joey was almost choking with anger. 'Ever since you told me, I thought it must be him. I could see he was obsessive about you when he tried to warn me off at Lichfield. What the hell are you going to do? Have you told the police?'

'No . . . no. I couldn't do that, not to all my friends. If he was arrested, the circus would close and they'd all be out of a job – at least for the rest of the season.'

'But you can't let him get away with it!'

'I may have to. But you never know, maybe sometime I'll get even.'

'But you can't stay on at the circus.'

'No, I know. I never want to see him again, after what he did . . .' She shook her head and Joey saw that she was shaking at the memory. 'I couldn't believe how strong he was, even though he was so drunk. It was disgusting . . . horrible.' She shuddered.

'Do you know why it happened now? After all these years of knowing you.'

'But he's been much keener on me recently, and with you turning up, I think he's become jealous.'

'There's no reason why he should be jealous of me, is there?'

Nina held his gaze for a moment. 'Don't be dumb, Joey.'

'I thought at first he was warning me not to talk to

you about what happened to your father and Mischa.'

'But, Joey, why should he? What *did* happen?'

He shook his head slowly. 'I can't tell you anything else, but some people are trying to implicate me.'

She stared at him. 'But why, Joey? Why now? After so long?' She stopped abruptly, gazing at him. 'I know – it's because you're famous now . . . and you've got a lot of money.'

'Nina – I can't tell you, I'm sorry.'

She tried to look behind the sparkling blue eyes, to see if she could detect any fear or guilt. Joey smiled sadly back at her, his face unreadable.

'You know you asked me if I wanted to come and see you in Newmarket?' she said.

He nodded.

'Is the offer still open?'

'Of course it is.'

'I'll come back with you tonight, then.'

Nina took a taxi to the circus pitch. She sneaked in and found the Spaniards to make arrangements for the horses. Half an hour later, she met Joey in the car park of the Little Chef with a single tote bag for luggage and a smile on her face.

On the drive to Suffolk, she seemed determined not to be crushed by the ordeal of the night before. Almost as if it hadn't happened, she asked Joey about everything he'd done since he'd left the circus. She listened, enthralled, to the story of his climb to the upper ranks of one of the world's most competitive sports.

They stopped at a pub outside Cambridge for dinner. It was a quiet Sunday evening with little to distract them from each other.

As Joey carried on talking about his love of racing and natural affinity with the horses he rode, Nina was ready to concede, for the first time in her life, that the world outside the circus might have something to offer.

Joey was glad to be side-tracked into telling her the story of his racing career. Resolutely, he pushed to the back of his mind the fact that his whole future was being threatened by one ill-judged action in his distant past. He was expecting another demand any time now, and dreading it. Besides everything else, it was getting difficult to get his hands on the ready money.

But with an effort, he ignored his own problems and played the easy-going, story-telling jockey he liked to be.

As they drove the few miles further to Newmarket, he could feel that the attraction between them had reached a point where something was about to happen, and the first move would be up to him.

Joey drove his car into the yard in front of his house. The buildings were bathed in a glow of orange floodlighting and Nina fell silent for a moment, dazzled by such opulence.

'My God, Joey, this is like something out of the films.'

He grinned. 'It's pretty modest by Newmarket standards, I can tell you.'

He opened the front door for her, ushering her through to the small sitting-room.

'What do you want to drink?'

'Anything,' she answered with a grin, 'I don't care.'

Joey put a CD on his player and went through to the kitchen for glasses. As usual, his answerphone was flashing at him. He hesitated a moment and reluctantly gave in.

There was only one message that mattered: a short

promise from the blackmailer that he would be in touch again that night.

Joey tried to pretend that he hadn't heard it, tried to push away his certain knowledge that the call would come. He didn't let Nina know, though, and kept her talking. He was longing for the moment when they might go to bed together, but sensed that she needed time to get over the ordeal she had suffered.

And then there was the next phone call. How could he focus on Nina, give her the love and attention she needed, when he was waiting for the next demand from his blackmailer?

The call came at last, after midnight; before Joey had been able to consider making love to her with a clear conscience.

He started when the phone rang. Nina noticed his unease as he went to the kitchen to answer it, carefully shutting doors behind him as he went.

'Go to your front door.'

The line went dead. The caller was taking no chances on being traced, or on Joey's phone being tapped.

Guiltily, he crossed his hall on tip-toes so Nina wouldn't gather what was happening.

He wasn't surprised to see a plain white envelope lying on the coconut mat in the hall. If Roger had still been alive, he would have barked the house down at anyone walking up the drive, but then, these people knew the dog was dead.

Joey picked up the envelope and took it back into the kitchen where he tore it open.

This time it had been produced by word-processor.

'If Colombian Prince wins tomorrow, the police get the tape and you'll be banged up within a week.'

Joey's knuckles whitened as he stared at the letter, seething with dread at the demand he'd prayed would never come.

He had been asked – subtly, occasionally overtly – to stop horses in return for various rewards, sometimes huge. But he had chosen never to take that route. It could only be a one-way street once you'd started down it.

There was to be no reward this time. He was being offered the stick instead of the carrot: Do as we say or the tape gets shown around. Joey felt sick.

He walked slowly back into the sitting-room where Nina was waiting for him. He couldn't pretend any more that nothing was up.

'I'm sorry,' he said. 'I've got a couple of things to deal with. Do you want to go to bed?'

Nina looked at him, confused. She didn't know if he meant his bed or not.

'I'll show you where to go,' he said regretfully, and led her up to an immaculately decorated spare bedroom which had seldom been used. He said goodnight and left her there without so much as a kiss.

Downstairs he put his head in his hands, wanting to weep.

Later, alone in his room, he barely slept. He had arranged to ride work for Seabourn at half-past six the following morning. He got up early and went into Nina's room. She was still asleep, her clothes draped neatly over a button-back chair. Joey saw a pair of small, pink pants on top and guessed she must be naked between the white linen sheets of his spare bed. He longed to get in beside her.

'Nina?' he said quietly.

She stirred and gave him a long, curious look. 'Hello.'

'I'm sorry,' he said simply. 'I've got to go out for an hour or so. We'll have breakfast when I come back, okay?'

She didn't answer.

When Joey came back from the Heath ninety minutes later, Nina wasn't in the house.

He looked all over for her, feeling foolish at first, then starting to panic. He had a sudden wild idea that the blackmailers had decided to strengthen their hand by kidnapping her.

Cursing his crazy fantasies, he nevertheless hunted for her all round the garden, even drove up and down the lane a few times to see if he could find her, until, angry with himself for mishandling things, he went back to Barry's office above the garage.

'Morning,' the Irishman boomed. 'Who was that lovely creature I saw leaving just now?'

'Did you see her go?' Joey asked, sharply enough for Barry to know something was wrong.

'Did you blow it, or what? That's not like you, Joey boy. Especially with a girl who looks like that.'

'Well, I did blow it. How did she leave?'

'She went off in a taxi from town.'

'Oh.' Jocy felt utterly deflated, but at the back of his mind was sure she'd be back sooner or later. Once he'd dealt with his own problems, he'd go looking for her again.

He checked his calendar with Barry and found he wasn't committed to anything before the three-ten at Kempton that afternoon. He made two phone calls, climbed into the Ferrari and drove to London, now prepared to try anything, however remote a chance, to discover who was hounding him.

Joey had never visited his solicitor's in London's West End. He had often wondered how they could justify charging a hundred pounds for twenty minutes' work; when he saw their offices and the bevy of female assistants, he understood why their bills were so large.

But he had often met Bruce Trevor in Newmarket and was inclined to trust him. He hadn't told him much over the phone – just that he needed some discreet enquiries made and a first-rate investigator to do it.

'Good morning, Joey.' Bruce Trevor greeted him with a firm handshake and waved him to a chic little sofa in a corner of his Georgian panelled room, while he went back behind his gleaming mahogany desk. Discreetly, he glanced at his watch and scribbled a note of the time on the pad in front of him.

'So, how much do you want to tell me?'

Joey looked into the lawyer's shrewd eyes. 'No more than I have to.' He had thought this over on the way down from Newmarket; all his instincts told him to trust nobody more than he had to. 'Basically, I'm being blackmailed – for something I didn't do. Trouble is, they've got a videotape that makes it look as though I was to blame, and the only two people who could say what really happened are both dead.'

The lawyer's eyes opened a fraction wider. 'Recently?'

Joey nodded. 'One died of AIDS at the beginning of June. The other was beaten up and died of a heart attack – last Tuesday.'

'Mmmm,' Trevor murmured with studied impartiality. 'He was . . . murdered?'

'There's an inquest to come, but the police are treating it as murder in the meantime.'

'Do you think it's connected with this blackmail?'

Joey shrugged and shook his head. 'I don't know. Probably.'

'Presumably the police don't know anything about that?'

'No, they don't. The fella who had the heart attack was an old clown I used to know at the circus. He was working in a holiday camp in Yarmouth. I was racing there and went to see him, the day after he was killed. The police interviewed me then.'

The lawyer leaned back in his big Chippendale carver chair. 'If, as you say, you were entirely free from blame over whatever happened, why don't you either call your blackmailer's bluff or take your chances with the police?'

'I told you – the evidence on the tape would be hard to disprove and the scandal would finish me. I'm not going to go into details, but I've worked my butt off to get where I am. You know the score in my game; it's not just a matter of being a little bloke with a good sense of balance. People need to be able to trust me: owners, trainers, punters. I'm not going to let anything come along and rock the boat, or put my licence at risk.'

'No. I quite understand.' The solicitor didn't press for any more details. 'As you asked, I've arranged for a very discreet private investigator to see you. He will have arrived by now. Would you like to talk to him in here?'

'Yes, that's fine.'

Trevor buzzed his secretary in the adjoining room. 'Ask Mr Allen to come in, please.'

Nick Allen wasn't anything like Joey's idea of a private detective. He had long black hair and was wearing jeans and an Italian leather blouson. When Bruce Trevor introduced them, he took off dark glasses and shook Joey's hand. 'Pleased to meet you,' he said with a faint South London accent. 'I've won a few bob on you over the years.'

'Well, if you can do what I want you to do, you might be able to save me a few.'

'I'll do my best. What's the story?'

Joey sat down on the sofa and Nick dropped into an armchair opposite, while Trevor stayed at his desk.

'I'm being blackmailed. You don't need to know the details. I have to pay the money into an account at the Southern Counties Building Society. Their head offices are down in Croydon. I want you to see if you can find someone there who can tell you the identity of the account holder.'

Nick nodded. 'I know the place. I'm sure I'll find someone who *can* tell me; whether they *will* or not is another matter. I've had dealings with the building societies before, and I wouldn't hold out a lot of hope. The only people they'll open up to are the Inland Revenue, Customs and Excise, and the police. But I'll see what I can do. Then what?'

'Let's get the name first.'

'Frankly, Joey,' Nick said with easy familiarity, 'it's a perfect scam he's organised. He can pull out five hundred quid a time, as many times a day as he wants from holes in the wall at any of two hundred branches all over southern England. He'd be almost impossible to catch, even if the police were involved. And suppose I do manage to extract a name – it's bound to be an alias, isn't it? Probably with a false address. But let me have the number and I'll get on with it.'

Nick stood up.

Joey took out a pen, wrote the account number on a slip of paper and handed it to his investigator. 'What do I do about paying you?'

'I bill Mr Trevor, and report to him. You pay him. Saves a lot of hassle. Right, good to meet you.' He stuck out his hand again and was gone as quickly as he'd arrivcd.

Joey drove on to Kempton feeling satisfied that if anyone could get the information he wanted, Nick Allen could. He always rated people who kept the talk to a minimum and acted fast.

Joey's mount in the three-ten, Colombian Prince, started odds on in a field of eight, and finished second. There were a lot of surprised faces in the paddock as Joey steered the horse towards the second slot.

On the walk back to the weighing room, Barry Mannion could barely contain himself.

'What the hell happened?' he hissed.

Joey tried to look him in the eye, but had to resort to fiddling with his silks. 'He just didn't have anything left.'

'But he was still well on the bit when he hit the furlong post, and you never moved!'

'He just wasn't going,' Joey hissed back, hating himself. 'Sorry if you've dropped a packet, but you're a big boy now.'

Later, he was walking across the car park to his Ferrari.

'Joey. Joey Leatham.'

He spun round and found himself facing Mike Wade. He was about to spin right back and carry on, when Wade said, 'That was an interesting ride you gave Colombian

Prince this afternoon. I didn't know he wasn't supposed to win. You really should tell your colleagues, you know. Still, I'd heard you'd got problems.'

'And you standing here in front of me is one of them.' Joey was startled by Wade's last statement but didn't let it show.

'But maybe I can help,' he went on, oozing insincerity. 'And maybe you can do my associates a little favour in the King George and Queen Elizabeth.'

'Listen, and try to remember so we don't have this conversation again: I don't have any problems. Colombian Prince got beaten fair and square. There's nothing you can do to help me and I'm not doing you any favours – ever, in the King George or any other race.'

This time, Joey turned on his heel and headed for his car. He wouldn't even look in Wade's direction as he drove out of the racecourse.

Driving back, he reviewed the day's events.

For one thing, he had decided he was never, ever going to stop a horse again, no matter how much pressure was put on him. It had been bad enough with Barry, and he'd hardly been able to look the stewards in the face after Colombian Prince's race. He would rather lose all his money than an ounce more of his integrity.

Which brought him back to the unremitting problem of the blackmailer. He had decided to tackle things from the inside through the building society when he'd realised that almost everyone he could think of was a potential suspect, including Mike Wade. He was no nearer knowing who it was – apart from eliminating Ginger and Giulio – than he had been since the first demand had arrived through the post.

At the same time, he knew he was dealing with people

ready to go to almost any length to maintain their threat. They had known exactly what effect they would achieve when they'd killed Roger, and Joey didn't doubt that Giulio had been attacked to stop the old clown from coming to his defence.

He wished he had seen Nina before she'd gone that morning; wished he'd had the guts to tell her the truth. He was concerned that by keeping this from her he'd threatened the rapport that was steadily growing between them.

But he couldn't help that – not yet.

For the next two days, every time the phone rang, Joey sweated.

But the three calls he was dreading or wanting didn't come.

The blackmailer's – to make more demands, and give him the name of the next horse to stop.

Bruce Trevor's – with any news from Nick Allen.

Or Nina's.

But on the third day, when he arrived home feeling fleetingly pleased with himself after scoring an unexpected double on a pair of two-year-olds, there was a message from Nina on his answerphone.

He had resisted the urge to call her over the last couple of days. Now he picked up the phone and rang her back before he played the rest of the tape.

'Hello, it's Joey.'

There was a moment's silence before she spoke. 'Sorry I left without saying goodbye.'

'I don't blame you. I'm sorry, too. I've been having the kind of hassles that make you forget about other people sometimes. What have you done?'

'I've left the circus. I haven't seen Wimsatt.'

'But you can't just let him get away with it.'

'I've told you, Joey, I'm not dragging the police into it. I won't see all my friends out of work. They know I'm leaving because of Wimsatt, maybe they can guess why. They know what a complete bastard he is – that'll do for me.'

'But, Nina, what are you going to do with your horses?'

He was astonished to hear her laugh. 'I've sold them to the Spanish boys. They reckon they can run the act themselves.'

'Then what the hell are you going to do?'

'First, I'm coming to see you. It sounds to me as if you could do with a bit of help. I've got some things to sort out first, but I'll be in Newmarket tomorrow. You needn't worry about putting me in your spare room, I've sent one of the boys on with my trailer. He'll find somewhere to pitch it.'

Joey thought of the immaculate verges at the sides of the roads for miles around Newmarket, and thought of Nina trying to find somewhere to park a wagon which no one would be able to distinguish from an out and out gypsy's.

'I've got a couple of paddocks. You can put it in one of them.'

'No thanks, Joey. I like my independence too much.'

'Don't stay too fond of it if you don't find anywhere to park! They're not too keen on people turning up and parking caravans all over the place round here.'

'I'll let you know.'

'But why are you coming?'

'Don't you want me to?'

'Of course I do. But what are you going to do?'

'Try and sort out my life, for a start. Also,' she paused, uncertain of his reaction, 'I thought I might have a go at this racing game.'

'What?'

'I was looking at the state of some of those horses out on the Heath; I could produce fitter animals than that, and have them better ridden. Some of those lads I wouldn't let sit on a garden wall. And I thought I might have a go at riding racehorses, instead of my Lusitanos.'

Joey was taken aback, but supposed it wasn't such a crazy idea. She certainly knew how to get the most out of her horses and she'd been doing it a long time.

'Why not? I'll give you a few lessons.'

'I taught *you* to ride, remember?'

He laughed again. 'I remember.' He wondered what Newmarket would make of a jockey who'd learned her trade riding bare-back, wearing a sequinned leotard with an ostrich feather headdress. 'I think you could have a lot of fun.'

For a while, after he'd put the phone down, Joey felt as carefree as a teenager, and all the hassles of the last month seemed suddenly less important.

Chapter Ten

When Nina turned up on Saturday evening, Joey felt as if he'd been holding his breath for the last forty-eight hours. He hadn't really believed she would come – it had seemed too improbable that she would go as far as chucking in her old career. It was more than understandable that she wanted to get away from Wimsatt, but she could easily have taken her team of horses to any other circus in Europe.

It was clear, though, from the moment she arrived at Three Elms Farm that whatever else she may have lost, she didn't intend to give up her freedom.

She arrived in the passenger seat of a horse-box. Joey guessed she must have hitched a ride; he was watching her from the window of Barry's office where they'd been reviewing a successful day's racing over a bottle of wine. She jumped down from the cab, waved a sunny goodbye to the driver and vaulted over the post-and-rail fence.

'Jesus, Joey. That's an athletic bird you've got yourself,' Barry observed over his shoulder. 'Are you up to the job, man?'

'I doubt it,' he laughed. 'But I'll give it a damn good try.'

He went downstairs to greet Nina and brought her

back up to the office to be introduced to Barry. He gave her both barrels of his Celtic charm, and even had the good manners not to laugh when she told him she wanted to take up training and race riding.

'She's serious, by the way,' Joey said. 'Would you get her fixed up with an amateur rider's licence?'

'No problem. I might even be able to fix a ride or two,' he added. 'If it's not a cheeky question, what's your riding weight?'

'I haven't decided yet,' she declared grandly.

Barry roared with laughter and looked her up and down. 'Nine stone, two pounds, with a breast plate, I reckon.' And she'd need a hefty one of those, he thought appreciatively.

A look from Joey told him to keep the thought to himself.

In the house, Joey made coffee and they sat at his kitchen table.

'So,' he asked, 'where's your trailer? I thought you were bringing it with you.'

'Not far from here. In a field on one of those big flashy studs you pass coming into town. I found a young toff who goggled like a rabbit and said I could park there for a few days. I told him I wouldn't make a mess.'

Joey couldn't help being impressed with her brazenness, a trait which always went down well in Newmarket, especially in long-legged blondes. 'But how did you get it there?'

'One of the Spaniards towed it for me.'

'Oh. Where is he, then?'

'Sanchez? He's gone.'

'And you haven't got a car?'

'No. I haven't even got a driver's licence.'

Joey laughed. 'You're crazy. You'll be really stuck, out on some stud with no car. I know you want to be independent and all that, but at least park your caravan on my land, then there'll always be someone to take you around.'

Nina looked at him consideringly. 'I need privacy, and water, too.'

'There's a great spot at the bottom of one of the paddocks, well tucked away about three hundred yards from the house, and right by the brook.'

'If you show me tomorrow, I'll make up my mind then.'

He accepted that was as far as he was going to get for the time being. 'How do you feel now?' he said, changing the subject.

Nina pushed her black coffee across the table. 'Put a bit of brandy in it, please.'

Joey found some Cognac and sloshed a generous measure into her mug.

She took a long swig, and spoke in her low, husky voice. 'I tell you, now it's happened I'm so happy. For years I've wanted something to force me out of the circus. It was beginning to seem like a prison. But, you know, I was scared to leave. I've lived in a circus all my life – I was born in a bloody circus trailer! And to the circus people it's sacrilege to want to get out. But when Wimsatt attacked me the other night – that was enough.'

Joey nodded. 'It must have been horrible, but I still don't understand why you don't want him to pay for it? I can hardly believe he'd do such a crazy thing.'

'Believe me, he *is* crazy. He kept saying he loved me, yet what does he do? Try and rape me! He risked the police, and me leaving his circus – even when he knows how many people come to see me ride.'

'There may have been more to it than that,' Joey said, not wanting to scratch Wimsatt from his list of suspects too soon.

'What are you saying?'

'I'm not sure yet. Nothing, probably.'

He struggled with his conscience, wishing he had the guts to tell her about all the guilt and confusion that weighed him down.

Since his visit to Lichfield and Wimsatt's attack on Nina, Joey's suspicions had turned in a new direction. For a while, after he had seen the tape which had been sent from France in Wimsatt's trailer, he had been utterly convinced that the ring-master was his blackmailer.

But now, in trying to rape Nina, the circus boss had committed what was obviously the act of an insanely obsessive man, not a calculating extortionist. Reflecting on Wimsatt's reaction when he had asked about that tape, Joey had to admit to himself that he hadn't shown the slightest sign of guilt.

He felt gloomily that his reluctance to confide in Nina was weakening the bond between them. But as she was leaving shortly afterwards, he was encouraged when she told him the name of the stud where her caravan was, and asked if he would come and get it the following day. She would take his word on the quality of his site.

Joey came and watched her walk out of the gate, impressed that she insisted on making her own way back.

The phone started to ring as he went into the kitchen.

'Hello?'

'Is that Joey Leatham?'

'Yes.'

'It's Nick Allen here. We met at Mr Trevor's.'

'Yes, of course.'

'Can I come up and see you?'

'What? Now?'

'Yeah, if it's convenient.'

It was a rare free Saturday evening, which Joey had hoped to spend with Nina. 'Sure,' he said gloomily.

'Great. I was hoping you'd say that. I'm only forty minutes away.'

The private investigator turned up just after nine. He declined Joey's offer of a drink, opted for strong black coffee and sat down at the kitchen table.

'Right,' he said, opening a folder. 'I made contact with an employee of Southern Counties Building Society. A young clerk, male, about twenty-five.'

'Great! What did you get?'

'Nothing. I explained who I was and what I was doing, though of course I couldn't reveal your name. I offered him a monkey if he could come up with a name and address from the account number you gave me.' Nick paused. 'I had a second meet with him this afternoon, and I'm afraid he was scared shitless of getting caught. Like I said, unless the police ask, there's no way the building society will identify the account holder.'

'So?' Joey asked impatiently. 'What do you suggest?'

'Tell the police.'

'I've told you, I can't.'

'In which case, these guys can carry on milking you and getting their hands on the cash without coming up for air as long as they like, until you run out of money.'

He stopped, and glanced up sharply. 'Is it only money they're looking for?'

Sitting at the table opposite him, Joey looked down at his hands. 'Not entirely.'

Nick gave a dry laugh. 'I guessed as much. Look, if these people are asking you to stop horses, isn't it likely they're in the business?'

'Not necessarily. It's pretty obvious that's one way of exploiting what they've got over me.'

'As long as they think you'll do it.'

'How do I convince them I won't?'

'Just don't – next time they ask – and see what happens.' Nick started shoving pieces of paper back into his folder and stood up.

'Listen, they've already killed my dog and gave another friend of mine such a hiding he died afterwards. He was the only person who knew the full story. But these guys got him, and then they followed me over to France and gave me a serious hammering. I don't think I want to see what happens next.'

'They'd be crazy to do you any serious damage because then you'd stop riding and lose your income. People don't kill the goose laying golden eggs or maim it either. That's bad for the laying process.' Nick picked up his folder. 'Anyway, sorry I couldn't do a lot for you – as far as the building society's concerned. If you think you'd like some more intensive work done in tracing these people, let me know and I'll be happy to oblige.'

'What else could you do?'

'I'll tell you that when you've agreed to take me on. Do you want to talk about it now?'

'No, but I'll let you know. Have you got a card?'

'You can get hold of me through Mr Trevor. He'll send you a bill for the couple of days I've done.'

The three-week spell of fine weather had come to an abrupt end. Thunder storms on Saturday night and a steady downpour which followed into the middle of Sunday morning were either too much for anyone who had planned a barbecue lunch, or too little for any trainer with horses that needed a cut in the ground.

Joey was giving Dick and his wife a drink on their way to lunch with one of their bigger owners who lived nearby. Di Lambert was with them.

'I hope you don't mind?' she said. 'I'm not going on to lunch afterwards. What are you doing?'

Joey noticed a slight and uncharacteristic raising of Veronica Seabourn's eyebrows. This was the first time he had noticed anything critical in Veronica's attitude to Di. He wondered what was causing it; whether, perhaps, Dick had told her about Joey and Di sleeping together.

He opened a couple of bottles of Krug, and caught himself wondering what his strait-laced, teetotal, penny-pinching foster-parents would have thought if they could have seen him filling his guests' glasses with such an expert hand.

He was just passing the glasses round when a short rap on the front door was followed by Barry's entrance.

'I'm sorry to interrupt your party, Joey, but I need a word with Mr Seabourn and Di.'

'Sure,' Joey said, surprised. 'Use my study.'

'If you don't mind, Dick,' Barry addressed the trainer, 'could we go over to my office? We've got into a real mix-up over next week's rides and we need to sort it out now.'

Seabourn agreed. 'Di, have you got your organiser with you?'

'Yes, it's in the car.'

They went out, leaving Joey and Veronica alone together. 'I can't think how Dick managed in the old days without Di and her little organiser.'

Joey picked up a hint of bitterness in her tone, which surprised him. 'I suppose when you had to keep everything in your head, you just did.'

'I always used to. It was one of the things that kept us close.'

Joey didn't like the direction the conversation was taking but guessed if Veronica needed to talk, he should be flattered to be her confidant. 'Aren't you still involved in the running of things?'

'Hardly at all now. My sole contribution seems to be providing meals for owners when they come.'

It was strange, Joey reflected. On the face of it, most women would have found Veronica's life-style thoroughly enviable. She lived in a large, comfortable and beautiful house with plenty of help. Her husband was handsome, charming and successful in his field. She had a busy social life, and a bright, good-looking daughter.

She had had the will and the money to age very gently, and was still an attractive woman. Yet now it seemed to Joey she was deeply unhappy.

'Maybe Dick felt you deserved a break from all the stress of running the yard?' he suggested.

'I'm afraid to say that would be unusually considerate for him.' She lifted her chin defiantly. 'Anyway, let's not talk about it. Why don't you sneak us another glass of champagne before they get back?'

A few minutes later, Seabourn and Di returned with

all the booking problems sorted out. Veronica showed no further signs of the anxiety she had expressed privately to Joey, and they carried on talking much as usual about racing and the horses in the Crowle House yard.

As they talked, Joey found himself wondering what Nina was doing and wishing she were here with them. He wanted to show her off to the Seabourns, and everyone else in Newmarket.

Later, they were getting up to leave when there was a flurry of gravel in Joey's drive. He went across to the drawing-room window and looked out to see a bright aquamarine Bentley skidding to a halt.

Ivor Wimsatt burst from the driver's door and strode purposefully towards the front of the house.

Joey went and opened the door to him and was slammed back against the wall almost before he turned the deadlock.

'Right, you little sod, where is she?' Wimsatt bellowed. He wasn't a tall man but he towered over Joey and his eyes bored into him with undisguised hatred.

'D'you mean Nina?'

'Of course I fucking do!'

'She's not here.'

'Yes, she is. The Spanish boy who brought her told me.'

'He didn't bring her here.'

'Where did he take her trailer then?'

'I don't know, and if she'd wanted you to know, she'd have given you a forwarding address.'

Wimsatt puffed out his chest. His sharp black eyes narrowed. 'Listen, you jumped up little tit, I know where you came from, remember. So just get out of my way!'

'She's not here!' Joey shouted back, close to losing his

own temper. 'Do you seriously think she wants to see you after what you did to her? You must be mad even to think of coming to look for her here!'

'What's she been saying, then? Look, I gave the ungrateful bitch a ring worth ten grand, for Christ's sake! *That's* what I've done to her. And I know she's here!' Wimsatt lunged forward so suddenly he caught Joey by surprise. He barged past him and looked around the hall before charging into the empty kitchen.

Joey stood and watched while he checked the other rooms until he reached the drawing-room, where Di and the Seabourns sat with drinks in their hands, trying to suppress their astonishment.

'You can look upstairs, too,' Joey invited, feeling in control in the face of Wimsatt's obvious derangement, 'as long as you don't make a mess.'

Wimsatt glared at him, then at the others.

Abruptly, he let fly a left hook which caught Joey on the tip of the chin and sent him staggering back into a drinks table. Bottles and glasses crashed and tinkled across the room. Joey stumbled to his feet, rubbing his jaw.

'She's far too good for you, you little wimp,' Wimsatt roared at him in his ring-master's voice. 'God help you if I ever find her here.' He turned on his heel and strode from the room.

Nobody spoke until they heard the car pulling away with a noisy scattering of gravel.

'Who on earth was that?' Dick asked.

'Believe it or not, he used to be my boss. He owns the circus I was in.'

Dick's eyebrows raised. 'Your old boss? But why's he suddenly turning up here? And who was he looking for?'

'Nina Korsakov. She had a riding act in his circus.'

'But what did he do to her?' Di asked excitedly.

The Bentley had gone, but a movement outside caught Joey's eye. 'I'll tell you another time. She's just arrived.'

The front door-bell rang. He went to answer it. A few seconds later he showed Nina into the drawing-room.

'This is Nina. Nina, this is my boss, Dick Seabourn, his wife Veronica, and this is Di Lambert who runs the office for Dick.'

Dick looked at Nina with open approval; Veronica with curiosity. Di, at first sizing her up like a jealous rival, quickly assumed a friendly smile and came over to take her hand in greeting. 'We've just been hearing all about you.'

Nina glanced at Joey. 'What have you been saying?'

'Only that you've come to set the racing world alight,' he said quickly.

He gave her a glass of champagne and soon the others were questioning her, fascinated by her bizarre career and plans to move into racing.

While the Seabourns were there, no mention was made of Nina's eccentric living arrangements and the proposal to move her into Joey's paddock, but once they'd gone, she asked, 'Do you still want to bring my trailer here?'

'What's that?' Di asked with a grin. 'Have you brought your horses with you? They'll stand out from the crowd on the Heath.'

'No, I've sold them, but I've brought my living trailer – my home.'

'And you're going to park it *here*? What a laugh, Joey! The locals will go crazy. They'll think you're starting a caravan site.'

'Well, I'm not,' he said sharply and turned to Nina.

'We could go and get it now, if you like?'

She nodded. 'That would be great.'

'Provided Danny hasn't gone off in the Range Rover.'

'D'you need a hand?' Di asked.

Joey could see she'd be hard to dissuade. 'It's stopped raining and it looks as though the sun's here to stay for a bit, so if I light the barbecue you could get everything ready to cook when we get back. We'll only be gone half an hour or so.'

'Fine,' Di said brightly. 'Let's get on with it.'

While they were fetching the trailer, Joey was able to tell Nina about Wimsatt's whirlwind visit. When he mentioned the punch he'd taken on the chin, she looked at him with deep concern.

'Joey, I'm so sorry you've got caught up in this.' She put a hand on his arm.

'It's okay,' he said, 'but we've *got* to teach the bastard a lesson – make sure he doesn't come round pestering you again.'

'Just so long as other people in the circus don't suffer.'

Nina loved her new pitch. It was a quarter of a mile from Joey's house, screened by a belt of birch and oak. Even in high summer the brook gushed and tinkled crystal clear over a small weir a few feet away. It was on the far side of a flat pasture, a hundred yards from a road gate, tucked in among the trees.

'This is so beautiful,' she said. 'Thank you very much, Joey. But I must pay you rent.'

'If it was a grazing horse, I'd charge twenty quid a week, so we'll call it that, okay?'

She pulled a note from her purse and made him take

it. 'And don't think that just because I'm pitched on your land, you can come round any time you like. Only when I invite you.'

'Fine. When can I come, then?'

'I'll see,' she laughed.

Although Joey had been irritated by Di's inviting herself to hang around, when he got back to the house, he decided she'd earned her lunch. Everything was prepared and the barbecue was glowing like a furnace.

Joey was also impressed by the canniness with which she treated Nina. Nina was more beautiful, almost certainly more talented and with an obviously more impressive physique, but somehow Di managed to present herself as more worldly and sexually aware.

A lot of this was lost on Nina – at least, if she saw it, she wasn't prepared to be affected by it. Nevertheless, the feeling prevalent was that they were two women of equal attractiveness and knowledge of the world, and on the whole Joey was relieved by this. It was better than out and out competition.

The sun was beginning to gleam through the clouds and they decided to eat outside. It was an enjoyable al fresco lunch, helped by two bottles of Burgundy.

After a couple of hours of eating and talking lazily, Di rose decisively to her feet.

'Okay, Joey, I expect you've got lots of dreary phone calls to make – at least for an hour or so – so I'm going to whisk the lovely Nina away and show her the sights of HQ.'

'HQ?' Nina questioned, not objecting to the idea in principle.

'Newmarket is HQ to anyone in flat racing,' Joey said.

He wanted to tell Di to go away and leave Nina with him. But that would have upset the good humour of the lunch party.

'What a good idea,' he said instead. 'There are several things I need to do this afternoon.'

He walked around to the front of the house, where Nina and Di climbed into Di's Peugeot 205 and shot off up the drive.

Joey went inside, switched on the answerphone, and set off for a walk across the broad flat fields of pasture that surrounded his house. Once he issued a sharp, tremolo whistle and listened for the sound of Roger, rustling and snuffling through the undergrowth, until he remembered with a sharp pang of grief that he would never again feel the dog's wet nose barge into the back of his hand.

And as he walked, he nursed his bruised chin and hoped the women's conversation didn't reach the point where intimate details were swapped; although he guessed Di wouldn't be able to resist the temptation.

Di drove at ninety-five with half a finger on the wheel as she extracted a cigarette from a packet of Silk Cut. She poked it into her mouth and managed to light it without taking her eyes off the road.

'How are you getting on with Lord Tewkesbury?' she asked.

'Who's Lord Tewkesbury?'

'He's a well-known breeder – the man who let you park on his stud. I saw him yesterday evening. He'll be very disappointed you've left.'

'Oh. He told me his name was Gerry. He was very nice to me. I went to look at his mares this morning and he gave me some eggs. He said I could stay as long as I liked, but I told him I was moving to Joey's.'

After a long drag on her cigarette, Di shot a glance at her passenger. 'So, I suppose you and Joey had a mad passionate affair when he was riding with you in the circus?'

Nina gave a husky laugh. 'No way! You're not going to believe this, but in those days I thought he was gay.'

'Joey gay?' Di exclaimed, appalled. 'That's the last thing he is.'

'You know from personal experience?'

Di answered with a grin.

Nina felt a sudden surge of envy for the English girl. Then reminded herself she had no justification. It was absurd to expect Joey to have stayed celibate for ten years, and she'd only reappeared in his life three weeks before.

'But what on earth made you think it?' Di was asking.

'Because when he first arrived, he lived in a trailer with a strange little Czech clown who'd always liked other men. And my father told me too, though I guess that was just wishful thinking on his part.'

'My God! Was your *father* like that?'

Nina shrugged. 'Sometimes.'

'What a life you must have had.'

'Maybe, but for me it was normal. Coming here, where everyone has so much land and big houses – that's much more peculiar for me.'

'I hate to disillusion you, but not everyone has big houses here. The trainers – some of them – a few of the top jockeys, like Joey, and some of the big owners and breeders, but for every one of them there are a hundred humble souls like myself, living on a pittance, lurking in grotty cottages and flats. The lowest of the low, the young lads, often live in grim little hostels on no money at all.'

'But not Joey's brother,' Nina said.

'No. Danny's lucky. Luckier than he deserves to be, really. I sometimes wonder why Joey puts up with him.'

'Are you fond of Joey?' Nina asked point blank.

'Yes, I'm not interested in a long-term scene with him, though. He can be a bit too intense, you know.'

'Intense? What do you mean?'

'Well, he can brood a lot, especially lately. I suppose he takes his job very seriously. My boss says he does, anyway. But I've always rather fancied him.'

'Do you have a lover?'

'Sort of,' Di said quickly, turning her attention back to the road. 'Was that madman who turned up before lunch your ex?'

'You mean Ivor?'

'Yes.'

'Of course not. No way! He wanted to be, he kept giving me presents and promising he was buying a great big place where we could live in the winter, but he was full of shit. I loathed him. It was just that I'd got stuck in his circus and didn't seem to know how to get away. It was a sort of inertia. Then last week he . . . well, he tried to rape me.'

Di took her foot off the accelerator and turned to Nina, shocked. 'But surely, if he threatened you with rape, you must do something about it?' Nina was the only person she'd met who'd ever come close to being raped.

Nina tossed her head. 'What? I could never prove anything. It would just be a waste of time and would only cause problems for my friends still at the circus.'

'But you can't just let him get away with it! Listen, if you need help dealing with him, promise me you'll let me know, okay?'

Barry Mannion didn't go to the Brighton races with Joey next day. Joey knew that was probably because he didn't think they'd have a winner. It turned out he was right.

Despite the demands on his attention from the blackmailer, and from Nina, Joey's urge to win was as strong as ever. But that day, not one of his mounts remotely deserved to win a race. It happened like that sometimes, and it often shook Joey's self-confidence.

Driving home, he phoned Barry, in need of reassurance; he wouldn't have admitted it, but his friend knew.

'Joey,' Barry butted in as he was trying to justify his performance, 'you don't need excuses – not like you did with Colombian Prince. It was all their fault today – you'd five rotten horses. I'm sorry. If anyone's to blame, it's me. But frankly, all the winners were tied up. You know how it is sometimes.'

'It wasn't your fault, Barry, and you know it.' Joey recognised he was being humoured. 'Anyway, what's been going on back at the ranch?'

'I've had your Miss Korsakov here in the office, haranguing me for not having her licence yet. She says she's already got three or four rides lined up. I tell you, Joey, that girl's taking this town by storm.'

'Did she leave any message for me?'

'She asked when you'd be back, and I told her. She watched a couple of your races on the box then disappeared.'

Joey said goodbye, put down the phone and drove the

rest of the journey in a state of expectation and frustration. When he got home, he was almost ashamed at how delighted he was to find Nina back in Barry's office.

Barry poured them both a drink. After a few minutes, Joey knew he couldn't evade it any longer and slipped over to the house to see who had rung him during the day.

Among the normal, everyday communications there was just one ominous message, delivered over the phone in that familiar, distorted voice.

'I'll ring again after eight. Make sure you're in.'

It was ten to. Joey went back to Barry's office, where a couple of his friends had turned up and were flirting outrageously with Nina. He managed to take her to one side.

'Do you want to have dinner with me tonight?'

'Oh, yes. Can we go somewhere called Le Picasso? Di told me that's where you took her and it's the best place to go.'

'What else did she tell you?'

Nina grinned. 'Nothing to put me off!'

'In that case, of course we can. The only thing is, I'm expecting a call soon, so we'll have to wait until it's come through. D'you mind?'

Nina shrugged her shoulders. Time had never been much of a factor in her life.

Joey glanced at Barry's friends. They'd be more than happy to entertain her till then. 'I'll get back and wait for this call, then we'll go, okay?'

'Sure,' she nodded. 'Barry says he'll show me some tapes of the ladies' races.'

After twenty minutes of waiting in his house for the

phone to ring and to hear the familiar, eerie voice, Joey didn't know whether to be relieved or alarmed that it hadn't come. As he walked back up the outside stairs to Barry's office to fetch Nina, he put on his best smile and decided to forget things for tonight.

Le Picasso was buzzing. It buzzed even louder when Joey walked in with Nina. In a town where gossip was the staple diet, a new dish was always welcome. During the evening, several people passing their table stopped on some pretext to talk to Joey, but really wanting to take a closer look at Nina.

Between these unsolicited interruptions, they talked, and Joey felt they were recovering some of the ground lost since they'd last been together. At the same time, he could see that she was flattered by all the interest the racing world was showing in her.

'Di says racing is a sexy business,' Nina said.

'I suppose it is,' Joey acknowledged with a wry smile.

'But you don't have a lover?'

'No. I've been waiting for you.' He grinned.

Nina laughed. 'I bet you've had women in and out of your bed the whole time.'

'Only if they reminded me of you.'

'Did you sleep with Di?'

'Did she say I had?'

'No.'

'There you are then.'

'But I don't believe her. She wants to be a friend to me, I think, but I don't trust her.'

'Why not? They don't come much straighter than Di.'

'Is that what you think? She must have a rich boyfriend somewhere.'

'I don't think so. Why do you say that?'

'When I was in her flat yesterday, after we drove around Newmarket, I was in her bedroom and she showed me her jewellery. She's got some fantastic stuff – and yet she doesn't seem like a very rich person.'

'There are lots of girls like that in racing, from posh families with loads of assets they won't sell and no readies. Di's family live in some bloody great house with a thousand acres the other side of Thetford, and her father drives around in a clapped-out old Volvo and wears jackets with elbow patches. You'll probably find the jewellery was left to her by her granny or some great-aunt.'

Nina bowed to Joey's greater knowledge of the arcane code of people like Di Lambert, while he found himself wishing he could buy some jewellery for Nina – if only all his money wasn't being raked in by blackmailers as fast as he made it.

With that thought, the magic of the evening disappeared for him. He tried not to let his disappointment show, but knew he wasn't ready to take her home with him tonight.

She looked surprised when he suggested he would take her straight back to her trailer, but didn't try to change his mind.

'Have you got everything you need in there?' Joey asked.

'Yes, of course. For me a trailer is home, remember?'

'Okay, but is there anything I can do for you?'

'Yes, there is. Fix for me to come and ride with you tomorrow.'

Joey wondered what Dick would think about Nina's turning up to ride out. 'Sure,' he said, with a grin. It would certainly shake up the lads. 'I'll pick you up at seven.'

Nina opened the car door but stayed where she was for a moment. Abruptly, without saying anything, she leaned across and gave Joey a soft kiss on his mouth before she climbed out and disappeared into the blackness of the oak spinney with a backward glance and a wave.

He sat in his car and watched her go, cursing the malign influence of his blackmailer.

Nina's eyes opened wide at the sheer magnificence of Crowle House, the fifty-yard square of fine, brick-built Edwardian stables, the venerable clock-tower, and the time-honoured, organised chaos of morning duties.

Joey parked his Ferrari among the dozen or so cars belonging to Seabourn's lads and work riders and took Nina round to introduce her to the yard.

Dick barely raised an eyebrow when Joey walked into his head lad's office with Nina. He declared that he was more than happy to put her up on a young filly for a little light work.

For once, the lads were dumbfounded. A lot of girls rode work, but none who looked like Nina. Joey noticed that the string was unusually talkative as they walked up to the Heath.

Several versions of who Nina was and her background had already swept through the yard before they had even pulled out.

'What a dream to ride these horses! But more difficult than my Spanish stallions.' She grinned as they pulled up at the end of the all-weather gallop.

'I should think it is,' Joey laughed. 'These little things haven't had ten years' tuition from you, for a start.'

Together they turned to ride over to where Dick

Seabourn stood watching with an owner.

'You can come and ride work any time,' he said to Nina, 'just as long as you don't distract my jockey too much.'

'I try not to,' she said with a look at Joey.

They hacked back to the yard and after a quick debrief over coffee in Seabourn's kitchen, climbed back into the Ferrari to drive home.

Joey never locked his car. That morning someone had left a copy of the *Sporting Life* and an envelope with his name on it on the passenger seat.

With a faint feeling of foreboding, he stuffed the envelope into the pocket of his leather jacket and drove Nina back to his house for breakfast.

The angry weather of the last two days had passed. It was a fine, warm morning and they laid breakfast on the cast-iron table under the laburnum tree.

As they ate, Nina talked happily about the horses that had been out that morning – what they had done and what they might be expected to do. She was entranced by them.

She was in mid-flow when the mobile phone beside Joey rang.

He tried to control the trembling which now afflicted him every time he heard it.

'Hello.'

'Joey Leatham, please.'

He sighed with relief. It wasn't the blackmailer. 'Speaking.'

'Oh, great. This is John MacClancy – sports producer for the BBC. We wrote to you about appearing on our quiz show and we haven't heard anything. We were wondering . . .'

'I'm sorry,' Joey said, trying to disguise his impatience. 'There's no way I can do the show right now.'

'But I understood from your agent . . .'

'My agent books rides for me, not TV shows.'

'Fair enough, but would you consider it? I know our audience would be very excited to see you on it.'

'Look, I'm sorry, I have far too many other commitments at the moment. I'll be in touch. Okay?'

'Okay, Mr Leatham.' The TV producer sounded so dejected that Joey almost felt sorry for him as he put down the phone. If the man had rung three weeks earlier, Joey knew he would have said yes.

As soon as he had put it down, the phone rang again.

It was Barry, already in his office, wanting to see him urgently.

Joey pulled a regretful face at Nina, leaving her to top up her coffee and read the racing papers.

While he was up in Barry's office, the phone in the garden rang once more.

Nina picked it up.

'Hello?' she said in her husky Russian accent.

'Oh, hello? I wanted to speak to Joey Leatham.' It was a young female voice, uncertain, obviously thrown by having to talk to a woman. 'Is that his number?'

'Yes, but he's not here.'

'Oh. When will he be back?'

'He won't be gone long.'

'Tell him Laura phoned, and wants to see him. It's urgent.'

'I'll tell him. Goodbye.' Nina switched off the phone with a flourish, poured herself more coffee and settled back in her chair. She had just seen Joey coming back through a trellis arch at the side of the house.

'One of your lovers just phoned. She must see you *urgently*,' Nina said with a broad smile.

Joey shrugged. 'She's going to be disappointed. Did she have a name?'

'Yes. Laura.'

Joey stopped in his tracks. 'Laura?' he repeated.

'Oh? So maybe she won't be disappointed.'

Joey shook his head. 'Laura's not a lover, but she could be a problem. She's Dick daughter. I think she feels that as I work for her dad, I ought to be at her beck and call. And I found her drunk with Danny the other night.'

'The old ugly sister routine,' Nina laughed.

'That's not fair on Danny.'

Nina looked at him closely. 'You don't think you're sometimes just a little too protective of that brother of yours, do you?'

'If I am, it's because blood is thicker than water.'

When Nina had gone back to her trailer, Joey went straight round to Danny's cottage. There was a Mercedes Joey didn't recognise parked in the courtyard, as well as both his own cars. Danny should not have been still at home at this time of day, but it looked as though he was and Joey wanted to find out what had been going on with Laura Seabourn. He was just about to ring the bell by the front door when it opened and Lenny Williams came out. Joey backed away instinctively, as if to avoid contamination.

''Morning, Joey. I hope you can talk some sense into that brother of yours. Things are getting out of hand.'

'They'll get more than out of hand if I see you round here again. Do you realise what you could do to my reputation?'

Lenny grinned coldly. 'Of course I do, and I hate to embarrass you. But maybe you can help me – your brother didn't seem to know. You're riding a horse called Tap Dancer tomorrow, aren't you?'

Joey froze. 'What of it?'

'What's the matter, Joey? I just want to know if you think he'll win.'

He looked at the bookie with utter disdain. 'Just get out of here. If you come here again, I'll call the police.'

Lenny burst out laughing. 'You? Call the police? Yeah, why don't you do that?'

Still laughing, he walked across to his car and climbed in. He gave a couple of farewell toots as he skidded off up the drive.

Joey turned and went into Danny's cottage.

'Dan? Where are you?'

There was a croak from the small living-room. Joey went in. His brother was lying on a sofa bed, unshaven and pale.

'What's wrong with you?' Joey asked.

'I've got a dose of 'flu, that's all.'

'Yet another hangover, more like,' said Joey with a sigh. 'Why did you let Lenny Williams come here?'

'I didn't let him. He just turned up. I owe him a bit, that's all.'

'Oh, Dan! Take my advice and stick to cash betting. At least then you know when you've run out of money. I can't keep on bailing you out, it's bad for both of us. And what have you been doing to Laura Seabourn?'

'Not enough,' Danny said, turning his face to the wall.

'Oh, well, we'll talk about it another time.' Joey stared at his brother's back, wishing Danny didn't find it so difficult to cope with life, knowing that his own success was part of the problem.

As he walked back to the house, he thought about his achievements and the downside it could bring; then, with a sudden sinking in his stomach, he remembered the envelope which had been nestling in his pocket for the last hour.

He wanted the protection of his own four walls, so waited until he was inside before shoving his hand in his pocket and pulling out the unwelcome letter. He extracted a single sheet of paper, printed like earlier ones in Letraset.

'TAP DANCER better not win.'

The name of his best ride the following afternoon at Sandown was highlighted in bright orange.

Chapter Eleven

Joey was booked to ride four races at Leicester in the afternoon. He set off in his Range Rover just after midday with Nina and Di.

As they cruised across country on the A14, he tried to push to the back of his mind the thought of stopping Tap Dancer next day. Meanwhile, his companions were discussing the best way to pay back Ivor Wimsatt.

'You can't just let the bastard off,' Di urged. 'Men like that have got to be shown that they simply can't abuse women as and when they feel like it.'

'But I've told you, I won't go to the police – I don't want him sent to jail; too many other people would suffer as a result.'

'Okay, but there must be some other way of punishing him, mustn't there, Joey?' Di appealed.

He agreed that Wimsatt had to be taught a lesson – one he would not easily forget.

And something Danny had recently done gave him an idea.

In the early-evening, on his own, Joey sat at his kitchen table gazing at a list of all the branches of the Southern Counties Building Society. The money he'd been pouring into it could have been drawn from any one of them, scattered across the south of England, up towards the Midlands. There was even a branch nearby in Cambridge.

For a few irrational moments, Joey considered a plan to stake out the Cambridge branch and watch to see if anyone he knew turned up there to draw money from the 'hole-in-the-wall'. But he knew he was clutching at straws. Nick Allen had made it clear enough that even the police would have had trouble homing in on whoever was taking Joey's money.

He got up and put on the kettle. It was just coming to the boil when the phone rang. He picked it up.

'Hello, Joey. Did you get my note?'

He didn't reply.

'Sounds as though you did. Remember what will happen if you don't do as you're told.' There was a brief pause. 'And we want another fifty thousand, by Tuesday.'

'I can't do it by Tuesday.'

'Yes, you can. And you'd better if you don't want this tape sent to the press and the police. And don't forget, we're watching you.'

As usual, the line went dead as soon as the speaker had finished.

Joey stared at the phone. He was beginning to sense something faintly familiar about the voice. Or was it his mind playing tricks?

He wondered if the threat that he was being permanently watched was just a bluff. Although they'd had no trouble tracking him in France, there'd been no mention of his visits to Lichfield or Chester.

But then, they'd known when he'd been to Yarmouth; Giulio's corpse was testament to that.

Joey stood up and stretched. Determined to take some control over his life, he went and changed. The sponsors of the big weekend meeting at Newmarket were holding a reception at the racecourse, to which everyone was invited. He had asked Nina but to his surprise she'd turned him down; she'd already been asked to a party herself.

In a moment of desperate insecurity, Joey wondered if she had been annoyed by the call from Laura this morning. Perhaps she hadn't believed his woolly explanation about Danny's involvement. But he dismissed the thought as unworthy, and hoped that the reason was Nina's fierce sense of independence.

The reception was in a large, elaborate marquee behind the stands at the racecourse. Few people noticed when Joey walked in; at four foot ten, it was hard to make a grand entrance.

Expensive scent mingled with the smell of cigar smoke and champagne. The indecipherable babble of a few hundred voices talking loudly all at once enveloped him without giving him the buzz it usually did. Occasional camera flashes reminded him of the publicity purpose of the function, and Joey wished he'd never come.

He squeezed his way through the crowd, nodding at most of the people he passed. He hadn't ventured far inside the canvas cavern when he noticed a small group gathered around the man who was currently the town's most fashionable trainer: a philanderer with good connections and an uncanny eye for a horse.

It was natural for Charles Rettingham to be surrounded by rich, laughing men and beautiful women. But on this occasion at the centre of the circle was Nina.

Joey felt a sharp stab of jealousy at her presence. He saw Di, too, bathing vicariously in Nina's popularity. He deliberately skirted round the group, not wanting to be part of it.

'Hello, Joey!' Laura Seabourn greeted him with an extravagant hug and a generous kiss on his lips.

He returned the greeting with as much enthusiasm as he could muster. 'Hello, you wicked little creature.'

'Little? That's rich, coming from you!'

'You won't argue with the "wicked" though?'

'I'm sorry about what happened the other week. You were right, I was being stupid. Poor Danny.'

'I hope you haven't been driving him crazy ever since. Anyway, why did you ring me this morning?'

'I just needed to talk to you,' she said defensively.

'Here I am,' Joey said with a friendly smile; she wasn't much more than a child after all.

'It's just that . . .' Laura was suddenly less sure of herself. 'Well, Mum and Dad . . . Oh, it doesn't really matter.' Her voice trailed off and she reddened.

Joey guessed that the real reason for her call was that she'd heard about Nina from her parents and wanted to find out what she meant to him. Now it looked as if she were too embarrassed to ask. Pretending he hadn't noticed, he managed to get her chatting about horses for a while, until someone caught her eye and she took the cue.

'Joey, I'll see you later.' She leaned down to kiss him on the lips, ignoring a photographer's flash. She may only have been seventeen, but she was a very attractive girl. The next moment, she was gone.

He heard Nina's voice in his ear. 'Hello, I can see you're busy, but aren't you going to talk to me?'

'I didn't think you'd noticed I was here.'

'I hadn't, Di told me.'

'Your new friend.'

'I've got lots of new friends since I came to Newmarket.'

'Who brought you tonight?'

'Gerry and Charles.'

'Well, don't pay too much attention to Rettingham, for a start.'

Nina laughed. 'He already told me that breaking in fillies is his speciality.'

Joey grinned with relief at her evident disdain. 'And has he offered you any rides, yet?'

'You could say that. And he says he has a horse to win a ladies' race called the Newmarket Plate or something.'

Joey nodded. 'The Town Plate. You wouldn't be popular if you won that.'

'Hello, Joey,' a loud, aristocratic voice boomed over his shoulder.

Joey turned round to face a tall man in his early-forties, lean, fit and fine-featured. 'Hello, Rupert.'

The tall man's eyes flickered from Joey to Nina. 'Any chance of an introduction?'

'Nina Korsakov, this is Lord Leamington. He used to be a jockey.'

Leamington looked approvingly at Nina. 'Are you Russian?'

'Of course,' she said in her low voice.

'How interesting. Where are you from?'

'The circus.'

Lord Leamington laughed, already hooked by her unique combination of the bizarre and the beautiful.

'How is Lady Leamington?' Joey asked.

'She's fine.' He nodded over adjacent heads. 'Just over

there, talking to your boss. We've just bought a horse in your yard – Tap Dancer. You're riding him at Sandown tomorrow, I believe?'

Joey couldn't speak at first. What was this? A conspiracy? Fate playing with him, or what? He had been trying desperately to forget the instruction to stop Tap Dancer, and Lenny Williams' subsequent interest.

'You are riding him, aren't you?'

'Yes, I think I am. He should go well.'

'Worth a punt?'

Joey nodded. 'On the form. I haven't ridden him for a while, though. I don't know how well he is. You'd better ask Mr Seabourn.'

'Dick says he's jumping out of his skin.'

Joey's heart sank, but he was saved from making any more inventive excuse by someone else catching Lord Leamington's eye. 'Best of luck then, Joey. I expect we'll see more of you?' He gave Nina a winning smile and walked away.

'My God, what a fantastic-looking man,' she said, and just as abruptly changed the subject. 'But why were you so fidgety when he mentioned Tap Dancer? Don't you think he will win?'

'Was it that obvious?'

'Yes.'

'I don't think he's up to it, but the man's only just bought the horse. I couldn't say, "Well done, you've got yourself a donkey".'

Nina looked at him.

He was irritated to feel himself blush.

She shook her head. 'Joey, you wouldn't ever cheat anyone, would you? You were such an innocent, honest boy when you first came to the circus.'

'I'm still an innocent, honest boy,' he protested.

'Who's this you're talking about?' Barry said, coming up behind them with a grin.

Joey didn't want to repeat the conversation he'd just had with Tap Dancer's new owner. 'Can you convince this woman I wouldn't lie to her?'

'Nina,' Barry said with elaborate earnestness, 'yer man here is probably the straightest jockey in Christendom, but of his qualities as a liar, I know nothing.'

He beamed at them both.

Joey tried to detect some double-entendre from his agent's delivery, but the Irishman's smile was as inscrutable as ever.

'Now, Nina,' Barry went on, 'there's someone over here I'd like you to meet. He may even have a ride for you.'

Joey watched them go, cursing the way this woman had him trembling like a teenager. Why the hell, he asked himself, did this have to happen when he was in the middle of saving his career – his liberty even – from a cunning, opportunistic blackmailer?

He'd already realised he'd need all his wits about him to handle Nina, and had to remind himself of this later when he decided to leave.

He went to find her and she greeted him with a big grin and a warm kiss on his cheek, as she laughed with the group surrounding her.

'Can I tear you away yet?' he asked.

'No, you can't. Di and I have a job to do tonight, remember? And I'm afraid you'd only get in the way.'

'Are you doing it tonight, then? You've worked fast.'

Nina nodded with a grin. 'We strike while we're hot.' Her eyes flashed. 'We got hold of your brother's friend.

Di's been over to Cambridge to get him.'

Joey was impressed. He wished he could do more to help with the plan he'd helped formulate, but Nina had objected. Wimsatt knew him, and that would blow the whole thing.

'Keep out of trouble, if you can,' he told her. 'Come round tomorrow and tell me how it went. I'm going to bed early. I've got a living to make in the morning.'

If you could call this living, he thought to himself as he walked towards the exit from the marquee.

Di was already in the car park, waiting for Nina in her small Peugeot. She had been home briefly to change.

'My God!' Nina gasped. 'You look fantastic! I've never seen anything so tarty in my entire life. He'll love it!'

'Let's hope so. He sounded pretty doubtful when I said I wanted to see him after the show tonight. Said he liked to look at new acts with a clear head in the mornings.'

'Don't worry, as soon as he sees you, he'll forget about that. And when he thinks you're going to sleep with him to get the booking, he'll do whatever you want. He's one of those men who just loses his mind as soon as his prick hardens. Believe me, I know.'

'Right, let's hit the road to Banbury.' Di glanced in her mirror. 'Danny and the chap from Cambridge are right behind us.'

Ivor Wimsatt walked back to his trailer with eager little strides. Over the phone, there had been a husky confidence about the woman's voice which suggested she had more to offer than just a juggling act. He wasn't particularly interested in that, anyway; he already had one of the best female jugglers in the country. But, as his father had always said, it cost nothing to look – especially if there could be a bonus for him in it. And it wouldn't be the first time that such a bonus was on offer.

It had been a good show tonight. Bringing the lion act back had certainly boosted the rural Oxfordshire crowds. Inside his trailer, Wimsatt poured himself a large brandy and tried to stop his hands from quivering at the prospect of his interview with the juggler.

He had left the door open to let in the warm evening air. He caught a waft of her powerful scent before he heard the tap on the door.

'Come in,' he said in a gruff, dry voice.

Long legs in knee-high boots drew his attention first. Then dark tan stockings with black tops showing below a scanty black leather skirt. Above this was a short expanse of exposed midriff, and a slinky, shiny short top barely covering a black lacy bra and big, round breasts.

Only then did the ring-master look at his visitor's face.

Di had enjoyed going to town on her appearance. The make-up methods of the professional seductress were tried, tested and devoid of subtlety. She hadn't attempted to improve on them: a warm foundation, long false lashes, dark kohl around the eyes. Her hair fell in long, loose waves to her shoulders.

'Hello, my dear,' Wimsatt said breathlessly.

Di knew she'd reached first base. 'Mr Wimsatt?'

'Come in, come in. Would you like a drink? Brandy? Champagne?'

'Brandy, please,' Di said in a voice her mother wouldn't have recognised, and sat down on a comfortably sprung, built-in couch.

She saw Wimsatt gulp as she hitched up her skirt and flashed her scarlet knickers at him. She took the large balloon glass he offered her and pretended to drink a mouthful of brandy.

He did the same, and positioned his squat, ungainly body beside hers. He put one podgy arm around her and squeezed. 'Well, my dear, if your juggling is anything as good as the first impression you give, I think we might be able to come to some arrangement.' He cleared his throat. 'Are you married, by the way? I forgot to ask on the phone.'

'No. I was once, but I like a bit of variety, know what I mean?'

'Of course.' Wimsatt tried for a debonair tone. 'I quite agree.'

'Is the circus all yours, then?' asked Di.

'Oh, yes. And my father's before me.'

'Is that big blue Roller outside yours too?'

'Yes, though it's a Bentley.'

'D'you fancy taking me for a spin in it – give us a chance to get acquainted, like?'

Wimsatt hesitated for a moment, balancing up the probability that if he complied he would be rewarded against the certainty that he was over the drink-drive limit.

Lust – enhanced by Di's stretching her legs and offering him another glimpse of her red knickers – took about five seconds to overcome prudence.

'Come on, then. Bring your glass and I'll bring the bottle.'

With obvious glee, he shepherded her down the steps to his gleaming, aquamarine limousine. He opened the passenger door for her and his jaw sagged with excitement as she tucked her long legs under her on the white leather seat.

He scuttled round and climbed into the driver's seat. There was still a faint hint of sun in the western sky, but there was no moon rising and soon it would be pitch dark. Di chose a soul album from the rack in front of her, pushed it into the CD player and lay back in her seat, praying that Nina and the boys were following close behind.

Nina sat beside Sean Delaney, a recently acquired friend of Danny's, who was driving his small Renault van. Danny was crouching in the back, peering between the front seats at the tail lights of Wimsatt's Bentley.

In the Bentley, Di took a deep breath, gritted her teeth and snuggled up beside Wimsatt. Given the reason for the whole exercise, she considered it worthwhile, and it wouldn't last too long. Anyway, she enjoyed giving her performance, and knowing she was playing her part in securing a triumph for Nina.

She had fixed the wing mirror so she could see the lights of Sean Delaney's van.

Three or four miles west of the old market town where the circus was playing, Di slipped one arm around Wimsatt's ample waist and squeezed, while her other hand massaged his upper thigh. He smiled smugly at his powers of seduction – and Di marvelled anew at a male vanity which was so predictable and easy to manipulate.

She gently tugged Wimsatt's arm. 'Let's turn down this lane and find somewhere to stop. I'm beginning to feel very horny.'

Wimsatt nearly overshot the turning in his excitement,

but hauled the big car round at the last moment and nosed into the narrow lane between tall trees.

After another fifty yards, Di pointed. 'Look, there's a little track. No one's going to disturb us there.'

Wimsatt nodded eagerly and recklessly turned the Bentley on to the narrow earth track where it lurched a dozen yards into the woods.

It was nearly ten and night had fallen. Nina, Danny and Sean sat in the van with the window open, listening to the evening calls of the birds and the screech of barn owls waking for the hunt while they waited for Di to work on Wimsatt.

After five minutes, they climbed out, Sean carrying a small case containing the tools of his trade. They trooped in single file down the secondary lane until they reached the point where the track headed off into the woods. They stopped and listened. The Bentley's engine had been turned off and they could clearly hear the CD player now, still belting out soul.

They peered up the rutted track. Out of some strange instinct, Wimsatt had left on the side lights and switched on the interior lighting.

'S'pose he likes to see what he's doing,' Danny whispered.

Nina put a finger to her lips and signalled them to keep still while she set off up the track, comfortable in the knowledge that the khaki waxed jacket she wore over her party dress would make her hard to spot in the dark.

When she was within ten feet of the Bentley, she stopped and waited a moment before creeping forward, right up to the car, crouching with her head well below the windows. She listened to the noises from inside. As far as she could judge, everything was going according to the ad hoc plan she and Di had worked out, giggling over a bottle of Chardonnay at lunch today. There was a rock track playing now and the murmur of two voices – Di's husky and false, and the more intermittent growl of Ivor's, fuddled with drink.

Nina took out the pocket knife she had brought with her and groped around until she had located the nearest of the four big tyres.

She unfolded the well-sharpened blade and began cautiously to press it into the side of the tyre. Quivering with fear and excitement, she started to apply pressure with her finger alongside the blade. As soon as she felt the first hint of escaping air, she pulled back the knife. Within a few minutes, Nina had all four tyres deflating gently. Then she crept back the dozen yards to where the two men were waiting.

Di wasn't particularly enjoying her part of their stratagem, but was at least gaining some satisfaction from seeing it.

Wimsatt eagerly activated a reclining mechanism until both pristine white hide seats were near horizontal – more than flat enough for a comfortable snooze.

Di was quick to take the initiative.

She was getting a buzz from the power that her sexual hold over the man gave her, and submitted to his clumsy pawing of her breasts. The music didn't completely drown the grunting and snuffling sounds he made as his excitement mounted.

'Ivor!' Di said in mock affront. 'You're so keen – like a boy in a sweet shop! Slow down, you're getting overheated. Let's get you undressed first, then you can undress me – nice and slow.'

'Oh, yes!' he grunted as Di unbuttoned his shirt, unbuckled his belt and unzipped his flies. He fumbled around, helping her to slip down his pants to reveal an unimpressive erection.

Di was careful not to laugh; she knew he was capable of violence if she did anything to injure his pride. She carried on pulling the clothes off his tubby, inebriated body until he was completely nude against the white leather upholstery.

She gritted her teeth and put a hand on his naked thigh, massaging it as much as she could bear, while with her spare hand she picked up the bottle of brandy and put it to her lips. She tilted back her head, carefully ramming her tongue in the neck of the bottle before she lowered it with a contented gasp and passed it to Wimsatt.

He took it in the same spirit of abandon and, less carefully than Di, also tilted it back. The brandy dribbled from the side of his mouth as he gulped down as much as he could.

As he drank, Di scooped up his shoes and all the clothing she'd removed. Wimsatt, busy with the bottle, didn't notice. She quickly let herself out of the driver's door.

'Just going to have a pee,' she said over the noise of the CD, and shut the door. By the dim light of the car's interior, she peered into the gloom of the bushes beside the track.

'Danny!' she hissed.

He came out of the undergrowth, crouched over, a coil of rope over one shoulder. Sean was beside him, with his box of tools. 'Hi,' Danny whispered. 'Having fun?'

'I will be when I see what you can do.' Di dropped the pile of clothes into a plastic bag Danny had brought for the purpose, and opened the car door.

'Hurry up,' Wimsatt bleated. 'I don't think I can hold out much longer.'

Di climbed back into the car and pulled the door shut.

Meanwhile, Danny crept round to the driver's side of the Bentley with Sean, who had been prepared to broaden his usual sphere of activities for the extra hundred pounds he'd been promised. Danny clutched the handle, looked at Sean and opened the door against which Di had managed to press the ring-master's flabby body.

She quickly backed away while the two young men grasped Wimsatt's doughy flesh with gloved hands and heaved him off the reclining seat. It took some strength to manoeuvre his eleven flaccid stones from the car and on to the grass verge between the track and the woods.

For the first few seconds Wimsatt had no idea what was happening. As soon as he started to struggle, half-way out of the car, Danny gleefully punched his fist hard into the flabby, white midriff, and Wimsatt collapsed into a quivering heap.

Di turned off the lights in the Bentley. In the sudden darkness Danny and Sean swiftly dragged Wimsatt a few yards further into the wood to the sturdy trunk of an oak tree. They heaved the naked man against it. Sean propped him up and flicked on a powerful torch while Danny took the coil of rope from his shoulder and lashed Wimsatt with his back to the tree and arms splayed around it behind him.

The ring-master was jabbering with a mixture of terror and fury that he'd been set up. But every time he struggled, Danny punched him and he soon got the message.

'What the hell do you want?' he gasped, blinking into the beam of Sean's torch. 'If it's money, just say so. You don't have to go through all this charade.'

'It isn't money.'

Wimsatt glared into the darkness, not sure if that was Nina's voice he had heard.

'Who's that? Nina? What do you want?'

He shivered as the air grew perceptibly cooler and his penis shrivelled into obscurity.

Nina stepped into the dim torchlight, and laughed. 'You'll find out soon enough.'

Once they were sure that he was securely tied, Sean fetched his tool-box from the other side of the car.

He came back and handed Danny the torch while he placed the box on the ground and opened it to reveal his collection of needles and syringes.

Wimsatt saw them and quivered in terror. 'What the hell are you going to do? You can't kill me . . .' he cried.

Sean looked up at him and smiled. 'We're not going to kill you, Mr Wimsatt,' he said softly. 'It's not drugs in here, it's dye. We're going to tattoo you.'

Wimsatt's face registered complete horror.

'What do you mean? What kind of tattoo?' he asked in a strangled whisper.

'A warning to others,' Nina told him coldly. 'So you don't get a chance to hurt anyone else the way you tried to hurt me.'

Sean stood up with the first needle ready. 'I'm going to do this free-hand, so it won't be the best I've ever done. But then, I don't suppose you'll be showing it off too much,' he added with a humourless grin.

He took a pace nearer and placed the needlepoint on Wimsatt's bare, hairless chest. 'I think here, just above the nipples.'

Wimsatt flinched, and the needle caught his flabby pectoral. He squealed with pain. 'For God's sake!' he pleaded.

'The more you move, the more it will hurt,' Sean said calmly. 'Now, I'm going to do the outline in black, but you can choose the infill colour. What would you like?'

'Fuck you! I'll make you pay for this, you bastard!'

Sean carried on smiling. He was enjoying himself. 'All right. If you won't choose a colour, I will. I think a nice turquoise, to match your car. That'll look good, won't it?'

Twenty minutes later the job was done. Nina, who had been watching silently from the shadows, stepped forward. She raised an automatic camera to her eye. It flashed half a dozen times on the trembling naked figure of Ivor Wimsatt, lashed to the tree, with the word RAPIST emblazoned in two-inch letters across his chest.

He kept up a muttered barrage of abuse and self-pity as he realised they were going to leave him. They had taken his car key, and his spare wouldn't be any use with four flat tyres. Besides, it looked as if they weren't going to untie him from the tree.

'You can't leave me here like this!' he wailed.

Nina reached into the back of his car and pulled out a rug folded on the rear seat. She passed it to Danny. 'Wrap this around him. If he gets much colder, his cock's going to disappear altogether.'

Di and Nina crammed into the little van with Sean and

Danny. As they drove away, they crowed with triumph and relief.

'My God,' Nina said. 'I never actually believed you'd get him to drive you into the country.'

'Didn't you? O ye of little faith,' Di laughed. 'It was easy. Once his blood was up, he would have done anything I wanted.'

'I think that'd work with me too,' Danny guffawed.

'Yeah, well, you're not getting the chance to find out. And don't you dare tell *anyone* what we did tonight, or I'll have your bollocks.'

'Yes, please,' he tittered.

'I mean it.'

Danny didn't miss the steely edge to Di's voice.

'But thank you very much, Danny,' Nina said to mollify him. She was glad she'd asked him to help. He'd done his bit well; the whole operation had gone better than she'd dared to hope, and they had inflicted just the right amount of humiliation on Wimsatt in retribution for what he had done to her.

With a great deal of expense and embarrassment, he would eventually be able to get the letters on his chest removed, but there would always be a faint scar to remind him.

They soon reached the circus site, where Di and Nina transferred to Di's Peugeot. She gunned it into life and they headed back to Newmarket.

After a couple of miles, she stopped and pulled into a lay-by. She picked up her mobile phone and dialled the Banbury police.

When the call was answered, she adopted the voice of an upper-crust sexagenarian and told them where they would find a man acting very strangely, almost certainly up to no good, maybe even murder.

Then she put down the phone.

'Do you think they'll go?' Nina asked.

'They're bound to. They couldn't ignore a call like that, just in case it turned out to be genuine. I don't suppose they'll do him for much more than being drunk in charge of a vehicle, but that and the tattoo should keep him away from you for the foreseeable future, shouldn't it?'

'I don't know, but he's the sort of man who hates to look a fool so I guess it'll work.' Nina laughed. 'And it was fun doing it. I should think he's going crazy now. Either I'll never see him again, or he'll come back and try to kill me.' She shrugged her shoulders fatalistically.

Di had started the car again and was driving more slowly now. 'Was it hard to persuade Sean to take the job?'

Nina grinned. 'Not too hard.'

Di glanced at her. 'You're amazing. You've only been here a week, and you've got people running all over the place for you. I'm sure Gerry Tewkesbury fancies you, and he's one of the most eligible men in Newmarket.'

'Well, I don't fancy him.'

'Just Joey?'

Nina nodded. 'Just Joey.'

When they reached Newmarket, Di stopped the car near the centre of the town, outside a large Edwardian red-brick house that had been split into flats. Hers was on the top floor. 'Come on up and have a drink.'

'Thanks, I need one.'

In the small, pretty apartment, Di took a bottle of champagne from her fridge and filled two slender glasses. 'Here's to Operation Ivor.'

They both laughed and drank. Di put on a CD and they settled down on her squashy calico-covered chairs.

'So, tell me all about Joey and the circus?' she invited.

'Have you ever seen Freddie Fielding's Circus?'

'No. Never.'

Nina told her about circus life and Joey's early days there; how he had been taken into her mother's Cossack Riders, then her father's trapeze troupe, and how he was learning to fly when her father and brother had been killed.

'Soon after that, my other brothers left, leaving me and my mother. Ginger moved on, then Joey. I assumed he was going to look for Ginger.' Nina shook her head at her misjudgement. 'Of course, we got a new trapeze troupe – a Mexican family called the Flying Ferraras. I don't think they'll stay with Wimsatt much longer, though, they're a brilliant act.'

Di nodded. 'Yes, I've seen them . . . I think. Or heard of them.'

'Anyway,' Nina went on, 'I never saw Joey again after he left until he turned up in Nottingham two and a half weeks ago.'

'Really?' Di said. 'He just turned up out of the blue, without any warning?'

Nina nodded. 'Yes.'

'What made him suddenly do that?'

'I'm not sure. He said he was looking for Ginger. I gave him the address of Ginger's old partner, Giulio. He went to see him, but a week later the old chap was attacked and died. It was terrible.'

'Do you think Joey's visit had something to do with it?'

Nina didn't want to tell her what she thought. She'd already said too much. She shook her head emphatically. 'No, but Joey was very upset.'

'He must have been. Do you know, he never really talks about the circus. Of course, most people know that's where he came from and where he learned to ride, but I've hardly ever heard him speak about it. It's as if he's trying to forget it.'

'I don't think so – not entirely,' Nina said. 'Though I do know he wasn't always happy there.'

Di got to her feet. 'Refill?'

Nina nodded.

After a couple more glasses of Di's champagne, she turned down the offer of dinner and took a taxi back to her caravan. She climbed into bed, satisfied with her evening's work, and grateful to Di for her help. At the same time, she had an irrational but nagging hunch that there was more to Di's assistance than simple good nature; and she wondered, not for the first time, if the girl still harboured stronger feelings for Joey than she was prepared to admit.

The next day, at Sandown races, Barry found Joey in the weighing room. The agent could barely contain his anger.

'Why the hell aren't you riding Tap Dancer? He'll waltz it – look at the field. There's nothing to touch him. What's going on?'

Joey stood by the rails behind the weighing machine and stared at the large brick fireplace. He couldn't look his friend in the eye. 'Barry, I tell you, I've done something to my ankle. It's bloody agony. I'll have to go and see the quack.'

'But what have you done to it, for God's sake?'

'I don't know. Twisted it jumping down, I think. Does it matter? It hurts like hell, that's all I know.'

'Look, Joey,' Barry pleaded, 'I've backed the horse, and there's no one else much around to ride him.'

'Graham hasn't a ride,' Joey suggested. 'But anyway, it's up to the guv'nor – not you or me.'

'I'll have to go and see Dick and sort it out, then.'

Joey watched Barry rush off and wondered just how much money he had on the horse to make him so anxious for Joey to ride.

Or – he paled as the thought struck him – did Barry just want Joey to have the ride to be sure the animal *didn't* win?

Nothing had happened to eliminate anyone else from his long list of suspects and he had to accept that Barry Mannion's name was still on it.

He walked to the racecourse doctor's office, hobbling conspicuously, trying to be consistent in which leg he was favouring.

The duty medical offer felt Joey's ankle and shook his head. 'Can't feel a thing.'

'Maybe you can't, doc, but it's my leg and I bloody well can!'

'Just try walking on it again,' the doctor asked.

Joey swung his legs over the side of the couch and took a few paces, limping heavily and wincing.

'Oh, well,' the MO said, 'if it's that bad, I'd better sign you off for the rest of the day.'

'Thanks, doc. My agent didn't believe me, I'm afraid.'

'Didn't he? I don't think I do either, but there it is. Please try not to twist your ankle like this again.'

Joey left with a certificate forbidding him to ride

that day and until he'd seen another doctor to pass him fit. He went to look for Dick to tell him the bad tidings. As he'd expected, Barry had got to the trainer first. Seabourn looked livid. 'Do you know where the hell Graham is?'

'I don't know, guv'nor. He was here, and he's got a ride in the last, I think.'

'Well, he's nowhere to be seen now. If you see him in the next few minutes, tell him he's needed. Otherwise there's a young claimer I could put up.'

'Lord Leamington won't mind who rides him, as long as he wins.'

Dick looked at him hard. 'I hope to God there's something seriously wrong with your ankle, Joey.'

'Thanks a lot, guv'nor!'

Joey didn't stay at the races. He couldn't face seeing anyone else and pretending to be injured. The whole incident was making him feel genuinely sick, but at least he'd avoided having to pull the horse.

He found his Range Rover and drove out of the car park. He listened to the race commentary on a premium rate service over the phone, glad for the new owner when Tap Dancer sounded as though he'd won easily.

He didn't want to think about what the consequences would be for him. Instead, he thought of Nina.

He had been hoping to see her that morning, to hear how she and Di had got on with their scheme to deal with Wimsatt. But when he'd rung, she hadn't answered her mobile.

Although usually he didn't believe in revenge, he had never been subjected to the kind of demeaning assault that Wimsatt had inflicted on Nina, and could see how she might well feel purged if the culprit was made to suffer a similar ordeal. Di's eagerness to be involved he attributed to her taste for adventure.

When he got back to Three Elms Farm, Joey ignored his flashing answerphone. Instead of playing his messages he went straight upstairs to lie in a bath with a large tumbler of vodka, and tried not to think about what could happen next.

At last, he forced himself out of the womb-like security of the water to face raw reality. Wrapped in a towelling robe, he went downstairs and played through his messages, dreading the alien tone of the blackmailer.

But the only call was from Laura, asking him if he'd seen the papers and telling him to call her as soon as possible. He decided to deal with her later. Right now, he needed to concentrate on identifying the party or parties who were holding him to ransom.

Like Nick Allen, he was coming round to the view that he must be dealing with someone involved in racing. It could have been anyone who at some point had had access to Ginger's tape, and the opportunity to play and copy it.

He stared at the list of names he had already made a dozen times and willed one to jump out at him.

Graham, Barry, Mike Wade, maybe Lenny Williams through Graham; any of these was still a possibility. So, for that matter, was Ivor Wimsatt. Even though he had no direct connection with racing, it was more than likely he had friends who had.

Joey banged the table in frustration. He had already been up and down this road a dozen times, proposing and rejecting suspects on the flimsiest evidence.

He was still gazing angrily at the names when a soft thud from his study caught his attention.

He stood up slowly and wrapped his robe tighter around him. He padded silently across the hall. The study door was ajar, far enough for him to see into part of the room. He stopped, waited, listened.

There were no sounds from inside the house besides the tock of the grandfather clock behind him. He stood for another ten seconds in complete silence before he pushed the door wider and walked into the room. At first, he saw nothing odd or out of place until he noticed that the door of the long cabinet behind his desk was open a fraction of an inch.

It should have been locked, and he kept the keys to it in his bedroom. This was his gun case, where he stored a twelve-bore for occasional forays across the meadow after teal and pigeons.

Abandoning caution, he walked quickly across the room and pulled the oak-panelled door wide open. The gun wasn't there.

'Looking for this, Shorty?'

Joey spun round.

An anonymous male figure stepped out from behind the curtains. He was wearing a cheap checked shirt, jeans and Timberlands. On his hands were leather gloves and his face was obliterated by a black, three-hole balaclava.

Even in his fear and confusion, Joey recognised the voice at once. It was the man who had beaten him up in France.

'That gun won't be much use to you without any shot,' he said defiantly.

'Maybe, but this way I know you won't be using it either. Now, we want a word. Outside.'

Someone grasped Joey viciously from behind. His arm was rammed up between his shoulder blades. He was spun round and marched to the front door, out across the gravel forecourt towards the spreading shrubbery on the other side of the drive.

'Looks like your ankle's better,' the man with the gun said from behind him.

Summoning up all his strength and speed, Joey jerked round and tried to wriggle free from the grip on his arm. The stock of his own shotgun was smashed into his side as he caught a glimpse of a second hooded man, who twisted him back violently to face the front and frog-marched him towards a wall of lush, full-leaved laurel.

When they reached the bushes, his captors carried on propelling him straight in among the branches, pushing through to a clearing on the inside. They were no more than twenty feet from the public highway, but Joey knew that only two or three people a day walked along it.

Without warning, an iron-hard fist drove brutally into his side, deep between his lower ribs and pelvis.

'We don't want to damage you so much you can't ride. You owe us a lot of money and you need to be able to earn it. But I promise you, this is your last warning.'

The bile that rose in the back of his throat emphasised the bitterness of Joey's defeat. The frustration he felt was almost worse than the pain.

A second blow slammed into his other side, bruising his kidneys, making him retch and gasp again.

'Understand? Next time you're asked to stop a horse, you fuckin' stop it, see? Unless you want to end up like your mate Giulio. I wonder who the Old Bill would look for then? Someone wanting revenge for the death of two men on a trapeze, I should think. The daughter . . . the sister. What d'you reckon?'

For a third time a fist was pummelled into Joey's side, already almost anaesthetised by the previous punches. 'That's who they'd look for: the daughter of the man you killed. They'd be looking for Nina Korsakov – your pretty friend. Wouldn't they?' The man hit him again, laughing.

Joey came close to fainting. Through the mist of pain and fury that dimmed his vision, he could see splashes of a blue-gold evening sky between the blurred edges of dark waxy leaves. The next day seemed a hundred years away, and his house a hundred miles. He wondered if he would ever see either again.

When they hit him once more, he gave up and waited for oblivion.

But it didn't come.

Slowly he realised that they had gone – abandoned him on a carpet of rotting leaves beneath a green canopy of laurels. The sharp pain in his sides had diminished to a dull ache of bruised muscles, and a shameful fear.

Joey heard them go. There was a noisy snapping of branches and rustling of leaves. Then a car revving up out in the road; a faint squeal as it roared off.

He didn't know how long he lay there, but with the return of his strength came a new resolution.

He had to get to these people before they asked him to pull a horse again. And he had to confess to Nina how and why her father and brother had plunged to their deaths ten years before.

If she didn't forgive him or accept the innocence of his involvement, at least he would have had the satisfaction of telling her himself, and not allowing her to hear it from the thugs who had just beaten him.

It was another couple of minutes before he was strong enough to clamber to his feet and push his way out of the laurel thicket. He took the same route as the men who'd beaten him and found a gap in the fence where they had clambered through on to the roadside. On the verge was a trail of skid marks and gravel spewed from the road across the scrubby grass.

He scrambled through the fence and limped back down the road towards his gate. He was opening it when Barry's Porsche appeared at the end of the straight and slowed down to turn in.

Joey hobbled back to the house before his agent could see the state he was in. He'd just banged the front door shut behind him when Barry pulled up outside and walked across to knock on it.

Joey got himself upstairs and opened a window in his bedroom, overlooking the courtyard.

'Hello, Barry. I was just lying down to rest my ankle. I'll come across later if you're staying?'

'Joey, what the hell's going on?'

'I'll tell you later. Nothing to worry about. Tap Dancer won, didn't he?'

'But *you* should have had that winner.'

'Well, you backed him, didn't you?'

'That's not the point. I need to know what's going on.'

'I'll be up in your office in ten minutes, okay?'

'Okay.'

Relieved, Joey watched him go, praying that he hadn't just been sold an elaborate double-bluff. If the agent was genuinely happy at the outcome of the race, he couldn't have wanted Joey to stop the horse – which in turn meant he was nothing to do with the blackmail plot.

Joey wondered if, after all the years he had known him, he could really be sure of Barry.

When he was out of the shower, he picked up the phone by his bed and dialled Nina's number which he already knew by heart.

This time she answered.

'It's Joey. How've you been?'

'I've been having fun. Last night was brilliant! And today I was schooling some horses for Charles Rettingham.'

Joey winced. There could be only one reason why Rettingham should want Nina to school his string – and it had nothing to do with the horses. But he refused to let himself be jealous.

'I'll come over later and you can tell me all about it,' he said.

'Great. I'll make you dinner. Bring some wine.'

'How's the ankle?' Barry asked as Joey walked into his office over the garage a few minutes later.

Joey didn't have to pretend to be lame.

'Bloody sore.'

Barry suddenly looked at him more closely, noticing the cuts and bruises on his face. 'Are you okay, Joey?'

'It's okay. I'm fine.'

'But what have you done to your face?'

'Nothing. I walked into a stable door, that's all.'

'Lucky you didn't do it yesterday.'

'Why's that?'

'Haven't you seen the *Mail* today? There's a lovely picture of you on the gossip page.'

Joey remembered Laura's message and pulled a face. 'No.'

Barry handed him a copy of the paper. There was an eye-catching photograph of Joey and Laura kissing at the reception the evening before; underneath it the caption, 'Joey Leatham: retainership?' and an article speculating about possible marriage plans.

Joey groaned.

Barry laughed. 'They do write the most terrible drivel, don't they? I suppose it stops them getting bored.'

'Never mind that. What will Dick Seabourn think?'

Barry shrugged. 'Who cares? He's not going to get rid of you, whatever you do. Not now. He needs you too much to worry about his daughter rutting below her station.'

'She's not rutting – well, not with me.'

'Not while the lovely Nina's around anyway,' Barry chuckled.

Joey froze. There was no chance that Charles Rettingham would have let the day pass without drawing the article to Nina's attention, and milking it for all it was worth. 'Oh, shit,' he muttered, and sat down at Barry's desk to read the piece in full.

Barry stood up. 'I've left some stuff in my car,' he said. 'Just hang on a minute while I fetch it. There's a couple of things I wanted to talk to you about.'

He hurried off down the stairs. Joey finished reading the fiction about his nuptial plans and glanced at the papers on Barry's desk. His eye was caught by an official police notification of a speeding offence, registered by camera.

It was for Barry's Porsche, on the M56, between the M6 and Chester on Sunday, 7 July.

The day Joey had been up to get Nina.

The wording dissolved into a blur and swam in front of Joey's eyes.

Coincidence?

Joey thought wildly. What could possibly have taken Barry to Chester on a Sunday?

He heard his agent climbing back up the stairs and quickly walked across to the sofa and sat down, as if still reading the paper.

Barry came in. Joey let him carry on with finalising a few arrangements before he said casually, apropos of nothing in particular, 'Did you go to the evening meeting in Chester last Friday?'

'No. Why?'

'When were you last there?'

Barry looked at him, slightly bemused. 'God, I haven't been in two years. Why do you ask?'

'I just wondered.'

Barry looked at him askance and checked two more dates with him before Joey got up, glancing at his watch.

'I'm sorry, Barry, I've got to go.'

'Nina?' He grinned.

'Yes.'

'Best of luck. Dick says you're working Scaramanga early tomorrow. I'll see you on the Heath then.'

Nina had asked him to bring some wine. Joey picked up two bottles of Barolo from the rack in his kitchen and walked down to the paddock in the evening sun, his mind busily turning over the implications of Barry's trip to Chester.

Of course, being caught on the M56 didn't mean he had been to Chester, but near enough for him to have mentioned it when Joey asked – if he'd had anything to hide.

Barry had been one of Joey's closest friends since he had arrived in Newmarket.

Against that, there was no denying that he liked making money as much as anyone else in this town of brazen opportunists.

The only thing to do – and Joey should have done it there and then this evening – was to confront him directly over the speeding ticket. Resolved that he would do just that the next morning, Joey clambered stiffly over the stile, through the belt of trees, and climbed up the wooden steps to Nina's front door.

When she opened it to him, he saw at once that she had made an effort to look as good as she could, and was glad he hadn't let his bruises prevent him from coming. It made him feel better just to see her.

The inside of Nina's trailer looked as it had on Joey's first visit to Nottingham – the time she'd invited him in to eat goulash. He was struck that a mobile home should have such an air of permanence about it. He guessed it was the plethora of ornaments and free-standing domestic objects that achieved the effect, as well as the length of time Nina's family had occupied it.

Joey was impressed to find her already quite at home in Newmarket after just a few days. It seemed that everyone was offering her help, advice, jobs – anything to make her life easier. He was under no illusion that any spectacular-looking woman of exotic background could fail to attract a lot of interest, but couldn't help feeling a little cheated nevertheless.

However, he couldn't blame her.

Nina had carefully made up her eyes, accentuating their brightness. She was wearing a hand-worked lace blouse, full at the shoulder and close at the waist, and a multi-coloured tiered skirt. If it hadn't been for her fair colouring, she'd have looked like a Hollywood gypsy. As it was, Joey thought, she looked like a proud and knowing peasant, about to seduce a young squire.

Her manner was more compassionate. She immediately saw the bruises he'd acquired. 'Joey, what happened to you?'

'If you give me a corkscrew to open this wine, I'll tell you.'

'It wasn't Wimsatt, was it?'

'No, it wasn't your old boyfriend. Why should it be?'

Nina laughed. 'I should think he's mad as hell over what we did to him last night – and ready to take it out on anyone.'

'Do you think it was such a good idea?'

'I don't care whether it was or not. I had to do it, and I'm sure it worked. Anyway, it was your idea, remember?' she added with a grin.

'I'm not so sure how good it was, though – not if you think he's going to come back and make trouble.'

'He was already doing that, wasn't he?'

'I suppose so. Was Danny any help?'

'Sure, he was fine. So was Di, but I still can't see why she's so friendly to me. I think she still wants you.' Nina nodded her head knowingly.

'How's helping you supposed to achieve that?'

'Some women like to be devious,' Nina told him gravely.

Joey jerked the cork out of the bottle and glanced at her. 'So I've heard. But you're okay?'

'Of course I am.'

'But if he does come back, he's not going to be in a good mood, is he?'

She dismissed the problem. 'I'll deal with him if he does. Anyway, it seems to me you're the one who needs protecting. If it wasn't Ivor who came and beat you up, who was it?'

'I wish I knew.' Joey filled two glasses and put them on the polished mahogany table fitted between two upholstered benches. He slid on to one of them, opposite Nina. He smiled then groaned at his own folly. 'There were two of them, both with balaclavas over their heads. I know who sent them – the guy who tried to make me stop Tap Dancer.'

'Lord Leamington's horse? No wonder you thought it wouldn't win. What happened to it?'

'I didn't ride it – I got myself declared unfit. The horse won. These people weren't too happy.'

'Were they going to pay you to stop it?'

'No.' Joey breathed in deeply. 'They said they were going to send a videotape – to you, and to the police, if I didn't.'

Nina stared at him. 'To me?'

He nodded.

'Why to me?'

He refilled their glasses and pushed one across the table towards her. 'I should have told you about this weeks ago, when I first came to see you; and I won't blame you if you never want to see me again after I've told you.'

Nina sat quite still, gazing intently at Joey. It was as if she could see right into his soul. She said nothing.

'It was a tape of us practising on the trapeze the day your father fell.'

Nina's eyes opened even wider. 'You, my father and Mischa?' she said in a whisper.

Joey nodded. 'It's fuzzy and dark, but it clearly shows what took place.'

'But I remember, when it happened, Ginger said there was no . . .' She stopped abruptly. 'You wanted to see him. That's why you came back, isn't it? And why you wanted to find Giulio.'

'Ginger had recorded it – though he'd promised me he wouldn't.'

'Why? Why did he *promise* you? I know he always used to record rehearsals. My father used to bully him into perching up on the poles to get the best angles. And that was going to be a very important rehearsal. That was the day Sol Werner was coming to see the act, don't you remember?'

Sol Werner.

Joey held his head in his hands for a moment until a feeling of nausea had passed. He was telling Nina the truth now, and it might be the only chance he would get. He didn't want to blow it.

'I remember it all right,' he said, not allowing his eyes to waver from hers. 'Ginger promised me he wouldn't make a tape. Said he'd give an excuse to Ivan, say the tape bust – anything – but he wouldn't record the rehearsal because he'd asked me not to catch your father . . . to drop him – as a joke, a cruel joke – to humiliate him in front of Sol Werner.' Joey took a swig from his glass.

He glanced away; couldn't look at Nina for a few moments. 'Ivan had been terrible to us, me in particular; I never knew why. But he'd also upset Ginger – he'd pinched Giulio from him. I didn't know that then, of course, but I didn't care what he'd done. I was quite happy to see him made to look stupid, especially in front of this agent, and maybe put a stop to that crazy idea of his for two flyers to catch him. We didn't want to do the act; it was never going to look great, but he wanted it, so badly, like he was jealous of his own sons for being able to fly.'

Joey lifted his eyes and looked straight across at Nina. 'But I swear to you, I never knew about the nets . . . and I *never* thought he'd take Mikhail with him.'

Nina stared back at him. 'This is all on a videotape?' she asked huskily.

Joey looked closely at her, searching her eyes for any sign of forgiveness. 'Yes. Ginger sent me a copy just before he died. I found the hospice in France where he'd been. The nuns there said he'd seen me on telly, when that mad stallion went for the girl on French Derby day. Up until then he didn't even know I was a jockey.'

'But why did he send it?'

'I don't know. But a few weeks after the tape arrived, I got a blackmail letter, posted from Nottingham, and, of course, I assumed it was from Ginger. It was only when I went to France that I realised he'd died a week or so before the letter was sent. Then I started getting phone calls and notes demanding money, masses of it. A hundred grand!'

'A hundred thousand?' Nina gasped. 'What did you do?'

'I paid it, and a lot more since.'

'Why? How could you pay so much?'

'They threatened to send the tape to the Jockey Club, the press, the police, and then to you.'

'Joey, I believe what you say – that Ginger asked you to do it. I don't blame you. Of course I was sorry to lose Mischa – heartbroken – but so far as you were concerned it was an accident.'

Her words lifted a weight from Joey's mind.

'But if you saw the tape, you might doubt it, which is why I don't want it sent to anyone. The only people who knew the truth were Ginger and Giulio. And they're both dead.'

'Ginger wasn't murdered?'

'No. He died of AIDS. But whoever is blackmailing me found out that Giulio knew I'd been put up to it by Ginger. And Giulio saw him loosen the pegs on the net guys.'

'And now they ask you to make horses lose?'

'That's almost worse than any money, though I've really run out of that too. The blackmailer who calls knows more or less how much I've made every week, and he always wants a percentage.'

'But don't you have *any* idea who it is?'

'No, not yet. I've got a few ideas, but . . .' He shook his head.

'But you *must* find them, stop them – get rid of them!'

Joey looked at her eyes, fiery with indignation, and knew he had been right to tell her. He wished he'd come clean before; but he hadn't known a few weeks ago just how strong and resourceful this woman was. Now he couldn't help smiling.

'Sure,' he said. 'I'm trying to find them, believe me. But at the moment I'm getting nowhere. All I have discovered is how they're getting the money. I pay it into an account at the Southern Counties Building Society, and somebody draws it out in cash. They can do that at any branch, up to five hundred pounds a time, several times a day.'

'Joey!' Nina said, devastated at the scale of the extortion. 'You must find these people, before they really harm you!'

'Why? Would you mind so much if they did?'

'Don't be such a fool! Of course I'd mind. I'd hate it if anything or anyone took you away from me, like that skinny girl who was crawling all over you at the party last night.'

'You saw the paper? I suppose Charles Rettingham showed you.'

'Yes, he did.'

'Nina, that was Laura Seabourn, Dick's daughter. I told you – I think Danny's after her. But yesterday she said she wanted to talk about her parents – and, well, I suppose they're friends of mine.'

'That was Dick's daughter?' Nina laughed out loud. 'I was so jealous!'

Joey's heart missed a beat. 'You were?'

'Of course. Don't you know that?'

He shook his head slowly, and a broad grin spread across his face.

'Of course,' Nina said, 'since you came to my trailer that first time in Nottingham, and I realised you weren't gay. Why else do you think I've come here?'

'Because you wanted a career in racing?'

'I do, but I want you more.' She stretched her hand across the table, took Joey's and squeezed it.

Joey dried the dishes while Nina washed up in a tiny enamel sink. She had put some Russian folk music on her stereo. Joey felt as if they were a couple of gypsies. They drank the second bottle of wine, and Nina turned down the wick of the oil lamp which had illuminated the caravan since the sun had buried itself among the trees on the other side of the paddock.

At one end of the trailer, taking up its entire width,

was a high brass bed, covered with an elaborate quilt of satin and broderie anglaise.

'I want you to stay, Joey,' Nina said with a shyness he hadn't seen in her before but which didn't surprise him.

'Only if you promise to massage my bruises?'

'Every square inch of your body, if you want,' she promised. She was standing very close, facing him. She linked her arms around his neck. He wrapped his about her waist until their bodies were pressed tightly together. Her open mouth found his and their tongues entwined hungrily in their first real kiss.

The gypsy music on the stereo became quieter, so that they could hear the wind rustling the birch leaves outside in the summer night. Joey leaned back on the bed while Nina, silhouetted against the warm golden light of the lamp, began slowly to undress, swaying in time to the wild cadenzas of the Romany violin.

The faint smell of musk and a haziness induced by heavy Italian wine lent a strange, other worldly quality to the scene. The light gleamed off Nina's earrings and her pale soft flesh as she slid her lace blouse over bare breasts. She wriggled her hips free from the tightly hugging upper tiers of her skirt and slipped it down her bare legs.

When she was completely naked, she sat on the bed and swung her leg over to kneel on either side of Joey's hips. Dexterously, she unbuckled his belt and slid down his jeans.

When he was naked too, they lay side by side for a while, wrapped around each other.

Then she knelt beside him and with her fingers gently caressed the tingling surface of his bruised flesh. The curls of her pudenda gleamed in the lamplight between firm, flawless thighs and the gently dimpled curve of her haunches. Her breasts, like a pair of harvest moons, shone down on him as he flickered his tongue around her stiffening nipples.

He reached up and drew her down on to him. As their bodies met, all Joey's pain and worry melted away and he lost himself in a place he'd dreamed of but never known before. He never wanted to leave it and deliberately delayed his orgasm, prolonging her pleasure, drawing his own from her sighs and gasps and ultimate surrender.

Later as they were lying side by side in her big brass bed, Nina was suddenly struck by a thought and sat up, shattering the mood of intimacy.

'Joey.' She propped herself on one elbow to speak and looked steadily into his eyes. 'You can't let this blackmail go on. How do you know they won't send the tape because you didn't stop that horse?'

'First, I didn't ride the horse. And second, I was calling their bluff. After all, the minute they send the tape, they stop the money coming – and if they damage me, they damage my earning capacity. Anyway, I've made up my mind: I'm not shelling out any more. My biggest fear was what would happen when you found out. I mean, I have to tell you – on the tape it's absolutely clear that I deliberately dropped your father. I still feel terrible about it, even though I'd no idea what Ginger had planned.'

'Don't feel terrible. No one was sorry my father went – you know that. And I've already told you, I don't blame you for what happened to Mischa. I just want to help you, Joey. What can I do?'

He smiled slowly and reached under the bed clothes to

stroke the soft curves of her thighs. 'I'll tell you what you can do.'

She shivered and gasped. 'Joey!' A big grin spread over her face. 'What are you doing, Joey . . .'

Chapter Twelve

It was strange, he thought; he'd slept less than an hour, yet despite all the pressure being brought to bear on him, he'd never felt so alive and positive as when he jumped down from Nina's trailer to go to Dick Seabourn's early the next morning.

Driving out to the gallops with him, through wisps of early mist, Dick noticed it too. 'You look brighter than you have for a while, Joey.'

'Maybe it's because I stayed with Nina last night,' he said with a grin.

Seabourn looked at him sharply. 'Did you? After that photograph of you and Laura in the *Mail* yesterday, frankly I'm relieved.'

'I presume you don't object to Nina?'

Seabourn gave him what was intended to be a worldly smile. 'Of course not. What you do in your own time is entirely your affair. It's only when it spreads over into my territory that I get worried.'

'Laura's not causing you too much trouble at the moment, then?' Joey asked tentatively.

'No, no. Not as far as I know,' the trainer answered airily. 'Anyway, as I say, it looks as if your new girlfriend's doing you good. I hope it lasts,' he added.

'Ah, excellent. Here comes Scaramanga. There are only nine days to go to the King George. I'd very much like your opinion as to whether we should run him. Personally, I'm not entirely happy.'

They climbed out of his car and waited for the string of twelve horses to reach them.

Joey looked around for Barry, who'd said he would be there to see the gallop. There was no sign of the Irishman. Joey thought with a shiver that maybe his agent was avoiding him, anticipating a confrontation.

Once he was on the back of Scaramanga, he gave the job his total concentration. He had the ability – essential to any top-class sportsman – to clear all other problems from his head and give one hundred percent of himself to the task, whether he was racing or working a horse to assess it for a major race.

Although Scaramanga had run so close in the English Derby, he would have to prove himself in one of the other Group One races if he was to achieve the best possible value at stud the following year.

The King George and Queen Elizabeth Stakes, run over twelve furlongs at Ascot towards the end of July, was a race with almost as much kudos in the breeding world as the Derby itself, pitting the current year's three-year-olds against those of the previous year's classic animals that were still in training.

What was more, Joey had a deal with the colt's owner that if he won the King George on it that season, he would get a nomination to the horse when it went to stud. A nomination would give him the right to send one mare to the stallion each year. And that right could be worth as much as fifty thousand pounds a year – a useful pension if the horse prospered as a stallion and lived a long, fertile life.

But if he ran in the King George and gave a mediocre showing, a lot of the merit achieved by his impressive performance at Epsom would be lost.

Joey was only human; he'd worked like a slave to get where he was, and these personal financial considerations were bound to concentrate his mind. He gathered up the reins and hacked down to the bottom of the gallop.

Seabourn had told him to gallop seven furlongs alongside the stable's most experienced miler, to stretch Scaramanga a little.

'How fast shall we go?' the rider on the lead horse asked as they arrived at the start of the gallop.

'A good strong canter and then quicken up from the three-furlong marker. I'll come and join you for the last two.'

'What do you think?' Seabourn asked as Joey returned.

'He feels fantastic – better than he did at Epsom.'

Joey drove home for breakfast leaving Dick Seabourn in a much happier frame of mind and himself feeling buoyant about his chances in the King George, and ready to launch a fresh strategy in the search for his blackmailers.

First he wanted to see Nina. He parked his car at the farm and walked across the paddock to her caravan.

There was a small Ford in the field beside it. Joey climbed up the steps and knocked on Nina's door.

'Hi.' She beamed at him, making his heart thump faster at the thought of the night they'd spent together. 'This is Harry.' She waved to a slight young man of twenty or so, already installed on one of the benches at the mahogany table. In front of him, scattered so that they covered most of its surface, were several photographs and a copy of the *Banbury Star*. 'Harry's a groom at Gerry's stud, but he says he's really a photographer, so – I gave him the chance to prove it by developing all my shots from the other night. I didn't want to take them to the chemist,' she added with a giggle. 'Take a look!'

A quick glance showed Joey that most of the photos were of Ivor taken from various angles.

'And look at this, Joey!' Nina picked up the paper and leafed a few pages into it until she found a short report which stated that the boss of the circus currently playing in the town had been charged with drink-driving.

No reason was given as to why Wimsatt had been found with three times the limit of alcohol in his blood, naked by a Bentley with four flat tyres.

'You'd have thought they'd have mentioned that he was tied to the tree,' Joey remarked.

'Danny loosened the ropes,' Nina said. 'Just enough so he wouldn't have too much trouble getting out of them. And we left him with a car-rug to wrap round himself. But look at the rest of the story.'

The last paragraph offered the information that Essex police were also investigating a fire at Wimsatt's winter quarters in Canvey Island, in which he claimed hundreds of thousands of pounds worth of equipment had been destroyed, and his eighty-year-old mother had been killed.

'He never kept anything at that place,' Nina said. 'It was just a ruin of a house and a few tumble-down barns where he used to store a bit of hay in the winter. And I never knew his mother was still alive. The funny thing is, none of us in the circus heard a word about this.'

'I don't suppose it made it to the nationals at the time,' Harry said. 'Not a big enough story.'

'I remember him saying how rich his mother was,' Nina speculated. 'Maybe that's how he bought the car and the jewellery he gave me. And he was talking about buying a massive farm near the old one. I'm sure the circus wasn't making enough for all that.'

'I bet he put in a bloody great insurance claim for the fire, too,' Joey said. 'He must be mad at himself – scaring you off by trying to rape you, just when he was thinking he probably had enough bread to land you.'

'The arrogant pig! As if I'd have gone anywhere near him just because he had a lot of money.'

Joey laughed at her indignation. 'Anyway, at least you've got the justice you were after. He seems to be in all sorts of trouble now, as well as having to explain away that tattoo every time he takes his shirt off! I don't think we need worry about him showing up round here again. Serve the bastard right for what he did, especially if the police arrest him for arson, and possibly murder, as well.'

When Harry had gone, leaving the pile of photos with Nina, she and Joey walked back to Three Elms Farm. Joey made some coffee and busied himself cooking a breakfast of eggs, bacon and toast that few jockeys could have got away with. As he ate, out of habit he looked around for Roger to give him the bacon rinds. The old spaniel's absence brought him back down to earth with a vengeance; Nina may have savoured the sweet taste of revenge, but his own problems were far from over.

She sensed the change in his mood. 'Have you heard anything new?'

Joey shook his head, reluctant to involve her any more than he had while at the same time longing to share his troubles.

'I wish I could help you,' she sighed.

'There's not a lot you can do. I'll have to get that private detective back and ask him what he thinks; I'm getting nowhere on my own. If they ask me to stop another horse and I don't, there really will be trouble. And if they ask for any more money, I'm either going to have to hock this place or sell it.'

'But, Joey,' Nina almost whispered, 'you can't! You've worked so hard for all this, you don't deserve to lose it. It's not as though you had any intention of killing Mischa and my father. I could tell that to any court.'

'I wish it would carry some weight if you did, but you weren't even there. And, besides, you haven't seen the tape.'

After breakfast Nina left saying she had some business to attend to, but she refused to tell Joey where she'd been when she arrived back at Three Elms Farm a few hours later. When they set off for Sandown that afternoon, he pressed her to tell him.

'No, I won't. I've been following up some suspicions of my own, that's all. I don't know if I'm on the right track yet. But I'm going to find out.'

As they drove into the jockeys' car park at Sandown, Joey groaned. 'Oh, God. Not again.'

'What is it?'

'See that man leaning on a BMW? That's Lenny Williams. One of the bentest bookies in the business. He's always trying to fix races. I thought he might have been involved in the blackmail at one point, he seemed very interested in Tap Dancer's race, but I think now he must have taken a few large bets on the opposition.'

They passed the car and Joey stiffened. 'Crikey! That's Barry's old BMW and the guy in the driver's seat is Graham Street. There's no way he could afford the ten grand Barry was asking for it – not on what he's been earning recently.'

'But why does that bother you?'

Joey hadn't slowed or done anything to let Graham know he was taking any special notice of him. He carried on, parked and climbed out, leading Nina towards the weighing room. 'Because I've been going round thinking anyone who was in Barry's office the day the tape arrived could be involved. Graham was there, test driving that BMW.'

'Nina! Hi!' Di Lambert had spotted her walking into the Members' Stand and came over to greet her with a hug. 'I didn't know you were coming today. Are you going to have lunch with us?'

'Am I invited?'

'Of course you are! Come on up to the box.'

Once they were inside, there was no scope for private discussion, with people coming and going and Dick being expansive with owners and guests. Nina joined in, alert to any nuances in Di's conversation that related to Joey.

But it wasn't until everyone else had finished lunch and gone off to the paddock to see the runners for the first race that they were alone again.

Nina easily managed to steer the conversation around to the difficulty she was having in getting a particular type of make-up which she liked in Newmarket.

'They said I might be able to find it in Cambridge. Trouble is, not driving, I don't know when I'll be able to get over there. Maybe I can get Joey to give me a lift some time, but he's always so busy.'

'I'm going in on Saturday morning,' Di volunteered. 'Write down what you want and I'll get it for you.'

'Would you? Thanks a lot. You've been so kind to me since I got here.'

'It's no hassle; don't worry about it.' Di waved aside her thanks. 'I'm just pleased it's going so well with you and Joey. It still is, isn't it? I mean, no signs of stress yet?'

'To tell you the truth, Joey does seem to be worrying about something, but I don't think it's anything to do with me. Of course, he says it's nothing. He wouldn't tell me anyway.'

Di looked at her, concerned. 'I wouldn't have thought he had too many problems at the moment,' she remarked. 'He's having a fantastic season.'

'Yes, I suppose he must be.' Nina nodded at her and smiled, looking forward to Saturday when Di would go to Cambridge.

She left the box to place a small bet on Joey's horse in the next race. Nina preferred to deal with the bookies out on the front, rather than the unpredictable, anonymous Tote. On her way back to the stands, from the corner of her eye she caught sight of a profile that was as familiar as it was distinctive, and definitely out of context.

She swivelled her head and found herself looking at a short man wearing a silver mohair suit, a dark red shirt and silver tie. A pair of heavy, black-framed spectacles rested on the bridge of his over-sized nose and his thick, silver hair was brushed straight back from a low forehead. She turned away before he saw her and carried on back to Seabourn's box, contemplating the fact that this particular man was the last person she'd expected to see at the races.

Joey's next horse didn't win, nor had any of his earlier rides. He didn't have a ride in the last race and wanted to get back to Newmarket. After he'd showered, he found Nina in Seabourn's box and they left before most of the crowds. Once they were out of the racecourse and heading for the M25, Nina said casually, 'Guess who I saw today?'

Joey wasn't in the mood for a guessing game but suggested a few obvious racing names.

'No,' she said. 'It wasn't anyone you'd expect.'

'Who then?'

'Sol Werner.'

'Good God!' he gasped, taken by surprise. 'What the hell was he doing there?'

'I don't know. I didn't speak to him. In fact, I only just recognised him; I hadn't seen him for a few years.'

'Are you absolutely sure it was him?'

'Oh, yes. His isn't the sort of face you forget.'

'I wonder why he showed himself now?'

'Why shouldn't he?'

'I didn't tell you the other day because it seemed so crazy, but I thought *he* might be one of the people blackmailing me. And now he's turned up at the races.'

Nina looked at Joey as she considered the possibility. 'Maybe. I certainly never trusted him.'

She was still working on her own ideas, while Joey wondered about a possible connection between Sol Werner and Barry Mannion.

Barry hadn't turned up on the Heath in the morning,

he hadn't been at the races, and Joey hadn't been able to get hold of him on the phone. His secretary said he would be at home in the evening.

'I've got to call round at Barry's place as soon as we get back to Newmarket. That may open a couple of doors for us.'

'Barry? What's he got to do with it?'

Joey told Nina about the speeding ticket issued the day he'd been to see her in Chester. 'I was going to tell you last night, but I thought you'd had enough surprises for one evening.'

'You could say that.' She gave him a wide smile. 'But I'm really surprised if Barry's part of it. He told me he was one of your oldest friends.'

Joey winced. That was what troubled him most. 'I wish I was wrong, but it can't just be a coincidence he was up there the same day I was. He must have been following me, to see what I was doing. That's how they knew about Giulio.'

'Maybe you should go to the police and tell them the truth now, Joey.'

'I can't. I've told you, if they look at that tape, they'll say I killed two men. There's no one left to tell them about Ginger's part in it, and I'm bloody sure the CID won't let it lie.'

'But the blackmailers – Barry, Sol, whoever – would they have gone and killed Giulio themselves?'

'Not a chance. It will be the same people that have already had a go at me twice, and they know what they're doing.'

Joey left Nina at her caravan. She insisted that she would cook dinner if he promised to come back later. He went home first, to check his messages and faxes.

There was nothing unusual waiting for him. He rang Barry and got him at his flat. Without any preamble Joey said he wanted to see him and was on his way round. It wasn't an unusual request, and Barry seemed to take it in his stride.

Joey knocked on the door, and Barry let him into his big, newly built, fourth-floor flat. He showed him into a large, light kitchen/dining-room with wide views over the Heath to the west, dominated inside by an over-sized television and two vast piles of racing journals and sale catalogues. Otherwise, it was unexpectedly clean, tidy and well equipped, with an elaborate espresso machine already spluttering on the work-top.

The Irishman greeted Joey and made him some coffee. 'Did you see what's happened to the price of Scaramanga?' he asked, before Joey had a chance to say anything.

'No. I haven't looked yet.'

'They've cut him from fives to five to two.'

This made the colt favourite over the Derby winner. Several pundits had already expressed the view that it was the shape of the Epsom track that had beaten the colt. But this dramatic drop in price meant that news of how well he had worked was already out.

They talked for a few more minutes about Scaramanga, while Joey tried to detect any suspicious undertone in Barry's voice or manner. Despite his apparent glee at winning on Tap Dancer, Joey didn't underestimate the Irishman's ability to act. He'd seen him in action too many times for that. Listening to him now, Joey realised he was never going to get anywhere by pussy-footing around.

Angry with himself for not coming to the point sooner, he braced himself.

'By the way,' he said, during a lull in Barry's almost incessant talking, 'do you know why I asked you if you'd been up to Chester the other day?'

Barry looked at him blankly and shook his head. 'No. Haven't a clue.'

'You got caught on camera speeding up there, on the M56.'

Barry stared back as if Joey had lost his reason. 'What the hell are you talking about?'

He had to force himself to battle on in the face of Barry's obvious indignation. 'When I was in your office last night, I saw a speeding ticket, for your car on the M56 on the seventh of July. So you must have been there, right?'

'You saw a speeding ticket? Good God! Is that what this is about? And why the hell shouldn't I have been on the M56 on July the whatever?'

'Well, were you?'

Barry shook his head in disbelief. 'I wish I knew where the hell you were coming from, Joey. What's got into you?'

'Barry, it's a simple question. Were you driving along the M56 that day?'

'If you're talking about that speeding ticket, I didn't even notice where it was from. I'm just going to pass it straight on to Graham.'

'Graham?'

'Yes, Graham Street. He was using the car. I sold him my old BMW, and it broke down. He came round here whingeing about it, saying he needed a car desperately, and I told him he could take the Porsche. I wasn't going anywhere.'

'So you're absolutely sure it was him who was speeding on the M56?'

'Yes, yes, for God's sake, I told you – I haven't been up there for years. And anyway, what the hell is so important about it?'

'It doesn't matter. I'll tell you another time.' Joey tried to defuse Barry's annoyance. 'But did you say you'd sold thc BMW to Graham?'

'If you can call it "sell". I've only seen ten percent of the money so far – I'm too bloody soft, that's my trouble. I should think it'll be a long time before he comes up with the necessary.'

Joey looked away and took a gulp of his coffee, convinced Barry was telling him the truth.

Whether he was or not, Joey guessed there was no point in further confrontation that evening.

'Okay,' he said, with an attempt at a careless smile. 'That clears up the mystery. Sorry if you thought I was accusing you of anything.'

Barry fixed bright blue eyes on Joey's. 'It hurts, you know, when I feel there's a lack of trust between us, Joey. Next time you've something on your mind, just level with me, okay? You must know by now you can trust me.'

Joey gave a small sigh. 'Yes, of course I do.' He swallowed the rest of the coffee and put the cup down. 'Right, someone's cooking me dinner so I'd better get back.'

'Some spicy hot Russian dish, I shouldn't wonder,' chuckled Barry.

Joey drove a few hundred yards from Barry's flat, round two corners into a road of small Victorian terraced houses which ran along the back of the High Street.

This was a part of Newmarket occupied by the lower rungs of racing's pecking order. Graham had recently moved there with his wife and three children, after his smart bungalow on the edge of the town had been repossessed.

Joey managed to find a tight slot for his Ferrari outside a snooker club opposite Graham's house. He climbed out to a chorus of greetings from local children and walked self-consciously to the front door and rang the bell. There was no sound from inside. After some time he knocked and a moment later the door was opened by a girl of three or four with a grimy dress and a nose that needed blowing. Her eyes were replicas of Graham's.

Joey smiled at her. 'Hello. Is your dad in?'

Before the child made any response, a harassed woman, no more than thirty but already worn out, shuffled through from the back of the house in a T-shirt, a pair of grey leggings and dirty pink slippers.

Even in her unkempt condition and obviously devoid of self-esteem, Joey knew that Angela Street could be – certainly once was – a surprisingly good-looking woman. He hadn't set eyes on her for several years. Graham must have let her down badly to bring her to this, he thought, feeling unexpected compassion for her.

'What do you want, Joey?' she asked ungraciously, registering the Ferrari parked on the other side of the road.

Joey didn't blame her for resenting him. He tried a smile on her. 'Just looking for Graham,' he said lightly.

'He's not here.'

'Any idea when he'll be back?'

'No, and if I had, and told you, he'd go ape-shit.'

Joey pulled a regretful face. 'Could you tell him I called, then?'

'Yeah, s'pose so.'

Joey looked at the small girl who by now had wrapped her chubby arms around her mother's skinny legs. 'Would she like a little present?'

'Like what?' her mother asked suspiciously.

'I was just going to give her something to buy some sweets with.'

'No thanks!' the woman said, pulling the girl closer to her. 'We don't need your charity.'

Joey couldn't think of an appropriate response. He gave the child a small smile, turned and walked back to his car, depressed by the encounter and frustrated that he hadn't had the chance to confront Graham with the speeding ticket from Cheshire.

He drove home, turning the new development over and over in his head. Since he had first come to the conclusion that it must be someone in racing who was extorting money from him, Graham's name had never been far from the top of his list of suspects.

Yet now that it looked to be a distinct possibility, he couldn't understand why, if Graham had been getting his hands on the money, his family weren't looking a lot better provided for.

It seemed to him that no man would willingly let his wife get into that state if he could afford to do something about it. But then, Joey knew from his own experience that human nature was capable of infinite variation.

He would just have to be patient until he got Graham on his own and could study his reactions.

★ ★ ★

The phone was ringing as Joey walked back into his house. Out of habit, he ran to catch it before the answer-machine cut in.

'Hello?'

''Ello, Joey.'

Joey held his breath for a moment. This was a new voice – new in this context, but not unfamiliar.

'Who is it?' he asked calmly.

'You've been talkin' to my colleagues . . .' The voice left the statement hanging, not requiring confirmation, while Joey ran back through his memory bank to identify it.

'You was workin' a horse this mornin' – you know the one I mean?'

'What about it?'

'Worked well, didn't 'e?'

'What about it?'

''E won't win 'is next race, will 'e?'

'He might.'

'If 'e does, you're fuckin' dead. And your girlfriend will take the rap – I'd make sure of that.'

Joey was still absorbing the full horror of what had just been said when the line went dead. Trembling, he slowly put the phone back in its cradle.

And as he did, he knew whose voice he'd just heard. It was the man in the balaclava, who only the day before had beaten him up and stolen his shot gun.

Joey didn't doubt that he'd just heard a genuine threat. His murder, with the crime clearly attributable to Nina, was a far more effective use of the tape from the blackmailers' point of view. However heroic he might have chosen to be in risking his own life, to risk Nina's being charged with murdering him out of revenge for the death of her father and brother wasn't even a remote option.

Scaramanga was due to run in the King George and Queen Elizabeth in eight days' time, which gave him that long and no more to find the blackmailers.

Determined not to be cowed, he pulled a bottle of champagne from his fridge and walked to Nina's trailer.

'To celebrate.'

'What?'

'I just had a call from my friendly neighbourhood extortionist and he didn't ask for money.'

'But, Joey, if they didn't ask for money, what did they want?'

'They want me to stop Scaramanga in the King George.'

'But surely there are other horses that can win it – the Derby winner, Nureyev, he's running too.'

'This isn't about placing bets – it's about laying them. Some big bookie will ease his price, once he's sure Scara won't be winning, and he'll take tens of thousands on it from the punters, and lay it for a few hundred other shops, knowing that he'll keep the lot. He'll be prepared to pay for the certainty that Scara isn't going to win. Trouble is, he *will*.' And Joey grinned at her.

Later, their love-making was even more passionate and profound than the night before.

In the morning Joey woke with Nina still in his arms. At her first slight movement, the excitement returned and they were lost in each other again until it was time to go.

Nina went with him to ride out. He was trying a horse

for Charles Rettingham, for whom he sometimes rode when Dick didn't have a runner. Rettingham was more than happy that Nina had come, and immediately proposed that she should ride too.

It was a perfect morning on the Heath and to Joey it was one of the finest sights in the world. Racehorses had been galloping up the grassy slopes for so many centuries that they were an integral part of the place. A gentle breeze rippled the long grass beside the mown gallops and a haze was lifting gently off the broad horizons of the low-lying landscape. This place gave him a sense of freedom that he would have gone to almost any lengths to defend.

Forgetting all his other troubles for the moment, he smiled at Nina as he leaned forward to give her horse a gentle pat on the neck.

She smiled back and drew in a deep breath. 'I can see why once you came here, you stayed,' she said. 'Do you know, it's amazing the way a shy little boy like you has come to this place and become a king.'

Joey laughed, hoping no one had overheard. 'I'm no king. The trainers are kings here, and the pompous stiffs in the Jockey Club are gods. Rettingham there,' Joey nodded to the trainer, strolling long-legged and languid towards them, 'is at the top of the heap. I just ride what he produces. Even the best jockeys in the world call trainers "sir".'

'At least you get paid for your skill and courage. In the circus we risked our lives, night after night – for peanuts.'

'Well, you've left now,' he said. 'So make the most of it.'

Thanks to her, Joey was feeling in much better spirits

as they later drove over to Seabourn's yard.

Dick Seabourn greeted Nina with his usual, old-fashioned good manners but refused to talk about horses in front of her. 'Have a look round the yard,' he said with an expansive gesture. 'You'll probably find a few animals better suited to the circus than the racecourse,' he added, joking against himself.

He took Joey into the house, to the office, where his manner changed abruptly. 'There's a rumour going round that someone doesn't want Scaramanga to do his best next week.'

Joey froze. He attempted a laugh. 'What! In a Group One race? They'll be lucky.'

'Joey, has anyone contacted you to . . .' Seabourn was evidently having trouble completing the question.

Joey stared back at him, registering horror that Seabourn could even consider such a thing.

'Bloody hell, guv'nor, I'd have told you if they had – you know that. Just don't worry about it. As long as I'm on him, the horse will win.'

'That ankle of yours is all right now?'

'Yes, thanks, more or less.' Joey didn't like having to lie to Seabourn, but he had no choice.

The trainer looked distracted, glancing out of the window every few seconds. Joey followed his gaze to where two surly men in anoraks were walking through the yard with clipboards in their hands.

He and Seabourn talked for another twenty minutes about the horses entered over the next few days. As Joey left, Di walked into the office and gave him a broad smile. 'Are you okay, Joey? You look as though you've been in the wars.'

She was looking at a small cut he'd got on his jaw

during his tussle in the shrubbery. It was healing badly and looked worse than it was.

'It's nothing. Just a scratch. Coming to Newbury today?'

'No, the boss won't let me. Too much to do.'

Joey left the house and went down to the yard. He looked into the office beside the tack room where he found Martin, the head lad and the man who managed the day-to-day running of the yard.

'Morning, Joey,' he said. 'Did Billy go well for you yesterday?'

'Yes, improving all the time.'

'Unlike other things in this yard,' Martin said grimly.

'What are you talking about? We're having a great season.'

'I'm talking about money. This yard is suffering from severe sterling deprivation. Some of the owners who took their horses away last year after the virus struck refused to pay. There's one big one still arguing the toss, says we never did the job properly. Of course, I don't know about these things, that's not my job, but I do know the boss was late with the VAT last month, and the bailiffs turned up this morning.'

'Those two miserable-looking blokes in anoraks?' Joey asked.

'Yes. They're not taking anything away, apparently, but they will if they haven't had the money in a week or so.'

'Good God. Poor old Dick.'

'I don't suppose it's a problem, really. I'm sure his missus will bail him out if it comes to that. They say her dad left her a few million.'

'As long as our jobs aren't on the line,' Joey said lightly.

'No chance,' Martin replied.

'I hope you're right. Anyway, I was looking for Danny.'

'He's already left to go to Thirsk.'

Joey knew Dick had a runner at the Yorkshire track, but didn't know Danny was looking after it.

'Is that one of his, then?'

'No, but he's put in for a lot of travelling recently and the other lad didn't want to go.'

'That's new,' Joey said. 'Where was he yesterday?'

Martin thought for a moment. 'God, we've had so many runners and lads away lately.' He called across to a girl carrying a muck-sack round to the heap. 'Where did Dan go yesterday?'

'Chepstow,' the girl shouted back. 'Came back with a pile of cash, the jammy sod!'

Joey's face paled. In his present suspicious state, the idea of Danny with a pile of cash struck an unpleasant chord.

He rebuked himself for his disloyalty. 'Tell him I was asking,' he said, 'otherwise he feels neglected.'

Martin grinned. 'Yeah, sure. I'll tell him.'

Joey found Nina chatting to two of the girls. As they walked away, he talked normally to her until they were in the car and out of anyone's hearing.

'Danny!' he burst out as they left the yard. 'He went to Chepstow yesterday and came back with a load of cash.'

Nina looked at him, appraising the information. 'So, he took a horse to Chepstow and he won some bets. Is that so unusual?'

'Yes, for Danny. He's a terrible punter.'

'But once in a while he could get it right, couldn't he?'

'I suppose it's possible,' Joey sighed. 'But Martin said

Danny's travelling much more, too. He says he likes it. He's already gone up to Thirsk today.'

'Is there a Southern Counties branch there?'

'No. Not that far north.'

'Then if he comes back with another bundle tonight, that will be from the bookies.'

'Or some punter he's selling information to,' Joey said disdainfully.

'But not your money at least.'

Joey gave a short grunt of frustration. 'Yes,' he conceded. 'You're right. It may not mean anything, but I can't pretend that it's impossible Danny could do something like that.'

'I think you don't realise how loyal he is to you,' Nina said. 'He's just an awkward boy, you know, and lives in your shadow. I think he copes with it pretty well.'

'But he's always been mates with Graham, right from the start, and now he's in with people like Lenny Williams. He hangs around with a lot of dodgy people.'

'But you haven't even seen Graham yet. He might have some perfectly good reason for being up near Chester that day.'

'Do you really think that's likely?'

'No,' Nina admitted. 'But that still doesn't mean Danny's done anything.'

'I hope you're right. Anyway, I'm going to find Graham now. Then we'll know what's going on there. Do you mind waiting in the car for a few minutes?' He had turned the Range Rover into the top of Graham's road and once again found a space near the snooker club. 'I think it'll be easier if I do this on my own.'

'Okay,' Nina agreed. 'I'll stay here.'

He walked across the road and knocked on the door.

This time Graham's wife opened it with a mutinous look in her eyes. 'If you're looking for him, he's over the road.'

Joey turned. 'In the snooker hall?'

'Yes. He's always there, the bastard, or in some slag's bed.'

'Thanks.' He hesitated a moment before taking a fifty-pound note from his top pocket. 'Get something nice for the kids,' he said and offered it to her.

This time she took the money, showing her gratitude with a faint smile, and Joey was glad he had taken the risk. Nodding a brief goodbye, he turned and walked across the road.

He pushed open the swing doors into the dingy stucco-covered building. The snooker hall had been converted from a Methodist chapel in the early-sixties and now helped fill the long leisure hours of the town's less busy men.

There were eight tables, all being used at half-past nine in the morning. Joey spotted Graham about to play a shot on the farthest one and made his way towards him. Everyone in the room recognised Joey and most greeted him cheerfully – apart from Graham who glowered as he glanced up from missing an easy pot.

'I heard you'd been sniffing around. What do you want?' he growled.

'Maybe we should talk somewhere less public.'

Graham stood back while his opponent, ignoring Joey, leaned over the table to take a shot. 'I've no secrets from anyone here.'

'Okay. I want you to tell me what you were doing in Chester three Sundays ago?'

'Why the hell should I tell you what I was doing at any time?'

'Because if I find you were there, I can guess what you were doing and you'd better believe, I'll have you for it!'

Graham straightened up from slouching against the table. 'I don't know what the fuck you're talking about! It looks like success has gone to your head, mate. I'm not doing anything to you, and Sunday three weeks ago, I was here all day, playing a tournament which I bloody well won. You can have a look at the results over there.' He nodded at a noticeboard on the wall, on which a knock-out competition chart was displayed. Joey didn't bother to walk over and check. He already knew from Graham's eyes that he was telling the truth.

'Then who the hell was driving Barry's Porsche? He lent it to you, and got sent a ticket for speeding on the M56.'

Graham looked at him in amazement. 'On the M56? She said she was going to Windsor, for the polo.'

'Who?' Joey asked hoarsely, sweating at the prospect of the information he was about to receive.

'Di. She wanted to borrow my car, but that was buggered, so I got Barry to lend me his.'

'But you didn't tell him Di was going to drive it?'

'No,' said Graham defensively. 'I was borrowing it because the pile of junk he sold me was knackered. It wasn't his business who was going to use it.'

'But why did Di want to borrow your car in the first place?'

'I dunno. Maybe that little thing of hers was off the road. But she asked me, and I said yes; she never said she was going to Chester.'

'And you're sure it was that day?'

'Of course I bloody am. Anyway, what's this all about?'

'Don't worry. If it was Di, it's no problem,' Joey said as lightly as he could. 'I'm glad I cleared things up. Sorry to interrupt your game.'

Graham shrugged his shoulders, apparently mollified. 'Yeah, well. I'll let you know when I need a favour.'

Joey walked out of the snooker hall with a friendly smile on his face and his head spinning.

Outside he had to stop himself from running to the car. But he held in his news until he'd driven down the road and was heading for the country when it burst out of him. 'It was Di! She must have followed me up to Chester.'

'Di?' Nina nodded with an ironic smile.

'Yes,' Joey said. 'You were right about her. I can hardly believe it!'

'Why? Why shouldn't she be a blackmailer, as much as anyone else? Just because she has an upper-class accent and a fresh face doesn't mean she's honest.'

Joey glanced at her ruefully, knowing she was right.

'I've never trusted her from the start,' Nina went on. 'She let slip she'd seen the Flying Ferraras, but also said she'd never been to Freddie Fielding's. That's impossible. Then suddenly she changed her mind and said she'd only heard of them. Anyway, I've already arranged to follow her into Cambridge tomorrow. I'm dropping round to her flat tonight to give her a list of make-up I'd like her to buy. We might get lucky and catch her withdrawing money from a building society.'

'You've planned this?' Joey said with amazement.

'It was just an idea.'

'But, Nina, she'll see you a mile off.'

'That's why I got myself a grey wig and a pair of glasses, and one of Gerry's lads is driving me in his old car. If she even notices, all Di will see is a little old lady and her son going shopping.'

Joey smiled at her. 'Of course, she may not go near the Southern Counties, but you're right, it's worth a try. Do you know, when I saw her at Dick's this morning, she asked me quite innocently if I'd been in the wars – made a good job of it too. I just wouldn't have believed she was part of all this.'

The following morning Joey had arranged to be at the yard early. A fresh strip of grass was being opened, and Seabourn wanted to be first on it.

When he arrived, the yard was full of excitement; the feeling was that they might pull off a treble that afternoon. Joey wanted it, not just for him but for Dick and all the team. Since hearing about his problems, Joey had made a few discreet enquiries. Moves to sue recalcitrant owners had already cost the trainer nearly a hundred thousand pounds for debts of just under a quarter of a million, and neither sum was likely to be recovered.

And Seabourn was a mere tenant of his wife's family trust. Factor in the general downturn in the racing business since the nineties recession started, and the informed view was that poor old Dick was suffering, and too proud to ask his wife to bail him out.

Joey could believe it. Dick Seabourn had always seemed to him the epitome of honour – the kind of man who would die rather than ask for help.

He wondered what the trainer would think if he knew he was harbouring a blackmailer in his yard; someone whom he trusted completely, and who was cold-bloodedly arranging for his best horse to fail in one of the biggest races of the year.

★ ★ ★

Nina had left Di's flat after one the night before and had taken a taxi back to her caravan. Joey had called in on his way to work the next morning. He wanted to hear what she'd found out, but she'd learned nothing new beyond the fact that Di's first sexual experience had been with a boy who had come up from London to pick vegetables on her father's farm.

Nina had a feeling this might be one of the men they were looking for.

'But why do you think he might be helping her now?' Joey asked sceptically.

'She talked about him as if he had been on her mind recently,' Nina told him. 'You know, remembering in a way that was connected with the present.'

'It certainly isn't Sol Werner who's been ringing. His German accent's so strong you'd hear it through the fuzz-box or whatever it is he's using. Not just the accent but his grammar, too. I'm sure the guy who calls me is English; and the bloke who came and thumped me is definitely an East Londoner.'

'How do you know they're not the same person?'

'I don't, but when the heavy phoned, he didn't even bother to disguise his voice – maybe because he knew I'd heard it already.'

Joey left Nina in her caravan to change into her simple disguise and wait for Gerry Tewkesbury's lad who was going to pick her up and drive her round to wait near Di's flat.

The King George was now seven days away. He still hadn't told Nina the full story of the last threat that had been made. It was more than he could do to admit to her that if Scaramanga won, and they still hadn't found the blackmailers, there was the threat he'd be killed – and in such a way that the evidence of the videotape and whatever else they could plant would make her a very strong suspect.

He had prepared a document to lodge with his solicitor, giving every detail he knew of what had happened since he had first received the tape. For whatever pressure was put on him, he intended to ride the horse, and ride to win.

That afternoon, to prove to himself and anyone else who might have been interested that he wasn't allowing the threat creeping up on him to affect him, he produced the trio of winners the yard had been hoping for.

For a few hours, being the most popular man in Newmarket helped him forget his troubles. He only wished he could have put a bigger smile on Seabourn's face as the trainer collected his trophies.

Still, Joey reasoned, it could only be a matter of time before everything came right for his boss. For a start, they were going to win the King George next week.

Nina arrived at the course halfway through the afternoon, transformed from a morning spent as a frumpy fifty-year-old. She called Joey from the changing room.

Outside, she said quietly: 'Di went to the building society.'

'Did she take anything out?'

'Yes.'

'How much?'

'I'm not sure. I was too far away from her when the money came out, but it looked like quite a lot to me.'

Joey found he was trembling but beamed at the news.

At last!

At last he knew with whom he was dealing. The connection with the man who had been relaying the demands they could deal with later. At this stage it was enough to know it was Di who'd been behind extracting the money – though part of him still found it hard to believe.

'She must have got her hands on the tape somehow,' he said. 'Probably made a copy of the one Ginger sent and put the original in the office for me to find that evening when I came back from York. If she did, the chances are she's keeping the copy hidden at home.' He thought for a moment. 'I wonder if we can get into her flat somehow,' he said, keeping his voice to a whisper. 'We'll have to do it when we know she's away for a few hours.'

'That's no problem,' Nina said. 'I'll find out what her plans are. She said she was coming here to give me the make-up she bought for me.'

Joey grinned at her. 'What would I do without you?'

'I'm doing it for me, really,' she said. 'I want you all to myself, with no distractions.'

Joey had one more ride, in which he passed the post halfway down the field.

Nina was waiting for him outside the weighing room.

'Did you see Di?' he asked as they walked towards the car park.

'Yes. And guess who I saw her talking to?'

'Not another guessing game, please – not now,' Joey protested.

'It's the same answer as last time.'

He stopped. 'Sol Werner? I knew it! I knew he had to be in on it too.'

'Di told me he'd been pestering her to see Dick about sending him some apprentices from the circus. He got the idea from you, he told her, and I suppose he thinks there's more money in handling jockeys than trick riders.'

'Why did Di tell you about him? Did she know you'd seen him?'

'No, I don't think she did, but I guess she was just covering herself because she knew I'd recognise him.'

'They must be working together to rip me off.'

Nina agreed. 'Anyway, we can have a look in Di's flat tomorrow; she's going off to Norfolk to stay with her parents.'

'Are you sure?'

'Yes. She asked if I wanted to come too.'

'And did she remember your make-up?'

'Yes, she did,' Nina said thoughtfully.

Joey rang Di's number several times on Sunday morning, but got no reply. This didn't prove she had gone to Norfolk, so Nina rang her parents' number and asked if she was there.

She wasn't but had phoned her mother to say she was coming to lunch.

'I wonder where she was last night?' Nina said. 'We'd better wait till nearer lunchtime before we go to her flat.'

The uncertainty that they wouldn't be disturbed made them nervous but didn't put them off. Joey had a plan for getting into her flat without breaking in. He knew there was an old caretaker who lived in two small rooms in the basement. He went round to the back of the building and knocked on the old man's door.

'Mornin'. What can I do for you?' If the janitor recognised Joey, he didn't show it.

'I've a birthday present for Diana Lambert on the third floor. It's a great big plant and I want to leave it in her flat as a surprise. I wondered if you could let me in?'

The old man looked him up and down, assessing him for criminal tendencies. Joey was hoping he would simply hand him the key and tell him to help himself, but the old man took it off a rack behind him and shuffled out.

'All right then. I'll let you in.'

Joey's plan two would have to be implemented. 'Perhaps you could give me a hand with the plant?' He jingled some coins in his pocket to underline the request.

The caretaker nodded and followed him to the Range Rover where an oversized yucca in a heavy terracotta pot was crammed into the back.

Nina was nowhere to be seen.

The two men heaved out the plant and carried it into the building and up the three flights of stairs. When they reached the door to Di's flat, the porter unlocked it and pushed it wide to let them in.

'Can you give me a hand carrying it through to the kitchen, do you think?' Joey asked.

The old man grunted, apparently in the affirmative, as he bent down to take up his side of the pot once more.

As soon as the two men were halfway down the hall, Nina, who had flitted up the stairs behind them unseen, darted in through the front door and into Di's sitting-room, just in time to hear Joey and the old man walking back, the porter making a performance of pulling the door firmly behind him to ensure it was locked.

She heard two sets of steps clattering down the stairs, and a few minutes later a single set ascending much more quietly. She went to the door and opened it. Joey slipped in.

'Okay,' he said. 'We'd better be quiet, just in case she's got nosy neighbours.'

'What sort of people live in flats like this?' Nina asked.

'I can tell you exactly who lives here. There's a young bloodstock agent, a journalist from one of the racing mags, and a junior vet, but I don't know how public-spirited they are.'

'Okay. Where shall we start?'

'I'll do the living-room, you do the bedroom. I wouldn't feel right rummaging around among her knickers.'

'I wouldn't mind if you did, as long as she's not wearing them,' Nina said in a whisper and let herself into the bedroom.

Fifteen minutes later she came into the living-room where Joey was prodding desperately under the corner of the fitted carpet. He looked up. 'Any luck?'

She shook her head. 'Nothing, not even a dirty love letter.'

'Okay, try the bathroom. I'm just going to run the first few seconds of these videotapes to check they're what they say on the sleeve.'

There were twenty or so tapes. When Joey had checked them and found nothing, he went through to the kitchen and searched all Di's cupboards, making sure he left everything as he'd found it.

Nina came in, shaking her head in disappointment. 'I've searched her spare bedroom. There's nothing in there, either.'

'I've got a few more things to check here. But you could have a look through all the books on that shelf in the living-room. I forgot to do it.'

Ten minutes later, he admitted defeat in the kitchen and went to see how Nina was doing.

In a corner of Di's sitting-room there was a small, tidy desk with a fax machine and a word-processor on it. Joey had already searched the contents of its single drawer, but Nina was sitting at it, studying a piece of paper.

'What's that?' he asked.

'It's the last bill for Di's phone card.' She passed him the itemised call breakdown. 'Do you recognise any of the numbers?'

Joey ran his eye down the long list. The only one that registered with him was Dick's. 'Let's take a copy of it and we can check them out later.' He fed the document into the fax machine and set it to copy.

Nina was rummaging in the drawer. Something caught Joey's attention which hadn't the previous time he'd looked – a small packet of Letraset type, partially used.

He leaned over Nina's shoulder and picked it out. 'Two of the notes I've had were written with this stuff. I wonder if there's any way of proving they came from these sheets?'

Nina nodded. 'There could be. Let's take it and check.'

'No,' Joey said. 'We've got to leave everything exactly as we found it. Now we know it's her, we have the advantage. Did you find anything in the books?'

Nina shook her head regretfully. 'No.'

'Too bad. We'd better get out of here, then. You go down to see the caretaker and keep him chatting for a few minutes while I get that plant back into the car. If I look out of Di's kitchen window, I'll be able to see you at his door.'

'Okay, see you back in the car.'

Joey went back into the kitchen and craned his neck to watch her coming round to the back of the house and knocking on the caretaker's door. Once he could see her talking with her usual animation, which would keep the old man happy for as long as she chose, he heaved the big plant on to the landing outside Di's front door. He went back in to make sure they hadn't left any sign of their search before firmly clicking the door shut and carrying the yucca down to his car.

Back at Three Elms Farm, Joey and Nina looked at the list of phone numbers Di had called.

Most of the Newmarket calls were to her boss. Some were to Barry, others to Graham and several racing people whose numbers Joey verified from his own address book.

That left a few dozen calls to other parts of England which struck no immediate chords.

'I bet one of those numbers is Sol Werner's. When I rang you from Paris the other week, you gave me his number. I think I wrote it in my diary.' Joey reached across his desk for his Filofax and leafed through it. When he found Sol's number, he ran his eye down the list on Di's bill.

'That confirms it!' The London number cropped up twice, towards the bottom, dated ten days previously. 'Di Lambert and Sol Werner!' He thumped the desk with glee. 'Now we'll get them.'

'What about the man who beat you up and rang you to stop Scaramanga?'

Joey gave a pained smile. 'And the guy who was ringing before that.'

'How can we check these other numbers?' Nina said.

'I tell you what. With that sexy voice of yours, no man's going to hang up in a hurry. You dial them and when they answer, keep them talking. I'll turn up the speaker on the phone, and see if I recognise any of them.'

They were rewarded with several unanswered calls and two female voices, similar to Di's, who dealt brusquely with Nina's enquiry: 'Is John there?' These were interspersed with several business answering services and followed by a man who denied there was anyone called John on the premises, but wondered if he would do.

Joey, listening, shook his head, and Nina put the phone down.

The next one was also answered by a man, to a background of heavy metal.

'Is John there?'

'John who?'

'He never told me his other name.'

'And what's yours, darling?'

'Maria,' she lied. 'Can I speak to John?'

'What d'you want to talk to him about?'

Nina glanced at Joey, who was straining his ears to hear the voice over the music. He grimaced and shook his hand from side to side to indicate his uncertainty.

'Maybe I'd rather talk to you,' said Nina.

'If you came round here, I'd make sure of that.'

Joey stiffened. Exactly that phrase had been used by the man who had phoned telling him to stop Scaramanga; the accent and intonation were identical. He glanced at Nina and gave her a thumbs up.

'I bet you would,' she laughed into the phone. 'I'll be round later.' She put the phone down then let out a gasp and looked at Joey. 'Was that him?'

'I thought it was from the start, and then he used words identical to ones he used to me on the phone the other day. I'm sure it's him. Di must have been communicating with this guy so it's more than likely his number would be on her bill, right?'

'Okay,' Nina said. 'If you're right, we've got a number for one of the men working with Di and possibly Sol. What do we do next?'

Joey flipped open his Filofax. 'We call in the pros.' He picked up the phone and dialled his solicitor's home number.

'Bruce Trevor.'

'Hello, Bruce, Joey Leatham here. Sorry to call you on a Sunday afternoon. I need to get in touch with Nick Allen.'

'Nick? Sure. No problem. I'll get him to call you. Are you at home?'

The private investigator rang within fifteen minutes. He cut Joey short from telling him any details over the phone, saying he would report for duty at eight sharp the following morning.

Joey and Nina knew there was nothing useful they could do about pursuing Di and her accomplices until then. Instead, they cooked dinner on a fire beside the stream and pretended they didn't have a care in the world. As the last glimmer of daylight left the sky to the stars, they went to bed in the caravan and happily lost themselves in each other until the first thrushes whistled their alarm call.

Chapter Thirteen

Next morning, after riding first lot, Joey found it hard to concentrate on what Seabourn was saying to him. He was too impatient to get out of the yard and into his car so that he could phone Nina at the farm.

'Is Nick there yet?'

'Yes. And I've just spoken to Di. She told me she'd been home to see her parents and got back late last night.'

'Okay. What are the chances of keeping her busy for a couple of hours this morning, well away from the flat?'

'I can try. She did say we should get together soon.'

'Tell Nick, and say I'm on my way home. I'll get out of doing another lot.'

Joey rang off, confident that Nina would manage to find some way of distracting Di. In the short time since he'd got to know her again, he'd learned that if Nina said she was going to do something, it was done.

He arrived to find her sitting with Nick at the kitchen table, with a large pot of coffee before them.

Nick jumped to his feet and shook Joey's hand.

'Nina's told me most of what's been going on. I've already got someone tracing the name and address of the guy whose voice you recognised.'

'And, Joey,' Nina added, excited, 'Di wasn't at home so I phoned the yard and Dick told me she's already gone to Lambourn with some horses for him. She has to do some paperwork or something, he said.'

'Do you know where in Lambourn?' Nick Allen asked.

'Yes.'

'Get the number and leave a message for her. Ask her to call you on your mobile when she gets there.'

'What are you going to do then?'

'Search her flat, of course.'

'We already have,' Joey said, 'every square inch of it.'

'I know.' Nick smiled. 'I hope to hell you didn't give yourselves away.'

'Nina says we didn't.'

'Maybe not, but as soon as we know she's well away, I'll go in there and do the job properly. Did you happen to see if she had a second VCR in the flat?'

'No. Just one.'

'So if she made a copy of the original, she probably did it in your agent's office – where there are two?'

Joey nodded. 'Yes, that seems the most likely possibility.'

'Okay. I'll need to take a second VCR with me and a blank tape.'

'No problem. I'll sort them out for you now.'

While they were waiting for Di to return Nina's call, Joey went over to Barry's office and tried to pretend this was just another Monday with a big race to look forward to at the end of the week. That afternoon, he had two rides in Bath. If they hadn't been good ones, he might have passed them up. As they were he arranged to fly down so he wouldn't be away from Newmarket for too long.

He was still talking to Barry when, through the window, he saw Nick Allen walk from the front door with a video recorder under his arm and get into a small BMW. A moment later the car was heading up the drive and out of sight.

Joey excused himself and hurried back to his own house.

Nina was waiting for him.

Di had just rung her back.

'She's in Lambourn now. I asked her if I could have lunch with her, but she said she wouldn't be back until around four. I told Nick and he went straight off. He said he'll call if he needs anything.'

'Great. I hope he does better than we did.'

'What do we do now?' Nina asked.

Joey grinned, wrapped his arms around her and drew her to him.

'Something to make the time pass quicker while we're waiting.'

Nick Allen had entered hundreds of private residences illegally, and had never been caught yet.

When he saw the mellow red-brick Edwardian building, he didn't think this would prove to be the exception. With Joey's VCR and a blank videotape stowed in a suitably anonymous khaki rucksack slung over one shoulder, he let himself into the main door of the block with a rudimentary skeleton key.

Three flights up, he took one look at the simple lock and flipped open his wallet. From half a dozen credit cards he plucked out the least worn and slipped it between the door jamb and the curved face of the bolt until it had been pushed back into the lock far enough to disengage and let the door swing open.

He closed this quietly behind him and, in almost complete silence, started his search.

Twenty minutes later, he was considering ringing Joey to ask why he was so certain Di Lambert was the blackmailer. Apart from the Letraset sheets, which were inconclusive, Nick had found no sufficient evidence to support their claim.

He sat down at the desk and hunted through it for a third time.

He flipped open the spring-backed telephone directory and checked all the numbers in it against those on the itemised phone bill. He couldn't find the one which Joey and Nina had identified as belonging to the man who had beaten up Joey.

Flipping through it for a final time, his eye was caught by a nine-figure number, written in isolation on the reverse of the "A" card.

He stared at it, knowing it was out of place. It wasn't a phone number – there was no "01" at the beginning – and he knew he'd seen it before somewhere.

'Yes!' he hissed to himself as he pulled his notebook from his jacket. He leafed through a few pages, until he found it – the number of the Southern Counties Building Society account where Joey had been instructed to make his payments.

He stood up. This was all the confirmation he needed that Di was involved.

And if she was, all his professional experience told him there must be something else in the flat to link her with the blackmail plot.

He resumed his meticulous search again, overlooking nothing.

After half an hour, without anything to show for it, he started on the kitchen for the second time. He had already checked all the cupboards and the fridge-freezer, but this time he took all the packets out of the deep freeze and placed them on the draining board by the sink.

He picked up and checked each of them until he found a couple that had already been opened. An apple-pie carton that seemed a little more tightly packed than it should have been caught his attention, and an under-weight slab of folded puff pastry.

He took the cling-film wrapping off the pastry, but it was too frozen to pull apart. He ran it under the hot tap for a while to make it more pliable. Then, carefully, he unfolded it until he was rewarded with the discovery of a bundle of fifty-pound notes.

He extracted them, counted them and found around five thousand pounds in five-hundred pound batches of consecutively numbered notes. He jotted down the serial numbers in his notebook and carefully folded up the money again and rewrapped the outer casing of puff pastry.

He turned his attention to the apple-pie carton, from which he pulled a videotape, tightly packed in bubble wrap and cling film. And with the tape was a single folded sheet of cheap squared paper on which a letter had been written in a spiky hand.

Nick carried the tape and the note through to Di's sitting room. He quickly connected up the VCR he had brought with him and used it with Di's player and the blank cassette to make a copy of the tape he had found. After a few minutes' more activity, he ejected Di's tape from her player. He made a copy of the letter on the fax machine, and put it back with the tape into the apple-pie carton exactly as he had found them.

He repacked the freezer and wiped down the draining board to remove any trace of his presence there.

In the sitting-room, he disconnected the second VCR and replaced everything in the room as he'd found it. Satisfied, he tucked the VCR and the copy-tape under his arm and headed for Di's front door.

He had his hand on the small metal catch of the lock when he heard footsteps coming up the stairs.

Knowing the lay-out of the flat, he slipped into a tiny spare bedroom, scantily furnished in pine and Laura Ashley chintz. He let himself into an empty built-in wardrobe and shut the flimsy door behind him just as a key was turned in the lock.

'How did you manage to get back so quickly?'

Nick heard the voice clearly through the thin partition walls. It was a man's voice, but it had neither Sol Werner's thick German-Jewish accent nor the heavy's East London, both of which Joey had described to him.

'I left the lorry driver with the paperwork. He knew what to do.' Di Lambert's confident tones rang out clearly as she and the man walked past the spare room and into the sitting-room. 'I drove back like a hare with a pair of lurchers on its tail.'

'Lucky lurchers,' the man chuckled.

'You're the lucky lurcher,' she said.

No one spoke for a few moments.

Nick guessed they were kissing and fondling. To his practised ear, they sounded like two people in the middle of a lustful affair.

'Do you want a drink, you horny beast?' Di asked.

'No, let's get to bed while we've got the chance.'

Their footsteps moved from the sitting-room to the main bedroom next door.

The two bedrooms had evidently been constructed from one larger room, and the dividing wall was simple studding and plaster board. The sounds of full-blooded love-making seeped through the flimsy partition. Nick listened dispassionately as Di Lambert and her lover reached a vigorous, noisy climax.

There was a lull in the noise, then a quiet murmuring which rose to a normal conversational level.

'That was fantastic!' the male voice said. 'What a succulent, wicked little creature you are!' The voice became more downbeat as it went on. 'But if we want to keep this up, we're going to have to find another really big injection of cash from somewhere soon. What we've been getting out of Joey doesn't go halfway to what we need.'

Nick carefully opened the door of the cupboard just enough to let some light in.

'Don't you worry,' Di was saying. 'I've got a couple of other irons in the fire that'll bring in plenty. Then we can start our own yard and really show those cynical bastards.'

'What else have you got going?' The man sounded concerned. 'You never told me about that.'

'Don't worry. Billy's handling it.'

'Billy? Do you have to use him?'

'There's no point in being snotty about him. He's been bloody useful and you know it.'

'I hope you've got him under control?'

'Of course I have. As long as he can get his bets on, he's happy to do what's necessary.'

'Why did you have to get him involved any further?'

The man seemed alarmed at the prospect. 'I suppose you have to use him for threatening and so on, but I wish you hadn't got him so mixed up in it. I really don't trust him.'

'Don't be so bloody pathetic!' Di said with an icy scorn which didn't fit Joey's description of an affable, easy-going Sloane Ranger. 'He'll be okay. As long as the money keeps coming – he'll do anything for money.'

'Yes, well,' the man sighed. 'Won't we all?'

'I'm not doing *this* for money.'

Nick guessed what she was doing from the man's contented sigh. A few moments later, the sounds of energetic sex reached him once more through the wall until suddenly the man seemed to panic.

'Christ! Look at the time. I've got to get back.' There were sounds of someone jumping out of bed and stumbling about, getting dressed in a hurry. 'People will smell a rat if I don't turn up for lunch.'

'Some rat!' Di laughed. 'Maybe you're right. I'll see you later.'

In his cupboard Nick prepared to leave. The man made a hurried exit and ran down the stairs. The faint bang of a car door being slammed echoed up from the street outside.

Di seemed to be taking her time, though. Nick heard her go through into the kitchen and evidently prepare something to eat. He listened intently for any sign that she'd noticed things had been moved, but after ten minutes of normal activity she walked back down the corridor to the bathroom where she spent some time in the shower.

An hour and a half after she and her lover had come in, she left the flat – Nick presumed to go back to her duties at Dick Seabourn's stables. Cramped and stiff, he slowly stepped out of the cupboard, keeping an ear cocked for sounds of Di returning. But from one of the bedroom windows he could see her, getting into her car and driving off.

He let himself out of the flat carrying Joey's VCR and the copy-tape in his rucksack. Making sure that no one saw him leave, he walked to his car and drove back to Three Elms Farm.

Half a mile from the house, he stopped and punched in Joey's number on his mobile phone.

Nina answered.

'Is Joey there?'

She recognised his voice. 'No. He had to go racing. We thought you'd have been in touch much earlier?'

'I'll tell you about it later. Is anyone else there?'

'Only Barry.'

'Ring me as soon as he's gone. And tell Joey to ring me if he can.'

Joey pushed the Ferrari hard on the way to his house from Newmarket racecourse where his plane had landed. He was edgy with frustration. Nick Allen had already been at the farm more than two hours, and Joey had made him promise not to let Nina see anything – the videotape or the note – until he got home.

At the same time, his heart was pounding with excitement now they had definite, unequivocal proof that Di was one of the prime movers in the conspiracy to blackmail him.

At first, when Nick had told him over the phone that he'd found the tape, Joey had been more shocked than angry. He realised that until that moment, he'd refused to believe that anyone from Di's background could possibly be a criminal.

When he drove into the farm's courtyard, he was relieved to see that there was no sign of Barry or anyone else in the office. He parked right outside his front door and ran in, to be greeted with a kiss from an excited Nina.

'My God, Joey! It feels as if we've been waiting days for you to get back, and Nick won't show me anything.'

They walked into his study where the private detective was waiting. 'Hi, Joey. Shall we get on with it?'

He nodded, and sat down on the sofa. He was dreading what their reactions were going to be when they saw the tape, dreading Nina's response most, despite all the understanding she had expressed to him.

But this moment had to be faced.

They laughed at the first sequence of the Cossack Riders: a nervous, waif-like Joey, aged sixteen going on twelve, riding round the arena in an oversized *feska*; a chubbier eighteen-year-old Nina, with blonde hair even longer than it was now, flowing behind her.

Joey looked down at her, sitting on the floor with her back against the sofa. It seemed astonishing that so much had changed in the ten years since the film had been shot. She glanced up at him, and smiled, thinking the same thoughts.

The riding sequence came to an end.

All Joey's muscles tightened, as if to withstand the shock of what he knew was to follow.

After a few seconds of flickering static, the interior of the circus big top came into view. Joey had watched this scene on tape only once before, but every second of it was etched on his memory so clearly that he was pitched right back into the whole terrible nightmare.

★ ★ ★

Joey's knees quivered as he gazed down at the safety net, ten feet by forty, stretching the distance of the arcs of the trapezes to either side of the big top. It was suspended under tension between eight angled poles at the sides and each corner. The poles were secured with wire hawsers which disappeared beneath the banks of raked timber seating where they were anchored to the ground. The net was there to save lives, but it still had to be treated with respect. If you landed wrongly, you could do serious damage. No trapeze artist ever ate for several hours before a session, to avoid choking if he hit the net.

Joey and Mikhail, side by side on the specially made wide trapeze, swung themselves up together, keeping perfect time between them, maintaining the balance and precise momentum needed to be at the exact spot when Ivan would let go of his own swing and hurtle down towards them.

At the top of the arc, they turned themselves over and swooped back, hanging from the rail by their knees.

Ivan stood perched like an eagle on a cliff top, watching them, counting the timing of each swing. As Mischa and Joey were halfway down their return swing, he stood on tip-toes, lifted his own trapeze and launched himself, diving with none of an eagle's grace towards the centre of the tent.

Joey and Mischa were already swinging back towards him as he started to drop. They had performed the cycle once more when Ivan gave a low grunt at the top of his swing; Joey braced himself for the violent tug when both his hands would grasp one of Ivan's large fists.

The young men had done the routine so many times they knew instinctively what each other was doing; there was no need for them to see or hear.

Ivan, swinging by his hands, let go of his bar halfway up its forward curve and dropped like a lead weight towards his pair of pint-sized catchers.

Together they took the sudden massive strain of Ivan's weight as his hands slapped their wrists and instinctively clutched them.

They swung back with Ivan dangling below them. His weight sent them hurtling down and back up, almost to the crow's nest on their side.

The strain on their shoulder muscles intensified at the top of the swing as Ivan's sixteen stones were whipped out by centrifugal forces. The three of them careered through another half-circle. When they reached the top at the apex of the tent, they released Ivan, who twisted through a hundred and eighty degrees and caught his original trapeze as it came up to meet him. Two seconds later, he placed his feet with a thud on his home base.

Mikhail and Joey had spun themselves over to sit on their bar and carried on swinging. Ivan turned and growled across the upper void of the canvas cathedral. 'That was okay,' he admitted grudgingly. 'Did you get it, Ginger? I want to see it afterwards.'

'Sure I did, Ivan,' the clown piped from his perch in the darkness. But Joey knew he hadn't; he had promised he wouldn't.

'Good,' Ivan bellowed. 'Now Mr Werner has arrived, so we do it again.'

Joey's pulse quickened as they began the routine again. He and Mischa tipped themselves over to hang by their knees and launched themselves towards the summit of the big top.

The air rushed through their hair and pressed against

the flesh of their cheeks. They swung twice. Ivan launched himself again.

The catchers swooped back. At the bottom of their arc, Ivan reached the top of his. He let go, and dropped like a boulder towards them.

Joey gritted his teeth and uttered a short prayer. When the precise moment came to extend his hands for the catch, he held back, withdrawing them a few inches until the critical fraction of a second had passed.

He heard Ivan's big right hand slap into Mikhail's wrist while the other groped wildly in the air in front of Joey's face, seeking the absent hand. He even saw Ivan's eyes, angry, black, terrified, and knew that the punishment for his betrayal would be vicious.

Joey shouted at his partner: 'He missed me, Mischa! Let him go!'

Too late. The slender young Russian had taken all his father's weight, which tore at his shoulder for a moment of excruciating pain. He had tried to release the large hand, but Ivan wouldn't let go. His left arm flailed furiously just short of Joey's grasping hands.

Mikhail's only option was to drop from the swing. He straightened his legs at the top of the arc, detaching himself from the swing, and tumbled down to the net, pulled by the wrist still in his father's grasp.

Joey saw the double fall as he swung back. Passing over them, in the split second before he was hurtling up to the top of the tent, he saw them hit the net . . . and carry on, as if it didn't exist.

It felt like minutes before he swung back and turned himself over to land on the platform where they'd started. He dropped the trapeze and left it dangling above the terrible spectacle below where the net had collapsed into a heap of knotted nylon cord over two broken bodies.

His heart stopped for several seconds. He didn't breathe until the full implication of what had happened hit him and he exhaled in a long, loud gasp. 'Jesus Christ!'

Just then, Ivor Wimsatt walked briskly through the curtained door into the arena and stopped as if he'd walked into a stone wall. He immediately started yelling for help in a voice that was surprisingly loud and clear in the still aftermath of the fall.

Within moments, people were running in and scurrying around the tangled net, opening it out to reveal the bodies of the two fallen men.

Joey watched from above, trying not to believe what he saw, until he heard Tatyana wail: 'My God! Mischa, my little Mischa . . . Dead . . . Dear God, he's dead!'

More calmly, Wimsatt's voice echoed through the shocking stillness of the great tent. 'So is Ivan.'

It was Nick Allen who picked up the remote control and turned off the VCR.

Joey carried on staring at the blank screen. He didn't dare look at Nina, until he felt her hand on his knee giving it a gentle squeeze. Her eyes were brimming with tears of compassion, not accusation.

'I understand,' she whispered. 'You didn't know about the net.'

He gazed back at her silently.

'Is that true?' Nick asked.

'Yes,' Joey replied. 'I told you, it was all Ginger's idea – just to make Ivan look a fool in front of Sol Werner.'

'I've got to tell you, anyone looking at that sequence

would say you'd deliberately dropped the guy, and it would be hard to convince people you didn't know the net was sabotaged.'

'I know,' Joey said grimly. 'And the only people who knew that Ginger rigged it, were him and Giulio. Di and her mates worked that out pretty quickly. Anyway, thank God you've got their copy of the tape now.'

'I haven't. This is a copy of their copy.' Nick explained what he'd done at the flat, and the importance of Di's not learning they had found her tape.

'But I don't care if she knows we've found it! I just want her to stop the blackmail and give me my money back.'

'What?' Nina said indignantly. 'You don't want her punished?'

'Listen,' Nick said to Joey, standing up to make his point. 'You're the client, and you give the orders, but I can tell you, there's enough evidence here for the police to get a conviction – at least against her. And I guess it wouldn't be too hard for them to get a case against whoever murdered Giulio too.'

'But Giulio wasn't murdered, he died from a heart attack.'

'Any court would say that was a direct result of the attack, though. She could get ten to fifteen for conspiracy to blackmail and murder.'

'And what would I get if I'm found guilty?'

'You'd be charged with manslaughter, not murder, and if they convicted, you could be looking at five years.'

'Five years!' Joey exploded. 'I've struggled too hard to risk all that. I'm not doing five days, never mind five years.'

'But, Joey,' Nina was looking at him, 'you *can't* let Di

get away with it. She was a friend of yours, and tried to be a friend of mine. You trusted her.'

'I don't care. I'm not risking my freedom and my career for the sake of revenge.'

'Okay,' Nick said, in a mollifying tone. 'We'll deal with that later. There's also this note I found with the tape.'

He passed Joey the Xerox he'd made of the sheet of cheap, squared paper. It took Joey a few moments to recognise the sloping, foreign hand.

It had been sent from the hospice in France, dated 3 June, the day after the French Derby.

Dear Joey,

It's been a terrible long time since I saw you. I thought about you often, and wondered what you were doing. Then I saw you on the television, saving the girl at the racecourse, and I see you are a hero and a great jockey.

I am very proud for that.

But I am dying now, very close. I want you to have this tape. There is something on it you won't ever want to see again, but it is the only one, and you can destroy it yourself. It was my fault what happened. I have terrible guilt about it always. I unhooked the guys for the net. I knew what would happen. Ivan had been very cruel to me but I did not want his son to die.

Forgive me, Joey.

With much love from your old friend,

Ginger

(Heinrich Calaval)

Joey read the letter twice. He could do nothing to stop

the tears welling up. He passed the piece of paper to Nina without a word. She read it, and looked at him. Her eyes showed that she understood without any further explanation what it all meant. His story had been corroborated from beyond the grave.

'How did Di get the tape and this letter?' she asked.

'It came in the post – in a padded bag. I was out, so it went up to the office. It had a French post-mark on it; I guess everyone assumed it was the Prix du Jockey Club video. Barry said he didn't have time to watch it. There were other people in and out all day. Di must have picked it up, opened it and realised from the note that it wasn't the race and might be worth watching. She could easily have been in there on her own long enough to have a look and make the copy which she took home. And she obviously realised it was worth something.'

'And she was right,' Nick said. 'But I haven't made the connection with Sol Werner yet.'

'What about the other guy?' Joey asked. 'Did you get anywhere with the phone number?'

'Yes. He lives in Epping and his name's Billy Duckett. I think you were right; he's your thug, but Di Lambert's much more involved with someone else. They talked about setting up a yard. She spent an hour showering and messing about after he'd gone,' he said. 'That's why I didn't get back before you left for Bath.'

'But who the hell was she with?' Joey said. 'Has she told you about a new boyfriend?' he asked Nina.

'No. Nothing. But it's not so surprising, and it must be someone who knows you.'

'That could mean anyone in Newmarket,' Joey said without vanity.

'It has to be someone in racing,' Nick nodded. 'Someone who would consider taking up training.'

'A jockey, maybe.' Joey shrugged. 'A bloodstock agent; another trainer's assistant. You say he had an upper-class accent?'

'Yes, same as Di's.'

'There are plenty of those round here,' Joey said thoughtfully. 'But I can't think of any involved with Di, or who's bent enough.'

'You never can tell,' the private detective said.

'Yes,' Joey agreed ruefully. 'I realise that now, thanks to Di.'

'She sounds a right scheming bitch to me,' Nick commented.

Joey clenched his fists and looked at Nina. 'The bastards! How can people like that, with so much going for them, sink so low? I wouldn't blame them so much if they'd had nothing – if they'd had to fight their way up from nowhere.'

'They're weak, and they're cowards,' she said, voice husky with anger, 'and they're greedy. We *must* take back everything they took from you and more. And they must pay for killing Giulio.'

'All the evidence is there, Joey,' Nick said. 'The tape, the money – you'll find they can prove that's come from branches of Southern Counties. The account number is in Di's writing on her phone directory. Then there's Ginger's note and the Letraset sheets, in conjunction with the notes you've had. Also it's an odds-on chance this bloke Billy dealt with Giulio, and he seems dozy enough to have left something behind in Yarmouth.'

'Maybe we could get them done for that, without

bringing the blackmail into it?'

'I doubt they could pin anything on Di Lambert without it.'

Joey stared at a large oil painting of a group of horses behind the start on Goodwood racecourse. But he didn't see it.

Why had these people tried to tear his life apart like this?

What had he ever done to them?

In the silence, the phone on his desk rang. The answer-phone was on so Joey let it ring.

There was a click as the tape finished and the caller came in with a message, amplified over the speaker.

'Oh, hello, Joey. Dick Seabourn here. I tried to get you earlier but I couldn't get through on your mobile. Well done on the filly; she went much better than I'd hoped.' The trainer's cultivated voice conveyed his customary charm. 'I'd like to chat about her, and a couple of things for tomorrow. Could you give me a ring, please, as soon as you've a moment? Thanks. 'Bye.'

'I never asked,' Nina said. 'Did you win?'

'I did, as a matter of fact.'

'Never mind that.' Nick was staring at them in agitation. 'Who was that?'

'That was my trainer. Why?'

'That's the guy who was in bed with Di Lambert!'

There was complete silence in the room for a few moments.

Joey felt his jaw drop. 'Don't be crazy. That was Dick Seabourn. He's a respectable, middle-aged man, old enough to be her father and happily married.'

'All that may be true, but it's never stopped anyone before. I heard him in bed with Di Lambert and they weren't playing tiddlywinks. Plus he's involved in what's going on.'

'My God!' Joey strode back and forth across the room. 'I can't believe it! Dick, for Christ's sake! The whole world's going crazy!'

'If he's your trainer, why would they be talking about getting their own yard?' Nick asked.

'Crowle House belongs to Veronica, Dick's wife. He rents it from her trustees. He's never had a lot of money of his own.'

'And now he's having a steaming affair with his secretary.'

'I just can't believe it,' Joey said again.

'It's probably happened a million times before,' Nick said. 'It's the weak, middle-aged men, flattered by some young girl's attention, who do the craziest things – quite out of character. But what do you want to do about it?'

Joey picked up a salt pot from the sideboard and fiddled with it for a moment as he thought. 'Now we know Seabourn's part of it, that makes it even harder.' Joey turned the problem over in his mind. 'I don't want Veronica to go through the embarrassment and disgrace of seeing him sent to prison.'

'He wanted to speak to you, didn't he? If you rang him back and asked him to come round here, would he?'

'Maybe.' Joey glanced at his watch. 'They'll be starting evening stables soon, but he sometimes leaves that to Martin.'

'See if you can get him over,' Nick urged.

Joey looked at the phone for a moment before picking it up and dialling Seabourn's number.

Veronica answered.

'Evening,' Joey said as calmly as he could. 'Is the guv'nor there?'

'He's just out at the yard.'

Joey detected an unusual breathlessness in her voice. 'Are you all right?' he asked.

'I'm fine.'

There was a pause. Something in her voice told Joey she was far from fine, but he didn't press her.

'Dick wanted to see me,' he said, 'and I was wondering if he'd mind coming round here? There're a couple of things I need to show him.'

'I don't see why not. He'll be in any moment, I'll get him to go straight round.' She said it in a way that left him in no doubt her husband would come.

Joey put the phone down, not looking forward to the imminent confrontation. He knew, though, that they had to talk to Seabourn before Di. Of the two, the trainer was most likely to capitulate under pressure.

He turned to Nick. 'What are we going to say when he comes?'

'You leave that to me.'

'My God!' Joey said, striding up and down the room again. 'When I think of all the people I suspected were in on this – and I never once considered Dick! Bloody hell! I thought it was everyone but him. I even thought it might be my own brother!' He stopped and looked at Nick. 'But Sol Werner could still be a part of it.'

'The circus man you told me about, the one Nina saw at the races?'

'Yeah. It was him who told me to go to that place in France where I got beaten up.'

Nick shook his head. 'That doesn't mean he had you thumped. Di obviously had Billy following you around, when she couldn't do it herself. I would say it's more than likely she found out about Giulio and realised he had to be bullied into keeping his mouth shut, but her mate Billy overdid it. As for Sol Werner –' Nick shrugged '– from what you've told me, and what I've seen and heard myself, he's not involved at all. Di was – probably in some kind of partnership with your Dick Seabourn, and with a bit of hired muscle from this Billy Duckett.'

Dick Seabourn arrived twenty minutes later. Joey saw as soon as he opened the front door that the trainer was apprehensive.

'Ah, hello, Joey. Veronica gave me your message.'

'Thanks for coming.' Joey ushered his boss across the hall. 'I thought it might be better to talk here.'

Seabourn stiffened and half turned as he walked into the study. 'Something confidential, eh? I hope you're not thinking of going freelance again?' He attempted a chuckle which died when he saw Nina and Nick Allen standing in the room.

'I might have to,' Joey kept the conversation going, 'if what I've just heard is true.'

Seabourn stopped dead just inside the door to the study. Taking in Nick's no-nonsense expression and Nina's obvious scorn, he turned and looked at Joey like a nervous stag which knows it has just been cornered.

'What . . . What have you heard?'

'I heard it, Mr Seabourn,' Nick said matter-of-factly. 'I heard a conversation you had while I was searching Miss Lambert's flat this afternoon.'

Seabourn, who had taken a few steps further into the room, visibly sagged at the knees.

'Why not sit down?' Joey waved him to a chair. 'Do you want a drink?'

'Yes . . . yes, please. A whisky,' the trainer said faintly as he lowered himself into one of Joey's deep, wing-backed chairs.

'I've been working for Mr Leatham,' Nick went on dispassionately, 'trying to find out who's been blackmailing him.'

Seabourn's head, already hanging, dropped lower while his eyes lifted. He looked at Nick, then, wincing with shame, at Joey. He said nothing.

The detective walked across the room and sat behind Joey's desk. Without any further announcement, he retold Seabourn and Di's conversation to Joey and Nina.

Seabourn's specific reference to Joey caused the trainer to close his eyes and shake his head remorsefully.

He straightened his back, sitting bolt upright in the chair. He turned to Joey. 'I will never be able to express my shame and regret for what I've done.' He walked across to the window and gazed out silently towards the meadows behind the house, where the sun had started to lengthen the shadows of the alders by the brook.

When he spoke, he didn't turn to face his listeners. 'I never wanted to get involved, but Di's a lot sharper than you might think. And, you see, I was obsessed with her. Of course I love my wife, and respect her deeply. It's just in recent years she seems to have lost any interest in the physical side of our marriage. I understand it happens sometimes and I shouldn't take it as any reflection on myself. But it's very hard not to. I have the usual male urges, and Di is a very attractive, very physical woman.'

Nick, seated at the desk, nodded. 'What my client

wants to know is, where's the money?'

'The money?' Seabourn said vaguely, as if that were the least of the problem. 'Di was transferring it to another building society account, drawing it out from the one where I'd told Joey to put it.'

'*You* told him?'

Joey was nodding. 'Now I know, I can tell Dick made the first phone calls. Not from his accent, nor through that voice-distortion box, whatever it was, but from the words he used and the way he phrased things.'

'Yes, it was me,' Seabourn said quietly.

'Asking me to stop those horses?'

'What horses? What are you talking about?'

'Colombian Prince. Tap Dancer. Scaramanga.'

'No! No, I never asked you to stop them. I'd heard a whisper that someone had, or at least I had a suspicion from something Di once said. But of course I wouldn't have asked you to lose a race.'

'Who was it then?'

Seabourn said nothing.

'Come on. We know, but give us a name: confirm it for us.'

'He's a chap Di knows. Nothing to do with me. I never got involved with him or wanted him to do anything.'

'Like beat the shit out of me in France, and then again right here in my own garden?'

'That was Di's idea. I didn't know what she was up to but she said it was to encourage you. She said it was just like you were paying an extra tax – half your earnings was no worse than paying for an ex-wife after a divorce. She made it sound quite reasonable.' Seabourn's voice was breaking by now. 'I don't know how I let myself be carried away by it all.'

'You still haven't told us the bloke's name,' Nick reminded him.

'Billy,' Seabourn sighed. 'Don't ask me his surname.'

'Billy Duckett,' Nick said. 'The muscle from Epping; one of Di's previous bits of rough. Give her her due – she has a catholic taste in men. What about Giulio?' he snapped suddenly.

Seabourn blinked. 'Giulio? Who's he? What's he done? She never said she had anyone else helping her.'

'All right,' Nick said. 'We'll forget Giulio for the time being. Let's get back to the money.'

'I haven't got it,' Seabourn said. 'We decided it would be too risky if I had anything to do with the account. There are already enough people snooping around trainers' finances. But anything I can do to get it back, I will.'

Nick shook his head with a cynical smile. 'It's a bit late to start offering to give it all back and trying to do deals.'

Seabourn turned around to face them across the room – Nick at the desk, Joey leaning against the fireplace and Nina sitting on the edge of the sofa.

Drawing together the tattered remnants of his dignity, he looked Joey straight in the eye. 'I have behaved abominably. You've been utterly loyal to me . . .'

'No, I haven't,' Joey said. 'I stopped Colombian Prince.'

'You didn't have much choice, by the sound of it. Anyway, I suppose I was to blame – indirectly.' Seabourn sighed and gazed down at the carpet. 'What's going to happen now?'

Joey stared at him. 'We'll see,' he said quietly. 'Go home now. We'll let you know.'

★ ★ ★

From his study window, Joey watched Dick Seabourn climb back into his Mercedes. It gave him no pleasure to see the older man suffer and he hoped that Seabourn's fears for his future would not come true.

Exhaustive discussions with Nick had convinced Joey that he and his blackmailers were at a stand-off.

If he wanted to see Di convicted for blackmail and conspiracy to murder, he would have to let the police see the tape with which she was blackmailing him.

However he then argued his own innocence, there was a strong chance he himself would be charged with killing Ivan and Mikhail, and suffer all the ignominy which Dick Seabourn now dreaded. And besides, although he wouldn't have fallen from such a height within the racing establishment as the trainer, his high public profile would make him a much more newsworthy subject.

And bringing down Di meant bringing down Dick Seabourn. Which would inevitably involve Veronica.

Billy Duckett was a different matter.

As soon as Seabourn had driven away from Three Elms Farm, Nick Allen dialled a number Joey had given him.

'Detective Inspector Jacobs? . . . Hello, Inspector. I'm told you're dealing with the death of Mr Giulio Santini . . . The man who did it was Billy Duckett of 15 Pychard Way, Epping. I expect your colleagues there know him.'

Nick put the phone down with a grin. 'That's him dealt with, we hope. Now, what about Miss Lambert?'

'Nina's on the phone, arranging to meet her.'

'Does she trust Nina?'

'As soon as Nina turned up here in Newmarket, Di latched on to her – presumably to keep a close check on me and divert suspicion. As it happened, she got that all wrong. Nina thought there was something wrong about her from the start.'

Nick grinned. 'I learned a long time ago not to underestimate what they call "female intuition". Of course, it's not intuition, just a natural cynicism more highly developed than ours!'

As they spoke, Nina came into the room. 'Okay. She said she'd meet me at the stable where she keeps her horse. I told her I wanted to see him.'

'What horse is this?' Nick asked.

'An old racehorse she keeps,' Joey said. 'She likes to hack around the Heath on him.'

'Where's the stable?'

'On the edge of town. It's just a couple of boxes and a small paddock she rents.'

'Sounds ideal. How are you going to get there, Nina?'

'Danny just came in. He says he'll take me.'

'Okay. We'll follow.'

'Good-looking woman,' Nick observed appreciatively.

He and Joey were in Nick's car, under the cover of a great, spreading oak. They watched Di park her car twenty yards away and walk down a short track to a small block of two timber stables and a tack room.

Nina was waiting for her, leaning over the post and rail of an over-grazed paddock beside the stables, in which a big, handsome chestnut horse was nudging at an empty feed-bowl.

'What do you think of Hector, then?' Di asked proudly.

'He's lovely. Was he a good racehorse?' Nina asked, glancing over the animal with an expert eye.

'Yes, he was a useful stayer – won over two miles. He'd have made a good jump stallion if they hadn't cut him.'

'He's still got the look of a stallion about him.'

They admired the horse and talked about him until Di suggested they go into the tack room while she mixed his feed.

'Right,' Nick said from the cover of the car. 'That looks an ideal place for the little chat you're about to have. Let's get down there and get on with it.'

Joey pushed open the door of the ten-by-ten wooden tack room.

Di was leaning over a feed-bin with a scoop in her hand. She glanced up at him, startled.

Nina feigned surprise. 'Joey! What are you doing here?'

'I came to see her.' He nodded at Di.

Her eyes narrowed in a hint of alarm. She glanced at Nina to see how she was taking what could be construed as an act of infidelity on Joey's part.

Like Joey, Nina smiled. Di grew visibly nervous.

Nick appeared in the doorway behind Joey.

'This is Nick,' Joey told Di. 'He's what you'd call a private investigator.'

'Oh?' Di said. 'What are you investigating up here? An equine paternity suit?'

'No. Someone's been extorting money from Joey with a threat to send a potentially incriminating videotape to the police. He asked me to look into it, so I searched your flat today.'

Di looked away sharply to conceal her reaction. Apart from a sudden tightening of her jaw and fists, little showed. She picked up a bridle and fiddled with it for a few seconds until she'd recovered. Then she turned back and addressed Joey.

'What on earth's he talking about?' she asked in a self-righteous tone. 'Why should he be searching my flat?'

'What would he have found, Di?'

'Nothing. He didn't find anything.' She turned to Nick. 'Did you?' she challenged.

He didn't answer. The very fact that she showed no indignation at having her flat broken into was a de facto admission of guilt.

Joey calmly sat down on a corn bin and folded his arms. 'He found the number of the account I've been putting all my money into. Over a hundred and fifty grand I've paid in! How much is left?'

Di stared at him, defiant and scornful. 'I don't know what you're talking about.'

Joey shrugged.

'He found the sheets of Letraset, matching up with the notes you sent me.'

'What does that prove?' she asked contemptuously.

'What could it prove, Di?'

'Nothing. I don't know what the hell you're talking about.'

'Let me explain something to you. Just for the moment, you can take it we've got so much evidence we could drive you round to the nick in the High Street and have you banged up tonight – for blackmail, conspiracy to defraud, and murder.' Joey grinned at her encouragingly. 'The only problem is that I'd have to let the police see a video of an accident which happened ten years ago, which makes it look as if I deliberately allowed two men to fall to their deaths. Even though I didn't have any intention of doing that and thought they'd land safely in the net below, it would be hard for me to prove, and the publicity would finish me as a jockey.' He paused. 'I don't know why I'm telling you,' he added. 'You obviously realised it all as soon as you found the tape and the letter in Barry's office.'

Di sat down on a saddle rack and stared back at him. She clearly wasn't planning to admit anything yet.

'Unfortunately the only two people who knew who had sabotaged that net were Ginger, who did it, and Giulio – his lover. Luckily for you, Ginger died just after he sent me the tape, and you had Giulio killed. So, it looks like a stand-off. Nick, you tell her the score.'

'It *is* a stand-off, but not an even one.' Nick spoke authoritatively. 'I can tell you, even without any witnesses for the defence, if Joey gets convicted at all, it'd be of manslaughter and he'd get about five years. But you would definitely go down for what you've done, for something nearer fifteen.'

Joey looked closely at Di as Nick spoke. Her hands were shaking.

'So I suggest,' Nick went on, 'you listen very carefully to what Joey has to offer.'

'It's simple enough,' he took over. 'You give me back my money and your copy of the tape, and we'll do nothing. You'll get off scot-free.'

Di tilted back her head and laughed.

'That's absolutely pathetic! Just the sort of thing I'd have expected from a tight-fisted little shit like you.' She stood up and walked across to the door, opened it and looked outside. Evidently satisfied, she closed it and turned back to them.

'I see your dozy brother's standing sentry for you.' She

shook her head. 'Anyway, listen to me. You can't pin a thing on me. The account's not in my name. All I've got is a card and the PIN number to get the cash out. Your private detective here may have found the Letraset, but he didn't take it, and I burnt it when the caretaker told me this afternoon he'd seen someone snooping around. And you don't think I did it all on my own, do you?'

Joey grinned. 'No, of course not. Dick was round at my place earlier. He left half an hour ago. By the way, he asked me to tell you he's posting your P45 and a cheque in lieu of notice – no need to go in to pick them up.'

Di's face contorted into an ugly mask of fear and spite. 'The despicable, cringing bastard!' she hissed. 'Of course, Veronica'll always have him back and forgive him, because she feels guilty she never lets him screw her.'

'Probably,' Joey agreed.

'Listen, even though he was going to end up with a yard of his own, the cowardly shit didn't have much to do with it – apart from making a few phone calls. You won't find much on him.'

'Maybe, but I haven't told you everything. Nick also found a telephone bill in your flat, listing a string of calls to someone called Billy Duckett.' Di squeezed her eyes tight shut for an instant. 'He's an old boyfriend of yours, isn't he? The police from Yarmouth will be picking him up – just about now – for killing poor old Giulio.'

Di's healthy colour faded from her face.

'B-but even if they pull Billy, he'd never tell them about me.' Her confidence returned. 'And they can't do anything without the tape, and I've still got my copy. I can take a punt too, Joey. From where I'm standing, it looks like you've a lot more to lose than me.'

'That depends,' he said with a shake of his head, 'on how many copies you made.'

Her eyes shifted uneasily.

'If the only one you had was the one in your deep freeze,' Joey went on, 'I'm afraid you'll find it's been wiped. Isn't that right, Nick?'

Di was quivering with rage now. 'What? What the hell are you talking about? You didn't find it . . . It's still there. Why didn't you take it? You didn't wipe it – I checked this afternoon. I played it!'

'All of it?'

Suddenly limp, Di stared at him and didn't answer.

'He didn't erase the nice footage of Nina and me as Cossack Riders – there was nothing very embarrassing about that. But if you'd bothered to play it all, you'd have found the bit I don't want anyone to see isn't there any more. And we've got the serial numbers of the five grand in notes in the pastry packet. They'll be traced straight back to Southern Counties – or do you want to take a punt on that too?'

She took two hesitant paces towards the door. Joey stood aside. 'If you want to go and have a look at that tape and get the money, Danny'll take you. He'll make sure you don't come to any harm.'

Di opened the door stiffly and stepped out like a sleep-walker. Joey followed and signalled to Danny. The Range Rover roared into life and rolled down the track towards the woman walking slowly towards it.

Barry was waiting in his office when Joey arrived back at Three Elms Farm with Nick and Nina.

'Will someone tell me what's happening?' he asked plaintively. 'Dick Seabourn sounds so miserable, you'd think every damn' horse in his yard had just died. And then you ring me demanding my presence, as if you were going to read a will.'

He waved his three visitors to the sofas in the middle of the room and got them drinks.

'So, what's the big occasion?'

Joey took a grateful slug of the vodka Barry had poured him and launched into an account of the complicated chain of events which had led to his suspecting almost everyone in Newmarket of blackmail – and the extraordinary developments that had taken place since he'd found the speeding ticket on Barry's desk.

His friend was dismayed, though eventually realistic, when he heard that even he had fallen under suspicion. 'I tell you, though, I'm almost relieved to know you stopped Colombian Prince. I was seriously worried about your competence for a few days after that. Of course, I always knew Dick would be feeble under pressure.'

'But can you believe it?' Nina asked. 'Joey couldn't accept that people like Seabourn or Di would stoop to blackmail.'

'I do find it hard to believe,' Barry admitted. 'And when we Irish decide to be cynical, we're good at it.'

They were interrupted by the sound of a car pulling up outside. Nick went to the window and looked down into the yard. Danny was opening the door for Di – not, it appeared, out of an excess of politeness.

A few moments later, he was ushering her into Barry's office.

When she walked in, Di seemed to Joey like an entirely different person from the one he'd always known. There was a resentful hardness about her he'd never seen.

A few steps inside the door, she stopped and gazed at him with undiluted hatred.

He stood up to face her, acutely conscious of the eight-inch difference in their heights.

A second later, a pale object flew through the air, caught him hard on the side of his head and thudded to the ground behind him.

'There's five grand, gift wrapped in puff pastry!' Di advanced a few more steps and flung a videotape at him. 'You miserable little bastard!' She was screaming manically now as she pulled an envelope from a pocket of the cotton jacket she was wearing. She scrumpled the paper into a ball and hurled it at the floor.

'You sort it out. I opened the account in the name of Jennifer Hartwell. I've signed a blank draft. All the money's still there, except the five grand in the pastry and ten more that's gone, and you can bloody well piss in the wind for that.'

She stopped and glowered at Joey, shaking her head. 'My life's ruined now, thanks to you, you selfish *dwarf*! What do you need all that money for anyway? You've got no one to spend it on.' She shot a spiteful glance at Nina. 'No woman's going to hang around long for a lousy little prick like you! Think you're a star in bed, don't you? Well, let me tell you, a boy-scout on beginner's knots could do a better job than you.' She tossed her head, spat at the documents on the floor and walked from the room.

There was a stunned silence in the office, broken only by the sound of her footsteps clattering down the wooden stairs outside.

'Jesus!' Barry hissed. 'I wouldn't have believed she could change like that.'

'She never changed,' Nina said in a low voice. 'She was always a bitch, kidding she was a good old jolly-hockey-sticks type. Joey, you can't let her get away with it! Ten thousand pounds – stolen from under your nose.'

'Leave it,' he said, struggling to keep his voice even. Di's scathing reference to him as a dwarf had hurt him as much as her theft of his money.

'She's bloody mental,' Danny said. 'But like Nina says, you can't let her get away with it.'

'It's my money. And provided I get the rest of it back without any trouble, I'm not going to stir anything up. That's the way I want it left.'

'You must be crazy.' Barry was looking at him in amazement. 'If anyone ripped me off for ten grand like that, then abused me the way she just did, I'd not only want her guts for garters, I'd want every sinew in her damn' body. You *can't* let her get away with it.'

Joey looked at him. 'Barry, I don't give a damn what she said to me. She's barking mad and I'm happy to lose ten thousand quid if that's an end to the whole business. So let's leave it.' He turned to Nick Allen who, with professional impartiality, had not expressed a view. 'Nick, thanks. I'll let you know if I need any more help.'

The private detective thought of saying what was on his mind, but Joey had made his intentions clear, and that, Nick guessed, was that.

Barry drove Joey back to Newmarket the evening after the King George and Queen Elizabeth Stakes. Joey had just ridden the race of his life, Scaramanga looked set to become one of the great horses of his generation, and Dick Seabourn had been acclaimed for a supreme display of training.

Joey tilted the passenger seat of the Porsche as far back as he could. 'God, what a wonderful feeling!' he sighed.

'Winning the King George at last?'

'No. It's great but I wasn't thinking of that.'

'Is it knowing you'll be going home to a lovely Russian tonight?'

Joey laughed. 'I'm just getting used to the idea of not having to worry about phone calls and threats and who's going to see that video.'

Barry chuckled. 'You looked very pleased with yourself, burning that last copy of it the other night.'

'I was. That was all I wanted – that and getting the money back.'

'All bar ten grand,' Barry growled.

'I've told you, I can live without that.'

'I don't know how you can stay in the same town as that woman, after what she did.'

'There's not a lot I can do about it, not without stirring up more hassle than it's worth for ten grand.'

'Well, I won't tolerate you being treated like that.'

'What's it to do with you?'

'What's it to do with me? You're my best friend, for God's sake! I have a vested interest in your well-being, and that includes your pride. So you'll understand when I tell you that Nina and I, and Danny, all felt Di deserved a little something for what she did to you.' He glanced at his watch. 'As a matter of fact, Danny should have delivered it by now.'

Joey sat up in his seat. 'What? What the hell are you talking about? What have you done?'

'None of us have to do anything now – that's the beauty of it.'

★ ★ ★

Di Lambert parked her car near the stables where she kept her horse. It would be dark soon and a sharp night was forecast. An unseasonal northerly wind was blowing.

She hurried down the track to the tack room and opened the wooden door. Inside, she rummaged around, moving a stack of blankets and sweat rugs to uncover a well-used jute rug. As she gathered it up, she took little notice of the strong, vinegary smell which lingered on it.

Out in the cold night, she made her way round the side of the stable block to the paddock. The horse had his front end in a lean-to, eating hay. She climbed over the fence and walked towards his strong chestnut quarters. The evening breeze gusted behind her and rippled the jute rug on her arm.

'Hector,' she called. 'Come on, old man.'

The horse lifted his head and turned towards her.

She knew at once that there was something wrong. This was not Hector. The animal's nostrils were flaring; he was showing the whites of his eyes and he was wearing a leather head-collar.

A second later, he had pirouetted his half-ton weight and was charging towards her with his head down.

The horse lunged forward in a frenzy of fear, triggered by memories associated with the acrid odour of the disinfectant spray in which the rug had been soaked.

As his head rose up, the dying light caught the brass name-plate on his head-collar and, etched on it, two words: Sudden Spin.

False Start

Chapter One

Kate Scanlan peered through the window of her warm office into a dark, blustering night. Raindrops drummed on the glass, making it difficult to see what was happening outside. She leaned forward. In the weak glow of an old security light, she could just make out the figure of her head girl, Sandy Jennings. It was six o'clock, going home time, and Sandy was heaving shut the large sliding door to the stable block.

Kate sat back and looked at her reflection in the window. She wasn't sure if she liked her new short bobbed hair. It made her look older, more like the twenty-six she really was. She became nostalgic and thought longingly of the time when closing up had been her job. She'd been happier then, taking hands-on care of the animals at the Rescue Centre. Organising the staff and the day-to-day admin was much more of a chore, but when the chance of promotion had come, she couldn't turn it down; the mortgage on her recently purchased small cottage had decided it for her.

The North Wiltshire Animal Rescue Centre (or

NOWARC, affectionately known as Noah's Ark) was part of a highly efficient national charity with an annual turnover of tens of millions. It had been set up originally to deal with the thousands of farm animals which were found each year abandoned or abused by their owners. The centres were called in by the public and other agencies to house, cure and find new homes for a wide variety of victims, though NOWARC dealt mainly with horses, cattle and sheep.

While the animals always came first, the trustees of the charity were adamant that their donors' money should not be wasted and they demanded thorough accountability from the leaders of the centres, which meant showing where every penny had gone. Maths had never been one of Kate's strong points and she loathed this side of the job. She'd had enough office work for one day. She closed the accounts book in front of her and rummaged in her bag for a packet of Marlboros. The girl who helped in the office hated the smell of tobacco smoke, but she'd already gone home. Kate lit her cigarette. She had taken a couple of contented drags when the phone rang. She glanced at it, prepared for a moment to ignore it, but she couldn't. Working at the Rescue Centre was a vocation, like being a doctor or a priest; being needed was the point of your existence.

She picked up the phone. It was Richard Stanley, head of the local branch of the RSPCA.

'Kate, I'm sorry to do this to you on a night like this, but I've got three men off with some bug and its pandemonium here.'

'You're sorry to do what?' Kate asked as she looked out at the blustering rain with a sinking stomach.

'The police have just phoned. They've had a call about some cattle making a hell of a racket on a farm a mile or so up the hill above Ramsbury. They want someone to take a look . . .' He left the sentence hanging in the air.

'And you haven't got anyone spare,' Kate said helpfully.

Richard Stanley uttered a guilty sigh. 'I suppose you couldn't send someone over, could you?'

'Yes, I suppose I could,' Kate said with a grin. Through the window she caught a glimpse of the tail lights of Sandy's car disappearing through the gate of the small car park. 'Damn!'

'What's the matter?'

'Oh, nothing,' Kate said. 'I've just missed Sandy, that's all. I'll go myself.'

'Great. Thanks, Kate. I owe you one.'

'And I won't forget it. What's the farmer's name and how do I get there?'

'Cyril Barton. Apparently he's in his eighties, lives on his own.' He gave Kate the name of the farm and rough directions. 'Give me a ring if you have any problems.'

When she'd put the phone down, Kate got up and walked across to look at the Ordnance Survey map on the back wall of the office to see exactly where she was going. She knew most of the farms within half a dozen miles of the centre, but she'd never had any dealings with this particular one. When she'd worked out the best route, she locked up the office and went out to her old Renault in the car park.

Twenty minutes later, her car headlights picked out a rotting sign on which the words 'Lodge Farm' were just discernible. The post from which the sign hung had long since broken off at the bottom; now only a thick, black hawthorn hedge supported it.

It was surprising that anyone had complained, she thought. The farm – more of a smallholding – was a good quarter of a mile from the metalled lane and, as far as she could tell from the map, some distance from the nearest neighbour.

Kate's headlights lit the muddy, puddled track beyond the entrance. She shivered. She dreaded what she might find. Once on a similar mission, she'd discovered fifteen starving horses. She had wept hopelessly at the sight of them and the memory still haunted her.

Without much enthusiasm, she drove her car through the entrance and cautiously along the deep ruts. She had covered three hundred yards and was beginning to wonder if she had somehow gone wrong, maybe missed a turning off the track to the house, when round a bend her headlights swept across a three-sided courtyard and reflected off the wet stone of a dilapidated house and the ancient buildings clustered round it. She drove into the yard and parked her car just inside the gate. The house loomed darkly, unlit on the far side. She turned off the engine and waited, wondering what to do. Something about the place gave her the creeps. She locked the car doors and picked up her mobile phone to call Sandy, but the orange light showed she was out of signal.

The wind had dropped and the rain diminished to a silent drizzle.

Abruptly, the quiet was shattered by a furious bellow from one of the barns. Kate froze, startled out of her normally collected wits. She knew almost at once that the noise wasn't human, but it took her a few seconds to register that it was an angry, probably very hungry bullock.

The bellowing was joined by a rasping regular bark of an old dog. Kate looked at the house for a reaction. No light, no human sound marked the owner's presence. He could have been out, or asleep, or ill. But that wasn't her problem; at least, it wasn't her priority. Her job was to look after the animals, and by the sound of it, they needed it. Every instinct told her to drive away, but instead she leaned over to the back seat and found her torch. She got out and directed its powerful beam into a large, ramshackle timber-clad barn. The big wagon door had been blown open, and inside she could see a jumble of straw bales, muddy farm tackle and empty paper feed bags. She picked her way across the remains of the cobbles that had once covered the yard until she stood in the doorway.

The dog's barking crescendoed to a manic yelp as her torch picked it out, crouched, too arthritic to want to move from a bed of filthy sacking under a long-abandoned Ferguson tractor. She moved cautiously into the barn, flicking the torch's beam into every crevice, searching for hidden danger. When she reached the dog, she looked behind her, then bent down to offer it her hand to smell. The bark became a pleading whimper as she stroked it and murmured gently until the silence was fractured again by the angry bellowing.

Kate looked around and saw the source of the noise. In an old stable to her left, behind high iron bars, were two half-ton bullocks. She left the dog and went across to them. She hauled back an ungreased bolt which squealed in protest. Cautiously, she let herself in. The animals nuzzled her roughly, desperate for food, as she searched around their quarters. The manger was empty; the water trough was bone dry.

What these animals needed most was water. There didn't seem to be any reaching the inflow valve of the troughs. Filling them would be a tap and bucket job. She searched the yard until she found them both outside the back door of the house. Carrying her torch under her arm, she trekked back and forth until she'd heaved five bucketfuls which the big beasts sucked up almost as fast as she could pour the water into the iron tank. Filling the buckets eased her earlier fear, and she began to move about with more confidence.

In another stall, she found a ewe with a pair of weak, spindly lambs. She watered them all, then the dog. There were no more animals in the first barn so she crossed over to the next.

It seemed colder and wetter in this one. A sweep of the torch among the trusses and bearers showed large gaps between the roof slates which looked as though they had been letting in the weather for years. Under this scanty protection was a suckler cow with her two-month-old calf. The cow was lying on her side, weak from lack of food and liquid. The water trough and manger were empty. The straw had been trampled into a filthy paste of mud and slurry. The calf could barely open its eyes. Kate made a few more drenching trips with the buckets across the yard then looked around for some food. Besides the hay in the first barn, she could find nothing else. She'd have to come back up in the morning with some supplies.

As she worked, she wondered angrily how things could possibly have reached such a state and rehearsed the lecture she was going to give the owner.

Where the hell was he, anyway? He had no right just to go off and leave his stock unattended.

She marched back across the yard and shone her torch on a back door which hadn't seen a paintbrush for forty years. She looked for a bell. There wasn't one. She hammered and heard only the hoot of an owl for an answer.

She waited half a minute before she turned the old iron ring handle and pushed impatiently. The door creaked open.

She considered leaving; after all, she'd done her job for the moment. Then she found herself calling out, 'Hello! Anyone in?'

She was answered by a profound silence. She shivered, gritted her teeth and stepped through on to a cold, flagstone floor. Her nostrils were filled with the damp, musty smell that belongs only to very old houses which have never known central heating or damp-proofing. It was a smell which in her line of work she associated with old people – people who had grown too weak or too crippled or too poor to look after the animals which they'd been used to having around them all their lives, and which they refused to give up.

She flashed her lamp around a messy hall, cluttered with old yellow newspapers, Wellington boots, stout hazel thumbsticks and decrepit furniture. A dusty, unshaded bulb hung on a length of fabric-covered flex. After some searching, she found a switch. She wasn't surprised when it produced no light.

There were four closed doors off the hall. Kate opened the first and shone her torch into a large room, some kind of formal sitting room, tidy and furnished with good, solid old pieces. It looked as though no one had sat in it for years.

She tried the door at the back of the hall. A short passage led to a room which her nostrils told her was the kitchen. On a large pine table, among stacks of unopened *Farmers' Weeklys*, there was an old oil lamp with a box of Swan Vestas beside it. Kate lifted the glass, turned up the wick and lit it. In the more general glow that it cast, she saw a bowl of rotting fruit and a loaf of bread that was growing a thick coat of grey-green woolly mould.

Wrinkling her nose, Kate carried the oil lamp with her back to the hall. The silence and the lack of response were beginning to make her jumpy again. She tried another door, this time opening on to a flight of steep, narrow stairs. She called out again, not really hoping for a reply, and, summoning all her courage, started up the creaking steps.

They led her to a wide, bare-boarded landing. Ten feet from the top of the stairs, in a heap of crumpled old pyjamas and a threadbare dressing gown, a very old man lay curled up like a baby.

Kate's heart thumped as she took a few steps towards him. Holding the lamp high, she looked down at a small, white face then she jerked backwards, transfixed by the face's expression cast in complete and utter terror.

Holding her breath, Kate knelt down to listen. Not a whisper of air escaped the wrinkled, slightly parted lips. Trying to control her fear and revulsion, she stretched out a hand to touch the white forehead. It was dry and as cold as stone.

Kate snatched back her hand and wiped it on her jeans. In twenty-six years of rural life, she had never seen a human corpse at first hand. This one certainly hadn't died peacefully. As she looked closer, she noticed the purple-brown bruises round the loose-skinned turkey neck. Her heart missed a beat.

Instinctively, she glanced over her shoulder with wide horrified eyes in the lamplight, although she knew that the man must have died hours, days before, and the killer would be long gone.

She scrambled to her feet, tilting the lamp in her haste. The glass fell to the floor and shattered, snuffing the light as it fell. The torch and the matches were in the kitchen. Kate stood rooted to the ground in panic and total darkness. Clenching her fists she tried to pull herself together.

She forced herself to breathe normally. When she was ready, she felt her way back to the top of the stairs. She stopped and listened, ignoring the calm voice of logic trying to tell her that no one would still be in the house. She forced herself down the narrow stairs and groped her way into the kitchen, to the table where she had left her torch. Gasping aloud with relief, she found it and flicked it on.

Nervously, she flashed it around the filthy room, vaguely looking for a telephone. She must get someone up here, quick – the police, anyone, to deal with the wrinkled, strangled corpse upstairs.

She began to search in earnest but she couldn't find a phone in any of the downstairs rooms. She couldn't bear to go upstairs again. Maybe the old man simply didn't have a phone. She went outside into the still drizzling night and shone her torch around the gables of the house. There wasn't a sign of an incoming telephone line. She'd have to go for help. But where? Drive to Marlborough, or find a phone-box?

There must be someone living near enough to have heard the distressed bullocks and alerted the police. She ran out of the yard and looked south, down the hill towards the river valley. At the bottom of a grass field was a belt of woodland and through it, like a beacon of welcome, glowed a light from a cottage window.

She clambered over a gate into the field. She slithered down the wet grassy hillside, unconcerned about scratches and bruises as she slipped and stumbled between thistles and molehills.

It was further than it looked, five or six hundred yards, and when she reached the bottom, she had to get herself over a barbed wire fence between the pasture and the woods beyond. Panting, scratched and soaked to her skin, she pushed her way through a thicket of rhododendron until she reached a clearing in the birch wood where the cottage stood.

She had approached it from the back where there was no entrance. She ran round, found the front door and rapped a tattoo on it.

A moment later it was opened by a small, neat woman who looked with alarm at the soaking, bedraggled young woman on her doorstep.

Kate gasped with relief at the sight of a kind, normal-looking woman, not unlike her own mother. 'I'm so sorry to burst in on you like this, but I need to phone the police.'

'My goodness! You'd better come in.' The woman opened the door wider and beckoned Kate. 'What's happened? Are you all right? Is someone after you?'

'No, no. I've just come from the farm at the top of the hill. There's no phone. I found the farmer there. He's dead. I think someone killed him!'

'What? Old Cyril Barton at Lodge Farm?' The shock in the woman's voice conveyed that she'd known him.

Kate nodded urgently. 'Yes. I nearly fell over him lying there. Please, let me use your phone.'

They were in a small, brightly lit hallway. As Kate was

speaking, a door opened and a tall, grey-haired man in his sixties appeared. 'What's happened?'

'Oh, David. This girl's found Cyril Barton dead in his house. She thinks he's been murdered!'

'Why do you think that?' the man asked without any sign of panic or alarm.

'He's just lying on the landing, in his pyjamas . . . It's the look on his face, and there are horrible bruises on his neck.'

The man nodded. 'Right. Don't worry. I'll call the police.'

He went back into the room he'd come from. Kate and the woman listened through the open door while he gave an operator precise details and directions to the farm.

When he had put the phone down, the woman asked Kate if she would like anything – a hot drink, a change of clothes?

'No. I need to get back up there. I was called in to check the animals. Someone complained.'

The woman nodded. 'That was me. I should have gone up to check first, but my husband wasn't here.'

'I've dealt with most of them but on my way down here I thought I heard something in the field – a horse cantering around making a fuss. I didn't see it, but I really ought to check. None of the animals had been fed or watered for days as far as I could tell.'

'I'll run you back up there,' the man offered.

'That would be great. Thanks.' Kate had been having serious second thoughts about going back on her own.

When they were in his car, the man told her he was

called David Patterson and that he and his wife, Pru, stayed in the cottage most weekends.

'I'm Kate Scanlan. I run the NOWARC centre.'

'Who called you in?'

'The RSPCA. They hadn't anyone spare.'

'And you dealt with the animals before you went looking for the farmer?'

'Yes. They were making such a racket when I got there, I had to get on with it. Besides, there weren't any lights on in the house. But I went to look for the owner, to give him a piece of my mind.'

'That must have been quite a shock for you.'

'God, yes. I've never seen a corpse before and I'm sure he was murdered.'

'So you said.'

Kate considered what the man had said. She was struck by his lack of any sense of crisis. There was a certain confidence about him, yet his eyes were cold as ice.

'You're not a policeman of some sort, are you?'

'No, though I was a soldier once. This won't be the first time I've seen a corpse.'

When they reached the farmhouse, a mile or so by road and track, Kate didn't want to go in again. 'I really just want to see what's in that lower field. Do you think you could wait up here while I have a look around?'

'Of course. Do you want me to come with you?'

'No, that's okay. It shouldn't take long to see if there's anything there.'

She didn't relish the thought of wandering around an

unfamiliar field in the rain on a pitch dark night, but knowing this very calm ex-soldier was watching, she felt happier about it.

She found a rope in the big barn and clambered back over the gate. She cast her torch around the field. It wasn't large, six or seven acres, and hedged with untrimmed hawthorn.

She had been right. Within minutes, she picked out the shape of a nervous horse with a tattered jute rug half twisted under its belly. Using all her skill and persuasion, she managed to get near enough to loop the rope round its neck. Close to, she saw that the animal, although it was muddy and out of condition, was an obviously well-bred mare. Looking at the shivering horse, Kate decided to bring it in out of the cold for the night. She could have a proper look at it in the morning. The mare fretted and fussed, unwilling at first to come, but Kate gently led her up to the yard and into the stable next to the cow and calf.

David Patterson was waiting by the gate. 'Well done! Can I do anything to help?'

'No, thanks. If there are any more out there it's too bloody bad.' She settled the horse on to some clean straw, filled its water trough and stuffed a hay net. As she came out, the shrill wail of a police siren was carried up on the breeze. A moment later a blue light flashed round the bend in the track.

'Do you want me to stay around while they deal with the old boy?' Patterson asked.

'Would you? That'd be great. I've got to get back and

change out of these clothes.'

'You'd better just stop and tell them how you found him, then I'm sure they'll let you go.'

'Who was the old geezer, then?' Jason asked from the back of Kate's Renault.

'A farmer called Cyril Barton. Lived alone in the farmhouse. Really squalid.' The cloud and rain from the previous night had completely blown away. Kate was peering into the rising sun ahead. Although she'd found it in the dark the night before, it would be easy to miss the narrow turning up to the farm.

'How big's his place?' Darren in the passenger seat beside her asked. He came from a farming family himself – measured people by their acreage.

'Not much. Thirty, forty acres, maybe. I went round one of his fields with a torch last night. Most of the animals were already in, but I found a lovely mare still out.'

Jason and Darren were on a work experience scheme at the Rescue Centre. Kate had brought them along to help with the feed bags and to make up the animals' bedding.

'Who rang up, then?' Jason asked.

'His nearest neighbour. She told the police she could hear some cattle bellowing. They rang Dick Stanley, and he rang me.'

'Did you go up on your own, then?'

'Yes,' Kate nodded.

'And you found the old boy, like?'

'Yes, I did,' she said with a shudder.

'Bloody hell! Wasn't you scared?'

'Of course I was – bloody terrified. I've never seen a real live corpse before.'

Jason laughed. 'Well, you wouldn't, would you,' he said, labouring the joke. 'What did he look like?'

'Like a piece of wrinkly old putty. I touched his face to make sure he was dead. It was all cold and dry. Ughhh.' Kate spotted the old sign to Lodge Farm and turned on to the muddy cinder track, driving carefully over the ruts. They rounded a corner and she had her first daylight view of the farmhouse and its outbuildings.

'Is that it?' Darren asked. 'What a dump!' Darren's grandparents lived in a similar house; most of their lives they had looked forward to moving into a tidy little bungalow.

'It's got loads of character – three or four hundred years old, I should think,' Kate said. 'It could be really nice with a bit of money spent on it.' She hoped she'd end up in a place like this.

They reached the top of the track where a pair of lopsided gateposts with no gate marked the entrance to the yard. On the far side, the house loomed with its back to the sun.

Kate turned off the engine. She and the two boys got out into a deep rural silence. Even now, at the start of a bright winter's morning, there was an eerie, other-worldliness about the buildings.

Jason shivered. 'What a creepy place. When's this vet coming?'

'He should have been here by now,' Kate said. She had phoned Mike Pengelly before she left at eight that morning, and he had less far to come. 'Anyway, we'd better get on with it. Start with watering them. It's a tap and bucket job, I'm afraid; there's nothing reaching the valves in the troughs.'

The rasping bark of the arthritic dog echoed from the big barn on their left. This was joined by the furious bellow of one of the bullocks. Jason jumped. 'Christ! He sounds pissed off.'

'Start with him, then,' Kate said. 'There's the tap, by the back door.'

Jason nodded and walked off to quench the thirst of the angry bullock.

Kate told Darren to unload the bags of cattle feed, corn and beet they had brought up from the centre while she made a more thorough search for food among all the buildings, under every lean-to and tarpaulin. She found nothing. She was surprised. She had expected to find something special for the horse, at least. She had been impressed by it, even in the dark and covered in mud. It was unusual for anyone with quality horses not to look after them.

Kate shrugged philosophically. After two years at the refuge, she had seen more than enough evidence of people's callousness and stupidity where livestock were concerned. She would arrange transport for all the animals to the centre later that day. In the meantime, they'd get as good a feed as she could give them.

She walked into the smaller barn. The cow looked up

brightly. Darren had already refilled her trough and manger and the calf was on its feet, sucking happily. Kate smiled at the fruits of their efforts. 'Well done, Darren. They're looking a lot happier than they were last night. Have you had a look at the mare yet?'

'I have. I've done her water but she still looks miserable.'

Jason and Kate walked across to the box which contained the mare. She gave them a wary glance and carried on pacing around the box, apparently anxious and distressed.

'I wonder what's wrong with her,' Kate said.

'Maybe she's missing a friend,' Darren suggested.

Kate looked at him sharply. She knew from experience that his intuition as far as animals were concerned was highly developed and often right.

'But there weren't any other horses around last night.'

'It was dark, wasn't it, and you didn't check all the fields.'

'I was going to have another look this morning anyway. We'll do it now.'

Kate and the two boys walked out into the yard. Kate sent the boys to look down the hill and headed for the field above the house. When she reached the gate, she clambered over the five bars into a four-acre meadow hemmed in by a ragged hawthorn hedge. The grass was well-grazed but dotted with patches of docks and nettles. At first glance it appeared empty. She walked along the hedgerow, looking for holes or gaps. But despite its unruly appearance, it was well wired. At the first corner there was a ditch, damp at the bottom. Kate worked her way along it, parting the lower branches where they were splayed across it. She found an abandoned plough and a few oil drums, but no sign of a horse.

She approached the next corner where a group of pollarded willows marked a larger watercourse. The ditch widened to meet a permanent stream which ran off the chalky downland behind. Water had backed up to make a patch of boggy ground between two fallen willow boughs which had sprouted new wands of their own. On the far side of the ditch the mud was churned up and there were long marks where horse's hooves had slithered and dug in. Beyond it, a rotten post and wire fence lay flat on the ground.

Kate drew in a breath and looked at the uninviting muddy slope.

'Katie, come quick! For God's sake!'

She turned sharply and looked back towards the gate by the house.

Darren was standing on a lower bar, waving frantically. Kate set off at a run across the meadow. When she reached the gate, Darren was hopping around on the other side of the yard at the entrance to the lower field. When she caught up with him, she found she was in the field she'd run through in the dark the night before. It was below the one she'd been searching, with the fallen fence visible at the top of a steep slope. Darren headed for the lower corner where a drinking bay had been carved in the bank which dropped down towards the brook, partially hidden by a group of three whiskery old willows.

Only when Kate reached this crude access point to the stream could she see the young horse which had become trapped there. The animal, no more than a yearling, had tangled its legs in two strands of barbed wire and the pig wire below it, which was intended to stop any animals wandering off up the brook. The posts had collapsed and left the wire suspended a few inches off the ground.

Kate slithered down the muddy ramp. As she came within a few yards of it, the horse panicked. The whites of its eyes rolled up, its ears flattened down its neck and it struggled frantically to release itself.

Kate stopped short and stood a few feet away, talking gently, trying to calm it. Darren watched with admiration from the top of the ramp, impressed by Kate's capacity for winning the animal's trust with just a few words. When he had tried to get near it, the creature had flailed around so that it was now held even tighter by the brutal wire.

Kate could see fresh blood oozing over the congealed remains from the savage lacerations in the fine-boned legs. The young horse stopped thrashing long enough to let Kate lean forward and offer her hand. Its ears twitched forward tentatively and its large eyes settled in their sockets. Kate moved another couple of inches and softly stroked its nose with the tips of her fingers.

Ignoring a thick layer of sticky mud on the ramp, Kate settled on her haunches to talk to the horse where it lay on its side. She was grateful for the sunshine; waiting for the animal to trust her sufficiently to let her unravel the wire round its leg could take a long time.

Slowly, she eased herself down the slope towards the brook and the collapsed wire fence. She could see that the horse had somehow got its leg between the two barbed strands and, hopping around, had put a slender hoof through two squares of pig wire, tightening it every time it struggled.

Kate turned to Darren who'd been joined by Jason and was still watching from the top of the ramp. 'One of you go and see if you can find some wire cutters. And bring some feed.'

Jason ran up the field and came back a few minutes later with a pair of sharp edge pliers. 'These should do the job,' he said, panting, and slid them down the slope, along with a scoop of horse nuts, to where Kate was still comforting the young horse. She picked them up, let the youngster nuzzle a few nuts, then, taking her time, she began a continuous rubbing motion with her hand over the soft brown hair of the horse's neck. Gradually, Kate worked down to the shoulder, flanks and finally to where its hind legs were trapped. All the time she talked, gaining the horse's confidence. Each time she felt it resist her hand moving to a new part of its body, she'd move backwards and start again.

There was a lot of tension in the barbed wire. Somehow she would have to move the animal back down towards the brook to slacken it and avoid the wire whiplashing as soon as she cut it. Slowly, by heaving gently, she eased the horse down until there was no strain in the wire. She cut the first barbed strand as close to the leg as she could. The horse flinched as a loose end scratched its leg. The second strand came free as easily but whichever way they moved, the pig wire was still tight round the fragile limb.

Kate decided to cut through from the top of the fence, four strands away, to give a clear opening for the horse to remove its leg.

She had cut through the first two when a pheasant, lying low in the dead bracken on the far side of the brook, abruptly decided it had taken enough risks for one day. With a clatter of wings it launched itself from the cover into the air while its frantic honking ricocheted through the still morning air. In its eagerness to get away from the alarming disturbance, the horse tried to propel itself up the ramp with its three free legs. A flailing hind leg caught Kate a passing blow on the temple, knocked her off balance and sent her slithering down into the brook and three feet of icy water.

Ruefully, she heaved herself out, sodden, frozen and weak from the bang on her head. The horse had stopped thrashing, though, and this time it didn't take so long for Kate to talk it back into a state of calmness. Shivering now with cold and nausea, she worked her way through the rest of the pig wire. The last strand fell away and eased the tourniquet on the horse's leg. Kate could sense the animal beginning to realise that it was no longer constrained. When the knowledge had sunk in, it scrambled to its feet, slipping and sliding on the muddy ramp and barely able to make use of a weakened off-hind leg.

Kate left it to get up as best it could and shouted to

the boys to give her some space. 'We'll catch her in a minute.'

The young horse scrabbled up the slope to the thick green grass of the paddock.

The two lads stepped aside and the filly trotted unevenly into the freedom of the big field while Kate painfully limped up.

'Nice looking filly,' Jason said.

'Yeah,' Kate panted. 'All yearlings look lovely. I just hope the wire hasn't done too much damage.'

'You reckon she's a yearling?'

'She's certainly too big to be this year's foal.'

'D'you think she's out of that mare, then?'

'More than likely. No doubt we'll find out. But it's going to be quite a job to get that leg right without any permanent damage. Look, she's hardly using it at all.'

'I think we should catch her now, before she runs around on it too long.'

'Yes. You're right. Go and see if you can find a head collar in one of the barns.'

Darren ran off as Jason and Kate slowly worked their way across the five-acre field to corner the nervous filly and keep her away from the damaged fence at the top.

They put the yearling in the box next to the mare.

'Keep an eye on her,' Kate told the boys. 'I'm going to see if I can find out who her dad is.' She left Jason and Darren and walked across to the house. It wasn't locked; no one had been able to find a key and the police hadn't been back to secure the place yet.

As the mare looked to be a thoroughbred, Kate

thought it likely she'd been covered by a thoroughbred stallion. It would be interesting to know the father of the plucky yearling filly she'd rescued from the tangle of wire.

Kate quelled any guilt she might have felt about prying into a dead man's things as she rummaged through the piles of paper on the grimy old kitchen dresser and table. But she found nothing about the horse. She went into the front sitting room and plunged into a bureau crammed with dog-eared documents. This produced a horse's 'passport', which confirmed the registration of a mare at Wetherby's. It gave details of colouring and markings, including whorls, of a horse called Stella Maris which matched the horse out in the stable. It showed that she was respectably bred by a very fast, flat-race stallion which had died some years before.

What Kate really wanted was some correspondence with a stud which would tell her the name of the sire of the filly.

Half an hour's search had produced nothing when she was interrupted by Mike Pengelly, the vet, arriving to keep his appointment with her.

Mike, dedicated, forty and innocently unaware of his own good looks, made a thorough examination of all the animals, beginning with the yearling, and pronounced them all in reasonable health. The damage to the filly's rear leg wasn't as bad as it looked though it still needed half a dozen stitches.

'I'll give her a tetanus,' Mike said as he worked, 'but keep your eye on it; keep it clean and keep her on the move to stop it swelling up. Insofar as I'm any judge of these things,' he added, standing up, 'she looks like a nice little filly.'

He and Kate stood in the box, gazing critically at the young horse. 'I'm a hopeless judge,' Kate admitted. She wrapped her arms round the animal's slender neck. 'All horses look wonderful to me at this age. I wonder why the old boy bred her. What was he going to do with her? And I wonder when she got caught in the wire. The police weren't sure how long the farmer had been dead. There's virtually no grass out in the meadows and there was practically nothing in here. I'm amazed they look as well as they do. By the way,' Kate went on, 'I tried to see if I could find out who the sire is, assuming the mare's her mother. But I couldn't find a thing.'

Mike Pengelly, used to Kate's seamless monologues, had crouched down to continue his examination of the filly. He half turned and spoke over his shoulder. 'I dare say some paperwork will turn up sooner or later.' He ran his hand gently down the damaged leg. 'There'll be a bill from a stallion owner somewhere.'

'Maybe, but I'll have to find a home for all these animals and the executors will want to know we've got a fair price.'

'You'll definitely need details of paternity for that,' Mike said. 'But aren't there any relations to take them on?'

'No. According to the police, the only one they could trace was a niece who lives in Liverpool. Apparently she's coming down to identify the old boy formally, though she hasn't seen him for over fifteen years. He was a real old recluse. Even the neighbours didn't see him often and the house is like something out of *Cold Comfort Farm*.'

The vet stood up and stretched. He looked at the ill-kept, mouldering house and the buildings falling down around it. 'Not without a certain amount of charm. Certainly, no one could accuse it of being over-restored. How old was the farmer?'

'In his eighties, I think. Cyril Barton he was called.'

Mike chuckled. 'Cyril Barton, eh? I haven't heard of him for years. He used to be a bit of a force in pointing round here when I was a small boy. Fancy him still keeping brood mares. It's amazing how some people just can't kick the habit.'

'What habit's that?' It was a new voice, not one of the lads from Noah's Ark. Kate and Mike looked up. David Patterson, in a tweed jacket and burnished brown brogues, walked into the barn.

'Oh, hello, Mr Patterson. This is Mike Pengelly, the vet. We were just talking about racing. Mike was saying Mr Barton was keen on it for years. He must have wanted to keep his hand in. We found this filly, tangled in wire down by the stream. I'm fairly sure she's out of the mare I found last night. Mike reckons she's pretty good.'

David Patterson walked over and looked at the quivering animal. He shrugged his shoulders. 'They all look the same to me, but what happens to them in circumstances like this?'

'Usually, after we've sorted them out, they ask us to find homes, or buyers for them if possible. This one might be worth a bit.'

'If you can discover her breeding,' Mike Pengelly interjected.

'I don't know if I'm talking out of turn, but my stepson is in the racing business, near here at Lambourn. He might be interested in the filly. Can I tell him to get in touch?'

Kate glanced at Mike. 'Why not? What's he called?'

'Charles . . . Patterson, like me.'

'Tell him to ring me at NOWARC. He can come and have a look at her there if he likes. We're taking all the animals over today.'

'Right,' Patterson nodded. 'I will. Anything else I can do to help?'

'No, thanks. We're all under control here now.'

'Well, let me know if there is.' Patterson left the barn and they heard him start up his Mercedes and drive out of the yard.

'Funny him being Charlie Patterson's stepfather.'

'What about it? Do you know the son?'

'No, but I know his partner well.'

'Who's that?'

'A chap called Nick Ryder, cousin of mine.'

'What's his interest in horses?'

'He's an assistant trainer with Charlie at Robert Aylestone's yard. Racing mad.'

Kate, although not obsessed with racing, took an interest. Her parents were members at Newbury and had taken her regularly since she had been strong enough to hold a pair of binoculars.

'Robert Aylestone's not much of a recommendation.'

'No,' the vet agreed, 'but Nick and Charlie are trying to get some money and horses together to start their own yard. And as long as they're at Aylestone's, they'll learn a lot.'

This was true. Robert Aylestone had a fearsome reputation for gambling, among other vices, but at least he usually backed his own horses and knew how to get them to peak for the races which he cannily selected for them.

'Are they honest?' Kate asked, down-to-earth.

'I don't know about Charlie, but Nick certainly is. He'd be interested in the horses.'

'I can see why he might be in the yearling but what about the mare?'

'I think he'll like her. If he takes them, you can be sure they'll be well looked after and you could keep tabs on the filly if you wanted. You're obviously rather attached to her.'

'Okay,' Kate said. 'I'll let you know what's going to happen to them.'

Wistfully she watched Mike Pengelly go. Though he probably didn't know it, it was he who had originally inspired her to try to be a vet herself, but she'd got bogged down with all the science involved and given it up. He certainly didn't know that as far as she was concerned, he could do or say no wrong. If Mike thought his chap Nick Ryder should have the horses, that was good enough for her.

★ ★ ★

It was a fortnight before the Rescue Centre heard from anyone about the dead farmer's animals. A solicitor in Marlborough telephoned to say that Mr Barton's sole heir, Mrs Cora Lenigan, would be coming to the refuge to see the animals and decide what to do with them.

Cora Lenigan arrived two days later. She had come by taxi from the solicitor's office in Marlborough. It was clear from the diffident way in which she dealt with the taxi driver that it wasn't a normal mode of transport for her.

Kate came out to greet her in the mild winter morning.

'Good morning, Mrs Lenigan. I'm Kate Scanlan.'

'Call me Cora, pet, or I'll feel like a granny.'

Kate smiled, liking the look of the woman and her lazy Liverpudlian drawl.

Cora gazed around at the sheds and compounds which held the various animals passing through the centre's hands. 'Which ones are mine?' she asked.

Kate took her on a short tour and showed her the dog, several cats, the cow and her calf, the ewes and their almost full-grown lambs and, finally, the horses which had come from Cyril Barton's farm.

'Crikey, they're big,' Cora said.

'She's a lovely filly,' Kate said enthusiastically.

'She certainly looks nice,' Cora said.

'You should keep her,' Kate said spontaneously. 'Put her in training yourself.'

'What? Me?' Cora laughed. 'I wouldn't know anything

about having racehorses. That's a bit out of my league. They wouldn't even let me have a budgie when I were a kid. It's going to be bad enough trying to get used to having a few bob when they sell that old house. It's funny really. I don't suppose I'd even thought of Uncle Cyril for months before the solicitor's letter came. And I'd never thought about him leaving anything to me – not that he did, really, he just never made a will and I'm the only relative he had left.' She shook her head with a slightly puzzled grin. She was evidently finding it difficult to come to terms with her good fortune. Kate liked her for that. 'You know what else is funny? You saying keep the racehorse when my husband, God rest him, Johnny Lenigan spent every penny he ever earned – and that weren't a lot – betting on horses that never won.'

'You're a widow, are you?'

Cora nodded. 'Johnny was a waster but he was a lovely bloke. He must be going mad up there, seeing me getting all this from Uncle Cyril when he can't get his hands on it,' she reflected without malevolence.

'Well, what would you like me to do with the animals?'

'Make sure they go to good homes.'

'That's no problem, Mrs Lenigan. If you don't want to keep them, we can arrange to sell them for you and certainly make sure they all go to good homes.'

'Would they be worth much?'

'Not the dog or the cats but we'll get a bit for the sheep, and the cattle might be worth a few hundred each; the horses a lot more probably. Of course you can always arrange for the lawyers to sell them for you.'

'Those slimy buggers? You must be joking. No, I can see just from your face you wouldn't cheat me. You get what you can for 'em and let me know, okay, pet?'

Chapter Two

'There's a gorgeous bloke here says he's come to look at your precious yearling,' Sandy bellowed across the yard at the Rescue Centre.

Kate glanced up, not expecting to share Sandy's eccentric opinion of their visitor's attractions but, she admitted to herself, the man strolling towards her with his hands in his pockets did have a particularly striking set of features.

He was in his late twenties, a shade over six foot, lean and energetic in a battered sheepskin jacket and a pair of faded jeans. Large pupils rimmed with blue in slightly short-sighted eyes gleamed a challenge from beneath a pair of dark brows. Kate sensed there was more than mere politeness in the smile that parted his well-shaped lips as he came up to her.

'Hello. Mike Pengelly told us about a yearling and a mare you've rescued.'

'Are you Nick Ryder?'

'No. I'm his partner, Charles Patterson. I think you met my stepfather.'

Kate nodded. 'Yes, I did.'

'Nick Ryder will be round later. He just asked me to have a look first.'

'As long as you know I'm supposed to dispose of these animals not only to good homes but at market price, and I promised the woman who owns them now that I'll get as much as I can, so I don't want any clever tactics to keep the price down.'

Charles Patterson looked wounded. 'Do I look like the sort of man who'd do that?'

Kate appraised him frankly. 'I should think you're the sort of man who's used to getting away with plenty.'

Charles laughed. 'I'd better leave negotiations to Nick, then, but can I have a look at them now?'

'Okay.' Kate led him into the barn which held a dozen stables used to house the larger animals that passed through the centre. Cyril Barton's mare, Stella Maris, was looking out through the top door of the first box. Her ears pricked at the sight and sound of Kate and she willingly backed away from the door to allow her visitors in.

Charles raised an appreciative eyebrow. 'Mum looks quite useful. Did she ever race, do you know?'

'To tell you the truth, I haven't looked her up yet.'

Charles nodded his dark, curly head thoughtfully and turned his attention to the next box where the filly was poking her tiny nose through the bars, desperate for Kate's attention. He went in, knelt down and felt the slender legs, picked up the small hoofs and inspected them. He stood up to gaze without speaking at the nervous creature.

'Well?' Kate asked anxiously. 'What do you think of her?'

'I think she's a lovely filly. But then,' he turned to look at Kate, 'aren't they all?'

'But you're in the racing business. You're supposed to be able to judge.'

'Judging a yearling tends to be a matter of guesswork. Especially,' he added, 'when you only know half the parentage. As you may know, you can't race a horse without a thoroughbred pedigree. Of course, if we wanted to take it eventing it wouldn't be a problem.'

'Don't worry. Cora, the farmer's niece, found the invoice. Apparently she's by quite a good jumping stallion called Nunsfield.'

'Is she?' Charles was impressed. Nunsfield had been a Group Class stayer on the flat and had sired plenty of good jump winners.

'The problem is,' Kate said, 'it looks as though Cyril Barton never paid the stud fee. There's four thousand pounds to pay.'

'That takes the gilt off it a bit,' Charles said flatly.

Kate looked crestfallen. 'But surely, if that was the stallion's fee, she must be worth at least that.'

Charles laughed. ''Fraid not. Nothing's as simple as that in bloodstock breeding. The quality of the mare and the animal itself are just as important, some would say a lot more. But don't look so worried. This filly's a nice enough looking animal, well worth a second look,' he said, genuinely appreciative and unconcerned that the smile on his face might adversely affect his bargaining stance. 'What happened to the leg?' he asked.

Kate was standing behind him. 'I found her with it tangled up in wire.' Charlie smiled at the compassion in her voice but he didn't let her see. 'It was quite badly cut,' she went on, 'but Mike Pengelly did a good job on it.'

'This was how long ago?'

'Just over two weeks.'

Charles crouched down to run his hand over the leg where it was still scarred below the hock. He nodded. 'I think it's probably over the worst.' He straightened his legs and looked at Kate with shining eyes. 'If you don't want too much for her, we'll have her.'

'What are you offering?'

Charles grinned again. 'Steady. I thought we'd agree that Nick would talk terms. I'll tell him what I think, then he can deal with you.'

'What about the mare?'

'Maybe we could do a package deal, but you'll have to appreciate that it may not be much more than the outstanding stallion fee. You'd better talk to the executors, though I'm sure we'll offer you as good a price as anyone. I'll look the mare up; see what she's done and if she's ever bred anything.'

When Nick Ryder came to the centre next morning, Kate couldn't imagine him and Charles Patterson as friends. Nick appeared to have none of Charles's self-assurance, none of the charm or infectious cheerfulness. He was the same age as Charles, but his brown hair was already thinning, and the old-fashioned spectacles he wore did nothing to enhance his plain features. But he shook her hand with a firmness which surprised her.

She looked at him. Perhaps there was hidden substance beneath the diffident exterior.

He examined the yearling, registering no reaction. He spoke little and without embellishment. 'Have you any idea what she's worth?'

Kate shrugged, and plucked a figure from the air. 'Fifteen thousand?'

'Fifteen thousand?' Nick raised his eyebrows with no sense of aggression. 'But I understand that there's a stud fee of four thousand to be settled.'

'I meant fifteen thousand including that.'

'I see. I'm afraid the best we could offer is ten, all in. Her mum was only a moderate race mare and, according to the stud, this is her first foal.'

'But that only leaves six to the estate.'

'I know,' Nick said apologetically, 'and it's probably the best offer you'll get. I'm only making it because Charlie's very keen on her.' He shrugged. 'I can see you're disappointed. I'm sorry.'

'It doesn't really matter. It's not my money, but I just feel she's special.'

'I've seen dozens of better bred horses knocked down in the auction ring for a thousand or two. It's heartbreaking for the breeders, but dealing in young stock is subject to market forces, pure and unadulterated. I tell you what; as you're so keen on the animal, we'll grant you permanent visiting rights, as long as she's in our yard.'

Kate perked up. 'Where is your yard?'

'Ah.' Nick glanced away then back again. 'There's the rub. We haven't got one yet. We're both still working for Robert Aylestone, until we've got enough money together.'

'But how are you going to pay for the filly?'

'Charlie will think of something, or so he says,' Nick added with a shake of his head, and Kate liked him for his honesty and for his loyalty to his friend, obviously against his better judgement.

'Okay,' she said. 'Provided I always know where she is. It was me who actually rescued her. She was stuck so tight in some wire that she wouldn't have got out in a month, and her owner had died, and she was in a field miles from anywhere, up above Ramsbury.'

'So I hear. I'd say that definitely entitles you to special visiting rights.' Nick smiled at last. 'I promise we'll keep you posted. If she's any good, we'll be training her ourselves next year.'

'She'll be brilliant,' Kate said.

'Maybe, but we'll still only pay ten for her.'

Kate looked resigned, though privately she was delighted to have got so good a price; she was relieved, too, that it was Nick and Charles who were taking the filly; she knew she'd enjoy seeing them both again. 'What about the mare?' she asked.

Nick shrugged apologetically. 'Unless you wanted to throw her in, we haven't got any more money to spend.'

'Oh well,' Kate said, making up her mind. 'I think I can get her sorted out all right.'

★ ★ ★

Charles Patterson – Charlie to his friends and thousands of punters who had followed his successful amateur riding career – came out of the long left-handed bend at Worcester racecourse and gave his reins a sharp tug. The big old gelding beneath him shortened his stride for a couple of paces and met the open ditch just right, standing back from it, gaining half a length in the air on the horse in front.

There were three more plain fences to jump in the final straight before the winning post. Charlie knew if he wanted to win he mustn't let his horse get its nose in front until the last moment or it would pull itself up. He had carefully saved the animal's speed for the last half-furlong of the run in. He had no doubt that the very amateur rider on the horse in front had already squeezed every bit of energy he could from his splendid old campaigner. He was happy to close the five-length gap which still separated them stride by stride until they were well beyond the final fence.

Charlie didn't need his whip. The old horse knew it was time to go, and he went, until he had his head in front a few yards before the post.

Charlie slowed to a trot and slackened to a walk as the favourite he'd just beaten jogged up beside him. Charlie turned to the other jockey. 'Sorry to sneak up on you like that,' he said with a grin. 'But it's the only way I can get this old bugger to win.'

The other jockey gave him a sour smile and said nothing. He wasn't looking forward to the greeting he would get from his father who'd paid well over the odds for a horse to give his son a win.

Charlie, on the other hand, could not have had a more exuberant greeting from his trainer, who was also his boss.

Robert Aylestone was a good trainer, no one denied that, but he was incurably devious. He had marred his reputation and discouraged a lot of otherwise admiring owners with his persistent urge to beat the bookies whenever an opportunity presented itself. As far as he was concerned, a hunter chase at an evening meeting at Worcester was as good an opportunity as any. The horse had been entered as trained by his permit-holding brother-in-law, but it was Robert who had got him right and knew when he would perform. Charlie was always going to give the gelding a good ride; he had the experience and the talent.

Robert Aylestone limped on the ankle he'd broken in a fall twenty years before, barely conscious of the residual pain as he stretched up to take the gelding's reins.

'Well done, Charlie! You rode that perfect! I'll have a little present for you later, after I've collected.'

Charlie wasn't going to say no to some cash, but what Aylestone seemed unable to grasp was that he would have ridden the race exactly the same without any inducement or reward, because he liked to win. At least, Charlie thought, Aylestone had never been stupid enough to ask him *not* to win.

Charlie drove the lorry back to Lambourn with Kenny, the lad who had brought the gelding and another runner to Worcester that evening. Aylestone had gone off for a drink with his brother-in-law.

'The guv'nor won't be out first lot tomorrow,' Kenny remarked drily as they left the lorry park.

Charlie laughed. 'He doesn't usually let a hangover stop him.'

'No, but he'll have a hell of a hangover tomorrow. D'you know how much he had on that horse?'

'Nope.'

'Well, how much did he give you?'

'Actually, I haven't looked yet. Fifty or a hundred, I should think.' Charlie felt his pocket for a crumpled envelope. Aylestone had handed it to him in the lorry, with instructions to 'Have a drink on me, Charlie'. Charlie squeezed it between his fingers and grinned. 'Unless it's old one pound notes, you're right. He must have had a monster punt. This'll come in handy for our new yard fund.'

'How's that going?' Kenny asked.

'Slowly. But don't you worry, we'll have got enough together by the end of the year.'

'D'you still want to train flat horses?'

'Yes. That's what I've always wanted to do, since I was about twelve. Of course, it's trickier than trying to get going with a jumping yard, but I want to deal in the cream.'

'You should be so lucky,' Kenny laughed. 'But I'll still come with you. I don't know how long I could stick it with old Aylestone, the bad-tempered sod. Did you go and see that yearling at the animal rescue place?'

Charlie smiled as he remembered the guileless, flawless features of the Rescue Centre's manager, and her pleasure at their decision to take the filly. Of course, ten grand was plenty for a Nunsfield filly, but in all the big yearling sales Charlie had attended, this one would have fetched at least what they had offered. But the sales were over and that option was no longer available to Cyril Barton's executors.

'We did,' he told Kenny. 'All we've got to do now is find the money to pay for her.'

'What do you want to go buying yearlings for before you've even got a yard?'

'I just liked her. She's a lovely looking filly, already got plenty of back end. Her sire and both her grandsires were good winners. Her dam wasn't much, but she looks useful.'

'Who's the filly by?'

'Nunsfield.'

'But he's a bloody jumping stallion!' Kenny scoffed. 'I thought you wanted flat horses.'

Charlie laughed at Kenny's scorn. 'We do, and this one's dam line is all sprinters. Mike Pengelly told me the old boy who bred her always put sprinting dams to long-distance sires, and you don't get much more long-distance than Nunsfield. But this particular individual has all the characteristics of a sprinter. Anyway, wait till you've seen her before you start criticising.'

Kenny grinned. 'All right, all right.' He was the first to admit that Charlie had an eye. Besides, he certainly didn't want to be in Aylestone's yard after Charlie and Nick had gone.

★ ★ ★

Charlie and Nick had a room each in a cottage on the outskirts of Lambourn. Their landlady was unashamedly fascinated by their private lives, especially Charlie's. She had a clear view now, through the window of her sitting room, of the young woman walking up the path to the front door.

'Never make one of them supermodels,' she observed to herself. 'Bit too well-covered and too short, but fresh enough to get most young men excited.' There was an assertive jauntiness in the way the girl had opened the gate and walked which the old lady behind the curtain knew would appeal to her good-looking tenant.

Kate shook her short mop of glossy black hair from her round face and rang the doorbell. The old lady was there to open it almost at once.

'Oh, hello,' the girl said in a light, husky voice. 'Does Nick Ryder live here?'

'Oh,' the old lady said before she could hide her surprise. 'You've come to see Nick, have you?'

'Who else would I have come to see then?'

'Mr Patterson, I thought.'

Kate's expression became evasive. 'He lives here too, does he?'

'Do you know him?' the old lady asked.

'We've met,' Kate said curtly, in a way which made the woman think that next time she came round, she'd be asking for Charlie.

'Mr Nick's room is at the top of the stairs and turn right. They're not really allowed females in their rooms but as it's so early . . .' She waved Kate towards a narrow staircase whose walls were crammed with shelves of accumulated mementos and gifts from previous tenants.

Kate hadn't stepped through the front door but she could already guess how this household was run. She shook her head. 'It's okay. Just tell him I'm at the pub, and I'll see him there.'

She had ordered herself a pint of cider when Nick came in. He was with a young golden Labrador, apparently fixed by some invisible means to a point two feet behind his heels. Nick was full of apologies about his landlady.

Kate laughed. 'I'm sure she thought I'd come round to have it off with you.' She watched with guilty satisfaction as Nick blushed.

'Would you like a drink?' he mumbled.

'I've already got one, thanks.'

'Oh, so you have. I'll just get one for me and Hercules.' Nick went to the bar and came back with a pint of beer for himself and bowl of water which he put on the floor for his dog. He turned to Kate. 'It's more likely that my landlady thought you'd come round to have it off with Charlie.'

'As a matter of fact, I think she did at first. That's what I objected to most.'

'Charlie's okay,' Nick said, evidently in the habit of defending his friend.

'How long have you known each other?'

'Since we were thirteen. I was always the brains and he was the brawn. We make a good team.'

'You don't need brawn now, though, do you?'

'No, but the confidence that goes with it is useful. Anyway,' he went on, 'have you spoken to this woman about our offer for the filly?'

'Yes. That's why I'm here. She says that's fine, and so do the executors. You have to pay them. I've got the address here and an official bill of sale.' She handed him an envelope.

'Great,' said Nick. 'Now all we have to do is find someone to pay for it.'

'What?' Kate said, alarmed. 'You mean you can't?'

'No. I told you, we're trying to get enough money together to set up our own yard. Don't worry, Charlie's pretty sure his stepfather will take her on.'

'Major Patterson, you mean? God, I hope so, now I've persuaded everybody it's a fair price.'

'A fair price,' Nick protested. 'Over the odds, if you ask me.'

'Have you thought about naming her yet?' Kate asked.

'Not really. There didn't seem much point until the deal was done.'

'Well, now it is, do you mind if I make a few suggestions?'

At that moment, Hercules leaped to his feet and waved his long feathery tail across the table, sweeping a small tin ashtray to the ground with a clatter and knocking Kate's glass so that only her swift reaction and nimble fingers stopped it from smashing on to the stone floor. She glanced up with annoyance to see what had caused Hercules's excitement.

'Ah,' Nick followed her glance. 'Here's Charlie.'

Kate took a deep breath and looked down at the table as Charlie made his way across the bar, acknowledging greetings on the way. He nodded at Nick and smiled at Kate's head.

'Hello, Kate. I take it this isn't a social visit.'

Kate lifted her head. Her eyes met his with chilly reserve.

Charlie took it in his stride. He didn't know why some women took this line with him, but when they did, he found that the less he worried about it, the sooner it softened. And in Kate Scanlan's case, he felt, the sooner the better.

'No, purely business,' Kate answered.

'Okay,' Charlie nodded. 'Do we get the yearling?'

'Once Cyril Barton's executors have the money.'

Charlie was standing opposite her now. 'I've been working on that. Can I get you another drink? Nick, are you having one?'

When they all had full glasses in front of them on the battered oak cricket table, Nick asked Charlie how he had got on in the race at Worcester.

'I managed to get the old boy's nose in front a few inches from the line. I didn't give him enough time to realise he was there until we'd passed the post.'

'Charlie rode in a hunter chase today,' Nick explained to Kate. 'The horse hates being in front, so you have to time your run exactly right.'

'Well done,' Kate said flatly, refusing to be impressed.

'The horse is a brilliant jumper, hardly needs any help

at all and he can still produce a turn of speed after three miles,' Charlie said, disowning any credit for the win. He turned to Nick. 'Aylestone had a serious punt.'

With a faint nod, Nick acknowledged what Charles was saying, but he didn't ask for more details. 'Kate was wondering,' he said, 'if she could help us choose a name for the filly.'

'My father won't want the hassle,' Charlie agreed.

'Is he definitely buying her then?' Nick asked.

'Oh yes. I haven't had a chance to tell you. He phoned at lunchtime to ask me who he had to pay.'

'Great,' Nick said with undisguised relief. 'He was bloody surly when I last phoned. Anyway, here's the invoice and all the details.'

Charlie picked up the paperwork and leafed through it. 'I'm sorry he still gives you such a hard time,' he sighed. 'You'd have thought by now he'd have accepted we've been friends for fifteen years. I wish I knew why he found it so hard to be polite to you. You're not alone, though, if that's any consolation. Right.' Charlie turned his attention to the filly's pedigree. 'The mare's called Stella Maris, isn't she?'

Kate nodded. 'Star of the Sea.'

'And you found the filly, didn't you?'

'Yes, trapped by a stream below a stand of old willows.'

'Something to do with the willows, then, or water?' Nick suggested.

'How about Pussy Willow?' Charlie said with a grin.

Kate looked at him with a dismissive toss of her head.

'I don't think so. What about Star something, after her mother?'

'Star Pussy?' Charlie suggested.

Kate ignored him. 'Why don't we call her Willow Star?'

'Sounds a bit corny,' Charlie said.

'But it rather suits her,' Nick answered thoughtfully. 'And anyway, Kate found her, so let her decide.'

'Willow Star it is, then,' Kate said. 'Even sounds like a Guineas winner.'

'An Oaks winner,' Charlie laughed. 'No. Wrong tree.'

'Here's to her, then.' Nick raised his pint of murky bitter. 'To Willow Star, the founding member of the Ryder-Patterson yard.'

Kate and Charlie joined the toast and there was a moment's silent harmony.

'Morning, Dad,' Charlie said cheerfully into the phone. 'We've named this filly for you. All we need now is your cheque.'

After only a moment's hesitation, David Patterson answered. 'Yes, of course, as you still seem determined to set up your own place. But don't go away with the idea that I'm going to buy every horse in the yard for you, if you ever get it. By the way, you'll have to make arrangements for the filly until she's ready to come to you.'

'No problem. We'll have our own yard any time now.'

'And how are you going to pay for it?' Patterson asked warily.

'We'll think of something,' Charlie said. He realised he

wasn't going to get any more backing from his stepfather. Perhaps it had been a mistake to use up what goodwill there was from that source on a damaged, unproven filly. But it was too late to change tack now. 'I've got an invoice from Noah's Ark, on behalf of Barton's executors. I'll send it on to you today. Listen, Dad, I really am very grateful to you.'

'I'm glad to hear it,' Patterson replied drily. 'I'll leave the rest of the arrangements to you.'

'Fine. I'll look after all the paperwork. By the way, how's Mother?'

'Oh, fine. Busy with her charity work. She's taken up visiting people in prison again.'

'Has she? Why?'

'I'm not entirely sure. You'll have to ask her. She runs a writing class, says it's good for them, gets things out of their systems.'

'And what do you think?'

'Don't ask.' Major Patterson didn't expand.

Charlie knew better than to expect him to. His mother had always thrown herself into any good deeds that were there for the doing. Charlie suspected it was out of a perverse guilt caused by her husband's lack of overt affection. He wished his stepfather a brief goodbye and put the phone down.

Nick was standing beside him. 'Well?'

'He says he'll do it, but he didn't sound as enthusiastic as I'd hoped.'

'Can he put his hands on ten grand easily?' Nick asked.

'Yes, I'm sure he can. He's just naturally very cagey. He's never told me anything about his affairs, but I think he's made a fair bit of money in his time. Especially when he was out in the Middle East.'

'After he left the army?'

Charlie nodded. 'He was on a massive tax-free salary out there.'

Nick pondered this. 'I suppose if he wasn't spending much, it could have grown quite impressively. But when I last saw him, in that shop of his in Kensington, he didn't strike me as being all that happy about business.'

'It's his habit not to strike anyone as being all that interested in anything. At least he's agreed to buy this filly. I just hope we can win a race with her.'

Chapter Three

'Do you know,' Nick said, leaning on a paddock rail, gazing fondly at Willow Star, 'I think we were mad to persuade your father to buy her but I'm bloody glad we did.'

Charlie, beside him, nodded. 'Yes. I think he's got himself a bit of a bargain.'

With the right diet and a bit of tender loving care, the handsome filly had thrived. Ivor Thompson, an old and well-respected trainer who was fond of both Nick and Charlie, had agreed to let them lodge their filly with him for a few weeks while they nursed her back to health and broke her in during their spare time – not that Robert Aylestone allowed them much free time these days. Ivor was sure that Aylestone suspected something and was making it as difficult as possible for either of them to fly the nest.

Robert Aylestone, short of really top-class horses, relied heavily on his skill in choosing the right races for his eighty charges. He had managed to come fifth in the National Hunt trainers' league table the previous season with eighty-five winners. He owed this comparative success in no small way to the dedication of his young assistants. Charlie had helped further by riding eleven hunter chase winners for the yard.

Aylestone had also pulled off a couple of large gambling coups and the partners had discreetly ridden on his coat tails. Charlie and Nick had managed to scrape up winnings and savings now amounting to a little over ten thousand pounds. Although this was a fraction of what they needed to start up their own yard, Ivor Thompson had assured them that his attractive set of racing stables on the edge of Upper Lambourn would be available whenever they needed it. The partners were now determined to get in there by February at the latest for the following flat season, with as many horses as they could muster.

Charlie and Nick could see the yard across the meadow where Willow Star was grazing in a borrowed rug.

'Has Ivor come back with a price yet?' Charlie asked Nick.

'Yes. It's fair enough. Thirty grand a year for the yard and these twenty acres. He's staying in the house but we can use the bungalow – the lads' hostel.'

Charlie made a face. 'I'd almost rather stay at Mrs Phipps.'

'It'll be okay; we can get someone to do it up a bit. And we've got to be on the spot.'

'Maybe we can get Kate round to give us a hand.'

Nick groaned. 'Are you still trying to pursue that one?

Haven't you heard the old adage about flogging a dead horse?'

'I don't think you can reasonably describe Kate as a dead horse and I've got no intention of flogging her, but I'll get through to her some day. I know she fancies me.'

'That's just what she doesn't like about you.'

Charlie assumed an air of bafflement and shook his head. 'I'm beginning to think that the only way I'll get anywhere with her is if I get Willow Star to win the Oaks.'

'Yes, well, the way things are going, we're not going to be in business in time. I've tried all the banks. They're quite happy to put up half if we provide a hundred per cent security and put up the other half, so that's no good.'

'And I've drawn a blank with my stepfather. In fact he was quite shirty about it when I asked him. Asked me what I thought he would get for the filly.'

Nick's face whitened. 'Oh no!'

'Don't worry. I talked him out of it, said she'd be worth three times as much as soon as she's had a few runs. But he certainly won't come across with any more.'

'What about the other people you went to see?'

'I've tried most of the owners we thought might come in with us. They all said we should spend a few more years at Aylestone's, then they might put a horse or two with us if we get a yard.'

'I've got a few more irons in the fire,' Nick said, 'but

everyone's still bloody cautious. This recession's gone on so long.'

'Maybe we should have been bolder with our punting,' Charlie said. 'We're about five grand ahead at the moment.'

'Sure, but only on Aylestone's touches.'

'Okay, but maybe we should go in a bit heavier next time. After all, that's what keeps him in new Mercedes.'

'Let's wait and see.'

Robert Aylestone limped out of his office into his tidy, brightly lit yard. The light from the stable windows glowed through a freezing rain which made no impression on his hard, ruddy features. As usual, he was carrying around too many plans, campaigns, schemes, and deals in his head to worry about external elements. His only concern about the weather was the effect it might have on the running of his horses. The top doors of all the boxes were closed tight. Inside, the lads groomed vigorously with their jackets off, dressing over each horse for evening inspection. By the time Aylestone began looking around at five thirty, everything would be immaculate. Hoofs would be grassed, mangers scrubbed clean and a neat twist of straw laid in each doorway.

Aylestone caught sight of Charlie coming out of the feed house.

'Oi! Charlie!' he bellowed as he might have done at a new apprentice. Charlie tensed up angrily. He stopped where he was and let Aylestone limp across to him, hoping his annoyance would be registered. It wasn't.

'Get Nick to look after tomorrow's first lot. You're going to take Percy to Newbury. I want him to have a good work-out.'

Persimmon Way, or Percy as he was known in the yard, was a well-built bumper horse which Aylestone had bought at Ballsbridge in the summer. He'd looked half starved when he'd first arrived. Nick and Charlie had both questioned their boss's sanity in buying him but then, as had often happened with similar horses that had passed through the yard in the four seasons they'd been there, the animal began to flourish.

Charlie had ridden him in his only race to date, a moderate contest at Ludlow where he'd scrambled home by a neck. Since then he'd improved almost beyond recognition and there were now few better horses in the yard.

'What time are you sending him?' Charlie didn't disguise his annoyance. 'I've a ride booked at Warwick at three thirty; I'll need to be on my way by one.'

'I've fixed it for nine o'clock sharp.'

Since he had worked for Aylestone, Charlie had only once known him to send horses away to gallop, and that had been after a long cold spell when there'd been no racing and the gallops at home refused to thaw. He wondered why Aylestone was sending Percy now. Until something else occurred to him. 'Who are you going to work him with? The only suitable horses we've got are either running or about to run. You won't want to use one of them, will you?'

Aylestone shot him a withering look. 'No, son. I won't.' He turned and hobbled back to his office.

As Charlie started on his round of the horses, he considered what Aylestone could be up to. As much as he despised the man, he recognised that he had a rare understanding of horses, an intuition that you couldn't learn from books. If he and Nick were going to survive when they started training on their own, they would have to learn to think as Aylestone did.

Charlie thought through all the possibilities. He was sure about one thing; whatever Percy was going to gallop against would need to be very useful. He had been riding Percy out most days and the horse never seemed to stop improving.

By the time Charlie had organised the work board for the following morning and arranged a visit from the blacksmith, it was after seven. When he arrived back at Mrs Phipps' cottage, Charlie slammed his keys down on the table.

Startled, Nick looked up from the form book in his lap. 'What's the matter with you?'

'The sooner we start on our own, the better. We work our balls off for that bloody trainer and the conniving little rat won't even tell us what's going on.' Charlie told Nick about Aylestone's arrangements for Percy's gallop. 'What do you think he's up to?'

'If Percy isn't working with one of ours, he's obviously working with someone else's.'

'Well done, Sherlock Holmes,' Charlie said sarcastically. 'What I want to know is who the other horse is, and why the secrecy. If he's planning a gamble, we ought to know about it. What's the point of being his bloody assistants otherwise?'

Nick put down his form book. 'Okay then. Let's work it out logically. Percy's the only bumper horse in our yard and we haven't got anything else to work him with. He needs a good gallop to put him spot on if Aylestone is planning a touch with him. So, what does he do? He works him with a good bumper horse who's already shown some decent form. And you can assume he's planning to run him soon, or he'd wait and gallop him with one of our own.'

The pair discussed several other possibilities. In the end, they accepted that they'd just have to wait until the next day to find out exactly what was going on. But characteristically, Charlie wouldn't let it go. He sat up in bed with a pen and pad on his knees, determined to figure it out. He was the same with a crossword; he'd keep on going back until it was finished.

If Aylestone was hatching a coup, there had to be a way he and Nick could make some money too. Another twenty thousand and they'd have enough to get their own yard started. With the incentive of getting away from Aylestone, Charlie was even more determined to work it out. He'd almost fallen asleep when he suddenly remembered a bumper horse he'd seen win at Ascot three weeks before. He couldn't think why he and Nick had missed it earlier. The horse had trounced a number of well-fancied rivals without ever coming off the bridle. More significantly, it was trained by Aylestone's ex-head lad, Oliver Baring.

Charlie remembered now that, after the race, Baring had told the press the animal's main target for the season would be the bumper at Aintree. In between, it would run at Sandown. Charlie looked at the date on his watch. The Sandown race was a week tomorrow.

Charlie put his head back on the pillow and smiled. If he was coming to the right conclusion, there would certainly be some money to be made, maybe a lot more than he and Nick had ever made before.

In the morning, Charlie drove the horsebox into Newbury Racecourse. A light frost lit by a weak wintry sun glistened on top of the ground. Aylestone, wrapped in a bulky sheepskin coat, was already waiting beside his Mercedes. A Dutch cigar was jutting from his mouth.

'Get him tacked up, son. They'll be here in a minute.'

Charlie dropped the ramp and went up into the box. He was getting Percy ready when he heard another lorry pull in and draw up alongside. He was itching to see if his theory was right. He pulled the saddle down over the foam pad, finished tugging up the girths and stood on the tips of his toes to peer through the side window.

A ripple of excitement ran through him.

Parked beside him was a dark blue two-box. On the back, in large white letters, were the words 'Oliver Baring'.

Charlie watched as Aylestone walked over to greet the young trainer who was jumping down from the cab. While they talked, a lad got out of the other side. Baring issued some instructions and a few moments later a tall, angular bay was being led down the ramp. It was Paymaster, the horse Charlie had seen win at Ascot.

Paymaster had travelled with his tack on and was ready to go by the time Charlie had dragged Percy down the ramp. The two geldings, glad of the company, briefly touched noses and snorted. Their hot breath billowed in the crisp morning air. Paymaster seemed almost embarrassed by Percy's immaturity and threw his head in the air. Charlie pulled Percy away and let Aylestone leg him into the saddle.

Aylestone's orders were simple enough. Charlie and the other lad, a conditional jockey called Tony Hellier, were to warm up both horses for twenty minutes or so, after which Tony was to lead them along at a good swinging canter for a mile before letting them run along up the straight.

'Make sure he has a good blow, but don't overcook him,' Aylestone added. 'If he can't get to the other horse, don't worry. I'll be watching from the stands.'

'What's all this about then?' Charlie asked Tony Hellier as they walked out of earshot.

Tony shook his head. 'Don't ask me. All I know is this horse is supposed to be running at Sandown next Friday and the guv'nor says I can ride him again. He also said if anyone gets to hear of this gallop, I'll be looking for another job.'

Charlie hadn't registered that Tony had been the jockey when Paymaster had won at Ascot. Now it emerged that he looked after the horse at home and saw him as his main chance of making a name for himself.

He also told Charlie that the horse had improved since his win.

The two jockeys chatted as they jogged and hacked for a circuit of the course. Despite an awkwardness in his appearance, Paymaster had a definite presence about him, a confidence which Charlie didn't think Percy had yet. The longer they were out, the less he fancied Percy's chances of winning the gallop.

He and Tony pulled up to let the horses catch their breath. After a few minutes, they set off in earnest, keeping to the outside of the hurdle course where the ground was seldom used. There was always room for manoeuvre when a trainer wanted a good, swinging gallop and it was obvious from the way Tony set off that he planned to take no prisoners.

In the past, Percy had sometimes been difficult to settle, but now it was all Charlie could do to lay up. He sat quietly on the horse, talked to him, tried to make him think he was travelling faster than he was.

They tracked Paymaster for half a mile before Charlie felt Percy gradually find his feet and his breathing became less strained. As they swung wide into the straight, Charlie squeezed Percy firmly between his legs, taking him up to join the horse in front. He shortened his reins to take a firmer hold of Percy's head, keeping him balanced, at the same time getting him to lengthen his stride.

Percy lacked experience; it took him a while to understand what he was supposed to do, but then it clicked and Charlie felt him respond.

As Percy quickened, Tony let out a reef on Paymaster and they passed the three-furlong marker both flat out, with Paymaster shading Percy by the length of his neck. The two stayed locked together for another two furlongs before Charlie felt Percy begin to lose his action; the strain of laying up with Paymaster was taking its toll.

Charlie kept his hold on Percy's head but stopped pushing. He let Paymaster ease away until he was some six lengths ahead when he passed the winning post.

Walking back towards the exit from the track, Tony Hellier had a big smile on his face. 'I told you he could go a bit. What do you think?'

Charlie reckoned that Percy could have kept within a length of the other horse if he'd really pushed him, but he agreed that Paymaster was something a bit special.

Charlie didn't see Nick again that day until he got back from Warwick later in the evening.

'Well?' Nick asked excitedly. 'What happened?'

'Percy got beaten. That's what happened.'

Nick's face registered disbelief. 'By what?'

Charlie took him through the whole gallop in detail.

'He must be some tool to beat Percy,' Nick said with disappointment. 'I really thought he was the best we'd got in the yard. So, what do we do now?'

'I'm not sure. Presumably now the guv'nor and Baring know which is the best horse, they'll run them both and back Paymaster.'

'And so will we,' Nick said, hitting the arm of his chair with his fist. 'I took another look over Ivor's yard today.

It's perfect for us. I reckon by the time we've paid a year's rent and insurance, bought some tack and rugs and paid a few weeks' wages, we're going to need at least forty thousand. At the moment we've got just over five in our punting fund.'

'Okay, let's put the lot on.'

Nick gaped at his partner. 'You must be joking.'

'Why not? Come on, let's do it. Shit or bust, unless you still want to be working for Aylestone in ten years' time.'

It took Charlie three days to persuade Nick to go for broke. It was entirely against his friend's prudent nature, but in the end he gave in to Charlie's relentless campaign. When the five-day entries appeared, Nick dived into his form book, checking which of the other runners in the race at Sandown were likely to bother Paymaster. After two hours, he came to the conclusion that unless one of the newcomers was exceptional, Percy was the only danger. And they both knew now that he wasn't good enough.

Two days before the race, Nick and Charlie worked out their plan. Charlie had ridden Percy every day since the gallop and once again had the ride on him at Sandown. Nick was worrying that the two trainers might have a different plan from their own.

Charlie tried to reassure him. 'If they were planning something else, Baring wouldn't have warned Tony Hellier not to mention the gallop to anyone.'

In the four years that Charlie had been riding as an amateur, he'd accumulated a number of punters of varying wealth and success. Common sense told him that the only punters who could get a large wager accepted were those who regularly bet in large amounts and were net losers. Bookmakers didn't keep winners on their books.

Charlie didn't know any really big gamblers, but he knew a handful who, given the right information, would bet a thousand. Normally when he had a ride or the yard a runner which they all fancied, he would tell his punters and they would put him on the odds to a hundred pounds. This time, Charlie would need to go to them with the money, but it would need to be placed as close to the race as possible so that only those who were meant to would know what was going on.

As he discussed the details, Nick tried once more to get him to halve the stake.

Charlie put his arm round Nick's shoulders and gave him a confident squeeze. 'By five thirty on Friday we'll have enough for that yard. You draw the cash out tomorrow; I'll organise the punt.'

Except for those with a vested interest, the seventh and final race on the card that Friday in January was an unimportant event: a National Hunt flat race; twelve runners, five of whom had never appeared on a race-track before. Apart from Paymaster, those that had run didn't offer much promise of high-class sport. The rumours circulating about the débutantes were the usual unreliable lads' stories. The bookies had no strong views about Persimmon Way who was quoted at six to one; the form of his Ludlow success hadn't impressed anyone.

Charlie and Nick still didn't know for certain if their boss was gambling on the race, but the right result would mean they could phone Ivor Thompson that evening to confirm they'd be taking on Oak Hollow Stables within a fortnight.

For most of the afternoon, a damp westerly had been carrying in a cargo of thick grey clouds which had started to drop their load on the Esher track. The going had changed from soft to heavy by the time the runners for the bumper had left the paddock and headed along the tarmac road towards the course. None of them had ever raced on anything worse than good to soft. Charlie began to worry that he'd made the wrong decision. If he'd had the chance now, he'd have called off the bet; that's what a cool-headed professional gambler would have done.

But it was too late.

The lad leading Percy wished Charlie luck and pulled the lead rein from the horse's bit. Charlie and Percy set off through squelching mud downhill towards the start.

Percy floundered slightly as he tried to adapt to the new, unfamiliar conditions; Charlie kept a good hold of his head to help him to stay balanced. He looked at the horses going down in front and derived some consolation when he saw that Paymaster and the others appeared just as lost.

Nick watched anxiously as the runners walked around at the start. The picture on the screen in the bookies' shop in the village was blurred by the pouring rain, but through the clouds of steam rising off the horses he could just make out Percy's colours. Three lads from Aylestone's yard were standing beside him. He wondered if they knew that Percy wasn't supposed to win.

As they came under orders, Charlie had Percy positioned on his own, wide on the outside. Nick assumed that Charlie had walked the course and found the going heavier there – anything to make it more difficult for him.

The starter let them go and they set off through the driving rain with Paymaster leading them as they laboured up the hill and turned right-handed away from the stands. The palms of Nick's hands began to dry as he watched Paymaster bowling along some five lengths clear of the pack, with Percy not even in the picture.

The camera angle changed as they swept wide into the long back straight, giving a view of the whole field. Percy was still wide of the others with only a couple behind him. Three or four of the jockeys were already beginning to scrub away at their horses, trying to lay up with the leader. They made no headway; if anything, Paymaster was increasing his lead.

Charlie sat quiet as a mouse. Nick couldn't tell how well he was travelling, but he was a good distance behind. As the horses galloped round the long bend into the straight, it was clear to Nick that nothing could beat the horse in front; he was the only animal with any running left in him.

Nick glanced at the starting prices superimposed on

the screen. Paymaster had gone off eleven to eight favourite. He calculated that would contribute fifteen thousand pounds to the kitty – not enough for a full year's rent but they'd certainly be able to pay for the yard for six months.

A burst of excited shouting beside him jolted his attention back to the race. The Aylestone lads were beginning to cheer. Paymaster was inside the final furlong, but he was staggering like a drunk.

A sudden intense nausea welled up inside Nick as he saw one of the other runners come from nowhere to mount a challenge. He gulped as the picture cleared and he realised that it was Percy, still on the wide outside, catching Paymaster with every stride. Charlie was sitting motionless while Tony Hellier on Paymaster was pushing with everything he had. He went for his stick, but his horse seemed to be going backwards.

As Percy collared the leader, a raucous cheer from Aylestone's lads bounced off the drab grey walls of the betting shop.

Nick forced a tight smile in an attempt to seem happy about the result. He couldn't sustain even a vague pretence. Doing his best to cover the depth of his anguish, he left the shop feeling as if the earth had opened up beneath his feet, ready to suck him down into eternal destitution.

Why, why, why? Why had they risked so much of their funds on one race? It was absolutely crazy! He couldn't think what had possessed him to go along with Charlie's plan. He cursed his own weakness in letting his friend's absurd optimism get the better of him. 'Trust me.' Charlie's words of misguided confidence rang in his ears as he opened his car door. It occurred to him that the loss of a week's wages to the local bookie hurt him almost as much as the loss of their hard-gained nest egg. Furious, he screwed up his betting slip and drove back to the stables wondering what vain madness had driven Charlie to win the race.

Robert Aylestone struggled to hide his anger as Charlie rode an exhausted Percy into the winner's enclosure. Percy's owner, a retired banker, patently had been told nothing about the intended coup as he stood waiting under the winner's board smiling excitedly at anyone who came near and looking proudly at his horse. Ten feet away, Paymaster's connections stood in a small shell-shocked huddle.

Charlie slid from the saddle wondering how vicious his reception would be.

Aylestone sidled up to him, on the pretext of giving the winning horse a pat on the neck. He looked as if he would rather have strangled it.

'I want you out of my fucking yard by the morning,' he hissed from the corner of his mouth. Charlie slowly stopped undoing his circingle and stared defiantly at the trainer.

He was going to protest, but he snapped his mouth shut before the words came. A slanging match in front of the owner and in full view of the press would do neither of them any good. He turned away and carried on taking off the sodden tack. He gave Percy a grateful rub on his nose and after a few words with the owner, hefted his saddle off to the weighing room.

Nick was sitting, staring blankly at the television when Charlie arrived back at their digs a little after seven. He didn't look up or move when Charlie came in, dropped his kitbag on the floor and flopped into an armchair beside him. 'What the hell have you done?' he asked flatly.

Charlie didn't answer. He was waiting for Nick to see his face. When Nick eventually did look up, he found Charlie grinning back at him.

'What's so bloody funny?'

'You are. I've never seen you sulk before. I hope you're not going to be like this when we're running our own yard.'

Nick was feeling far too sorry for himself to be humoured. 'With you investing our funds, I should have plenty of time to cure myself of the habit,' he said sourly.

Charlie laughed, a great gale of laughter as he leaped out of his chair. 'Cheer up, you miserable bugger. We've done it!' He yelled. 'We've bloody well done it!' He stooped down and put his hand into the inner pocket of his kit bag. With a flourish he plucked out an enormous parcel of fifty pound notes.

Nick's heart leaped like a salmon up a spring river. 'Where the hell did you get that?' he whispered huskily.

Charlie waved the package under Nick's nose. 'Thirty-five grand, my old son, and it's all ours! Five big ones on wonderful Percy at six to one.'

Nick's body collapsed with relief as the world turned the right way up once more. 'Jesus Christ! When the hell did you decide to switch?'

Charlie grinned with a hint of rare conceit. 'Since that gallop at Newbury.'

'But you came back and told me Percy had been well beaten.'

'He was. But considering I'd put a two-stone weight cloth underneath his saddle, he worked like a Derby horse.'

Nick got to his feet, shaking his head to convince himself the nightmare was over. 'I don't believe it,' he gasped. 'You sneaky bastard. Why on earth didn't you tell me?'

'Because I thought your highly developed and unselective sense of loyalty might make you feel deceitful towards our oafish boss and if Aylestone had been in on this, we'd have been lucky to double our money.'

Nick was grinning too now. He nodded.

'By the way,' Charlie went on, 'he sacked me in the winner's enclosure. I shouldn't think that happens often.'

They both laughed as the tension of the last few weeks drained away. Ten minutes later, they were in the pub, celebrating with the lads whose loyalty bets had brought home their weekend's drinking money.

The following evening, Charlie dialled Kate Scanlan's number at her cottage. There was no reply. He tried her parents in Marlborough. She wasn't there, but Charlie asked them to pass on a message if they spoke to her.

Kate rang Charlie at Mrs Phipps' the next morning.

'Hi,' she said. 'I got a message you'd called.'

'Just keeping my half of our deal.'

'What half of what deal?'

'When we got Willow Star, one of the terms was that we must always tell you where she is.'

'I know where she is. She's in a paddock at Oak Hollow.'

'Okay, but I thought you might like to come over and take a look at her and discuss her future.'

'But I'm not her owner; your father is, isn't he?'

'I still think of you as part owner. After all, you saved her life, didn't you?'

'Well,' Kate said with tantalising indecision, 'I suppose I could come over, tomorrow morning.'

'It's a deal,' Charlie said. 'Meet me at Oak Hollow at twelve thirty. Then we'll have lunch.'

Kate hesitated a moment. 'It'd better be a bloody good one.'

Kate checked her hair and make-up just one more time before she left to drive to Lambourn. As she turned her Renault into the drive that led down to the pretty old red-brick yard, she stopped and checked once more.

She parked behind the stables, which she noticed were empty now. Outside, it was warmer than it had been for the last few days, and quieter. She listened to the sounds of the small valley, the plaintive winter bird calls, the distant sound of a tractor rolling and the whinny of a young horse nearby.

There was no sign of Charlie or his battered Range Rover. Kate shrugged. It was just like him to be late.

While she waited, she walked round to take a look at the yard. She was always interested in other people's stables. She opened the top doors of the first two boxes. They were empty and spotless, as if they had just been swept.

She wondered idly why there were no horses in the yard. She wasn't sufficiently well up on the local racing scene to know whose yard she was in. She was aware that the owner had let Charlie keep Willow Star here for a few months and the filly had done well here. She was already broken in and beginning to canter.

Kate wandered up past the rest of the boxes and opened the door to the tack room at the end.

The tack room, like all the stables, was spotlessly clean and empty, save for two chairs and a small table. It was a moment before she took in that the table was covered in a white cloth and lavishly laid for lunch. Beside the table stood a black rubber feed bucket full of ice from which protruded the top of a bottle of champagne.

As Kate gazed with amazement at the unlikely spectacle, a door on the far side of the tack room opened and Charlie walked in with a welcoming smile.

'Happy New Year. Welcome to Oak Hollow.'

Kate frowned. 'What are you doing here with all this? And why aren't you racing today?'

'I wanted to give you lunch. I couldn't do this at Mr Aylestone's. He sacked me.'

Kate felt suddenly guilty. 'Oh Charlie, why didn't you say so? I wouldn't have accepted lunch if I'd known.'

'I'm glad you did. I wanted to celebrate our acquisition of Oak Hollow.'

'Your acquisition? You and Nick?'

Charlie nodded gleefully. 'Yes. Poor Nick hasn't had the sack yet so he's had to go racing, but he sends his warm regards. Now,' he pulled the bottle from the bucket, 'a drink?'

Kate submitted to Charlie's skills as a host and didn't pretend that she wasn't enjoying it. Anyway, she defended her attitude, in some way she couldn't quite put her finger on, Charlie had changed.

'How did this all happen?' she asked.

'Thanks to Percy.'

'Percy who?'

'Persimmon Way, to be precise. A very handsome four-year-old, whose owner I hope will send the horse to me to run on the flat. He could be really useful – a long-distance handicapper, maybe even a Cup horse.'

'Whatever that is.'

'Don't worry, you're going to have plenty of time to get used to racing terminology.'

'Why's that?' Kate asked, already knowing.

'As Willow Star's surrogate mother, you'll be entitled to,' Charlie said.

'But what did this Percy do for you?'

'Won at six to one. Unfortunately – very unfortunately, I suspect – my ex-boss backed the opposition and blamed me when it lost, for some reason or other.'

'You bet on Percy and won enough to set up your own yard?'

Charlie nodded. 'That's about it. The toast is,' he said, topping up her glass and raising his own, 'Willow Star, Oak Hollow, and Percy!'

Chapter Four

With a display of reckless confidence which he didn't feel, Charlie swung his mud-spattered Range Rover up the narrow concrete ramp of a car park near Portman Square. He found a vacant space and slotted into it. He switched off the engine and turned to Nick.

'Okay. How are we going to do this? Shall we spoof or toss a coin?'

They had to decide once and for all which of them was going to hold the licence to train. The Jockey Club wouldn't mind which of them applied, but under its rules a licence could only be held in a single name. Charlie and Nick both fulfilled all necessary conditions as far as experience and references were concerned. And thanks to Charlie's natural charm at attracting owners, they had no problem in complying with the rules regarding the minimum number of horses they would be training. For a simple flat or jumping licence, the minimum was nine. Charlie and Nick were going to concentrate on the flat, but they also wanted to be able to send out a few jumpers. For that, they'd have to keep at least twelve;

they were expecting over twenty horses from the owners they'd already spoken to.

Nick would have loved to have held the licence himself and seen his name alongside their runners, but it was obvious to him that it should be in Charlie's name. Charlie was already quite well known and he had the ability to draw in and encourage owners, which was a trainer's principal task. Without owners, there'd be no horses to train. And it was absolutely vital to Nick that the yard should succeed commercially; the money he was putting into the partnership represented every penny he owned.

Although Charlie thought Nick was probably right, he was reluctant to admit it. He insisted that they each had qualities which were different but of equal importance in running a yard.

Nick fished in his pocket and pulled out a ten pence coin. 'All right. Heads it's me; tails it's you.'

Charlie nodded.

Nick flicked the coin into the air, caught it and slapped it down on the back of his left hand.

'Good luck,' he said. He lifted his right hand just enough to look at the coin without Charlie seeing it. 'Bollocks! You win.' Nick shook his head and slipped the coin back into his pocket.

'Hang on,' Charlie protested. 'I didn't see it.'

'Well, I did, and I'm the loser.' Nick was offering a *fait accompli.* He was sure it was the right decision. 'Come on or we'll be late and we won't have a licence at all.'

Charlie shrugged his shoulders. He knew Nick well

enough to know when he wouldn't be budged. They climbed out of the Range Rover. It looked shabby and lacklustre between a pair of gleaming BMWs. With a dismissive nod, Charlie led the way out to the street and 42 Portman Square.

The granting of the licence to train was more or less a formality at this stage. Oak Hollow had already been visited by the Jockey Club inspector. He'd reported that he was satisfied that everything was up to standard. Access to gallops and security had been his priorities. Every stable had to be fitted with a lock so that horses could be left overnight in the certainty that they couldn't be got at. Charlie and Nick knew well enough that this was only a theoretical certainty; if someone was determined to dope a horse, there was no way, short of having a full-time guard, that it could be stopped. Besides, the ruling made no mention of securing the windows which were always left at least partly open. As for the gallops, there were communal training facilities next to the yard, which included schooling hurdles and fences. Nick and Charlie had already received a letter from the owners confirming their right to use them.

All Charlie needed to do now was to go in and convince the trio of committee members that he was a fit and proper person to hold a licence. If he could do that, they'd be in business.

The interview took place in a panelled room on the first floor. As far as Charlie could tell, it started well enough. He stood and confidently answered a string of routine and technical questions put to him by the three Jockey Club stewards.

After ten minutes or so, Charlie was aware of a slight awkwardness in the proceedings. The questions stopped and an embarrassed silence developed. The senior member, sitting in the middle, was looking down, uneasily shuffling his papers. When he looked up, Charlie could see the discomfort in his eyes.

'Mr Patterson,' the distinguished old peer was finding it hard to get the words out, 'in normal circumstances we would grant your licence straightaway.' He paused. Charlie's heart thumped as his mind raced for a reason why they should be turned down. 'Regrettably, we've received a letter casting doubts on your integrity. I'm afraid we'll have to postpone the granting of your licence until we're satisfied there's no truth in it.'

Charlie was dumbstruck. Why? Who on earth would wish him and Nick any harm?

He burst out without thinking, 'For God's sake, you can't—' He caught the eye of one of the men in front of him and stopped. He'd suddenly realised who the letter must be from. 'I'm very sorry,' he mumbled quickly, 'but if the letter is from Mr Aylestone, I can explain it.'

'Mr Patterson,' the senior member cut in, 'we've no intention of revealing who this letter is from. But as soon as we've investigated, we'll let you know.'

Charlie recognised that arguing about it now wouldn't help their case. Apparently, the interview was over. He thanked them without much warmth and left the room.

Outside, Nick was admiring one of the huge equestrian paintings in the anteroom. He turned as he heard the door open.

Charlie walked straight past him to the lift and pressed the button. 'Come on. We're going.'

The lift arrived and they stepped in. 'Fucking Aylestone!' Charlie hissed as the door closed behind them. 'He's been sticking his oar in, trying to screw things up for us.'

Nick listened in silence as Charlie cursed his way through his account of the interview. He was right, Nick thought. Aylestone probably had sent the letter. No one else had a motive for doing it. But whoever it was, there was nothing they could do except wait.

The lift reached the ground floor and the partners walked out of the building into the grey morning.

'If we don't get a licence,' Nick said to ease the tension, 'Kate'll be more disappointed than either of us.'

'Kate? Kate Scanlan?'

'Yes,' Nick answered defensively.

'Why should she be disappointed? What's it to her?'

'She's really looking forward to us training Willow Star.'

The thought of Kate's interest helped to lift Charlie's depression. 'Is she? I haven't seen her for three weeks. I produced a gourmet lunch for her up at the yard the day Thompson gave us the keys but I haven't been able to get hold of her since. Have you seen her?'

Nick looked embarrassed. 'Well, yes, last week. She wondered if she could have a look at the filly. When I asked her if she wanted to have dinner with me, she accepted.'

Charlie looked away and bit his lip. He knew it was absurd to be jealous. He hardly knew the girl, and Nick was his oldest friend. 'How did you get on?'

'We had a great time.' Nick nodded his approval. 'She's a bright woman, great sense of humour.'

'Did she mention me at all?'

'Not really.'

Charlie opened the door of the Range Rover. 'Let's hope we don't disappoint her, then. With luck, we should have our licence within a week.'

'That depends on what Aylestone had to tell them.'

'We'll just have to hope they don't take any notice of him.' Charlie said, without convincing himself.

A week later, Nick found the letter on the table when he came back for breakfast in the cottage. It was addressed to Charlie but he knew at once where it was from. Although he had as much right as Charlie to read it, he didn't open it at first.

Since Charlie had told him about the letter the Jockey Club had received, Nick had made up his mind they weren't going to get a licence. There were so many accusations Aylestone could have made, however unfounded, which would be impossible to disprove and which would be bound to cast doubts in the stewards' minds. Charlie, predictably, had persisted in dismissing the whole thing as a red herring. 'Those old boys may look as though they don't know what's going on but, believe me, they know exactly what Aylestone's like. When we applied, they were probably expecting him to hit them with a bunch of sour grapes. Don't worry; they'll chew it over for a day or two, then they'll spit it out.'

Nick wished he had that kind of confidence, though he wondered whether Charlie really felt it. Perhaps he was just putting on a face. He dropped the letter back on the table and sat down to pour himself a cup of tepid coffee. He observed, as if it was someone else's, that his hand was shaking. If the envelope contained the right message, he and Charlie would start moving out of Mrs Phipps' house today and their life would instantly accelerate into a faster lane. If not, they'd be condemned to a few more years as assistants to whoever would take them.

He took a gulp of coffee, picked up a knife, slit open the envelope and pulled out a single sheet of paper.

'Charles Patterson Esq . . . After due consideration . . . the Stewards of the Jockey Club have decided to grant you a licence, upon receipt of a list of the horses you propose to train . . .'

Nick read the letter through twice, not absorbing all the details; they could be dealt with later. The main thing, the only thing that mattered, was that at last he and Charlie could set up their own yard.

Charlie had been right. Whatever Aylestone – if it was Aylestone – had said had not swayed the stewards. There were no reservations or provisos in their permission. But that didn't take away from the fact that somebody, before they had even taken the first step in their new career, wanted to see them fail.

Nick read the letter once more to reassure himself. This time, he put it down and let out a great sigh of pent-up anxiety. 'Fantastic!' He got up from his chair and ran back up the stairs to hammer on Charlie's door.

'He's not there.' Mrs Phipps' voice floated up from her kitchen.

Nick's euphoria dimmed for a moment. Sharing the news with Charlie was all part of it. He came back down more slowly. 'Where is he? Did he go out early?'

'No. I don't believe he came back at all last night.' Mrs Phipps pursed her lips at the scandal of it.

'I expect he went to see his mother and stepfather, and ended up staying the night,' Nick said, just to spoil her fun.

'He didn't,' Mrs Phipps said with satisfaction. 'His mother's already been on the phone.'

'Well, I'm sure he's not lost, Mrs Phipps, but if he comes back here, tell him to meet me up at Oak Hollow as soon as possible.'

Nick let himself into the bungalow that stood a hundred yards from the stable block where Ivor Thompson had housed his string of racehorses for the last twenty-five years. The place hadn't been lived in since Ivor's head lad had moved out before Christmas. The lack of heat and furniture had already given it a depressing, damp, unlived-in smell. The cramped little house hadn't anyway been decorated for ten years or more and the removal of pictures and shelves had left a messy scattering of brighter patches on the faded wallpaper. It wasn't much of a place to call your own, Nick thought, but he couldn't have been more pleased at the prospect of moving in.

In the still air he could hear an ominous dripping noise from the kitchen. He walked into the dank little room where the cold tap above the sink was depositing fat drops, thudding like a metronome into the stainless steel sink. A quick twist of the tap quietened it. The silence which followed was interrupted by the rasping scrape of the back door being opened. Footsteps clumped on the bare linoleum and Charlie walked in.

'Morning,' he said. 'What's brought you here?'

'Didn't you get my message from Mrs Phipps?'

'No. Haven't seen the old witch. I left at half six this morning. Went out to meet Charles Gordon.'

'Charles Gordon? The owner?'

Charlie nodded. 'Percy's owner.' He left the statement dangling.

'Well?' Nick asked impatiently. 'What for?'

'To talk about Percy coming to us. I told him ages ago that I thought Percy should be in a flat yard. I'm sure he could win good handicaps. Now I think I've talked him into it. Aylestone will be livid.'

'You mean he's coming to us?'

Charlie nodded again.

'That's brilliant!' Nick laughed. 'And, by the way, we're in business. We got a letter from Portman Square this morning.'

'I guessed that when I saw your car out there. I knew you wouldn't come up otherwise.'

Nick grinned at Charlie's perceptiveness. 'You're right. I didn't want to tempt fate.'

'Right. Let's go over to Ivor and sign the lease before he changes his mind.'

Ivor Thompson beamed at his two new tenants. He remembered the day thirty years before when he had been granted his trainer's licence. He guessed these two were experiencing the same emotions. He looked at his watch. 'I know it's only half past ten,' he said, 'but I think we have ample excuse to open a bottle.' He walked across a fine antique Baluchi rug to a large oak cabinet in which a small fridge had been cunningly set. He opened it and took out a bottle of champagne. 'Krug seventy-eight okay?' he asked with a grin.

He eased the cork from the bottle and filled three glasses. 'The very best of luck to the pair of you. You've got as good a chance as any and better than most of making a go of it. You've got the front and the bottle,' he said, lifting his glass to Charlie, 'and you, Nick, you've got the brain. Looking after the finances is as important as anything else. I wish I'd had a partner to do that in the early days. I'd be a much richer man by now if I had.'

Nick nodded sagely and Charlie hid his smile behind his glass. Ivor Thompson was reputed to be one of the richest men in Lambourn.

'Now, sit down and tell me what your plans are. What are you doing about staff, for instance?'

Charles and Nick had no objection to telling Ivor how they intended to set up their yard. He wasn't a rival; he was on their side.

'We've got Kenny Ford and three more of the best lads coming from Aylestone's – all good work riders.'

'The old scoundrel won't be happy about that, but I dare say you've worked that out for yourselves.' Ivor had very little regard for Robert Aylestone.

'He won't be too happy when he hears one of his horses is coming to us too.'

'But he hasn't got any flat horses, has he?'

'There's one which won a bumper for us a month ago.'

'Oh yes, I remember. Persimmon something, one of Charles Gordon's. I gather you had a bit of a touch on it.'

Nick, startled, glanced at him. No one should have known at all. 'Who told you that?' His tone confirmed what the older man had said.

'Don't worry. Just a discreet little bird. You can never have a touch without people getting to know. As long as it's after the event, you'll be all right. But why do you want this particular horse?'

'I'm certain he could win a few staying handicaps, if we get him on the right mark,' Charlie said. 'I've ridden him and I know what he's got under his bonnet.'

Ivor looked doubtful but made no comment. 'What about the rest of your staff?' he asked.

'We've seen and liked half a dozen girls,' Nick said. 'Charlie's reputation helped there.'

'Reputation for what?' Ivor chuckled.

'They didn't say,' Nick said drily.

'Head lad?'

'We're not sure yet. We think Kenny may do. Though he's young, he's really dedicated. Anyway, we've only got about twenty-four horses to start with, so we can do a fair bit ourselves.'

'Just as long as you don't forget that one of you should be spending at least half your time out finding new owners and new horses. Without a steady flow of those, you'll run out of steam before you've done a couple of seasons. It may sound obvious, but it doesn't matter how much you know about training horses if you haven't got any to train. I can tell you that for the last thirty years most of the training in that yard was done by assistants and head lads.'

The two nodded, though they were not sure that they believed him. They had anyway decided between them that they were going to do as much as possible themselves.

'Any particularly promising horses to start with?'

'Apart from Percy, we've a couple of three-year-olds that might be useful. They're well bred but they've been backward and just had a couple of runs. And we've got a two-year-old filly called Willow Star who looks the part. I think there's enough to get us started.'

Ivor was sceptical. 'You'll find that you need ten horses with potential for every one that actually goes out and does anything. That's why it's essential that you spend time drumming up business to keep your numbers up. And don't forget, the fuller the yard, the more you make on each horse in it. We'll have to see what others we can get for you. Several of my old owners will want my advice. As soon as you're up and running, I'll come and have a look.'

The partners left Ivor's manor house half an hour later encouraged by the older man's enthusiasm. Suddenly the whole thing was real. Horses would soon arrive to be bedded and fed; they would have to get to know them and try to assess their potential. Races would have to be studied and chosen; training programmes and diets worked out.

The Range Rover crunched over the gravel, through the high brick pillars either side of the gate. As he drove into the lane, Charlie turned to Nick. 'Well, we've done it! I think I believe it at last, now we've actually got a licence and a lease in our pocket. We ought to have a yard-warming party or something.'

'There'll be opportunities for parties when we've had a few wins to celebrate,' Nick said with his usual caution.

'At least we could have a few friends round for a drink. I guess I'd better ring my stepfather and tell him; I don't think he really believed we'd get the place. And you could ask Kate Scanlan – Willow will be one of the first horses to move in.'

'Yes,' Nick said, 'maybe I could.'

Within a month, there were twenty-six horses in the yard and they had spent almost four thousand pounds on tack alone. Apart from saddles and bridles, they had to buy rugs and exercise sheets, muck sacks, pitchforks, grooming tools, feed buckets and countless other bits and pieces, all of which were absolutely necessary. While they had been working at Aylestone's, they'd experimented with every type of bedding on the market, from newspaper to peat; they'd come to the conclusion that, provided it was disinfected every day, straw was still the best. It was warmer than paper and cleaner than most other bedding. It was also freely available and cheaper. But it was beginning to look as though this was the only item whose cost they had over-estimated. Everything else, even the insurance, seemed to have gone up since they'd made their original plans and, once they'd started, blacksmith's fees, vets' accounts, and bills for feed and saddlery repair seemed to arrive in an unstoppable flow. Their overdraft was hovering dangerously close to its limit.

On the last Friday in March, as they drove up the gallops, Nick outlined their financial problems.

Charlie was sanguine. 'Look, Nick, it doesn't matter if you and I don't make a lot of money this year. We've got no dependants, as far as I know,' he added. 'And we're going to be too bloody busy to spend any money on ourselves.'

'It's all very well you saying that, but I can't see any point in working our arses off for no money.'

'When Percy starts racing we'll make plenty,' Charlie said confidently. 'Don't worry.'

'Let's hope so.'

'I know so. You watch him work this morning.'

Up at the gallops, Nick stayed in the Range Rover and

Charlie climbed out to meet the string winding up from their stables. When Percy reached him, Charlie took over from Sally, the girl who'd ridden him up. 'Kept the saddle nice and warm,' he grinned down at her when she'd legged him up. She smiled back and reddened while Charlie reminded himself that he'd vowed not to get involved with any of the stable girls. He thought of Kate instead.

She had been up for a drink at the bungalow when Nick had rung to ask her, a couple of days after they'd moved in. She had seemed to want to make it clear that she considered Nick her point of contact, and while she hadn't ignored Charlie, she'd done nothing to encourage him. She'd been round a few times since, quick visits to have a look at Willow Star, nothing more.

Charlie told himself it was only a matter of time before she became interested. Just once – it only needed once – he'd caught her gazing at him with a quite different look in her eyes. She'd turned away almost immediately, but it had been enough.

Charlie took a deep breath and trotted off towards the bottom of the gallop, pushing Kate from his thoughts. Girls would always come second to horses while the likes of Percy were around. The gelding hadn't stopped improving since the day he'd beaten Paymaster. He'd be ready for his first real flat race soon. Charlie gave him a good piece of work over a mile and a quarter with two other horses, and he galloped all over them without coming off the bridle. Charlie pulled up, throbbing with excitement at the thought of Percy's prospects. And Percy was by no means the only exciting horse in the yard.

The day of Willow Star's first race promised to be a cracker from the moment the sun appeared over the curve of the downs, a balmy, May day, the first real summer's morning.

Kenny Ford whistled as he strolled down the lane from his digs to the yard shortly before six that morning. He was looking forward to a day out at Goodwood and seeing his favourite charge run for the first time. Not only was Willow Star a supremely good-natured filly, she was willing, quick to learn and the fastest horse he'd ever ridden. It was partly at his urging that Charlie had entered her. She had been a late foal and conventional thinking suggested she should make her debut later in the season. But though she was quite small, she was well-developed and a six-furlong gallop wasn't going to do her young limbs any harm.

Kenny reached the yard before any of the other staff. He took each horse a small feed and checked their legs and temperature, part of his duties as head lad. When he was satisfied there were no problems, he walked down to the bungalow where he knew Nick and Charlie would be in the kitchen. He let himself in through the back door.

'Do you want Willow to go out for a walk this morning, Charlie?' he asked.

'No. I don't think so. But when you get to the races, just remember to get her out in plenty of time before you take her into the parade ring.'

At that moment the door from the small hall opened. The three men looked up. Kenny gave a knowing grin and Nick looked startled as Kate Scanlan walked in.

'What on earth are you doing here so early?' Nick asked.

'I just wanted to wish you all luck with Willow today. I'm going to give her a big kiss.'

'Aren't you coming?' Nick asked.

'No. I can't. Sandy's going to a funeral so I've got to be on duty. I'll listen to the race on the radio.' She leaned over and touched Charlie's forehead with her lips before she left in her habitual rush.

Nick looked after her. 'I didn't hear her car this morning,' he said, sounding defeated.

'No,' said Charlie. 'She followed me back after dinner.'

Nick raised an eyebrow.

'Cracked it at last, eh, Charlie?' Kenny chuckled.

Nick clenched his fists and stared at the entry forms on the table in front of him.

Nick travelled to Goodwood in the lorry with Kenny. Charlie was picked up later by his stepfather in his Mercedes, a twenty-year-old model but still gleaming.

Major Patterson was handsomely correct in a linen suit and regimental tie. He opened the passenger door from inside for Charlie and greeted his stepson with a brief smile. Opaque grey eyes shone guardedly from beneath his carefully groomed grey-blonde hair. His handsome, clean-shaven features gave away as little as possible. Beyond a few formal words of greeting, he didn't utter a word for the first half-hour of the journey and seemed to feel no discomfort at the silence.

Charlie had never had a communicative relationship with him. For most of his young life, his stepfather had been away, posted abroad. He had never felt any affection for the man, but he respected him and was grateful to him for giving him a home and his name. He knew nothing about his natural father; his mother had offered no information. Patterson had agreed to take him on, completely and without reservation, as his own. Prudence, Charlie's mother, was unable to have more children. Charlie felt that even if he had been Patterson's natural son, he would have evoked no more affection from him and he had taught himself not to resent its absence.

David Patterson was reputed to have been a highly effective soldier. But something had gone wrong when he had reached the age of forty. Charlie had never found out what, but his stepfather had left the army earlier than expected. Soon afterwards he became security adviser to a Saudi Arabian arms dealer, a lucrative but not highly respectable post. Patterson had never told Charlie anything about it. He was by nature a silent, secretive man who offered little about himself. Now, it was only after they had covered the first twenty-five miles of their journey that he made any attempt at conversation. He asked a few questions about his filly, scarcely seemed to hear Charlie's answers, and relapsed into a long silence until they were within a mile of the racecourse.

'We're in Michael and Veronica's box for lunch,' he said abruptly.

Michael Russell was David Patterson's brother-in-law, also an ex-soldier who had come out of the army to make a more than good living from his own security business. He and Patterson's sister, Veronica, had one daughter, Imogen. Despite the absence of any blood ties, Imogen was like a sister to Charlie. Both only children, they had been thrown together from an early age and had remained close.

'Good. Will Immy be there?'

'I dare say.'

'And how is Uncle Mike?'

'As prosperous as ever,' Major Patterson answered. There was a distinct sourness in his voice.

Charlie wondered why, but knew that asking would yield nothing. He extracted a little information about his cousin's activities. She had been in Italy for the last few months. Charlie hadn't seen her since he had moved into Oak Hollow.

As they joined the queue for the car park on the wooded downs behind the racecourse, Patterson asked, 'Who's riding the filly?'

'I told you, Dad. Owen Williams.'

'Yes, so you did. He's useful, isn't he?'

'He's as good as anyone on a two-year-old filly. Doesn't fuss them. He's got a very quiet pair of hands.'

'And the filly? Showing any promise?'

'God, don't you listen to anything I say? I told you, she's better than average. I'm quite hopeful.' Charlie was deliberately low key when dealing with his stepfather.

'If she made a showing at this stage, would she be worth much more than I gave for her?'

'As I got her so cheap for you, almost certainly.'

'How much more?'

Charlie was struck by the naivety of the question but didn't let it show in his voice. 'That would depend on the quality of any races that she won. If she got a good group race, like the Queen Mary, she'd be considered a potential Classic filly – worth maybe a hundred thousand.'

'You'd be doing me a good turn if you could pull that off,' Patterson murmured.

Charlie detected an undercurrent of nervousness which he hadn't come across before in his stepfather. But then Patterson had always been unpredictable and hard to read. Charlie mentally shrugged his shoulders and climbed out of the car.

For most of the crowd on that fine spring morning at Goodwood, it promised to be another day's enjoyable, possibly profitable racing. For Nick, Charlie and their small staff, it was the biggest day in their career so far. Willow Star was the best horse in their yard. If she didn't win or at least come close today, their chances of scoring any important victories in their first season would look depressingly slim.

Nick and Kenny had already been at the course for a couple of hours when Charlie and his father arrived. Charlie went straight round to the stables to check that the filly had travelled all right. He also wanted to be sure that Nick had declared her.

There were no problems, and Willow Star looked better than ever. With a confident bounce in his stride, Charlie made his way to the stand and to Michael Russell's box.

He walked in to an atmosphere of palpable tension between his stepfather and Michael. Imogen wasn't there. Veronica was glancing impatiently between her husband and her brother. Charlie grinned at them and sensed that they all felt some relief at his arrival.

'Charlie!' Michael said in his role as host for the day. 'Let me get you a drink. How's the filly?'

'She's travelled well. That's something. She hasn't kicked herself in the lorry, and she ate up her breakfast this morning. So far so good.'

'It's hard to tell what the opposition's like,' Veronica said, holding the day's card in front of her. 'At least half of them are débutantes.'

As she spoke, the door opened and Imogen walked in. Charlie greeted her with a kiss and inspected her with detached appreciation. 'Immy, how are you? You look outrageously well.'

'So do you. But you look much too young to be a trainer.'

'It's a sign of age, Immy, when policemen and racehorse trainers start looking young.'

They enjoyed their customary banter as Charlie brought her up to date on the change in his status since they had last seen each other.

'Uncle David doesn't seem particularly excited about his runner,' Imogen said.

Charlie followed her eyes. His stepfather's reserve did seem more pronounced than usual. He was used to the lack of communication, but today it was worse; and there was definitely something uncomfortable between him and Michael Russell. Charlie had no idea what. He wished his mother had come to the races; it might have livened up the party a bit; but she'd gone to a meeting of prison visitors.

He made sure he sat beside Imogen at lunch but left as soon as he could afterwards to check Willow Star. Her race was the fourth on the day's card and he knew he was going to find it hard to fill in the time.

Charlie walked into the parade ring with his stepfather and Imogen. Kenny was already proudly leading Willow Star. The filly was walking easily with a long, loose stride. She looked in perfect condition and was undoubtedly catching the eye of the cannier punters. Her price on the bookies' boards shortened steadily.

The jockeys burst into the paddock, bright splashes of shining silk against the deep green turf. Owen Williams, wearing David Patterson's colours on their first ever outing, approached Charlie.

'Good afternoon, sir,' he said, his Welsh accent pronounced. 'How do you want her ridden?'

'Sensibly. It's her first race and I want her to enjoy herself. I want her to learn something, too, so don't just sit on her.'

Kate Scanlan drove her dusty Renault into the car park as the horses left the paddock to go down to the start of the fourth race. Sandy had got back to Noah's Ark from the funeral before lunch.

'I didn't feel like hanging around,' she'd said, adding generously, 'You bugger off and watch your precious filly run.'

Kate bought herself a badge and rushed through to the Richmond enclosure in time to see the runners being loaded into the starting stalls at the far end of the straight course. She would have liked to watch the race with Charlie, but she guessed he would be in a box with his uncle, whose name she couldn't remember. While the starter was seeing the last few difficult young horses installed, Kate swept the stands with her binoculars to see if she could identify Charlie in one of the boxes.

On the second sweep, she got him.

He was standing beside what, to Kate, looked like a ravishing, slender goddess of a girl. They were both laughing, looking down towards the start, and she had an arm locked into his.

Kate tore her eyes away from the sight. She tried to concentrate on the horses down at the start but her stomach churned at the bitter unfairness of her timing. Only the night before, after months of telling herself not to, she had let herself go with Charlie, convinced that there was real depth beneath the lightweight charm and macho banter. She'd been sure she'd judged it right, and it had been a beautiful night. But what the hell was he doing, the very next day, with his arms round a girl who looked like Claudia Schiffer without a squint?

She couldn't stop her glasses drifting back to rest on the box. She winced, and her eyes clouded.

Down at the start, Owen Williams sat calmly on the stocky bay filly. Her manners so far had been perfect. She had walked into the stall without a hint of objection and was standing quietly but alert to everything going on around her. Her long ears were twitching like radar scanners. When the last runner was in, Owen tightened the reins and squeezed her gently to let her know they were about to go. The starter wasted no time in raising his hand and pulling down the lever to spring the gates.

Willow Star leaped out of the narrow entrance, delighted at the sight of the long, clear stretch of deep green turf in front of her. A couple of runners alongside her bumped together as they left the stalls. They had to struggle to find their balance but once they had, the race settled into a sensible pattern.

Willow Star found herself in her element. She was small and compact, ideal for the grassy switchback that lay ahead. The gentle rise of the first furlong gave her time to settle into a sharp but reassuring rhythm.

She was so much better than anything else at home that she always worked by herself. Now she was surrounded by other horses going a really good gallop, and she loved it. As they skimmed the brow of the hill, past the five-furlong marker, the pace quickened and a gap opened up in front of her. She pricked her ears and surged forward, eager to show how good she was, until she felt the tug of the bit in the soft corners of her mouth. She eased back for a few strides, throwing her head in the air. She desperately wanted to please but now she was confused; she didn't know what was wanted of her and, throughout the next half-furlong, became unsettled.

The field was travelling fast now and Willow Star saw the grandstands looming in the distance to her left. Suddenly, she felt her jockey urging her forward. They were still racing downhill, but her balance was returning. She had never galloped so fast in her life and the effort was beginning to burn up the muscles in her adolescent legs. There seemed to be no end in sight to the uphill run to the line, but despite her tiredness, she saw that she was catching the half-dozen horses in front.

Above her she could feel the rhythm of Owen pushing and squeezing her. Helping her to maintain her balance, urging her forward. But she didn't need any encouragement. She was straining every sinew in her body. She wanted to win for herself, and also for Kenny and Kate.

The oxygen in her lungs was beginning to run short. As she raced on through the pain barrier, the months of hard training were paying off as one by one the horses in front faltered and came back to her.

With fifty yards to run, a shift in her jockey's weight told her that he'd raised his arm; a split second later, a sharp pain stung her quarters as his whip cracked down on her tender skin.

For an instant, she was going to object and dig her toes in, but an even stronger instinct made her stretch out her neck for one last effort.

As she stormed across the finishing line, with her ears lying flat against her neck, she knew for the first time what it was like to win, and she liked it more than anything else she had ever done.

Kate, almost faint with excitement, only lowered her glasses when Owen Williams had finally pulled up Willow Star a hundred yards past the finishing post and was wheeling her round to come back. For a few moments, Kate had forgotten the misery that had been tearing her apart before the race.

Now, with horrible inevitability, she raised her binoculars again and trained them on the box.

The sight that met her eyes almost made her retch.

Charlie had wrapped the girl in his arms. They were hugging each other as if they'd only just discovered it could be fun.

Kate dropped the glasses from her blurred, smarting eyes and turned away. She felt utterly betrayed, and a complete fool. Hurt, angry, confused, she came to an abrupt decision. She walked straight to the exit and out to the car park.

Robert Aylestone was feeling nauseous too. He lowered his glasses as Willow Star passed the post and allowed his dislike of Charles Patterson to reach new depths.

Everything seemed to have gone wrong at his yard since Percy had won his bumper. He'd sacked Charlie; he'd had to. His guts had told him, and gossip had confirmed, that his young assistant had worked the whole Percy episode to his own advantage. Then Nick Ryder had gone.

Aylestone thought he must be slipping when he heard that his two assistants were taking Oak Hollow. He should have known weeks before. The parcel of invective he'd sent to the Jockey Club hadn't brought a result. Now, to cap it all, the cocky bastards had talked Charles Gordon into moving Percy to their yard.

It was more than humiliating, it was character assassination. Aylestone had also heard that morning that Charlie had entered Percy for a long-distance condition race at the end of June.

Nick was jubilant at the yard's first big win. He thought it only right that as a partner in the yard he should go up and congratulate the winning owner. With some misgivings over Major Patterson's reaction, he walked into Michael Russell's box. Charlie wasn't there. Nick considered backing out, but he'd already been spotted by David Patterson.

Veronica was friendly enough. Nick had known her since his school days when sometimes she had come and taken him and Charlie out for the day.

'Well done, Nick! Brilliant effort. You even managed to get a smile out of David.'

'I think you'll find,' Patterson said in his quiet voice, 'that Charlie does most of the actual training at Oak Hollow.'

Nick tried not to flinch. He'd had to deal for some time with this kind of oblique attack from his friend's stepfather. He still didn't understand why.

Veronica rushed to his defence. 'Really, David, don't be so ungracious. Nick's in it with Charlie; the licence may be in Charlie's name, but they're equal partners, isn't that right, Nick? Charlie was telling me at lunch he couldn't possibly have got it all together on his own.'

Nick nodded, embarrassed.

'Charlie always made sure Nick was on his team,' Patterson remarked.

Veronica, genuinely upset by her brother's rudeness, took Nick by the arm and led him towards the front of the box. 'Don't take any notice of him. He's one of those people who's not just a bad loser but a bad winner, too. Let me get you a drink.'

Nick wished he'd never come to the box, but as he was here he was glad to be able to get a good view of the next race, which he wanted to see. He found himself standing beside Imogen. She gave him a warm smile which made him tingle and think of Kate, then, unhappily, of her spending the previous night with Charlie.

He smiled back at Imogen, painfully aware that he held no interest for her. 'How are you, Immy? I gather you've been in Florence.'

They laughed and carried on a comfortable conversation discussing the charms and appeal of the medieval city. Nick knew that their enthusiasm would have been lost on the less erudite Charlie. The horse he had his eye on won the next race, as he had hoped. He left the box feeling less sorry for himself, acknowledging that it wasn't Charlie's fault that Kate was attracted to him and his stepfather was so damned rude.

Chapter Five

Nick couldn't get Kate out of his head. He knew he'd been a fool to let himself imagine she was attracted to him but he was still finding it hard to accept.

Being honest with himself, he knew she'd never been anything more than friendly towards him, but a few kind words from a pretty girl was all it had taken to arouse romantic ideas in his normally rational head; ideas of warm relationships, love – even marriage. He hadn't much experience of love; just two short-lived affairs with girls who didn't begin to compare with Kate.

His physical attraction to her was compounded by a mental affinity he felt they had. They shared the same dry sense of humour and taste in music; they read the same books and, of course, they both had an unquenchable fascination with horses. It seemed, just now, a terrible shame that they also shared an affection for Charlie. But at the back of Nick's mind lurked the hope that maybe, when Charlie finally lost interest in her, which on all known form he would sooner or later, he could resume his pursuit of her.

The season got into its stride and the yard became busier with more runners. Nick's hurt at losing Kate began to ebb, made easier by the fact that Charlie never mentioned her and she herself hadn't been to Oak Hollow since the day Willow Star first ran at Goodwood.

On a hot June day, when the sun baked the tops of the rolling downs and no wind stirred the long coarse grass that covered them, Nick was sitting in the poky little room in the bungalow which he had commandeered for his office. Looking through the ever-changing list of the yard's inmates, he thought of Ivor Thompson's advice about the need to find new owners. Of the twenty-six horses they'd started with, only sixteen were left. Of those that had gone, just one had broken down – an older horse who'd had leg problems with his previous trainer; the others had just been no good. Nick and Charlie had decided as a matter of policy wherever possible to move on any horse they thought incapable of winning a race. Their practice of being honest with owners looked as though it would pay off in the long run; they, not their rivals, were being asked to find the replacements. But good horses weren't easy to find mid-season.

As Nick turned to his current balance sheet, he reflected that having orders to buy was no help in paying the rent. Six new horses had restored the number to twenty-two, but that wasn't enough to break even, let alone pay the partners a wage for their toil.

Despite these fiscal worries, and his disappointment over Kate, Nick had to admit that he'd never been happier. He was his own boss. The horses they had were running well and prospects were bright. The advantage of weeding out the slow horses was that it allowed them to be positive about those that remained. They didn't need to believe that their geese were swans, and they could afford to aim only at goals they had a realistic chance of reaching. Each horse had its own training programme with specific targets. If one failed, Charlie and Nick meticulously drafted another.

Countless hours spent between the form book and the racing calendar had yielded other rewards. The partners had already earned tidy sums from gambling, for themselves and their owners. This, though, never showed on Nick's balance sheets; gambling winnings, as far as he was concerned, were the icing on the cake. The yard had to support itself on its training income.

The biggest encouragement to potential owners was the fact that the yard was producing winners. Charlie's high profile gave them more than their fair share of publicity and though their numbers were down, a lot of outsiders were beginning to show an interest in the new tenants at Oak Hollow. Even Nick, without Charlie's natural optimism, thought it only a matter of time before they filled the yard and really took off.

So, despite the financial knife edge along which they seemed sometimes to teeter, there was never any question of corners being cut where the welfare of either the horses or the lads was concerned. Nick and Charlie agreed that the most important ingredient of their success to date was that the yard was a happy one and discerning visitors saw that reflected in the horses as they came squealing from their boxes each morning.

Kenny and the other lads had already made a significant contribution. They never complained when there was extra work to be done, and the two young bosses weren't above mucking in with them. Because of their age, Nick and Charlie had a more informal relationship with their stable staff than most trainers. Racehorse training was generally an industry steeped in traditions of old-fashioned master-servant relationships. The lack of this obstacle to communication at Oak Hollow allowed the lads to put their point of view knowing they'd be listened to and taken seriously. The more responsibility they were given, the better they seemed to respond.

Nick leaned back in his chair, stretched his arms high above his head and let out a long yawn. He reached down and picked up the well-thumbed form book which he seemed to spend most of his life studying, searching for the easiest races for their intended runners. The dilemma facing him and Charlie that morning was whether or not they should run Flitgrove in a seller. Flitgrove was a filly moderately bred for the flat. She belonged to Percy's owner, Charles Gordon. Mr Gordon was slowly building up a small band of brood mares and had bought Flitgrove as a present for his wife, Sarah, for their wedding anniversary.

Although she had worked well at home, the filly had failed to show any form on the racecourse. After three disappointing runs, Charlie and the girl who looked after her felt she needed to gain some confidence. A selling race should be well within her capabilities and just one success, however lowly, could make a great difference to the price of her offspring when they came to be sold. The risk of running her in a seller was that someone might run the price up at the auction afterwards if she won. An even worse scenario would be that they lost her altogether to an outside bidder. Mrs Gordon adored the filly. She brought a big bag of titbits for her every Sunday morning. She was a large, domineering woman with a voice like gravel. Nick couldn't even contemplate the possibility of having to give her the news that her darling had been sold.

In the meantime, an hour's study of the other entrants' form convinced Nick that if Flitgrove ran, she would win. He was glad that the final decision to run her would be taken by Mr Gordon with help from Charlie.

Nick eased himself stiffly from his desk chair and walked out into the sunshine to find Kenny. While he was up at the yard, he saw Charlie arrive back in the Range Rover and go into the bungalow.

When Nick got back to the office, Charlie was sitting in his chair with the phone pressed to his ear, pleading. 'I can promise you, Charles, that nobody will bid for her, but even if they do, all you have to do is outbid them. It's not a problem, I give you my word. Let her run; let her win a race and we'll see if she can win a little handicap somewhere after that.'

Nick gathered that the owner was deliberating, experienced enough to weigh the pros and cons, but Charlie was at his most persuasive, almost irresistible. After a couple more minutes of optimistic enthusiasm, Charlie put the phone down and turned to Nick with a triumphant grin. 'Another winner coming up, Nicky boy. He's agreed to let her run in the seller at Bath on Monday.'

Nick greeted the news with a wary smile. Although he agreed that the filly would probably win, he was still uncertain about running her. He doubted that Charlie had thought beyond the race. 'Let's just hope nobody does bid for her. If we lose her, I can see us losing Percy as well.'

'Bollocks,' Charlie laughed. 'You're being too bloody cautious as usual. Who's going to bid for her?'

'I don't know. Anybody could,' Nick said. Privately, he thought that Robert Aylestone might, but he didn't say so. He was still sure that it was their old boss who'd written the letter to the Jockey Club objecting to their licence application. But Charlie, after his initial anger and once the licence had come through, had pushed the event right out of his mind. Nick wished he could too. Aylestone might not notice that the filly was running, he told himself; he was only interested in jumpers. He might be away on holiday. Nevertheless, in the days leading up to the race, Nick couldn't write him off as a threat when they were in such a potentially vulnerable position.

During those three days, Mr Gordon phoned constantly. Each time Charlie managed to convince him there was nothing to worry about. He told Nick that Mr Gordon had chosen not to explain to his wife what the outcome of a selling race could be, knowing she wouldn't agree to the filly running if he did. Mr Gordon, in the end, trusted Charlie and he wanted the stud to pay its way as far as possible. A win for Flitgrove would do a lot to enhance her paddock value. Once she had won, though, that would be it. No more sellers.

Mr Gordon also announced with some regret that he and his wife wouldn't be able to come to watch the race themselves. Charlie promised to take care of everything and ring them the moment the race was over.

Monday turned out to be a comparatively quiet day in the office. Nick had worked most of Sunday so he decided to indulge himself and go racing for a change. Besides, Bath was less than an hour away down the M4; Flitgrove's race was the first on the card. He and Charlie would be back by four.

They set off in Nick's car, a ten-year-old BMW which looked as if it had left the showroom that morning.

When they had run through the risks and returns of the afternoon's race for what must have been the twentieth time, the conversation turned to Willow Star and her next race at Royal Ascot in ten days' time.

'Will your stepfather be coming to see her run?' Nick asked.

'I don't know. I told him he should, but frankly I don't think he's that interested. I think he only bought her to help us out.'

'He wouldn't have done it as a favour.' Privately, Nick didn't think Major Patterson was capable of a considerate act.

'Yes, you're probably right. He was certainly keen to know how much he might get for her if she carried on showing some form.'

'You don't think he'll sell her?' Nick asked.

'Hard to say. I don't think he needs the money, but he never talks to me about that sort of thing.'

'He was bloody rude to me at Goodwood,' Nick said reluctantly. It was the first time he'd mentioned it to Charlie.

'I know. Immy told me. I'm sorry, but that's what I mean. He's been getting very tetchy lately.'

'My father told me he'd had some bad luck at Lloyd's.'

'Is he his agent?'

'I think so. He certainly introduced him to a few syndicates.'

'Anyway,' Charlie said after a few moments' silence, 'I don't know what he's thinking of doing about Willow. My guess is he'll hang on to her for a couple of seasons. At least, that's what I've told my mother to persuade him to do. To me, she's just the sort of filly that will improve as a three-year-old, and Goodwood was promising.'

'Ascot will be a better indicator. Do you suppose Kate Scanlan will be there to see her run?'

'I don't know,' Charlie said. 'Don't you?'

'Me? Why should I?'

'I thought she was such a great friend of yours.'

'The last time I saw her, she'd just spent the night with you, remember?' Nick said quietly.

Charlie didn't answer at once. He looked down at the racing paper in his lap. 'Look, Nick, I'm sorry. She's a bloody good-looking girl – I'm sorry we both fancy her. But she'd given me such a hard time, I couldn't believe it when she suddenly eased up and came out to dinner, and it all went brilliantly. Then I don't know what happened.'

For a few moments Nick stared straight ahead, concentrating on his driving. 'She said you were lousy in bed; that's what happened.'

'What?' Charlie spluttered. 'How the hell could she say that?' Stammering with agitation, he began to describe his night with Kate until Nick stopped him with a burst of laughter.

'It's all right,' he said. 'She didn't say that. At least, if she did, I didn't hear her. I haven't seen her either, to be honest.'

'You bastard!' Charlie laughed with relief. 'You had me going then.'

'I know your weak points,' Nick said. 'Did you see her at Goodwood?'

'No, but she told me she'd been. I've spoken to her a couple of times, but she's been ice-cold, said she was busy – you know, washing her hair.'

'Maybe she's embarrassed; I mean, she knew I was interested in her.' Nick sighed. 'I suppose I knew she didn't fancy me but we got on so well; she knows a lot about music, and we've read the same books.'

Charlie laughed. 'She didn't tell me that.'

'Well, she wouldn't,' Nick said with the ghost of a grin. 'Anyway, it looks as if we've both blown it.' He seemed satisfied that this was, if not ideal, at least fair.

'Yeah,' Charlie nodded, only half-agreeing but relieved

that the air had been cleared. He looked back down at the day's runners. 'I hope to God we've done the right thing, putting this filly in a seller.'

'It's not too late to take her out. You could always say she's off colour.' Nick knew this wasn't what Charlie wanted to hear. He sensed that his partner was getting cold feet and wanted reassurance which he couldn't honestly offer.

Charlie stared out of the window, hoping for some flash of inspiration. He wanted winners and Flitgrove should win. Even if the unthinkable did happen and they lost her in the auction, it wouldn't be the end of the world. As far as he could tell, she would never be more than a moderate horse. But he didn't want to lose Percy. He was certain there were plenty of good races to be won with him. His problem was that he could judge a horse's reaction to a situation better than a human's. He didn't know how well he would manage Mr and Mrs Gordon if things went wrong. He wound down the window and leaned back to let the cool air rush over his face.

After a while, he turned to Nick. 'Let her run,' he said decisively. 'We'll never get anywhere if we don't take a few chances.'

'All right,' Nick nodded. 'But I tell you what. I'm going to ring Aylestone's yard to find out where he is.'

'Aylestone's? Why?'

'Because if he's away on holiday, I think we'd have a lot less to worry about.'

Charlie didn't answer at once. He looked at Nick,

knowing what he was saying, reluctant to admit its relevance. Slowly, he reached out and picked up the phone. 'I'll do it,' he said, starting to dial Aylestone's number. The trainer's secretary answered and recognised Charlie's voice at once. It took only a few flattering words to discover that the boss was out for the day but she didn't know where.

Bath racecourse is the highest in the country, perched over the small city, nearly eight hundred feet above sea level. On a fine day like this it was possible to see across Somerset to the Mendips. As Nick drove into the racecourse, with two hours to go before the first race, the vast green car park was already filling up with picnickers taking advantage of the sunshine for a pre-race lunch.

Charlie went off to check that Flitgrove had arrived safely and that she'd been properly declared. Nick sat and read the papers.

The conditions for Flitgrove's race stated that the winner was to be sold for not less than two thousand guineas. The race itself carried a two thousand pound prize to the winner so if someone did decide to have a go at buying her, they could bid at least that much before the expenses began to mount. Above the minimum selling price, the racecourse kept fifty per cent, which meant that if Flitgrove sold for four thousand, Charles Gordon would receive only three. Or if they had to bid four thousand to buy her in, it would cost them a thousand to keep the filly. It would be money well spent. The value that winning the race would add to Flitgrove's progeny at the sales would be much more.

Nick dozed off in the warm summer sun. He woke with a start only twenty minutes before the filly was due to run. He half ran to the course and made his way to the front of the stands where the bookmakers were doing their best to drum up some business over what looked no more than a moderate contest. The best price he could find for Flitgrove was six to four. While Nick cursed that he couldn't find anything longer, he knew that if he were a bookie, he wouldn't have been as generous. He and Charlie had planned to put a thousand pounds on the filly, provided she wasn't odds on.

Discreetly, Nick pulled a wad of fifty pound notes from his pocket, split them into five bundles and placed two hundred pounds with each of the biggest firms on the rails. Satisfied that he'd done the best he could, he walked to the owners' and trainers' stand to wait for Charlie.

The runners emerged on to the course down to his right. There were fourteen in all. Flitgrove came out in a small group of three. Her dark brown coat glistened as she strode on to the course. She looked, Nick thought, in a completely different class to the rest of them. As the field turned and cantered back towards the one-mile five-furlong start, he lifted his glasses to take another look at the bookies' boards.

'What are you grinning about?'

Nick lowered his glasses and turned to Charlie who had slipped in beside him. 'I'm grinning because we've got six to four about an odds-on shot.'

'I've told that little jockey not to win by too far,' Charlie leaned over and whispered. 'And to make sure he jumps straight off her and leads her back in as if she was totally knackered. I think if we get away without having a bid for her, we'll have had a result. The rest of these look rubbish.'

Almost as soon as the horses had sprung from the stalls, there was never much doubt about what was going to happen. Flitgrove was always travelling easily and from the turn into the straight the only question was how far she would win by.

Charlie wanted to kick himself as she romped home by an easy five lengths with the jockey unable to make it less. On that performance, she looked as though she could have won just about anywhere. As he and Nick climbed down from the stands, he made a quick reappraisal of her value.

Although he'd convinced Charles Gordon that no one would make a serious bid for her, he had privately estimated that the most anyone would go to was five thousand. After such a convincing and obviously effortless win, it could well go to a lot more. If the worst came to the worst, he and Nick would have to help out on the repurchase because, whatever happened, they had to hang on to her now.

Despite the jockey's pantomime of jumping off her as she came to a halt, there were plenty of people pushing against the rail of the winner's enclosure to get a better look at her and see what promised to be a good, active auction.

As soon as the 'weighed in' had echoed from the tannoy, the Clerk of the Course, who doubled as auctioneer on these occasions, climbed on to a rostrum to deliver a crisp, upbeat summary of Flitgrove's racing career and breeding. Charlie bit his lip and shook his head angrily as the auctioneer eulogised over the filly, making her sound like the best thing on four legs since Pegasus.

Nick had slipped away somewhere quieter where he frantically tried to get hold of Charles Gordon on the phone. He wanted to tell them that the horse had won. More important now, he wanted to be in contact in case the bidding escalated to silly money.

'Who'll start me off at two thousand?' the auctioneer began confidently. 'Come on! You all saw her win. There are plenty more races in her – and not sellers either.'

Charlie cringed at the accuracy of his words. A coating of clammy sweat seeped through the pores of his neck and forehead.

The auctioneer was looking around, waiting, not too impatiently, for the first bid when a man – a farmer by the look of him – thrust a hand in the air and offered one thousand. The bidding was slow to start, rising in increments of two and three hundred. The farmer dropped out after two and a half thousand. Someone else had taken it up, but Charlie couldn't spot the other bidder. When the price reached five thousand, he thought he had the filly.

'All done then?' the auctioneer asked testily. 'She's bought in and you're letting a bargain go, I'm telling you.'

'I'll shoot the bastard if he doesn't hurry up and sell her,' Charlie hissed at Nick. 'Haven't you got hold of those bloody owners yet?'

Nick didn't reply. He'd just seen Robert Aylestone.

The trainer had appeared from nowhere. Now he was standing directly opposite them. He nodded at the auctioneer.

'Thank you, sir. Five thousand five hundred; that's more like it.'

Charlie gritted his teeth as the Clerk of the Course stared straight at him.

'Come on now, you don't want to let her go for the sake of a bid,' he cajoled. 'She's better than you thought, I'll wager.'

Charlie raised his index finger for one last bid as the auctioneer's gavel reached its zenith, ready to knock the filly down to Aylestone.

Aylestone gave a short, quick nod and a bland smile spread over his craggy face. He looked at Charlie and Nick with an insolent shrug, daring them to take him on.

At fifteen thousand pounds, Nick still hadn't made contact with the Gordons. Swallowing bitterly, Charlie turned away. The filly just wasn't worth that much, even allowing for Mrs Gordon's extravagant affection for it.

'What the hell do we do now?' Nick said, close to panic.

Charlie was about to launch into a vicious verbal slating of Robert Aylestone when the auctioneer's excited voice rose in pitch. 'Fifteen thousand five hundred guineas. A new bidder. Thank you, sir.'

Charlie and Nick looked at each other in astonishment. Charlie glanced across the ring. Robert Aylestone's weatherbeaten face was creased with uncertainty. The bidding had been rising by a thousand pounds a time. Aylestone pondered a few uncomfortable moments before nodding again. The auctioneer turned to his right. Charlie and Nick followed his eyes. They were resting expectantly on a well-known bloodstock agent. Mike Dubens was still in his early thirties but he had already made a name and a lot of money by constantly being one step ahead of the rest of the pack. With a barely perceptible movement of his head, the bidding jumped again.

'Come on, don't lose her now,' the auctioneer gleefully urged Aylestone.

'What the fuck is Mike Dubens doing?' Charlie muttered hoarsely to Nick. 'She's stones below the type of animal he deals in.'

'I don't know, but he's going to get her. Aylestone's just walked away.'

'All done then at sixteen thousand?' The auctioneer's voice suggested he was more than pleased, in fact rather bewildered at the price he had achieved. His eyes made one last sweep around the small crowd and he brought his gavel down firmly on the front of his rostrum. 'Mike Dubens. Thank you.'

Charlie grabbed Nick's sleeve. 'Come on. Let's go and see what the hell that was all about.' He turned and made straight for the young bloodstock agent who was signing the sales docket.

Charlie and Nick knew Mike Dubens, but not well. If

they'd known him better, he'd have let them know beforehand that he was planning to bid for the filly. It was a recognised courtesy.

Mike looked up and smiled as they approached. Charlie brushed aside his friendly greeting.

'Look, we know why Aylestone was bidding, and it had nothing to do with wanting the filly at that price. But I can't see any reason why anyone as sharp as you should want to pay way over the odds for her.'

Mike looked embarrassed and put his hands in the air. 'Look, I'm sorry. I didn't know you were that keen to buy her. I wanted her, but I wouldn't have bid if you hadn't dropped out. I thought Aylestone was going to get her.'

'Aylestone was trying to run us up just to make life difficult,' Charlie said. 'The bastard's pissed off at us setting up on our own. But why the hell do you want her? It's not as if she's related to anything special.'

Mike's eyes slithered uncomfortably to one side. Charlie and Nick stared at him for an answer.

He shrugged his shoulders. 'Until three o'clock this morning you'd have been right about that.' Charlie felt as if someone had punctured his lung. He had a horrible feeling he knew what was coming. Mike went on, 'Her full brother had his first run on dirt at Santa Anita last night and knocked nine-tenths of a second off the course record. The trainer says he's the best he's ever had. It was just lucky for me I heard about it, knowing his sister was running here today.'

Nick and Charlie shook their heads in resignation.

They recognised that they'd been pipped by a pro who did more homework than any other agent on the circuit. Mike seemed genuinely sorry when Nick told him that Flitgrove had become Mrs Gordon's special pet, and Charles Gordon also owned Persimmon Way.

'Look, I'd normally let you have her back for a small profit but something tells me she's capable of a lot more than she did today. She might even be like her brother and improve again once she gets on the dirt.'

Charlie heard from a distance. He was grappling with the problem of how to break the news to Charles Gordon. It was bad enough to have lost the filly but then telling him she was closely related to a potential star in America, just as he was expanding his stud, would make him justifiably furious.

'I'll tell you what I'll do,' Mike was saying. 'I don't want to sell her to you, but you can go on training her. Mind you,' he added with a grin, 'I don't want her running in any more sellers.'

This didn't do much to ease the partners' concern about the Gordons but they thanked the agent and had a brief discussion about training fees and future plans. When Mike had gone, Nick and Charlie went to the stables. They told the lads what was happening and walked back to the car park.

Nick was pulling away when they saw Mike Dubens again. He didn't see them; he was too preoccupied. He had an arm wrapped round Kate Scanlan's waist.

'I don't believe it!' Charlie spluttered. 'First he nicks our horse, then he nicks our girl as well.' He burst out laughing. 'Oh well, at least we haven't got anything to fall out over now.'

Nick didn't laugh. 'We wouldn't have done anyway.'

On a sunny Thursday, two weeks after Flitgrove's race at Bath, Willow Star was entered to make her second public appearance in the Chesham Stakes at Royal Ascot. The Chesham was traditionally one of the weaker two-year-old races of the meeting. Nevertheless, it carried Listed status and was a coveted prize. The form of her first win at Goodwood had worked out well. A couple of those who had finished well behind her had won since. And a win at Ascot in any race would do Oak Hollow's reputation a lot of good. Everyone involved was getting excited at the chance to show what they could really do – everyone, that is, except the two people Charlie had most expected to show interest and enthusiasm.

David Patterson gave no sign of pride or pleasure in his first racehorse, and Kate still hadn't been near Oak Hollow since Goodwood. Charlie had wanted to ring her, prompted by the thought of Mike Dubens moving in on her, but pride wouldn't allow it. Privately, though, he hadn't given up hope. He was bound to run into her sooner or later and get a chance to advance his cause. He would admit only to himself that he found her rejection and decamping to the bloodstock agent a lot harder to handle than he'd thought he would.

He refused to let it get him down. Everything at the yard was going well. He had managed to placate Mrs

Gordon over the loss of Flitgrove with a lot of heartfelt apology, throwing himself at her mercy and promising to find a replacement soon. Charles Gordon had been less easy to deal with. Although in the end he'd been persuaded to leave Percy at Oak Hollow, a definite rift had opened up between them, which wasn't going to be cured in a hurry.

Besides this, they'd managed another two wins which brought their total so far to thirteen. For the size of their yard, at that stage of their first season, it was a perfectly respectable score, with the chance of a listed winner with Willow Star.

Charlie had booked Owen Williams again to ride her. This was Oak Hollow's only runner at the meeting. With runners elsewhere, Charlie had missed the first day. On the Wednesday he had treated himself to a day out and took his cousin Imogen.

She didn't have to make much of an effort to stand out, even at Royal Ascot. She was a natural target for the army of photographers and TV cameras who had come to cover the fashion rather than the racing. On a hot day, in deep maroon silk and a pink straw hat, she was a picture editor's gift.

Kate stared at the photograph in the *Daily Mail* next morning as she drank a cup of coffee in her cottage kitchen. She picked up the telephone and dialled the number at Oak Hollow. To her relief, it was Nick who answered.

'Hello,' she said. 'It's Kate here.'

'Kate who?' Nick asked.

'Scanlan,' she started to say, before she heard Nick laughing.

'What's made you break your silence after so long?' he asked. 'We thought you'd forgotten all about us.'

'Of course I haven't. Look, Nick, I just wanted to ask you something. Who is Imogen Russell?'

'Immy? Oh, I suppose you've seen that very flattering shot of Charlie with her in the *Daily Mail*.'

'Yes, I have.'

'And you'll have noticed how, with typically shoddy reporting, they haven't wanted to spoil a good story with the detail that Charlie and Imogen are first cousins and like brother and sister to each other.'

There was a silence at the other end of the line, until Kate asked quietly, 'If they're like brother and sister, why were they hugging and kissing at Goodwood?'

'When?' Nick asked, genuinely astonished.

'After Willow won.'

Nick really laughed now. 'Didn't you want to hug and kiss the person nearest to you when she crossed the line? I certainly wanted to.'

'I bet you didn't, though.'

'No,' Nick admitted, 'I didn't. But anyway, who says brothers and sisters can't hug and kiss?' He paused a moment. 'Is that why we haven't seen you at the yard since then?'

'Yes,' Kate said in a small voice.

'Does that mean,' Nick asked kindly, 'that we might start seeing you again?'

'Maybe.'

'God, I hope so. We might get Charlie back to normal. Are you going to come racing today?'

'Mike Dubens invited me but I didn't want to come so I haven't got a badge.'

'No problem, I'll leave one for you. It won't get you into the royal enclosure but at least you'll be able to see Willow in the flesh.'

'How is she?'

'I don't think you'll be disappointed.'

Although he was head lad and responsible for the overall running of the yard, Kenny Ford still managed to look after Willow Star himself. In his eyes, the filly could do no wrong. He knew the time would come when he'd have to let someone else do her, but for the moment he was making the most of it.

The filly's race at Ascot was the last on Thursday's card, at five thirty, which meant that after he'd ridden out first lot, he'd had time to lead her down the road for half an hour to stretch her legs. Away from the gallops she behaved like an old hack and ambled along quietly at his side. Occasionally she would nuzzle his arm and pocket, looking for a mint, but for the most part she seemed glad just to be out in the open. Kenny had given her a small feed of oats first thing that morning. He'd let her have a few fistfuls of hay and, apart from water which she could drink until two hours before her race, that would be all until she arrived back home for her supper.

The horsebox was due to leave at one o'clock. At

midday, Kenny gave Willow a thorough brushing and greased her feet. When he had dealt with the others' lunchtime feeds and checked that there were no problems in the yard, he went home to change into his best suit. He groomed himself with a perfunctoriness he wouldn't have tolerated in one of the horses and rushed back to the yard.

He wrapped Willow in a light travelling sheet and loaded her into the lorry with his kitbag and a hold-all containing Major Patterson's silks. When he was sure she was happy and comfortable, he clambered into the cab beside the driver. They set off far earlier than they would normally have done, to allow for any delays they might meet.

At two fifteen, Willow Star walked safely into her stable at Ascot, overlooking the lawn beside the driveway. It was hot and airless in the confines of the stableyard. Even with her sheet off, it was too hot to keep the door closed. Kenny heaved a bale of straw from the lorry and put it against the stable door, where he sat for the rest of the afternoon, keeping watch over her as the other lads and horses came and went.

Results from the earlier races filtered down from the canteen nearby. The first three all went to horses trained at Newmarket. A lad bringing news of the fourth shouted to him, punching his hand in the air. 'Four out of four, Kenny,' he jeered. 'I told you, Lambourn's only got slow old jumpers.'

Kenny smiled and lifted his hand to stroke Willow's nose. She had her head over the door, taking in everything that was going on. 'You'll soon show 'em who's best, eh?' Kenny's fingers tickled her delicate skin. She lifted her nose high in the air and curled back her top lip, baring her teeth and gums. It looked for all the world as if she was smiling. Kenny wondered if they'd both be smiling after the race.

At four forty-five, he gave her a final rub over with a brush and cloth and greased her feet again. He pulled on her racing bridle and clipped on the leading rein with its smart brass chain. He led her from the stable and joined four other horses from her race on their way up the hill and across the main road into the racecourse.

Of the nine horses declared to run in the Chesham, only two were fillies. As they walked quietly round the pre-parade ring, Kenny and the other filly's lad were careful to keep them at the back, away from the randy advances of the colts. It was hot and there was no shelter where they were. A few flies were buzzing around Willow Star's eyes and she started to sweat. Kenny kept talking to her, keeping her as relaxed as he could, but he was relieved when Charlie arrived to put on her saddle. Once it was on and he'd sponged her mouth out with cold water, Kenny was able to lead her down into the main paddock. It was much cooler there in the shade of the tall beeches. By the time the jockeys came strutting into the parade ring, Willow had dried off completely.

'How is she?' asked Owen as he leaned down from the saddle to adjust the length of his irons.

'I'd say she's improved at least ten pounds since Goodwood. She knows what the job's about now.'

Willow Star had woken up. She knew she'd soon be

racing. She was too well-mannered to jig-jog but the excitement was almost too much for her. She began walking with an exaggerated movement which made Kenny laugh and pat her neck. Owen cracked her smartly down the shoulder to stop her.

Kenny reached up sharply and squeezed the jockey's leg angrily so that it hurt. 'Do that again and I'll drag you off and slap you.'

Owen tried to justify himself but Kenny cut him short. 'All she's doing is letting you know how well she's feeling. In the next ten minutes she's going to run her guts out and earn you the best part of two grand. So keep your whip to yourself.' Kenny forced himself to wish the jockey luck as he released the lead rein. He watched Willow Star bound away across the green turf, eager to get on with things.

When she'd passed the Silver Ring, Kenny walked the short distance to the small concrete stand reserved for stable staff. It was a good viewing point and there was a large TV set in front of the guard rail to let the lads watch the proceedings until the last few furlongs when they could follow the race with the naked eye.

Kenny found himself sitting next to a lad with whom he'd once shared digs. The lad's horse had run poorly in an earlier race and he'd lost all his week's wages. He was anxious to know if he could recoup them on Willow Star.

'You could have done, but you're too late.' Kenny pointed to the screen as the commentator's voice calmly let spectators know that the race had started. Kenny leaned forward eagerly. He watched as Willow Star broke quickly from the stalls. She was the least experienced in the field but while most of the others struggled to find their feet, she began burning a trail up the middle of the course. She led for over three furlongs with her ears pricked, until a horse with a big white blaze pulled its way alongside her. His long easy stride contrasted starkly with hers. For a few moments it looked to Kenny as if she'd been headed. He could see her struggling to hold her place. Owen started to pump away on her, head down and hands running up and down her neck like someone using a washboard. For a brief spell it looked as if the whole field would swallow her up.

'She's had it now,' said the lad beside Kenny, thankful he hadn't got a bet on. Kenny told him to shut up and moved in closer to the screen. He heard the large crowd packing the stands beginning to bellow. He switched his view down the course where a multi-coloured blur was galloping towards him. He picked out Major Patterson's bright red silk, but couldn't judge how Willow was travelling. He darted back to the TV and a side view. His heart suddenly thumped with excitement when he saw she was almost upsides again. Both his feet left the ground as he launched himself into the air, bellowing his lungs out. 'Come on, Willow! Come on, my girl!' His head flicked from the screen to the course and back again as he watched her battling her way to the front. There were three horses in a line and everyone around him seemed to be shouting for a different one. With only fifty yards to run, a photo finish looked certain, until a brave little nose began to edge ahead of the rest.

Kenny didn't care who saw the tears which trickled down his face. It was the proudest moment of his entire life. Watching her outfight the others right up to the line was something he would never forget. He leaped from the stands amid shouts of congratulations from the other lads and ran to greet her.

'This is one tough filly,' beamed Owen.

Kenny forgot their earlier friction and heaped praise on the pair of them. He threw his arms round Willow's neck and gently pulled her ears. 'She's the best bloody filly in the whole country.'

In the morning, Charlie woke without the thumping hangover he deserved. He opened his eyes, took in the morning suit scattered around the floor of his bedroom, the simple white cotton frock and Kate's gentle features, serene in sleep, a few inches from his face. He closed his eyes and refused to think about his duties for the day just yet. After yesterday and last night, there didn't seem anything else left to achieve.

He eased himself closer to the soft, warm body beside him and felt a pair of arms wrap themselves round him. As he and Kate snuggled closer and her fingers crept up between his thighs, something told him he was going to be late for work.

After the autumn sales at Newmarket, twelve yearlings arrived at Oak Hollow ready for breaking in. The owners of the seven two-year-olds they had run that season confirmed they would be leaving them there. Only four horses moved on.

Kenny was now too busy as head lad to give Willow Star the attention she merited and a young Scottish boy called Titch had taken her over.

Willow had come home from the Chesham Stakes with sore shins. Charlie and Nick decided to rest her for the remainder of the season. For the next two months she did nothing more than light exercise. Each day Kenny smoothed soft clay on to the front of her canon bones to keep them cool and gradually she returned to total fitness. By late October she'd resumed a normal training programme with the others. Titch now rode her out every day – a responsibility he relished. He rode well but had never 'done' a really good horse. For him, it was a thrill just to canter her and he spoiled her as much as Kenny had. As 'stable star', she was now housed in the best box in the yard, next to the feed house where the lads all congregated, and she was guaranteed plenty of attention. If no one took any notice of her at feed times, she would bang her feet on the door until they did.

Throughout the winter she developed well and though they were reluctant to admit it even to each other, Charlie and Nick both thought she had real Classic potential. It was a lot to hope for, and there was always the danger that she wouldn't train on or wouldn't stay beyond the six furlongs at which she had already won. But, if anything, she looked as if she'd improve at a longer trip and as the year opened, everything was in front of her.

Willow Star's first major target was the One Thousand Guineas at Newmarket. Nick had spent many long winter hours absorbed in the form book and calculated that she had to improve by at least five pounds to have a realistic chance of a place. The top fillies' race at the back end of the last season had produced some talented youngsters. One in particular, a filly called Lightbeam, had been very impressive winning at Newmarket and was already three to one favourite for the Guineas. As Willow Star hadn't run since June, she could be backed at almost any price and Nick and Charlie were worried that she might have become ring rusty after such a long lay-off.

The main prep races before the first Classic of the season came only a couple of weeks before it. It would be taking a risk to let Willow have her first run in one of them. If they found she needed another run for experience, it would be too late then.

They thought about taking her to a racecourse for a full-blown gallop but that was never quite the same. The cut and thrust of a race could never be simulated. In the end, they opted for the unusual step of taking her to the south of France, to Cagnes-sur-Mer on the Côte d'Azur where competitive racing and good ground happened earlier. They phoned to find that the going was good and there was a suitable race for her. What was more, if she won, she would more than cover the expenses of getting there. And, just as important, she seemed to love travelling.

To save money, Charlie went as a groom with Titch

and flew in the plane with the horses. They arrived with their own supply of hay and water two days before the race, to give her time to settle down. The following morning, Titch took her for a spin round the outside of the track while Charlie stood on the rails and watched through his binoculars.

'How did she go?'

Titch shrugged his shoulders. 'I don't know. It's difficult to tell. I couldn't say that there's anything wrong with her.' He hesitated slightly. 'It's just she doesn't seem as perky as normal. Maybe it's being in a strange place.'

'Oh hell,' Charlie muttered. 'I hope this wasn't a bad decision. My father'll be livid if I've brought her all the way here and she doesn't win anything.'

Titch jumped down and plucked a handful of grass and offered it to the filly. She took it, then, uninterested, let it fall to the ground.

'Maybe she'll be better tomorrow,' the lad said doubtfully.

When he returned to the lads' hostel where he and Titch were staying, Charlie phoned Nick. He needed reassuring that they were doing the right thing for the filly. He couldn't decide whether he should withdraw her or not, or how much damage she might do to herself if he let her run when she wasn't well. Her temperature was normal, but as Titch had said, she just didn't seem a hundred per cent.

After a long, rambling discussion, they decided to let her take her chance.

In the morning, a warm drizzle drifted in off the

Mediterranean. Charlie felt as grey as the thick clouds above as he and Titch ate their breakfast in the canteen.

'She seems a bit perkier today,' he said.

'I wonder if they'll even run if this rain keeps up all day.'

'I bloody well hope so. Having come all this way, I'd like us at least to have a crack.'

Willow Star had eaten up well. Charlie gave her a little water and a couple of scoops of rolled oats first thing. 'That's your lot, darling, until you've gone out and won this poxy race,' he said.

At eight thirty, Titch led her out to stretch her legs.

Ideally, Charlie would have chosen Owen Williams to ride the filly again, but the Welsh jockey was committed to a winter riding contract in India. Instead, Charlie had booked Jean-Yves Ribello, a swarthy native of the Midi who specialised in the southern French tracks. Charlie had seen him ride a few times and despite the Frenchman's lack of finesse, he was confident he would give her a good ride.

Charlie spent the morning at the stableyard with Titch. He wasn't interested in going anywhere else or out to lunch. By the time the race was due to be run, he felt as if they had been on the racetrack for a week.

Jean-Yves appeared in the parade ring looking dapper in Major Patterson's colours and leaped on to his mount with a confident grin. Willow Star left happily for the start with her short, energetic stride and her two connections began to feel more hopeful.

Two furlongs from home, their hopes collapsed.

Jean-Yves Ribello had put her in front, as instructed, and she had pulled two lengths clear at five furlongs. In the next three, the rest of the field had moved up and eclipsed her. Major Patterson's red and gold diabolo was clearly visible at the back of the field.

Before the winning horse had reached the post, Charlie and Titch had lowered their glasses. The race had ceased to hold any interest for them.

Chapter Six

A misty March sun rose over the Berkshire Downs as Charlie, Nick and Kate walked towards the crest of a treeless hill. They stopped and turned. A distant rumble, a sound which a hundred years before might have augured the advance of a hostile army, floated up the empty slopes through the still, spring air. Growing in volume, it wasn't yet loud enough to drown the long liquid trill of a curlew circling above his nesting ground in the valley below.

Kate, ankle-deep in dewy, dark green grass, shivered in her sheepskin coat; the sound of galloping hooves still thrilled her. She raised a pair of binoculars to her eyes.

A moment later, the first horse broke the skyline, moving in a fluid, unrelenting gallop. A bright red exercise sheet flapped lazily over the shining golden bay of its rippling quarters. Kate shivered again. She shook her crop of short black hair and a smile spread across her face. Charlie had been right. Willow Star was back to her best. She had arrived home from France with a temperature, though nobody knew what had caused it.

Within four days she'd recovered. As they watched her now, she was pulling away from her galloping companions while her jockey struggled to hold her.

They didn't speak as seven horses thundered close by them, past the six-furlong marker and on to the end of the broad strip of mown turf on the grassy hillside.

As the horses began to pull up into a steaming circle, Kate lowered her binoculars. She turned to Charlie and grinned.

'She's brilliant! I've never seen her work so well.'

Charlie nodded. His blue eyes gleamed confidently, but not complacently. 'And she'll get quicker. Maybe she'll peak in May, at York.'

'Let's hope,' Kate said, breathless in the crisp air. 'You're still sure she likes six furlongs best?' Over the last few months, Kate had been following Willow Star's career much more closely. She hadn't actually moved in to Charlie and Nick's bungalow, but she was there more often than at her own cottage. She got on well with the lads and knew the form of every one of the thirty-two horses at Oak Hollow.

Charlie put his arm round her shoulder. 'I'm not sure of anything now; I don't think she'd mind ten furlongs, but she'll shine more at six.'

Nick, silent until then, joined the conversation. He'd been meaning to say what he was thinking for weeks. 'I hope she wins something big soon, then maybe your stepfather will settle his bills.' The words sounded harsher than he'd intended.

Charlie was astonished. 'How much does he owe?'

'About six months' worth.'

'Including Cagnes?'

Nick nodded.

'Why the hell didn't you tell me before?'

'I didn't want to embarrass you, and anyway, people like him only don't pay if they can't.'

Nick was right, Charlie reflected. It was very out of character for Major Patterson to owe money to anyone – especially his stepson. For her first six months' training the previous year, Willow Star had paid for herself with her winnings.

They made their way back to the yard. When the horses filed in, wrapped in a misty haze of sweat and hot breath in cold air, Kate held Willow Star while Titch washed the mud from her feet and sponged off the sweat marks around her girth. When he'd led her into her freshly strawed box, he stripped her off to let her roll.

The next lot were only cantering, not working. Charlie, Kate and Nick walked the hundred yards from the handsome three-sided brick yard to the unprepossessing pebble-dashed bungalow.

Inside, the place was beginning to look more like the country cottage they wished it was. Nick had always had a good eye at an auction and in his spare time, he enjoyed stripping down and restoring old pieces of country furniture. Although Charlie's stepfather dealt in high quality antiques, he had given them nothing. His mother, though, had produced a few handsome old kilims, and the walls were crowded with undistinguished equestrian oil paintings in battered frames, photographs of horses racing, rugby teams, college groups – an edited pictorial history of their lives. New curtains and well-chosen paint had transformed the feel of the place and when the wood-burner in the kitchen was going in the early morning, it was positively cosy.

Soon the kitchen was filled with the smell of fresh coffee and grilled bacon. Nick, with Hercules his dog weaving hopefully between his legs, cooked and served up breakfast on the worn elm table which doubled as their office desk.

They were discussing plans for one of the two-year-olds when the phone rang. Nick leaned back in his chair and picked it up from among the clutter on the oak dresser behind him.

'Hello?' He was still munching a piece of toast. 'Oh, good morning, sir . . . I'm sorry to hear that.' He choked slightly on his toast and a worried look spread across his already serious face.

Kate glanced at Charlie, asking with a gesture what it could be about. Charlie shook his head and shrugged.

'Oh . . . Oh. I see,' Nick said. 'Do you really think that's a good idea? It might be helpful if I ran through the likely outcome if you keep her in training with us for the rest of the season . . .'

Nick sounded calm enough but Charlie noticed with sudden alarm that his face was reddening and the pencil he was holding snapped in his hand. Charlie hadn't seen his partner look so angry since they were both at school, when a notorious bully had picked on him all term. On that occasion some inner force that had never shown itself before seemed to burst out of Nick. He'd flung himself on his tormentor and thrashed him senseless. It had taken four boys to pull him off, and no one had ever pestered him again.

He was angry now but he hadn't lost control. He was speaking in a quiet monotone whose menace might have been lost down a telephone line. 'If you don't mind my saying so, I think you're making a serious mistake.' Nick waited while the other party apparently ranted at him. 'Yes, sir,' he went on as if he was talking to a dim child, 'but at the end of this season she could be worth twice that. And of course we could come to some arrangement about your outstanding fees.'

Charlie, beside himself with impatience, got up and walked round the table to switch on the telephone loudspeaker. He immediately recognised the angry voice that burst into the room. 'How dare you patronise me. For a start, I've agreed terms with Jarvis. Secondly, she's my horse; I paid what I was asked, to help out my son, and you too. Now I think I have the right to do what I want without seeking your permission. I've done quite enough already, and I did it for Charlie, not for you. I'm sorry if you're having trouble making ends meet, but I blame you for leading Charlie into it when he's too young, not ready for the responsibility of looking after other people's expensive horses.'

Nick, shaking with anger, was holding the phone with a white-knuckled fist. All the colour had drained from his face, he was sweating and breathing in short gasps. He tried to speak but the disembodied voice went on.

'You've always had too much influence over Charles. You're brighter than he is; you've always known it and taken advantage of his good nature and loyalty, riding on the back of his personal popularity, using his gifts to supplement your own weaknesses. Now, I've told you what's happening. I don't want to discuss it further.'

A click followed by a dialling tone echoed from the phone's speaker. Nick slowly lowered the receiver, placed it back in its cradle. He let out a long hiss. 'Fuck you, you arrogant bastard!'

'For God's sake,' Charlie barked. 'What did he say first?'

'He's sold Willow Star to Robert Jarvis – for eighty grand! And you know Jarvis won't let anyone but his brother-in-law train for him.'

'Shit!' Charlie thumped the table and stared angrily at two fried eggs on his plate. He glanced up at Nick. 'Eighty grand for a filly that cost ten! And he didn't even have the decency to tell me himself.'

'But surely,' Kate joined in, 'she'll be worth much more than that if she goes well this season.'

'Of course,' Charlie said, 'if she does. But there's a school of thought that advises taking a profit on a horse whenever it's on offer. And if my stepfather hasn't been paying his training bills, he must be desperate.' He shook his head. 'It's pathetic. There's a man who commanded a squadron in the SAS, must have been responsible for taking out dozens of terrorists and other human dregs, probably not giving a shit for his own life. And now he's being eaten alive by a bunch of grasping hyenas at Lloyd's.'

Nick nodded, resigned. 'He says Willow will have to go some time in the next couple of weeks. He'll let us know and settle any outstanding bills from the proceeds. You'll have to try and persuade him to hang on to her. Tell him how much more she'll be worth.'

'He's not going to take any notice of me.'

'Maybe he'd listen to your mother.'

Charlie was doubtful. 'He might, I suppose. But he's almost impossible to turn once he's made up his mind.'

'I'll go and see him,' Nick volunteered. 'See if I can patch things up.'

'Don't be crazy, Nick. You've done enough damage already. You just couldn't stop yourself trying to lecture him, could you? You really should know by now how he'd react.'

'For God's sake, Charlie. What was I supposed to say?'

'You should have handed him straight to me.'

'He didn't want to talk to you. He didn't want to be the one to tell you he was taking away the best bloody horse in the yard. And I don't know what the hell you think you could have done better.'

Charlie glared back at Nick. In the fifteen years they'd known each other they had seldom argued; when they did, it seemed all the harsher. 'You pompous arsehole! You always think you're bloody right!'

Kate looked on, horrified. She'd never heard the two friends insult each other like this. 'Charlie, for heaven's sake, calm down.' She grabbed his arm. 'Come on. Come outside with me before you say something you'll regret.'

With an angry snort and a toss of his head, Charlie followed her through the back door and slammed it behind him.

Nick looked after him, quite still.

Patterson's words had cut him more deeply than his friends could have guessed. Charlie's lack of support had made them worse. And besides all this, just as the yard was looking as if it had a real chance of succeeding, their best animal was going.

Nick leaned over and pulled a bottle of whisky from the back of the dresser and sloshed a long measure into a glass.

He blamed himself. He'd panicked and completely mishandled Major Patterson; Charlie was right, he'd been ridiculously pompous and put the man's back up. Now it was up to him to put it right. It would take guts, patience and a helping of humble pie.

He took another swig of whisky and gagged. The phone rang on the dresser behind him. He leaned over and grabbed it.

'Hello,' he said with gruff curtness.

'Hello. Mr Patterson or Mr Ryder?' An ingratiating, nasal male voice. Nick wondered what it was trying to sell.

'This is Nick Ryder.'

'Oh, great. Geoff Haslam here, *Racing News*.'

Nick was immediately on his guard. He said nothing.

'I was wondering if there was any decision over the filly, Willow Star?'

Nick guessed the journalist wanted to know if she was

still aiming for the first of the Classics.

'About the Guineas?'

'Yeah.'

'No.' Nick said.

'There's no decision or no she's not running?'

'No decision,' Nick said, wanting the man to get off the phone.

There was a moment's pause before the next question. 'Is she staying in your yard?'

Nick felt a nasty lurch in the pit of his stomach. 'What are you talking about?'

'I've heard she might be going.'

'Who from?'

'From her owner – her ex-owner.'

Nick couldn't believe Charlie's stepfather had compounded his disloyalty like this. 'What do you mean? Who told you?'

'Major Patterson. I heard a rumour, I phoned the major. He confirmed it.'

'The bastard!' Nick spluttered before he could stop himself.

'Oh dear,' the journalist murmured gleefully. 'Been a bit of bust-up then?'

'I'm not going to talk about it.'

'You don't need to, Nick. Thanks for your help.' The journalist put the phone down before Nick could.

Nick crashed the receiver back into its cradle, furious with himself, with Charlie, with Patterson, and with the nasty little shit of a journalist who was going to make Willow Star almost irretrievable for them.

★ ★ ★

Willow Star took her nose from her manger for a moment, glanced up and gave a quick snort of recognition.

Kate leaned on the bottom door of her stable and gazed at the small, robust filly. She vividly remembered the misty morning, eighteen months before, when she had first set eyes on her, trapped in the wire by the brook on Cyril Barton's farm. And it was almost as long since she'd first set eyes on Charlie Patterson. Now it was hard to imagine there had ever been a time when she hadn't known him. She still thought he was vain and devoid of any intellectual ambition, but he was also optimistic, vital, kind-hearted, funny and a good, strong lover. On balance, she thought she was lucky.

The filly nuzzled her. Kate gave her another carrot and stroked her nose with vigorous affection. It was, after all, Willow who had brought her and Charlie together. Kate wished it was in her power to do something, anything, to keep the animal at Oak Hollow.

Prudence Patterson stepped down from the double-decker bus which had carried her from the grey-brown, windswept open spaces of Wormwood Scrubs to the pulsing, vibrant-hued crowds swirling around Notting Hill Gate.

A session at the prison always left her in a confused state of elation and depression. There were moments of triumph to be gained from the occasional successes she felt she had achieved, when she could see the light of new hope and aspiration beginning to spark in the eyes of one or other of the inmates she had been working with. Sometimes, she would be rewarded with a piece of writing so remarkable it would have made the hardest of hardened publishers cry. But too often these turned out to be flashes in the pan, unrepeatable one-offs. She wondered, not for the first time, why she did it and as usual failed to come up with a thoroughly satisfactory answer.

A quiet, grey speck among the cacophony of colour and energy all around her, Pru was just fifty, small, neat, sturdy and easy to look at. She turned off the main road into one of the back streets which led up the gentle hill towards the upper part of Kensington.

In a road that lay parallel to Church Street, near its highest point, she let herself through a door in a dun brick wall. It gave into a small yard which someone had attempted optimistically, perhaps twenty years before, to turn into a garden. Now it contained a rusty bicycle, some discarded pieces of Formica kitchen furniture and a rotten hammock strung between the single small horse chestnut tree and a ring in the wall. Facing her was the disorganised paraphernalia of additional plumbing and central heating flues that had been tacked on to the back wall of the large, mid-Victorian terraced building in which she and her husband lived.

The building faced Church Street and the ground floor had been converted into a shop, or showrooms, as people in the antique trade liked to call their premises. The basement served as an extra stockroom, which meant that in the ten years Major David Patterson had been in business it had become stuffed with his mistakes.

Pru opened the back door of the house, planning, at first, to creep upstairs without disturbing her husband in the showroom. But she heard his voice, and paused to listen.

'Well, I'm sorry, too,' he was saying. 'But there it is. I can't magic the money out of thin air, and you people have already had nearly everything I own. I'm afraid you've reached the bottom of the barrel. There's nothing left but the dregs.'

There was a pause in his voice as the other person replied. Then he spoke again. 'The cottage is rented to me for a peppercorn by an old regimental friend. This building's on a lease, with no capital value. Most of the stock in the shop belongs to clients, in here on sale-or-return. The only stock I own is more or less worthless. Frankly, you might just as well write me off as a lost cause – a burnt-out case. There's nothing else to take.' Though he spoke quietly, there was no escaping the bitterness in his voice. 'I wish to God I'd never given you anything. I know now I should have struck out like all those other Names. I thought they were whingeing and dishonouring their pledges at the time but, I have to say, if they get you shown up for the bunch of crooks you are, I'll be right back in there with them, suing for every penny you squeezed out of me . . .'

Pru had sidled up the corridor to the door which opened into the showroom by the bottom of the stairs. She couldn't see her husband directly where he sat at an inlaid escritoire towards the back of the shop, but she could see him clearly reflected in a large ormolu-framed mirror. He had stopped talking and from the way he was staring at the telephone she guessed that the other party had hung up. He put the phone back and leaned forward on his elbows with his head in his hands.

Pru tiptoed up the stairs to the flat into which they had moved when David had been forced to sell their London house the year before. She longed to help him, but he wouldn't allow it, wouldn't even discuss it. She knew from hard experience that she couldn't push him into revealing any more than he wanted to. It had been a regular feature of their strange life together that when he felt the world closing in on him, he would simply disappear, sometimes for a day or two, sometimes for weeks without giving her a clue where he was. When it had first happened, Pru had been hurt and wanted to be angry. She worried that he was being unfaithful but in time she had convinced herself this wasn't the reason for his absences and she became used to them, even understood them. He always came home calm and free of whatever demon had been pursuing him.

David Patterson lifted his head to gaze at the framed photographs propped on the desk in front of him: Pru, who had made only the smallest demands on him throughout their marriage, and who never complained now that even these small demands could not be met; Charlie, his adopted son and only child, whom he had brought up at long distance while the army, then the job in Saudi Arabia, had kept him away from England. Charlie who had gratefully accepted a substitute father, called him 'Dad' and, as a boy, had treated him with the informal affection of a real son.

Next to the picture of Charlie was a photo he had sent of the filly, Willow Star. She was a very handsome animal, Patterson thought. It was a shame she had to go. Charlie would be shattered, let down again. Patterson knew perfectly well that the filly had provided the only real taste of success in Charlie's first year as a public trainer. It was a cruel irony that this success had made the filly already worth appreciably more than he'd paid for her. If she had performed only moderately, or inconclusively, she wouldn't be worth selling.

He was deeply ashamed of himself for telling Nick but he just hadn't been able to break the news to Charlie himself. Besides, he admitted to some satisfaction in hearing Nick so uncomfortable. It was as if in hurting Nick, he was hurting his father. And it was Nick's father, Roland Ryder, who was responsible for much of his troubles. It was Roland Ryder who had suggested he should join a number of Lloyd's syndicates in which he had an interest. The Ryders had invited him and Pru to lunch, shortly after the boys had left school and he'd come back from Saudi. At the time, and on Lloyd's past record, it seemed madness not to join and you didn't even have to put up much of the money, leaving your capital free to work twice for you.

Now he despised Ryder senior for making a fool of him, for standing by while he went bust. And that spite had spilled over on to Nick whom he had never liked anyway, and who had always had far more influence over his stepson than he had himself. He knew Nick had done nothing wrong and sometimes cringed with guilt that he should be so unpleasant to Charlie's oldest, most loyal friend.

And he hated letting Charlie down. There had been a time, he knew, when his own code of personal conduct wouldn't have allowed it. He just hoped that Charlie would understand. He and Pru had to survive.

Charlie rattled home to Lambourn through the late spring sunset in his rusty Range Rover. Despite the looming crisis over Willow Star, he was pleased with himself; it showed in his handsome, honest face, and he didn't mind who saw it. He'd saddled two of their three jumpers at Stratford and sent home a winner and a third. If the tapedeck in the car hadn't been broken, he would have played something festive on it. The yard still wasn't making much of a profit yet but at least it was, as they say, washing its own face and providing him and Nick with a sort of living. There was the real prospect of a future shared with Kate and he was even prepared to kid himself that they might find a way of hanging on to Willow Star.

Nick had obstinately insisted that it was up to him to make amends for the disastrous phone call. Charlie had half convinced himself that Nick could persuade his mother to talk his stepfather out of selling the filly. Surely it was obvious that the potential long-term profit to be made was far too great to cash her in now.

Charlie parked his Range Rover behind the red-brick

boxes and walked round into the yard. Evening stables were just finishing. Heads of horses eager for their supper protruded from most of the thirty boxes.

Charlie strode across to a storeroom in one corner where Kenny was mixing the evening feeds. When he'd checked that nothing in the yard needed his urgent attention, he walked down to find Nick in the office.

Nick looked up as Charlie's cheerful face appeared and regretted that he was going to have to dowse the sunbeam smile.

'Well done,' he said first, acknowledging their winner. 'Did you have a punt?'

Charlie nodded. 'I did, as a matter of fact. They both looked absolutely outstanding so I had some on each. But we still made a profit.'

Nick nodded his older, wiser head. He wasn't in fact older but he thought in a more responsible way than his partner. It was his function to provide financial stability in the business. 'I think we've made more money punting than we have training so far this year.'

'A bit of inside knowledge is a trainer's perk. Silly not to use it.'

Nick was prepared to agree with him. 'We could do with a big hit just now. The prize money kitty isn't looking great, and a lot of it last year came from Willow Star. Now I'm afraid it looks as though we're definitely going to lose her. Your father rang again.'

Charlie gritted his teeth, annoyed at having his day's success soured by the reality of Willow Star's imminent departure. 'What did he have to say this time?'

'Not a lot. Told me I was a complete amateur for talking to the press. Thank God Haslam didn't make too much of the story. I think your father was worried that some of his creditors would pick it up, but fortunately I don't think that's happened. Anyway, he's had confirmation of Jarvis's offer of eighty grand.'

Charlie still couldn't quite believe that his stepfather was about to sell the filly. He hadn't spoken a word to him about it.

'I think I'll go and see him, grovel, apologise, do whatever it takes,' Nick said eventually.

Charlie looked at his friend and raised an eyebrow. 'I think you'll need to do more than grovel. What we need is a plan – a leaseback, maybe, that'll let him keep the horse. We really need her if we're going to get noticed this year.'

Nick got up from his desk. 'Okay, I'm not too hopeful but it's worth a try.' He walked to the door. 'I'm going up to find Kenny to check this vet's bill,' he said waving a light green invoice. 'I'm sure they've been charging us for things we haven't had.'

Charlie followed him out of the bungalow and watched him for a moment, walking away with his awkward, unathletic gait. Nick might lack charm and good looks but he was his own, secure man. He knew his weaknesses but he knew his strengths, too, and built on them. Charlie was in no doubt that Nick was a better man than he was, a good counter-balance to his own exuberance and tendency towards bad judgement.

Charlie turned and went back into the bungalow,

thinking about Kate, Willow Star, and his father's cold aloofness.

David Patterson made one last trip to the shippers to make sure the consignment had been correctly packed.

There were twenty-eight pieces in all, one of the biggest single collections in the world of furniture by François Linke. This would be the biggest, most impressive deal Patterson had ever done, and it was happening just when he most needed it. In a way, he was sorry that no one but his client was ever going to know about it, but the client didn't want any publicity, and nor did he.

The furniture of François Linke had always been something of a speciality of David Patterson's. He had been fascinated by it ever since his father had told him about the staggering lengths to which the furniture maker would go to achieve what he considered perfection. The style was too ornate for some tastes but in the right setting and to someone who appreciated craftsmanship at its very zenith, it was in a class of its own.

Born to a poor family somewhere in Czechoslovakia in the late 1800s, François Linke eventually made his way to Paris and set himself up in a small workshop beside the Seine. He was well established by the time the Exposition Universelle was held in Paris in 1900, on which he staked his reputation and every sous he possessed to build and exhibit an outstanding collection of furniture. Each piece was made from tulip wood and mounted with sculpted brass in the style of Louis XV. The centrepiece was a *grand bureau*, measuring almost five feet in height. It was the most elaborate project Linke had ever undertaken and, as was his normal practice, he kept a minutely detailed record of the work involved. The chiselling for the cast bronzes alone took his men six thousand nine hundred hours, and another three thousand six hundred to mount them.

Like most men at the time, François Linke was in the habit of rolling his own cigarettes. When he was inspecting a piece, he would take out one of his cigarette papers and if he could pass it between the wood and the moulding, he would send it back to be refitted. In all, the *grand bureau* took thirty-one thousand eight hundred and ninety-three hours to complete. It was acclaimed as the finest piece he had ever made and was quickly snapped up by one of the Romanovs. Not to be outdone, King Wilhelm II of Prussia ordered an identical one. The castle where it stood was destroyed by German troops in 1942 and most of the furniture was destroyed with it or stolen. No one was sure of the fate of the *grand bureau.*

When Major Patterson informed his old employer, Sheikh Sala Mahmoud, that he had found an original *grand bureau*, along with a large collection of other Linke pieces, the Sheikh had agreed to buy the lot, provided the deal attracted no publicity. Patterson had been given some of the money in advance, which had paid for the goods. The balance would be paid into an account he had opened in Switzerland specifically to accommodate it, as soon as the furniture arrived in France. He knew Sala Mahmoud wouldn't let him down;

at least, he hoped to hell he wouldn't, but to have asked for all the money up front would have killed the deal – the only good thing that had happened to Patterson in four devastating years.

He had been the Saudi sheikh's chief security adviser for several years after he left the British army. Sala Mahmoud had taken over where men like Khashoggi had left off. He dealt in arms and military hardware with anyone who could pay. He had shown his appreciation of Patterson's skills and experience with a substantial salary and a more than generous package of perks. But, even with his well-known talent for detachment, Patterson found it hard to work for Sala Mahmoud. He had been pleased enough, though, when his ex-employer had turned up to see him in London the previous autumn. It was the first time he had seen Sala Mahmoud in nine years, but it was clear that the Arab had kept himself informed of his activities.

Sala Mahmoud was based, to the French authorities' impotent frustration, in a large estate outside Paris. Guarded like a fortress for other reasons, it also provided a safe setting for the priceless objects for which the sheikh had developed a collector's taste. He had discovered that his mansion had once housed a large collection of François Linke furniture and he was obsessed with the idea of re-establishing it. He had gone to Patterson because he knew the ex-soldier was as knowledgeable as anyone about Linke. He had asked him to get as much of it together as he could, keeping him informed of the prices as he did so. The added bonus of the *grand bureau* had completely hooked the Arab.

The sea of Patterson's financial troubles was just about to close above his head when the deal was agreed. And this time he was going to keep the profits for himself. He had taken elaborate precautions to obscure his identity when he had arranged the purchase of the furniture and its shipment. If word got out in the trade, it might well find its way back to one of the institutions to whom he owed money. He should see a profit of a little short of a million pounds on the whole transaction. Provided he kept it to himself, he could live out his days with Pru in comfort, somewhere quiet and warm and a long way from England. If he didn't do it, there was no way out; they would be left with nothing.

He didn't have any difficulty keeping his activities from Pru. He'd never discussed his work with her, since the days when he was specifically banned from doing so by his military bosses. But now he would have to tell her certain details of his plans, or she might let something out inadvertently. In any event, he was absolutely certain of her loyalty.

The last pieces of furniture were now being wrapped for carriage to Sala Mahmoud's mansion in the Forest of Fontainebleau.

Patterson checked the documentation with the shipper, confirmed the arrangements which would trigger his payment and drove his elderly Mercedes back to Kensington through the late afternoon rush hour.

Once in the flat, he assumed the air of impecuniousness that had become habitual when dealing with creditors. Pru regarded him affectionately. Guiltily, he wondered why she put up with him and the string of financial disasters he seemed to have attracted. But she seemed to know him almost better than he knew himself and to appreciate him for qualities which he considered less than desirable – his aloofness, his total aversion to depending on others.

In the small sitting room on the first floor above the shop, Patterson opened a drinks cupboard – a good Georgian bow front – which contained two bottles of cheap Scotch, a bottle of sherry and a few bottles of Bulgarian red wine. He sighed and hoped fervently that within a week or so he'd be in a position to buy some serious claret without having to look at the price.

'Sherry?' he asked his wife.

She nodded.

He poured one, and a large Scotch for himself. 'How have you been?' he asked.

'Okay.' Pru realised he didn't want to talk about his own problems and related that she'd had a letter from one of her ex-inmates, wanting to talk about his writing.

'Who's that?'

'A chap called Brian Tennent. You may remember, he was supposed to come down and do a bit of decorating at the cottage – well over a year ago now. He never turned up though.'

'Was that the chap who rang later and said he'd got lost and gone home?'

'That's the one. He's an odd specimen but quite bright, with a fascinatingly macabre perspective on life. Not without humour, either.'

'What was he in prison for?'

Pru explained rather ashamedly that he had killed two schoolchildren while being chased in his car by police, having just robbed a building society.

The major tutted and shook his head. 'Well, if you want to help him, that's up to you.' He wanted to add 'but you're a fool' but didn't.

Later, over a supper of pasta and Bulgarian wine, he told her about the piece that had appeared in the *Racing News* and of his recent phone conversations with Nick.

Pru's face fell. 'Oh, David. Poor boys. Did you have to? After Charles did so well with the filly last year.'

'Frankly, it's only a matter of time before one of my creditors latches on to the fact that I own the animal, especially if she does as well as everyone hopes this year. If I sell her to Jarvis, he can pay me abroad where Lloyd's can't get at it.'

'But are you sure that's safe? And is it strictly legal?'

'It's safe enough, and it's strictly illegal.'

'But David, won't you get into trouble? I mean, it's rather unlike you to do that sort of thing.'

'It might have been once, but quite frankly I haven't got much choice. I've been a complete fool up until now. I've played it by the book while the people who conned me grabbed my money and laughed. But don't worry, I won't get into trouble. I was thinking it would be warmer and a lot cheaper if we moved out to Cyprus. You liked it when I was posted there, didn't you?'

Pru sighed. 'Up to a point. But I was jolly glad to settle in England when we finally did. Still, if that's all we can afford, I suppose I could cope.'

'It just might be expedient for other reasons, too,' Patterson said.

Chapter Seven

Nick drove his new red Subaru estate car slowly between the high banks of a lane which ran down towards the River Kennet; the lane was barely wide enough to accommodate his car and, since he'd set out, he was less eager to reach his destination. He was looking for the turning to Birch Lodge, the cottage where Major Patterson and his wife usually spent their weekends.

Lying below the high grassland hills of the Downs, it was one of several houses on a small estate belonging to General Sir Peter Sheridan, ex-CO of the Irish Guards as well as the 22nd SAS Regiment at Hereford at the time David Patterson had commanded his squadron there. The general had told Patterson he would be welcome to a cottage, at a peppercorn rent, provided he kept the place in good order. Patterson, knowing he'd meant it, had taken him up on the offer without embarrassment as soon as he had settled back in England.

Nick glimpsed the general's big Edwardian house through a screen of trees, carefully planted a hundred years before. He turned in at the next entrance. There was a rough drive leading away into the dense woodland to the left immediately inside the gate. Nick drove in through the tunnel of trees as Charlie had told him to that morning.

A hundred and twenty yards along the track, round a slight bend, the cottage came into view, tucked in a clearing ringed with spindly birches.

Major Patterson's Mercedes was parked outside. According to Charlie, they had driven down separately, Pru having returned from a visit to her parents in Devon.

Nick wasn't sure that he could handle Patterson without Pru there to mediate. On the other hand, if he was going to do anything to keep Willow, it had to be done now, before Jarvis finalised the deal.

He parked the Subaru on a patch of rough ground beside the cottage and walked across to ring the bell at the front door.

It was a few moments before Major Patterson appeared. He looked as spruce as he always did, in a soft tweed jacket, crisp beige shirt, cavalry twill trousers and gleaming conker-brown brogues. When Nick saw him, his heart fell. Patterson was patently angry at the unexpected interruption.

As Nick was stepping into the cottage, Pru Patterson was finishing her shopping for groceries in Hungerford. Thirty minutes later, she pulled into the drive of Birch Lodge, parked her car next to her husband's Mercedes and went inside.

The moment she shut the front door behind her, she

could sense that something was wrong. She put her bulging shopping bag on the table in the hall and walked nervously through to the small sitting room, calling her husband's name. There was nothing but an eerie silence for a reply. As she entered the room, she put her hand to her mouth and let out a gasp.

Papers were scattered all over the carpet, the contents of drawers had been tipped out on to the floor. The sofas and chairs had been ripped apart. Carpets had been pulled up and floorboards jemmied from their joists.

Then she saw the body.

The shock set her trembling.

Gazing at the blood-stained grey hair around the vicious headwound and the familiar clothes, she struggled to absorb what had happened. She wanted to be sick and forced herself to turn away.

Her first instinct was to phone Charlie. She rushed into the study, also in a state of chaos, picked up the phone and, with trembling fingers, keyed the number at Oak Hollow. Before it started to ring, she dipped the plunger to cut it off.

She started again; this time she pressed 999. 'Hello? Emergency services? Police, please . . .' Pru was amazed at how calm she sounded. 'Hello? Yes. My husband's been killed – murdered . . . Yes. I've just found him . . . Please, please come now!'

They asked for the address and, once Pru had given them directions, told her they'd be there in a matter of minutes.

Pru took a deep breath, and dialled Charlie's number again. It rang six, seven times before he answered.

'Mum,' he said, sounding out of breath. 'I was outside, on the point of driving over to see you.'

'Charlie, something awful's happened.' There was barely a quiver in Pru's voice.

A catalogue of potentially awful things ran through Charlie's head. There was silence. 'Mum, what! What happened?'

'Your father's been killed. I've just found him.'

'Good God! How? Why? What from, do you know?'

'Someone's broken in and killed him. The whole house is in a terrible mess.'

'What about you? Are you all right?'

'Yes, yes. I'm all right. I wasn't here. Someone must have been trying to burgle the house.'

Charlie's thoughts lurched abruptly to Nick and his planned visit. Only he knew that Nick was going to the cottage that day. They had decided it would be better if they didn't warn his mother or stepfather that he was coming.

But what had happened to him? Had he decided not to go through with it?

Or had he been and gone before the murderer turned up?

Or . . .

Charlie could scarcely formulate the thought.

No. It just wasn't possible. And yet . . .

Charlie remembered Nick's rare but very real outbursts of anger under intense provocation.

No, he thought again. Nick had neither the strength nor the skill to overcome his stepfather.

'Have you rung the police?'

'Yes, of course, they're on their way.'

A thought suddenly crossed Charlie's mind, and his stomach churned. 'Mum, whoever did it may still be hanging around. I'll come round straight away.'

'No,' his mother said, firmly. 'Don't. It's such an awful sight. I couldn't bear you to see David like this. I'll lock myself in until the police arrive.'

'Mum, what are you talking about? I'll be right over.'

'Please don't come until they've been. There's no reason why you should have to deal with this.' There was no mistaking the earnestness of her plea.

Charlie didn't press her. 'Okay,' he said, 'if you're sure. Ring me as soon as they've gone and I'll come over and stay.'

'Thank you, Charles. I'll ring you later. Goodbye, dear.'

Pru put the phone down and glanced at the embers of the fire. Looking around the room, distraught but in control, she noticed a beer tankard on a table beside one of the big armchairs.

David never drank beer.

She didn't touch the glass in case it had any fingerprints on it.

To calm her nerves, she took another glass from a cabinet and filled it with dry sherry. She sat down, sipped the drink and waited. When she heard a police siren approaching, she rose to her feet and rushed through to the kitchen to rinse out her glass and leave it on the drainer.

The siren echoed down the tunnel of trees and then the police car skidded to a dust-swirling halt where Nick's Subaru had sat earlier. Two uniformed men and a plainclothes officer leaped out and ran to the front door.

Pru let them in without a word and waved them towards the small drawing room where, among the mess and confusion, a blood-stained poker lay on the carpet beside the body.

Nick walked in through the back door of the bungalow at Oak Hollow, looking as if he'd seen a ghost.

'What the hell has happened?' Charlie stammered. 'What have you been up to?'

Nick didn't answer at once. He walked past his partner into the kitchen and sat down at the table.

'My mother phoned. She'd just found my father, dead.' Charlie stopped for a moment. He was finding it hard to get the words out. 'He's been killed . . . murdered.'

'I saw him too,' Nick said flatly, resting his elbows on the table and putting his head in his hands.

Charlie noticed that his friend's right eye was slightly twitching. 'What? Was he dead when you got there?'

Nick shook his head. 'No, he asked me in.'

'You mean you were there when it happened?' Charlie asked, incredulous.

'Yes, I was. Pass me that Scotch and I'll tell you.' He mixed plenty of water into his drink and then met

Charlie's worried, doubtful eyes straight on. He took a deep breath.

'When I got to the cottage, your mother's car wasn't there. I almost turned and drove straight out again but your father would have seen me and . . . well, I thought I had to go in and get on with it. He opened the door but he didn't look at all pleased to see me. I said I hoped he didn't mind me dropping in. Amazingly, he said no, and asked me in.

'We went into that small sort of study, on the left as you go in. He'd obviously been sitting there. The fire was lit and there were loads of papers scattered on the desk. He sort of shuffled them away, as if he didn't want me to see them. I don't know what they were. Anyway, he asked me if I wanted a drink. I said I'd like a beer. He told me to put some more coal on the fire and went off. He was gone for a while, looking for some beer I thought, then came back with a can of lager and a glass. He said he'd had to get it from the cellar. Anyway, he poured himself a Scotch and sat down, still looking fairly twitchy. He said, "I suppose you've come to talk about that wretched filly."

'I wish I'd waited for your mother. His manner put me right off my stroke. I got the impression he had something very heavy on his mind. But I started blathering, like I did on the phone to him. When I suggested we might carry on training Willow for nothing, he suddenly lost his temper. He went mad. Began roaring, said I was patronising him.'

'What was he so upset about?'

'I don't know. Maybe he hated my talking to him about money. He also said the horse was already sold anyway. But not to Jarvis.'

'Shit,' Charlie exclaimed, forgetting his stepfather's death for a second. 'Who to?'

'He didn't say.'

'Hell!' Charlie shook his head. 'What happened next?'

'Well, I was pretty pissed off I hadn't managed to stop him selling Willow, so I started telling him how stupid he was. I don't know why I didn't just accept it, but I couldn't stop myself. He was furious. He leaped out of his chair absolutely ranting at me and I thought for a moment he was going to hit me. God knows what would have happened if he had, but suddenly he stopped himself, as if he'd just remembered something. He walked out of the room, closing the door behind him. I couldn't think what the hell he was doing. I couldn't hear him but I was sure he hadn't left the house. I sat and drank my beer for a bit, hoping he wasn't going to come back and start attacking me again when I heard glass breaking somewhere in the house and your stepfather yelling.'

'Who was he yelling at?' Charlie asked.

'Me. He was shouting my name and he sounded in a real panic, as if he needed my help. I rushed out of the study into the hall. I heard someone in the drawing room. The door was ajar. I pushed it open and went in. The place was a complete shambles. It had been ransacked. I couldn't believe the chaos. Then I saw your father. He was lying prostrate in front of the fire. There was blood all over the back of his head and he wasn't moving. I just couldn't believe it. I must have stared at him for a few seconds, then everything went blank.'

'What do you mean?'

'I mean someone hit me from behind and I blacked out. I don't remember a thing until I came round about a quarter of an hour later. It took me a while to realise where I was, lying on the carpet with a headache. Then I saw your father's feet across the floor. I got up and took another look. The mess on his head was terrible, and there was a poker with blood on it lying beside him. Thank God whoever it was didn't use it on me, too.'

'But Nick,' Charlie was looking at him closely, 'if the guy had already killed my father, why didn't he kill you?'

'I don't know, for God's sake. Maybe because he knew I hadn't seen him. I'm not complaining.'

'How bad is your head now?'

Nick reached up and felt the spot. 'The lump's gone down already, thank God.' When he saw the disbelief on Charlie's face, his heart sank. 'Hang on a minute, Charlie. You must believe me, for Christ's sake. You don't think I did it, do you?'

'I don't know what the hell I think, but it doesn't look good.'

Nick held the palms of his hands up in a gesture of innocence. 'I know, I know. Don't think I don't realise that, but I swear I didn't do it. Why should I? You must know I couldn't have done it!'

Charlie looked at him, hating the dilemma that faced him.

'Charlie,' Nick pleaded. 'You're the only person who knows I was there. The police won't ever connect me with it. Let them concentrate on catching whoever it was. It must have been a burglar. The place had been torn apart, I told you.'

'Okay,' Charlie sighed. 'I won't tell anyone you were there. But are you sure no one else saw you?'

'No, I'm not, but I don't think so. I was very careful when I drove out. I stopped and listened a couple of times to make sure there wasn't anyone else around, and there weren't any other cars about when I drove into the lane.'

'You didn't leave anything or write anything, did you?'

'No.'

'What about fingerprints?'

'I wiped the beer mug I'd used and the handle of the fire tongs in the study, and all the door handles I'd touched.'

'Was there any sign of anyone else?'

'When I came round and went back into the study, it had been ransacked as well. Somebody had been through all the drawers there while I was out for the count.'

'I wonder what they were looking for. I'm sure Dad didn't keep anything particularly valuable at the cottage, assuming he still owned anything valuable.'

'Maybe it was just a chance burglar your stepfather caught in the act. The place is fairly isolated, far enough from any other house for no one to hear or see.'

'Maybe.'

'Charlie, you still don't believe me, do you?'

'I'm sorry, Nick, God knows, I really am. It just seems such a coincidence for it to happen the only time you've ever been there.'

'Yes, well, coincidences do happen.'

'Well, I don't fancy your chances if the police get on to you.'

'You didn't tell your mother I'd been round?'

'No. I wanted to hear from you first. But the trouble is, if someone says they recognised you there, it'll look a lot worse if you haven't told the police.'

Nick gulped down a mouthful of Scotch. 'Don't think I haven't thought about that. But if that happens I'll just have to say I knew how compromising it would look and I was frightened to own up. That's all I can do.'

Two forensic officers arrived at Birch Lodge. They spent three hours finding very little, besides a set of fingerprints on the handle of the poker which had killed the major.

DI Mike Ferrier who was in charge of the investigation came back when his colleagues had finished in the house. He wanted to go over the afternoon's events one more time with the victim's widow. He sat in the study with her, drinking tea.

'Let me get this right, Mrs Patterson. You went out at ten, leaving your husband here, and when you returned about midday you found him dead and the place pulled apart. As far as you know, he was expecting no one and the only casual visitor who ever calls is the general.'

Pru nodded.

The detective looked at her for a moment without speaking. He stood and walked across the small room.

'This glass had beer in it; the other one whisky. Your husband's prints are on the whisky tumbler, but the beer mug has been deliberately wiped, and so have the door handles. This suggests that your husband was at least prepared to entertain whoever came here, don't you think? Though I wonder why they didn't wipe the poker handle too,' Ferrier mused. 'Anyway, the forensic blokes are just having a look around outside and then we'll be off. I'll need to see you again, I'm afraid, but I'll try not to make it too soon. The minute we've confirmed the cause of your husband's death, we'll be able to release his body for burial.'

'But surely the cause of death is obvious.'

'On the face of it, but there may be signs that he died of a heart attack or something else.'

'I see. Will you need me to make a formal identification?'

'No. That won't be necessary. I would suggest you either go and stay with a friend or relative, or have one come here.'

'My son is coming over, thank you.'

'Good. Right then, I'll be in touch with you tomorrow.'

The police, the mess, the body and all signs of the fatal struggle had gone by the time Charlie arrived at the cottage.

Pru told him what the police had done so far, and Charlie privately thanked God no sign had been found of Nick's visit. He was ready to console his mother. He knew she had loved her husband, despite his lack of obvious affection. He also knew she'd been particularly worried about him recently, though she hadn't said why. She seemed, though, to be handling the whole business of his murder with remarkable composure. The real grief wouldn't begin until the shock of what had happened wore off.

Neither of them felt like eating much. Charlie found some bread and cheese and a bottle of wine. They were picking at the cheese when Detective Inspector Ferrier telephoned.

'Hello, Mrs Patterson. Just to let you know what progress we're making. I'm afraid it isn't much but we do have a sighting of a car leaving the top of your track at around midday, just before you got back, I should imagine. I thought you might be able to help me there.'

'Oh,' Pru said. 'What kind of car was it?'

'I'm afraid it's rather a broad description – a red estate car, possibly a Subaru. Any idea who that might be?'

The only other news was that they had still had no luck in matching the fingerprints from the poker. But, as the inspector said, it was early days.

When the policeman had rung off, Pru walked slowly back to the dining room where Charlie had finished eating and was impatient to hear what had been said.

Pru looked at him quizzically. 'Nick didn't come round to see us by any chance, did he?'

Charlie swallowed and slid his eyes from her gaze.

This confirmed her suspicions. Charlie had never been able to lie to her. She sat down. 'Why didn't you tell me?'

'How do you know he did?'

'Someone has reported seeing his car leaving the top of the drive just before twelve.'

'Did they take the number?'

'No. The police only have a vague description.' There was a worried look in her eyes as she gazed intently at her son. 'It sounded like Nick's car to me. The one he bought to replace the BMW.'

'Did . . . did you tell them?'

Pru shook her head. 'No. And I won't. I can't believe Nick would have had anything to do with it.' She caught the look of doubt in her son's eyes. 'Why? Do you?'

Charlie stayed the night at his mother's cottage. He rang Kate from there. He wanted to tell her what had happened, but he couldn't explain it properly. He arranged to see her the following evening.

Charlie didn't see his mother when he left at six next morning to organise the exercising of his string of horses. When he got back to Oak Hollow, Nick was up, trying to do his routine tasks as if nothing had happened.

Charlie considered whether or not to tell him about the sighting of the car, and decided against it. He told him that the fingerprints on the poker hadn't been matched and weren't Patterson's. He watched Nick's reaction carefully.

Nick seemed to be more concerned with Willow Star's

likely fate. 'We'll have to find out who's bought her and contact them to make sure she's staying here.'

'Presumably whatever arrangements my father was about to make will be on hold until the will's sorted out. Maybe that'll give us a chance to hang on to her.'

'No, he was definite about that. The deal's been done, paid up.'

'But why didn't he tell you who?'

'The conversation didn't last long enough.' Nick paused, remembering it and Patterson's vehement attack on him.

'So Willow's a hundred per cent sold?'

'That's what he said. I guess his solicitors will tell you who owns her now.'

Charlie spent the rest of the day in a confusion of emotions, trying to come to terms with his stepfather's death and worrying about his mother. At the same time, he was harbouring a gruesome wish to know why it had happened and who had done it, hoping desperately that it wasn't Nick.

Kate came round after evening stables. Since Charlie's phone call, she'd read the reports of the murder in the morning papers.

She had just arrived when a beige Vauxhall Cavalier drew up outside the yard and two men in their thirties, casually dressed, climbed out. They strolled down to the bungalow, taking particular note of Nick's car as they passed it. They walked up to the door and knocked. Charlie let them in. The shorter of the two pulled out his warrant card and tweaked it open. 'Evening, sir. We're from Thames Valley CID. Is that your car?' He nodded in the direction of Nick's Subaru.

Charlie's heart nearly stopped for a second. 'No, it's not,' he stammered.

The detective's eyes showed more interest. 'Is the owner here?' He consulted his notebook. 'Mr Nicholas Ryder?'

'He's up at the yard. Why? What's he done?'

'We just need to eliminate him from some inquiries we're making.'

'Oh. Right. I'll come up with you.' Charlie closed the door behind him and walked with the two policemen up to the stableyard.

'And who are you, sir?' the senior of them asked him.

'I'm Nick Ryder's partner. Charles Patterson.'

The two detectives stopped. 'Patterson? Was Major David Patterson your father?'

'Stepfather, yes.'

'I see. I'm sorry. We're investigating his murder. A red car, possibly a Subaru, was seen leaving the major's house shortly after the estimated time of death.'

'But there must be thousands of people driving around in red Subarus.'

'Not thousands, sir, and surprisingly few that have been bought from the local dealer recently. Do you happen to know if your partner visited your father yesterday?'

'You'll have to ask him that.'

'Or did you by any chance borrow his car to go there yourself?'

'No. I was here all afternoon, ask anyone. For God's sake, I wouldn't murder my stepfather.'

'I'm sorry, sir. But it does happen. Anyway, if you wouldn't mind hanging around for a while, we'd like to ask you some questions too. But we'll see Mr Ryder on his own first, thank you.'

Nick, coming out of the tack room, knew they were police as soon as they walked into the yard. Despite the jeans and the suede blouson, there was an inescapable air of officialdom in their manner.

He gulped quickly, before they were near enough to see, and lifted an inquiring eyebrow.

'Mr Nick Ryder?' one of them asked.

'Yes?'

'We're police officers, sir,' the other said, displaying his warrant card again.

'You want to see me?'

'Yes, sir. I take it you knew Major David Patterson, your partner's stepfather.'

'Yes. Of course I did. You're investigating his . . .' Nick let the word 'murder' die on his tongue.

'We are indeed, sir. And we understand you called in to see him yesterday.'

Only a small twitch at the side of his mouth betrayed Nick's nervousness. 'Yes,' he said. 'I did go round there to talk about a filly he keeps with us. His car was there. I rang the bell,' he shrugged, 'but there was no reply. Of course, now I know – it's terrible – he must have been dead inside.'

'What time was this?'

'About half past eleven.'

'And where were you at half past ten?'

Nick thought for a moment. 'I took my dog for a run in Savernake Forest.'

'Did you see anyone there?'

'No. You seldom do in the part I go to. That's why I go there. It makes a change from the open downland for him.'

'I see, sir. So you arrived and rang the bell. How long did you wait before you gave up?'

'A good five minutes. I thought if the major's car was there, he must be at home. I know he never lets himself be driven by Mrs Patterson in her car.'

'So you knew him quite well?'

'I wouldn't say that, but I knew about him from Charlie.'

'Right. Well, we may want to talk to you again. In the meantime, we'd like a set of your fingerprints – just to eliminate you from the murder inquiry.'

'Of course,' Nick said, confident that his prints weren't on anything incriminating. 'Come on down to the house. We'll do it there, not in front of the lads, if you don't mind.'

Later, when Kate had gone home, Charlie drove to his mother's cottage where her sister was already installed in the second spare room.

They were halfway through dinner when Nick rang, wanting to speak to Charlie.

'Hello, Charlie. I'm afraid you'll have to get back here and look after the horses.'

'Why?'

'The police are here again, a chap called Ferrier who's in charge of investigating your stepfather's death. It's crazy,' Nick's voice faltered, 'but he says my fingerprints match the ones on the poker that killed him.'

Chapter Eight

Nick put the phone down. He was in the small office in the bungalow; he felt like a rat in a trap. He looked up at Ferrier and his sergeant who stood in front of him, pleased with themselves for having found their man so soon.

The sergeant was fiddling with a pair of handcuffs. Nick glanced at his own hands; they should have been shaking but they weren't. He looked back at the officers; now was his last chance before they snapped the cuffs on him and took him to the police station.

He lumbered to his feet, then with a speed which his physique belied he took two steps towards the door. He was through it and had slammed it shut before either of the policemen could get a hand on him.

Normally, when he was out, he kept his office locked from the prying eyes of lads or anyone else who might have come to visit with dubious intentions. The key was in the lock now. Nick turned it just as one of Ferrier's fists closed round the knob inside. It wasn't much of a door; it would give him only a few seconds' lead, but that was all he needed.

He ran through the kitchen, out of the back door and into the damp night. The scrubby paddock behind the bungalow dropped away to the brook which ran along the valley bottom. Nick vaulted a timber rail fence and loped purposefully down the bank.

The stream at the bottom was full and flowing noisily. It was lined by a screen of small alders and willows. When he reached it, he stopped for a few seconds to look back. The policemen were searching around the front of the house, shouting angrily, waving torches around.

It was half a minute before they came round to the back. Nick was already up to his waist in the stream, ignoring the chill of the water that sprang from high in the chalk downs. He waded downstream until he'd passed a thick thorn hedge on the far side and clambered up the bank into a field of permanent pasture. Grazed by sheep most of the year, the going was good despite a recent downpour.

Nick was no athlete, but he didn't smoke and he was fit. He ran with an easy stride up the rising field, tolerating the squelch in his shoes and damp cotton chinos clinging to his legs. He guessed he'd already put a quarter of a mile between him and his pursuers.

He decided that the last place the police would expect him to hide was in the local pub. And he could position himself so that he would see their car if they did turn up.

Five or six hundred yards behind him, still on the far side of the stream, he spotted the flash of a torch. He carried on to the lane, jumped over the wire fence and travelled a hundred yards down the hill on the road until he came to a gate in the hedge on his left. He clambered over and ran easily down the gentle slope.

Ten minutes later he was sitting between the fire and the window in the front bar of the Goat with a pint of bitter in front of him while he tried to concentrate on a discarded copy of the *Sporting Life*.

No one noticed him look up sharply at the sound of a wailing police siren racing by.

There were no signs of police near the pub when closing time was called. Nick walked out with the crowd and set off on foot along the main road through the village. After a hundred yards, he slipped through a gate into a silent courtyard. As he'd known there would be, two lorries were parked there. He tried the small side door of the newer horsebox. It wasn't locked. He clambered in and quietly closed the door behind him. He felt around, knowing what to expect, grateful for the blankets when he found them in the Luton above the cab. He crawled in among them and made himself comfortable.

In Birch Lodge, at the moment Nick made his decision to run, Charlie put the phone down with a shaking hand. His mother looked at him with wide-eyed concern.

'What on earth's happened?'

'The police have arrested Nick.'

'But they can't have! That's absurd!'

'His car was seen; he couldn't deny he'd been here. The fingerprints on the poker were his. I'd say the police think they've a pretty strong case.'

Pru put her head in her hands. 'Oh my God! Why on

earth did it have to turn out like this?'

'What do you mean, Mum?'

'I mean . . . Nick being involved.'

'He wasn't,' Charlie said, trying to fight back his doubts. 'He wants me to organise a lawyer for him. I said I'd get a solicitor down to the police station right away. Then I've got to get back to Oak Hollow. You'll be okay with Aunt Sue here, won't you?'

'Yes, of course. You get back to your horses. I'll be all right. I'm just so worried about Nick. Will you go and see him in the morning?'

'Go and see him where?'

'Well, in prison, I suppose, if they've arrested him.'

Until then, Charlie hadn't let himself acknowledge that was where Nick was going. 'Shit! What if they don't let him out or give him bail?'

'You must go round first thing and see what you can do.'

Charlie drove his father's old Mercedes back to Oak Hollow, scarcely noticing the road as he drove. He was locked in a mental struggle over Nick. As his oldest friend as well as his partner, Nick merited all his loyalty, but the evidence against him was so damning. If only the police had found something, anything that pointed elsewhere. But with such a hot suspect, would they even look now?

Nick had sounded calm enough over the phone and didn't seem to be panicking. But that was Nick's way.

Charlie was very conscious of his partner's rare lapses of control, but even allowing for that, he couldn't bring himself to believe he would kill anyone. But if Nick didn't do it, there had to be something somewhere that would point to the real culprit.

Charlie pulled up in front of the dingy little house. All the lights were still on but he went up to the yard first to check his horses.

Everything was calm there. The horses for the most part were keeping away from the damp night air outside their stable doors. Charlie shone his torch into each. When he was satisfied that there were no problems, he went back down to the bungalow.

As he took out his key to open the front door, a police siren wailed up the lane from the village, coming towards Oak Hollow. He saw the flashing blue light swing off the road on to the concrete drive that led to the bungalow. The car skidded to a halt and two uniformed police leaped out. Charlie stood and waited.

'Who are you?' one of the PCs asked aggressively.

'Charles Patterson. I live here.'

'Oh. You're Major Patterson's son, are you?'

'Yes. What are you doing here? I was told you'd already arrested my partner.'

'He escaped.'

Charlie's heart dropped to the pit of his stomach. He didn't trust himself to speak for a moment. He tried his key in the front door to find it wasn't locked. The sight of the office door hanging off its hinges seemed to confirm what the police were saying. They followed him into the house.

'Has he been in touch with you?'

'No, no, he hasn't. I'd no idea he'd gone. I spoke to him on the phone maybe half an hour ago. I was at my mother's house. He told me he'd been arrested and asked me to get a solicitor down to your station, which I did. I've just got back.'

'We'll take another look round anyway.'

'I can't think why he's done a runner,' Charlie went on, aware as he said it how unconvincing he sounded. 'I'm certain he didn't do it. He had no reason to and he didn't have the strength, for Christ's sake!'

'I wouldn't know anything about that. We've just been told to look for a man escaped from police custody. If you think your friend is so innocent, the sooner he produces himself, the quicker he can prove it.'

'Sure. If I hear from him, I'll try and persuade him to give himself up.'

The PC looked at him hard for a moment.

Charlie shifted uncomfortably under his scrutiny.

'Has DI Ferrier had you in yet?' the policeman asked, struggling with the temptation to show up a plainclothes colleague.

'No.'

'Well, he will.'

Down in the village, in the deserted yard, Nick had slept fitfully. He awakened fully when the lorry's engine started up. The vehicle trundled out of the yard. Nick moved himself right to the front, burying himself in the blankets. He had purposely chosen the newer of the two lorries. Thanks to his regular painstaking study of race entries, he had guessed it was the one that would be taking the trainer's three runners to Doncaster, provided he hadn't sent them up in other transport the night before.

Nick looked at his watch and saw with relief that it was only five thirty in the morning. They wouldn't be moving off this early to get to Folkestone where the only other meeting was being held today. He guessed he was safe where he was for the time being. The lorry would be on its way up to the trainer's yard to pick up the runners.

Five minutes later, after some manoeuvring, the lorry came to a stop and the engine was turned off. Nick remained hidden. The ramp was dropped noisily. A rush of cold damp air penetrated to the front of the box. A lad and a girl clambered on board, sleepily chiding each other as they opened up the partitions to let the first horse on. Shortly afterwards, the clip of aluminium shoes across rippled concrete announced its arrival. There was a sudden cacophony of prancing hooves and rich cursing as the animal objected to going in. A moment later, with a thumping of metal on timber and rubber, the horse leaped in and was quickly confined in a stall.

With much the same performance, the other two runners were loaded. The lads tied them up and the ramp was banged home. The side jockey door clicked shut and beneath him Nick heard the driver and the lads clamber into the cab. The motor was gunned back into life and the lorry lurched out of the yard.

★ ★ ★

Charlie had meant what he said when he'd told the police he would try to persuade Nick to give himself up, but when he heard from him, shortly after eight next morning, he was beginning to see his point of view.

'Look, Charlie, I can't give myself up. You must believe I didn't kill your father, but right now the evidence is all against me.'

'Your running doesn't help.'

'Please, do whatever you can to get the police to look for someone else. They've got to listen to you. I mean, your father was the victim, for God's sake.'

'The guys who came last night after you'd gone behaved as if they thought I'd done it. I'll do what I can, but you were crazy to run.'

'The longer I'm running, the more chance there is of someone turning up the real villain.'

'Maybe,' Charlie said, unconvinced. 'Are you okay?'

'I'm fine. I'll be in touch.' Nick cut off without giving a clue where he was.

Charlie shook his head, deep in thought. He picked up the phone and dialled Kate at Noah's Ark.

When she answered, he got straight to the point. 'Nick was arrested last night,' he told her without preamble.

'My God! What for?'

'If you can believe it, for my father's murder.'

'But that's crazy!'

'It's worse than that. He managed to get away before they could get him into their car. He's done a runner and he's still missing.'

'But . . . but surely he wouldn't have done that if he didn't—'

'Not necessarily,' Charlie said.

'But it looks so much worse, Nick taking off like that.'

'Of course it does. I'll have to see what I can find to get him off the hook.'

'What on earth can you do that the police can't?'

'God knows, but they think they've got their man; they're not interested. Look, I'm going to do it but I need your help. Is there any chance you could leave Sandy in charge for a bit and come over here to help Kenny at the yard?'

'Yes,' Kate said quickly. 'Of course I'll come. There aren't many animals in at the moment anyway. When do I start?'

'Now?' Charlie asked.

'See you at midday.'

Charlie's next call was going to be more difficult.

Roland Ryder, Nick's father, had scarcely spoken to Nick since he had left Cambridge and gone into racing. He had always expressed the view that it wasn't an occupation for a serious man. Nick, without a mother since he was a boy, hadn't even attempted to justify his decision to his father, and the two had seldom seen each other in the past five years. But Roland Ryder had to be told.

Charlie got through to his office in Lloyd's where Ryder headed a large underwriting syndicate. He was put through without any delay.

'Good morning, Charles,' Ryder said unemotionally. 'I

was sorry to hear about your stepfather.'

'It's all been an awful shock, especially for my mother.'

'I can imagine. As I expect you know, he was on some of my syndicates.'

'I'd heard.'

'I'm afraid there'll be some considerable claims on his estate,' Ryder went on, without a hint of regret.

Charlie realised now why he had been put through so promptly. 'That's not why I've rung,' he said. 'I'm afraid Nick's been arrested . . . for my father's murder.'

A short burst of indignation spluttered down the line, resolving itself in a strangled yell.

'He only went there to talk about a horse my father had with us.'

'But how the hell could he end up killing him? It's crazy!'

'He didn't kill him, Mr Ryder. It just looks that way.'

'Where have they taken him? He'll want bail.'

'He escaped,' Charlie said, deriving some satisfaction from delivering the news.

'My God! This is going from bad to worse. Which police are handling it?'

Charlie told him. Roland Ryder rang off without another word.

Charlie took a deep breath and started to make a string of phone calls to racecourses, jockeys and owners. Most of the time he was talking, his mind was miles away.

Nick judged that the lorry had left the M25 and was

heading north up the M1. That meant they should reach Doncaster around eleven.

The lorry's destination at the South Yorkshire racecourse was crucial to his plans for the next few days. The only place in the country where he was absolutely certain of receiving an unquestioning, warm welcome was no more than twenty miles from Doncaster.

When Nick was a boy, Harold Amory had always treated him with kindness and equality. Amory, already in his sixties even then, had been his parents' gardener. Since he had retired fifteen years before, the old man had moved back to his native Lincolnshire, to live in a small cottage on his son-in-law's farm. When Nick's mother had been killed in a car crash outside Monaco when he was just twelve, he had written to Amory before anyone else and, receiving a beautifully written reply, had kept up a regular correspondence with him ever since.

After a couple of long hold-ups, it was eleven o'clock before the lorry reduced speed and swung off the M1 on to the M18. They didn't pull into the racecourse lorry park until shortly before midday.

Nick listened carefully as the ramp was lowered and his three fellow passengers were led down. When it had been banged back up, there was a period of comparative silence while Nick gave them time to move away. With luck, the lorry would be parked out of sight of the stables. There was, anyway, at least a fifty-fifty chance that the small side door from the box wouldn't be visible. If he didn't want to arouse anyone's suspicions, he would just have to get out quickly and confidently, as if he belonged with the lorry.

He clambered down from the Luton, opened the door, and jumped straight out. He took a quick look around to get his bearings, closed the door behind him and started to walk towards the back of the stables. After a few yards, confident that no one was taking any notice of him, he veered off towards the main exit to the road.

Charlie was giving Kate a final briefing. They had a runner in a small race at Folkestone. Charlie ought to have been going with it, but he had more pressing plans. Kate offered to go, but he needed her at the yard. In the end, they decided their travelling head lad would have to deputise and hoped the owner didn't kick up a fuss. When he felt Kate knew enough of what was going on to cope without him, Charlie gave her a quick kiss, got into the Mercedes and went to see the police.

DI Ferrier eyed him sourly. 'And where do you suggest we start?'

'You're the detective, not me. All I can tell you is my partner was physically and temperamentally incapable of doing it.'

'I understand your loyalty to your friend, but I'm afraid he was there and he was the last person to handle the murder weapon. You've admitted it was possible he and your father argued about this horse, and he's got a history of violent anger.'

Charlie stared at the policeman. 'Who the hell told you that?'

'The headmaster of his old school.'

'For God's sake,' Charlie said, feeling he'd lost control of this conversation, 'I was there with him. He never did anything more than lose his temper now and again, and that was over ten years ago.'

'Well, there it is. And he's done a runner.' The policeman nodded with a cynical smirk.

'Only because he knew it looked so bad for him.'

'He's told you, has he?'

'No,' Charlie snapped, caught on his back foot. 'But I know how he'd be thinking. Anyway, what about outside the cottage? Did you search there?'

'Of course.'

'Wasn't there anything?'

'I think you'll find what there was will just confirm your friend was there.'

'Why? What did you find?'

'We've got some good clear footprints on the ground outside the front door. We haven't been able to match them yet – Ryder was probably wearing the shoes when he ran.'

'You checked all the ones in the house?'

'We did.'

'Was there anything else?'

The detective shrugged. 'Not really. A pack of Rizlas.'

'Cigarette papers?'

'Yes.'

'Nick didn't smoke; and Dad certainly never smoked roll-ups. Where did you find them?'

'Outside, where the cars were parked.' Charlie felt a

lurch of disappointment. Ferrier dismissed the papers as trivial. 'Could have been anyone's.'

'Have you checked?'

'You mean have we called in everyone in the district who uses green Rizlas? Quite a few of them wouldn't want to come. Maybe your friend liked the odd bit of wacky baccy.'

'No, he never liked dope,' Charlie said as if it would help Nick's case. 'I take it you can't stop me asking questions if I want to?'

Ferrier laughed. 'As long as you don't break any laws or cause any complaints. But there's no point; there's nothing you can do to help your friend except maybe get him a good brief once we've got our hands on him again.'

Charlie found as he drove out of the police station car park that in trying to convince the cynical detectives of Nick's innocence, he'd gone some way to believing that the police might be right. But until Nick's guilt was proven beyond reasonable doubt, he would do everything he could to help him.

He decided to start back at Birch Lodge, or rather, on the general's estate, by asking anyone if they had seen anything unusual.

The general himself was out. His housekeeper, a silent, unsmiling woman, was prepared to accept that the son of the victim had a right to ask questions though she pointed out that she'd already told the police she knew nothing and had seen nothing.

'Who else might have been around that day?'

'Saturday? No one, really. Tom Skyrme might have been in; he sometimes comes for an hour or two on a Saturday, but I didn't see him, and I haven't seen him today.'

'Who's he?'

'The general's gardener. Lives in the West Lodge.'

The West Lodge was on the other side of the estate from Birch Lodge. Certainly the gardener wouldn't have seen any comings or goings there from his house.

Tom Skyrme turned out to be a small, wiry man in his late fifties, with a weather-beaten face beneath a worn cap. When Charlie found him he was scraping the mud from his boots on to the top of his spade. He told Charlie he'd been among the rhododendrons by the track to the major's cottage on Saturday morning.

'Did you see anything unusual, anyone around you didn't know?'

'No, not in the grounds.'

'What do you mean, not in the grounds?'

'Well, your father had someone with him.'

'How do you know? Could you see into the house?'

'No. I mean in his car. I saw him driving down the track and he had a bloke with him.'

'A bloke? Who was he?' Charlie asked with much more interest.

'I don't know. Never seen him before. Didn't look much like a friend of the major's.'

'Why not?' Charlie urged, bursting with frustration at the old gardener's ponderous delivery.

'Scruffy bugger, he were. I saw him get out of the car

wearing old jeans and a tatty sort of bomber jacket.'

'How old was he?'

'Oh, hard to say. Fifty, sixty.'

'How tall?'

'A good height.'

'What? Six feet?'

'Maybe more.'

'What else?'

'That's it, really. I didn't pay too much attention. Not my business who the major saw.'

'What did you tell the police?'

'I haven't told them nothing.'

'Why not?'

'They didn't ask me, and anyway I've been away for a few days.'

'But didn't you think you should go to them, after what happened to my father?'

The gardener shrugged. 'If they comes looking for me, I'll tell 'em. I hasn't got time to go sticking my nose in otherwise.'

Charlie spent another five minutes pressing for any small detail. He soon realised he'd got all he was going to get, but he drove away feeling triumphant. Half an hour into the job, he told himself, and he had something new. He was eager to inform DI Ferrier and let the police get on with it, but first he wanted to take a closer look inside his father's car.

He wasn't surprised when the ashtray yielded up the fag ends of two roll-ups.

Charlie continued his search, concentrating on the

front of the car where on the evidence of the gardener and the fag ends, his stepfather's passenger had been sitting.

After ten minutes, he had found nothing. He gave up and sat back in the driver's seat, feeling deflated. But there was no doubt that there had been someone with his father, by consent, on Saturday morning. And the police knew nothing about this man. But what had he got to offer them? The gardener's reluctant evidence, and two roll-up fag ends. His mother clearly didn't know that his stepfather had driven someone to the house after she had gone out to do her shopping. She hadn't mentioned it to him or the police.

Charlie sat in the car trying to decide his next move. The dull morning had cleared and was maturing into a fine early summer's day. He started the handsome old car and, in the absence of a more constructive plan, headed for Oak Hollow. Whatever else was going on, he still had to keep his eye on the yard.

There were only six policemen on duty at Doncaster races that day. There was no tradition of serious trouble there. Only the usual drunken exuberance or morbidity caused by gambling successes or failures.

PC Mike Withenshaw adjusted his helmet more firmly on his head as he walked from the police minibus that had brought them up from the station. On his way to the main lorry entrance, he was thinking about the Yankee accumulator he'd put on four of the day's races and how he would spend the money when all four horses came in.

The briefing before he and his colleagues had left the police station had been the usual two-line injunction not to hit back and a message circulated to all stations with a local horse-racing connection: keep an eye out for a young Lambourn trainer called Nicholas Ryder, absconded while being taken into custody to be charged with murder.

PC Withenshaw had read a profile on Oak Hollow in the *Racing Post* and he knew exactly who Nick Ryder was – not a trainer, that was for sure. Charlie Patterson did all the training in that yard. He had produced some useful winners in his first year and a small profit for PC Withenshaw.

Why the hell anyone should think Ryder would turn up at the races if he was on the run, God knew.

The constable reached his post at the gate to the lorry park and looked across at the stables. There were already several lorries parked and horses being led to their temporary accommodation. He tried to identify a few of them, but even if he had been able to consult the *Racing Post* in the pocket of his tunic, he would have been no wiser. He envied the lads, scurrying about, doing what they loved – though not so well paid, mind, he added to himself. One of them was walking towards him now. Or maybe it wasn't a lad. He was wearing a tweed jacket and a pair of rumpled cotton trousers.

The man was walking briskly, with his head down. As he got near the gate, the policeman greeted him. 'Morning. What's happened to you? Lost your horse or what?'

The man looked up sharply, barely slowing his pace. 'Looking for a phone.'

'There's some back in the grandstand,' PC Withenshaw said helpfully.

'I saw one just down the road,' the man replied, and hurried on.

The policeman watched him go and tried to remember if there was a public phone anywhere near. He couldn't think of one. And he was trying to think who the man was. He'd seen him before somewhere.

A few seconds later it dawned on him and he gasped. He looked at the man's back. This chap had already given two blokes the slip. No point him going after him alone and losing him. He reached for his radio.

Nick was shaking as he walked out of the gate. He couldn't believe the policeman on the gate hadn't seen his fear. But there was no shout, no challenge as he walked away up the empty road.

The further he got from the racecourse entrance, the more he relaxed. Now all he had to do was to travel as inconspicuously as possible to the small village outside Gainsborough where Harold Amory lived. Then, secure in the knowledge that none of his friends or connections were aware of Amory's existence, he would be safe to sit and watch developments from a distance.

Three hundred yards from the racecourse gates, a row of terraced houses was broken by a small newsagent-tobacconist. Nick was feeling the effects of twelve hours without food. He went in and bought crisps, biscuits, chocolate and a can of Coke to keep him going. He was anxious to get out of the busy outskirts of the town as quickly as he could.

He stepped out and had walked on a few paces when he heard a car roar up behind him and squeal to a halt outside the shop.

He turned, wondering idly who was in such a hurry, and too late saw two police patrolmen leap out and run straight towards him.

He spun round and looked down the empty road, enclosed on either side, offering nowhere to run or hide.

He turned back as his pursuers reached him, shortly joined by the PC he had seen on gate duty.

'Nicholas Ryder, you're under arrest. Don't attempt to move or we may be required to use force to apprehend you.'

Nick shrugged. He understood odds. Running last night had been a reasonable risk. This time the odds against getting away were somewhere in the order of five hundred to one.

'Okay. I'm coming,' he said.

When Charlie arrived back at Oak Hollow later that morning, he almost wished he'd stayed away. Kate was staring blankly at the screen of Nick's computer.

She glanced up when she heard Charlie walk into the office. 'I don't suppose you know how this bloody thing works, do you?'

Nick kept all their accounts, all their entries, form information, everything to do with selecting races, on the computer. Charlie had assumed it was just a simple database. 'Why?' he asked.

'I can't seem to get into this entries file.'

'I thought you knew how these things worked,' Charlie said, immediately regretting the irritation he showed.

'I do,' Kate came back bitingly, 'but Nick's obviously got a password which you've failed to tell me.'

Charlie reddened. Kate was right, and he hadn't a clue what the password was. 'God, I'm sorry,' he said. 'We'll just have to wait until he contacts me again. I wonder where the hell he is.'

'Ah,' Kate said. 'That's the other disaster. They've caught him again.'

'Where, for God's sake?'

'In Doncaster. I've already phoned that solicitor who was going to see him. Apparently they're bringing him back to Marlborough to charge him.'

'Oh God! Poor Nick. When can I go and see him?'

'They said he wouldn't be back until late tonight. You'll have to wait until tomorrow when they'll charge him or ask to remand him for a few more days.'

'I'll have to go and see him then. At least I'll be able to get that password for you.'

'I expect we can manage from the paper records in the meantime.'

'I can probably remember what's going on over the next few days anyway. Get the calendar out and we'll have a look. I'll go and get my diary from the car.'

Charlie had left the car up at the yard. As he opened it to get the old-fashioned A5 diary that was his lifeline, one of the more energetic lads walked over to admire the old Mercedes.

'Lovely model, that,' he said.

'Yes. My stepfather was very proud of it. He had it for years.'

'It's a shame it's in such a six-and-eight. It could do with a bloody good clean.'

'Are you volunteering, Jimmy?'

'Yeah. I'll have it looking like new, in and out. I done six months' car valeting in Reading before I come here. Fiver, okay?'

Charlie agreed and left the lad going for the hosepipe they used to wash down the horses' legs. Back in the office, he sat down with Kate to establish exactly what Nick had entered where over the next seven days. But as he worked, Charlie couldn't get Nick's arrest and his stepfather's last visitor out of his head.

'Look,' he said abruptly, 'I can't handle this, Kate. Can you try and make head or tail of it? Get Kenny in to help. I've got to go and see my mother. I think we may be able to get Nick out of this sooner than we thought.'

'How?' Kate asked eagerly; she had been reluctant to talk about it while she knew Charlie was still uncertain.

Charlie told her about his chat with Tom Skyrme. 'It looks as though DI Ferrier and his men have been bloody useless, but I want to be sure of my ground before I rub their noses in it.'

Pru Patterson was packing a suitcase when Charlie arrived at Birch Lodge.

'Where are you going?' Charlie asked, approving.

'I'm not sure. Probably to Michael and Veronica. They've been very sweet and asked me to stay as long as I want.'

'When are you thinking of going?'

'Not for a day or two, but I just thought I'd get ready.'

Charlie had already noticed that the whole cottage had been thoroughly tidied – a kind of occupational therapy, he guessed, for his mother while she came to terms with her husband's death. He admired her for the stoicism with which she was handling his death and he was reluctant to probe her over it. But now that there was a real chance of an alternative suspect to Nick, he had to follow it through.

'Mum, I've discovered something the police don't know.'

She looked up sharply from her packing. 'What's that?'

'Dad was seen driving someone back to the cottage on Saturday morning.'

'Really?' The surprise in her voice was genuine. 'Who saw him?'

'The gardener, Tom Skyrme. The police never even spoke to him, for God's sake.'

'But who does Tom say he saw?'

'He just had a glimpse of a man in Dad's car. Someone scruffy and tall. I found two roll-up fag ends in the ashtray and the police had already told me they'd found a Rizla packet outside. As soon as they establish exactly who it was, it might get Nick off the hook.'

Pru straightened up and started to tidy up bottles on her dressing table. 'I'm really sorry about Nick, but I'm afraid the man you're talking about won't help. I was here when he came and when he left.'

Charlie's elation collapsed like a burst bubble. 'Oh, no! Who was he?'

'He was a chap who served in the regiment with David. He was just passing and called in for a chat.'

'What was he wearing?'

'I don't remember really.' Charlie could see his mother searching for an answer. 'A type of bomber jacket, I think. David picked him up from the station, they went into the study and talked for a while, then he left.'

'How?'

'Well, I suppose he must have walked,' Pru said vaguely. 'I don't know, unless David called him a taxi.'

'But Dad didn't drive him anywhere?'

'No. I went out shortly afterwards, but he'd already gone.'

'How do you know he didn't hang around and come back?'

'I'm sure he didn't, darling. He was perfectly happy when he left. David had given him whatever he'd come for and that was that. There wasn't any question of his getting violent. I wish I could give you better news for Nick's sake, but there it is.'

Charlie sat down on a small buttoned chair and put his head in his hands. 'Bugger!' he muttered. 'I really thought I was getting somewhere; opening up a lead even the police couldn't ignore.'

'Come on, Charlie.' Pru put a hand on his shoulder. 'I'm sure they'll turn something up.'

'Not if they're not looking, they won't.' Charlie glanced up at his mother. 'God, I'm sorry. Here I am worrying about Nick, when you've lost . . .'

'It's all right,' Pru said firmly. 'I can cope, and I understand your loyalty to a friend.'

'But you don't think he did it, do you?'

'No, darling. Of course I don't.'

Charlie drove back to Oak Hollow in a deep depression. He couldn't rid himself of the idea that his mother thought exactly the opposite of what she'd said. And with his alternative suspect accounted for and eliminated, Nick's position looked as bad as ever.

Chapter Nine

Charlie shivered as he looked at his partner across the small courtroom and listened to the magistrate issuing instructions.

Nick Ryder had now formally been charged with the murder of Major David Patterson. There was no question of bail being granted. He would be remanded in custody for two weeks pending further inquiries before committal.

Nick's pale face was empty of expression as a policeman led him through a small door at the back of the dock to the cells below.

Charlie still found it almost impossible to absorb the fact that the police thought Nick had murdered his stepfather. And yet, with the *prima facie* evidence of the fingerprints on the poker, Nick's admitted presence at the scene of the crime, compounded by his attempt to abscond, the magistrate had accepted that they had a sufficiently strong case.

Charlie drove to Birch Lodge to tell his mother what had happened.

'I still think it's absurd,' she said with indignation. 'There is not the slightest possibility that Nick did it. David would have eaten him alive, even if he was forty years older.'

They were sitting in the drawing room of the small house, the room where Major Patterson had been battered to death. Charlie looked at the fire-irons, neatly placed by an empty grate.

'But the prints on the poker? What if he crept up and hit him?'

Pru gave Charlie a look of despair. 'I don't know, I just don't believe he could do it.'

'Are you really sure about that, Mum?'

'Yes, of course. Aren't you?'

'I think so; I don't know. I was so certain he hadn't when I heard about the man who came to see Dad. Now I don't know where to look.'

'What are you going to do?'

'I can cope at the yard. Kenny's been marvellous and Kate's helping.'

'I suppose that means she's moved in.'

Charlie grinned. 'Just a temporary arrangement, I assure you, so that she's on hand if I'm away late.'

'Away late? Doing what?'

'God knows. Looking for something to help Nick.'

'Surely the police should be doing that, shouldn't they?' Pru asked, alarmed.

'But they're not. They're convinced Nick did it. Everything looks right so far and the article in *Sporting Life* describing Nick's feelings about Dad taking Willow Star away seems a good enough motive.' Uneasy about this theory, Charlie changed tack. 'What about you? How are you going to manage? Financially, I mean.'

A faint smile turned Pru's mouth. 'I'm afraid I haven't been left much. I think quite a lot of things may have to be sold to cover your father's liabilities. Things had become rather tricky recently.'

'Yes, I guessed they had when he told us he was going to sell Willow Star. Was it Lloyd's that did all the damage?'

Pru nodded. 'Lloyd's and a number of other investments he let himself be talked into. Did he know Nick was coming round that day?'

'No,' Charlie admitted. 'We thought it would be better if he turned up without any warning.'

'But why was Nick coming, not you?'

Charlie winced guiltily. 'We thought you'd take more notice of him than me.'

Pru threw him a bleak glance and shook her head. She eased herself from her chair and walked to the window where she stopped and looked out at the naked branches of the birch trees swaying in the wet March breeze. 'I've arranged the burial,' she said, without looking at her son. 'It'll be at midday on Friday, at Putney Vale. It'll only be us and a few family.'

'Won't a lot of his old army colleagues want to come?'

'I've tried to put them off, as far as possible.'

'Why?'

'I just don't think I could stand a crowd, all reminiscing and telling me how marvellous David was.'

★ ★ ★

'Maybe I *did* do it.' The normal pallor of Nick's face was accentuated by the stark white light of the naked neon tubes above. He stared forlornly at Charlie and heaved his shoulders hopelessly. 'I've told you, I haven't got a clue what happened. I certainly didn't have any conscious wish to do him harm, although he'd annoyed me.'

Charlie thought about the fingerprints on the poker and tried to envisage Nick creeping up on his father. Somehow he just couldn't picture it.

They were sitting at a bare table in a visiting room at Bullingdon jail, about eight miles north of Oxford. A wary-eyed warder was keeping watch over them.

'What did my father say?' Nick asked flatly.

'Hasn't he been to see you yet?'

'No. He phoned to say he'd come as soon as he could,' Nick answered without any detectable emotion.

'When I spoke to him he just huffed and puffed. As a matter of fact, at first he thought I'd phoned to talk to him about my stepfather's debts at Lloyd's. He told me there wouldn't be much left of the estate. Dad was on some of his syndicates, and several other bad ones as well. And there were other deals that went wrong.'

'No wonder he wanted to sell Willow Star. Though he was too proud to mention his financial problems the day I went to see him.'

'And you didn't see anyone else while you were there?'

Nick looked blank. 'No. Not a soul.'

Charlie told him what he'd learned from the general's gardener, and his excitement at discovering the cigarette ends in the ashtray. 'But Mum said he was just some old soldier on the touch and he'd gone quite happily before she'd even left the house. But look,' Charlie leaned forward and put a hand on his friend's shoulder. The warder stepped forward, shaking his head. Charlie scowled at him and removed his hand. 'Look, Nick. I'll carry on doing everything I can to get you out of here. I know you didn't do it, and I'm not going to stand by and watch you go down for it.'

Nick looked grateful but unconvinced. 'Thanks, Charlie.' He then forced a smile on to his face. 'What's the news on Willow Star?'

'She's fine. She worked very well this morning.'

'I mean, about her ownership.'

Charlie shook his head. 'I don't know for certain, but I hope she'll be staying.'

'You mean your stepfather really *had* sold her to someone else?'

'Yes, he did, that morning. What's more, he wrote to Wetherby's at once to confirm it. They got the letter yesterday saying she was to be transferred to a nominee owner.'

'So you still don't know if she'll stay with us?'

'No, I don't. In the meantime, Dad's executors said we should keep her and run her in the normal way in their name and they'll look after the fees from the day Dad died. But I'll try and get the whole thing sorted out when I go up and see them after the funeral.'

'When's that?'

'The police have released the body. My mother's

arranged his burial at Putney Vale on Friday.'

'Charlie,' Nick said, showing some animation for the first time, 'whatever happens, you must hang on to Willow, she's our best prospect. It might be a long time before we get another like her.'

Charlie shook his head with a smile. 'You're amazing. You're in the shit up to your ears and yet you're still worrying about the horses. Don't worry,' he said. 'I'll sort it out. We won't lose her.' He looked behind him at the expressionless warder, and a woman with a tear-streaked face who was leaving the room. 'Look, I'm afraid I've had enough of this place. I'll come back tomorrow. Is there anything you want that I can bring?'

'A high quality solicitor would be a help.'

'It's the quality of the barrister that counts. And Nick,' Charlie said, standing up to leave. 'I know you didn't do it. I don't want you ever to have any doubt about that.'

When Charlie arrived home, Kate was still working in the office. 'How's Nick?' she asked anxiously as he walked through the door.

'As well as can be expected. Come on,' he said, putting up a hand to stem the flow of questions. 'I'll tell you everything over dinner somewhere. That prison has really got me down.'

Kate obviously had a firm grasp of what went on in the yard and what needed doing. As they ate, she told him that she'd had the vet round and he'd confirmed that two of their charges had contracted ringworm. There was a good chance that some of the others had already picked it up too, so she and Kenny had decided to isolate the six most important horses in the yard. Charlie's initial alarm was calmed by her pragmatic approach and the damage limitation she'd already put into action. 'It's good to know the place is in sound hands while I do what I can for Nick.'

'I've told my regional boss that I need a few weeks off – to learn about keeping bloodstock,' Kate said with a hint of guilt.

'Are you thinking of turning Noah's Ark into a training establishment then?' Charlie laughed.

'I might be, you never know.' Kate delved into her bag for her cigarette pack. With it she pulled out an envelope. 'By the way, this is from Jimmy.'

'Jimmy?'

'Yes. The new lad. He cleaned your father's Mercedes. He said you asked him to.'

'Oh him. He seemed so keen I didn't want to disappoint him. What's that, a bill?'

'No, just all the bits and pieces he found while he was doing the interior. He said he thought it was all rubbish, but left it for you to decide. He gave it to me just as I was on my way to the village.'

Charlie glanced inside the envelope before he tucked it into his pocket.

Later, when he and Kate were sitting in the kitchen at the bungalow, running through the evening's messages, he took the envelope out and tipped the contents on to the table. There was a business card from a firm of art shippers, a couple of bookies' tickets, presumably from

Goodwood, a slip of paper with the message 'Hungerford, 9.37' written in Major Patterson's neat hand, and a shoe repair ticket, dated the previous week, from a heel bar in Kilburn High Road.

Charlie looked at each in turn. 'It's amazing,' he said, shaking his head. 'I thought I'd been through that car with a fine-tooth comb. How did I miss all this?'

Kate looked sceptically at the motley collection. 'Just looks like litter to me.'

Charlie shrugged. 'Probably. The bookies' tickets are unlikely to yield a lot, I admit.'

'Or the shoe repair ticket, unless you think your stepfather left a decent pair of shoes to be picked up somewhere.'

'He wouldn't have had them repaired in Kilburn.'

'Maybe it was the guy who came to see him.'

Charlie shrugged in resignation. 'I suppose you're right. And this other bit of paper must be the time of the chap's train; that fits in with when the gardener saw him.'

'Charlie, I don't want to discourage you, but wouldn't the police forensic people have been through the car if they'd thought it was worth it?'

'Yes, but I'm going to follow up this shoe ticket. You never know, this friend of Dad's could have seen something.'

Kate agreed but part of her remained unconvinced.

Charlie sat with his mother in the back of a long black Ford. He stared straight ahead at the hearse they were following to London along the M4. In the hearse, between dark-coated, stripe-trousered men who chatted about football and their own domestic problems, was one of the cheaper coffins from the undertaker's catalogue. Charlie thought of his stepfather's once hard, efficient body lying in it among the folds of white silk.

His mother showed little emotion. Charlie supposed this must be the result of years of marriage to a man who, if he accepted the need for human emotion at all, saw no reason to display it.

He tried to identify what he was feeling within himself. Sadness? Nostalgia? Disappointment? Grief? Nothing?

He was acutely conscious that the man in the coffin had been no more than an acquaintance to him, an acquaintance for whom he had the same awed affection he might have for a favourite view of a distant mountain. His stepfather had been aloof but, until recently, he had always been consistent. He had sometimes said that he considered it a complete waste of breath and not worth the energy required to open his mouth to make statements which he wasn't completely prepared to stand by. Charlie reflected that it had made for dull conversations, when ideas and conjecture were precluded.

As they reached the outskirts of London, the hearse turned off the motorway and headed south, over the River Thames at Kew. They crossed Richmond Park in convoy. Charlie looked out, detached from the walkers, runners, cyclists and horsemen indulging in their everyday pleasures. The deer grazed gracefully at a distance while stags kept guard. The sun, making its first appearance for several days, gleamed weakly orange above the

Mies van der Rohe tower blocks on the edge of the park. To Charlie, everything outside seemed part of a surreal, unattainable world.

The small gathering outside the anonymous chapel brought Charlie back to reality. Despite his mother's discouragement, a couple of dozen men – old military connections, Charlie deduced from their ties and deportment – stood a little to one side of the relations: Pru's sister, Sue, David Patterson's only sister, Veronica Russell, severe and unsmiling beside her emotionless husband. Sadly, Charlie noted, no sign of Imogen. A pair of more distant cousins, seldom spoken of, almost never seen. In the background, David Patterson's old commanding officer, General Sir Peter Sheridan, stood quietly observing, speaking to no one.

The undertakers carried the coffin into the chapel. With no great eagerness, the party followed slowly. Charlie sent his mother in ahead so that he could greet any late arrivals. He watched the last of the old soldiers walk in and was about to follow when he was stopped by the sight of a convoy of three cars, two Mercedes and a Rolls-Royce, sweeping up the avenue of grey-green conifers to the chapel.

The Rolls pulled up directly in front of the door. A chauffeur got out smartly and opened the rear door for his employer – a black-bearded Arab in a Western suit of shiny mohair.

The Arab saw Charlie and acknowledged him with only the faintest narrowing of his eyes. He walked straight past him into the small chapel. From one of the

Mercedes, two more Arabs in jellabas and headcloths emerged. They did not enter the building but stood outside the door with the wind flapping their white garments around their silk ankle socks.

Two more men, swarthy, Middle Eastern, got out of the second Mercedes. They were dressed in jeans and leather jackets. They stared at Charlie. One of them took a pack of Marlboros from his pocket and they both lit up and leaned against the car.

Charlie was still wondering who they were when he took his seat beside his mother in the front row, a few feet from his stepfather's coffin.

A vicar who found it hard to sound concerned about one of the constant string of strangers who were brought here to attend their last service intoned the prayers of burial, the regrets and thanks for a life past, perhaps fulfilled, possibly worthy and not too sinful. The clergyman had no idea from the scanty notes he had made in a brief discussion with Pru what the man he was burying was really like.

And, Charlie thought, not for the first time, nor had he. But while he was confused by his own emotions, he was deeply puzzled by his mother's. She stood beside him, responding to the prayers in a quiet, firm voice, with no hint of a quaver to it. As the last prayers were said, the final hymn tunelessly droned and the timber-boxed body carried out by the undertakers' bearers to a deep, neatly cleft trench, Charlie thought that at least now she would show her grief.

But there was no dampness in the corner of her eyes,

no wringing of her neat hands, no trembling of her lower lip, even as the box was lowered into the ground and the vicar said the final prayers and invited the widow and son to cast a trowel of earth on to the coffin. Maybe she hadn't loved him at all.

Charlie, with his mother on his arm, led the way back to the chapel. He noticed that the three Arab cars had already gone. The man in the suit, the putative boss, had not come to the grave. Charlie wondered what a Muslim had thought of the simple, undemonstrative Christian burial. He also wondered who he was. He turned to his mother and asked her.

'That was Sheikh Sala Mahmoud.'

'David's boss in Saudi?'

Pru nodded.

'I didn't know he was that fond of him.'

'He thought a lot of David but I admit I was rather surprised to see him here.'

'Who were the others?'

Pru shrugged. 'Just members of his entourage.'

'You didn't speak to him.'

'No, but that's quite normal. He came. I suppose we're meant to be grateful for that.' Pru turned to talk to several people waiting to see her, their faces full of earnest sympathy.

Charlie walked away and nodded at one or two mourners he knew. One man made a point of walking over to him. Charlie recognised Guy Helmsley-Barret. He held out a hand. 'Hello, Charles. Very sad.'

Charlie nodded. The man facing him was in his late

fifties, thick, grey-haired, in a rumpled but expensive suit and still good-looking in a raffish way.

'He was an extraordinary man,' Helmsley-Barret murmured. He had been a fellow officer of Major Patterson's.

Charlie nodded again, though he didn't know if he agreed.

'Look, if you don't mind,' the ex-soldier said, putting a hand on Charlie's forearm, 'I'd like to talk to you about him, get a couple of things off my chest. Could we have lunch together?'

Charlie glanced at his watch and his mother, chatting calmly to the cousins. He had planned to go to Kilburn to visit the shoe repair shop. But he thought Helmsley-Barret might well be able to shed light on some aspects of his father's activities.

'Yes,' he said. 'Why not? I'll just tell my mother.'

He arranged to go round later to the flat above the now closed shop in Kensington Church Street. She made no objection to his lunching with someone else.

Helmsley-Barret drove them in his oldish Daimler to a small, busy restaurant, halfway down the Fulham Road, where he appeared to be known by the Italian staff and by a gathering of over-ripe women who were lunching together.

They were shown to a table in a corner where, Helmsley-Barret explained, they would not be overheard.

When a bottle of Frascati and plates of antipasti had been placed on the table, Charlie's host spoke in the same quiet, confidential tone he had used earlier.

'I dare say your mother's very upset. I mean, he could

hardly have gone in more horrible circumstances.'

'She's coping surprisingly well, as a matter of fact,' Charlie replied. 'I think my father had trained her for years that it wasn't the thing to let one's emotions show.'

'Well, I must admit, she did seem to be taking it pretty calmly, which is something to be glad of.' He poured more wine for them both. 'You know, your father and I had some business dealings together.'

Charlie nodded. 'Stepfather,' he corrected. 'I vaguely knew about it. He referred to it once, some while ago. I . . .' Charlie considered his words. 'I got the impression there was some kind of problem.'

Helmsley-Barret glanced away, smiled fleetingly at a woman who was trying to catch his eye and took another gulp of wine. 'He was a sort of partner in a venture of mine. He wasn't involved in the day-to-day running of it but he was a director.'

'What was the business?'

'It was a chain of restaurants and wine bars. We established a very effective *modus operandi* in the early eighties, and we wanted to take advantage of it when business really took off after that. We had fantastic opportunities for growth but not enough capital, and the banks wanted usurious rates of interest or a hundred and fifty per cent security.'

'So my father invested in it, did he?'

'Only in so far as he gave some fairly sizeable guarantees for our bank loans.'

Charlie, reading Helmsley-Barret with a sickening surge of concern for his mother, was beginning to see where this was leading. 'And what sort of state is the business in now?'

His companion lifted a shoulder to show that matters were beyond his control. 'This bloody recession. We hadn't had the time to put on any fat before it hit. And of course the banks started to run around screaming like stuck pigs.'

'What does the business consist of now?'

'Nothing. We ran out of operating capital and unfortunately we're locked into one or two long leases.'

'What exactly does that mean?'

'It means that although the company has stopped trading, we still have to pay the rent – or perhaps I should say we're still liable for the rent.'

'And was my stepfather involved in these leases?'

'I'm afraid he was but he seemed extremely reluctant to honour his commitments.'

'I suppose,' Charlie said, 'the landlords will be looking to the estate for the rents.'

'Yes, I'm afraid so. I was wondering if you knew yet what sort of estate he left?'

'Were you?' Charlie nodded. 'What happens if there's not enough there?'

'You don't think that's the case, do you?' The man sitting opposite him looked alarmed. 'After all, your father came back from Saudi a wealthy man.'

Charlie ignored the man's panic. 'Who do the landlords pursue if they can't get it from my late father?'

'Any other personal guarantors.'

'In this case you, I suppose.'

Helmsley-Barret nodded.

'And how are you fixed?' Charlie asked.

'Frankly, boracic.'

'Who the hell's paying for lunch, then?' Charlie asked.

Helmsley-Barret shifted his well-dressed frame uneasily on the rush-seated chair.

Charlie stood up. 'If I'm paying, I'd rather eat with someone who's company I'd appreciate.'

'Hang on,' the ex-officer said with an effort at smooth bonhomie. 'I'll get it. I have a sort of arrangement here.'

'Why's that?' Charlie asked.

'It used to be one of ours.'

Charlie shook his head and glanced around the busy restaurant with a cynical grin. 'Used to be?' he said before turning and walking out.

In the crisp wind funnelling up the Fulham Road, he walked east until an empty taxi cruised by. He flagged it down and asked the cabbie to take him to the Kilburn High Road.

In the half-hour it crawled through clogged London streets, Charlie tried to piece together what his father's position must have been by the time he was killed. He knew there had been cash calls from syndicates at Lloyd's but he had no idea of the size of them. He also knew that the antiques business was doing badly, like almost every other antique shop in London; his mother had told him that much but, again, he had no idea of the scale of losses. He could only guess from Helmsley-Barret's agitation that the liabilities on the restaurant company weren't small.

Charlie sighed. He hadn't expected to get anything himself from his stepfather's estate but he had assumed there would be something left for his mother. He was certain of one thing, he was in no position to support her if there wasn't.

O'Grady's Lightning Shoe Repairs operated from a narrow-fronted shop on the High Road near the tube station. The quiet sound of a rasp and the pleasant leathery smell seemed to contradict the 'Lightning' of the shop's title.

When Charlie entered, a bell above the door pinged and an oldish man looked up from the heel he was filing. Charlie took the repair ticket from his pocket and put it on the worn lino counter.

'What have we here?' the old man said, rising from his seat and picking up the ticket. From his undiluted west of Ireland accent, Charlie assumed it was O'Grady who addressed him.

'I wondered if these were ready yet.'

O'Grady turned to the shelves across the back of the shop and fingered his way through rows of brown paper parcels. He stopped and stood back a moment, staring at the ticket. He turned slowly and confronted Charlie. 'What is it you're trying to do? Yer man already picked these up. Friday it would have been, just as I was closing. He couldn't find his ticket, but I recognised him so I let him have them. Are you telling me they were yours?' It was clear that O'Grady didn't think this likely.

Charlie offered the Irishman a winning smile. 'No. I

thought I was doing the chap a favour. I was going round to see him. He left the ticket in my car, so I thought I'd pick them up on the way round.'

'He's a friend of yours?' Clearly an unlikely proposition.

'No. He served in the army with my father, though.'

'I'd be surprised if ever he was in the army. Nasty piece of work, if you ask me.'

'Do you know his name?'

'I do not.'

'Could you describe him to me?'

'Why?'

'I just need to be sure it's the same chap.'

O'Grady shrugged. His description of his customer was very similar to Tom Skyrme's. Charlie, though he couldn't have justified it, derived a tingle of satisfaction from discovering this much.

'What repair did he have done?'

'Why do you want to know?'

Charlie knew from the man's voice that he was just as curious now. 'I wish I could tell you, but it's out of the question. If you don't tell me, though, I'll have to get the police round.'

'I'd rather tell you.' O'Grady nodded. 'Let's have a think now. It was a straight re-soling job.'

'Any idea what sort of soles?'

'I'd be pretty sure it was the standard composition sole, heavy duty.'

'What does that look like?'

O'Grady turned and crouched to rummage on the lower shelves. When he stood up he was holding a rubber sole with a deep tread, distinctively patterned in diamonds and double Us.

'Can you remember what size?'

'Ten, eleven.'

'Can I buy one – a size ten?'

'Sure. Did you want me to stick it on a shoe?'

'No. I want to match it to a footprint.'

Charlie left the shop with his prize and started walking towards Marble Arch with his head over his shoulder, searching for a cab.

He was satisfied with the meagre fruits of his journey. If all he had done was find the shoe that matched the footprint DI Ferrier had found, he had removed one small piece of potential evidence against Nick. It wasn't much, but it was in the right direction.

A taxi dropped Charlie in Kensington where he rang the bell on the back door of the shop in Church Street.

His mother opened it and let him in. Without speaking, she showed him up to the drawing room on the first floor. When she went into the small kitchen to make some tea, Charlie looked around at the comparative comfort of the apartment and wondered how this could be sustained in the face of all his stepfather's business creditors.

But if his mother was worried about it, it didn't show. She seemed to be far more concerned about Nick being in prison, though she was fatalistic about Charlie's chances of finding out anything that might help him. Charlie didn't tell her about his visit to the shoe menders, or the slab of thick rubber in his pocket. He didn't want her dismissing it from the equation just yet.

'I don't see what you can do that the police can't,' she said as if she'd read his mind.

'Quite a lot, as they're not doing anything,' Charlie said. 'There had to be someone else there, besides Dad's soldier. But the police think they've got their man and they're not too worried.'

Pru sighed. 'Surely they ought to be following up other lines.'

'Of course, but it's no use telling me.'

'If only he hadn't turned up just when he did,' Pru said, mostly to herself.

Charlie stayed that night in the London flat. In the morning, he and his mother had an appointment with David Patterson's lawyers.

They were met in the Lincoln's Inn offices by a partner with a harassed, disapproving manner.

'Your late husband's will was all in order, Mrs Patterson,' he said. In the still, dusty air of a book-lined meeting room, he read aloud a document which left everything to Pru. There were no other personal bequests.

'We are handling probate,' the lawyer went on, 'but I'm afraid we've already had some alarming claims on the estate. It seems your husband issued a number of guarantees to banks and property companies which are being called. On top of this there was an outstanding Lloyd's liability. We've been involved in fighting this for him, but that's all a very grey area and will be for some time to come. Did your husband make any separate, life-time provision for you?'

Pru shook her head.

The solicitor looked worried. 'Oh dear. I'll see what we can do but I'm afraid it looks as though it's a case of trying to salvage what we can from the wreckage. I do hope I'm not being too depressing when you've only just buried him.'

'That's all right,' Pru said quietly.

Charlie was disappointed to hear that the solicitor had no good news about Nick's predicament but went on to ask the question he most wanted to.

'Can you tell me what the situation is with the filly, Willow Star?'

'Ah, yes. The racehorse. Your father did have an offer for it which he indicated he wanted to accept.'

'I understand he confirmed it with Wetherby's.'

'Wetherby's only received his instruction after he had died.'

Charlie bit back his frustration. 'Have you had any other offers for her?'

'We have had one and we have accepted the best offer.'

Charlie's heart raced, anticipating bad news. 'So, who's the new owner?'

The lawyer hesitated a moment. 'It's a small nominee syndicate.'

'But who are they?'

'I'm afraid I'm not at liberty to say.'

Charlie took a deep breath. 'What are they going to do with her?'

'I dare say it will please you to hear that they wish the filly to stay where it is, in your yard at Oak Hollow.'

Chapter Ten

With ten days to go before the one thousand guineas, Willow Star's work programme was going well, but that was about all it was for Charlie.

In the two weeks since Nick had been arrested nothing had turned up to improve the prospects for his release.

Charlie was finding it difficult to concentrate on the yard while his partner's future was still in jeopardy. Barely a day passed without some speculation in the tabloid press, and Nick's resilience was fading fast.

Kate was at the yard all the time now. Without waiting to be asked, she had taken over the bulk of the paperwork which Nick normally handled and she was completely at home with the computer programme. She understood the complicated emotions afflicting Charlie as a result of the death of his stepfather and the arrest of his partner. Having looked at the balance sheet for the yard, she also realised just how important it was for him to succeed on the racecourse. The tensions in his life were palpable and potentially self-destructive, but she was learning how to defuse them.

She appointed herself guardian to Nick's dog, Hercules, who, for a time after his master's absence, had lacked his usual spark. He still wasn't quite back to his old self, but a couple of nights spent sleeping on Kate's bed, and with some regular titbits, he had perked up no end. Kate was also riding out most mornings; she was now fitter, leaner and losing the hint of chubbiness she had carried when Charlie had first met her.

Today, Kate had gone to Salisbury with a couple of runners. Charlie was still thinking of her as he waited in his office to see a potential owner with a lot of horses and a tight diary.

His visitor, a North London property dealer, turned out to be about fifty with a narrow, neatly trimmed moustache. He wore a camelhair coat, a navy trilby and a deep tan. There were large gold rings on six of his fingers and a Rolex oyster dangled on his wrist.

It normally took Charlie about fifteen seconds to weigh someone up, and another fifteen minutes to be proved right. If he wasn't mistaken, the character sitting opposite him would be a bad payer and an even worse loser. But he needed the horses. The meeting went well enough, at least to the extent that a couple of cheap two-year-olds, in which his other, grander trainer showed no interest, would be coming to Oak Hollow.

After the owner had driven away, the yard was deserted. It was two o'clock and the lads had either gone shopping for the afternoon or were in the hostel. They weren't needed now until evening stables. Charlie wanted a few things from the village. Kenny had taken his Range

Rover to collect some peat-moss, so he took the VW Golf which Kate had recently bought to replace the old Renault. He was just getting into it when he saw a large Mercedes swing off the road and creep down the drive to the stables.

Charlie temporarily abandoned his plan to go to the village and got out of the Golf to walk back to the bungalow. He didn't recognise the vehicle and watched its approach with interest. He was almost at the front door when the car swung down towards him and pulled up on the gravel.

Two men climbed out, one from each side. Charlie waited to greet them. They looked familiar. He groped a moment for their identity until it snapped into place. They had been part of Sheikh Sala Mahmoud's entourage at his father's funeral two weeks before.

Why should Sala Mahmoud be sending emissaries to Oak Hollow? Charlie barely knew about the Saudi merchant's activities but as far as he was aware the man had done little more than dabble in British racing. Maybe he had developed a taste for it.

Charlie smiled. 'Good morning.'

The two swarthy men did not smile back. They started walking towards him.

There was a hostility in their approach which made Charlie take a step back to the door, instinctively seeking the shelter of the house.

The larger of the two put his hand on Charlie's chest and shoved him with sudden violence against the partly open door. Charlie sprawled backwards into the house, he tried to save himself as he fell but before his hands touched anything, the back of his head connected with the corner of a stone umbrella stand. Lightning flashed in his head as he blacked out. When he came round a few moments later, he had been dragged down the narrow hallway into the kitchen. He was propped on one of the chairs. A handkerchief soaked in vinegar was being held to his nose, making him gag.

The older of his two aggressors was slapping his face. 'We want to talk to you,' he growled with guttural Arab consonants.

Charlie snatched the handkerchief away and struggled to regain some of his senses. 'What's the point of trying to smash my brains in first?'

'We smash more than your brains if you don't talk.'

'What the hell do you want?'

'Your father.'

'What about him?'

In a flash the man grabbed hold of Charlie at the throat. 'Your father cheated Sala Mahmoud. Where is the money now? You tell us what we need to know, or we start to do you harm. Where is your father?'

Charlie could hardly breathe, let alone talk. He'd always thought himself more than capable of fighting his own corner. But something about these men frightened him. Suddenly the hand was removed from his windpipe. 'I don't know what the hell you're talking about! My stepfather was murdered.'

The second man, who hadn't spoken at all, grabbed both Charlie's arms and brought them back behind the chair. He pulled a coil of cord from the pocket of his leather jacket and bound Charlie's wrists tightly to the chair slats. The cord sliced into Charlie's skin until he couldn't move his arms without agonising pain.

The man who had tied him leaned over him. Charlie smelled his rancid breath as he bent forward and put his hands between his legs to clutch both his testicles in a vicious grip, a crude technique for extracting reluctant information which was probably as old as man and always worked. The problem was, Charlie didn't have anything to tell his torturers.

They tried burning him with cigarette stubs; they put him on the floor and bent him nearly double backwards until he thought his spine would splinter. His face was hit so ferociously and so often that he could scarcely mumble his denials through thickened, bleeding lips.

His whole body ached. He was nearly unconscious with pain when, abruptly and without warning, it was over.

He became aware that he was alone and tied to the chair again. He was dimly conscious of the sound of a car starting and skidding away. A few minutes later, he heard someone walking down the passage from the front door.

'Hello? Guv'nor?' It was Kenny Ford. 'Jesus Christ! What the hell's happened?' The head lad stared with disbelief at his boss trussed to a chair, his face swollen and bruised, his mouth bleeding. Kenny was already taking a penknife from his pocket to untie him. 'Was it those blokes in the Merc?'

Charlie nodded as Kenny severed the cords binding his wrists and helped him to his feet. He flopped back on to the chair.

'I'll get you a drink.' Kenny went out into the office and came back with a tumbler half full of brandy.

Charlie gingerly put the glass to his swollen lips. 'God,' he spluttered. 'I never touch this stuff.' He took another slug and let the warming, softening, anaesthetising liquid sting his lips, dribble down his throat, through his chest into his battered guts.

Kenny sat down on the other side of the table and watched anxiously. 'What the hell's going on, guv'nor?'

'I wish to God I knew.' Charlie ran his tongue over his teeth, checking for damage. Fortunately, none was broken. 'They work for my father's old boss.'

'What did they want?'

'They said my father had stolen some money from Sheikh Sala Mahmoud, the man he used to work for. They thought I'd know where it was. At least they know I don't now. I haven't got a clue. Oh my God!' Charlie leaped to his feet. 'What about my mother?'

He picked up the phone and rang the flat in Kensington, but a recorded message announced that the line was not in service. Then he phoned Veronica and Michael, whom his mother had said she wanted to visit, but neither of them had heard from her. Finally he dialled the number at Birch Lodge. He let it ring for at least a minute before hanging up. 'I'll have to go round there,' he said to Kenny. 'If I'm not here when Kate and the others get back, tell her I'll ring later.'

★ ★ ★

The lock of the front door at Birch Lodge had been forced and the door was swinging on its hinges. Charlie pushed it open and walked in. Every room had been thoroughly and messily searched. Drawers were open with their contents scattered all over the floor. Upstairs it was the same. There was no sign of Charlie's mother. The case she had been packing a few days before and all her personal things had gone. That reassured him a little. But it could be she had them in London. If it was Sala Mahmoud's men who had broken in, it didn't look as though they had taken anything. And there was nothing to suggest that his mother had been here when they came.

He tidied up a little and realised he should arrange for the door to be mended. He ought also to tell someone what had happened.

He phoned a local locksmith and then drove round to the general's house.

Charlie didn't know General Sir Peter Sheridan well, but he was aware that the old soldier was one of his father's few close friends. He found him pruning roses in front of his handsome Edwardian house.

'Afternoon, sir.'

'Afternoon, Charlie. What on earth have you been up to? Fallen off one of your horses or what?'

'Nothing serious, sir. I was wondering if you'd seen my mother recently?'

'Not for a couple of days. Isn't she in London?'

'She may be, but the phone doesn't seem to be working.

The cottage here has been broken into again.'

The general straightened his back. 'Really? When?'

'Within the last twenty-four hours I should think. Did you hear anything?'

'Not a thing. And there's no sign of your mother?'

'No.'

'Have you told the police?'

'No.'

'Right. Let's get down there.' He looked closely at Charlie's damaged face. 'And you'd better tell me what happened to you, too.'

On their way back to the cottage in the woods, Charlie told General Sheridan about the Arabs' visit to Oak Hollow.

'They must have been under instructions from Sala Mahmoud,' the general said. 'I'm afraid they may be justified.'

Charlie gaped at him. 'You mean my father *did* cheat the sheikh in some way?'

'I don't know, but I'm certain he was up to something. He never told me directly, but I've known him a very long time, and I could read him as well as anyone. He was in serious financial trouble – you must have known that. He'd had a lot of bad luck and made some frankly poor judgements. I warned him before he joined Lloyd's I thought the party was over there. After all, they wouldn't have wanted to go out signing up thousands of new members when they could easily have written more business themselves and kept the profit. They knew they were in for a rough time and wanted some outside punters to carry the can. That's when I got out, after fifteen good years.'

'But it wouldn't be like him to run away from a few debts.'

'I don't think it was a question of a few debts; it was total wipe-out. Besides that, as I say, I think he pulled off a questionable deal just before he died. That's almost certainly why those Arabs wanted to talk to you.'

'What kind of a deal?'

'I don't know specifically. My guess is that it was something to do with that furniture he used to deal in. Occasionally he handled some very expensive pieces. He knew a lot about it and did quite well from it sometimes but every penny he made went to paying off his debts.'

They had reached the cottage now. The locksmith Charlie had rung was waiting in his van. The general confirmed that he should go ahead with fitting a new lock. He and Charlie went inside to inspect the damage. Afterwards he urged Charlie to drive straight to London to check on his mother. 'Ring if you need me and let me know that she's all right.'

Charlie drove away trying to make sense of the day's events, unable to reach a rational conclusion.

The break-in at the flat in Kensington had been a lot cleaner. Charlie found no sign of the lock being forced but the place had been ransacked; as he entered each room he held his breath, half expecting to find his mother lying beaten-up on the floor but there was no sign of her. He was now desperate to discover her whereabouts.

Charlie spent half an hour going through the piles of papers in his father's desk. A lot of these confirmed what the general had said about his father's current financial state. There were dozens of letters delivering draconian ultimatums. There was a letter from Nick, pleading with Major Patterson to think again about selling Willow Star.

Charlie thought of the filly for a moment. He had now received the lawyers' written instructions about the horse. The new owners had decided to remain anonymous. The bills would continue to be paid by the solicitors, and Charlie was to communicate all news through them. He wondered if the new owners had paid as much as Robert Jarvis had offered. Not that it mattered. The main thing was that the animal was to stay in his yard. And as every day passed, he became more convinced they still hadn't seen the best of her.

Charlie brought his mind back to the present problem. He found the keys to the shop below and let himself in. Apart from a few light fittings and some broken pieces in the basement, the place was empty. The landlord's 'To Let' sign was already up outside the shop.

After two hours, Charlie gave up.

He drove back to Oak Hollow, worried about his mother and wondering whether his father really had been involved in some kind of serious crime when he was murdered.

Kate was horrified at the state of his face. Kenny had

told her only that Charlie had been attacked, but not to what extent. He played down his visitors' brutality and insisted that she should tell him how she'd got on at the races before he talked about the day's bizarre events at the yard.

Charlie smiled at her enthusiasm as she described each of the races, stride by stride. Neither horse had been placed, but they had both shown promise and the owners had gone home more than satisfied. Charlie was painfully trying to eat his way through a steak when the telephone rang. He picked up the mobile beside him on the table.

'Hello? Charles?'

He nearly choked on the piece of meat he was swallowing. 'Mum! For God's sake, where are you?'

'I can't tell you. But I must see you.'

Charlie immediately thought that she must have been kidnapped and he imagined someone holding a gun to her head. 'Are you all right?'

'I'm fine, but I need to see you. By the giant rhubarb.'

Charlie knew exactly where she meant. 'What time?'

'Could you manage nine o'clock tomorrow morning?'

'Okay. I'll see you there. Are you *sure* you are all right?'

'Yes, and Charles, make certain you come alone.'

Next morning he drove into London via the A4 and didn't turn off until he had passed the Natural History Museum. He headed up Exhibition Road into Hyde Park and found a space for his car by the bridge over the Serpentine. He climbed out and looked around. He couldn't help his nervousness after the previous day's attack. He half expected somebody to know that he was arriving here, although anyone overhearing his conversation with his mother would never have guessed where they were to meet. There was a favourite spot in the park where she had often taken him as a small boy, near a clump of monster-leaved water plants which he had referred to then and always since as the 'giant rhubarb'.

She was waiting for him on a bench, neatly wrapped in a Burberry raincoat. She wore dark glasses against a watery sun. A Hermes scarf depicting scenes of implausible rustic tranquillity covered most of her head.

Charlie gave her a quick kiss of greeting and sat down beside her. She saw his battered face and gasped.

'Charlie, I'm so sorry,' she said, guiltily. 'I should have warned you.'

Charlie stared at her. 'You knew they were coming?'

'Not for sure, but I thought it was possible.'

'What's going on, Mum?'

His mother reached out a small, nervous hand and clutched his tightly. 'I'm not entirely sure.'

'But you have an idea? You knew Dad was up to something?'

Pru looked out across the placid ornamental waters. She set her face firmly. 'Yes. He felt he'd been betrayed by a number of people he had trusted. He hated the fact that he had ever relied on them in the first place. Instinctively, as you know, he was a loner.'

Charlie nodded.

His mother guessed what was going through Charlie's mind. She put a hand on his arm. 'Don't think harshly of him. He always tried to think of you as his own son, he genuinely did. He was very fond of you.'

'He had an odd way of showing it.'

'Why do you think he bought that filly?' Pru defended her late husband. 'He certainly couldn't afford it at the time. He just wanted you to know he was interested in your career.'

Charlie didn't answer for a moment. 'What was he up to, before he . . . died?'

'I can't tell you. However hard you try to make me, I shan't tell you anything for the time being.'

'For God's sake, Mum. You must tell me. I had a rough time yesterday.'

Pru dried the corner of her eye with a small handkerchief. 'I can see that, darling, and I'm sorry, but they went, didn't they, because they realised you didn't know anything. It's better that way.'

'But what about you? They've been to the cottage and the flat.'

'So I gather.'

'It's bloody lucky you weren't there. God knows what they might have done to you otherwise. Where were you?'

'At Veronica and Mike's; I told you I was going there.'

'But I phoned and they said they hadn't seen you.'

'I asked them to. Oh my God!' Pru gasped. 'I hope those people don't go there.'

'Would they know that Veronica is Dad's sister?'

'It wouldn't be hard to find out, would it? I'd better warn them.'

'But what about you, Mum? You can't go back to the flat, and certainly not to Birch Lodge. You should go and stay somewhere these people will never find, at least until things have quietened down.'

Pru nodded as if she was grateful for his support for a decision she had already taken. 'Yes. I'd thought of that. I'm going up to Scotland.'

'Thank God,' Charlie said. 'Where?'

'It's probably better that you don't know,' Pru said quickly.

'But what if I want to get in touch with you?'

Pru sighed. 'I'll give you a number where you can leave a message for me but if you do ring don't say it's you, say you're . . .' She puckered her forehead and looked around for inspiration. 'Peter Pan,' she grinned. She took a biro and a notebook from her bag and scribbled a number.

Charlie knew he'd find out approximately where she was by looking up the code. The thought seemed absurd. 'Mum, it'd be a lot simpler if you just told me what's going on, then I could go to the police.'

'Oh, no!' Pru said anxiously. 'Don't do that. It wouldn't help at all.'

'For God's sake, what is happening?'

'I can't tell you,' Pru pleaded. 'If we just ignore these people or they can't find us or learn anything, in the end they'll go away.'

'They seemed pretty determined to me,' Charlie said.

'But they won't press you, as long as they're sure you don't know anything.'

'I must know if there's anything that could help Nick.'

Pru looked away and closed her eyes. 'How is he?'

Charlie thought back to his last visit. 'Desperate.'

Pru turned back to face her son. She forced a look of encouragement that she didn't feel.

'Tell him not to worry. I'm sure he'll be released soon.'

Charlie wanted to question her further, but he knew it was pointless.

'I'm going now. Don't try to find me. Just ring if there's a serious emergency.'

'Mum, I hope you're not involved in whatever Dad was doing.'

She smiled with resignation. 'I'd rather not be, too. Now, are you sure no one followed you?'

Charlie got up from the bench, nodding. He had checked half a dozen times on his way from Lambourn.

'Good. I'll be in touch. In the meantime, don't tell anyone you've seen me.' She stood on tiptoe and gave him a kiss on the cheek. 'And don't worry about me. I'll be all right.'

Charlie looked at her. He knew it was probably pointless to ask her again, but he caught her arm and gave it a gentle squeeze. 'Mum, you must tell me. What did Dad do to Sala Mahmoud?'

His mother looked at him with grey eyes that held steady, despite the anxiety in them. 'All I can tell you is that just before all this happened, he was involved in a reckless scheme which he should never have started.

Trust me, Charlie, and understand that I must protect myself too.'

Charlie sighed.

His mother touched his cheek with her hand. 'Go now.'

Charlie turned on his heel to walk back to the car park, three hundred yards away beyond a dense shrubbery.

When he reached the far side of the bushes, he ignored the signs requesting the public not to disturb the plants and dived in to push his way back through to see what his mother was doing.

She was still standing where he'd left her. He hoped she wasn't going to wait until she saw his car drive away.

After another half minute, she started to walk briskly across Kensington Gardens towards the gate at Notting Hill. Charlie slipped out from beneath the laurels and followed her.

At first it felt somehow immoral, spying on his own mother, but then he saw himself more as a discreet bodyguard and it became a matter of duty.

Pru reached the Bayswater Road and hurried west to the tube station at Notting Hill Gate. Charlie almost had to run to catch up so that he didn't lose her in the labyrinth of passages. He managed to keep sight of her as she took an eastbound Circle Line train.

At Euston Square she got out, crossed Euston Road and made her way to the mainline station. Charlie tagged along at a distance. She walked on to the main concourse and looked at the departure board before heading for the Edinburgh train.

She didn't buy a ticket. She must either have got one earlier, or she had a return. Charlie bought himself a ticket through to Aberdeen and a *Sporting Life*. His mother had been born on an estate some twenty miles up the River Dee from Aberdeen and Charlie guessed that she would go to ground somewhere up there.

He found a seat in a carriage halfway down the train where he could keep an eye open in case his mother got off anywhere unexpectedly. For the rest of the journey, he settled back with his newspaper and fended off a couple of approaches from self-avowed racing fans.

At Waverley Station he saw his mother get out and head briskly for the Aberdeen train, as he'd predicted. Keeping his distance, he did the same. He knew that once they reached Aberdeen, his task would be more difficult. It was unlikely that his mother would be staying at her family's house or any of the several cottages that belonged to it.

When they arrived there, he almost lost her. She walked straight from the station building to the car park and Charlie's heart sank as he watched her get into her small Rover saloon. It was like discovering that a girlfriend was cheating on him.

She must have been up here all the time, nowhere near Veronica and Mike. Why had she lied to him? Surely she knew he wouldn't have betrayed her?

He turned and walked back briskly towards the cab rank. His wounded feelings would just have to wait until he'd discovered what was really happening. There were two taxis, and two sets of customers already waiting.

When they had gone, Charlie was looking around desperately for an alternative when an old black cab rattled into the station forecourt. Charlie had the back door open before it had stopped and leaped in. His mother's car had disappeared. Charlie took a calculated chance. 'Take the Banchory road,' he said. 'And hurry, please.'

They were leaving the sparser outskirts of the city, driving into the thickening dusk, before Charlie saw his mother's car.

'That's it!' he shouted through the opening in the glass partition. 'Can you follow that grey Rover?'

The driver was an Aberdonian who fancied he knew the ways of the world.

'Aye, no problem. It's not motoring too quick. D'you want them to know we're behind?' He looked at Charlie in his mirror on the windscreen.

'No, not if you can help it.'

The driver grinned. 'They won't.'

At first it was easy to keep several cars between them. But it became more difficult as they headed out into the country. It was after the equinox; the northern days were already longer than in the south but it was nearly dark by the time Pru drove through Banchory and turned off the main road into the heavily wooded hills to the south. After a while, she slowed and turned east on to a narrow stone track which led up a valley through the trees. Charlie paid off his taxi and waited by the road until its lights had disappeared on the way back to Aberdeen.

A damp westerly moaned through the trees, interrupted by occasional long hoots of a tawny owl in the oak woods of the lower slopes. Beside the road, a brook gurgled noisily. There wasn't a sound of his mother's car.

Charlie walked a few yards up the track in the thick, black night, peering through the trees ahead of him. There was no sign of a light. Finding his way was as much a matter of feeling with his feet as seeing with his eyes, though he was beginning to discern the gap in the trees which marked the track.

He stumbled on, his thoughts plagued with guilt that he hadn't rung Kate to tell her what he was doing or to find out how she had got on. He couldn't guess what his mother's plan was. Taking herself out of circulation to avoid any communication with Sala Mahmoud was certainly only part of the story.

The ground was rising now and Charlie was concentrating on the way when he heard a car coming. He looked up. Between the serried trunks of young pines, he saw the flash of headlamps coming towards him down a winding track.

He left the track and pushed his way several yards into the cover of the trees. As the vehicle passed, Charlie made out a short wheel-base Land Rover such as was used on every other farm in the country but he couldn't see who was driving it. He watched it bounce on down to the road then turn north and speed off towards Banchory.

He stepped out and carried on up the track. The low clouds were beginning to release some of their moisture in a thick, steady drizzle and the rutted woodland road was doubling as a stream for the run-off.

Another twenty minutes' trudging brought a reward in the form of a light glimmering a few hundred yards ahead. Quickening his pace, he almost slammed straight into the wooden garage that marked the top of the track. Cautiously, he found the door, opened it and slipped in. He flicked his lighter and by the quivering flame saw his mother's car.

He extinguished the flame and let himself out of the garage. He cast about until he found a footpath which led up to the house.

He approached cautiously, planning to find out who was in the house before making his presence known.

It was a small, stone-built farmhouse. Once, before the heavy reforestation of the last thirty years, it had stood in a dell among an open expanse of rough grazing. Several barns and animal sheds still clustered around the building, neglected and seldom used. Charlie carried on past them to the house where two uncurtained windows glowed. A mile from the road, no one had been concerned to close the shutters.

Confident that the wind and darkness would cover his approach, he walked towards the first window and peered into a sparsely furnished kitchen. As he looked, his mother walked into the room, put the kettle on the stove and started to prepare a meal. She tuned the radio to a classical station and strains of Mendelssohn seeped out through the window into the blustery night.

Charlie crept past the low doorway to the next lighted window. He stopped and peered into a small empty sitting room.

When he had worked his way round the whole house, he returned to the door and knocked on it.

From the other side he heard his mother's voice, calling above the wind. 'Who is it?' Even in the noise of the night, Charlie detected her panic.

'It's Charlie,' he shouted back.

The door was opened and his mother's face appeared. She looked at him and peered into the darkness beyond him. 'Charles! What on earth are you doing here?' For an instant, she seemed reluctant to let him in. Then, as though thinking better of it, she pulled the door wide open with a flourish.

Charles stepped over the threshold into the comparative calm of the small house. Without waiting for an answer, his mother led him through to the kitchen where the gas stove had already warmed the room.

'You look frozen,' she said. 'Let me give you some soup.'

At her suggestion, he peeled off most of his damp clothes which she hung off the backs of chairs around the room. 'They'll soon dry in front of this stove,' she said. She took a jug of broth from a larder cupboard and poured the contents into a pan on the stove. Before it started to bubble, she filled a big white bowl and put it on the table with a hunk of fresh bread. 'There you are.'

Charlie took a spoonful and relaxed in the comforting warmth of the place. The house was in good order, considering its remoteness. There was no electricity and he guessed that all the lamps and the cooker were fuelled by gas bottles.

'What is this place, Mum? Is it your father's?'

'No. It belongs to a neighbour, Archie Bell. We used to come up here often when we were children. It was more or less derelict then. Archie had it done up when the first rush of oilmen arrived up here, looking for places to rent not too far from Aberdeen.'

'Why have you come here?'

'Archie's an old friend. I haven't been in touch with your grandparents, and Archie will be discreet. I told you, I have to protect myself. I don't think anyone will come looking for me here.'

'I found you easily enough,' Charlie pointed out.

'How did you get here? I mean, actually up to the house. I didn't hear a car.'

'I followed you in a taxi from Aberdeen and got it to drop me at the bottom of the track. If I'd known it was so far, I'd have got him to drive me halfway up.'

Charlie looked around, crossed to the window and closed the shutters. 'Okay. I suppose you'll be safe enough, but for how long? Whatever this deal was that Dad did, the guys who saw me were very serious about Sala Mahmoud wanting his money back.'

'Yes, I know, and if I knew where it was, I'd give it back.'

'Don't you have any idea?'

'No. None at all. Your father did make a transfer to my account the day before he died. But I'll have to use that to live on for the time being. What he did with the rest, I just don't know.'

The fact that his mother had lied to him already was

still agonizingly fresh on his mind. 'Mum, for God's sake, come clean. I'm caught in the middle here. You *must* tell me.'

'I would, Charles, if I could, believe me.' She met his gaze steadily, defying him to disbelieve her.

Charlie took her wrists and clutched them tight for emphasis. 'You're going to have to find that money,' he said. 'Or you'll never live your life in peace.'

'That depends on where I am.'

'But, Mum, you won't be safe anywhere. And they'd still be watching me, waiting for me to come and see you.'

Pru's eyes clouded over and for a moment Charlie had a glimpse of the bleakness she was trying to hide. She had trained herself and developed the strength to subjugate her own vulnerability and sensitivity to the emotional needs of the moment. Charlie yearned for her to release herself and let it all out, but he knew how stubborn she could be.

'Charles, please don't press me,' she said firmly. 'Do you think I like being in the position your father's left me? Do you think I approve of what he did?' A hint of anger crept into her voice, which she hadn't intended. 'I understand, of course, because he'd become utterly desperate. He was completely broke, and no one would advance him a penny – not that he asked many, but the banks were totally unreasonable and I hated to see him so humiliated.' She shook her head. 'He felt that everyone had betrayed him, friends, Lloyd's, the bank, the whole establishment, everyone pressing him for money he simply had no hope of getting. He felt very strongly that he'd let me down; you too, when he had to sell Willow Star. All he did was pre-empt the bank, who had already written to him asking about her,' she said resignedly.

'If I'd known, we could have registered her in your name.'

'Charlie, my name is on all of the guarantees as well.'

Charlie was momentarily stunned. Her side of the family weren't enormously wealthy, but she was due to inherit part of a large estate in Scotland. He couldn't believe she had been so naive as to risk all of it for her husband.

'It's probably hard for you to understand but privately David was surprisingly insecure. It was this insecurity and his tremendous strength of personality that made him so secretive and self-reliant. He was brave, but he was careful – careful not to expose himself to ridicule or even criticism. Anyway, I loved him and loved him more when I realised he was ready to admit he needed me. I'd have stood by him no matter what he did.'

She cleared away Charlie's plate and bowl sensing some kind of admonishment from her son. 'Now, I think it would be a mistake for you to stay here,' she said. 'As soon as your clothes are dry, I'll drop you back to Aberdeen. Then you must promise me you won't come here or try to contact me again, under any circumstances. I beg of you,' she pleaded. 'Or sooner or later those people will follow you here.'

Chapter Eleven

Reggie Pymer shook his head in frustration and stood back to look at the ceiling he was working on. He didn't need his tape measure to know that the last piece of cornice lying at his feet was a couple of inches too short to finish the job.

Reggie had been in the business of repairing and fitting new plaster mouldings for most of his working life. He specialised in deep Victorian mouldings. Most of them, like the one he was replacing in this mid-nineteenth-century house in Kilburn, were handmade, using the original patterns. It would be at least two weeks before he could get hold of another length.

'Bollocks!' He blamed himself. He had left Matthew, his apprentice, to carry on without him while he'd gone to the dentist. The youngster had wasted as much cornice as he'd fitted.

He turned and looked at Matthew. 'You're a useless twat, aren't you?' he said mildly, as he pushed his worn cloth cap to the back of his bald head. 'The painters are due in 'ere tomorrer.'

Matthew shuffled his feet and his spotty cheeks twitched remorsefully. Reggie gazed from the floor to the ceiling and back, looking for a solution. For Matthew's benefit, he gave a long, groaning sigh. 'I tell you what we'll do,' he said. 'You go out to the skip. Find the best piece of cornice we chucked away and I'll see if we can mitre it in to make the job look half decent. If you can't find a piece, don't come back.'

The boy nodded, eager to make up for his mistake. He clattered out of the building. Reggie sat on his toolbox and waited. He'd run short of material hundreds of times and had always been able to make good with something. It wouldn't do Matt any harm, though, to sweat for a while.

He pulled a pack of cigarettes from his pocket and poked one between his lips. He was just about to strike a match when he heard the front door slam back against the inside wall and the thud of panicked feet racing down the hallway. Matt came rushing in. His normally bovine eyes stared wildly and his face was as white as a hospital sheet.

'Quick! Come quick!' he yelled, dragging Reggie to his feet. 'There's a body in the skip.' They both ran outside to the large iron container filled to the brim with discarded materials.

Matt leaned over it and lifted a piece of broken plasterboard. Reggie peered over his shoulder.

A man's head, grey-white, with glazed and staring eyes, nestled on the rubble in which the rest of his body was buried.

★ ★ ★

'Probably just a tramp,' suggested Reggie to the first police patrolman to arrive in answer to his 999 call. 'I should think he just curled up for the night and never woke up.'

The policeman shook his head. 'No. He's too tidy for a tramp. Look at his hair,' he said. He fingered the man's soft melton jacket. 'I'm not saying he's dressed for the City, but his clothes are clean, and he doesn't smell like a tramp.'

A second police car drew up with squealing tyres, followed almost immediately by an ambulance.

Reggie, his problem cornice forgotten for the moment, stood back and watched while photographs were taken and he and Matt answered questions. It wasn't until the body had been slid into the ambulance to be ferried across to the mortuary that they started to rummage around in the skip for lengths of cornice. They soon found some and went back inside to finish their job.

Later, as they were packing up for the day, one of the policemen came back.

'We need to check a couple of things.'

'What for?' Reggie asked, delighted that he was still involved in the drama.

'The geezer you found was murdered.'

Charlie never enjoyed the constrictions of flying tourist class. He stepped from the Aberdeen-Heathrow shuttle with relief. It was half-past twelve the day after he had followed his mother to the cottage in the hills outside Banchory.

Self-conscious and feeling slightly paranoid, he made two circuits of the airport terminal before he was satisfied there was no one following him. He took the tube to Hyde Park Corner and walked across to the Serpentine car park to find that his Range Rover had collected two parking tickets but not the clamp he'd been expecting.

He drove impatiently out of London, catching up on his business over the phone as he squeezed his way through the crawling traffic. To his relief there had been no dramas at the yard.

'You should disappear more often,' Kate said. 'Everything runs a lot smoother without you sticking your oar in and telling everybody what to do.'

Charlie took the banter well. Just then it was what he needed to take his mind off his worries about his mother's safety and Nick's freedom, as well as his father's activities. He was almost glad to see Detective Inspector Ferrier climb out of his car just before evening stables. At least the detective was someone to talk to about his current crisis, and he wanted to present him with the rubber sole he'd brought back from the shoe repairers.

As Ferrier strolled across the yard towards him, Charlie had the impression he was making an effort not to appear too aggressive.

'Evening, Mr Patterson. I need another chat with you. Is it convenient now?'

'Yes, sure. I've got a few questions for you, too. Come into the house and I'll get you a drink.'

The DI accepted a generous measure from a bottle of twelve-year-old malt Charlie had bought at Aberdeen airport that morning.

'So,' the detective started. 'What did you want to ask me?'

Charlie leaned back in his chair and took a brown paper parcel from the dresser top. He tipped the deeply moulded shoe sole on to the table in front of him.

The policeman looked at it, unimpressed. 'Well? How's this supposed to help us?'

'I think there's a good chance it will fit the footprints you found outside Birch Lodge.'

'Been visiting your friend's cobbler then, have you?' the policeman said with a faint grin.

'No. It came from a heel bar in Kilburn – that's North London.'

Ferrier's eyes narrowed abruptly and the grin faded from his lips. 'I know where Kilburn is.'

'My father was seen driving someone else to the cottage on the Saturday morning – one of his ex-squaddies.'

'How do you know?'

'Unlike you, I spoke to General Sheridan's gardener. He told me he'd seen someone with him in the car. You found a pack of Rizla papers on the ground outside. I found a couple of fag ends in the ashtray of the car, and my father never smoked roll-ups. I also found a shoe repair ticket.'

The detective's curiosity overcame his annoyance at Charlie's tone of voice. 'Why didn't you tell us this before?'

'When I told you I was sure Nick Ryder hadn't killed my stepfather, you almost laughed, remember? I also told you I was going to make my own inquiries and you said I'd be wasting my time. I wanted to be pretty sure before I came back to you with anything.'

'How did the gardener know it was an ex-squaddie who'd come to see the major?'

Charlie suddenly didn't want to answer this. 'Well, it must have been.'

'Why?' the detective asked impatiently. 'Someone must have put it to you. Was it your partner? He never told us he saw anyone else.'

'No.' Charlie knew he was backed into a corner. 'It was my mother. She said they often came to see him.'

'Why do you suppose she didn't tell us about him then?'

'Because he'd gone away before she'd left to go to the shops that morning.'

'I see. She didn't think it was worth mentioning to us.'

'I suppose she just thought it wasn't relevant.'

'I'd like to talk to her about it myself. Trouble is, I don't seem to be able to find her.' Charlie didn't miss the edge to the detective's voice. 'Do you know where she's gone?'

'She said she was going to stay with my stepfather's sister and her husband.'

'Mrs Veronica Russell?'

'That's right.'

'No. She hasn't been there. I sent someone from the local force.'

'I'm not sure where she is then. I had a meeting with her at the lawyers the day after the funeral but I haven't seen her since. She's rung me a couple of times, I assumed from the Russells.'

'Did you?'

Charlie knew that Ferrier didn't believe him.

'I'll tell you something else about Kilburn, shall I?' the detective went on.

'What's that?'

'Someone from Kilburn rang your mother a few times.'

'My mother?'

'Yes. After the major was killed. Do you think that's the same person whose footprint you say you can match?'

'How the hell should I know? But he obviously came from Kilburn or somewhere nearby, or why would he have his shoes repaired there?'

'Indeed. As a matter of fact, though, it wasn't the same man. The chap who phoned was called Miles Latimer. He was found dead as a kipper in Kilburn, yesterday morning. Someone had chucked him in a builder's skip; half buried him in rubble.'

'How do you know it wasn't the man I was told about?'

'I'm afraid I'm not sure I believe in your man. But Latimer was real enough, and he certainly didn't wear a size ten shoe.' Ferrier nodded at the rubber sole on the table. 'He'd been lodging at his sister's. She was pretty long-suffering. He'd not been out of jail long and she'd lent him a lot of money. But he kept telling her not to worry, he'd soon be able to pay her back. He'd found a goose that laid golden eggs.'

'He was going to rob someone?'

'No. Geese lay eggs regular, not one offs.'

'What are you saying?'

'Blackmail.'

Charles could feel his mouth drying up as the pieces of the jigsaw slotted into a different pattern. Did this man Latimer know that his stepfather had been involved in some illicit deal before he died? Was he trying to extort money from his mother?

'How do you know he rang my mother?'

'The number shows up on his sister's phone bill – three times – a few days after your stepfather was killed.'

'But why should that mean he's blackmailing her? And for what, for Christ's sake?'

'If we could talk to her ourselves,' Ferrier said pointedly, 'I'm sure we could sort it all out.'

Charlie stared back at him. He couldn't see which way to go next. He took a step back. 'About this shoe. Will you check it against the print you took? If it fits, I've got matching descriptions of the man who went to Birch Lodge that day, from the gardener and from the cobbler.'

'All right, Mr Patterson. We'll do that. But first you've got to tell me where your mother is.'

Charlie shrugged his shoulders and did his best to appear totally mystified. 'I wish to God I knew.'

The policeman gave Charlie another long, hard stare.

'If this other person did come to the house, only she can testify to it.'

'If I hear from her, I'll let her know.'

'If you hear from her, you let *me* know, p.d.q.' Ferrier gazed steadily at him, making it clear this wasn't a polite request. 'And are you going to tell me who came looking for you?'

'What do you mean?'

The detective tapped his mouth, nodding at the bruises on Charlie's face.

'Oh, that,' Charlie gave a light laugh. 'I just tripped on the ramp of the lorry leading a horse out and fell flat on my face.'

Ferrier raised an eyebrow but didn't comment.

Charlie looked back innocently.

Ferrier drained the last drop of whisky from his glass and stood up. 'All right,' he said. 'You can stop the amateur detective stuff now. We'll follow up your heel bar and the gardener.' He nodded and walked out of the front door. Charlie followed and watched him get back into his car.

'Don't forget,' Ferrier said before he closed his door. 'If you hear from your mother, let me know, for her own good. Thanks for the Scotch.'

Charlie watched the Vauxhall drive up the track to the gate. He guessed he wouldn't be able to make a move now without someone reporting back to the detective – or to the Arabs. But he would have to see his mother and warn her that the police were as keen to find her as Sala Mahmoud was.

* * *

The next day dawned bright and blue-skied for the first time in a fortnight. Charlie woke alert and positive about what he was going to do.

There was no sign that he was being watched but he didn't take any chances. He rode out of the yard with the first lot, reaching the bottom of the gallops shortly before seven. He watched Willow Star cantering and then set off towards a clump of beech trees a few hundred yards away where Kenny was waiting to take over. While the head lad rejoined the rest of the string Charlie slipped through the trees to the far side of the copse where a hedge straggled along the brow of the hill. He walked quickly in the shadow of the hedge for a quarter of a mile until he found Kate's new Golf which she'd left for him the night before. She had agreed to his using it, but he hadn't told her he was planning to drive to Scotland in it.

He had the key to the car in his pocket. He let himself in and drove quietly down the track towards the Wantage road. Within half an hour he was on the far side of Oxford, heading across country for the M1, and by three o'clock that afternoon he left the A90 at Laurencekirk and headed up the road for Banchory.

He reached the gap in the woods where the track led up to the house. He didn't turn into it. He drove straight past and on to the next village where he pulled up outside a small dusty general store. Looking in the driving mirror of his car, he could see no other vehicle coming up behind him, but he waited five minutes and watched two local cars drive past before he was satisfied there was still no one on his tail. He certainly didn't want to be caught now, when he was so near his destination. He got out and walked into the shop to buy a paper before getting back in and turning south.

When he reached the spot where the taxi had dropped him two days before, he drove off the road and up the stony, gullied track. He was impressed again by the remoteness of the place. He guessed that as long as his mother's own family, who anyway lived ten miles away over the hills, didn't know she was here, she would be quite safe for the time being. But sooner or later someone would recognise her and tell her family. And it would probably be only a matter of time before her whereabouts was known to everyone.

He stopped his car halfway up the track at a muddy passing place. He got out to listen. A chain saw whined faintly and intermittently somewhere across the valley. Otherwise he could hear only the emptiness of the conifer woods. Ignoring the track, he walked on up the hill through the trees. From now on caution was paramount.

He reached the barn which served as a garage without seeing or hearing anything to alert him. His mother's car was still there.

For a few minutes he remained concealed, his eyes fixed on the house beyond. There was nothing about the place to alarm him. A wisp of smoke curled reassuringly from the chimney. He took a deep breath and walked across the grassy clearing.

The front door was ajar. He was about to call out

when he heard a voice from inside the house. It was his mother's, on the phone, Charlie guessed. Something about her tone that sounded not quite right, out of place, made Charlie hold back a moment. Then it struck him – it was too light-hearted, too cheerful. He paused in the hall to listen a little longer before he let her know he was there.

From the small sitting room on his left he heard her give a quick, warm laugh. 'I'm looking forward to seeing you too,' she said with unmistakable tenderness. There was a pause while the other party spoke, then Pru's voice became more serious. 'Yes, I will take care. Apart from Charlie – and Archie, of course – no one knows I'm here and Charlie's not going to tell anyone.'

Charlie racked his brain trying to think who might be on the other end of the line.

'I'm sure he has no idea,' Pru was saying now. 'Anyway, I'll see you tomorrow morning . . . No, I won't be late, midday, but I wish I could stay with you . . . All right. I understand. Goodbye, my darling, and look after yourself, too.'

Charlie had to decide then and there what he should do. An appalling thought had entered his head – appalling, but a rational explanation of a lot of contradictions since his stepfather had died.

Before his mother had replaced the phone, Charlie had slipped back out of the house. By the time she reached the hall on her way to the kitchen, he had run across the clearing and was already hidden among the pine trees.

That his mother should have a lover wasn't, on the face of it, so strange; David Patterson had always been a difficult man. But Charlie had never doubted that his mother had stayed loyal to him despite that and it was beyond his comprehension of her that she could have concurred in the murder of her husband. Yet it explained her strange calmness and lack of emotion at the time of his death. It explained her reluctance to talk to the police or to see that Sala Mahmoud got his money back.

His mind shied away from his thoughts. The implications were too awful to contemplate. He was jumping to conclusions. First he had to find out who she had been talking to. She was due to meet him next day; he would simply wait here until then, and follow her in the morning.

Charlie managed a few hours' uneasy sleep in the reclining seats of the Golf with a horse rug wrapped round him. But he'd been awake for two hours, longing for a coffee, when finally he saw his mother's Rover emerge from between the trees at the bottom of the track.

He was parked three hundred yards away at the side of the road, confident that his mother wouldn't recognise the Golf. He took care not to get too close to her. If he lost her, he lost her; she would always come back to the cottage. But if she discovered he was following her, he might never get to the bottom of this mess.

He still found it impossible to reconcile his knowledge of his mother with the actions of a woman who could connive with her lover to murder her husband just when he had made an apparently huge illicit profit through a deal with an Arab who was prepared to torture her son to regain his money. And what about Nick? Charlie's hands tightened on the steering wheel. No wonder his mother had been so sure Nick was innocent.

Charlie had no idea how he was going to deal with her and the man she was meeting, but he had to do this himself. He couldn't simply hand his own mother over to the police.

As he drove, now seeing her, now letting her get ahead, Charlie tried to convince himself that there might yet be an innocent explanation for the phone call he had overheard, but as they crossed the snow-draped Grampians and the Spey at Grantown he still hadn't managed to come up with one.

At Inverness, Pru headed south-west along the bank of Loch Ness. The bright spring sun glittered on the narrow length of the loch as they followed the northern shore to Fort Augustus. It was half-past twelve when they reached the small town. Charlie hung back, as he had in Inverness. He let a couple of cars in between him and his mother although he was confident that she had no idea he was behind her.

When she parked in the main street, Charlie drove on by and found a space further up. He stayed in his car and surveyed the sleepy high street through his rearview mirror. Pru got out of her car and crossed the road with her short, busy stride. She walked into a pub and disappeared from sight.

His heart thumping, Charlie climbed out of the Golf and crossed the road a hundred yards from the large inn. Taking care not to be seen from inside it, he sidled along until he could steal a glance into the bar.

Pru was sitting, facing the door. The man she was talking to had his back to Charlie. He was wearing a scruffy donkey jacket. His dark hair was long and untidy.

Charlie ducked back before his mother looked up. He couldn't go in and confront them there. He would have to wait until they came out. If they split up, he would follow the man.

He bought a paper and walked back to his car. He angled the driving mirror so that he could watch the door of the pub; he could see his mother's car in his wing mirror. He opened the paper and pretended to read, glancing up every minute or so.

He didn't know how much later it was that he jerked awake to see his mother's car pulling out.

He was in time to see her drive past him and he frantically searched up and down the street, hoping to catch a glimpse of the man she'd been with. Angry with himself for having missed his chance, Charlie started the engine and was about to move off when the man who had been drinking with his mother appeared from the bar. At a distance of fifty yards, the man seemed vaguely familiar. Charlie was beginning to think that he was looking at the person who had been described to him by Tom Skyrme and Mr O'Grady in the heel bar. And he realised with a physical jolt that this would explain something which had been worrying him for weeks: why his mother hadn't told the police – hadn't even told him, for God's sake! – about the earlier visitor that Saturday morning. Nick turning up when he had must have been an unexpected piece of luck for them, a ready-made red herring.

The man hauled himself into an old Land Rover and set off towards the village of Invermoriston with Charlie following him. Here the Land Rover branched off to the left along a road which swooped and curved through a shallow river valley. On either side, the craggy mountain peaks stood out crisp and white against a clear blue sky and no wind disturbed the thick forests of the silent valley.

The road was empty and Charlie had to hang well back from the slowly moving vehicle. After twenty minutes, another small loch came into view. The Land Rover carried on along the northern bank on a straight, flat road. It was travelling even more slowly now. Charlie almost came to a standstill until he was about half a mile behind his quarry. The road took a dog-leg turn past a stand of Scots pines and Charlie lost sight of the Land Rover. He quickened. When he reached the trees, he was confronted by the sight of half a mile of lonely road.

He stopped and gazed at the grey strip. His lips tightened in frustration, and he swore. He set off slowly, glancing from left to right, praying for a glimpse of the vehicle. On his left there was only a thin swathe of land between the road and the loch. On his right, the ground was well covered in heather, bracken, and stunted, scrubby trees, sweeping up to a stark rocky edge. There was no sign of the Land Rover or any other human intrusion. And yet there hadn't been time for the vehicle to reach the far end of the road. Charlie drove on to a point where the road curved left again to present another empty landscape.

Angry with himself, he turned and drove back. He stopped halfway along the straight and climbed out. Nothing broke the sea of purple, green and dun that swept up the mountainside. The wind moaned gently, carrying a few bird calls which emphasised the absence of man.

Cursing his incompetence, Charlie got back into the Golf and headed back down the loch. He thought about his mother and how he should confront her. When he reached Invermoriston on the shores of Loch Ness, he still hadn't decided what to do. He didn't even know what he would have done if he had found her lover. She was obviously implicated in the death of his stepfather, but whatever she had done, all his instincts recoiled from handing her over to the police.

He stared at the narrow lake for a few minutes, took a deep breath and turned his car south.

It was midnight when he drove in through the gates at Oak Hollow. A few minutes later he slipped into bed beside a soft, sleepy body which welcomed him with arms that wrapped round him. Kate's body arched in answer to gentle fingers feeling the warm, damp recesses of her bushy mound. Soon, Charlie's problems and tensions had melted away, not to disturb him again until morning.

Chapter Twelve

The prison visiting room smelled faintly of disinfectant and depression. Despite the authorities' efforts to soften the experience for visitors – brightly painted murals, and smiling women from the WRVS serving tea – the walls seemed to ooze anguish and the tears that had been shed here. Charlie could see that his attempts to cheer Nick weren't working. His partner's jaw was set, not with determination but with hopeless resignation to the inevitable. His depression was tangible. He'd resigned himself to his fate. Not even the news about the body in Kilburn or the man spotted in his father's car had stirred him. There was an awkwardness between them, brought on largely by Charlie's failure to mention his mother's involvement, and after a short while Charlie muttered an embarrassed farewell, leaving his friend more miserable than ever. But he knew now that he had no option but to get straight back to Scotland and find the man responsible for Nick's incarceration.

Charlie pulled up beside the loch, turned off the Golf's

engine and got out. The water shimmered in the light of a young moon. Only the distant gurgling of a capercaillie broke the deep mountain silence and there was not a glimmer of light or sign of human habitation to be seen.

Neil MacPhee, the landlord of the pub in Fort Augustus, had told Charlie that the man he was asking about was David Urquhart – a writer, he thought. He didn't know him, but he'd heard that sometimes he stayed in the croft by Loch Cluanie. The directions he gave were vague, but Charlie couldn't find anyone who could pinpoint the place more precisely.

Standing looking up at the empty, silent slopes, Charlie knew that the house, croft, cottage, whatever it was, was no more than half a mile from where he stood. The small cairn of stones by the roadside was the landmark he'd been told to look for. There was no road, just a track which might be viable with four-wheel drive. He had to find somewhere suitable to leave Kate's car. The edge of the forest was a few hundred yards along the bank of the loch. Charlie got back into the car and drove until he reached a piece of sheltered verge. He parked the car there and left it, confident that there was a negligible risk of its being stolen in such a deserted spot. Carrying a small rucksack he had packed in Lambourn early that morning, he walked back to the cairn which marked the point where he had to leave the road.

In the scanty, silver light, Charlie could make out the faint track which led due north towards the Pole Star. He set off cautiously, stopping to listen every few yards. Once he heard the sharp scream of a barking fox. From several miles away to the east, the breeze wafted the sound of a car coming up the side of the loch.

After three hundred yards, when he met the rising ground, the path turned forty-five degrees and dropped down into a dell with a small copse of Scots pine and oak. The place he was looking for should be just north of the copse, sheltering in a small gully in the hillside.

Charlie reached the copse. Just behind it, in the growing moonlight, he caught sight of a building of lime-washed stone. Relieved that he had arrived, he stopped and listened again. There was no sound of the car. Reassured, he set off cautiously over the last fifty yards. He could see now that the building was definitely a dwelling – one-storey, with a fat chimney in the middle of a broad-slated roof and two small windows on either side of a simple front door.

There wasn't a hint of light from inside. Charlie approached one pace at a time, his heart thumping. Was the man away? Asleep? Alert and already waiting for him?

He stopped to listen again. He had seldom heard such silence; his own heartbeat was the loudest sound.

He took the last few paces to the front door. It had a simple wooden latch and a bolt which could be secured with a padlock.

Charlie pushed down the latch with his thumb. The door swung open and he stepped inside, dark as pitch, but for a glimmer of orange light glowing through the blackened glass doors of a large stove. The low-ceilinged room harboured a strong smell of peat smoke. He groped by the door for a light switch until, feeling foolish, he realised there wouldn't be any electricity in a place like this. He struck a match. There was an oil lamp standing on a table in the middle of what was a small living room and kitchen combined. He lit the lamp, keeping the wick as low as he could, and pulled a pair of shutters across the window. He turned up the flame a little. The walls were whitewashed stone and the floor was flagged. There were two side chairs at an old pine table and a large old oak carver opposite the peat-burning range.

He was about to start looking around, to get some idea of who he was dealing with, when a sound from outside froze his blood.

He had heard a distinct rustle, the sound of the scrubby bracken and heather being disturbed. It could have been a fox, maybe, or a deer, but all his instincts told him it was a human. He stepped across the room so that he'd be behind the door when it opened.

A second later, it flew back, letting in a gust of heather-scented evening air and two powerful torch beams. The door was pushed shut and one beam swung round and found Charlie pressed against the wall like a rabbit in a trap. He hadn't even started to make a plan.

He held his breath and in the few seconds that followed a torrent of thoughts rushed through his mind. He could see no one behind the lights but he knew there were at least two of them. The man he had seen in Fort Augustus, David Urquhart, his mother's friend? And who? His mother?

It seemed unlikely that his mother would be running around the glens in darkness. He wished someone would speak.

'So.'

Charlie quaked. He recognised the voice at once.

'Why have you come here?'

The wick of the oil lamp was turned up. The torches were clicked off and the smoky room was filled with the warm yellow glow of the lamp. Charlie found himself looking at the distinctive features and glistening black beard of the man who had done all the talking when he'd been tied to a chair and tortured at Oak Hollow. Behind him was the even less forgettable face of the man who had tortured him. Both men were holding pistols, aimed directly at him.

Charlie's guts heaved and sweat prickled the palms of his hands. 'What do you want?' he croaked.

'Sheikh Sala Mahmoud would still like his money, and he is getting impatient.'

'I don't know where it is. I told you before. I know nothing about it.'

'Then why have you come here?'

Charlie didn't answer. He couldn't think of a plausible lie. The second Arab, silent up till now, grunted and stepped forward. He lifted his gun, turned it round and smashed the metal butt on to Charlie's jaw.

Charlie's head jerked back, lolled forward and came to rest on his chest, feeling as if it was filled with cement. He couldn't even contemplate what was going to happen to him. He had no experience of this kind of violence and had no idea how to cope with it. He wanted to fight back but he was a complete amateur, and he knew it.

He felt himself grabbed and a hard, sinewy forearm was jammed across his windpipe as he was manhandled towards the centre of the room. For the second time he was shoved brutally on to a chair and his wrists bound with cord.

The memory of the pain he'd suffered last time surged through him. He closed his eyes and prayed that he would faint before it started again.

The bang of the door crashing back against the wall reached him with a gush of fresh air. He jerked his eyes open. He was facing the door. Standing in the frame, with a gun in his hand, was the man he'd come to find. In the time it took Charlie to form the thought, orange flame spurted twice from the short barrel of the weapon. The shots followed so close on each other they mingled into an extended single report. Without seeing them, Charlie was aware that the men either side of him had slithered to the ground. Involuntarily he closed his eyes and waited for the next shot.

Nothing came.

He was dimly aware of activity behind him and felt the cord round his wrists loosen. He flicked his eyes open and turned round to find himself staring into the eyes of his stepfather.

'Are you all right?'

Charlie blinked hard, feeling a mixture of relief and bewilderment. 'Dad? Dad! What the hell . . .'

David Patterson cleared his throat. 'I've never known you to be stuck for words.'

Charlie was still staring. 'But . . . For God's sake! We buried you!'

There was a hint of shame in the major's voice. 'I know.' Then, unaccustomed to such guilt, he reverted to his military tone. 'But what the hell are *you* doing here?'

There was a short silence as he helped his son from the chair. Charlie felt his blood begin to flow again as he walked around the small room, avoiding the still, silent figures splayed grotesquely across the floor, but unable to take his eyes from them.

It was like a scene from a film. He looked around in bewilderment at the simple room. The peat smoke was hanging like a cloud below the low roof. He coughed to clear his bruised windpipe. His father stepped over one of his victims and opened a cupboard. He reached in and took out a bottle of whisky and glasses.

Charlie gratefully took a large gulp. Patterson sat down opposite him and drank more slowly.

'What are you going to do about these two?' Charlie asked.

For an answer, Patterson stood, leaned down, grasped the first of them by the collar of his expensive leather jacket and heaved it up until he could sling the limp body over his shoulders. 'I'll get rid of them now.' Charlie was astonished by the ease with which his father hefted the first corpse outside and kicked the door shut behind him.

Charlie took another slug of whisky. He looked with

horrified fascination at the remaining Arab. There was a small, neat hole, scarcely any blood, in the centre of his forehead. Charlie had never seen his father fire so much as a twelve bore in all the time he'd known him. He supposed he'd always known he was a first-class marksman – it was part of the job in the regiment – and he'd always assumed that he had killed people. But to see it happen so coolly and so efficiently had somehow made the actual event less horrific than he would have expected. Even the entry wounds were tidy. And now his stepfather was calmly disposing of the bodies.

The front door opened and Patterson came in. Without a word, he heaved the second body over his shoulder and went outside again.

Charlie felt the tension in his muscles ease now that the dead men were gone. The whole thing – his stepfather coming back from the dead, the abrupt denial of his belief that his mother and a lover had been responsible for killing him – seemed like the jumbled recollection of a crazy nightmare, until Patterson came back in as if he'd just been for a quiet walk. He gave Charlie a quick, remorseful glance. 'I'm sorry you had to see that. I really didn't have any choice. Anyway, no one will ever see them again.' He picked up his whisky and sat in the chair by the range. 'Now, I must know how you got here. I suppose you persuaded your mother to tell you.'

Charlie shook his head. 'No. She didn't even tell me you were alive.'

For the first time since he had walked in, Patterson

looked worried. 'Oh my God. They must have found her,' he said.

He hastily took a mobile phone from the pocket of a jacket hanging up behind the door and keyed a number. After a few seconds, a look of relief spread over his face. 'Are you all right? . . . That's great. Something happened . . . It doesn't matter. We've dealt with it . . . Yes, Charles is here. It's a long story. I thought you'd given directions, but he must have been followed. Everything's under control now. Stay there. I'll be in touch.'

Patterson turned to Charlie. 'She's seen no one. I'll have to get back and check out the house, though. And this place will already be insecure if our visitors passed on their position before they came in.'

'But I don't see how they can have followed me. I checked dozens of times.'

'They could have put a bug in your car.'

'I came in Kate's car. She's using mine.'

'Okay. We'll check it out. But how did you find me?'

'I met up with Mum and followed her back to Scotland.'

'Yes. I saw you arrive. I was driving out.'

'That was you in the Land Rover?'

Patterson nodded. 'But if your mother didn't tell you, who did?'

'I came back up to Banchory again, twenty-four hours later. She didn't know I'd come. When I reached the house, the door was open and I overheard her talking to you on the phone, arranging to meet you.' Charlie laughed and shook his head at the absurdity of what he'd deduced. 'I thought she was talking to a lover – a lover she'd persuaded to kill you. I waited outside until she left and followed her over to Fort Augustus in the morning. I saw her meet up with you and when she left I followed you back as far as the loch. Then I lost you. Of course, I didn't know it was you, with the beard and the dark hair and glasses.'

'So, how did you find me? That was two days ago.'

'I went back to Lambourn and went to see Nick in prison. He was in a terrible state. He looked as if he was about to top himself. I promised myself I'd come straight back up here and try and track down the man I'd seen with Mum. I asked in the pub where you met her. They told me you were a chap called David Urquhart who rented this place, and they told me roughly how to get here. I wish to God Mum had let me know what was going on; it would have saved a lot of hassle.'

'We wanted to keep you at arm's length from the whole business, but I hear Sala Mahmoud's men had already visited you.'

'Yes,' Charlie said ruefully.

'Those two?' Patterson nodded at the door through which he'd carried the dead men.

'Yes.'

Patterson looked more closely at the injuries still visible on his stepson's face. 'What did they say?'

'They were looking for money.'

'Did they sound as though they thought I was still alive?'

'I couldn't say for sure.'

'And you had no idea?'

'No, of course not.'

'Do you think the police have?'

Charlie tried to think of DI Ferrier's attitude two evenings before. 'I don't think so. The DI who's been handling your . . . case turned up at my place a couple of days ago, just when I'd got back from here, and told me they'd found some guy called Latimer dead in a skip. He'd been murdered, and they knew from some phone bills that he'd spoken to Mum a few times just after you were supposed to have been killed.'

'They did, did they? And who do they think put him there?' Patterson's eyes rested coolly and steadily on Charlie's.

'They didn't say. But presumably it wasn't the man who came to see you that morning.'

Patterson didn't answer; his expression gave nothing away.

'Come on,' Charlie said. 'For God's sake. That had to be the man who was dead in your drawing room. I understand, if he was threatening you or something.'

'What he was,' Patterson said quietly, 'was a man who was quite prepared to kill young children who got in his way, and never showed a sign of remorse in the fifteen years since.'

Charlie thought of a dozen retorts but it wasn't the moment for a debate on moral justice. He took a gulp of whisky. 'Dad, you've got to tell me.'

Patterson shook his head. 'No, I haven't. The less you know, the safer you'll be.'

'That's not going to stop the police looking, and they

are. I think you underestimate them.'

'Do I?' his father said sourly. 'And what are you going to do about it?'

'Me? Nothing as far as the police are concerned. But somebody's going to come looking for those guys, aren't they?' Charlie waved a hand towards the door. 'Sala Mahmoud's not going to give up until he's had some kind of satisfaction from you. They said he's very upset; he's been taken for a ride, and now you've killed two of his men. He isn't going to like it. He'll want revenge.'

'He wants revenge and I wanted repayment, Charlie, I'd been swindled by people I'd known and trusted for years.' Patterson's voice cracked. He grunted to cover it up. 'I'd been brought to my knees. It wasn't going to make any difference to Mahmoud, and he got what he wanted. God knows how he ever found out the stuff wasn't right. They were the best fakes I've ever seen.' For a brief second, his despair showed. 'God, I'm sorry to have dragged you into it. I suppose it was a damn stupid thing to do, but I can't go back on it; not now.'

Charlie had never seen his stepfather ready to admit a fault or so prepared to let his true emotions show. He wanted to let him know that he understood, whatever he'd done, then an image of Nick in prison stopped him short.

'Running and hiding isn't going to achieve a thing,' he said. 'There are some very heavy people after you. There's a limit to how long you can hide in a place like this.'

'Maybe not here, but I'm quite used to looking after

myself in these sort of conditions.'

'Dad, it must be twelve years since you saw anything like active service.'

'Don't knock it, Charlie. There are some things which you never forget.' Charlie remembered the calculated manner in which he'd shot the two armed men. 'In the meantime, there are only three people who know I'm here. Your mother, me, and you.'

'What about the locals?'

'I've been coming here on and off for years. I pay forty pounds a year rent for this place in the name of David Urquhart. They think I'm a romantic Scottish writer who misses his homeland and enjoys a bit of quiet fishing.'

'I've never heard you mention this place.'

'I never did, to anyone, not even your mother. It was absolutely private, a place where I could assume an alternative identity when I needed it – until now.'

Charlie looked at his stepfather's handsome face beneath the beard and the glasses – strong, forceful, unassailable. He recognised more clearly than ever that there were whole areas of this man's psyche he had never known; that he had no idea what he was really capable of.

'Dad, what are you going to do? If they don't find you, they may find Mum, and I don't suppose they'll leave me alone.'

'Did they do that damage to your face?'

Charlie nodded.

'What else did they do?'

Charlie told him.

Patterson showed his sympathy with a curt nod. 'They were undoubtedly Palestinians. Saudis are often too lazy or too stupid or too damned uneducated to do most things in life, and though they hate it, they rely on the Palestinians to carry out a lot of essential jobs.'

'Including revenge.'

'Including that,' Patterson agreed.

'But you can't just sit and wait for it. What about Mum? What about me?'

'Nobody will do much to you, as long as they think you know nothing. And your mother's secure where she is.'

'For the time being.'

'I'll move her from there shortly. I just didn't want to risk her being here with me yet. I knew if I was found, it would get nasty and I wouldn't go without serious resistance. When I'm sure the trail has gone cold, I'll leave the UK and she can join me. Now,' he said standing up. 'As you're here, you'd better stay the night, but tomorrow you must leave, and forget you ever came.'

Charlie decided he would do better to save his arguments until the morning. He took another glass of whisky. 'How come you were outside when I came?' he asked.

'I've got trip wires all round the place.' Patterson nodded at a khaki metal box housing a row of monitoring dials, a British Army surveillance field system.

'What about power?' Charlie asked.

'Batteries and a generator fifty feet inside the cave

behind this place. I've also got a few microphones in the trees on the way up from the road. The bloody sheep keep triggering them every time they cough,' he added with a laugh, a sound which Charlie had seldom heard.

'What else have you got to protect yourself?'

Patterson patted the automatic in his pocket and pulled open a drawer in the cupboard behind him. 'This is a Heckler & Koch MP5 automatic assault rifle,' he said. Charlie admired the gun along with a stock of magazines and half a dozen bush knives and throwing blades. Patterson pushed the drawer back. 'Those should cover most events,' he said. 'Now, what have you done with your car?'

'I left it about a quarter of a mile west of the pile of stones, in the woods.'

'Visible from the road?'

'Not easily.'

'Okay. We'll deal with it first thing in the morning. And we'll have to do something about our visitors' vehicle. Now, we'll eat.'

Patterson produced a bowl of mutton and barley stew from the range and spooned some on to two plates. As they ate, he refused to discuss the deal he'd done with Sala Mahmoud, or why he had done it. And on the question that Charlie wanted answered most, he offered nothing. Every time Charlie tried to draw him on the identity of the dead man at Birch Lodge, he shook his head in dismissal.

'But for God's sake, Dad,' Charlie pressed. 'What about Nick?'

'He'll be all right. They'll let him go sooner or later, when they dig up the truth.'

'What the hell do you mean?'

Patterson raised an eyebrow. 'Just believe me, Charles. Your friend won't suffer more than a few weeks on remand. And I dare say the experience will do him good.'

Charlie looked at him, shocked by his stepfather's apparent indifference to what Nick was going through and his total lack of remorse for the murders he had committed.

Patterson produced a palliasse and some blankets from an oak chest and made a space on the floor. 'You'll be comfortable enough on that,' he said to Charlie. 'I want you up early and away in the morning so you may as well turn in now.'

Charlie was far from ready either to sleep or to end his discussion with his father, but he wasn't offered an alternative.

To his surprise, he slept well and was feeling fully restored when his father shook him at six next morning. The smell of freshly brewed coffee hanging in the atmosphere also helped to wake him.

'Go back to the road the way you came. I'll give you ten minutes before I follow. Don't let anyone see you coming out of the track. If possible, I don't want anyone to know I've had visitors. They don't have a lot to talk about round here and the smallest unusual activity will get them gossiping.'

Charlie gulped down some coffee. Before he had fallen

asleep the night before, he had firmly resolved to confront his stepfather again about his activities and future plans, but as he looked into his father's emotionless grey eyes, he knew he'd be wasting his time.

At half-past six, with the sun making its first appearance over the top of the mountains to the east, David Patterson unlocked the door of the simple house.

'Go carefully,' he said as Charlie walked out. 'I'll meet you by your car in fifteen minutes.'

Charlie sniffed in the intoxicating dawn smell of damp heather and bracken as he walked briskly along the track. He looked for his father's trip wires and microphones but, not surprisingly, saw no sign of them. Before he reached the road, he dropped to his hands and knees and crawled behind a bank of heather. In the still air, he guessed he would hear a motor from half a mile away, but there was no sense in being hasty. Carefully and slowly, he parted the wispy branches to survey the road beyond.

There was no moving traffic, but parked, hastily by the look of it, on a wide verge of coarse grass was a silver BMW. Charlie's heart stopped. He recognised it, he was sure. He scrolled back through his memory trying to place it. At last it came to him. He'd noticed a BMW the afternoon before in Fort Augustus. He even remembered checking that it hadn't followed him out of the town.

Coincidence was out of the question. God knew, he thought, wracking his memory for where he'd gone wrong, he hadn't seen a sign of the car trailing him yesterday. His stepfather must be right; the Golf must have been bugged.

When he was confident there was no one in it or near it, he emerged cautiously from his cover and walked across to the BMW. He put a hand on the grille. It was stone cold. The car was locked and there was no one inside. Satisfied that the only occupants had been the two dead men, he set off at a brisk walk towards the forest where he'd left the Golf.

David Patterson was already waiting for him when he arrived. He was holding a small, muddy metal object. It had taken him less than half a minute to find the tracking device.

'Maybe they bugged every vehicle in your yard,' he said.

'No. I know what happened. When they first came to see me, I was just about to drive down to the village in Kate's car. They must have seen me getting out of it and assumed it was mine.'

'You should have thought of that.'

'I haven't had the benefit of your training.'

'No,' his father agreed. 'Did you see their car?'

'Yes. A Silver BMW. Just by the track down to the croft.' Charlie paused guiltily. 'Actually, I saw it in Fort Augustus yesterday, when I was asking around about you. I even checked to see if it had followed me.'

'Well, there's nothing you can do about it now. I'll get it out of here before the police find it and start asking questions.' He pulled a key on a hire company fob from his pocket. 'I'll take it with me to my next billet.'

'Do you want me to come?'

'No. You get back to your place. If you're away too long without notice, whoever takes over from our friends back there will think you know more than you did. And the police may sniff a lead.'

Chapter Thirteen

Charlie tried to analyse the expression on DI Ferrier's face as he walked into the office at Oak Hollow. It had all the smugness and elation of a hunter lining up a kill.

'We've made what you might call a bit of a breakthrough,' Ferrier said, deliberately low-key. He was leaning back in the office chair. 'You'll be pleased to hear that we've established that Nick Ryder didn't kill your stepfather.'

Charlie leaped to his feet with delight. 'I told you that two weeks ago,' he said, smiling uncontrollably. 'But what made you change your mind?'

'I think that'll become clear in a moment. You can go and pick him up as soon as you like.'

'That's great. So who killed my stepfather? The man who went to see him that morning – the man I told you about?'

'We've found him, but it wasn't him.'

'But surely if it wasn't Nick, it must have been him.'

'I doubt it, Mr Patterson. He's dead.'

'Good God! Where did you find him?'

'Where do you think?'

'Where do *I* think? How should I know? Where was he?'

'In a coffin labelled "Major David Patterson".'

Charlie gaped at him. 'Two of them? In one coffin? But that's absurd. How did they fit?'

'Major Patterson wasn't among those present.'

'You mean he wasn't there?'

'Yes. Just the other bloke, with the back of his head damaged exactly as it was when we first found him at your parents' cottage.'

'Are you saying this man was killed at Birch Lodge, not my stepfather?'

'Yes, Mr Patterson,' Ferrier hissed impatiently. 'That's exactly what I'm saying.'

'But my father was identified.'

'By your mother. And I have to tell you, we're getting nowhere looking for her. We should have had her permission to exhume the body. As it turns out, it wasn't hers to give or refuse anyway, seeing as it's not her corpse. But as you may imagine, we are more anxious than ever to see her now.'

'My God, yes. I can see that you must be.'

'Well? Where is she?'

'I wish I knew. I've lost track of her. I can't find out where she went in Cornwall and she hasn't been in touch with me at all. Do you suppose she's all right?'

'I should think she's being very well looked after – by your father.'

Charlie did his best to look astounded.

'Surprised, Mr Patterson?'

'Yes. I mean, if my stepfather isn't dead, where is he?'

Ferrier looked at him for four or five seconds. 'I don't know where he is. That's what I'm hoping you're going to tell me.'

Kate appeared at the door of the office with cups of coffee for them. Neither of them spoke until she had gone.

'I'm sorry,' Charlie said. 'This isn't making any sense. As far as I'm concerned, my mother and I buried him six weeks ago. I suppose I've got to believe you when you say he wasn't in the grave, but the whole thing sounds crazy to me. I mean, who killed this man?'

'Who do you think, Mr Patterson?'

'Not my stepfather.'

'Why not?'

'Why, for God's sake? Why should he kill some old soldier?'

'He wasn't an old soldier. He was an ex-con called Brian Tennent, one of your mother's writing protégés. He'd been inside with Latimer, the bloke we found in the skip. We think Latimer was the only person who knew where Tennent was going that Saturday morning – apart from Major Patterson who'd arranged to meet him.'

Charlie stared back at Ferrier. 'You're seriously suggesting Dad had something to do with Tennent's death, and that he's done a runner, with my mother? That's crazy. He's not that kind of man. He's too honourable, too conventional. There has to be more to it.'

'If there is, it wouldn't do him and your mother any

harm to come in and talk to us, would it?'

'I can promise you, Inspector, if either of them contact me, I'll tell them to get straight on to you.'

'No you won't, son, unless you want to be charged with aiding and abetting. You don't mention me, and when you've finished talking to them, you get in touch with me, understand?' He banged his mug down on the table and stood up. 'Why don't you go and pick up your mate from jail? I think he's been there long enough.'

Driving back from prison in the April sunshine, Charlie told an incredulous Nick what had happened.

'What are you going to do about it?' Nick sighed.

'God knows. I can't turn my father in. I can hardly believe it, but it looks as though my mother's involved, at least to some extent. She'd be up on a charge of aiding and abetting at least.'

'How the hell did she let herself get talked into it?'

'My father's a very domineering man. He thinks people like Tennent and this other guy, Latimer, are totally worthless. He wouldn't have any feelings at all about killing them.'

'But doesn't he see that in a civilised society, individuals can't dole out arbitrary justice?'

'I wish I could tell you what was going through his head,' Charlie grunted. 'God knows how this whole thing is going to end. Still, you're out of jail and off the hook.' He leaned across and slapped Nick on the shoulder. 'You can start concentrating on the horses now.'

Nick grinned. 'I can't wait. I hear they all look great and Kate's been a star.'

'Who did you hear that from?'

'Kenny came up to see me. He says all the lads really like working with her.'

'Yeah,' Charlie said thoughtfully. 'She's not going to want to go back to the rescue centre in a hurry now. I think she's caught the racing bug.'

'I'll leave that one with you, then,' Nick said with a laugh.

'Don't worry. She knew it was only a temporary job, covering for you until you got out.'

'I still can't believe it. I thought I was in there for good.'

'Can you believe what my father said? He thought the experience would do you good, and he seemed certain the police would never make it stick.'

'That's not the impression I had. But what are you going to do?'

'I'm not going to shop him but I've got to try and persuade him to give himself up and let my mother off the hook. And he'll have to give the Arab his money back or they're going to be hounded for the rest of their lives.'

'Your father seems well able to hide himself away if he needs to.'

'It's okay for him. He's not a very social animal, but my mother has friends and relations she cares about, and she won't dare get in touch with them in case they get caught up in it all.'

Nick looked at Charlie's exhausted, harassed face. 'I think you should tell the police. I don't think you've got a cat in hell's chance of persuading him to go himself.'

With Nick out of jail, an immense sense of relief had descended on the yard. Charlie should have been sleeping more easily, but he wasn't. As his mind conjured with the seemingly insolvable problems, the night passed slowly in a blur of fitful sleep and anxiety. Should he go to the police; attempt to persuade his father to give himself up and submit himself to British justice; or do nothing and hope that his parents would get away before either the police or another gang of Palestinians got to them first?

Despite his troubled night, he was in the yard at six o'clock.

Titch was working Willow Star. She galloped freely for half a mile while Charlie watched her through his binoculars. There was no doubt about it; her development had been immense since the early disastrous run at Cagnes. The sunshine would improve her yet again. He looked at Nick beside him. Hercules had been allowed up on the gallops as a treat and was still gambolling around his master like a puppy.

His partner was in a state of euphoria after sleeping in his own bed for the first time in weeks. He ought to have had a king-sized hangover from the quantity of champagne he'd drunk the evening before, but nothing could depress him this morning. He looked up at the big blue bowl of the sky edged with gold in the east and grinned at the pleasure of simply being free.

'Let's confirm her for the Duke of York Stakes,' Charlie said. 'The Guineas is too soon, but in two weeks she'll be spot on.'

Nick agreed. 'Perfect. A group race and a sixty thousand pound prize would go down very well at the moment. By the way, did the lawyers tell you how much this mystery owner paid for her?'

'No. They said it was none of my business. Our only concern is to train her.'

'Well, let's hope if they get a really good win out of her they'll have the decency to show themselves, and perhaps we can talk them into buying another.'

Driving back to the yard, Charlie found it hard to believe how normal everything seemed. Here he was watching his horses, doing his job as if he hadn't been anywhere near his father earlier that week, watching him shoot two Palestinian heavies without turning a hair.

He had been worried that someone might have circulated details of the Arabs' car, but he guessed that if anyone ever did report them missing, it wouldn't be until several days after, by which time Patterson would have got rid of the BMW or doctored it beyond recognition.

He thought of his mother and hoped for her sake she'd been able to join up with his father now. At least he would know how to look after them both. Having heard nothing from either his parents or the police, or anyone else for that matter, Charlie allowed himself to believe that no news was good news.

Then, two days later, his mother telephoned him. She

used his mobile number and briefly asked him to see her again where they had met last time, in two days' time.

This meeting in Kensington Gardens was very different from the previous one.

Charlie arrived late. He noticed a blue Ford Sierra behind him as he drove out of Lambourn. He spotted it again in Hogarth Road and dived off down Earls Court Road at the last moment.

The Sierra came with him, but he slipped into a small mews, parked and walked down a pedestrian alleyway before his tail had time to back up and turn into the narrow road itself.

He went the rest of the journey by tube.

When Charlie saw his mother, he could tell at once that she was under pressure. Her face was drawn and she fidgeted nervously.

When she spoke she was close to tears. 'Charlie, I don't know what we're going to do. David told me about the people who followed you to Scotland and Glen Shiel. Thank God they didn't come up to the lodge and find me. But it's all got out of control. He has no idea I'm seeing you. I didn't dare tell him, in case he moves us on again. But I can't persuade him to face up to what he's done. Do you think you could?' Her voice was pleading.

Charlie put his arm round his mother's shoulder and he felt her fight back a sob. 'I doubt it,' he said. 'I tried when I was with him, but he said the whole thing would blow over and you and he would be able to slip away somewhere where you'd never be found.'

'He just doesn't understand that I don't want to hide

for the rest of my life, live like this, with the constant threat of being found and murdered in our beds.'

'The trouble is, Mum, it's second nature to him. But surely you must have known something like this would happen when he faked his own death. It's not surprising Sala Mahmoud guessed he was still alive, is it? After all, it was a bit too much of a coincidence just after Dad had ripped him off.'

'Yes, but he didn't tell me about that, he just said if he didn't disappear, there'd be even more money problems. He was adamant, wouldn't take no for an answer. I didn't want to see Brian Tennent killed. God knows, he'd done a terrible thing and he'd shown absolutely no remorse for what he did, but he'd done his time, paid his penalty.'

'He would have done it again, sooner or later. You could tell yourself that someone else has probably been saved from him.'

'Maybe, but that's not how it works, and you know it.'

Charlie nodded. 'Look, the police are keeping tabs on me at the moment. The best thing for me to do is to get on with my job for a week or so. Let things settle. You and Dad, keep your heads down. If there's a sudden change of plan, let me know; if you're desperate and you need to, ring me and I'll try and meet up with you, maybe halfway, in Manchester or somewhere.'

His mother nodded, grateful that at least her son understood her state of mind. She put her hand on his forearm. 'Charlie, don't let anything happen to you. I don't want you to take any of the blame for what your father's done.'

Charlie took a deep breath. 'I'll be fine.'

Pru shook her head slowly. If anything happened to Charlie because of her, she'd die. 'We've got to bring this to a head. David's sure that we're all right at the cottage for a while. He's set up all his surveillance stuff and God knows what, but I'm convinced we should move.'

Charlie could hardly believe his ears. 'You mean you're both at the house by Banchory?'

'Yes. There's a sort of priest-hole there, and he's got rid of the Land Rover and neither of us goes out anywhere now. He'll be going mad, I just left a note for him saying I'd be away for the day.'

'Well, he may not want to stay there when the rest of the news breaks. I had Ferrier round the day I got back from Scotland. They've dug up the coffin.'

'Oh.' Pru looked away, wondering what to say. 'I knew it was too much to hope for but David was so certain that it would work.'

'It might have done if you hadn't disappeared. When the police couldn't find you, they assumed you knew something they didn't. And then they found this guy Latimer, dumped in a skip in Maida Vale.'

The blood drained from Pru's face. 'Oh, no! David promised me he wasn't going to do anything about that.'

'About what?'

'The phone calls I got from Latimer. He was trying to blackmail us. He said he knew what had happened.

Don't ask me how, unless he'd made some arrangement with Tennent which wasn't kept. He said he would tell the police that they wouldn't find Tennent alive, ever. I believed him. I asked David what to do. He said Latimer had no way of following it up and couldn't prove anything.' Pru's resolve was weakening. 'How on earth could he do it? I can hardly believe it.' Her voice was breaking, large tears were sliding down her cheeks.

Charlie glanced around but no one was taking any notice of them. 'And there were the two Arabs who followed me.'

Pru gazed bleakly across the glittering Serpentine. 'And what about Nick? If only he hadn't turned up that afternoon. I was very angry with David about it, but he said that they'd never convict him.'

'That's the one bit of good news. Nick's out now. They let him go as soon as they realised Dad wasn't in the coffin.'

Pru sniffed back her tears and forced a smile at the news. 'Thank God for that.' She let out a sigh and stood up to leave. 'I must go, or I'll miss my train. I'll be in touch if I need you.'

Charlie rose and hugged his mother tighter than ever before, pressing his cheek against her hair.

'Look after yourself.'

Charlie drove back to Berkshire, uncertain what to do. Ferrier was waiting for him in the office again. Nick had discreetly disappeared.

'Morning, Charlie,' the policeman said with a grin

which Charlie didn't trust. 'Heard from your mum or dad yet?'

Charlie met the detective's eyes straight on. 'I wish I had, at least from my mother. Whatever happened, it can't have been her fault.'

'I wouldn't be so sure. After all, she identified Tennent as your father.'

'Sure. He was wearing my father's clothes, lying face down with the back of his head smashed in. It wouldn't have occurred to her that it was anyone else, would it?'

'That's what we'd like to ask her. By the way, where have you been this morning?'

'I had to go to London, to see a new owner.'

'Who was that, then?'

Charlie casually plucked from the air the name of the property dealer who had recently sent him a couple of two-year-olds. Ferrier noted it down.

'He wasn't there,' Charlie went on. 'Apparently he'd forgotten the date we made.'

'I see. I hear you still have a horse here that belongs to your father.'

'Willow Star? She used to belong to him. His lawyer sold her to a new owner, when we all thought my father was dead.'

'And who's the new owner?'

'A syndicate, run in a nominee name. I've never met them; we get all our instructions through the solicitors.'

'Isn't that rather unusual?'

'Yes, but it's not unheard of.'

'I see. Did you get on with your stepfather?'

'Not really. He was a very distant sort of a man. Of course he was away a lot when I was younger – he was in the army.'

'Yes. We do know that. I should think if he wanted to disappear from sight for a while, he'd know how to go about it.'

'I dare say,' Charlie said.

'But not your mother. Do you suppose she's with him?'

'I haven't a clue.'

'Listen, Charlie, if one of them gets in touch with you, you'll be committing an offence if you don't tell us, make no mistake.' Ferrier had abandoned his chummy tone and replaced it with a quiet, hard edge. 'So make sure you do, okay?'

Charlie watched him drive away. He wondered how convincing his lies had been, grateful, at least, that it hadn't been one of Sala Mahmoud's men asking the questions.

Chapter Fourteen

It had been a fine afternoon at Newbury but now, as the runners paraded before the last race, the sun was losing the last of its warmth. A slight chill descended, dampening the grass, and the casual racegoers found the Pimms Bar held more interest for them than a moderate staying handicap.

But for Persimmon Way this was a big occasion. It was going to be his first race since chipping a bone in his knee three months earlier. It had taken only a small operation to remove the tiny fragment, but Charlie had thought it wise to be extra careful with his recovery training schedule. He had no experience of a horse with this particular injury but common sense suggested that the joint should be subjected to as little concussion as possible. He had asked Kate to take special charge of Percy, knowing that the gelding came second only to Willow in her affections. At sixteen hands two inches, Percy was a hand and a half taller than the filly, much more Kate's size. When she rode him out, she felt she was on a real racehorse.

Percy's re-training programme had started with long walks, always on the easier surface of the all-weather track and always when there were no other horses around to over-excite him. Gradually, Kate had started to hack gently over short distances, building up slowly until now they were cantering up to five miles a day. To this was added a daily swim in the local equine pool. Every afternoon, Kate led him down to the village for a work-out, rubbed him under a sun lamp until he was dry and then walked him back home. She was sure that he was fitter now than he'd ever been.

Charlie and Nick had invited Charles Gordon and his wife down to look at their fast recovering animal. As Percy walked round the paddock with muscles bulging under his shiny black coat, they all congratulated Kate on the wonderful job she'd done. She had never felt so proud.

On the peak of his form, the partners could have expected Percy to waltz home on this first outing since his recovery, but they were uncertain how much psychological damage the injury had caused. Some horses, having once suffered the pain of a chipped knee, were reluctant totally to commit themselves afterwards for fear of repeating the damage. Although Percy had always been a tryer before, Nick and Charlie wouldn't have blamed him if from now on he'd held a little in reserve. Jimmy Scaron, the jockey booked to ride him, was told that on no account was he to use his whip; whatever happened, Percy was to enjoy himself.

Charlie, Nick and the Gordons made their way to the

front of the grandstand. Kate had gone off to the tote to have a small bet on her charge – just out of sentiment. The others had decided there were too many ifs about him to risk their money.

As she waited for her ticket, Kate sorrowfully reminded herself that now Nick was back, she would have to return to the Rescue Centre. She was going to miss the excitement of working at Oak Hollow. But she had made up her mind that she wasn't going back to manage the place. Working with the animals was what she enjoyed; if she had to take a cut in salary, so be it.

She rejoined the others on the stand just as the fourteen runners were coming under orders. The gates flew open and Kate raised her binoculars to focus on Percy's dark green silks. Her hands trembled with a confusion of emotions. She wanted him to do well, to be back to his best, but more importantly she prayed for him to come back sound.

Percy had been drawn on the inside and Jimmy Scaron kept him there. As the runners came round the bend in front of the stands for the first time, Kate cursed out loud. The horse outside Percy had cannoned into him, making him lose his footing for a moment. It was the sort of thing that happened in every race, but Kate didn't want it happening to Percy. She was like a mother worrying over a son in his first point-to-point. Jimmy Scaron took a tight grip on the reins and in a matter of strides had him back on an even keel. He kept Percy in mid-division until they started the long turn out of the back straight.

Kate could see that some of the horses in front were tiring. Percy began to move through them slowly. His long stride seemed to be getting more powerful as the race developed.

They were heading for home and the pace quickened. When they passed the three-furlong pole, Kate began to jump up and down with excitement. Percy was going easily with his ears pricked and had cruised up to join the leaders.

Kate wanted to scream her encouragement but stopped herself before she made an undignified spectacle of herself. She compromised by giving Charlie a sharp jab in the ribs with her elbow. 'He's going to do it! He's going to do it!' Her gaze turned back to the track.

At that moment, Percy stumbled and almost fell. His nose crashed into the grass and then bounced up again. As Percy took his next stride to recovery, his jockey almost fell off and Kate stifled a desperate scream. Percy's near foreleg, which she'd spent months treating, was swinging limply beneath him. She turned to Charlie with wide, horrified eyes and grasped his arm with both hands. Her insides felt hollow.

Down on the course, Jimmy Scaron had pulled Percy to a halt and jumped off as quickly as he could. The magnificent animal stood bewildered, with his left knee outstretched and the lower limb dangling uselessly from it, like a weight on a crane.

In all her time at the Rescue Centre, nothing had prepared Kate for this. She had seen animals viciously burned, horses pulped in road accidents, any number of terrible injuries, but none of them came close to causing her the appalling anguish she felt now. Her closeness to Percy, all the time and care she had lavished on him, added another dimension to the pain.

Once the initial, numbing shock had passed, she galvanised herself into running with the others down to the course where the knacker's van was already heading.

By the time they arrived, a dark, canvas screen had been erected. Percy's lad was in there, wet-eyed, holding the reins while the vet examined Percy's leg. It was, the vet knew, a mere formality. He didn't need to be told what the injury was, or what he had to do. But no matter how many horses he shot, coping with the animals' pathetic look of innocence and their complete confusion over what was happening to them never became any easier. They were always so proud; dying like this seemed so pointless.

Charlie made Kate and the Gordons wait some distance from the screen. Jimmy Scaron walked over and explained to them what had happened, though one look at Percy's leg had told them enough to expect the inevitable. As the vet took his humane killer from his bag, he nodded an apology for what he was about to do. Charlie joined him behind the screen and took the reins from the lad who was weeping uncontrollably now. The vet moved round to Percy's head. Charlie gave the broad, dark neck a last, loving pat. A second later, it was all over.

Charlie watched hopelessly, barely able to speak. Losing Percy was a disaster in its own right; coming on top of all the other events crowding in on him, it was as much as he could bare.

It would have to happen to one of Charles Gordon's horses, he reflected bitterly. Typical Sod's Law. This was the first time the Gordons had been to the races in months. It had taken him the best part of a year to make it up with Mrs Gordon over the Flitgrove fiasco, especially when the filly went out and won three more races after Mike Dubens had bought her. And then Mrs Gordon had transferred her affections to the lovable Percy. Charlie grimaced at the unfairness of it, and braced himself to go and talk to her.

Later, after Kate, still fighting back her tears, had climbed up into the cab of the lorry with Kenny and set off for home, Charlie left the main enclosure and headed for the car park where he had arranged to meet Nick who was completing the formalities with the vet. He'd just reached the first line of cars when he became aware that a group of well-dressed, cosmopolitan olive-skinned men had fanned out behind and to either side of him. One of them, with a boyish face and a wafer-thin moustache moved against him.

'Come with us.'

Charlie felt a jab in his spine. If it wasn't a gun, it felt too much like one to take a chance. Sweat prickled his torso. He looked around for help, but there was nobody nearby. He let himself be guided towards the back door of a black Mercedes. It was opened from inside and Charlie was firmly pushed in between two of the burlier Arabs.

As the engine started, Charlie wished he'd made a run for it. Now it was too late.

They drove on to the M4 and headed east through the late afternoon traffic. After a few minutes on the motorway, one of the Arabs spoke to Charlie.

'Sheikh Sala Mahmoud wants to talk to you.' He barked in Arabic through the intercom to one of the men in the front. The glass partition slid back, and the man in the passenger seat passed back a mobile phone. The Arab on Charlie's right took it, spoke a few words and handed it to him.

Charlie took it apprehensively. Feeling slightly foolish, he said, 'Hello?'

'Your father has been a very stupid man. I trusted him.' The voice was deep, with a thick, throaty Arabic accent. 'Tell him he will not escape. I will not stop until I have found him and been repaid. If you are interested for him, you must tell him this. He should return my money to me.'

'W-what do you mean?'

There was a moment's silence. 'Perhaps you know; perhaps you do not. Just tell him what I say. And remind him, please, that unlike your police, my resources are limitless. We will find him. I wish you no harm, but if you get in my way, I will not be merciful. This is also true for your mother.'

There was a silence. Charlie didn't answer.

'Do you understand? I am a civilised man, but I will not be merciful.'

'I understand,' Charlie said flatly.

'Good.'

There was a click as the other end of the line was disconnected. Charlie slowly handed the phone back to the impassive man beside him.

At the next junction, the limousine swept off, swung through three hundred and sixty degrees and headed back the way they had come.

The man on Charlie's right turned to him. 'Where do you want to go?'

They dropped him where he asked, outside the pub in the village. Nick was there with Kate.

'Where the hell have you been?' Kate asked. 'We were beginning to get worried.'

Charlie, still recovering from what had happened, nervously explained.

'What are you going to do?' Nick asked.

'As soon as I think it's safe, I've got to go and see Dad again. Somehow I've got to convince him it'll be far better for him in the long run if he gives himself up to the police. And, more to the point as far as I'm concerned, safer for my mother. And she didn't know until afterwards what had happened to you, Nick. My stepfather just took the chance when he saw it.'

'He's a callous bastard.'

Charlie nodded, thinking of the four men his father had killed.

'I hope he gets a taste of his own medicine.'

Charlie sweated it out for another twelve days. He was certain that someone was still keeping tabs on him, and he didn't dare risk leading them to Scotland.

Then two days before Willow Star's race at York, he answered the phone to hear the distinctive sound of his mother's voice. She was desperate to see him. Charlie didn't waste any time. Half an hour later, he slipped into the horsebox while it was parked in the yard.

He told the driver to stop for a moment at the roundabout in Newbury. When they reached it, the driver banged on the back of the cab and Charlie opened the side door. He nodded at the lad he left in there and let himself out. He walked briskly to the station, confident that no one who might have had the yard under surveillance would have seen him leave or followed the lorry.

He changed to the airport bus at Reading, going through a couple of turns to check that he wasn't being followed, and did the same at Heathrow. He got a seat on the Aberdeen shuttle without any trouble and two hours later he'd hired a Ford Escort and was heading west out of Aberdeen. He had plenty of time to check again that he wasn't being followed. He left his car in the village and started plodding up the empty road, suitably clad in shorts and carrying a rucksack like any of the thousands of people hiking round the Highlands at that time of year.

Before he reached the point where the track down from the farmhouse gave on to the road, he turned off into the woodland and, for a third time, started to walk up the steep valley side to the hidden forest lodge.

Nothing warned him of the attack.

In a single motion, a hand covered his mouth, a knee was shoved into the small of his back and he was hurled to the ground like a day-old calf. As soon as he hit the ground, his attacker had a forearm across his windpipe and his arms pinioned behind his back.

The assault was so sudden, so efficiently achieved, that Charlie was beaten before he'd registered what was happening. As his mouth and nose were forced into the soft pine-needle mould, he knew he'd been jumped by a hardened professional. He felt the sharp pressure of a knee in the small of his back and didn't even consider trying to wriggle out of the hold he was in.

His head was lifted from the ground.

'Sorry. Boss's orders,' a throaty voice apologised. 'Are you Charles Patterson?'

Charlie nodded vigorously.

'I'm with your dad. Don't make a sound when I take my hand away.'

The hand was removed and Charlie gasped for breath. He turned his head to see a large, craggy head topped with short, cropped grey hair and a beard to match. The dazzling blue eyes of a much younger man shone from a wrinkled walnut face. There was the same stillness in them that Charlie had seen in his stepfather's eyes.

'Who the hell are you?' he whispered.

'Shoosh.'

Charles did as he was told.

Without a word, and scarcely another sound, the man led him up through the woods to the house. When they reached it, he stopped outside and spoke in a low voice. 'Your father's expecting you.' He opened the front door and nodded towards the small sitting room on the left.

Charlie opened the door and went in.

David Patterson was sitting in one of the armchairs, reading a book. He looked up. 'You met Hutch, then?'

Charlie pushed the door shut behind him. 'Yes, if Hutch is the old soldier who jumped me in the woods.'

'He was one of the best squadron sergeant-majors in the regiment. No one'll get near us as long as he's around.'

'Come on, who are you kidding? You can't stay here for ever.'

Patterson looked at him coldly. 'I didn't want you to come, Charlie. You've been dragged up here for no reason.'

'I wasn't dragged. I'd have come whether Mum had phoned or not as soon as I thought it was safe. I've had people watching me, just waiting for me to make contact with you.'

'I'm not planning on being here much longer.'

'Frankly, I don't know how you've survived so long with all the people who are after you. But that's your business. What I'm concerned about is Mum. She's put up with a hell of a lot all the time she's been married to you because she's a loyal woman. But this time you're asking too much.'

Charlie's stepfather made no reply.

'This operation's a fuck-up, and you know it. You're in danger of screwing the whole thing up and taking Mum with you. It's damage limitation time, Dad. You must see that.'

David Patterson still remained silent. He stared back at Charlie, not focusing on him, looking through him. He put a marker in the book he was holding, closed it and placed it on a table beside him. He lifted himself from the chair and walked across to look out of a small window at the thick evergreen woods that hemmed them in.

'There's no point your going on with this,' Charlie persisted. 'You've killed four people now.'

'More than that,' Patterson replied.

'What you did in the army was sanctioned. With these people it was straight murder.'

'What happened at the croft was self-defence. You can be sure that if they'd got to us first, they'd have killed us, whether or not they got the money.'

Charlie opted for another, less direct approach. 'Tell me about the money, Dad.'

'I told you, Mahmoud thinks I cheated him over some Linke furniture he bought from me – about a million pounds.'

'But you did cheat him. You told me the furniture was fake.'

Patterson shrugged. 'The pieces are so good, it's an insult to call them that. Very few people would ever know the difference. The cabinet-maker, Harry Thorndyke, specialises in Linke replicas and it so happened that he had quite a lot of what I wanted in stock, and he was prepared to pull out all the stops to make the rest. I think someone must have got to hear of it and tipped Mahmoud. I knew if I wanted to be left with anything at all for me and your mother to survive on, I'd have to disappear. I had no assets to leave, so if the money couldn't be found, there was no point in them suing the estate.'

'If things were so bad for you how could you afford to buy Willow Star?'

His stepfather took his eyes off the trees swaying outside to glance at his son. 'You have no idea how difficult that was to raise. But I knew it meant a great deal to you, with your plans for the new yard and everything.'

'But you never seemed that interested.'

'I may not have seemed it, but I was. I wanted you to have all the encouragement I could give you. I was really proud when you sent out your first winner.'

Charlie was amazed. His stepfather had never expressed an opinion or any particular interest in the performance of Oak Hollow. 'Who did you sell her to?'

The major put his finger to his nose. 'More than my life's worth to tell you.'

'Well, what will happen to the money that was paid for her?'

Patterson grinned. 'That'll all be a real mess, now they've dug up Tennent and know I'm still alive. I suppose the lawyers will hang on to it until they're forced to pay something to the hoard of creditors wanting to get their snouts in.'

'Where's the money Sala Mahmoud gave you?'

'It's safe, where it can't be got at by any of the bastards who've ripped me off.' Patterson stood up and walked to the fireplace. He picked up a bronze sculpture from the mantelpiece and studied it. 'Bastards,' he muttered again.

'Who?'

'People I thought I could trust. Brother officers.'

'Helmsley-Barret?'

Charlie's stepfather looked surprised at hearing his name. 'You've come across him, have you?'

'I had lunch with him, after your "funeral". He was anxious to know if there was any money left in the estate.'

'He's already had a good bit of it.'

'How? He said you'd agreed to give some guarantees for a restaurant business which has gone bust.'

'That business may have gone bust, but the restaurants are still there and he still owns half of them.'

'But if he defrauded you, surely you could have gone after him in the courts.'

'That would cost tens of thousands, take years, and there's no certainty I'd get a result. He knows that, so he let the banks come after me for my guarantees. There seemed absolutely no end to it, and at the same time, every year since I became a Name at Lloyds, I've been asked to cough up bigger and bigger cheques. I paid them for the first two years – seemed fair enough. It was what I had agreed to, and put my name to. Now, of course, I realise it was all an enormous fraud to let the insiders off the hook,' he added bitterly.

Charlie looked at his stepfather and understood his resentment and what this kind of financial ruin meant to him. It wasn't just the money, or even mainly the money, it was the knowledge that he'd made so many bad judgements. David Patterson was humiliated and, under the laws of a practical world, defenceless. Now he was dealing with the crisis in the only way his instincts and his training enabled him to.

Charlie was beginning to understand but he still thought his father's course of action was wholly misguided.

'You can't win, Dad,' he said. 'You're wanted for murder and on the run from the police as well as Mahmoud's people. Sooner or later you'll be caught, and my bet would be on Mahmoud getting to you first.'

'I appreciate your concern, Charlie, but I'm not turning myself in, and that's final. When I've laid low for a while longer and things have quietened down, we'll slip away. I'll let you know in due course where we've gone. In the meantime, I don't think you'll have too much trouble from the police or Sala Mahmoud's men. Just give the impression that you'd like them to find me as much as they would. Shouldn't be hard.'

'But how can you be so sure I won't let it out?'

'I may have been a lousy stepfather and I'd probably deserve it if you gave me away but I haven't got a choice and I trust you.'

'Even after what you did to Nick?'

'That was no big deal. I thought they'd arrest him and maybe charge him, I admit it, but they'd have been hard-pressed to make it stick. And anyway, once I was out of the country, I was going to contact you to tell the police to exhume the body in my grave.'

'There's no way you could have been sure that would have worked,' Charlie said, outraged by his father's complacency. 'The police found Nick's fingerprints on the poker. That's pretty damning evidence, though he said he couldn't remember touching it. Was that your doing?'

His father looked down guiltily. 'Yes, I swapped the handle of the tongs he'd used in the sitting room.'

'What about Brian Tennent? Why was he in the house?'

'Your mother first told me about him a long time ago. He was a complete bastard of a man but she'd tried to help him in prison. After he got out, about the time your girlfriend Kate found Willow Star, Pru arranged for him to come down and do a bit of decorating at the cottage. It was a very generous gesture of trust on her part but he never showed up; instead he got involved in a bit of chance burglary which went wrong.'

'Where was that? At your place?'

'Oh no. We never knew about it at the time. But last month your mother saw him in London. When she came home I could see she was worried, she said she'd noticed a watch he was wearing – a big gold hunter on a chain. She recognised it as old Cyril Barton's. The police had no way of knowing what was taken when the old boy was killed because he lived on his own and nobody had a clue what he owned.'

Charlie sat down at the desk opposite his stepfather. 'Are you saying Tennent murdered Cyril Barton?'

'I'm saying that he was supposed to come to our cottage that day. He must have got lost and found Lodge Farm, vulnerable and rich in pickings, and I guess the old boy caught him at it.' Patterson gave a characteristic shrug of his shoulders, exonerating himself from his subsequent actions. 'After that, I had no compunction about his role in my scheme.'

'You'd planned it already?'

'More or less. Your mother had mentioned that he was about my age and build. It was easy to construct a plan to make it look as though he'd murdered me and gone.'

'But did Mum know?'

'She had to. It took a lot of persuasion, but I think she accepted that Tennent's life wasn't worth a jot, and she knew we had to get ourselves out of the mess we were in.'

Charlie didn't believe she would willingly have accepted any such thing. 'But she can't have agreed with you doing what you did to Nick.'

'No, of course she didn't. She wasn't even there when he came. I collected Tennent from the station at Hungerford. I drove him home and took him into the drawing room. I knocked him unconscious, tied him up and when he came to, I questioned him about Cyril Barton. He admitted what he'd done, said it was an accident. Then I hit him with the poker on the back of his head. He went straight down; I didn't have to do anything else.

'That was when Nick arrived and started lecturing me

about how I should pay for training my horse. When I lost my temper, he was scared out of his wits. He started trembling and it suddenly occurred to me, if I could leave him at the scene of the crime and get his finger-prints on to the weapon, it would give the police another lead to follow besides Tennent, and generally keep them from working out what really happened. I went out, smashed a vase in the sitting room to sound as if someone had broken in, and called Nick for help. I just waited behind the door until he came in.' Patterson shrugged. 'After I'd messed up the study a bit and dressed Tennent in my clothes, I disguised myself and slipped out through the woods. I walked down to Marl-borough and away. All your mother had to do was identify Tennent's body as mine. And that was that.'

Charlie looked at his father, shaking his head. Part of him admired the cold-blooded ingenuity of the scheme; part of him was filled with disgust. 'Well, from the way I see it, you've got no choice. For Mum's sake, you *must* go to the police.'

Patterson glanced impatiently at Charlie and walked across the room to stand by the window. After a minute, he turned. 'If I give myself up,' he said, 'I'll be in jail for the rest of my life. If you mother can't take what's happening now, maybe she should go to the police herself, to demonstrate her own innocence. I could get out of the UK now if I had to, but she wouldn't ever see me again.'

Charlie knew how his mother would react to this plan. She would be incapable of deserting her husband; it would be against all her instincts.

'It's her choice. We either carry on running, together, until we find a safe haven – which we will, with plenty of money – or I give myself up, take all the blame and let her visit me in jail for the next twenty years. Or does she go back, proclaim her innocence, and never see me again? Those are the choices. I've told her, and I've told her I want her to stay with me. She'll be safe with me, I can guarantee that.'

'You can't guarantee anything and it's not much of a choice,' Charlie said sharply.

'It's all there is. I've got nothing more to say about it. And unless you want to be implicated, don't come here or try to find me again. Sooner or later you're going to lead someone here like you did to Loch Cluanie, and then there'll be trouble.'

'Look, if you give yourself up, with a good lawyer you could get as little as ten years, you might be out in seven.'

'What about Mahmoud?'

Charlie thought of what the Arab had said to him on the phone in the Mercedes. 'I will not be merciful.'

'If you gave him the money back, I think you could handle him.'

'If I gave him the money, I would be penniless. Your mother would never be able to cope with that while I was in jail.'

'You're underestimating her. And I'll be around to help her, if she needs it.' Charlie stood up and moved nearer to his father. 'Listen to me,' he said urgently, his anger bubbling just below the surface, 'if you're capable of listening to anybody. You're in a real mess! You need to resolve it. Now! You know it; I know it.' Charlie's voice became harsher. 'You're not on some SAS operation; you're talking about the life and feelings of a woman who's given you her life, for God's sake! You know what you have to do. Now bloody well do it!'

Charlie turned and walked from the room. He slammed the door behind him. There was no one in the hall. He went through the door opposite the sitting room. It opened into the kitchen where his mother sat at the table with Hutch. Behind him, he heard his stepfather walk through the hall and out of the front door, which he closed with a bang. Through the kitchen window, they watched him stride towards the woods.

Charlie sat down next to his mother. 'Look, Mum, I don't know if I've got through to him or not, but if he doesn't come round in the next few days, I think you should come back home, to the cottage, and tell the police everything you know. That way at least they might not charge you, if you convince them you genuinely thought the body you found was Dad's. They'd find it very hard to prove otherwise. That might at least jerk him into action, one way or the other. But you can't go on with this sword of Damocles dangling over you. He must realise it. I spoke to Sala Mahmoud last week. His men picked me up so I could speak to him on the phone. He's not pleased, but I don't think he's a complete savage. If honour is restored, he'll leave us alone.'

'What about his men who were killed?'

'I guess he'll have to take that in his stride.'

Hutch nodded. 'Yeah. He's right. If the major crawls back with the money, Mahmoud will consider the slate clean.'

They all knew that the major would never crawl.

Pru looked at her son. 'Thank you for trying, Charles. I'll let you know if I'm coming back.'

Charlie stood up. 'I've got to go.'

'You can't go already,' his mother protested.

'I'm not hanging around to see him again. If I said anything else, I'd probably undermine what good I may have done. Anyway, I've got to get to York. Willow Star arrives there tonight. She's running her first big race of the season tomorrow.'

Charlie walked back down the valley to find his hire car parked where he'd left it beside the road. He was back in Aberdeen in time to check it in that evening. British Rail delivered him to York before eleven o'clock the following morning.

Resolutely he switched his mind to Willow Star. He found Kate and Nick with Titch at the stables. Willow Star had been perfectly settled since her arrival. She'd eaten up her small breakfast, been out for some light exercise, and now had her head over the stable door, ears flicking with interest, obviously looking forward to the outing she knew was coming.

One of her opponents, a light chestnut colt called Hit the Canvas, who was trained locally, was led into a stable opposite. He looked magnificent, at least a hand taller than Willow Star, full of confidence and with a bounce in his stride. Charlie immediately began to doubt Willow Star's ability to win, but decided not to brood on it. 'Come on, let's go and get a cup of tea,' he said brightly, and set off across the middle of the course towards the main buildings on the far side.

They were almost there when they bumped into Imogen, who'd been looking for them. Charlie wondered why she hadn't told him she was coming. He greeted her and turned with a grin to introduce her to Kate.

'Hello, Immy,' Kate smiled.

'Have you two already met?'

'Yes,' Imogen said. 'Several times.'

'When Immy's been to the yard,' Kate added.

'I didn't know you'd been,' Charlie said, surprised.

'Nick's asked me round a few times. You just haven't been there.'

'Nick?' Now Charlie was amazed. Nick hadn't said a word about it.

Nick joined them and a smile spread across his face when he saw Imogen. She reached up and kissed him. 'How's your Star?'

'Well, aren't you the sneaky ones!' Charlie joked, quite taken aback by their obvious affection. He noticed the slight reddening of his partner's cheeks and not wanting to embarrass Nick he deftly turned the conversation to Willow Star's race.

Throughout lunch, in the Champagne Bar, they discussed little else. There had still been no communication from Willow Star's new owners. No one knew if they were coming to watch or not. Kate and Imogen decided that in their absence, they would deputise, so when Nick and Charlie walked down into the paddock, they followed.

The Duke of York Stakes was fourth on the card. Six furlongs straight, for some of the fastest horses in training. Apart from Willow Star and Hit the Canvas, there were eight other runners. They all looked fit, but Hit The Canvas just shaded them. His muscles ballooned beneath the glossy skin of his enormous frame.

It was impossible to be unimpressed, but Charlie and Nick were determined not to be put off. Instead, they convinced first the girls then Owen Williams that Willow Star could do it. 'The bigger they come the harder they fall,' Charlie said confidently as he legged the tiny jockey into the saddle. 'Try as hard as her and you'll win.'

Charlie gave Willow Star an encouraging pat on the neck, wished Owen and Titch good luck and then caught up with the others, who were making their way towards the front of the grandstand.

The commentator, perched high in his gantry, watched the runners canter down to the start, checking that their colours corresponded with the crayoning in his ledger. He had them down in the order in which he would see them leaving the stalls. Below him, the stands were full. A short while later, as he watched the last horse being eased into the stalls and readied himself for the next seventy seconds of furious action, with every pair of eyes trained towards the start, Willow Star set herself like a spring ready to uncoil. Every sinew in her body was tensed, every muscle in her quarters bulged ready to thrust her forward the very instant that the gates holding her in began to part. Her delicate nose was now jammed against her chest as she braced her neck, the steel of the bit still firm across the corners of her mouth. The noise from the main road running only thirty yards behind her was suddenly drowned as the ten iron traps released them on their way. Owen Williams was thankful that he'd grabbed a handful of Willow Star's mane as she flew out of the stalls beneath him. She was eager to show everyone just how good she really was.

At home she always had to wait for the others, and in France, where she'd had her last race, she'd been running a temperature. Her entire body had ached so much she doubted her ability even to finish. Every stride of the race had hurt her. Now, she was in peak condition. Above her, Owen Williams could only sit and steer as she took control and blazed away down the long carpet of green that lay before them.

He couldn't believe that this was the same animal he'd ridden at Goodwood. It was as though Willow Star had been programmed to reach the finishing line like a missile locked on to its target. The furlong markers flew by with not so much as a glimpse of another runner. He knew that she couldn't possibly sustain her speed, and about three hundred yards from home, for just a brief moment, he feared that she might be about to falter. Then, before he had time to react, and just as he sensed another horse at his quarters, Willow Star changed legs, picked up the bridle and was off again.

It was the most exciting feeling he had ever experienced. The sheer power of the horse sent a shiver down his spine. He glanced behind as the winning post flashed past. The others seemed a distance away. As he slowly eased her down, he lowered his right hand and patted her neck appreciatively. If she didn't turn out to be the season's Champion Sprinter he'd hand in his licence.

Kate rushed from the stand, taking the iron steps two at a time. She met Willow as they walked off the course towards the winner's enclosure and threw her arms around the filly's neck, hugging her as they walked, beaming like a child on a fairground ride, and kissing her wildly.

Charlie and Nick weren't far behind. As professional trainers, it wouldn't do to show as much excitement as Kate, but they were every bit as pleased. Nick had a lump in his throat and was pinching his leg to stop himself from crying.

The cheer from the enthusiastic crowd who packed themselves around the winners enclosure was deafening. Willow Star froze for a moment until Titch encouraged her to step forward into the limelight. Once she realised that the applause was for her, she jutted her head up proudly in the air and stood like a champion, allowing people to pat her and take her photograph.

There were no photo finishes or objections or stewards' inquiries to cast a shadow over the result. Charlie bore in mind the instructions he had had from the lawyers acting for the anonymous owners. In the event of the filly winning, he was to nominate someone to accept the prize on the owners' behalf.

Kate was the obvious choice. She was so thrilled by the result, Charlie thought she might drop the trophy that went with the winner's prize of sixty-five thousand pounds.

'Kate, you look as though you won the bloody race yourself.'

She turned to him, beaming. 'I have – at least, I feel as if I have!'

'You mean you backed her well?'

'Yes, of course I did, but it's more than that.'

Charlie grinned at her. He thought he understood. She felt she was a fully integrated member of the Oak Hollow team now, and she was right.

Chapter Fifteen

They were in the members' bar opening a second bottle of champagne when Charlie heard his name called over the Tannoy. His mind instantly began scrambling for reasons why the race could be taken away from him. He'd watched the jockey weigh in and there had certainly been no interference then, so unless someone had actually objected to something it was difficult to know what else could have gone wrong.

More concerned than he cared to admit, he offered his apologies to the group and quietly edged his way out of the bar. When he reached the weighing room, he turned left towards the tiny communication booth. The operator recognised him. 'There's someone here to see you.' He nodded towards a man whom Charlie had just walked past.

He was about thirty-five, slightly built and wearing a cheap suit. Charlie's relief that he wasn't a steward was tempered by the look of concern on the man's face. He walked over and tentatively introduced himself.

'Hello. I'm Charlie Patterson.'

The man offered his hand and gave his name as Sergeant Kenneth Foreman from York Police. He led Charlie into a small empty room adjacent to the changing rooms.

'I'm afraid it's about your father,' he said eventually.

Charlie instantly had an image of his stepfather arrested and incarcerated; then his thoughts flashed to his mother distraught, humiliated and confused.

'Stepfather,' he said automatically.

'Sorry, sir. But he's been involved in an accident.'

'What? Where?'

'On the A1M. Just south of Scotch Corner. I'm afraid he died on the way to hospital.'

'What about my mother?'

'He was on his own.'

The news was so unexpected, so contrary to anything Charlie had been anticipating that for a few seconds he felt as if he'd been hit on the back of the head with a sandbag. When he had recovered, he asked huskily, 'How did it happen?'

The sergeant looked down at the notebook he had opened on the table in front of him. For a few moments he said nothing, then he cleared his throat.

'He was being pursued by a police officer at the time. He had been reported speeding. The police driver was trying to catch up with him. He was travelling extremely fast along the raised section at Darlington when he left the carriageway and broke through the outer crash barriers. There's a drop of fifty feet to the road below. Fortunately, nobody else was involved.' He paused. 'I am sorry to have to give you such bad news.'

Charlie heard but he couldn't reply for a moment as he grappled with the image of his father being hounded by the police. What had been going through his mind? Where was he going? Could he have been coming to York? And if he was, why?

'How did you know how to contact me?' Charlie asked.

'From the front of his personal diary: who to contact in case of emergency. Durham Police rang your stables, and they told us you were here.'

'Can I see him?'

'We would like you formally to identify him. He's at Darlington. Have you got transport?'

Charlie knew that Nick would supply that. 'Yes. I'll go right away.'

Charlie left Kate, Nick and Imogen at the Post House in York. They were as shocked as he was and had offered to come with him, but he wanted to deal with this alone. When he told them he would be going straight on to Scotland to tell his mother, they agreed to go back to Lambourn in the lorry while Charlie took Nick's Subaru.

Charlie shivered in the hospital mortuary. A taciturn, white-coated official pulled out a body-sized drawer and stood back. Charlie and the police sergeant who had met him at the hospital gazed at the pale, handsome features. Beyond a few small abrasions, there was no sign of the accident on David Patterson's face. His torso, the policeman said, had been completely crushed. The police surgeon's report gave the information that he had died in the ambulance on the way to hospital. Every means of revival had been tried, but the damage was too serious.

Charlie tried to divine from the set of his father's lips and his closed, bloodless eyelids what his intentions had been as he drove his car from the road. He tried not to face the possibility that it had been a deliberate act to resolve the impossible dilemma he faced.

Charlie wasn't looking forward to breaking the news to his mother. And he knew his own involvement wasn't over. Maybe Sala Mahmoud would not want revenge now, but he would still want his money.

'Would you mind coming back to the station with me, sir? There are a few things we need to clear up.'

Charlie carried on gazing at his dead, adoptive father and nodded. He wondered if the sergeant had any idea just how much there was to clear up.

Charlie was treated with deference and consideration by the police. Interrogation was preceded by polite sympathy. A lean, earnest detective inspector sat opposite him to ask the questions.

'There's something puzzling us about this incident,' he said slowly. 'The police vehicle pursuing your stepfather wasn't marked and the officer wasn't wearing a cap. There was no way he could have known it was the police after him, and yet the driver reports that he was definitely trying to get away from him, as if he was expecting somebody to be pursuing him.' The detective opened his eyes wide with inquiry. 'Any idea who he might have thought would be after him?'

Charlie looked blankly back at him. He imagined his father had assumed that Mahmoud's people were on his tail. 'No,' Charlie said. 'I don't know who he might have thought it was.'

'But did you know the Thames Valley Police were looking for him?'

'Yes. They told me.'

'Did you know where he was?'

'No. But he phoned me,' Charlie lied. 'To tell me he was coming to see me.'

'Do you know why that was?'

'Not for sure, but I had tried to persuade him to give himself up.'

'You're aware of why he was wanted?'

Charlie nodded.

The DI looked at him for a moment before he went on. 'Thames Valley want to see your mother, too.'

'They told me. I can't help, I'm afraid. She went off to stay with friends, to get over everything, then I lost contact with her.'

The policeman looked at him with frank scepticism. 'Where will you be going when you leave here?'

'Back to my yard at Lambourn.'

'Yes, you're a trainer, aren't you? I gather you had a good winner today at York.'

Charlie nodded.

'I imagine this has all taken the gilt from the gingerbread,' the detective said with a hint of sympathy.

'Yes,' Charlie agreed. 'It has rather.'

'All right, we won't keep you here, but Thames Valley want to see you in the morning. There's one last thing, though.' The policeman flipped back a sheet of his spiral-bound notebook. 'When the driver of the police vehicle reached the car, he could see that your stepfather was still alive, but the car was so badly buckled by the fall that there was no way the ambulancemen were going to get him out on their own, so he called the fire brigade. They took a good quarter of an hour to cut him free before the paramedics could take over. While the fireman was working, Patterson spoke to him, quite lucidly. He asked him to give you this.' The policeman tore a page from his notebook and handed it to Charlie. 'He said someone should give it to you. That's not the original, of course, but maybe you can make something of it.'

Charlie stared at a strange list of figures, and a name:

60/60/24/7
ROGER.

After a few moments he looked back up at the detective, shaking his head. 'Doesn't mean a thing to me.'

'Maybe not right away, but I'd say he was trying to convey something to you in a way only you would understand. It may have no bearing on Thames Valley's inquiries, but if you can work it out, we'd like to know what it means.'

'My stepfather,' Charlie stressed the 'step', 'was an eccentric man. We didn't have much in common and I don't pretend to understand how his mind worked, but if I think of anything, I'll let you know.'

Charlie drove the Subaru up the track through the pine forest south of Banchory. He was certain that no one had followed him from the police station in Darlington. He hadn't seen another car for the last five miles.

It was a black night and 2 a.m., little more than twenty-four hours since he had last been here. Now his father was dead. The police and Mahmoud had been deprived of their quarry, but while his death had done away with some problems, it had also presented new ones. Where, for instance, was the sheikh's money? His mother evidently didn't know, and if the slip of paper from his father wasn't a clue then the money could easily remain undiscovered forever. He'd studied the numbers from every angle for the entire journey, and still they meant absolutely nothing. He'd also started to worry about how best to break the news to his mother.

Charlie stopped the car and parked it in front of the barn. He walked briskly up the moonlit path to the house, hoping he would be able to rouse his mother.

He had gone a few yards down the track when he was dazzled by the light of a powerful torch.

'What the hell are you doing back here?' Hutch rasped from behind the beam.

'My stepfather is dead.'

There was a moment's silence before the light was clicked off. Hutch thought of the man alongside whom he had fought for the past twenty years. The only person in the world he cared about.

As Charlie's eyes adapted to the moonlight again, he made out Hutch's bulky frame in front of the house.

'What happened?' the ex-soldier asked huskily.

'He drove off a motorway.'

Hutch turned and opened the front door of the house. Charlie followed him in. They went on into the sitting room where Hutch took a bottle of Scotch from a cupboard. He poured a glass for Charlie and filled one for himself. He took a gulp. 'Was he forced off?'

'No. It was an accident. The police were after him, but only for speeding. They hadn't caught up with him when he went over the side of the flyover outside Darlington.' Charlie took a drink of whisky. 'They said they couldn't see any reason why it happened.'

'He was going to York, to see you. Then he was going to give himself up.'

Charlie shook his head slowly, considering the irony of it all.

'I'll bet you that was no accident. People like your father don't have accidents.'

'But he was being chased by the police.'

'It was because you came to see him,' Hutch said accusingly.

'For God's sake, you can't blame me. I just told him what the choices were, for him, for my mother. He was living in a fantasy world, as if he was on some military operation, running from a bunch of Omani terrorists or something. He wasn't making sane judgements any more.'

Hutchinson's face twitched. 'He was doing what he knew best. He'd tried to play by the rules of the real world and they let him down.'

'Didn't he think what it was like for my mother?'

'Yes, in the end, he must have done – you must have convinced him. But that left him no choice.'

'Is my mother still here?'

'Aye, she is. She's been fretting terrible since he left. He never told her he was going.'

'I'll go up and break the news.'

Charlie knocked on the door of his mother's bedroom. As soon as she saw him, she knew something had happened to her husband.

'Let me put on a dressing gown,' she said sleepily. When she appeared in the sitting room half a minute later, she looked at Charlie's face again and flung her arms round him.

'What happened?' she asked.

There was no easy way to begin. Charlie took a deep breath and recalled the bare facts of the accident. He felt his mother quiver against his chest. 'It was quick,' he lied. 'He didn't suffer. I saw him; he looked quite calm.' That at least was true.

His mother gave an uncontrollable shudder. 'Oh God! He could never have coped with prison, or penury, even for me. The poor, stupid man. He felt hunted, like a fox.'

'Hutch said it was my fault,' Charlie said.

'Don't even think that. Someone had to tell him. It's been like living with a boy obsessed with some private code of behaviour. Hutch understood it. I recognised it, too, but he knew I couldn't bear it.' Pru pushed herself from her son's arms and stood back. She tried to regain some dignity, wiping her eyes, dabbing at her nose with a handkerchief. 'I'll make us all some tea. Come into the kitchen and tell me exactly what happened.'

Charlie saw the grief, the deep lonely grief, and was amazed again by the strength of her love; his stepfather couldn't have been all bad to have retained the loyalty of a woman like her.

'I'm not sorry to leave that place behind,' Pru said as they waved farewell to Hutch and Charlie drove them from the house next morning. In the back of the car were the few personal possessions she and her husband had brought with them to the small lodge. Pru had no intention of going back there again. First they were going to the croft by Loch Cluanie to pick up David Patterson's things. It was a fine day for a Highland drive, but both of them were living in a kind of numb suspension of time, hating to look back, unable to look forward.

Charlie had heard his mother in the night, sometimes letting the grief take over in huge, gasping, desolate sobs, but in the morning she'd been determined to cope, to pull through and deal with the mess that faced her.

'I don't know what it is about men like that,' she went on. 'They seem to derive a kind of child-like satisfaction from hiding themselves away as deeply as they can. I suppose there's an innate insecurity about them.'

'But you wouldn't call Hutch or Dad weak men.'

'No, of course not, but a very strong man with a single weakness is a bad combination.'

Once they had settled into the long journey across Scotland, Charlie handed Pru the piece of paper the DI in Darlington had given him. 'Dad gave it to a fireman who was cutting him from the car. What do you suppose it means?' He glanced at his mother.

Pru looked at it and shook her head. 'That's typical of him, obscure to the end. He loved all those lateral thinking games but I could never work them out. It's obviously a clue to where the money is.'

'Christ! What a mess!' Charlie exploded, as it sank in that if he didn't find the money, Sala Mahmoud would never believe David Patterson had gone without telling him where it was.

Pru put a hand on Charlie's arm. 'Please, don't blame him. He couldn't help the way he was. Do you think I'd have tolerated him if he could?'

Pru gazed with astonishment at the sparse, tidy contents of the croft in Glen Shiel. 'Until a few weeks ago, I had no idea this place existed,' she said. 'And then he only told me because he had to, in case of emergency. This must be where he used to come when things got on top of him.'

Charlie nodded. 'He would escape into another identity here, he told me. The locals thought he was just a romantic eccentric; there are enough of them around. No one ever bothered him.'

Charlie opened the drawers and began to remove the

objects his father had kept there. Pru begged him not to bring the weapons, so he took them out and flung them into the loch. Together, they gathered up all Patterson's portable belongings – books, papers, pictures and a few small pieces of Victorian sculpture.

When the back of the Subaru was full, they closed and locked the door of the croft for the last time and set off for England.

They stopped for the night at an anonymous motel outside Manchester. They ate for the first time that day and bought newspapers. Several carried reports of Major David Patterson's death while being pursued by the police, with the additional information that he was wanted for questioning over the deaths of two ex-convicts, Brian Tennent and Miles Latimer. There was no mention of any missing Palestinians.

Pru read the reports bleakly. 'My gosh, it sounds so sordid.'

They set off for Wiltshire next morning. Pru intended to present herself to the police before they started looking for her. Despite the fact that all her instincts were those of a law-abiding, conscientious member of society, she let herself be persuaded by Charlie that she should offer a restricted version of events. 'They won't understand anything you might have done out of loyalty to Dad,' he said.

Everything was quiet at Birch Lodge when they arrived there after midday. The door lock had been repaired and the house tidied by General Sheridan's daily since the Palestinians' visit.

For a while, Pru sat in the drawing room where only a few weeks before Tennent had been killed. When she had plucked up the strength, she rang the police and was immediately put on to Inspector Ferrier.

'I'm very glad to hear from you, Mrs Patterson. I take it your son was able to convey the news about your husband?'

'Yes, yes. He came and told me.'

'We understood he'd be back home yesterday morning. We were getting worried. Where were you, Mrs Patterson?'

'In Scotland, at a friend's house. I went there after I thought my husband had been murdered to try and get over it.'

'I see.' He paused. 'Obviously, I want to talk to you.'

'Of course. When shall I expect you?'

'I'll be there in about an hour, if that's convenient.'

When Pru had put the phone down, she looked at Charlie sitting opposite her. 'Will you stay?'

Charlie nodded. 'I'll ring Nick and tell him I'll be home later.'

'Thanks,' she said. 'I'll see if there's anything in the deep freeze.'

She found enough food to make lunch, which they ate at the kitchen table. There was an air of reassuring normality to it after the crazy events and turmoil of the last few days. Charlie took from his pocket the piece of paper with Patterson's last message. Again they studied the numbers and the name that he'd left for Charlie, but they couldn't make sense of it.

Pru was clearing away the plates when the doorbell rang. 'That must be Ferrier.'

'I'll let him in,' Charlie went to the front door and opened it.

A large man came in as if he'd had his shoulder to the door, followed by two more who suddenly appeared behind him.

Charlie had time to see that while one was Arab, the first two looked English. It was one of them who hit him, an almighty, breath-killing blow in the lower guts.

He lay gasping on the floor of the hall as they stepped over him and went through into the kitchen to find his mother. He heard a stifled scream. They dragged her out and pushed her through to the drawing room. Someone pulled Charlie up and propelled him into the room behind her and thrust him on to a chair.

One of the Englishmen pulled a small automatic from his belt and aimed it at Charlie's head. The other posted himself by the window that looked out on to the drive. Neither of them spoke.

The Arab stood opposite Charlie and hissed, 'Your father is dead, but he has not taken the sheikh's money with him, has he? Now it is you who has it, and you must give it back, or you will inherit the dishonour.'

Charlie recognised the man now as one of those who had picked him up in the Mercedes. 'Don't hurt my mother,' he pleaded. Then he was struck by a sudden thought.

'First, I should like to see the Sheikh Sala Mahmoud myself.'

The Arab narrowed his eyes. He was about to reply when the man by the window growled that a police car had arrived.

Within seconds the three men had disappeared, letting themselves out of the back door and heading straight into the woods.

Charlie made a quick decision not to mention their visit to DI Ferrier, who appeared at the front door with another junior detective. Charlie let them in. In the back of his mind an idea was forming.

'Hello, Mr Patterson. You've been very elusive over the last few days.'

Charlie shrugged his shoulders. 'I was racing at York. Durham Police got hold of me there and I went to identify my stepfather.'

'It was really him this time, was it?' Ferrier couldn't help saying.

'Your question is in poor taste, Inspector,' Charlie said. 'My mother's been through hell over what happened last time.'

'So you thought it was him, last time, did you, Mrs Patterson?'

'Of course I did. You were there. What can you expect? I came home and found a man, wearing my husband's clothes, same sort of size and shape and hair, lying face down on the carpet with his head bleeding.'

Ferrier looked at her and let his uncertainty show.

Pru turned away with her shoulders heaving.

'But why did you disappear, Mrs Patterson?'

'For goodness sake, Inspector, I was upset; I thought my husband had died. I wanted to get away. A friend in Scotland lent me a house, in a very quiet, isolated spot.'

'And now we're back,' Charlie said quickly. 'And I'd like you to tell me how the press got hold of the idea that my father was wanted for questioning over the death of this other man, Miles Latimer.'

'I don't think there's any doubt that your father was responsible for Tennent's death, though we have yet to find out why. It clearly had nothing to do with an attempted robbery. When Tennent's one and only friend, the only person who knew where he was the day he died, turns up buried in a skip, I think we have reasonable grounds for believing there might be a connection, don't you?'

Charlie sighed. 'I suppose so.' Conceding his father's crimes didn't much matter now. What did matter was concealing Mahmoud's involvement and ensuring that his mother wasn't implicated in Tennent's murder.

'Right, then. Your stepfather may be dead, but we've still got to establish how these other two men were killed, so if you don't mind, we'll sit down and go through the whole thing again.'

Ferrier stayed for two hours. At the end of the session, Charlie still couldn't be sure if the detective suspected him or his mother of playing a part in the two murders, but he didn't suggest that either of them should be detained. When he and his constable had finally left, Charlie and his mother relaxed slightly.

'It's not over yet, Mum,' Charlie said. 'And you can't

stay here in case Mustapha and his two heavies come back.'

'But surely we can't go to your house either?'

'No. But we could go to Kate's.'

Pru looked suddenly tired and defeated. 'I seem to have done nothing but run and hide for the last few weeks.'

'When we've worked out where the money is, we might get somewhere. And I think it would be worth going to see Sala Mahmoud in person.'

'But unless you've got something to give him, he's not going to make any concessions.'

'I'm not sure. Mustapha was just about to say something that might have been revealing when Ferrier turned up.'

'Thank God he did,' said Pru.

'I don't know. I'm not sure those guys had any intention of harming us. But we'll still keep out of their way,' he added hastily, seeing his mother's worried face.

Charlie phoned Nick and told him as cryptically as he could that he was going to go to Kate's cottage, and suggested he meet them there.

Half an hour later, after travelling round in circles, Charlie drove a hundred yards up a narrow track to Kate's tiny brick and flint cottage. He parked the car at the back of the house and pulled an old green tarpaulin over it.

He let himself and his mother in. They were making themselves at home when Nick turned up.

'Kate couldn't come; she's flapping about a minute

corn on Willow's foot. She said she'll be over later and she'll bring some food.'

Charlie nodded. He brought Nick up to date on everything since he'd last seen him in York, including his father's obscure message. 'I'll write down these numbers for you to have a look at, see if you can come up with anything.'

'I'll try. It was signed "Roger", you say?'

'It wasn't exactly signed. He just wrote the name, in capitals, under the numbers.'

Nick stared at the numbers for a few seconds.

'Well?' Charlie asked.

'I don't know, but I can't believe it's all that complicated. Is there a relation or an old family friend called Roger?'

Charlie looked at his mother, but she shook her head. The damned puzzle was beginning to irritate her.

Chapter Sixteen

Nick and Charlie were still talking when Pru came back into the kitchen. She had a piece of cheap, lined paper in her hand.

'I think this'll answer Ferrier's questions about Latimer. It arrived at Birch Lodge, and I passed it on to David.' She handed the paper to Charlie.

It was a scrawled note:

'B.T.'s dead. I know who did it. If you want to talk about it, come to the toilets on the corner of Warwick Ave and Clifton Gardens. Nine in the morning Monday or Tuesday. If you don't come, I know who to tell.'

Charlie read it twice. He nodded gloomily, his senses blunted to what his stepfather had done. 'You're right. This had to be Latimer.'

'He said he was going to ignore it,' Pru said.

'He couldn't,' Charlie said. 'I suppose we might as well give it to Ferrier, just to show willing.'

Pru agreed. 'There's no point in pretending David didn't do it, now he's gone. The quicker it's cleared up, the less there'll be in the papers about it.'

'Mum, you're going to have to face up to the fact that the media won't let go that easily. This story's a gift for them – an ex-SAS officer drives off the road while being chased by the police for speeding when it turns out he's already wanted for two murders? And he was buried a month ago with all pomp and ceremony. Now we've got to do it all again.'

'What happens to Tennent's body?' Nick asked.

'God knows,' Charlie said. 'Unless some relation appears, I suppose the state re-buries him at their expense.'

Pru was gazing bleakly out of the window. 'Charles, you're going to have to deal with that. I don't think I can cope with burying him twice.'

'But . . .' Charlie started to say, then changed his mind. 'Don't worry, I'll look after all that.'

Kate came later, with a clutch of grocery bags. She insisted on cooking dinner for them all. Nick left at ten – he had to be up for first lot – and Kate stayed. Pru took herself to bed.

Her husband had chosen his own solution to his problems. Although it had left Pru desolate, she would survive, and she would not have to tolerate the torture of her husband being either in hiding or in prison. And only they suspected that his exit from the flyover must have been deliberate.

That night, Kate and Charlie didn't sleep until the birds had reached the finale of their dawn chorus. Two hours later they were woken by a hammering on the back door.

Charlie stiffened, then relaxed when he realised that if

it were Sala Mahmoud's men, they wouldn't be knocking on the door. Wrapping a towel round his waist, he went down to investigate. He looked through the kitchen window and saw Nick and, behind him, Imogen. He opened the door to let them in.

'What are you two doing here so early? Has something happened?'

'It's half past eight,' Nick protested. 'I've just sent out the second lot. Kenny's got everything under control. Immy came round last night and I showed her your numbers.'

Charlie turned excitedly to his cousin. 'Have you cracked it?'

She laughed. 'No, sorry. Not yet.'

'Oh well,' Charlie said, disappointed. 'I'd better make some coffee.' He started to fill a cafetière. 'Dad had a weakness for cryptic things. I only hope he hasn't over-faced us.'

'What sort of cryptic things?' Imogen asked.

'Oh, I don't know,' Charlie said, trying to think of one. 'Oh yes. There was one about a man who had a square house with windows on all four sides and they all faced south. Where was it?'

Imogen laughed. 'That's easy.'

'Okay. So where was it?' Charlie said.

'At the North Pole, of course.'

'If you got that one so easily, why the hell can't you work out these numbers?'

Imogen sat down and wrote the numbers in a column on an A4 pad: 60, 60, 24, 7.

Nick leaned across. 'It's a question of finding a sequence.'

'There's definitely something familiar about them,' Imogen nodded. 'Just be quiet for a second.'

A moment later she shrieked. 'Got it! It's been on the tip of my brain since I first saw them. It's to do with time. Sixty seconds in a minute. Sixty minutes in an hour. Twenty-four hours in a day. Seven days in a week.'

Nick and Charlie stared at the numbers. 'That's brilliant,' exclaimed Charlie, hugging her. 'But what the hell was he trying to say?'

'I should think it's the word we end up with – weeks.'

'Weeks?' Nick said.

'Weeks and Roger. What's the connection?' Charlie asked. He stared at the paper and his head spun in frustration. Somewhere at the back of his mind among the charged grey matter of his memory cells, he knew there was a connection, but he couldn't get to it yet.

'Come on,' Nick said impatiently. 'Immy's right – weeks and Roger. Just think, will you?'

'I am bloody thinking,' Charlie protested. 'But I didn't get a lot of sleep last night.'

'I bet you didn't,' Nick said with a grin. 'But you'll have to try harder or those guys will smash you in the balls again and put a stop to your fun.'

'What are you all doing?' Pru's sleepy voice asked as she appeared in a white dressing gown. She rubbed her eyes and looked with some surprise at Nick and Imogen.

'Mum, Imogen's done it,' Charlie said, explaining the riddle to his mother. 'What we need now is a connection between "weeks" and "Roger".'

Pru sat down and poured herself a cup of coffee from the pot Charlie had made. 'It could be a sound-alike – the weeks.'

'How do you mean?'

'Something that sounds the same but is spelt differently.'

'Weeks? Weaks – W.E.A.K.S.? Weekes! With an E!' Charlie exclaimed.

'What?' asked Nick.

'The sculptor! A Victorian. Dad's got a few of his.'

'Of course he has!' said Pru. 'We brought some with us from the croft.'

'Roger,' Charlie said urgently. 'Which of them is Roger?'

'That's easy,' his mother answered. 'Roger, Second Marquess of Hampshire. He's still in the car.'

Charlie and Nick rushed out of the house together. Charlie pulled the tarpaulin off the car and opened up the back. Buried among the things they had removed from the tiny Scottish dwelling was a small bronze bust. It depicted the Victorian marquess as a Roman emperor, complete with laurel wreath and toga. It was an undistinguished example of the work of the period, not rare, and not valuable. Charlie tugged it out and carried it back into the house. 'This is him, isn't it?'

'Yes, of course. It says so.' Pru pointed out a small inscription on the base.

Nick picked it up and turned it over. The underneath was smeared with some dirty brown wax which antique dealers sometimes use to 'age' their wares. He scraped at it with his fingernail until a clear circular cut in the bronze emerged. 'This must come out somehow,' he said.

Charlie, who considered himself more practical, took it from Nick. For some frustrating moments, there didn't seem any way of unlocking it, but by applying pressure and a little oil, he suddenly found that he was unscrewing it. When a neatly threaded circular panel dropped out, he was able to insert his hand into the hollow bronze. With his fingers, he felt some fine velvet cloth inside and extracted what turned out to be a small drawstring purse. His hands were trembling slightly as he opened the purse and poured the contents on to the kitchen table.

Fifteen stones of several pastel colours scattered in a glittering display on the worn pine surface.

'Shit!' Charlie said. 'That's it!'

'It looks like it,' Nick agreed. 'I don't know much about gems, though, what they are or what they're worth.'

'He went abroad, just before he disappeared. He must have got them then. What do we do with them?' Charlie asked.

'I'd turn them back into money if I were you. It'll be a lot simpler when you're dealing with Sala Mahmoud.'

Charlie shook his head. 'Maybe, but I'm not so sure. The first thing to do is to find out just how much they're worth.'

Three hours later, Charlie parked his car in Sydney Street, Chelsea. An old friend whom he trusted and who had, at the age of thirty, already made a name for himself as a reliable jobbing jeweller, had a shop close by in the Fulham Road.

Billy Wiseman emerged from the back office of his premises and greeted Charlie warmly. 'Don't tell me you've found some poor victim who'll have you?'

Charlie couldn't think what he was talking about for a moment. 'Victim?' he asked cautiously.

'Some innocent little creature that's been taken in by your specious charms?'

Charlie laughed. 'You mean am I getting engaged? Good God, no.' He stopped abruptly. 'At least, I don't think so. Anyway, that's not why I've come to see you. Can we go into your lair in the back?'

Billy Wiseman looked at the pile of stones Charlie poured on to the desk in his small private office. 'My goodness, Charlie, what have you been up to? I thought the only crime you ever committed was doping other people's favourites.'

'Look, Billy, these aren't mine, but I need to know how much they're worth before I pass them on.'

'Worth? That's an elastic term. We're talking markets and the variability of jewellers' eyes. But I could give you a figure within ten per cent either way.' Wiseman shrugged.

'That'll do,' Charlie said.

An hour later, he left the small jeweller's shop with the bag of stones, a list of their approximate values, and an invoice from Billy Wiseman for £200 for the valuation. Charlie felt fortified by the knowledge that the contents of the little velvet purse nestling in the inside pocket of his jacket were worth between two and three hundred thousand pounds more than the million the Arabs had said they were seeking.

He found his car and headed for Carlton House Terrace. When he managed to find a place to park near the Turf Club, he slipped up to the room he had booked earlier in the day. He changed out of the jeans he had been wearing and went down to the bar where Nick was waiting for him.

'Where the hell have you been?' Nick asked nervously.

'You don't get a million quid's worth of stones valued in five minutes, you know.'

'I couldn't help thinking somebody had cottoned on to the fact that you're walking around with those bloody things and nobbled you. Where are they now?'

For an answer, Charlie patted the breast pocket of his suit.

'What are you going to do with them?'

'I'm going to repay Sala Mahmoud. At least I know what they're worth now. Dad seems to have bought them well.'

'The sheikh is going to want some kind of concession, too, for his men being killed,' Nick pointed out.

'I'll just have to hope he's civilised enough not to blame me for that and accept that the person responsible is himself dead.' Charlie wasn't at all confident that that would be the Arab's attitude to his missing men, but it was a risk he had to take. There was no other way to dispose of the threat hanging over him and his mother.

★ ★ ★

Kate arrived in London in time for dinner.

They ate in the club, the three of them, and talked about the horses at Oak Hollow. The two men found they were treating Kate as if she was a partner too. It was only when they were drinking coffee that the conversation turned to the business of Sala Mahmoud's million.

'So, what are you going to do now, Charlie?' Nick asked.

'I'm going to see Sala Mahmoud.'

'Face to face?'

'Yes. I think that'd be best.'

'Where are you going to see him?'

'I've got to find out where he is first.'

'I know his trainer's secretary. I may be able to find out through her. I'll try now.' Nick left the table to make the call in the lobby.

Charlie looked at Kate for a moment before he spoke. 'I wonder if you'd do me a rather big favour?'

Kate grinned and gave an exaggerated shrug of the shoulders. 'Sure. If you think I can do it, I'll do it.'

'I wouldn't admit it to Nick, but it's just possible somebody at Billy Wiseman's might have traded the information that I'm wandering about with a bagful of diamonds. I'd hate anybody to jump me and help themselves. I don't think I ought to leave here with them.'

Kate's eyes gleamed. 'I'll take them out, no problem.' Charlie gave her a look that made up for all the fear already bubbling in her guts.

'What a woman!' he laughed.

Nick had made his call and was walking back into the

dining room. He watched his friends clasp hands across the table and grinned to himself. There was no pain in it now.

As he came closer, he gave an exaggerated cough.

Charlie looked up. He could tell that Nick had the information they needed.

'So what's the story?'

Nick sat down in his place. 'It looks as though you're off to Paris,' he said, 'or, to be precise, the Forest of Fontainebleau.'

Chapter Seventeen

Charlie drove Nick's Subaru on to a late ferry from Dover to Calais. Before they had left the club premises, Kate had ordered a cab. It picked her up and took her to Waterloo where she bought a ticket for the next Eurostar to Paris.

Charlie drove off the ferry on the other side of the Channel and headed for the French capital.

He arrived as the birds woke and men were sluicing down the ancient cobbled streets in the early morning light. He found a café that was open, sipped coffee and drank in the unforgettable atmosphere of a city he'd always loved, until it was a respectable hour to turn up at the hotel where he had arranged to meet Kate. He had become accustomed to trying to shake off tails, and after a series of manoeuvres in London, he knew he hadn't been followed to Dover, let alone Paris. He was sure that he and Kate weren't at risk, at least until he exposed himself to Sheikh Sala Mahmoud.

Over an extended breakfast in a St Germain brasserie, he gave Kate a more detailed account of what had gone on over the previous two days. To her disappointment, he told her he would not take her to see the sheikh.

He knew roughly how to find Sala Mahmoud's mansion in the Forest of Fontainebleau, but when he reached the village of Bois-le-Roi, he had to ask for more detailed directions.

From the locals' reactions, he gathered that it was a well-known and awe-inspiring place. He drove the last mile through the forest with growing trepidation.

He identified the opening in the trees that marked the start of a long private road that led to the house. He crept up it until he crossed a small bridge over a railway line, and covered another four hundred yards of dead straight road until he came to a fifteen-foot gate flanked by a chainlink fence topped with razor wire. The drive beyond curved away into the trees. There was no sign of the house. Charlie waited a moment; he had spotted a TV camera on top of one of the massive stone gateposts. When nothing happened for a while, he climbed out and walked across to find a small push-button beneath another camera lens, and a loudspeaker.

He pressed the button and stood back. After a moment, a disembodied voice addressed him in clipped Cockney.

'Who is it?'

'My name's Charles Patterson. I need to see Sheikh Mahmoud.'

'Do you have an appointment?'

'No. But if he knows I want to see him, I'm sure he'll agree.'

'Charles Patterson, right?'

'Yes.'

There was a click on the loudspeaker and the connection went dead. Charlie waited and wondered who he had been talking to.

The gatepost hissed back into life. 'Right. Leave your vehicle parked on the hard-standing to your left. Come in by the personnel gate and walk up to the house.'

Charlie got back into the Subaru and parked it. He climbed out and walked towards the gates. He heard a slight click as a smaller gate set in one of the main ones was unlocked. He pulled it open, stepped through. It swung back and closed behind him.

When he rounded the bend in the drive, he understood why his stepfather had described the place as one of the most magnificent in the forest. It was a fine example of nineteenth-century French architecture at its grandest and most elegant. While it wasn't the largest of the *fin de siècle* chateaux, it must have been one of the most beautiful and it was spectacularly set in its parkland, surrounded by the ancient forest.

On one side of the house, a lake, perhaps ten acres and edged with every kind of rush and full of lilies, gleamed and reflected the blue-grey tiles of the roof and the shimmering cream of the walls.

At the bottom of the long, double sweep of steps to the square pillared portico, a silver Rolls-Royce Phantom VI was parked; a liveried European chauffeur was yawning in the driver's seat, reading a paper.

Charlie walked across the expanse of fine gravel and

up the steps. Before he had reached the front door it swung open and an Indian servant bowed him into a marble-floored hall. Apart from a pair of plain, upholstered benches, there was no furniture, but a couple of fine English equestrian paintings – Stubbs, Charlie guessed – hung on the walls to his left and right.

He was admiring them when a stocky, bald man in a lightweight fawn suit appeared, clicking metal heels on the floor as he walked towards him.

'Mr Patterson.'

Charlie recognised the voice which had spoken to him over the intercom. 'Yes. Good morning.'

'Morning to you.' The bald man held out a hand. 'I'm Bill Jackson, head of Sheikh Sala Mahmoud's domestic security.' The man's manner was almost welcoming. Charlie began to feel a little more at ease.

Jackson beckoned him to follow and spun on his heel. As he walked, he turned and looked over his shoulder. 'I was sorry to hear about the death of your father.'

'You knew him?'

'Of course I did. I was in his squadron, then he recruited me to the sheikh's team when I left the regiment.'

Somehow, Charlie had overlooked that the sheikh's personal security had been his father's responsibility for seven or eight years.

He was being led down a long oak-floored corridor now. He noticed that none of the furniture and fittings were of that garish, over-the-top bad taste which he had always been told was distinctively Arabic. He recognised some pieces of furniture as François Linke's designs, though presumably by the hand of Harry Thorndyke.

At the third door, Jackson stopped and showed him into a large room with full-length windows which looked out over the lake. 'Have a seat.' He waved Charlie to a high-backed oak chair. 'The sheikh will see you when he sees you. Don't hold your breath, though. I'll have some coffee sent in.'

Charlie sat where Jackson had suggested and tried to relax. Jackson had been friendly enough, but that was no guarantee that his master would be.

An Indian maid appeared after a few minutes with a tray containing a jug of coffee and a small cup. When she'd gone, Charlie poured out some of the thick, dark liquid. He had taken only a few sips of the bitter brew when Jackson returned.

'Sheikh Sala Mahmoud will see you now,' he said, while his eyes communicated that Charlie was very honoured to be seen so fast.

Charlie followed Jackson out of the room, back to the central hall, up a wide curving flight of shallow marble stairs with beautifully wrought iron banisters. A rotunda above the stairwell illuminated the sheikh's huge English canvases to great advantage, though possibly not to their long-term benefit.

Charlie was led along a thickly carpeted landing corridor, through another room and, after a sharp knocking, into a second room beyond.

'Charles Patterson, effendi,' Jackson said, bowing from the waist in a way that seemed inappropriate to his undisguised Cockney accent.

Charlie found himself facing the man he had seen at the funeral in Putney Vale. Sheikh Mahmoud was half sitting, half lying on a silk upholstered sofa, wearing traditional Saudi robes, white, elegant, not greatly adorned. He had a short, well-trimmed and shiny black beard with eyes to match. He lifted one hand no more than an inch in greeting. Charlie felt impelled to bow slightly as Jackson had done.

'Good morning, Mr Patterson.'

Charlie was struck at once by his soft articulation. It didn't tally with the guttural tones he'd heard over the mobile phone in the limousine.

'Good morning, Sheikh Mahmoud.'

'I am glad to see the son of my old friend.' Charlie detected no sarcasm in the statement. 'Although I am sorry his death has been so, how shall I say, controversial?'

Charlie couldn't think of an appropriate response. He nodded.

'However,' the sheikh went on, 'having attended his first funeral, I will not be able to attend the second. But please pass my respectful condolences to your mother.'

'Thank you, sir.'

'And why have you come to see me?'

'About the furniture.'

'The furniture?' the sheikh said with surprise. 'The furniture of François Linke which your father collected together for me most efficiently?'

'Yes.'

'You can see it all around you.' He waved a hand at

various pieces in the room. 'Doesn't it look magnificent?'

'My father told me it would be just right for the house,' Charlie ventured.

'Indeed, but that isn't why you came to see me, is it?'

Charlie couldn't tell from the Arab's voice if he was teasing him or genuinely didn't know what he wanted to talk about.

'No, sir,' he plunged in. 'I understand, though, that they are not genuine François Linke pieces.'

'What? What are you saying?' The sheikh sat up, his black eyes blazing. He swung his feet over the side of the sofa and planted them on the ground. He stared hard at Charlie, puzzled and angry.

'But surely, sir, you knew. Men came to see me to find my stepfather, saying that you were very angry about it and wished my father to return the extra profit he had made from selling it to you as genuine.'

'Men? What men?'

'They said they were your men, and I saw them with you at the funeral. Then, after that, some others picked me up in your Mercedes and I spoke to you on the phone . . .' Charlie didn't finish the sentence. It was clear that this was not the man he had spoken to from the back of the car.

'I don't know what you are talking about, Mr Patterson. I have not been told that these pieces are not what your father told me they were. I am very pleased with them. I have sent no people looking for your father or you. The men you saw at the funeral were not my men, merely functionaries of my country's embassy in London – bodyguards and so on.'

'But they said you had sent them.'

'So you say, but I tell you I did not send them. What is this about the furniture? Did your father admit to you that he had cheated me?'

Charlie looked straight back into the glittering ebony eyes. 'Yes.'

'And why do you come now to tell me, when your father is dead?'

'I have come to repay the excess profit my father made, in accordance with what I understood were your wishes. I tried to persuade my father to do it before he died, but he wouldn't, although he believed you had sent your people to demand it. That's why he faked his own death, and to avoid paying hundreds of thousands of pounds he owed in England.'

'Your father was having such difficulties? Why didn't he tell me? I have great respect for him. He was a strong and honourable man.'

'He was far too proud to do that, Sheikh Mahmoud.'

'Then why did he cheat me?'

'He said you would never know that he had.'

'And I would not have done, nor has anyone who has been here and seen the furniture. We must find out how these people who posed as mine knew and who they are.'

'But the people in the limousine that picked me up at Newbury, they must have been your men.'

The sheikh nodded. He clapped his hands and a figure emerged from the shadows. Sheikh Mahmoud spoke briefly and the minion bowed and swept silently from the room.

A moment later, Bill Jackson knocked and entered.

The sheikh spoke to him in Arabic. Jackson nodded when he had finished and replied, apparently fluently, in the same language. During a further exchange, and the sheikh's issuing of a final command, Jackson betrayed no signs of his reaction. He acknowledged the sheikh's instructions, bowed and left.

'Mr Jackson will deal with them,' the Arab said briskly. 'So, you wish to repay the fraudulent profit your father made.'

'Yes, sir, in the interests of preserving our family's honour. Alternatively, since I have been able to locate the funds my father acquired through his transaction with you, I could repay you in full and take the furniture back.'

The Arab leaned back on his cushions and looked at Charlie through narrowed eyes. 'I do not understand why your father has done what he has,' he said.

'He was desperate; he didn't know how to deal with the prospect of bankruptcy. It must be hard for you to understand, but he had been tricked into a lot of obligations. He honoured some of these although probably he could have proved he'd been deceived. He was a formidable soldier, a leader of men, but when it came to the real, corrupt world of business, he didn't know the rules.'

'But you, you can deal with it?'

'I don't know. My partner and I are trying to get our training yard off the ground. We took a few gambles to get started, but we always knew exactly what the downside was.'

'And now you are offering to return to me a sum of money, I don't recall how much, a million pounds or so, to recover your family's honour?'

'To be truthful, it was also out of fear of reprisals. These people who were after my father had turned their attentions to me now that he's dead.'

'I admire your honesty.' The Arab regarded Charlie with an enigmatic half-smile. 'Where are you staying?'

Charlie gave him the name of the cheap hotel where he and Kate were staying, not expecting it to mean anything to the sheikh. Sala Mahmoud repeated the name. 'My people will come for you. Please, stay in Paris until then. This is a serious problem.' Charlie was dismissed with a curt nod and a wave.

Jackson drove Charlie to the gates in a Mercedes which had been parked outside the front door. He and two more British ex-soldiers covered him as he climbed into the grimy Subaru. Jackson assured him that no one was following, apart from one of his own men. Charlie didn't doubt him.

When he arrived back at the hotel, Kate was sitting in the tatty old salon reading. She looked up and smiled with relief when she saw him walk in. 'What's the story?'

'I don't think the sheikh has any plans to neutralise me right away. I still don't have any idea if he wants his money back. He's bloody pissed off, though not with me. It looks as if someone on his own staff got hold of the news that the furniture was wrong, omitted to tell the sheikh and thought they'd go after Dad for the money on their own account, pretending they were acting for Mahmoud.'

'Did he know that the furniture was bogus?'

'No. Not at all. He was chuffed to bits with it. Still is, as a matter of fact. He bought the stuff to sit on, not as an investment. Still, I dare say he'll want his pound of flesh.'

'But what about those men who were after you?'

'There's nothing in it for them any more. Besides, I think he told Bill Jackson to deal with them – and that'll discourage them.'

'Who's Bill Jackson?'

'He's a man my father recruited into the sheikh's service, used to be in his squadron at Hereford. He's head of domestic security now and quite capable of quietly disposing of a few wayward henchmen without recourse to the law.'

'Thank God for that.' Kate gave a tremendous sigh of relief, and Charlie realised with a stab of guilt that she'd been a lot more worried than she'd let on.

They spent the rest of the day being tourists. They walked across the Seine, ambled up the Champs-Élysées, stopping to lunch in a small restaurant by the *rond-point*. Kate hadn't been to Paris before. She soon agreed that she wasn't immune to the legendary charms of the place, especially in the early summer sun. After lunch, she and Charlie took a taxi to see the racecourse at Longchamps. They found an official who, on learning who Charlie was, allowed them to walk the course.

'Just think,' Kate said, gazing at the empty stands,

imagining the roar of the crowds it could hold. 'One day, we . . . you,' she corrected herself quickly, 'may be unloading runners here for the Arc.'

'What do you mean, one day?' Charlie laughed. 'We'll find something to run here next autumn. Any excuse to bring you back here again.'

They fantasised happily as they strolled arm in arm back across the *périphérique*.

When they reached their hotel, footsore and pleasantly weary, they took a bottle of champagne up to their room. Charlie drew the curtains and lifted Kate on to the bed.

'At last!' she laughed, kicking her shoes to the ceiling and taking a quick gulp of champagne. 'Here's to Sheikh what's-his-name, whatever he decides to do to you tomorrow.'

That evening, before they went out to sample more culinary delights, Charlie telephoned Nick.

'What's going on?' Nick asked.

'I've seen Sheikh Mahmoud.'

'And you're still alive. That's good. Your charm worked then?'

Charlie filled him in. 'The main thing is,' he concluded, 'he'll put a stop to those thugs who've been threatening me. I should think he'll be in touch about the money quite soon. In the meantime, Kate and I are seeing the sights.'

'I bet that's not all you're doing. By the way,' Nick went on, 'I hope you'll be back here the day after tomorrow. Willow Star's owners are coming to see her.'

'Good Lord. At last. I thought that win at York might flush them out. Who are they?'

'I don't know, beyond the fact that they're two women.'

'Two women? One each, eh?'

'I should think you've got enough on your hands.'

'You could say that,' Charlie laughed. 'I'll ring you tomorrow, if I'm still alive.'

Charlie didn't feel very alive when he was woken by the phone beside his bed at ten o'clock next morning. He and Kate had left Regine's in an advanced state of euphoria at three that morning. Now he had some difficulty lifting his head from the pillow.

'Hello?' he croaked into the receiver.

'*L'auto de Sheikh Sala Mahmoud vous attend, m'sieur.*'

'What? Now?'

'*Oui, m'sieur.*'

Charlie put the phone down and looked at Kate. She was lying beside him, sleeping serenely. He slipped out of bed, showered, gulped down a fizzing glass of triple Alka-Seltzer and wrote a note for Kate. Downstairs, he was ushered into the Sheikh's Rolls-Royce.

Lounging in the back, Charlie wished he was in better shape to enjoy being driven through Paris like this. To his surprise, he found some whisky in a decanter in the drinks cabinet – he didn't think Saudis drank. But he rejected the temptation to swallow a hair of the dog and tried to concentrate on his imminent meeting with the sheikh.

The limousine eased its way effortlessly south along the autoroute from Paris. It turned off to glide through the great forest of pine and broadleaf until it swept through the gate into the grounds of the sheikh's mansion and pulled up outside the classical portico. The chauffeur opened the door and Charlie stepped out at the bottom of one of the flights of steps up to the front door.

Again, the door opened before Charlie had reached it. He was ushered inside by an Indian servant and straight to the sheikh's salon.

Sala Mahmoud was sitting in one of the François Linke chairs, behind a carved walnut writing table. He lifted his head and smiled when Charlie walked in.

'Good morning again, Mr Patterson. I hope you are well?'

'Yes, thank you, sir.' Charlie walked across and stood in front of the table.

'Good. They tell me you have a good future in training horses.'

'We hope so,' Charlie mumbled, surprised by the sheikh's sudden reference to racing.

'I have some horses in England,' Mahmoud went on. 'Only twenty or thirty.' He made a gesture to demonstrate the paltriness of his string. 'Now,' he went on. 'I have thought about what you told me yesterday. I must tell you that I have been made very angry by what your father has done to me. But you have been honourable. You have told me, and you have exposed a traitor in my own household. I thank you for that. Do you have the money?'

Charlie's heart sank. He had been quietly nursing the hope that Sheikh Mahmoud wasn't going to ask for it. He had, nevertheless, come prepared. He took the small purse from his inside pocket and poured the stones on to the table.

The sheikh looked at the glittering display with apparent approval. He picked up one stone and turned it in the light.

'These are fine diamonds, but why do you bring me gems?' he asked Charlie.

'My father bought them with the money you paid him. Before he died, he left me instructions where to find them. I've had them valued. They're worth over a million pounds.'

'We shall soon see,' the sheikh said. He clapped his hands. A manservant appeared like a genie from behind a screen at the back of the room. The sheikh uttered a few words in Arabic. The servant slipped away silently.

Charlie gazed at the sheikh, trying to read his mind.

Sala Mahmoud rubbed his shiny black beard. 'You have said you will take back the furniture your father sold to me. I will decide and you will be told.'

Charlie knew enough not to ask when. He also understood that the audience was at an end. He bowed slightly. 'Thank you, sir,' he muttered and left the chamber.

The servant waiting outside seemed to know exactly what was going on and showed Charlie to the front door and into the Rolls which was waiting outside. He was taken back to Paris in silence. Only when the limousine drew up outside his small hotel did the chauffeur speak.

'Sheikh Sala Mahmoud will send a messenger.'

Charlie watched the car drive away. He had been gone for only two hours, but it was as if he had been to another world. He was brought down to earth by a New Age tramp asking him for money. He had nothing on him. He shrugged and walked into the hotel.

Kate was still asleep. He undressed, climbed back into bed and gently woke her.

Charlie drove the Subaru on to Le Shuttle at Calais late the next morning. When they reached Dover, he headed for the M2 and London.

He turned to Kate with a wide smile. 'Sorry we couldn't stay longer, but it's good to be back.'

'I can hardly believe so much has been settled in forty-eight hours.'

Charlie laughed. 'I think you'll find there's more to come.'

Kate nodded. 'You're right. Nick won't know what's hit him. How much did you say Mahmoud was sending?'

'Basically, he's giving me back half the money. He's decided to keep the furniture and he feels honour has been satisfied.'

'What are you going to do with it?'

'Give it to Mum. After all, he's promised us four yearlings for next season and he's paying their fees up front. We're doing very nicely out of it.'

'But that means you're not getting anything personally.'

'Women are so practical,' Charlie laughed. 'We'll have

to break it to Nick gently. He's already fussing about where to put the extra horses; that's another reason why he was so keen for me to get back. Anyway, at least we'll be there in time to meet these women who bought Willow.'

'Yes,' Kate agreed. 'I wonder what you'll think of them. I bet you'll really fancy one of them.'

'Of course I won't,' Charlie laughed. 'At least, I'll try not to.'

Nick's greeting was predictably ambivalent. He was immediately concerned that there was no room for four new horses.

'Don't worry, Nick,' Charlie said. 'We'll find somewhere to put them. We'll build new boxes if necessary.'

'I'll believe that when I see it. It's a pity it's not the Sheikh who hands out planning permission.'

Charlie laughed. 'And when you check our next bank statement, you'll find he's already paid the four yearlings' training fees twelve months up front.'

Nick made a quick mental calculation. His jaw fell visibly. He didn't say anything for a moment, then he gulped, and shifted his feet. 'Good Lord. I owe you an apology, then.'

'Don't worry,' Charlie said. 'Am I in time to meet Willow's owners?'

'What? Oh yes, I'd almost forgotten about them. They haven't turned up yet.' He glanced at his watch. 'They're due any time now.'

They all walked back towards the yard, Charlie and

Kate anxious to see the horses again. Kate made straight for Willow Star's box and made her usual fuss of the filly.

They hadn't been there long when Kenny shouted that there was a car turning into the drive. Nick and Charlie hurried to see who it was.

A new but extravagant Ford was creeping down the track. As it came nearer, Charlie saw that it contained only the woman who drove it. 'I suppose that must be one of them,' he said. 'Perhaps they're coming separately.'

They watched fascinated as the car drew up and a curiously dressed woman of about fifty let herself out and walked carefully towards them.

'Hello,' Charlie said.

'Hello. I'm Cora Lenigan,' the woman said with a broad Liverpudlian accent.

'Have you come to see Willow Star?' Nick asked doubtfully.

'Of course I have,' Cora chuckled. 'I own half of her.'

'Well, it's very nice to meet you at last,' Charlie said. 'But I thought there were two of you.'

'There are,' Kate's voice said from behind them. They hadn't heard her come out of the yard.

Charlie and Nick turned sharply, reacting to her tone of voice.

'What?' Charlie asked suspiciously.

'Cora and I are joint owners of Willow Star, fifty-fifty.'

Charlie and Nick gaped at her.

'Good God! Why on earth didn't you tell us?'

Kate met Charlie's incredulity with a grin. 'A girl likes to have some secrets, you know. Besides, I didn't want to say until I was sure we wanted to keep her at this yard, otherwise it might have been rather awkward, mightn't it?'

'But you do want to keep her here now, is that right?'

'Yes,' Kate said thoughtfully. 'I think she may as well stay here.' She paused. 'As long as I do.'

'That's blackmail!' Charlie protested.

'Yes,' Kate said with a grin. 'I suppose it is.'

'In that case.' Charlie fumbled in his trouser pocket and pulled out his screwed-up hanky. He opened it. Inside, a pale violet stone, which he had kept from the Sheikh, glittered in the afternoon sun. 'I suppose you'd better tell me how you want this set.'

Inside Track

John Francome

'Thrills to the final furlong . . . Francome knows how to write a good racing thriller' *Daily Express*

When champion jockey Jamie Hutchison is released from prison, all he wants is to escape the past. He can't remember what happened the night his car went out of control – but he'll never forgive himself for causing a boy's death.

Jamie's sister Pippa, a top trainer, has troubles of her own. Owners are moving their horses to rival Toby Priest, and she can't understand how he's turning slowcoaches into express trains.

Meanwhile DI Jane Culpepper is investigating the murder of a girl who used to work at Toby Priest's yard. The word is that it was a drug-related execution, but Jane's not convinced. She won't rest till she's made sense of the loose ends, wherever that might lead her.

Ex-National Hunt Champion Jockey John Francome is a broadcaster on racing for Channel 4, and his electrifying racing thrillers have won him legions of fans. Don't miss the previous bestsellers from Headline.

'Francome brings authenticity to tales of the horse-racing circuit and, like Dick Francis, goes beyond the thunder of the turf to the skulduggery of the trading ring' *Mail on Sunday*

'Francome provides a vivid panorama of the racing world . . . and handles the story's twist deftly' *The Times*

'The racing feel is authentic and it's a pacy, entertaining read' *Evening Standard*

0 7553 0062 9

headline

Dead Weight

John Francome

'Thrills to the final furlong . . . Francome knows how to write a good racing thriller' *Daily Express*

There's no hiding place for a jump jockey when his courage deserts him. After a crashing fall, champion rider Phil Nicholas returns to racing, but though his body has healed his mind has not. Flashbacks of his accident invade his dreams, rob him of his sleep and freeze him in the saddle. The tough guy of jump racing has lost his bottle.

But when one of Phil's colleagues is viciously attacked after losing a race he should have won, the jockey can't sit on the sidelines any longer. If he wants to save the sport – and the woman he loves – it's time for Phil to recover his nerve . . .

Ex-National Hunt Champion Jockey John Francome has been voted TV's most popular racing commentator for his broadcasting for Channel 4, and he has established himself as one of the front runners in the racing thriller stakes. Don't miss his previous bestsellers from Headline:

'Francome provides a vivid panorama of the racing world . . . and handles the story's twist deftly' *The Times*

'Francome brings authenticity to tales of the horse-racing circuit and, like Dick Francis, goes beyond the thunder of the turf to the skulduggery of the trading ring' *Mail on Sunday*

'The racing feel is authentic and it's a pacy, entertaining read' *Evening Standard*

'An action-packed storyline that gallops to a thrilling end' *Racing Post*

0 7472 6608 5

headline

Lifeline

John Francome

'Francome provides a vivid panorama of the racing world'
The Times

Unlike some of his fellow jockeys, Tony Byrne has never taken a bung and never ridden a dishonest race. All the same, his career is heading for the rocks, dragged down by weight problems and woman trouble – and too many slow horses.

In comparison, star rider Freddy Montague has never been fussy about sticking to the rules, either on the racetrack or in bed with another man's wife. And if there's money on offer to fix races, Freddy's guaranteed to be first on the gravy train.

Unfortunately for both men, the guarantees run out once Freddy's train comes off the rails. That's when the gravy turns to blood . . .

Ex-National Hunt Champion Jockey John Francome is a broadcaster on racing for Channel 4, and has established himself as one of the front runners in the racing thriller stakes. Don't miss his previous bestsellers from Headline:

'Francome brings authenticity to tales of the horse-racing circuit and, like Dick Francis, goes beyond the thunder of the turf to the skulduggery of the trading ring' *Mail on Sunday*

'The racing feel is authentic and it's a pacy, entertaining read'
Evening Standard

'Thrills to the final furlong . . . Francome knows how to write a good racing thriller' *Daily Express*

0 7472 6607 7

headline

madaboutbooks.com